VEGAS
RICH

FERN MICHAELS

VEGAS RICH

Kensington Books

KENSINGTON BOOKS are published by

Kensington Publishing Corp.
850 Third Avenue
New York, NY 10022

Library of Congress Card Catalog Number: 96-076025
ISBN 1-57566-057-1

First Printing: August, 1996
10 9 8 7 6 5 4 3 2 1

Printed in the United States of America

For Doris and John Fernesic. Rick too.

PART ONE

~

Sallie Coleman

1923–1942

1

~

1923

The old attorney stared out his grimy windows and winced. His secretary had cleaned those windows yesterday. He'd watched her swish her soapy rag over them, then polish them until he could see his reflection. Now, less than fifteen hours later, they were dirty and grimy as though they'd never been cleaned. He looked down at his desk and saw the same grainy granules of desert sand. Irritably, he blew at them and wasn't surprised when the offending sand refused to move. He told himself he was in the desert; sand was to be expected.

Alvin Waring, attorney-at-law, worried as he shuffled the two folders—one thick, one thin—from one side of his desk to the other. Waring knew exactly what was in each folder. If he were pressed, he could rattle off the contents without missing a heartbeat.

He saw her then, and he thought about waterfalls, summer blue skies, picnics and wildflowers. He wished, in that single second of time, for his youth. The two folders on his desk made perfect sense now. He stood, his old bones creaking as he walked around the side of his desk, held out his hand and touched hers, softer than any flower petal. She smiled, her summer blue eyes crinkling at the corners.

"Mr. Waring, I'm Sallie Coleman. I received your letter several days ago. I would have come yesterday, but I . . . I had to . . . sort through some things. I don't have much money, Mr. Waring. I used all my available cash to pay for Cotton's funeral. I do have this," Sallie said as she withdrew a small burlap sack from her purse. "Cotton gave it to me the first day I started to work at the bingo palace. He said it was to be my nest egg if things didn't work out. I'm not sure how much it's worth. Cotton said it was seven ounces of pure gold."

"Nest eggs should not be touched. They're for the future." The attorney cleared his throat as he handed back the sack of gold. He wondered what it would be like to walk with this young woman through a green meadow filled with daisies. In his bare feet. Holding her hand.

Sallie backed up a step, but didn't reach for the little sack. The summer blue eyes were questioning. "I don't understand. It could take me years to pay off . . . The gold would help me get to the end quicker. Did I say that right?"

"It makes no mind. There is no need for you to assume payment for Cotton Easter's bills. First, he didn't leave any bills. His estate would have paid for his funeral. There was . . . is . . . no need for you to assume the responsibility."

"Yes, Mr. Waring, there was a pure need for me to be doing that. Cotton was my friend. It was hard for me here in the desert when I first got here. He helped me. He watched out for me. Cotton didn't let anyone bother me. He was a kind man, a good man. Sometimes . . . most times, he was down on his luck, but when he had money he always shared with me and a few others who were less fortunate. I don't regret paying for his funeral. If he didn't leave any bills, and you don't want my nest egg, why did you write me that letter asking me to come here?"

"Sit, Miss Coleman. I have some things to explain to you. I'm going to read you Cotton's last will and testament."

"Mercy, Mr. Waring, isn't a person's will a private thing? I don't know if Cotton would like you to be telling me his secret thoughts. Cotton always told me a man's life and his past belonged to him alone. He said that and a man's good name were all God gave him when he came into the world, and when he left this world, his name on his marker would be all that was left. Now that I told you that, Mr. Waring, I'll be getting back to work. I'm having his marker erected next Sunday afternoon. The preacher agreed to say a few words. I'm going to serve a meal at the palace for anyone who wants to come."

Alvin Waring couldn't believe what he was hearing. She was almost to the door when he barked at her to come back and sit. He gentled his tone and smiled when she perched herself on the edge of the hard wooden chair. The summer blue eyes were frightened.

"Now, little lady, you just sit there and listen to me read you Cotton Easter's last will and testament. Before I do that, I want to tell you about Cotton. If I don't, you won't understand the will. Cotton came here to the desert with his daddy many years ago. He was just a small child at the time. His daddy was an educated man whose wife died before her time. With a small boy to raise, he decided to come here to seek his fortune the way his own father had done. He was very successful, almost as successful as his father. He sent Cotton back to Boston to get educated, and the minute the boy finished his studies, he hightailed it right back here and took his place next to his daddy. The main reason his daddy came here was because his father had mined the Comstock Lode. That would be Cotton's granddaddy. The old gentleman left all he held dear to Cotton's father. And, there was a lot that he held dear. Cotton's daddy sold all the shares to the Comstock that his father left him at just the right time, and banked a fortune. Sold high, $22,000 a share, and he owned thousands of shares. Cotton's daddy was a gambler and won acres and acres of land in poker games. He never touched that money. He struck it rich time and again. He had a big, old ugly Wells Fargo safe made special, and he kept his fortune in it. Didn't trust banks or the stock market. A wise man. He bought up half the desert for fifty cents an acre. He grubstaked many a man who later paid back double for the stake. In some cases the veins and mines found their way back to Cotton's daddy. When he died, his estate went to Cotton, who didn't give a whit about the money. Cotton wanted his own strike. He amassed his own fortune, and it all went into the Wells Fargo safe along with his daddy's money, and his granddaddy's money. Make no mistake, Miss Coleman, Cotton knew exactly what was his, what was his granddaddy's, and what was his daddy's. I don't think he knew or even cared about the amount. I tried to tell him, but he simply wasn't interested. He wanted to be like all the other miners— spinning yarns and drinking rotgut, loving women on the run, gambling, and hitting the mother lode. He craved respect, and you were the only person who gave it to him, Miss Coleman. He said you nursed him when he came down with pneumonia, and that you fed him when he was hungry. He said you washed his clothes once or twice and said you were—ah, what he said was . . . you were, forgive me, a lusty bed partner."

Sallie blushed, but the summer blue eyes didn't waver.

"Cotton left all of his holdings to you, Miss Coleman."

"Me! Now, why would he do a thing like that, Mr. Waring?"

"Because you accepted him for who he was, and he said you respected him and asked his advice. He said nobody else, man or woman, ever asked for his advice. You followed it, too. That was important to Cotton."

"But . . . but—"

"You're a very rich woman, Miss Coleman. It's a short will. I'll read it to you, and you can ask me questions, if you want, when I'm finished."

Sallie listened to the old attorney's quivering voice, understanding only one word: rich. Other people were rich. People like herself were never rich. If she were rich, she could go back to Texas and help her family. She would have to ask how much money that would take. She wished then that her life had been different. She wished she could read and write well. Cotton had helped her a little, but she'd been too ashamed and embarrassed to let him know how ignorant she was.

The attorney's voice trailed off. He was finished. She needed to pay attention. He had said she should ask questions. He was staring at her expectantly. "Mr. Waring, I'd like to help my parents out if that's possible. These past few years I've sent little bits of money back home, but there are quite a few young ones to take care of. How much do you think that will cost? If there's enough I'd like to maybe move my family to a little house with a yard for the children. Maybe buy a toy or two and a new outfit. Schooling too. My pa, he . . . how much will all that take?"

"Compared to what you have, what you're asking is a spit in the bucket. You're rich, Miss Coleman. Let me put it to you another way. Do you know how much a million dollars is?" Sallie's head bobbed up and down. In her life she'd never seen more than fifty dollars at a time. A million had to be a lot more than that. She wished she'd paid more attention to Cotton when he was doing numbers with her. All she wanted was to be able to count the money at the end of the day and know it was accurate.

"Then you multiply that by about fifty and that's what you're worth, possibly more, thanks to Cotton Easter. That doesn't count the property. Right now it's not worth much. Possibly someday it will be worth a fortune. Cotton's daddy thought so, and so did Cotton. My best advice to you is to take some of that money and buy up the rest of the desert and sit on it until the time is right to sell it. It's going for about sixty-five cents an acre. I can arrange all that for you if you want me to handle your affairs. If you have another attorney in mind, that's all right, too. I'll be sending you monthly reports on your finances, which pretty much stay the same since everything is locked up. Later, I'd like us to sit down and talk about the stock market. Will you be wanting to move into the Easter house?

They gave it a name when Cotton was just a tad. His daddy called it Sunrise. You own the mountain it's sitting on." He dangled a set of clanking keys to make his point.

"What house is that, Mr. Waring?" Sallie gasped.

"Cotton's daddy's house up on Sunrise Mountain. A fine house it is, too. Cotton's granddaddy had everything sent here from Boston. The finest furnishings money could buy. Real plumbing. There's a well and an automobile. There's a couple who look after the place. You can live there if you like. It's yours."

A house called Sunrise. Sally wondered if she was dreaming. "How many rooms does it have?"

"Eleven. Four complete bathrooms. Beautiful gardens. Do you like flowers, Miss Coleman?"

"Oh, yes, Mr. Waring, I love flowers. Do you?"

"Wildflowers especially. Bluebells, and those little upside-down bells, the yellow ones. My mother used to have a beautiful flower garden. Where do you live now, Miss Coleman?"

"In a boardinghouse. I have a big room. It has pretty wallpaper and white curtains on the windows. I can't open the windows, though, because of the grit and sand. I'd like to see those curtains move in the early morning breeze. Window screens are frightfully expensive."

"You don't have to worry about things being expensive anymore. If you don't mind me asking, Miss Coleman, what will you do? If you have a mind to tell me a little about your background, I might be able to help you. Plan your future, so to speak. Cotton trusted me. I'd like it if you would trust me, too."

Sallie sat back in the hard wooden chair and stared directly at the old attorney. She spoke haltingly at first, and then, as she grew more comfortable with the truth and shame, the words rushed out. "I'm one of eight children. I'm the oldest girl. The boys, they took off as soon as they could. My pa, he drank too much. My mother took in washing and ironing. I helped. There was never enough food. I was never warm enough. I left when I was thirteen. I made my way here and sang for my supper. Cotton said I sang like an angel. He loved to hear me sing. The miners gave me tips sometimes. Cotton was always generous. He didn't care that sometimes, when there was no money, that I would ... take money for doing things that would shame my mother. That's just another way of saying I was ... am ... a whore. You didn't expect me to say that, did you, Mr. Waring?"

"No, I didn't. I'm not going to judge you, Miss Coleman."

"That's good, Mr. Waring. I won't judge you either. Now we can start out fair. I can read and write a little. Maybe I can get someone to teach me now. There was no time for school and no nice clothes back in Texas. The good ladies in town called us white trash. Nobody cared about us. I wanted better, the way my brothers wanted better. Someday I'm going to find them, and help them if I can. I'll be taking you up on the offer to move into that fine house. Do you know if the windows open?"

The old attorney smiled. "I'll make sure they do. Miss Coleman, I have an idea. Do you think you could find someone to take your place at the bingo palace, for say, six months? Maybe a year. I know a lady in California who operates a finishing school for young ladies. If you're amenable, I can make arrangements for her to . . . to—"

"Polish me up?" Her tinkling laugh sent goose bumps up and down the attorney's arms. "I suppose so. But first I have to go back to Texas. Family needs to come first, Mr. Waring. When I get back, we can talk again. Where's that safe you spoke about? Do you give me the money or do I just open the safe and take it? Do I have to write everything down?"

"Miss Coleman, you can do whatever you want. When would you like to visit the house?"

"Today."

"It's a two-day trip on horseback. I can make arrangements to have you taken up tomorrow if that's all right with you. Here is the combination to the safe and the keys to the house. These past few years a lot of the funds were put in banks once I felt it was safe. This box sitting here has all the bankbooks. They're yours now. All you have to do is walk into any one of them, sign your name, and take as much money as you want. You're agreeable, then, to my purchasing more desert acreage?"

"If you feel it's a wise thing to do."

"I do."

"Then you have my permission, Mr. Waring."

"How do you feel now, Miss Coleman? I'm curious."

"Sad. Cotton was such a good friend to me. I cannot believe that he would leave me all this money. Is there something in particular he wants me to do? I guess what I'm saying is, why? Why me? He had friends. There must be family in Boston. Are you sure it is meant for me?"

"I'm sure." Waring rose, walked around the desk, and held out his hand. He held her delicate hand a moment longer than necessary. "Enjoy your new fortune, Miss Coleman."

"I'll try, Mr. Waring."

Sallie held out her hands for the small wooden box containing the bankbooks.

Outside in the late morning sunshine, Sallie stared up and down the street. She wondered how things could look the same as they had looked an hour ago when she first walked up the steps to the attorney's office.

Sallie's eye traveled to the line of stores whose owners she knew by name. Toolie Simmons owned The Arcade where beer on draft was sold, The Rye & Thackery run by Russ Malloy, the Red Onion Club, The Gem Counter with the letter N backwards on the rough sign, and on to the Arizona Club, whose sign proudly proclaimed its whiskey was fully matured and reimported. Men sat in the small pools of shade on spindly chairs, tilted back at alarming angles, talking, smoking their cigars and pipes as they waited for the saloons to open at noon. Those men would work if there were work to be had. Maybe she could do something about that. Some of them waved to her, others tilted their straw hats in recognition.

"Gonna sing us a pretty song tonight, Miss Sallie?" one of the hard rock miners shouted.

"Not tonight, Zeke, I'm heading for Texas to see my family, and I have a lot to do. Soon, though. You just tell me what you want me to sing, and I'll do it just for you."

"Heard the Mercantile got some canned peaches yesterday, Miss Sallie."

"Thanks for telling me, Billy. Would you like some?"

"I purely would, Miss Sallie."

"I'll get some on my way back and drop them off. You gonna be at the Arizona Club?"

"Nope. Don't got a lick of money in my poke today. I'll be waiting right here for you."

Sallie nodded as she skirted the barrels of hardware and produce outside the Mercantile Company. She smiled at Hiram Webster as he stopped sweeping the sand from in front of his doorstep to let her pass. "Good morning, Mr. Webster. It's a fine day, isn't it?"

" 'Tis that, Miss Sallie. Lots of blue sky today."

Sallie was convinced no one knew about her good fortune. As she walked along she remembered the tents and the smell of frying onions that permeated the air the day she'd first arrived. The tents were all gone now, replaced with newer wooden buildings. It was still a rough town, a shoddy town, a *man's* town. She realized she could fancy up the town now if she wanted to. She could buy up whatever she wanted. She could knock down all the shabby buildings and start over. Cotton said if the price was right, a person could buy anything.

Sallie stepped aside as three ladies walking abreast passed her, straw baskets on their arms. They didn't acknowledge her in any way. Sallie smiled anyway, and said, "Good morning, ladies." The scent of sagebrush seemed to be all about her as she walked along, past the bakery, the icehouse, the pharmacy, and the milliner. A gust of sand swirled past her. She tried to dance away from the circular swirl that spiraled upward, but her shoes were covered with sand. She stomped her feet and shook the hem of her skirt.

"Mornin', Miss Sallie. What brings you to this end of town? Can we do anything for you here at the Chamber of Commerce?"

"Yes, you can, Eli. How much do you think it would cost to plant cottonwoods up and down this fine street, on both sides?"

"Why do you ask?"

"I'd like to donate them and pay for the labor to plant them in memory of my friend Cotton Easter. Maybe some benches under the trees for the ladies to sit on. I think they'll make the street real pretty."

"That they will, Miss Sallie. The town's coming back to life a little at a time. I like that."

"I do, too, Eli."

Sallie fought the urge to dance her way down the street. It was a dream—but if it was a dream, what was she doing with the box in her hands? Well, there was one way to find out for certain. She stopped in a shop doorway, stuck her hand into the box, and withdrew one of the bankbooks. She looked at the name of the bank embossed in gold leaf on the front. Sallie retraced her steps, walked around the corner, and continued walking until she came to the bank. She entered, walked up to the bank teller and handed him the small blue book. "I'd like . . . five hundred dollars, please."

Five minutes later, Sallie walked out of the bank in a daze, the five hundred dollars safe in her purse. It was real, it wasn't a dream. She tripped down the street, giddy with the knowledge that everything Alvin Waring had said was true.

The money secure in her purse and loose bills in the pocket of her dress, Sallie stopped first at the Mercantile Company for a bag of canned peaches that she immediately handed over to Billy along with ten dollars. She handed out money to all the hard rock miners, admonishing them to eat some good food and to take a bath before they spent the rest in the Red Onion.

Sallie opened the door to the bingo palace with her own key. In the bright sun filtering into the large room, it looked like a sleazy, smoky, rinky-dink parlor with rough furniture, a rickety bar, bare windows, a cashier's cage, and a small stage that doubled as the bingo stand, where the bingo numbers were called, and where she sang at the beginning and end of the evening. She walked around, touching the felt-covered poker tables at the far end of the room, sitting down and then getting up from the bingo benches. She straightened the stack of bingo cards into a neater pile. Maybe she should throw everything out and start from scratch. She sat down again and closed her eyes. How best to pretty things up? A real stage, small, with a red velvet curtain that opened and closed. Matching draperies on the windows that could be closed in the winter. Chandeliers over the tables for better lighting. Perhaps a spotlight for the stage. A new bar, the kind the Arizona Club had, shiny mahogany with a brass railing. Leather stools with brass trim to match the bar. A new floor with some sections of it carpeted. No more spittoons. Definitely a new front door with glass panels, maybe even colored glass. She'd have some trees planted around the building, flowers if they would grow. She walked over to the farthest corner of the room, where she sat when things were slow or when she just wanted time by herself. She sat down on a wobbly chair and leaned her arms on a table whose legs didn't match. She smiled when the table rocked back and forth the same way her chair did. Cotton said the man who made the chair and table had a crooked eye. She wondered if she would miss things the way they were now. Old things were comfortable. New things took some getting used to.

Sallie stared at the small stage where she called out the bingo numbers hour after hour. She was always happy when a grizzly miner won his four bits and whooped in delight, his dirty boots stomping on the floor, the other miners cheering him on.

The bingo palace didn't make a lot of money, barely enough to pay the winners and herself. The doors opened at noon for her regular customers. By paying close attention she was able to tell which customers were hungry, which customers came to gamble, and which ones just wanted to hear her sing. The hungry ones were her biggest problem. Jeb, the owner of the steak house, allowed her to run a tab for hard-boiled eggs and pickles that she handed out on a daily basis. Most days if she had thirty customers she was lucky. The three poker tables covered in green felt had dust all over them. Most of her customers didn't have enough money to start up a poker hand, and those that did had to extend credit and write IOUs. The bingo cards were safer. Often she sat at one of the tables with her customers, playing poker for dry beans. She always lost. On rare occasions when one of the miners had a little extra in his poke, he'd lay money on the bar for her. Right before she closed at midnight she'd slip that same money under Jeb's door to pay off her marker.

What she really loved about her customers was the fact that they did their best to act like gentlemen when they came into the palace. They'd spruce up by slicking their hair back, shaking the dust from their clothes and boots. Most times they washed their hands even though they didn't have enough money for a room and a hot tub. She could always tell when they trimmed their whiskers, and she'd always compliment them and tell them they looked like fashionable Boston gentlemen. They'd cackle with glee and then she would laugh, too, when she was forced to admit she'd never seen a proper Boston gentleman.

Things were going to change now. For the first time in her young life, Sallie felt fear of the unknown. If only she weren't so ignorant of the world. There wasn't much she could do about the fear of the unknown. She could get some learning, though. She wished again for her brothers, Seth and Josh. If only she knew where they were. All in good time or, as Cotton said, Rome wasn't built in one day, whatever that meant.

In her room at the boardinghouse, with the door closed and locked, Sallie opened the wooden box. Sitting cross-legged in the middle of the bed, she looked at all the bankbooks—red ones, blue ones, green ones, two brown ones. So many numbers. She tried to comprehend the number of zeros. Mr. Waring made it sound like she could buy the world. The world! She wept then at her ignorance.

When there were no more tears to shed, Sallie's thoughts turned to Cotton Easter, her benefactor. *I don't understand, Cotton, if you had all that money, why did you live like you did? There were times when you were hungry and didn't have the money to rent a room. You didn't have a dollar for a bath. Life could have been so much easier for you.*

I wish you had let me know what you were planning. What should I do with all your money, Cotton? I never knew there was so much money in the world. You must want me to do something. What? She looked around, half-expecting to hear Cotton's voice. She flopped back against the ruffled pillows, the wooden box toppling over. She saw it then, the crinkled piece of white paper. A letter. Maybe it was for her, from Cotton. She crossed her fingers and then blessed herself. *Please let it be printed letters. Please, God, let me be able to read the words. Don't let me be ignorant now. I need to know why Cotton was so good and kind to me. Please, God. I'll build a church. I swear to You I will. I'll call it St. Cotton Easter. Cotton was a religious man. He prayed every day. He taught me a prayer. I promise I'll say it every day.*

Sallie squeezed her eyes shut as her fingers played with the folds of the crinkled letter. When she was calm, she spread the single sheet on her lap. The block letters and simple language brought tears to her eyes.

DEAR SALLIE,

IF YOU HAVE THIS LETTER IN HAND THEN YOU KNOW I DIED. I'M LEAVING YOU ALL I HAVE. I DON'T CARE WHAT YOU DO WITH IT. I MEAN THE MONEY. IT NEVER BROUGHT ME ANY HAPPINESS, BUT IT WILL ALLOW YOU TO BECOME A FINE LADY. ALVIN WILL HELP YOU. HE'S A GOOD MAN AND YOU CAN TRUST HIM. SALLIE, YOU WILL BE THE RICHEST WOMAN IN THE STATE OF NEVADA. YOU JUST BE CAREFUL WHO YOU TRUST. DON'T EVER TELL ANYONE THE WAY INTO THE SAFE. NOW YOU CAN STOP SLIDING INTO OTHER MEN'S BEDS. THERE'S NO NEED FOR YOU TO TELL ANYONE YOU DID THAT. REMEMBER WHAT I TOLD YOU. DON'T SHARE YOUR BUSINESS WITH OTHER PEOPLE. SOME THINGS NEED TO BE KEPT SECRET. I LOVE YOU, SALLIE. DON'T GO LAUGHING ON ME NOW. I KNOW I'M OLD ENOUGH TO BE YOUR PA OR YOUR GRANDDADDY. A MAN CAN'T HARDLY STOP WHAT HIS HEART FEELS. I DIDN'T EVEN WANT TO TRY. I WANT YOU TO BE HAPPY, SALLIE. YOU HAVE A GOOD, KIND HEART. SOMETIMES YOU ARE TOO GOOD. YOU TAKE CARE OF YOURSELF AND WHEN YOU HAVE TIME, VISIT MY GRAVE AND TALK TO ME. I WON'T BE ABLE TO ANSWER YOU, BUT I'LL BE ABLE TO HEAR YOU. THAT'S ALL I ASK OF YOU, SALLIE. I HOPE YOU FIND A GOOD MAN WHO WILL GIVE YOU CHILDREN AND WHO WILL LOVE YOU THE WAY YOU DESERVE TO BE LOVED. DON'T SHARE YOUR PAST,

SALLIE, OR IT WILL COME BACK TO HAUNT YOU. I LOVE
YOU, SALLIE.

YOUR FRIEND,
COTTON EASTER

Sallie rolled over on the bed and burst into tears. "I never got a
letter before," she whispered into her pillow. "I'll keep this letter forever and ever. I'll read it every day and I'll do what you say. I'll visit
and we'll talk. I'll talk and you listen. That's what you said, Cotton.
You have my promise that I won't . . . you know, do what you said."
A moment later she was off the bed and out the door. She ran, skid-
ding around the corners, not caring who saw her or what they
thought. She had something to do. Something important. Later she
could worry about acting like a lady.

When she arrived at the cemetery she was breathless and di-
sheveled. Her eyes were frantic as she searched out the mound of
dark earth that waited for the marker. When she saw the dried
flower petals she knew she had the right grave. She'd spent the last
of her money on the small bouquet. Now she could bring fresh flowers every day if she wanted to.

Sallie sat down on the hard ground. She brought her knees up to
her chin and hugged them with her arms. "Cotton, it's me, Sallie. I
got your letter today. It was in the box with all the bankbooks. It was
real nice of you to leave me all your money. I'm going to take the
train to Texas and visit my family. I took some of the money out of
the bank. I'm going to buy my mama a nice little house and a new
dress. I'll get things for the young ones, too, and maybe see about
getting them some learning. I can't wait to see my mother's face
when I walk in the door. She always said Seth would be the one to
make a lot of money. Seth was the oldest. I never knew him because
he lit out before I was born. So did Josh. Ma was so proud of her two
oldest sons. Every day she'd say they're coming back and will bring
presents for everyone. They never did. Then Ma stopped talking
about them. I don't even know what they look like, Cotton. Ma said
they were the spittin' image of Pa. Maybe someday I can find them
and help them out. It don't seem right that I don't know what my
own brothers look like. All I can see, Cotton, is Ma's face. I know she
was pretty when she was a young girl, but Pa, he drained the life
out of her. I used to hear her cry at night, but she always had a smile
on her face in the morning.

"I haven't seen that house up in the hills yet. It must be a beautiful place to be called Sunrise. Maybe Mama will want to come here and live with me. That would be okay, wouldn't it, Cotton? I'll get her a fancy chair so she can just sit and do nothing. I'll bring her flowers and give her steak to eat every day. I'm going to get her the prettiest dress in the whole world. Fancy shoes, too, and stockings. A pearl necklace, Cotton. I'll rub glycerine on her hands, file her fingernails, and maybe put some polish on them. I don't know what I'll do about Pa. Maybe I'll just let him drink hisself to death. That seems to be the only thing that makes him happy.

"I'm going to buy a new dress, Cotton, for the trip. I want Ma to be proud of me when she sees me. I want to thank you for all this good. I promised God I was going to build a church and call it St. Cotton Easter. Maybe the preacher will let me sing on Sunday. I'd like that. I'll sing for you, Cotton. You look down on me, you hear. Do you have wings, Cotton? Jeb McGuire said angels have wings and they ring little bells. Course he was drunk when he said that. I like the way it sounds. I have so much to learn, Cotton. I don't hardly know nothing. I'm going to be twenty years old and I'm ignorant as some of them miners who never had any schoolin' at all.

"I know you wanted to be planted here, Cotton, but I been thinking. If I move into that house up in the hills, I won't be able to come here too much. I don't want you gettin' lonely here all by yourself. I'd be willing to dig you up and take you up there. Mr. Waring said there's all kinds of flowers and gardens. I could make you a cemetery and talk to you every day. I want you to think about that, Cotton, and when I come back the next time, I want a sign that you think it's okay. If Jeb is right, ring your little bell. It's going to be a couple of weeks till I can come back here. I'll tell you all about my trip to Texas on the train. Maybe I'll have my whole family with me when I come to visit next time. My mama will want to thank you personal like. She has manners, my mama does.

"I need to be going home now. I'll be here on Sunday when they put up your marker. I want you to know, Cotton, I paid for that with my own money, not yours. I don't like to say good-bye so I'll just say I'll be back. The sagebrush smells real sweet today. There aren't any clouds in the sky. It's dusty and dry." There was genuine concern in her voice when she said, "If there aren't any clouds in the sky, what are you resting on?"

Sallie stood, smoothed down her dress, and did her best to tuck her flyaway blond curls back into place. She sniffed at the sagebrush-scented air before she waved her arm in a jaunty little salute of happiness.

Sallie climbed down from the wagon that was loaded with her personal possessions. She savored the moment by squeezing her eyes shut and then opening them slowly, drinking in the sight of her new home. In her life she had never dreamed such a place existed. The flower borders surrounding the house were every color of the rainbow. She bent down to touch the dark soil. It was moist to the touch, and from somewhere she could hear water dripping. The lawn was springy underfoot and damp, greener than a carpet of emeralds. She looked to the left and then to the right. "Now I know why Cotton's granddaddy called this place Sunrise," she murmured.

She backed up until she was standing between a row of tall stately-looking trees that afforded her a better look at the house, which was now hers. Pristine white columns glistened in the sun. She thought about the tar paper shack she'd lived in with her family back in Texas, a shanty with no windows and a door that had to be nailed shut and stuffed with rags in the winter. The door on this house was stout and beautiful, with tiny diamond-shaped panes of colored glass at the top. A heavy brass handle was just as shiny as the windows. But it was the heavy quarry stone in muted shades of gray and brown that brought a smile to her face. There would be no drafts in this house in the winter.

Sallie meandered around the grounds. Benches circled trees, and stone ornaments of different animals dotted the little path that led nowhere. It was cool and dim, green and lush. She tried to imagine herself sitting in the gazebo with a frosty glass of lemonade, dressed in a frilly pink afternoon dress, with a book in hand she couldn't read. She giggled. "Oh, Cotton, you should see me now."

She was at the front door now. Should she lift the heavy brass knocker? Should she fit the huge brass key into the lock? She was saved from making a decision when the heavy door creaked open. A plump woman, wearing a white apron and a braid of hair that circled her head like a halo, smiled. "Please, miss, come in. Joseph will see to your bags. I am Anna. I cook and clean. My husband tends the gardens and takes care of the animals. Come, come, let me show you your new home."

"Can you open the windows?" Sallie asked.

"But of course. Would you like me to open them for you?"

"Oh, yes. Yes, yes, I would. I want to see the curtains flutter in the breeze. Do all the windows have screens?"

"Yes. I do not open them because Joseph and I don't use the house. We live in one of the cottages in the back. Is there anything you'd like me to do for you now?"

"I'd like to see my room and maybe take a bath. If you don't mind, I'd like to walk through the house myself and look at things."

"It is your house, Miss Coleman. Do you have anything in particular that you'd like me to make for your dinner?"

"It doesn't matter. I do like pie, though. Sweet pie. Very sweet." She smiled wickedly and patted her hips. "I like gravy and potatoes. I like most anything."

"Joseph has a garden he tends. I can the vegetables for the winter. We have a wonderful cold cellar. The special room is in the back. Joseph has the key. He'll turn it over to you at supper. Is there anything else I can do for you? Would you like me to draw your bath?"

"No, thank you. I want to do all that myself. Later on we can discuss your . . . duties."

Lordy, Lordy, Lordy, she was acting like a grand mistress. How wonderful it felt! She sobered almost immediately when she thought about how her mother waited on other people and wore herself down to nothing more than skin and bones. Sallie made a promise to herself that she would never take advantage of anyone who worked for her. Cotton always said you should treat people the way you yourself wanted to be treated. He was right. She'd learned so much from Cotton.

Sallie walked from room to room, her lips pursed in a round circle of approval. She didn't know how she knew, but she was sure that this house looked like houses in Boston. All of the shiny dark furniture must have belonged to Cotton's grandmother or mother. The rugs were thin, colorful, with fringes around the edge. Some were round, most of them square. There were big ones and little ones. Her mother was purely going to smile and smile when she described the brilliant bird in the center of one particular rug. But always, in each room, her gaze settled on the windows and the lace curtains.

She chose a room at the end of the long hallway that overlooked the lush green gardens. The small balcony leading off the dressing room made her squeal in delight. She loved the French doors and the fine wooden floors. The high four-poster with the three-step stool with its canopy of lace made her grin from ear to ear. "I can't hardly believe this," she whispered to herself. Two giant closets rested side by side on one wall. Plenty of room for her ricky-ticky saloon gowns and feather boas. A dresser with flowered marble drawer pulls on all nine drawers caused her to suck in her breath. She didn't have enough underwear to fill the deep cavities. She walked around the room, finally sitting down on a sky-blue satin chaise longue that looked like no one had ever sat in it. Well, she was going to sit in it every day.

Now it was time to open the windows. She pushed the lace curtains aside, stretched her arms to push and tug at the window, and reached down for the wooden screen. She waited for the lace curtains to billow inward. When nothing happened, Sallie rustled the curtains. Still they didn't move inward. She was so disappointed she wanted to cry. She marched over to the bed and climbed up. She sat, determined to wait as long as she had to, until the curtains moved.

Maybe she should lie down and rest her eyes. Within minutes she was sound asleep. The afternoon passed quietly, and she woke when she felt a warm movement of air. She wiped the sleep from her eyes, uncertain if she was truly awake or not. A smile that rivaled the afternoon sunshine stretched across her face when she saw the lace curtains dance in the breeze. "Ohhhh," was all she could think of to say. "This is the happiest day of my life," she said aloud. "Thank you, Cotton, thank you from the bottom of my heart."

Sallie forgot about the step stool and slid off the bed, landing on her backside. She laughed then, peals of joy, as she kicked out with her legs, banging the heels of her shoes on the carpeted floor.

Time for her bath. She looked around for the doorway and saw her bags and boxes stacked neatly to the side. Anna must have unpacked while she slept. The door to one of the closets was slightly ajar. The garish saloon dresses looked out of place. The feathered hair ornaments she wore with her colored boas rested on the top shelf. They, too, looked out of place. A warm flush crept up to her neck and cheeks. She checked the dresser and wasn't surprised to see that her worn underwear and stockings filled only half of one of the drawers. She wished she had been the one to unpack her belongings. The flush of shame and embarrassment that someone else had seen her threadbare underwear deepened. Her shoulders stiffened. Everything was clean and mended. There was no need for shame.

In the huge, galvanized tub full of bubbles, Sallie leaned back, one long soapy leg extended. She eyed the red polish on the tip of her toes. Decadent! "Who cares!" She scrubbed and rubbed with a cloth that was softer than feathers until her skin was red. The length of

toweling was just as soft, and long and wide enough to wrap completely around herself. She loved the way it made her feel. She stared
at her reflection in the mirror. Her blond hair curled in ringlets
around her ears and neck. She smoothed it back until it was slick
against her head. When she wore her hair pulled back like this she
looked older, more experienced. When her curls tumbled about her
face she looked fifteen.

She thought about her mother again as she dressed. Her mother's
hair was like her own, but dull and usually greasy. She wore it
pulled back from her sweet face with a string. Sallie was going to
buy her a pearl necklace and some earrings. She'd take some of the
soap that smelled like roses and wash her mother's hair and fix it
the way the ladies in town wore their hair. She knew how to do these
things now. Her mother was going to be a queen, and her little sisters would be princesses. She could make it happen now that she had
all the money in the world.

Tomorrow she was going back to town. Tonight, when she got
ready to sleep in the high bed, she was going to make a list of things
to do when she got there. She wasn't going to wait one minute longer
than necessary before she returned to Texas to see her family.

Sallie felt every inch the grand lady when Anna served her supper in the dining room at the long table with the huge centerpiece
of fresh flowers. The meal was hearty and heavy—thick steak, fried
potatoes, gravy, sliced tomatoes, and bread spread with real butter.
She thought about the thin gruel and the hard bread spread with lard
that she'd eaten when she lived in Texas. Well, that was never going
to happen again. Never, ever. She dug into her rhubarb pie with a
vengeance and asked for a second helping. When she was finished
with her meal she asked for Joseph.

"Ma'am, how can I help you?" he asked respectfully.

"I want to go back to town tomorrow, early, before the sun comes
up. I plan on . . . going to Texas. I'm not sure when I'll be back."

"Would you like me to take you in the automobile, ma'am?"

"Why, yes, I would purely love that. Where did Mr. Easter get an
automobile?"

"Won it fair and square in a poker game. I learned to drive it all
by myself. Mr. Easter didn't want no part of something on four
wheels with an engine. He said it was the devil's own machine. I'll
be ready at sunup."

"So will I," Sallie responded smartly. "How hard was it to learn,
Joseph?"

"Not hard at all, ma'am. I could teach you when you get back. You need to practice so's you don't run into no trees and scrub along the way."

"You need to wear a hat, miss," Anna said. "Your hair will look like the end of a broom if you don't. Dust and sand get in your eyes. Joseph wears special spectacles when he drives that machine."

"Will you be wanting to see the secret room now?" The old man held out a key ring with a large brass key dangling from the end.

"Yes, I would, Joseph. Thank you for supper, Anna. It was real good, specially that pie. Who pays you your wages, Anna?"

"Mr. Waring. He comes up here on the first of every month. In the winter he pays us for three or four months at a time. Will you be thinking of changing that, ma'am?"

"No. But, maybe he should be paying you more now that I'm going to live here and you will have more duties. I'll speak to him. If you want someone else to help you, I can ask in town."

"I would have no objection to someone helping out. Joseph and me, we ain't young'uns anymore. Our bones creak a bit. Whatever you think best, ma'am." Sallie nodded, and followed Joseph out of the dining room.

"This be the room, miss." Joseph held out the key and withdrew discreetly. Sallie waited until the old man was out of sight before she fit the key into the lock. The door swung open. She stepped into a huge, bare room with no windows. Sallie held the lamp high in order to see better. Against the wall was the largest safe she'd ever seen. It went from floor to ceiling, an iron monster, shiny black with a huge silver eye in the middle and a thick iron handle.

It took Sallie six tries before she managed to open the safe. When she heard the final click on the dial, she yanked at the handle. The heavy door refused to budge. She dug her heels into the carpeted floor and pulled backward until she thought her head was going to explode right off her neck. The door creaked open. With her back against the inside of the door, she shoved with her backside until there was enough room to look inside. For the first time in her life she grew faint. Six long shelves, maybe six feet long, were filled with small burlap sacks. Each appeared to be the same size and weight. She opened three of the sacks. Gold. A wooden box full of papers sat square in the middle of the third shelf. Directly underneath was a second wooden box, this one with a lid. Sallie removed the lid and stared down at thick stacks of money.

Sallie sat down on the floor and hugged her knees. She stared at the contents of the safe, wondering what she was meant to do with this fortune.

A long time later, when the lamp started to smoke, Sallie pushed the massive door closed, twirled the knob, and backed out of the room. Her footsteps were sluggish as she made her way back to her room. Her shoulders slumped as she undressed and pulled on her nightgown. She wished suddenly that she could turn time backwards. She wished she'd never gone to Alvin Waring's office, wished Cotton were still alive, wished she were back at the bingo palace singing for her customers. In just three short days her life had been turned upside down. "I don't know what to do," she whispered into her pillow. "I understand, Cotton, this was a load on your shoulders, and that's why you didn't want it all. Maybe if I get more learning, it will be different. I don't think so, though. Is this what you meant when you said money was the root of all evil? Will I turn evil? I don't want to be evil. I just want to be me. The Lord, He must want me to be here. He must have placed His hand on your shoulder and told you to do this. I don't know why. Maybe I'll never know."

Sallie wept then, like the child she was. Eventually she slept, her pillow stained with tears.

The next four days passed like a whirlwind. Sallie shopped for new clothes, then purchased two valises and packed them with gifts for her family. She spent hours with Alvin Waring signing papers, making arrangements for the church to be built. She carried her plans one step farther and asked to have a town house built for herself so she wouldn't have to go back and forth to the house on the mountain. The last order of business was instructing Alvin Waring to buy the bingo palace and remodel it.

Sunday found her at the cemetery along with Cotton's friends. The preacher said his few words, she said hers, and Alvin Waring made a small speech that dealt with life and death, the Lord, and anyone else whose name he could remember. The preacher blessed the marker as Sallie placed her bouquet of flowers at its base.

The bingo palace was opened for the luncheon spread that Sallie paid her old landlady to prepare. Sallie sang song after song until her throat was hoarse. When it was over, she helped clear away the debris. Then she closed the door and didn't look back. In two hours time she was going to step onto the train that would take her to Texas and the family she'd left behind.

The last thing she said to Alvin Waring was, "I would appreciate it if you would increase Anna and Joseph's wages. I'd like it very much if you could find someone else to help out. There's a young Chinese girl at the laundry house who might be interested in the job. Her name is Su Li. She has a sister and a brother. If I bring my family back here, I'm going to need lots of help. They work very hard at the laundry. Children shouldn't have to work that hard. If they're interested, tell them I'll pay them good wages and they won't have to work on Sundays."

"I'll speak with them, Miss Coleman. Have a safe trip. I hope everything turns out the way you want it to. Call on me when you return; I'm at your service."

"Thank you, Mr. Waring, for everything. I'd like it if you'd call me Sallie. You won't forget to call the Pinkertons and have them start a search for my brothers Seth and Josh. It's mighty important for me to find them so I can share my . . . just share."

"I'll take care of it . . . Sallie. You take care of yourself."

"I will." The child in her bubbled over. "I can't wait to see my mother. I bought her all these fine things. I hope she likes them. She will, won't she, Mr. Waring?"

"Of course she will, child. I think, though, more than anything, she's going to be so happy to see you, she won't be thinking of fine presents. Your love and the fact that you're going back to help will be all she wants. Mark my word."

"What does that mean, Mr. Waring, mark my word?"

"It means what I said is almost certainly true."

"Oh. Good-bye, Mr. Waring." She reached up on her toes to kiss the dry, withered cheek.

Alvin Waring stood for a long time watching the train chuff out of sight. If he'd been younger, he would have run after the train. He sighed. He had a long list of things to do for Sallie, and there was no time like the present to get started. It would be a labor of love.

Tears of happiness dripped down Sallie's cheeks. She didn't care. *I'm coming, Mama. I'm going to make everything better for you. I'm coming, Mama.*

She was going home.

2

There was nothing pretty about the barren town outside of Abilene, Texas. It was just as hot and dry and miserable as it was the day she left six years ago with the medicine show. The only thing different, as far as Sallie could see, was that people were staring at her. When she'd gone through the town six years ago, no one had looked at her twice. She'd been one of those shiftless Colemans.

Sallie's shoulders stiffened, her head going up several degrees. She could stare them down today. She *would* stare them down. Six years ago she hadn't been able to do that. She paid the driver of the hackney and added a generous tip when he carried her bags into the town's only hotel.

Sallie walked over to the desk, aware that every eye in the lobby was on her. Not one person recognized her, she could tell. Well, they were going to recognize her in another second. She signed her name carefully and waited for the desk clerk to turn the registration book around to stare at her signature. Sallie smiled sweetly when the man's eyebrows shot upward, almost to his hairline. She fought the urge to laugh.

"Will you be staying with us long, Miss . . . ah . . . Coleman?"

"As long as it takes, sir."

"I see."

I see . . . it was something people said when they didn't know what else to say. A devil perched itself on Sallie's shoulder. "What exactly do you see . . . sir?"

"Well . . . I—"

"I see," Sallie said. This time she did laugh. Cotton always said if you laughed, the world laughed with you. He also said if you cried, no one cared.

Sallie turned around to look at the people sitting in the lobby filled with dusty plants. All men, of course, with nothing to do but play checkers and gossip like old women. They were speculating about her. She knew the moment she was out of sight, the desk clerk would tell everyone she was Harry Coleman's daughter. Well, he could shout it from the housetops for all she cared. What she cared about right now was getting a bath and a clean change of clothes. Then, she was going to head toward the Emporium and buy out the store for her mother and sisters. The pretty flowered dress with the lace collar for her mother was already packed in her bag, along with the strand of pearls and the gold and pearl earrings. She'd thought of everything, lacy underwear, something her mother never owned in her life. Hose, soft leather shoes, and a pair of bedroom slippers that were buttery soft. She couldn't wait to see the smile on her mother's tired face when she told her that from this day on, she was going to become a lady and people would wait on her. From this day forward her mother wasn't going to lift even her little finger as far as work was concerned. She thought about her father for just a second. Well, he could come with them, or he could stay behind. It would be his decision.

"Please arrange for hot water. I'd like to take a bath as soon as possible."

"Bath time is six o'clock."

"For other people. I want mine now, sir." Sallie placed a bill on the counter and watched it disappear faster than a lightning streak. She smiled. "Is there someone to carry my bags?"

"Zeke, grab hold of the lady's bags and take them upstairs. The water will be up in twenty minutes."

It was almost noon when Sallie, clad in a pumpkin-colored dress with matching shoes and handbag, walked down the steps to the lobby. She posed a moment so the occupants could get a good look at her pretty dress.

Outside in the hot, June sunshine, Sallie paused for a moment to get her bearings. She saw the bakery and remembered how heavenly the smells were. She made a mental note to buy a big sack of sweets for her mother. She'd eat some herself. She swore then that the money in her purse was starting to get hot. Time to spend it on her family. Lordy, Lordy, she could hardly wait.

Sallie was a shopkeeper's dream as she walked from one table to the next, picking, choosing, hoping she was getting the right sizes. The pile of merchandise on the counter mounted steadily. Toys, picture books, games, pencils, crayons, shoes, stockings, underwear, dresses, nightwear, sweaters. Bag of licorice, all-day suckers. In a separate pile she added toothbrushes, tooth powder, combs, brushes, sweet-smelling soap, and glycerine for her mother.

"While you wrap these things, I'm going over to the bakery. I'll need someone to take me to my parents' house. Can you arrange that? It's five miles or so. I'll pay for the trip. I'm not sure if we'll return with the driver or not."

"These things will be ready when you get back, miss. It's been a pleasure doing business with you. I have a man who will drive you. What'd you say your name was?"

"I didn't," Sallie said as she sashayed out the door.

In the bakery Sallie bought three of everything. In the glass case to the far left, she noticed crocks of homemade butter and jam. She bought two of each.

Now she was ready to go home. Ready to shower her family with her own good fortune. This, she decided, was the second-best day of her whole life. She was a child again, clapping her hands, pounding her feet on the floor of the wagon she was riding in. She started to sing, her young voice pure and sweet. The driver smiled. Who was this young girl with the voice of an angel?

Sallie's happiness came to an abrupt stop when she saw the row of mean-looking shanties the tenant farmers lived in. Even from a distance they were a blight to the land. She counted down, one, two, three, four. Her home for thirteen years.

"It don't look like nobody lives here, miss. Are you sure this is the right place?"

"This is the right place." Sallie clenched her teeth. He was right; most of the shanties were leaning so far to the side, a good wind would topple them. The doors on most of them were missing, except for number four in the row.

She saw someone, on the side of the shanty. Her sister Peggy.

Sallie didn't wait for the driver of the wagon to rein in his horse. She pulled up her skirt and jumped down, not caring that the heels of her new shoes would get dirty, or that they might break. She ran, shouting that she was home. She expected squeals of happiness, hugs and kisses. Peggy stared at her. "It's me, Sallie. Come here, give me a kiss and a hug. What's wrong? Look at the wagon, I brought presents. Where's Mama? Peggy, talk to me, honey. Is Pop in the fields, or drunk-asleep in the house? Mama, I'm home!" she shouted at the top of her lungs. To the driver, she said, "Unload the packages."

Sallie was almost to the door when Peggy reached for her arm. Tears rolled down her cheeks. "Pop died last year, Sallie. We buried him behind the shack. Mama died two months ago. Maggie got herself a man when Mama got sick. She left with him last month and took the little ones with her. I didn't try to stop her, Sallie. Maggie will take good care of them. I knew you'd keep your promise and come back. You look so pretty, Sallie."

Sallie's face drained as she fought to take a deep breath. A sick feeling settled in the pit of her stomach. "Was she sick, Peggy?"

Peggy screwed her freckled face into a grimace so she wouldn't cry. "She wasted away to nothing. Most times there wasn't enough food. This place . . . it robbed her of everything, Sallie. Me and Maggie, we did our best, but it wasn't good enough. I have a job in town and live in a boardinghouse. It don't pay much. They give me supper and I get a bath twice a week. I come out here once a week with a flower. I put it between both graves. Do you want to see the graves, Sallie?"

She didn't, but she said she did so Peggy wouldn't cry. "This place, it's all wrong. I'm going to look into seeing if . . . we can . . . move . . . It's not right, them being buried here in this god-awful place. Peggy, I want you to come back to Nevada with me. I have a beautiful house with lots of rooms. The windows open. There are flowers and a whole garden of green grass. You can take a bath every hour of the day. We can move Mama and Pa and make a . . . private cemetery. A family place."

"Oh, Sallie, I don't think I can leave. If Maggie or the others come back, they won't know where to find me . . . us. Maybe next year. Are you rich, Sallie?"

"I'm so rich it scares me. I just got all this money, or I would have come sooner. I did send money, Peggy."

"I know. Pa took it. Mama said you were a good girl to remember your mama. She said that, Sallie."

"Did you walk all the way out here, Peggy?"

Peggy nodded. "I don't mind the coming part. Going back is hard because I'm leaving Mama. I want to cry so bad, Sallie."

"Me too. Let's sit here by the graves and have us a real good cry. We have each other, Peggy. I'm glad you stayed. I don't know what I would have done if no one was here."

The sisters clung to one another, their tears mingling. They sobbed great heart-wrenching sounds, for their past and for the mother they both loved. When there were no more tears, Sallie helped Peggy to her feet. "I'm going to try and make this right for all of us."

"How, Sallie?"

"We're going to settle you in a house and open a bank account for you. I want you to get some learning so you can write me letters. I need to get some learning myself. I don't want either one of us to be ignorant. I'm going to buy you the finest of everything, and then I'm going to take you to the best restaurant. We're going to eat and eat and talk and talk until we're talked out. Would you like that, Peggy?"

"Oh, yes, Sallie, I purely would."

"Do you say your prayers every night and go to church? I sound like Mama, don't I?"

Peggy smiled. "You sound just like her, Sallie. I think that's good. I don't feel so sad anymore."

Sallie wrapped her arms around her sister. "We have a lot of things to do, so the sooner we get busy, the sooner I can get you settled. Do you like to shop?"

Peggy looked down at her faded dress. "I don't know. Everything I have is a hand-me-down."

"That's changing right now. Get in the wagon, Peggy."

The next five days passed in a flurry of shopping. A small three-bedroom house was purchased on a pretty tree-lined street. Furniture and rocking chairs for every room in the house and the front porch were placed reverently by both young women. The mercantile company delivered two loads of boxes—shoes, dresses, shawls, coats, hats, household goods, curtains, pillows, carpeting and anything else that appealed to young Peggy.

Sallie dusted her hands dramatically. "I think Mama would have loved this little house. I know she's in heaven smiling down on us. I feel her, don't you, Peggy?"

"I purely do, Sallie. Every time I sit in one of these rocking chairs I'm going to imagine Mama sitting across from me. I'll talk to her and tell her how good you are. I want to plant a garden, the kind Mama always said she wanted, with vegetables in the middle and flowers on the borders. I want to put some flowers in the window boxes, too. Can we do that, Sallie?"

"Of course we can. We'll go right now to get the plants and seeds and some buckets for you to water everything. I hope you don't love this place so much you won't want to come to Nevada."

"I'll come to visit. With all that money you put in the bank for me, I can visit you anytime I want."

"Sallie, if the others come back, you let me know right away, so I can do the same for them. Promise me."

"I promise," Peggy said solemnly.

The two young women worked side by side during the following days. Sallie finally asked in a hushed whisper for the details of her mother's death.

"She was worn-out, Sallie. Too many years of getting by with nothing so the rest of us could survive took its toll. When Pa died, she didn't care no more. She just plain gave up. Each day I could see a change in her. The little ones, they didn't . . . they cried all the time. That's why Maggie took them away. Mr. Rivers, he gave me my pay ahead of time so I could get a pine box and a dress for Mama. It was plain and she wouldn't of liked it, but it was the best I could do. All she talked about at the end was Seth. She kept asking if he was coming, and I kept saying he was delayed. She tried to hold on because she believed me. Mothers must love their firstborn sons more than the others. It broke my heart, Sallie. Maggie and me, even the little ones, we're the ones who did for her just like you did. She didn't say one word about us, just Seth and Josh. Seth broke her heart. She was dying, ready to go to heaven, and all she wanted was Seth. You best remember that, Sallie. Your firstborn son will break your heart if you let him."

Sallie's throat squeezed shut. "Did she *ever* say anything about me?"

"Only that you were a good girl for remembering your mama."

Sallie's voice was fierce when she said, "I'm hiring the Pinkertons to find Seth and Josh. And, when they do, I'm going to give them a piece of my mind. They never sent a penny home, never came back, not even once. That makes them no-accounts in my eyes." Sallie's voice grew more fierce when she said, "Mama loved us, I know she did. Pa loved us, too, in his own besotted way. If they didn't, I'd feel something in my heart."

Peggy's face set into stubborn lines. "They loved Seth and Josh best. Girls don't amount to anything. Mama said the sun rises and sets on boy babies. She said that, Sallie."

"That's not true, Peggy. You listen to me good now, you hear. I am going to amount to something, and so are you. Before that can happen we have to get some learning. We can go to college if we want. You know those willow trees that soak up water? Well, you and me, we're going to be like those trees, soaking up our learning till we are so . . . educated, we will be able to do whatever we want. Girls do account for something, and don't you ever forget it. I'm the richest woman in the state of Nevada. What do you think of that?"

"I think," Peggy said, throwing her dirty arms around Sallie, "Mama is in heaven giving you her blessing. Will being the richest woman in Nevada make you the happiest woman in Nevada?"

Sallie plucked a clump of marigolds from the box next to her. "I don't know. I was happy when I was at the bingo palace singing for my friends. It makes my heart feel good to help you. I don't know if that's the same thing as being happy. Look, we're done. It's going to be beautiful when the vegetables sprout and the flowers bloom. You be sure to always put flowers on the table the way Mama wanted."

"I don't know how to thank you, Sallie."

"You don't have to thank me, Peggy. I'm your sister. I just want one promise from you, that you and I will never drift apart. Can you make that promise?"

"I promise. I'm so glad you kept your promise to come back here."

"And I'm so glad that you had the good sense to stay on here to wait for me. Let's make dinner in your new house and then sit on the front porch and talk to Mama in heaven. Tomorrow I have to leave. I'll be back, though."

"I'm going to miss you, Sallie."

"For a little while. You're going to be busy now with all your schooling and taking care of this little house. Soon as you can, write me long letters."

Hand in hand, the two sisters walked through the garden to the little white house nestled behind a white picket fence.

On a clear summer day filled with blue skies and golden sunshine, Sallie Coleman laid to rest her parents, and her best friend, Cotton Easter, in the small cemetery that Joseph, her houseman, had prepared. It would be a special place with green grass and borders of flowers. A whitewashed rail fence surrounded the special place that rested under an ageless umbrellalike tree, with leaves greener than emeralds.

Sallie knew very little about death and dying. "Do you think they'll be happy here, Joseph? It's warm and sunny and the tree . . . the tree shades the . . . the plots. When the earth settles, you can plant the grass and flowers. This is . . . this is a family cemetery. It's my family. Someday, a long time from now, when it's time for me to join Mama and Pa, I can . . . I can be . . . planted here, too. That's a long way away, so I probably shouldn't be thinking about that right now. I want to say a prayer for my parents and one for Cotton, too. I am not going to think of this as a sad place. It's too pretty to be sad. It comforts me to know I can come here and talk to Mama anytime I want. The preacher said his words in town, so this is . . . private."

The burden of moving Cotton's body to this tranquil place rested heavily on her shoulders. She added a third prayer, asking God to make it right with Cotton.

"Should I start now, miss?" Joseph asked.

"Yes. Please, Joseph, you have to plant the sagebrush before the end of the day. Don't tire yourself."

"My two sons will be along soon to help me. They'll be bringing the brush with them. It will be finished by sundown, just the way you want."

"Do you believe in angels, Joseph?" Sallie's voice was fretful, uncertain.

The old man stared at her a moment. "I do, miss."

"So do I. I truly do. I do believe, Joseph, we have three angels here who are going to look after us. I worry sometimes that I might make a mistake. I don't want to do that. I feel . . . great comfort today knowing my parents and friend are here, so that must mean I was supposed to be doing this. Do you agree with me, Joseph?"

"Yes, miss, I do. It's a pretty place. I think now old Mr. Easter must have known you were going to do this when he had them people come to make his artesian well."

"How can that be, Joseph? Cotton's daddy didn't know me?"

"If he's an angel, he knows you. Angels see and know everything. He knew his son, Cotton, was going to be leaving you this place someday. He prepared it for you."

Sallie flushed a bright pink. She didn't know angels could see and hear everything. She was truly ignorant. She turned to leave. *"Everything?"*

"Everything," Joseph said sagely. "I hear an automobile, miss."

"That's Mr. Waring. Don't work too hard, Joseph. The sun is brutal today. Don't you have a hat?"

Joseph pointed to the tree and the shade it created. Sallie nodded as she made her way to the front entrance of the house. She arrived just as Alvin Waring climbed from his auto.

"The day's almost as pretty as you are, Miss Sallie."

"I do like to hear pretty words, Mr. Waring. Would you like to sit in the garden or in the house?"

"The garden is fine. I like to see all this green grass and flowers. Don't get to see much of it in town. This place is an oasis."

Sallie made a mental note to ask the old lawyer what an oasis was after their business was completed. "You must be parched. You get all your papers ready, and I'll fetch us some lemonade." She was jittery, her hands wrinkling the sash on her dress, then smoothing it out.

A long time later, Sallie looked first at her empty glass, then at the pile of papers in front of her. It could all be in some foreign language as far as she was concerned.

"Now, Sallie, we need to discuss your trip to California and the lady I spoke to you about. When do you think you can leave?"

Sallie licked at her dry lips. "I've changed my mind, Mr. Waring. I don't want someone teaching me to be a lady. I am what I am. What I would like is for you to find me someone who will come here and work with me on my reading, writing, and numbers. I want to learn to read the whole newspaper. I want to learn about the stock market and how that works. I want book learning. I want that person to come here and live in my house and teach me here. I can pay whatever they want. Can you arrange that?"

"Are you sure, Sallie? What about your business in town?"

"I'm never going to give that up. When my town house is finished, I'll stay there during the week and come up here on the weekends or . . . during the week if I decide to stay open on the weekends. I'm not sure yet. I have a friend who might be interested in working at the palace until I make my final decisions. I just have so many things in my head right now. Sometimes I think this is all a dream, and I'm going to wake up back in the shanty. I'm not smart enough to make good decisions yet."

"I think you've done amazingly well, considering the circumstances," Waring said dryly.

The summer blue eyes sparked and then blazed. "I don't think I need to make explanations or apologize for anything I do as long as my heart is pure."

"I think that about covers all our business, Miss Sallie. The church is coming along nicely. Another month or so if the weather holds, and it will be finished. Your town house should be ready by September. Oh, the help you asked for will be brought up here in a few weeks. The young girl had to find someone to take her place. She and her brother are most grateful for your job offer."

"I'm grateful to *you* for coming all the way up here. Do you know, Mr. Waring, where Cotton's daddy and granddaddy are buried?"

"In the church cemetery not far from town. Why?"

"Do you think I should bring them up here? For Cotton."

"Bless your heart, child. I think it can be arranged."

A bubble of hysterical laughter crept into Sallie's voice. "I keep digging up all these dead people—Mama, Pa, Cotton, and now his daddy and granddaddy. I just think everybody belongs together. What do you think, Mr. Waring?"

"You're right, child, families belong together. Now, Miss Sallie, are you sure you don't want to—"

Anticipating what the attorney was about to say, Sallie said, "No, I don't want to go to California. I don't want some teaching lady trying to make me into someone I'm not. I don't want to be a society lady. My mama, she'd purely turn over in her grave if I did that. She would, Mr. Waring. She wouldn't mind at all for me to get some learning, though. I haven't been able to sleep at night worrying about this. My mind's made up."

"Then it's settled," Alvin Waring said. "I applaud you, Miss Sallie, for standing by your convictions." At her puzzled look he said, "It means I'm proud of you."

Sallie's smile rivaled the sun for brightness. "Nobody ever said that to me, Mr. Waring. Even Cotton never said he was proud of me. It was a fine thing for you to say. Would you like to stay for lunch? Anna makes a meat pie that fair melts in your mouth. I saw fresh shelled peas and carrots no bigger than your finger. Her biscuits are the best I ever tasted."

"I wish I could, Miss Sallie, but after today's visit there is much work to be done. The next time I come up I'd be grateful if you'd invite me to stay over for the night. It's a long ride back to town. Now, is there anything else you can think of that you'd like me to do?"

"If something comes to me, I'll send Joseph to town."

"Always remember, you make the decisions, no one else. When you pay someone to do something for you, when you hire them, it's what you want. You can say or do whatever you want because you are in control. Control, Sallie. That's the key to success. Money gives you power. Power gives you control. Don't ever, for one minute, forget my words."

"I'll remember, Mr. Waring. Be careful going down the road."

Sallie stood in the bright sunshine watching Alvin Waring's car until it was out of sight. His words ricocheted inside her head. Money. Power. Control. She repeated the words over and over, until she was certain she would never, ever forget them.

Sallie walked out of the telegraph office with Alvin Waring at her side. "Thank you for sending the message to my sister Peggy. I can't wait for the day when I can come here and write the message myself."

"All in good time, young lady. Your sister is going to be just fine.

With your help she will make her entrance in today's world just the way you want her to. Trust me on this, Sallie."

"I know, I know. It's just so hard. All this money is a yoke on my back. Some days, Mr. Waring, I'm sorry I ever met you and Cotton. I swear before God that's a true saying."

"Speaking of Cotton. The church will be ready in about two weeks. The preacher wants to know if you'll sing the opening and closing hymn."

"Me! You want me to sing in church! Lordy, Lordy, I'll have to give that some thought, Mr. Waring."

"Think of it as your dedication to Cotton. I think he'll be mighty pleased."

"I think he'll laugh his head off. Sallie Coleman, saloon singer, singing hymns in church." Tears burned her eyes for a second time.

"Sallie, look at me." The old attorney gently tapped Sallie's chest with the tips of his fingers. "It's what's inside a person that counts, not the outer trappings. You are as beautiful inside as you are outside. Cotton knew that. He saw your goodness. I see it. You need to believe in yourself and put your past behind you. I'm not saying you should forget about your roots and all the bad things that happened to you. You've gone beyond that with Cotton's help. Now, you owe it to him to be the best you can be. Don't look back. Whatever came before is history."

"I'll try harder."

"Good. Come, Sallie, let's see how St. Cotton Easter is faring. I believe the pews were to be installed today. The stained glass windows are so beautiful they take your breath away. I'm sure the church will be full when the doors are open to the public. Think ahead, Sallie."

"I'm trying, Mr. Waring."

Overhead, a bird rustled in the branches of a tree. For a second, Sallie thought it was Cotton. She actually stopped in mid-stride, fully expecting to hear the tinkling sound of a bell. She blushed furiously when nothing happened. The midmorning sun seemed to drape Sallie in a golden light, while her shadow cloaked Alvin Waring.

Later, when Sallie was on her way home, Alvin Waring spoke with the preacher. "I swear to you, on my mother, I saw a halo around Sallie Coleman's head. It wasn't a trick of the sun and it wasn't because my eyes are old and tired. I saw it. It was radiant. I need you to explain what I saw, Preacher."

"God moves in mysterious ways, Mr. Waring. If you saw what you say you saw, He wanted you to see it. I guess this means I can expect to see you in the front pew with Miss Sallie when the church opens. Accept what you saw and go on from there."

Alvin Waring thought the preacher's voice mysterious, as though he knew something he had no intention of sharing. Goose bumps dotted the old attorney's arms. Cotton had said, on more than one occasion, that Sallie Coleman was an angel. Alvin tried to shake off his goose bumps as he headed for his automobile. Was it possible that a nearly twenty-year-old saloon singer and self-professed whore was an angel in disguise? He cleared his throat and decided the sun had tricked his eyes. A feeling of sadness washed over him. The few minutes he'd spent believing Sallie Coleman was an angel were happy moments. Now he felt like the crusty curmudgeon that he was.

Twice, on the drive to his offices, Alvin Waring thought he heard bells. He took his eyes off the road both times to see where the sound was coming from. He snorted, a manly sound of disgust. His hearing, like every other part of his body, was starting to deteriorate. He knew in that minute, had the devil appeared on the hood of his auto to bargain for his soul in return for his youth, he would have traded without a second thought.

Because of Sallie Coleman.

3

"Now, Joseph, do you really trust me to drive this vehicle? Are you sure I can do this? What if an animal runs in front of me? I'm too jittery. I don't like wearing these things over my eyes. What if people laugh at me? I never saw a woman drive a car. Lordy, Lordy, what if it breaks down and I have to walk?"

Joseph threw his hands in the air. "You said you were ready, Miss Sallie. It's just a machine. Human beings are smarter than machines. Animals will not run in front of the car, it makes too much noise. Animals run and hide when they hear it. If you don't like the special glasses, take them off, but you'll get grit in your eyes and then they'll get all red and painful. No one is going to laugh at you. I do believe they will envy you. If the car breaks down, you have to walk. It's all very simple, Miss Sallie. Sing while you drive. It will make the time go faster."

"Would you feel better, Miss Sallie, if I was to come with you?" Anna asked.

"Of course I would feel better, but no. I have to do this myself. How else will I get Su Li and her brother back here? And Mr. Thornton. Tell me again, Joseph, what I'm to do."

Five minutes later she was careening down the hill, the hot desert breeze blowing in her face. She started to sing and stopped almost immediately when her mouth filled with dry sand. She really didn't feel like singing anyway; she was too jittery. She squirmed uncomfortably in the leather seat. What would Mr. Philip Thornton think about a nineteen-year-old girl who could barely read and write? She tried to imagine the look on his face when she showed him what little she knew. Mr. Waring hadn't said how old Mr. Thornton was, only that he was from Boston. The name of the magical city of Boston was all she'd had to hear. "Hire him," she'd blurted.

Hours later, when daylight had given way to soft evening twilight, Sallie arrived in town. She parked her car in front of the Emporium and removed the goggles and wide-brimmed hat, brushing at her clothing as she did so. Tucking stray tendrils of hair behind her ears, Sallie walked across the street to the Chinese laundry. Su Li and Chue were waiting for her, four tightly wrapped bundles at their feet. They bowed respectfully, their hands folded in front of them. Sallie smiled. "We can leave as soon as I pick up Mr. Thornton," she said. "I hope you aren't fearful about driving in the dark. I need to be honest with you, I've never driven in the dark. There is a light," she added hastily. "Today was the first day of my driving career. I expect I'll get better with practice. Are you afraid?" The young girl and her brother shook their heads.

"That's good. You can put your things in the car. I'll walk over to the hotel and bring Mr. Thornton back here. We'll leave in a few minutes."

He was *young*. He was also tall, exceptionally so, impeccably dressed in a dark suit, white shirt, and tie. His face was thin, topped with finely arched brows below a thick head of curly dark hair that rested on his collar. It was unruly hair, she could tell, refusing to obey a brush. However, it was his dark eyes and his youth that caused Sallie's step to falter. He smiled, his teeth whiter than the pearls she'd bought for her mother. She felt in awe, inferior to this tall man with the unruly hair and angelic smile. He intimidated her. He was going to work for her, which meant she would pay him a wage. She was the one with the money, so that made her powerful and in control. That was what Mr. Waring said, wasn't it? "I'm Sallie Coleman. You must be Mr. Thornton. I hope I haven't kept you waiting?" Her words came out in a breathless rush.

"Not long at all. I like this time of day best, when daylight gives way to this soft purple evening. Everything seems softer, more gentle. Yes, I'm Philip Thornton. Please call me Philip. Am I to understand you are going to drive me back to your home in the dark?"

Sallie drew in her breath. Did he think she wasn't capable of driving in the dark? "The way I see it, Mr. Thornton, you can either take your chances and ride with me, or you can . . . walk."

"Have I offended you? That wasn't my intention, Miss Sallie. What I meant and obviously didn't convey very well was . . . I personally never saw a woman drive a car. I would imagine it's a feat in itself. Night driving, I also imagine, must be a . . . remarkable feat. I myself don't know how to drive."

So many words. Feat, convey, offended—what in the world did they all mean? His tone of voice suggested he was apologizing. Sallie turned her back on him to walk across the street. Over her shoulder she said, "Just because I'm a woman doesn't mean I can't do what some men can do. Maybe I'll teach you to drive."

"I rather doubt that, Miss Sallie. I am not the least bit mechanically inclined."

Damn, what did that mean? "Get in," she said curtly. "This is Su Li and her brother Chue. This is Mr. Philip Thornton."

Slowly and deliberately, Sallie put on her goggles and the wide-brimmed hat. She switched on the light.

"And then there was light!" Philip said jovially.

Sallie winced. Just how smart was this man? Of course there was light. She'd turned it on.

"Can you converse and drive this machine at the same time?" Philip asked an hour later.

Sallie's shoulders stiffened. What did converse mean? Obviously, it was a yes or no question. She opted for no. The evening silence fell around her and the occupants of the car. Maybe she should have said yes. Well, it was too late. If she had made a mistake, she would have to suffer with it.

It was a beautiful evening, the heavens blanketed with stars, the air warm and softly perfumed. She decided, at that precise moment, that she loved the desert and the sagebrush-scented air as much as Cotton had loved it. She made a promise to herself that she would never, ever live anywhere else.

Sallie let her mind wander to the young man sitting next to her. She thought he smelled faintly of camphor. He was a fine teacher with excellent credentials, Mr. Waring had said. Because of his excellent credentials and the fact that he was willing to come all the way from Boston, he was able to demand a high salary. Plus, she would be giving him free room and board. "You better be worth it, Mr. Philip Thornton," Sallie muttered under her breath.

Sallie turned the wheel sharply when a jackrabbit sprinted across the road. The occupants of the car shifted and slid down the length of the seat. Philip Thornton laughed and then righted himself. In the backseat Su Li and Chue clung to one another. "That was very good, Miss Sallie," Thornton said.

"Yes it was. I had no desire to hit a defenseless rabbit. My light must have blinded him for the moment."

"I applaud your driving skill."

Sallie could hear the smile in his voice. She knew what applaud meant. She got applause every night when she sang in the saloons, and then later at her bingo palace. "Thank you. Do you feel safer now?"

"I never felt unsafe," Thornton said gently. "Things are different here in the West. My knowledge is from books. Experiences such as this must be lived. I'm enjoying myself."

How sweet his voice was. It was deeper than a woman's, but not as hard and coarse as a man's She wondered why that was. Because he was educated, she supposed. "I think you'll like my home."

"How long have you had this tin lizzie?" Thornton asked.

"What?"

"This flivver, how long have you had it? Was it difficult to learn to drive? How fast can you go?" Thornton asked.

Sallie's feet itched to dance on the pedals. If it were daylight and if she were more familiar with the road, she'd give him the ride of his life. "Joseph said he can go forty miles an hour. I don't know if that's true or not."

"I would imagine that's true. It's got four cylinders. How much farther is it?"

"A few more hours. The sun is just starting to come up. It's beautiful, isn't it? We should be home by midmorning. If you're tired you can sleep."

"I'm too excited to sleep. I don't want to miss anything. The day I received Mr. Waring's wire, I knew I wanted to do this. I liked teaching in my school, but I wanted to see other parts of the country, and this job gives me the opportunity. One day I'll go back to Boston and resume my teaching career."

"Mr. Waring said you charge a lot of money. Are you trying to take advantage of me because I'm a female?"

"Good Lord, where did you get such an idea?" Thornton gasped.

"I know what you earned at the school where you were a teacher. You're charging me twice as much. I'll be giving you free room and board, and I did pay for your train ticket."

"What you said about me charging you twice as much is true. Don't forget my traveling time. When this job is over I have to return. I don't receive money for that. It was right that your solicitor should pay my train fare. He recruited me. I didn't solicit this job. I'm an excellent teacher and could get a job anywhere. I take my work very seriously. I'm patient and I'm understanding, and I'm an honest man. I work with you and no one else. That means you have my undivided attention. Neither one of us will have to worry about another student making demands on my time. When we part company, after my job is finished, you will be one of three things."

"What three things?"

"Either you will be smarter than I am, as smart as I am, or you will be almost as smart."

"If you were a gambler, Mr. Thornton, which one would you bet on?" Sallie asked sweetly.

"If you are as dedicated and determined as Mr. Waring led me to believe, then I'd wager you will be as smart as I am."

"I have common sense, Mr. Thornton."

"There's a lot to be said for common sense. That's a trait I lack. That's because my life is books. Nothing can take the place of book learning."

"And nothing can take the place of common sense," Sallie said tightly.

"I think we're both right. Perhaps you can teach me common sense, and I'll teach you from books."

"Perhaps. How much do you think I should charge you?"

"Touché, Miss Sallie."

Sallie wasn't certain about what he had just said, but she smiled in the early dawn.

"I would never have believed this was possible," Philip said as he stepped from the flivver. "Your home is beautiful. Actually, it's magnificent. What *is* that smell?"

"Sagebrush. Why don't you walk around and see everything for yourself. Anna or Joseph will show you to your cottage. They'll arrange for you to have a hot bath and some breakfast. If you need to take a nap, that's fine. Tomorrow will be soon enough for us to begin our lessons."

Sallie knew she looked like a ragamuffin as she ushered Su Li and Chue into Anna's kitchen. Anna beamed and embraced the brother and sister. "They speak some English. You may have to show them things instead of explaining. Su Li's legs are younger so you might want her to do the upstairs work. Please don't burden her, Anna. I don't want either one of them to think I'm a slave driver. They can share the cottage next to Mr. Thornton and take their meals here in the kitchen. Make sure they always have plenty of food. They like rice. Mr. Waring brought up two sacks on his last trip. See if you can get them to eat other food, too. I don't think it's too good for a person to eat the same thing every day. They might not be used to eating three times a day, so go slowly. When things are all settled, I plan on asking Mr. Thornton if he will teach them English in his spare time."

"I'll take care of things, Miss Sallie. You run along and take your bath. I turned down the covers on your bed and opened all the windows. There's a fair breeze this morning. I'll wake you for supper."

Sallie smiled gratefully. She hugged both Su Li and Chue. She pointed to Anna and said, "She's going to take care of you. Today is a day to do nothing but rest. You won't work sixteen hours a day in my house. When you go to sleep at night, you will look forward to waking in the morning."

Sallie climbed the stairs to her room. She was almost too tired to wash her hair and bathe. She did it because she knew she would sleep better, and she wanted to look presentable at supper for Mr. Thornton. She wondered, as she rinsed the soap from her body, what color Mr. Thornton's eyes were. She rather thought they would be puppy-dog brown. The thought pleased her.

Sallie slept deeply and dreamlessly until Anna woke her at five o'clock.

Sallie glanced out of the window to see Chue on his knees, weeding the flower beds.

Thirty minutes later, dressed in a pale blue dress with matching band around her curls, Sallie entered the dining room and took her place at the head of the table. The moment she was seated, Philip Thornton entered, freshly shaven. He wore a casual shirt, open at the throat, and neatly pressed trousers. "Good evening, Miss Sallie. I hope you had a good rest. I know I did. Your home is beautiful. I grew up in a house much like this one. Someday I hope you can travel to Boston to see the botanical gardens. Would you like to travel the country someday?"

"I don't think so. This is my home now. I had . . . a home . . . once. It was . . . terrible. I made up my mind the day I had my own home I would never leave it. I can't see myself changing my mind. Will we start our lessons tomorrow?"

"Yes. I have everything ready. We need to talk first, though. Perhaps after dinner we can sit in the garden and you can tell me . . . what you think I should know. In the summertime we always have our after-dinner coffee in the garden. It's a wonderful custom. Do you do that?"

"I have lemonade in the garden in the afternoon. Is a custom something you do every day?"

"Pretty much so."

"I'll ponder the matter. Do you like your supper?"

"It's delicious. I don't think I've ever had such tasty meat."

"Do you eat differently in Boston?"

"Yes. We boil things as opposed to roasting or frying. People in Boston make very tasty baked beans. It's good. You get used to eating a certain way. This is a robust meal to be sure, and I haven't even seen the sweet yet."

What was a robust meal? Sallie looked down the length of the table. Roast beef, mashed potatoes, gravy, corn, cranberries, a lettuce salad with crisp bacon bits sprinkled through it, fresh biscuits, yellow butter, and strawberry jam. "We're having chocolate pie for dessert. I like sweet things, especially licorice sticks."

"Really! I do, too. We have something in common, Miss Sallie. I like getting up early, before the sun comes up so I can watch it. I like to get a head start on the day. I usually retire quite early. Do you have a preference?"

If she knew what it was, she might. "I get up early. It's like a relief that I made it through the night. People die in the night. That frightens me. I go to bed early, too."

"As the days go on we'll find out we have other things in common. It's wonderful to learn things about people. You learn by asking questions. Don't ever be afraid to ask questions, Miss Sallie. By the same token, should I ask you something you don't wish to respond to, tell me so. I'll understand."

His eyes were the color of Anna's warm chocolate pie. Gentle eyes. Warm eyes.

"Is something wrong?"

"No. Why do you ask?"

"You were staring at me as though you wanted to ask me something, then changed your mind."

"I was thinking that your eyes are the color of chocolate pie."

Philip threw his head back and laughed. It was one of the nicest sounds Sallie had ever heard. "I'm going to take that as a compliment."

"And well you should," Sallie shot back.

"Your eyes are the color of the sky on a bright summer day. Did you ever see a bluebell? My mother used to have them in her flower garden. They were the same color as your eyes."

Sallie flushed. "Thank you."

"Chocolate pie and bluebells. A great combination," Philip said in a teasing voice.

Later, in the garden, Sallie said, "I think this is my favorite time of day. The day is over and supper is finished; the sun will set and the evening darkness hugs you. My mother always used to say that when I was afraid of the dark. You need to work hard during the day so you can appreciate the tired feeling when the night hugs you. Does that sound . . . strange to you?"

"Not at all. As a child I was afraid of the dark, too. I had a toy soldier I used to place on the floor by the door to protect me. I called him Ivan. I still have Ivan. If I ever have a son, I'll give it to him if he's afraid of the dark."

"Sometimes I wish I could see into the future and what it holds for me," Sallie said.

"I don't want to know," Philip said.

"I said sometimes. Not all the time."

"Life would be very dull if we knew what to expect from one minute to the next."

What he said was true. Because she didn't know how to respond, she nodded her head in agreement.

"If you don't mind me asking, Miss Sallie, how did you come to be so wealthy? Mr. Waring said you were the richest woman in the state, maybe in the four bordering states."

Cotton Easter's words rang in Sallie's ears: *There's no call to tell your secrets to other people. If you do, your past will come back to haunt you.* "I inherited my fortune. Mr. Waring handles all my legal affairs. I think he was wrong to tell you I was rich. That should be no concern of yours or anyone else."

"I'm sorry," Philip said. "Please, don't be offended. Mr. Waring didn't come out and say, 'Sallie Coleman is rich.' He implied it. It was what he didn't say that made me draw my own conclusions. He did nothing wrong. He certainly didn't betray any confidences. Please accept my apology. I had no right to ask such a personal question. Remember what I said, if I ask you something and you don't want to answer it, don't. You should have told me to mind my own business."

"Yes, I should have. I don't like to be rude."

"You aren't upset with me?"

"No. Tell me where we're going to start tomorrow. What will we do first? How long is it going to take before I can read a newspaper?"

"I don't think it's going to be long at all. Wanting to learn is half the battle."

"This is the month of July. Do you think I'll be able to read and write, say, by Christmas?"

Philip stared at his pupil in the early evening light. In his young life he'd never seen such an intent, questioning gaze, never heard such a pitiful plea. "It's up to you and me to make it all happen. My time is yours. If you're dedicated and determined, I think you'll be reading the *Nevada Sentinel* by Christmas. Maybe sooner. I'll make our lessons as enjoyable as I can, but you have to cooperate. Now, I suggest we take a walk around this lovely garden so we can digest that fine dinner. Do you know the names of the flowers?"

"No."

"The trees?"

"No. I just call them posies. My mama always said flowers were posies."

"Do you know how the artesian well works? Would you like me to explain it to you, or would you rather wait until our lessons are further along? It's a complicated process."

"The well doesn't interest me. You can tell me later. Mr. Waring did tell me that no one else has one."

"I can understand why. You need engineers, geologists, and the right rock formations. It's a very costly process. I'm surprised you have one. These flowers were planted with careful thought and precision. I wonder if a horticulturist designed the garden. The colors

all blend so perfectly. Yes, very careful thought was given to this garden. I imagine you will spend many happy hours here. I personally
can't think of a nicer place for us to work at our studies."

Sallie shrugged. "I think I'll retire now, Mr. Thornton. I usually
breakfast at six. We can begin our lessons right afterward. I enjoyed
our walk in the garden. Good night."

Artesian wells, engineers, geologists, horticulturists, designed
gardens. She felt so ignorant she wanted to cry. The moment her eyes
stopped burning, Sallie squared her shoulders. Cotton had told her
once that all things were possible.

Her intention had been to go in the house and prepare for bed,
but instead she found herself sitting on a small stone bench. In the
early evening light, with the stars twinkling downward, Sallie
thought her garden one of the prettiest places she'd ever seen. The
faint scent of a flower, whose name she didn't know, came to her.
One day she would ask Joseph the name of the flower.

Sallie looked up at the sky, wishing she could see between the
stars. She felt like a child who needed to talk to her mother and best
friend.

"I'm pure worried, Mama." She'd felt inferior with Philip. She
said so, her voice a bare whisper in the darkness. "I know you're in
heaven and can't do anything but listen. I'm going to work hard. I'll
stay up late with my lessons. I know I can never know everything
like Philip, but I can give him a run for his money. Cotton told me
that once. What that means, Mama, is, he's not expecting me to catch
on real quick. I'm going to fool him. He's going to have to run real
fast to catch me. I don't think he knows or understands how bad I
need this learning. I'll come out here each night before I go to sleep
and tell you how my lessons are going.

"It would please me greatly, Mama, if you'd whisper in God's ear
that I am mighty thankful for all the good He's showered on me. If
you see Cotton, tell him the same thing. Oh, I wish I knew if you
could hear me, Mama. I wish I knew what heaven was like. I wish
so many things. I'll say my good-night now."

In his room, which overlooked the garden, Philip Thornton
watched the young girl on the bench, looking as if she were talking
to the sky.

She was so beautiful and so very young. If she lived back in
Boston, she'd have every eligible young buck sniffing after her. She
might even be married with a child. The thought caused his heart to
pound until he thought it would burst right out of his chest. Sud-

denly, he wanted to kick off his shoes and socks and rush out to the garden to grab Sallie's hand and run about the way little children did when they were at play. He didn't know how he knew, but he knew that Sallie had never had the chance to play as a child.

Philip thought about his own childhood, his friends and his home. Compared to Sallie's life, he'd been rich and hadn't even known it. Anger coursed through him. It wasn't right. Sallie's mean beginnings, and he was just guessing that they were mean, would stay with her for all her life. She wasn't the type to forget anything. All the money in the world couldn't take away years of whatever it was Sallie had endured. He offered up a prayer that he could be the one to turn things around for Sallie Coleman. He wanted to be the one to drive the sadness and sorrow from her eyes. He wanted to be the one to make those bluebell eyes sparkle.

A wave of heat rippled through his body. What was he thinking? He'd known Sallie Coleman less than two days. He was the teacher, Sallie was the pupil. And that's the way it would remain.

For now.

Sallie danced around her room, her eyes sparkling with anticipation. She was finally going to school for the first time in her life. Her only regret was that she wasn't going to be in a regular classroom. Cotton had told her how he'd behaved in school and what to expect should she ever decide she wanted to go. Now, thanks to Cotton, she was going.

Tripping about the room, clapping her hands together, Sallie stopped long enough to admire her school attire. Navy blue skirt, crisp white blouse with long sleeves and a tiny navy bow at the neck, dark shoes, and thick white stockings. A bright red hair ribbon lay on top of the white blouse. She'd tried on her clothes so many times in the past two days Anna had to press out the wrinkles three different times.

She was ready.

Almost.

Sallie looked at the clock. Ten minutes to midnight. She should have been in bed hours ago. As if she could sleep. It wouldn't hurt to take one last look at the makeshift classroom she'd had Joseph prepare. She'd told him what she wanted, and, as if by magic, the furnishings had appeared. Thanks to Alvin Waring. She hadn't questioned anything. She wanted, she got. It was that simple.

In her bare feet, her nightdress billowing behind her, Sallie crept down the hall to the empty bedroom that was now her classroom.

Cautiously she opened the door and walked inside. The moonlight showed her everything was in place. The huge blackboard nailed to the wall, the single desk that was to be hers, Mr. Thornton's desk and chair directly beneath the blackboard. Open boxes of chalk, a cup full of pencils and pens, ink bottles, stacks of tablets, and three boxes of erasers. She'd ordered more than enough. Rulers, not just one but six, stood like soldiers in a separate leather cup.

She rubbed her hands over the shiny desk, imagining the moment when Philip Thornton told her to take her seat. She shivered with anticipation. The desire to write her name on the blackboard was so strong, she walked over to the desk and picked up a piece of chalk. She brought it to her nose to sniff the dry whiteness. It smelled wonderful.

At the door, Sallie turned for one last look at her schoolroom. After today, she would no longer be ignorant. After today, her life as she'd known it would never be the same. It would only get better and better, and then maybe it would be wonderful.

Sallie closed the door softly. "Thank you, Cotton. Thank you, God. I promise you I will learn everything there is to learn even if it kills me. I'm talking to you, God, because Cotton can't hear me. So tell him that for me. It's me, Sallie Coleman making this promise. Tell him I said good-night, too."

The dawn was blue-gray, laced with lavender shadows, when Sallie woke and dressed. Su Li, carrying a breakfast tray, tapped lightly on her door just as Sallie finished tying the red ribbon in her hair. She declined the food, and only touched some coffee.

When Sallie walked into the schoolroom, she was certain her heart was going to leap right out of her chest. She saw it all in one swift glance—Philip Thornton, letters already written on the blackboard, tablet and pencil on her desk.

Sallie's steps faltered when she saw the look of wry amusement on his face. A dark flush raced up her neck onto her face. Sallie knew she was dressed wrong. Philip Thornton was expecting to see the fashionable young lady he thought her to be. Was her schoolgirl outfit a mistake? Brazen it out. She damn well liked what she was wearing. She'd looked forward to this moment for a long time, and she wasn't about to let Philip Thornton spoil it. All she had to do was remember that she was the one paying his salary. "Good morning, Mr. Thornton."

"Good morning, Miss Sallie. May I say you look . . . proper."

"You may, but it would be a damn lie, and we both know it."

"I . . . what . . . ?"

"You're here to teach me. Start teaching."

"Be seated, Miss Sallie," Thornton said, his face red from her brisk words. "As you can see, I wrote my name on the blackboard. I want you to write your name underneath mine. I also want you to write the month, day, and the year. I want you to print as well as write. I want to see how advanced your penmanship is."

Her face crimson, Sallie walked on wobbly legs to the blackboard. She smelled her own fear, the newness of the blackboard, the flat scent of the chalk when she picked it up. She squared her shoulders and gritted her teeth. She printed her name, the letters different sizes, the a and the n in Coleman going downhill. She needed lined paper. She whirled around. "It's the best I can do, Mr. Thornton. I can read some if the letters are printed, but I can't read writing. I can't write the month or the day."

"It's a start, Miss Sallie," Philip said. "What this tells me is we will start at the beginning. Your tablet has lines on it. We'll do the ABCs first. All the letters except the capital ones will be the same size. Two pages of each letter. There are twenty-six letters in the alphabet. When you're done you'll have fifty-two pieces of paper to hand me. I'll give you a mark. If the papers are good, the mark will be red. If the papers are poor, the mark will be green. If you give me an outstanding paper at some point, you'll receive a gold star. I'm very stingy with my gold stars, so don't count on getting many of them."

"How many of them do you have, Mr. Thornton?"

"A dozen or so. Why?"

"I think you need to place an order for more. I'm waiting for the letters. You have to write them on the board for me."

"So you are. My apologies. I'm writing the date now. Each paper needs to have the date and your name on it. Today is July 26, 1923. Print your name at the top like this, then underneath, print the date. I correct papers at night and return them in the morning. Is that acceptable, Miss Sallie?"

"Yes. It does make for worry, though," Sallie muttered, her head bent to the task in front of her.

Philip, his face to the blackboard, smiled. He made a mental note to write home to his older brother, also a teacher, to have him send a box of gold stars. He wished he knew how this beautiful, rich young woman could be so uneducated.

It was nine o'clock when Sallie shuffled her papers into a neat pile and handed them to Philip. "Are the numbers next?"

"Yes. One through ten. Two pages each. Name and date on each page. When you complete the numbers we'll have recess."

"I'm not a child, Mr. Thornton. I don't require recess. I prefer to keep working. Su Li will fetch us some tea and coffee at ten o'clock."

"It's the law, Miss Sallie."

"This isn't a real school, *Mister* Thornton. You are tutoring me. I'm nineteen years old. The law doesn't work here in my house. In my house I'm the law, and I say no recess." This was all said as she painstakingly wrote the number 1 down the length of the page.

Philip snapped the ruler in his hand against the side of the desk. "Miss Sallie, look at me. We need to get something straight right now. In this room, I am the boss. I am the teacher. I will not put up with tantrums, tears, or womanly wiles. Furthermore, I don't care how rich you are. You will always treat me with respect, and I will show you that same respect. I will not, under any circumstances, allow you to dictate to me. Is that understood? If it is, we will have a twenty-minute recess commencing at ten o'clock when Su Li brings our tea or coffee. Tell me your answer." He watched, baffled, as a kaleidoscope of emotions showed on Sallie's face. Anger, fear, humiliation, humbleness. He felt like biting off his tongue for causing her one moment of discomfort. However, he held her gaze until she lowered her head.

"I saw your face when I walked into the room this morning, *Mister* Thornton. You didn't show me respect then. You were baffled at the way I look. I saw it on your face. I never went to school, as you well know. If I want to dress like a schoolgirl, I will dress like a schoolgirl because I *am* a schoolgirl. Your recess is a silly rule, but if that's what they do in a real school, I have no other choice, do I? Do *you* understand *that*, Mr. Thornton? If so, let me finish my work. In this room I will listen to you, but only in this room."

"Fair enough."

"Damn straight it's fair," Sallie said under her breath.

"A lady, Miss Sallie, never uses profanity," Philip said quietly.

"This lady does." The eraser she was using tore the paper. "See what you made me do!"

"You tore the paper yourself. You aren't scrubbing a floor, you use an eraser lightly. As I said, a lady never uses profanity. The choice is yours, Miss Sallie."

The rest of the morning passed quietly. Teacher and pupil retired to the dining room for a light lunch. The moment Philip folded his napkin, Sallie was off her chair and on the way to the second floor classroom.

"I want to read this afternoon," Sallie said.

"Reading is not in my lesson plan for today. We're going to do word association. I'll show you pictures and underneath the picture will be a word, sometimes several words. You will tell me what the picture or pictures are. We will then sound it out, and then you will print the word on a sheet of paper. We'll go through the entire alphabet. How many sheets of paper will you need, Miss Sallie?"

"Twenty-six. After we do that, what are we going to do?"

"We'll do the same thing with numbers. If you're going to be handling large sums of money in the future, this is going to be very important to you. I'm going to time you with my stopwatch. The timing is not important to you, only to me. I need to know if I have to slow or pick up my pace. Start!" At four-thirty, Philip gathered his cards into a neat pile. "That's it for today, Miss Sallie. Tomorrow we'll pick up where we left off."

"We still have several hours of daylight. I thought we were going to work till supper. I *want* to work till supper. I'm paying you a lot of money, *Mister* Thornton. I want to get my money's worth. Of course, if you're too tired to continue, I can sit here by myself and . . . and do other things. What that means, *Mister* Thornton is, I'm not going anywhere. Where you go is your choice."

"If you call me Mister Thornton in that tone of voice one more time, I'm walking out of here. School is over at four-thirty. Sit here if you want. Rome wasn't built in a day, Miss Sallie."

"What does that mean?"

"You can sit here and think about it, or you can walk in the garden with me and I'll explain it. There are a lot of things I can teach you outside this room. I'd like to read you some poetry, read to you from the classics, tell you about animals. I'd like to share some of my experiences with you, things I learned outside the classroom during my years of study. Your education needs to be well rounded. For instance, you like to sing. I heard you singing 'Poor Butterfly' the other night. I'd like to know how you learned that song. So you see, you can teach me at the same time. By the way, you have a lovely voice."

Sallie's face was set into stubborn lines. She looked down at her tablet, at the pencils with dull points. Her eyes ached as she stared at the erasers that were nothing but nubs. Would her papers have green marks on them tomorrow? Cotton always said not to cut off your nose to spite your face. A wise man always returns to fight another day. If Cotton were here right now he'd say . . . what would he say? Was she going through a power struggle with Philip Thornton? If so, she was not his match. Yet.

Sallie tapped her pencil with the dull point on the desk. She thought about power, money, control. Before she got up from her chair, she added a fourth word to her list: education. If she didn't go to bed until midnight, she had five full hours to repeat her lessons in the privacy of her room. The thought brought a smile to her face. She'd show Philip Thornton. He'd have to buy *three* boxes of gold stars.

A friendly but uneasy truce was established between teacher and pupil during the following weeks and months. When Philip looked at Sallie with suspicious eyes, puzzled at her remarkable progress during those same weeks and months, Sallie just smiled as she held out her paper for her gold star.

Eleven days before Christmas, Philip called a halt to Sallie's lessons. "School's out. You've done outstanding work, and I'm very proud of you. You not only deserve this break, you need it," he said jovially. "It's time to prepare for the holidays. I'm sure you'll want to decorate the house. It all takes time. You did say, Sallie, you wanted a Boston Christmas."

"But—"

"School is closed, Sallie. School always closes for the holidays. No books, no pencils, no lessons. After the New Year, lessons will resume."

"All right, Philip." Sallie smiled as she tried to recall the exact time and place when teacher and pupil had started using each other's first names. "What should we do first?"

"I think we should go to town. I'd like to buy presents for Anna, Joseph, Su Li, and Chue. I'd also like to get a box of cigars for Mr. Waring. If it weren't for Mr. Waring, I wouldn't be standing here with you right now."

"I was going to get him a new pipe and some tobacco. He likes to smoke his pipe when he drives. I seen him do that many times."

"Do you want to try that sentence again, Sallie?"

"I thought you said school was closed. No more lessons."

"I did say that, and yes, school is closed. If you aren't going to practice what you learn, what is the point of my teaching you? I wouldn't be a very good teacher if I didn't correct your use of words."

"You are absolutely correct, Philip. When do you want to go to town? Might I make a suggestion?"

"You might." Philip smiled.

"I suggest we stay in my town house for as long as it takes us to shop. We'll take Su Li with us. I also want to spend one evening in my bingo palace. My customers expect me to appear from time to time. I want to go to church on Sunday, too. Is that acceptable?"

"More than acceptable. Let's plan to leave at first light."

"I'm going to have Su Li ask one of her cousins if she wants the job of housekeeper in the town house so the house will stay clean. I don't like musty-smelling bedding."

"You don't like staying in town anymore, do you?"

"No, I don't. Later, I imagine that will change. I'm very contented right where I am, doing what I want to do. I have good employees at the bingo palace, so I don't have to worry about my little business. I'm never going to give that up. I might open another one if business calls for it. The town house is just a convenience. It is a long trip to town, even in the car, and I miss my friends sometimes. I like going to church on Sunday. My life will be settled soon, and, when that happens, I want to be ready to make . . . important decisions."

"You have the right attitude, Sallie. This might be a good time for me to compliment you. I'm usually fairly stingy with compliments. Before I give them I want to be sure in my own mind that they're deserved. You've done so well, Sallie. What I feel for your dedication goes beyond the word proud. You have worked like a Trojan. You're doing well in all your subjects, but you excel in mathematics. At first that surprised me, but then I started to think. You said Mr. Easter started your education with numbers, and later he taught you to write and read a little. I believe it's what you start out with first. You had a real interest in numbers because you dealt with money." He chuckled when he said, "Now you have even more money, and it's paramount that you learn how to take care of and protect your fortune. Don't depend on other people to do that for you, Sallie. At all times you need to know where you stand in regard to your finances."

"When will we be getting to that part?"

"We'll start on finances in a small way after Easter vacation. By this time next year you'll be ready if you keep progressing as you are."

"A whole year!" Sallie cried in dismay.

"Do you want to do it right, or do you want a slipshod course? If you don't understand what it is you're doing, you could make a costly mistake that will cost you thousands of dollars. Is that what you want? Understand also that I am by no means a financier. I understand the stock market, and I know a little about investments. However, I'm not an authority. You might want to have Mr. Waring engage someone in that particular field to help you. We don't need to think about that right now. We're on vacation."

"All right, Philip."

"Let's wash up and see what Anna has prepared for dinner. If you aren't too tired, might I suggest a game of checkers after dinner. No cheating!"

"Philip, a lady does not cheat at any kind of gaming."

"You do! I caught you three times in a row!"

"That's the way I play. It wasn't cheating. I simply changed my mind."

"You see! That's exactly my point. I tried teaching you the correct way, but you didn't have the patience. Oh, no, you thought you could do it your way. Well, your way was wrong, and you cheated."

"It wasn't intentional."

"Is that going to be your response when you make a big mistake in the stock market? *After* you lose your money?"

"I don't want to talk about this, Philip."

"That's good because I don't want to talk about it, either. What you need to do is *think* about it. I want you to do everything right. I know you have convictions and opinions, but if they aren't right, where does that leave you?"

"Having the last word, Philip. I'll see you at supper."

It was late, and the night was cold and brittle. Either he'd eaten too much at dinner, or he was about to come down with his yearly winter cold. Standing here at the window in his bare feet, staring at Sallie Coleman's bedroom window, certainly wasn't helping matters. The fire in the grate had burned low some time ago, and he hadn't replenished it. He did so now, his thoughts on Sallie and the light in her window. He was almost certain she was studying even though she'd given him her promise not to.

Sallie's obsession and her progress had startled him on a daily basis. When he finally realized she was carrying her studies far into the night, getting by on only a few hours' sleep, he tried everything he could to slow her down, but she was having none of his amusing chatter and caricature drawings. "You're here to teach me, Philip, and I'm here to learn. Don't be drawing pictures of how you *think* I look. It doesn't amuse me at all. All we're doing is wasting time."

Suddenly it was important to him to find out if Sallie had broken her promise and was studying. He ignored the cold evening, bundled up, and marched downstairs and out the door of his small cottage. He knew exactly where Joseph kept his ladders. He felt like a sneak, a Peeping Tom, when he quietly leaned the ladder against the house. Shivering, he climbed the flat rungs until he was able to peer into the room. He saw Sallie dozing, her head drooping into the crook of her arm. By squinting, he was able to see that she had been studying lessons that would begin after the New Year holiday. According to his calculations, she'd been up here since supper, which meant she'd been studying for six hours.

The urge to put his fist through the windowpane was so strong, Philip bit down on his lower lip and tasted his own blood. What he *really* wanted to do was open the window, crawl in, and gather Sallie in his arms and tell her . . . what? That he was falling in love with her, that he was concerned for her health? She'd tell him straight out to mind his own business. She might even laugh, that wonderful tinkling sound that sent goose bumps up and down his arms. So many times he wanted to say certain things to her, but her frosty gaze said, this is business, I want you to teach me and nothing more. Besides, how could he take care of her? She probably had more money than King Midas. She could spend more money on a dress than he earned in four months. He groaned with the thought, his foot slipping on the rung of the ladder. As he slid to the ground, the ladder toppling over, he heard Sallie scream. *Oh, hell,* was his last conscious thought before he hit the shrubbery that surrounded the house. Moments later, Sallie, Su Li, and Chue were standing over him, blankets draping their shoulders.

"Philip!" Sallie gasped.

"You broke your promise," Philip snarled, outraged that he'd been caught spying on his employer.

"Are you hurt? You were spying on me, Philip Thornton! That's despicable! I knew I'd get to use *that* word one day. I should fire you right now."

He was on his feet, but shaky. "Maybe you should! You gave me your word. Which just goes to show I can't trust you. I can pack my bags and be out of here in an hour. And, before you even think of asking how I'll get to town, I'll walk. You can mail my wages to Mr. Waring." He wanted to stomp off, but the pain in his ankle only allowed for a limping walk.

"Bring Philip into the house, Chue, so we can look at his ankle," Sallie said. "If he's going to walk to town, he's going to need a stout brace. It's a long walk." God in heaven, did she really say that?

What would she do without Philip? She trusted him. They got along well together. He never poked fun at her, never made her feel inferior. How would she fare with another teacher? What if she got a tart-tongued older woman with no patience? Philip had the patience of a saint.

Inside the warm kitchen Su Li bustled about, boiling water and mixing a poultice while Chue settled Philip on one of the kitchen chairs. He looked to Sallie for instructions.

"What should we do, Philip?" she asked quietly. He was, after all, the teacher.

"An apology would be a nice place to start. I twisted my ankle is all. Wrapping it tightly should work. I expect my bones will ache for a few days. I'll be off your property as soon as my ankle is wrapped."

"But you said if I apologize—"

"I said it was a good place to start. I didn't say I would stay. I can't trust you anymore. How many times did I tell you that a person's promise or that person's word is a measure of who that person is? You ignored the most important lesson in life, Sallie Coleman."

Sallie felt shaken to her soul. He had said that many times. She didn't want him to leave. She looked forward to waking and seeing him at the breakfast table. She loved spending the day with him, loved the crinkly smile in his dark eyes when she did something right. "I'm sorry, Philip."

"No you aren't. Sorry is just a word to you. You're wondering if tears will change my mind. Well, they won't, so don't bother."

"Why are you being so cruel to me?"

Because I think I'm falling in love with you. "I'm not being cruel. You want to believe that I am. What just happened is a lesson I taught you, gave you the opportunity to put it to use, and you failed the test. I guess I'm not a very good teacher after all."

"Oh, that's not true, Philip. You are the best teacher. You taught me so much. I'm sorry, truly sorry, that I failed the test. I know you're right. I'm wrong. It's just—"

"I don't want an excuse, Sallie."

"What the hell do you want?"

I want you to run your fingers through my hair. I want you to kiss me. I want you to whisper words in my ears, sweet words, words we both understand. "What I want is for you to tell me what you did wrong. Telling is one thing, understanding what you did is something else. Ladies don't curse."

"I never said I was a damn lady. You insist on calling me one. I don't give a hoot about being a lady. Get that straight, *Mister* Thornton. What I did wrong was promise you I would put my lessons aside. I broke that promise. It was wrong of me to do that. I thought . . . what I wanted to do was . . . go forward so that . . . when we started our lessons again, I would be familiar with what you were . . . I wanted you to be proud of me. I like it when you tell me I do good . . . well.

good . . . well. I really am sorry. I won't do it again, Philip. I will never, ever, break a promise to you. To anyone."

Philip smiled wearily. "That's good enough."

"Then you'll stay?" The relief Sallie felt was so overwhelming she grew faint.

"Can I believe *this* promise?"

"Yes, Philip."

"Then if you don't mind, I think I'll hobble on home and go to bed."

"You won't leave in the middle of the night, will you?"

"This *is* the middle of the night, Sallie. I promise you, I will not leave. You can trust *my* word."

Tears brimmed in Sallie's eyes. Not trusting herself to speak, she nodded. She watched as Chue offered his shoulder for the short walk back to Philip's cottage.

Upstairs in her room Sallie undressed for bed, tears rolling down her cheeks. She swiped at them with the sleeve of her nightgown. Her shoulders shaking, she walked over to the desk. Sallie stared down at her open book, at the pile of books and notebooks at the end of the desk. The cup of pencils and pens glared at her like a single malevolent eye. Sniffling, she closed her book, placed it on top of the stack of books. She piled the notebooks and tablets next to them. The last thing she did was push her chair under the desk. She wouldn't sit on the chair or open any of the books until Philip said it was time to resume her lessons.

Sallie thought about Philip and how fond she'd grown of him in the nearly five months he'd worked with her. Sweet, gentle Philip, who always had a smile for her even when her work was less than perfect. How many times he would smile and say, "Let's try that again, Sallie." Then he would smile again and praise her and say, "Perhaps I didn't explain it clearly enough," or something to that effect. She'd repaid that kindness and gentleness by deliberately ignoring his instructions. He was right about needing a break from her lessons. He was right about everything.

She climbed into bed, but sleep did not come. Only thoughts of Philip. Her heart thumped in her chest as she recalled how she felt when she heard Philip say he was leaving. Was it possible she was falling in love with Philip Thornton?

In the morning she put on a wool dress the color of ripe cranberries. She knew she looked fashionable with her matching shoes and purse. Philip would compliment her—he always complimented her when her hair looked particularly nice or she had on a new dress. Her wool coat was long with a fur collar and cuffs and nipped in the middle to show off her tiny waist. In the lamplight the color of her coat took on the look of burnished copper. She stuffed soft leather gloves the same color as her coat into one of the deep pockets.

In the kitchen, Su Li was making coffee. Sallie could see flapjacks bubbling on the griddle. A pot of blackberry jam sat in the middle of the table next to a crock of butter that was the exact color of spring daffodils. The coffee smelled heavenly.

"I was going to make my own breakfast, Su Li. You have to get ready for the trip. I don't think Mr. Thornton will be going with us."

Sallie walked over to the window to stare at Philip's cottage. All the windows were dark. She felt like crying.

Sallie stared at her full plate, at the thick syrup Su Li was pouring over her flapjacks. Suddenly her appetite was gone.

"Missy eat," Su Li said sternly.

Sallie cut a portion of the stack of flapjacks, then cut them again the way Philip had instructed her. She forced herself to eat daintily, the way he had taught her. What was it he had said? Oh, yes, ladies always walk away from the table with room in their stomachs. "Not this lady," had been her response. She'd gone on to clarify the statement by saying she would never, ever, be hungry again. If that meant she wasn't a lady, so be it. She pushed her plate away.

"Leave the dishes for Anna, Su Li. Make sure you bundle up, it's cold this morning."

Su Li pointed to the thick quilted jacket next to her sack of belongings.

"I'm going to buy you a long coat so your legs don't get cold. Would you like that, Su Li?"

"Like very much, missy. Time to go."

"Yes, it's time to go." By moving her chair to the left, Sallie was able to see through the kitchen window. The view was the same as it was when she'd looked out earlier. No soft yellow light glowed in Philip's windows.

"Missy look pretty," Su Li said, as Sallie settled a fur-trimmed, copper-colored hat over her blond curls.

"Thank you, Su Li. I think I'm going to get you a red coat. With your dark hair you'll look gorgeous in red. A red hat, too." Su Li smiled widely.

Outside, Sallie blew little puffs of air from her mouth. She burst out laughing as Su Li tried to imitate her.

"Climb in, Su Li. Use the lap robe over your legs. Ready?"

"Ready," Su Li said.

Sallie backed the car out of the barn. She switched on the headlights. Outlined in the piercing glow was Philip Thornton. He brandished a cane and shouted, "I hope you were planning on blowing that horn of yours. You know, I am a little incapacitated."

"Philip! How wonderful that you're coming. You are, aren't you?" Sallie said breathlessly.

"I promised, didn't I? I believe this trip was my idea to begin with. Of course I'm coming. May I say you ladies look particularly lovely this morning."

"You may say that." Sallie laughed. "Get in! We're going Christmas shopping! I never went Christmas shopping before."

Five minutes later Sallie took her eyes off the road for a moment to look across at Philip.

"Philip, I'm sor—"

"Sallie, I'm sor—"

Sallie thought she saw something strange in Philip's eyes, something she'd never seen before. Something wonderful, something she wanted to see more of. A slow rising heat crawled up through her body as her gaze swept back to the road.

Philip leaned back against the leather seat. What was that scorching look he'd just seen in Sallie Coleman's eyes? Certainly not anger. He blinked when the word passion skittered through his mind. He coughed to cover his confusion. He knew he should be saying something, but for the first time in his life, words failed him.

Sallie smiled. Her world was right side up. She wanted to look at Philip again, wanted to see that strange look, wanted to know if it meant what she thought it meant. Instead, she focused on the road.

A lot could happen over the holidays.

4

1924

Philip Thornton's voice was brisk, professional-sounding. "Date your paper with the new year at the top. Today is Monday, January 7, 1924." His voice was also chilly.

Sallie blinked at her teacher's tone. The tension was palpable. Had she done something wrong? What a silly thought. Philip had gone to town the day after Christmas and just returned late last evening. The last time she'd seen him was at dinner on Christmas day. The day he had kissed her under the mistletoe.

"There's no excuse for bad manners, *Mister* Thornton. You tell me that at least once a week. You could have told me you were going away. I realize you need time to yourself. A note would have been sufficient. I can read, you know." Sallie lowered her eyes and commenced writing.

"You're absolutely right, there is no excuse for bad manners. I apologize."

"I think your apology might mean more if you made it sound like you meant it. As far as I'm concerned, you just said words with no meaning. Sorry is merely a word that many people use at their convenience. Aren't those your exact words, Mister Thornton?"

"Again, you are absolutely right. For now it's the best I can do."

"It's not good enough. You're supposed to set an example. If I were the teacher, I'd *take away* all your gold stars."

Philip blanched. "I want a short essay on the meaning of Christmas. I'm going to grade you on your penmanship and your punctuation as well as content. Be aware of your commas. When you finish go right into the new year, set down your aspirations and your goals for this year. I want five hundred words in the essay. Begin."

He saw her eyes fill with tears before she lowered her gaze to the paper in front of her. He knew he'd get an excellent paper worthy of perhaps two gold stars. She would have no need of him after the summer months. Six months more at this house, and then he'd be heading back to Boston.

Philip thought about his week in town, about the hours he'd spent in Sallie's bingo palace listening to her employees extol her virtues, listening to the wild, wicked stories the patrons insisted on repeating for his benefit. One night he heard seven different versions of how and why Sallie acquired her immense wealth, none of them pleasing to his ears. He'd wandered the streets in the cold that night until he finally stopped at the Red Ruby brothel. Everything was a blur after that. The only thing he knew for certain was he'd stayed at the Red Ruby for four days. Last night he'd had a nightmare about all the fleshy, big-breasted women who'd paraded into his room. He'd had them all. At least Red Ruby said he did when she demanded payment on his departure.

According to most of the town, Sallie Coleman was a whore. According to the people who *really* knew her, she was a lusty saint. And none of it was any of his goddamn business. In less than six months he'd be gone, and Sallie Coleman would be a memory. He wished he knew what she was thinking about him, right now. Was he just her teacher? Did she feel the same attraction he felt? That kiss under the mistletoe had been his undoing.

"I'd like to kiss you again, Sallie. Right now, this very minute," Philip blurted. He told her then about his visit to town and what had transpired, right down to how much he'd paid Red Ruby. "Are all those stories true, Sallie? If they are, it's all right with me. I just want to know. I need to know. I'm falling in love with you. I don't know how you feel and I need to know that, too. I'm ready to marry you if you want me." Jesus God, had he just proposed marriage? By the look on Sallie's face, he had. His face and neck felt like a bonfire gone wild. He stood his ground, though, feet firmly planted, one leg and thigh smack against the desk because he felt weak in the knees.

Sallie stopped writing. Cotton's words roared in her ears. "My past or whatever you perceive to be my past, is mine," she told Philip. "You can believe whatever you want to believe. I will not deny anything you've said nor will I discuss it. I did not ask you anything about your past nor will I. I will say I am disappointed that you went to Red Ruby. Had you asked me, I would have recommended Beaunell Starr's establishment. Ruby robbed you." She paused for a moment, then blundered on. "I don't think I'm in love with you, but I like you very much. What happens if we do get married and I never fall in love with you? What if we aren't compatible . . . in bed? Did you think about that?"

"The girls at Red Ruby's didn't have any complaints," Philip said.

"They get paid not to complain," Sallie said sweetly. "I need to think on the matter overnight."

"You're making it sound like a business arrangement. I just asked you to marry me. It was a yes or no question."

"Philip Thornton, you told me nothing is black or white. You said there are always shadings of gray, and a person needs to make decisions based on facts. This is the same thing. Isn't it?"

"This is a matter of the heart. Emotions. It isn't a business deal. Do you care for me enough to marry me and bear my children?"

"I don't know. I have to think about it. You're complicating my life, Philip. Marriage to anyone was not something I planned on. I do want to marry someday and have children. Someday isn't right now. Do you still want to kiss me? If you do, I'm willing."

"Finish your paper, Sallie."

"You're upset, aren't you? Look at it this way, Philip. What kind of person would I be if I was less than honest with you? The kiss under the mistletoe was very nice. I dreamed about it. I hesitate to ask this, Philip, but ask I must. In my paper for my aspirations and goals, should I mention your proposal and what I feel?"

"Do whatever feels right for you. I've never censored anything of yours. I might make a suggestion, but that's as far as I will go. You're eating into your time by talking, Sallie."

"You didn't say there was a time limit."

"There's always a time limit. Don't make me use my green pencil."

"You're not indispensable, Philip Thornton," Sallie snarled.

"Neither are you, Sallie Coleman. Write! And don't bother to give me an answer in the morning. I don't want to hear it."

"Touché, Philip. I am writing. As for my answer, it would have been no anyway. You're my damn teacher. Act like one instead of pouting like a little boy."

Philip stared at Sallie's bent head, at the golden curls tumbling about her ears. He wanted nothing more than to hold her, to smooth back the curls and whisper in her ear. He looked away, but it didn't help.

Philip banged his fist on the desk. Sallie raised her head to stare at him. "You want a damn teacher? You got yourself the best damn teacher there is. Hand in your paper. Now!" he roared, his voice carrying all the way into the hall and down the stairs.

Sallie slapped her unfinished paper into Philip's hand. A second later she was off her seat and at his desk, reaching for the green pencil. "Here, let me hand it to you. Make no mistake, *Mister* Thornton, this is the last green mark you'll ever give me. I was wrong to call you a little boy. You're a jackass!"

"And you're a whore!" Philip shot back. He wanted to bite off his tongue the moment the words came out of his mouth. He was so distraught he didn't see Sallie leave her seat and stomp from the room.

How could he have said such cruel, degrading things? The urge to cry was so strong he was forced to knuckle his eyes. With his eyes squeezed shut he missed Sallie's return.

"Mr. Thornton, I'm ready to resume our lessons if you are. I'd like to think that both of us are mature enough to allow us to get past this . . . this awkward time. Why don't I leave the room again and return, and we'll start over. We'll pretend it's seven o'clock in the morning. We'll agree not to mention our respective outbursts. Do you agree?" Philip nodded, not trusting himself to speak. Sallie left the room and returned moments later to take her seat. She stared up at Philip expectantly.

Philip handed Sallie her papers. "Thirty minutes, Sallie."

The January incident, as Sallie thought of it, was never mentioned again, but the damage was done. Philip insisted on eating in the kitchen, doing his own laundry, and taking care of his quarters. Sallie, in turn, worked harder than ever, oftentimes getting by on as little as three hours' sleep. She waited for words of approval, for gold stars, encouraging words, none of which were forthcoming.

Weeks and months crawled by. Before Sallie knew it, it was early June, almost summer.

On a bright sunny morning, Philip handed Sallie a bound booklet. "This is your final examination, Sallie. It will take you all day today and all day tomorrow to finish it. I'll grade the exam tomorrow evening. On Wednesday I'll leave for Boston. I'm placing you on your honor for this examination. I'll be going to town to make my travel arrangements. I know you're going to do well, but I'm going to say good luck anyway. Remember to take your recess breaks."

The knot in Sallie's throat prevented speech. She nodded, her eyes miserable.

"There's no time limit on this examination, Sallie. You have all day. Take your time, think about the question, and try not to wear down your eraser. I'll see you tomorrow evening. If there are any messages at the telegraph office, I'll bring them with me." Sallie nodded again.

The moment the door closed behind Philip, Sallie burst into tears. She raced to the window to watch Philip cross the yard to his cottage. He was really going back to Boston on Wednesday. These past months she'd refused to think about this time, preferring to imagine that Philip would always be with her, teaching her forever. Now he was giving her a final examination. He would then walk out of her life and return to Boston, where all the ladies had unsullied reputations.

Sallie cried as she watched Philip greet Chue before he climbed into the car. These past five months had taken a toll on her both physically and mentally. She'd worked hard to make sure she didn't get a single green mark. If what Philip said was true, she now had the equivalent of a high school education.

The test booklet on the center of the desk seemed to glare at her.

She hated the thought of opening it and didn't know why. What would Philip do if she failed the test? If she *deliberately* failed, would he stay on? Would he assume responsibility? Would he think he was a failure as a teacher?

A short twenty minute catnap might help, she decided. Since there was no time limit to the test Sallie convinced herself that she would feel better, more refreshed after a brief nap. She didn't disturb the booklet on her desk as she left her seat. Maybe she wouldn't take the damn test at all.

Sallie flopped down on her bed and closed her eyes. She fell asleep immediately and didn't wake until the middle of the afternoon.

Refreshed, Sallie opened the booklet, read the instructions, and then closed the book. She squeezed her eyes shut, not understanding the strange feelings rushing through her. She felt like she could do anything she wanted to do. She'd never felt so alert. She knew her adrenaline was flowing at an all-time high. She opened the booklet again, her pencil poised.

Four hours later Sallie closed the booklet. She didn't check her work—there was no need. She'd known all the answers. Thank God for all the notes she'd taken during the year. Early on, Philip had said, "The faintest pen is better than the sharpest memory." Of course, she hadn't understood the meaning at the time. Now she did.

She looked up to see Su Li standing in the doorway. "I'm finished, Su Li."

"Test much hard, missy?"

"Very difficult. Mr. Thornton didn't go easy on me at all. I think I answered all of the questions correctly. I wouldn't be surprised at all to find the second half of the test even more difficult."

Su Li watched as Sallie walked to the front of the room to place her test on Philip Thornton's desk. She turned to see Su Li holding out a tall glass with ugly-looking dark liquid in it.

"Missy drink and then go to bed. I put cloths on eyes and massage neck and head."

Too tired to argue, Sallie did as instructed.

The crisp white curtains were billowing into the room when Sallie woke the next morning. She stretched luxuriously, taking a moment to discover how she felt. She felt wonderful, ravenous. She had a second exam to tackle. She tiptoed into the bathroom, and gasped when she saw herself reflected in the mirror. There was a sparkle in her eyes and a faint pink glow to her cheeks.

"Su Li," she called.

Su Li appeared at her elbow a moment later. "Missy very much hungry?"

"Very much hungry, yes. A big breakfast. Flapjacks, eggs, bacon, toast, jam with lots of butter. A big glass of apple cider and a huge cup of coffee with lots of cream. I'll be down as soon as I take my bath."

In the tub full of soapy bubbles, Sallie's good mood darkened. She could be as beautiful as the first spring flower, and it wouldn't change anything. Philip was leaving.

Sallie sat in the garden, her hands folded in her lap. She hated sitting alone like this in the quiet evening. Philip should have been back by now. She told herself she wasn't worried, but she was. She felt anxious about her test results, anxious about Philip's leaving, anxious about her future. She did her best to calm herself by taking deep breaths and listening to the cheerful sounds of the night birds and the crickets. While the deepening lavender shadows of twilight dropped around her, Sallie began to feel more comfortable. She watched a parade of ladybugs circle her shoe. Did bugs have intentions? Did they know where they were going? What was the point of circling her shoe? She wondered if Philip knew the answer. She made a mental note to ask him, then she remembered he was going away.

Even though they had been like polite strangers to one another these past five months, she was going to miss him terribly. She knew that Philip was still in love with her. Even though he kept a polite professional distance, she could read his feelings in his eyes. Cotton once said the eyes never lied.

Now that her education was fairly complete, she'd have to move back to town and take charge of her business. She could continue her education by reading. She could start up her own library. She could buy every book ever written if she wanted to, once she returned to town. She also had to decide if she was going to hire a financial person to help her understand the stock market. It was time her fortune earned more money.

The back porch light went on at the same moment she heard the car return. Carefully, so as not to disturb the ladybugs, Sallie moved her foot. She took her time walking back to the house so she wouldn't look anxious.

At the bottom of the stairs she saw him. She wanted her heart to beat faster at the sight of him, but it didn't. She wanted to feel the urge to run up the stairs after him, to beg him not to leave, but the only thing she felt was relief that he was back. She called his name. He turned, his face serious. He offered no smile.

"How did you find the examination?"

"More difficult than I expected. Were there any messages at the telegraph office?"

"None, Sallie. I checked. Excuse me."

"Philip . . . I . . ."

"Yes?" Even from her position at the bottom of the stairs she could see the hope in his eyes.

"Nothing."

"Is anything wrong?"

Was there? "I was wondering why ladybugs would circle a person's shoe. In the dark. Don't bugs, like people, sleep or hide or something, when it gets dark?"

Philip laughed. "I'm afraid I don't know the answer, Sallie. Perhaps your next teacher will know. I told you, I don't know everything. You like to think I do, but I don't." He smiled again, his eyes warm and soft.

Sallie's heart fluttered. "I see."

Philip laughed again. "No, you don't see at all. People usually say, 'I see' when they don't see at all. It's just a phrase. Is it important for you to know about ladybugs? I can look it up if it is."

"Not really. What time will you be leaving in the morning?"

"Around ten o'clock. I'll correct your test as soon as I get back to the cottage. If you prefer, I can do it in the classroom."

"Whatever is best for you, Philip."

"I imagine you're anxious, so I guess I'll do it in the classroom." He smiled again. "You look very pretty this evening, Sallie. Is that a new dress?"

"Thank you. Yes, it's new. I'm relieved that I don't have to wear that awful blue skirt and blouse anymore. I might just burn them tomorrow."

Sallie felt her heart flutter again. This was the first personal conversation between them in months. Suddenly she wanted to keep talking, to tell Philip how she felt, but the words stuck in her throat.

"That sounds like a smashing idea. Is there anything else, Sallie?"

"Well, I . . . no, Philip, there's nothing else."

Philip nodded, his eyes downcast. Sallie watched until he was out of sight.

It was close to midnight when she finally gathered up the courage

64 FERN MICHAELS

to venture from her room. She'd heard Philip in the hall and on the stairs an hour ago. That meant her test had been graded. All she had to do was walk back to the classroom and look at her grade. She felt a total, all-consuming rush of fear. It took every ounce of willpower in her body to make her legs carry her down the hall to the classroom. From her position in the open doorway, Sallie could see the test booklets on her desk. Next to them was a gift-wrapped package. A going-away present. From Philip.

Her hands clammy, Sallie advanced, and with one, wild, jerking motion, she reached for the booklets: A+, A+. The word Congratulations was printed in red letters across the top of each booklet. Sallie sat down at her desk and cried. When there were no more tears, she untied the yellow ribbon on the package. She stared at the contents for a very long time before she burst into heartbreaking sobs. Her very own official high school diploma! A small note in a crisp white envelope fluttered to the floor. Her hands shook so much she could barely open the envelope. She cried harder as she read the cramped script.

Dear Sallie,

While I was in town I spoke with the principal of the school. I explained your situation, told him how advanced you were, and showed him a copy of your final test. Of course I had no grade for you at the time. Mr. Brannigan told me if you earned an A, you deserved the diploma. As you can see, Mr. Brannigan, as well as the president of the school board, signed it, based on my word that you would pass with flying colors. It was left to my discretion, Sallie. I can truthfully say, no student deserves this diploma more than you. I wish there were an award for dedication. I would nominate you immediately. I want you to be proud of yourself because I am so proud of you I want to shout your achievements to anyone who will listen.

I'm sorry that things between us have been so strained these past months. It's my fault, and I am truly sorry. I want you to know and believe that I will miss you and will think about you every day. Please write to me and let me know how you are doing.

All best wishes,
Philip Thornton

The framed diploma clutched to her breast, Sallie ran barefoot in her nightdress through the house and out to the garden.

In his room overlooking the garden and the cemetery, Philip watched Sallie, his eyes misty with unshed tears.

How was he ever going to get through the days and get on with his life when he returned to Boston? How did one survive a broken heart?

Already bathed and dressed, Sallie waited for the dawn to creep over the horizon. She wanted to make sure Philip didn't sneak off without saying good-bye. All night long she'd agonized over his departure. She finally admitted to herself that she didn't love Philip, but she was more than fond of him. She should be able to shake his hand, kiss him on the cheek, and say good-bye. In her heart she knew it wasn't going to work that way. She was going to blubber like a baby and say all kinds of silly things.

How kind and wonderful he was. Someday he'd meet a fine Boston lady and get married and have children. She felt herself cringing at the thought. Philip would make a wonderful father. He'd play and romp with his children. He'd bandage their hurts and read poetry to them. He'd teach them right from wrong. He'd listen to their prayers at night and take them to church on Sunday. His children would grow up to be as kind as he was. The fine Boston lady who snared him would have no regrets. Philip would be a dutiful, devoted husband. Together they would watch their children grow, taking pride in their achievements along the way and finally growing old together, sitting on rocking chairs on the front porch where they'd reminisce about bygone years.

What would she be doing while they were living their lives? Working in her bingo palace, singing songs for her customers, counting her money, spending money on things she neither wanted nor needed. Where would she find a man as good and kind as Philip Thornton in Las Vegas? She flinched when she recalled the type of men she'd associated with in the past. Would she ever watch her own children grow and take pride in their achievements? Who would sit with her on the front porch when her hair was gray and her face full of wrinkles? Who would take care of her in her older years? What if she never married, and strangers were forced to take care of her? Who would inherit her fortune if she never married? She did want children. Golden-haired girls with big blue eyes. Girls always had a special affinity for their mothers. Girls would take care of her when she got older just the way Sallie would have taken care of her mother had she lived.

Her muscles were cramped and her joints ached as Sallie struggled from her cocoon on the window seat. Dawn was breaking and a new day was within her reach. What she did with the brand-new day was entirely up to her.

Sallie didn't stop to think, didn't weigh the consequences of her actions, didn't allow herself to look down the road into the future. Instead, she walked down the stairs and out the front door and around the corner to the small courtyard in back and then on to the three cottages. She rapped smartly on the door of Philip's cottage.

"Sallie! Is something wrong? What are you doing here?"

"I don't know what I'm doing here. What I do know is I don't want you to leave. I'd like it very much if you stayed, and if you still want to marry me, I'm saying yes. Do you still want to marry me, Philip?"

His eyes, sleep-filled, opened wide. "Do birds want to fly?" he asked hoarsely. "Of course I want to marry you. It's all I've dreamed of these past months. Are you sure, Sallie?"

"I'm sure that I want to marry you. I don't know if I love you. I've never been in love, so I have nothing to compare to what I'm feeling. What if my feeling isn't love? Is that fair to you, Philip?"

"Love is like a flower, Sallie. First you plant the seed, then it sprouts, and before you know it you have a bud that turns into a blossom. It's a gradual kind of awakening process. The best kind of love, in my opinion, starts out as friendship. We already have that. If we go forward, it can only get better. Besides, I have enough love for both of us. I need to ask you, though, what made you change your mind?"

"I couldn't bear to see you leave. My stomach churned each time I thought about seeing you drive down the road with your baggage. I couldn't eat or sleep."

"That's the first sign of love," Philip said. "Should I kiss you now, or should we wait? I have to get you a ring. It will have to be simple, I don't have much money. It won't be anything compared to those sparklers you wear."

"You can tie a string around my finger and I'll never take it off. The size doesn't matter. We do need to talk, though. About business, about my money, about what you are going to do and where we're going to live."

"I could live in a tent if you were at my side. I can provide and take care of you. I'm a good teacher. What I can't do is buy you jewels and fancy houses. Perhaps I can do that someday, but not right now."

"I already have all that, Philip. I told you once, I require very little. All I ever wanted was enough to eat, to know I would never go hungry, and to have a decent roof over my head so I wouldn't freeze in the winter and roast in the summer. A nice dress for church and good shoes. All the rest, Philip, is frosting on my cake. Right now, this very minute, I could walk away from here and not look back. You gave me something I never thought I would have, an education. I have my diploma. I can go to town to send a telegraph message to my sister Peggy."

"Speaking of that diploma, we have to take your test down to Mr. Brannigan. We're doing it as a courtesy. I also want him to meet you. When are we getting married?" he asked boyishly.

"Do you have a date in mind, Philip? I thought August might be good. I'll need to make some plans, get a wedding dress, that sort of thing. I would like to invite the people who work for me and a few of my friends. If you're agreeable, I'd like us to be married at St. Cotton Easter, and I want to sing at my own wedding. I miss singing, and I also miss working at the bingo palace. I want to get back to my old life."

"Does that mean you don't want to be a housewife? Who's going to take care of me? What about children?" His voice was light, teasing, but Sallie sensed a seriousness behind the words.

"I really don't have any experience in the housewife area, Philip. I'm not sure I want to get any experience, either. Su Li will take care of *both* of us. If we have children, a housekeeper will help us out. Su Li has many cousins. Are you going to be a demanding husband, Philip?"

"I don't know. Are you going to be a demanding wife?"

"More than likely. Will you like living in town?"

"If you're there, I will. I love you very much, Sallie."

"What about all those things we said? Will they haunt us? These past five months the whole thing just . . . just festered. If you have any doubts or if there are . . . certain things that you can't cope with, now is the time to talk about them. I don't ever want to go through something like that again."

Sallie's jaw tightened as she remembered how hurt she'd been. "If it happens again, Philip, I will leave you. I've had enough unkind words and gestures to last me the rest of my life. Just so we understand one another. I'm sorry I woke you. I'll tell Chue he doesn't have to take you to town. I'm glad we're getting married."

"Me too!" Philip said. "I'm very happy you decided to become my wife. I'll try to be everything you want in a husband."

Sallie wanted to say, "And I'll be everything you want in a wife," but the words wouldn't move off her tongue. In her heart, in her mind, and in her gut, she knew she was going to fall short of Philip's expectations.

On a bright, golden day in August, Sallie Coleman married Philip Thornton for all the wrong reasons. Philip Thornton married Sallie Coleman because he loved her with all his heart.

When he kissed the bride after the ceremony the guests heard him say, "I will love you forever and into eternity." Those same guests saw Sallie Coleman Thornton smile. Only the minister saw the unhappy shadows in her eyes.

5

1925

"Philip, why are you looking at me like that? I am not going to explode. I might *look* like I am, but it is a virtual impossibility. Pregnant women tend to look like this when they're about to deliver. Do you doubt me when I tell you I have this pregnancy under control?"

"Of course not. Is it wise to eat *so much*? You look so uncomfortable, so miserable."

Sallie stared across the table at her husband. It was all said so quietly she had to strain to hear the words. Words that irritated her. Philip irritated her. Su Li irritated her. The weather irritated her. "I don't know if it's wise or not. Actually, Philip, right now I don't care. I'm hungry, so I'm eating. If my eating habits bother you, I can take my meals in the kitchen. Yes, I am uncomfortable and miserable. There's not one damn thing I can do about it until this child decides to make his or her entrance into the world. If I had only one wish, it would be that I deliver this baby *right now!*"

"Is there anything I can do for you, Sallie? I can rub your back and feet if you like."

"Right now the only thing I want is another piece of pie. After I eat the pie I want to go to bed. Please, Philip, stop *hovering*."

"Is that what I'm doing?"

"It's what you've been doing since the day I told you I was pregnant. *Nine* months, Philip. It's been extremely difficult. I have constant indigestion. I throw up on a daily basis. I look like a giant puff pastry. It's hard to walk and harder to go up and down the stairs. I go to the bathroom at least a hundred times a day. In order to go to the bathroom, I have to go up and down the steps and walk down the hallway. I'm extremely tired and even though I sleep, it is not a restful sleep. Do you understand anything I've just said?"

"You're making it sound like you're blaming me. We talked about it, and both of us decided we wanted a baby. If you remember, I thought we should wait till we were more settled, and you said there was no point in waiting. I agreed. I'm truly sorry you're having such a difficult time. You know I would do anything possible to alleviate your discomfort."

"I know that, Philip. Men tend to say things like that. It sounds rather silly to me. There is nothing you can do, and you know it. Having a baby is something only a woman can do. You can offer all the help in the world and it isn't going to change a thing. I hate it that you are miserable. I regret that I can't sit still long enough to play chess with you. I also regret that I am not interested in hearing you read love poems to me. I'm focused on having this child. Right now nothing else interests or matters to me. God, I hope this baby is a girl. If it is a girl, I'm going to name her after my mother."

"Without talking to me first?" Philip asked.

"We did talk about it. You said it was all right. I agreed to you naming a son. Why are you talking as if we never discussed it?"

"We mentioned it in casual conversation. We didn't make a decision. A child's name is very important."

"Philip, I am not going to get into this right now. If you'll excuse me, I'm going upstairs to bed. Please, do me a favor and sleep in the guest room. You need your rest, too, and the skimpy amount of bed I allow you isn't fair. I feel like a damn elephant."

Sallie burst into tears before she trundled from the room.

Lying across the bed, she beat at the pillows with clenched fists. Her mother had never looked the way she looked now. Her mother had been thin with a small protrusion in her stomach when she was pregnant. She'd also been undernourished. Her long hours of work had never stopped because of her pregnancy. She had her babies and was up and about, taking care of the little ones. What was wrong with her that she couldn't be the same way? Daughters were supposed to take after their mothers.

Exhausted, Sallie slept, her dreams invaded by a procession of pregnant women, all of them looking like her mother. She woke in the early hours of dawn bathed in sweat, her stomach cramping unbearably. She knew instinctively that it was her time. Tears burned behind her eyelids as she struggled to roll over to the edge of the bed. It was a monumental task to swing her legs over the side. The effort made her light-headed. She called out for Philip and Su Li, her voice little more than a whisper. When there was no response, she made her way to the door. Along the way she picked up her hairbrush from the dresser, which she banged first on the wall, then the door. Su Li was the first to reach her, her long, fat pigtail flip-flopping against her back. She shouted something in rapid-fire Chinese that made Sallie swoon.

"Help me, Su Li," Sallie whispered. "God, I never experienced pain like this in my whole life. I never heard even a moan from my mother. I want to scream my head off. How can I be less a woman than my mother?"

"Each pregnancy is different, Sallie. Each person is different," Philip said quietly as he scooped her up in his arms. "The one thing you need to do right now is relax, hard as that may seem to you. You can't fight it, it will just make the pains that much harder."

"What do you know about having a baby? This is my body. I feel the pain, not you. Don't tell me what to do. Not now, not ever. Oh God!"

"I'll get the midwife. Here, let me put these pillows behind your head. I'll be right back. Su Li will stay with you."

Twelve hours passed, and Philip was ready to crawl out of his skin as he paced the long corridor outside Sallie's room. Her screams ripped at his soul. He looked at his reflection in the windowpane. Surely this wild-looking creature wasn't Philip Thornton, soon to be a father. He hadn't shaved or bathed. What in the hell was taking so long? He banged on the door to ask, and was told to take a nap. They wanted him to take a goddamn nap. Like hell. He wanted to be right here to hear his son or daughter's first cry. So what if he looked like a tramp. His firstborn would neither know nor remember in later years.

More hours crawled by, one after the other. He'd never heard of an eighteen-hour labor, but then he was no authority on childbirth. He remembered his brother's birth; his mother had been making cookies and he'd been sampling them in the kitchen. He'd seen the puddle on the floor where she was standing. She'd looked so pretty at that moment when she handed him two cookies and told him to go outside on the porch. He remembered a small amount of confusion when the housekeeper took his mother upstairs and then, lickety-split, he had a baby brother. When they let him see Daniel for the first time, his mother was holding the infant, her face wreathed in smiles. "He looks just like you did, honey," she had said. "I want you always to look after him until he's old enough to fend for himself. Promise me you'll love him." He'd promised because even as little as he was, he could deny his mother nothing. That's how it was going to be with his son.

He'd prayed daily for a son. He felt guilt and disloyalty because he knew Sallie wanted a daughter. He knew he could live with the disappointment if their firstborn was a girl, but he wasn't sure if Sallie could cope with a son. Which one of them was going to be disappointed? He wished they were back on the mountain, where things were calm and serene, but Sallie preferred living in town. He detested the house with its fancy furniture that was always covered with dust, no matter how often Su Li cleaned it. The windows were always dirty, and there wasn't a blade of grass to be seen. What kind of place was this to bring up a child? He could feel the anxiety start to build inside him when he thought of the grit that would cover the child's room.

Two hours later, the midwife opened the door and showed him his new son. He reached for the child, his eyes full of love and devotion. *His* son. His *first* son. The child looked just like Sallie. He knew the boy would have Sallie's summer blue eyes. He already had her blond hair. Philip felt his heart swell with love.

"He weighs almost as much as a sack of sugar, Mr. Thornton. It was a hard labor, but as you can see, that little bundle was worth it. He's a strapping, healthy young man. One day he will make you proud of him. I guarantee it. He's perfect, just perfect."

"Yes, I can see that."

"Time to give him back to me. I imagine you want to see your wife now. Don't stay long, she's very tired."

He'd forgotten about Sallie the moment he'd seen his son. Good God, what kind of man was he?

Philip tiptoed over to the bed. "Sallie," he whispered, "it's Philip. I've just seen our son. I am in awe. He's perfect. Have you held him yet? I did, but only for a minute. I felt so many things, the awesome responsibility, such love that I don't have the words to describe. I want to call him Ash. Ash trees grow tall and strong. That's how *my* son is going to grow, tall and strong. When will you start to nurse him?"

"I'm not. He's going to take a bottle. The first one is sugar water. You might want to give it to him."

"What do you mean? Mothers nurse their babies unless something is wrong."

"Twenty hours of hell is what's wrong, Philip. Babies are given bottles all the time. When you nurse you have to be available all the time, twenty-four hours a day. I'm not a cow. It's my decision."

"I think it should be *our* decision. I don't understand."

"Philip, I am very tired. I need to sleep. I don't want to nurse the baby. I plan to go back to work after a decent interval. I don't want to have to rush home to feed him."

"You'll change your mind after you hold him. I'll let you sleep now. I need to get cleaned up myself. We have a wonderful son, Sallie. Who knows, he might be president of the United States someday. Thank you, Sallie, for my son."

Sallie watched her husband as he left the room. Did her father act like Philip when her brother Seth was born? Did her mother dote on her firstborn the way Philip was doing? Of course she did. Firstborn sons. She tried to imagine Philip's reaction if the child had been a girl. She knew in her heart he wouldn't have said a word about bottle-feeding if the baby was a daughter.

It felt so wonderful, so blissful, to be free of pain. The midwife had told her a hundred times during her labor that the pain she was experiencing would be forgotten the minute the baby was born. "It's the easiest pain in the world to forget when you set eyes on your own child, the child you and your husband created."

That's the way her mother must have thought. Since her own labor was unlike any that her mother had experienced, that set her apart. She wasn't like her mother at all. She wasn't going to dote on this first son of hers. It would only bring heartbreak in the end, the way it had brought heartbreak to her mother. She wasn't going to be the kind of mother who gave her heart and soul to her child simply because he was a boy. No son of hers was going to break her heart.

I hate you, Seth Coleman, and I don't even know you. I don't care if you are my brother. Because of you I can't allow myself to love my son. It was your responsibility to take care of Mama. You were the oldest. I blame Josh, too. Mama gave you life, and then you turned your back on her. She's up there and she knows what you did. I purely hate you, Seth Coleman, I truly do. Someday I'm going to find you. I always do what I say I'm going to do, and I'm going to find you.

On what should have been one of the happiest days of her life, Sallie Coleman Thornton slept, her heart full of hatred for her faceless brother. When she thought about her son it would always be in relation to her brother Seth, and for that reason she would never allow herself to bond with her firstborn child.

Sallie Coleman Thornton had become a mother in name only.

On the fifth day of young Ashford Philip Thornton's new life, his mother left her bed for the first time and on wobbly legs ventured down the hall to his room.

Guilt overcame her when she stood over her son's cradle. The temptation to pick up the little bundle was so great, Sallie had to clench her fists to stop herself. She knew if she held the child, she would become the mother Philip wanted her to be. She would become her own mother all over again, raising a son like her brother Seth, who ended up breaking her mother's heart. Instead, she stared at the child, her heart hammering in her chest.

In the moonlight she could see how much he resembled her. For some reason she'd thought babies were born without hair. This child had a crown of golden ringlets. He was going to have blue eyes like hers, too.

Sallie looked around. Where was the baby nurse? And then she saw her husband, asleep on the floor, on the opposite side of the cradle. Father and son. She knew instinctively that Philip had discharged the woman she'd hired weeks ago. Philip was going to take over the care of their son. School was out for the summer and he had all the time in the world to be the father he always wanted to be. Again, guilt washed over her. She could change all that. All she had to do was bend over, pick up the child and walk over to where Philip was sleeping, nudge him with her toe. He'd wake instantly, a smile on his face. Her hands gripped the side of the cradle. She would not end up like her mother, she absolutely would not. "Oh, why weren't you a girl," Sallie whispered. "I so wanted a daughter."

The moment the door closed softly behind her, Philip was on his feet, his eyes full of pain. He bent over to pick up the sleeping baby. "I hoped, I prayed, that she would come in here to see you. I was so certain her arms would ache to hold you. I thought she just needed a few days to recover from her long labor. I don't think it's ever going to happen, son. I don't even pretend to understand, and I worry about how I'm going to explain all of this to you as you grow older."

Philip settled himself in the rocking chair, the baby secure against his heart. He rocked contentedly as the child sucked on his tiny fist. In ten minutes Su Li would arrive with the bottle of warm milk. "And now I'm going to tell you a story until your bottle gets here." His voice tender and soothing, Philip began. "Once upon a time there was a fairy princess named Sallie. . . ."

In her room down the hall Sallie curled herself into a ball on the window seat to watch the new day begin. She cried silently, her heart sore and bruised. She needed to be strong. There was no way in hell she was going to allow herself to turn into a broodmare whose only function was to deliver boy babies. She clenched her teeth so hard she thought her jaw would crack. When she couldn't stand the pain a moment longer, she made her way to the bathroom and, against the doctor's orders, drew a bath. She was going to wash her hair, lather up and soak. Then she was going to find a dress that fit and go downstairs for breakfast. After that, she was going to get on with her life. She would take her third cup of coffee out to the garden and study the recent stock market report. If she felt strong enough in the afternoon she would walk over to the bingo palace to check on things. If she felt too weak to walk, she'd call the livery to send a car for her. She might even do some shopping on the way back.

Bearing a son didn't mean the world stopped. At least for her. Life was going to go on and she was going right along with it. Regardless of what Philip thought or said.

"Sallie, how wonderful that you're having dinner downstairs." Philip's voice was cheerful, but his eyes were wary. "Ash is being such an angel. He sleeps so soundly. I remember when my brother was born. I seem to remember that all he did was cry. Ash is a good baby."

"Why didn't you tell me you discharged the baby nurse?"

"I didn't want to bother you. You needed your rest. If you recall, Sallie, you slept almost around the clock for several days. I wanted to take care of him. Believe it or not, we have a routine. Ash put himself on a schedule so Su Li can actually anticipate his waking. She has his bottle ready the moment he whimpers. I haven't actually heard him cry."

"He doesn't cry!" There was alarm in Sallie's voice.

"Of course he cries. I guess I should have said he doesn't wail the way most babies do. He's fine, Sallie. I do have a concern, though. It's so dry and dusty here in town. His room is full of grit no matter how often Su Li wipes it down. Would you object if I took him to

Sunrise for the summer? The air is so much cleaner, and the garden will be full of flowers."

Did she care? Of course she did, but what Philip said made sense. "We'll be out from underfoot and you can get on with your business at hand," he said. "I'd like to take Su Li, but the decision is yours, Sallie."

"I think it's a good idea. It will be better for Ash. Are you going to spoil him, Philip?"

"Absolutely."

Sallie laughed. "That's what I thought. Of course you can take Su Li. I think she'll be much happier at Sunrise. After all, Chue is still there."

"Will you miss us? Will you come up to visit?"

"Of course."

"How often?"

"I don't know, Philip. As often as I can."

"What did you do today, Sallie?"

"Everything I wasn't supposed to do. I feel fine for all my efforts. I hate it when doctors tell you not to do things because that's the way it is. Each person is different. I felt like I was able to go to the palace, so I did. I'm none the worse off. I sat in the garden. Now, that was a mistake. Everything is dry and burnt, the leaves of the plants are yellow. I think I'll ask Chue to come down to town temporarily and plant a garden indoors for me in the sunroom. We can put some shades on the windows to block out the noonday sun."

"What about the sand and grit?"

"It's a way of life, Philip, if you live in town. One of these days someone will figure out a way to prevent it from coming indoors. I can't live year round at Sunrise, Philip. I need to see people, I need to be where things are going on. Didn't you tell me no man is an island unto himself?"

"Yes, I did say that, but it was before I fell in love with you. I don't need anyone else but you and our son."

"I wish I could say that. I can't. If you want to move permanently to Sunrise, it's all right with me. We have enough money that you don't have to teach. You can take over Ash's education. That will be a job in itself. This might be a good time for you to write the book you've always wanted to do. It's a thought, Philip, and it doesn't require an instant decision."

"If I were to decide to do that, would you continue to live here in town?"

"Yes. I have some ideas for this town, and I have the money to put those ideas to good use. I'm going to schedule a meeting with the town council to see if any of it is feasible. I'd like to build a new school and the hospital, such as it is, could be expanded, and a library would be wonderful. I'm actually making money in the stock market. I want to turn those profits to good use. I also plan to build two more bingo palaces. The money I'm making on the first one is unbelievable. Anytime you want to give up teaching and become my partner, I would be quite pleased."

"That's not my forte, Sallie, but thanks for the offer. If you do build a new school, I'll be on hand for the dedication. Give some thought to building a college, too."

"That's a wonderful idea, Philip. I'll do it!"

"Just like that, you'll do it!"

"Yes. I have the money, so why not? You just said I should give some thought to building a college. I'll be . . . what's the word, Philip, a phil—"

"Philanthropist."

"Yes. That's going to be me. Isn't it wonderful?"

"Yes, wonderful," Philip said, his voice sour and cool. "It's almost time for Ash's bottle. Have a nice evening, Sallie."

Sallie sat alone at the table for a long time, her thoughts whirling chaotically. When she finally got up from the table, she muttered, "Tomorrow is another day. If I don't do what I want, it will be just a day like today. I don't want another today. I want each day to be newer than the one that came before." Her footsteps were heavy on the stairs as she made her way to her room.

Fourteen days later Sallie waved good-bye to her husband and son. "Take care of them, Su Li!"

"Very much good care," Su Li shouted in return.

A single tear trickled from Philip Thornton's eye to drop on his son's plump cheek. Had he seen his wife's moist eyes, he might have felt better, but young Ash chose that moment to squeal his displeasure a split second before he burped louder than a three-week-old baby should.

The Thorntons, at that precise moment, became a family divided.

With her family gone, Sallie spent every waking moment of the day doing business. She committed to building a hospital, a grammar school, and a college. In return for her generosity she would sit on all the boards, and have the final say when problems surfaced.

The *Nevada Sentinel* ran pictures of Sallie on a daily basis, extolling her virtues and praising her generosity. On little more than a whim and a stomach full of gut instinct, she bought up a freight company that had seen better days during the gold and silver strikes. She went with her gut instinct a second time and purchased fifty thousand shares of the Union Pacific Railroad because it was going to be part of the transcontinental run. The boom-and-bust cycle of Las Vegas would boom again. She crossed her fingers when she put the shares into the town house safe. The moment she twirled the knob, she forgot about them.

Weeks later Sallie bought a ramshackle building that at one time had been an icehouse, and contracted to have it restored and opened for business. She swooned when she calculated the profit the icehouse would give her in a year's time. Three days later she signed her name to a construction bill that guaranteed a modern laundry and dry cleaning plant. She knew the moment she signed the bill that all the Chinese laundries would be put out of business. She sent out the word to the owners of the smaller laundries, explaining what she had done, and offering them jobs and a percentage of the business. All six Chinese made their mark on the individual contracts.

On a quiet evening at her bingo palace, Sallie sat down at one of the round tables to play a hand of poker with some of Cotton Easter's old friends. Her mind wasn't on the game at first so she almost missed part of a strange conversation between two of the men.

"I'm telling you, if I knew how to get hold of Snowball Meiken, I'd go out there myself and buy that land he's holding. The man's older than God with no kin. If they go ahead and build that dam they be talking about, we could all retire and live in lux-youry."

"Are you telling me Snowball is still alive?" Sallie asked.

"Fer sure, Miss Sallie. Iff'n he dies before they build that there dam, his property goes to the state. Ain't fair, I can tell you that."

"Is it definite that they're going to build the dam?"

"Pretty definite, Miss Sallie. But first they have to buy up all the land. Snowball owns most of it. Ain't nobody who can find him. We tried. He's such an ornery cuss; he could be anywhere."

"Somebody must know where he is," Sallie said, her eyes alight with interest. "He came to Cotton's funeral. He was lighting out right after. He told me where he was going, but I can't remember where. Maybe it will come to me if I think on it hard enough."

"Think hard, Miss Sallie. He's sitting on a gold mine and don't even know it."

Sallie stared across the table at the grizzly old miners who still hoped one day to strike it rich. She knew none of them had ever had more than fifty dollars to his name at one time.

"If I remember, what do you want me to do?"

"Hell's bells, Miss Sallie, sweet-talk him and buy all his land. Then you sell it to the government and make a fortune."

"That wouldn't be very nice. I'd be cheating him. I can't do that."

"Why not? We told you, he's old as God. Old Snowball, he don't care. If you remember where he is, make sure you take a buggy full of whiskey and some good food. Some warm clothes would be good. He looked real raggedy at Cotton's wake. Did shave, though, out of respect. You gonna look for him, Miss Sallie?"

"I'll think on it. How about some food?"

"Have to be on credit, Miss Sallie. I'm plumb cleaned out," one of the miners mumbled.

"My treat. I think I can rustle up some ham sandwiches, hard-boiled eggs, and a pot of coffee." She slid some money across the table to the three miners. "That's for a hotel room and bath."

"Much obliged, Miss Sallie. We'll be paying you back someday. Don't know when, though." Sallie smiled. These old men, like Cotton, were dear to her heart. Like Cotton, they refused to give up hope of finding the big strike. Everyone knew the mines were dry now, all the tent cities gone, but if it was their dream, who was she to ruin it? When they left in the morning she'd make sure their wagons were full of provisions the way she always had in the past. Cotton would want it this way.

An hour or so before closing, with only a few patrons left in the palace, Sallie sat down alone at her private table in the back of the room, a cup of strong tea in front of her. She looked up, startled, when she saw the front door swing open. Red Ruby. She was walking straight for her.

"I didn't know the hour was so late. I see you're about to close. What's that you're drinking, honey?"

"Tea. Would you like some?"

"Tea! Honest-to-God tea! No thanks. I felt lucky tonight, so I thought I'd just come over and play a little bingo or faro."

Red Ruby, so named for her wild mane of fire red hair, was a voluptuous, blowsy woman who reeked of stale perfume. She wore outrageous theatrical eyelashes, and brushed her eyebrows upward until they stood up in little peaks. Round silver dollars of rouge colored her cheeks. Her thick, heavy lips were colored with a greasy lipstick that was also on her teeth. Sallie found herself wincing.

"It's been slow this evening. I was just about to close. If you really want to play faro, I can have Madison stay on for a little while." Red was, after all, a frequent customer, and regardless of whether Sallie liked her or not, business demanded she accommodate her.

"Now that you mention the word tired, I think I am, too. I've been meaning to come by and congratulate you on your marriage. For some reason, Sallie, I didn't think you were the marrying kind. And you got a kid, too! I heard about that just the other day. Well, maybe I can understand it. That husband of yours is one *wild* man. My girls smiled for a week after his visit. I also heard that he went up to Sunrise with the kid and left you here. Now, why would you let him do a thing like that, Sallie? Did it go sour already? The rumor in town has it that you have all the money in the world, more than the *government*. They're saying you don't need a man. Is that why you sent him up there?"

"I didn't send Philip anywhere. He wanted to go, not that it's any of your business or anyone else's business."

"That's worse yet, the fact that he *wanted* to go. I've been around a lot longer than you have, Sallie, so I feel free to offer you some advice. I wouldn't let too much of that Sunrise grass sprout under his feet. I'd hate to see him become a regular customer, and he will if you stay here and he stays up there. The advice is free."

"I think Philip learned his lesson that night. I can assure you he won't be back, so don't give it another moment's worry."

"A long time ago, Sallie, I learned a hard lesson. Never assume and never presume. Just remember something—there was a time when you were no better than me and my girls. All your money ain't never going to change that. Don't be forgetting where you got all that money to begin with. These people in town ain't going to forget it."

"I'll remember that, Red. You wouldn't happen to know where Snowball is, would you?"

"I sure do. He's at my place. He's got five bucks of credit left, then he'll skedaddle. We made sure he got a bath and we've been feeding him real good. He's happier than a pig in a mudslide. Why do you ask?"

"Jess Banes gave me ten dollars to hold for him. Said he owed it to him for a year," Sallie lied.

"I'll send him over first thing in the morning. He's about ready to light out anyway. He'll need that ten dollars for provisions. You planning to add to that little stake, Sallie?"

"If he needs it I will. Snowball is a proud man."

"Good night, Sallie. Thanks for the offer of tea. Don't drink too much of that stuff. It makes your hair stand on end." She offered her hand, and Sallie shook it. "No hard feelings, Sallie."

"None. Business is business."

"Now you're getting it." Red laughed. "See you around."

"Anytime. My doors open at four o'clock, seven days a week."

"Time is money, Sallie. You need to stay open round the clock like I do."

Sallie had the last word. "You forget, I don't need the money. You do."

Red chuckled, the sound sad and a little envious.

It was an hour past midnight when Sallie walked home along the quiet street, savoring the scent of sagebrush. She remembered how ugly the town had looked when she first arrived. She'd loved it on sight, even at its meanest, with the tent cities on every available patch of land. The helter-skelter of miners and those that fed off them as they all waited for the big strike, the desire to make and spend money, had made her a part of that same frenzy, fighting to breathe in the hot, dusty air. It was a hundred, a thousand times better than what she'd left behind.

The town had boomed and then busted wide-open. Then one day the tents were gone, and so were the people who'd inhabited them. She'd known fear then for the first time in her life as she scrambled to make a life for herself. This was the place she'd come to, believing there really was a pot of gold at the end of the rainbow. And, by God, she'd found the pot, thanks to Cotton Easter. She'd make this town boom again, now that she had the money to do it. *Cotton must be proud as punch,* she thought as she climbed the steps to her front porch.

Sallie's thoughts weren't of her husband and child as she prepared for bed. She fell asleep dreaming of the town of Las Vegas and how she could make it into what *she* wanted, knowing she had the time, the energy, and the resources to do it.

By midmorning, Sallie was ready for whatever the new day would bring. She'd finished her hearty breakfast, read both newspapers from cover to cover, and now it was time to go to her place of business.

The day wasn't breathlessly hot yet. Overhead the sun was bright; the cottonwood trees that she loved were greener than she remembered from the day before. At the far end of the street she heard a bird chirp, and then another. She hoped somebody was putting water out for the little creatures the way she did. "I could build a park and put in fountains," she murmured to herself as she walked past the shop owners sitting outside on their rattan chairs. She smiled or waved to each of them and received a smile and a wave in return. It was amazing, she thought, two years ago no one in town, not even Red Ruby, would give her the time of day.

"Snowball, you're here early," Sallie said as she fished in her pocket for the key to the bingo palace. "I've got your ten dollars under the counter. Did you have breakfast this morning?"

"Red fixed me some eggs and steak. Used up the last of my poke, so it's time to head for the hills." A fit of coughing left him gasping for breath, his face crimson with the effort.

"Are you taking anything for that cough, Snowball?"

"The doc gave me some elixir. Three bottles. On tick, seeing as how I'm busted. You want to grubstake me, Miss Sallie?"

"Of course. I can outfit you like a king, Snowball. Do you think you'll hit it this time?"

"Damn tootin' I will. This is my last winter, Miss Sallie. Doc says he don't know how I lasted this long. You outfittin' Boots and Corker? Jess, he still got some money left. Leastways that's what Boots told me."

"All of you. Cotton would do it if he was here. Since he isn't, I'll do it. I'm sure you'll be back in the spring if you take care of yourself."

"It don't pay to fool yerself, Miss Sallie. I know this is my last winter."

"Look, Snowball, if I buy that land you own at above the market value, will you stay in town and take care of yourself? I don't understand why, if you feel this is your last winter, you'd want to go up in those hills again and freeze."

"Because this time I'm going to hit it. Boots feels the same way. If my Maker decides to take me, they'll plant me under the cottonwoods come spring. I gotta do it, Miss Sallie. I'll sell you that worthless piece of land. How much?" he asked slyly.

"How much did you pay for it?"

"Didn't pay nothing for it. Won it in a poker game. Dunwoodie said he paid two bits an acre. Then he won some more shootin' craps. What do you think it's worth, Miss Sallie?"

"I don't honestly know, Snowball. How does three dollars an acre sound?"

"Mighty damn good. I'll take it. We can go over to that lawyer's office and I can sign the deed over to you. Damn, three dollars an acre will buy a lot of whiskey for those cold nights up there in the hills."

"Snowball, do you have any family anywhere? You know, cousins, brothers, sisters?"

"Not that I know of. Cotton, Boots, Jess, and Corker are my family. Why? You changing your mind, Miss Sallie?"

"No. There's talk the government might be interested in the land to build some kind of dam. If I own it and sell it to them, I might get more than I paid you. What seems fair to both of us now might not be fair later on."

"Jesus, Miss Sallie, I ain't gonna be here, so who cares? Just promise me you'll take care of the rest of 'em. If you do that, then we got ourselves a deal. Cotton said you were the only honest woman he ever met. That's good enough for me. He left you his poke, didn't he? Bet he had close to five hundred dollars when he up and died. Am I right, Miss Sallie?"

"More than that, Snowball."

"You funnin' me, Miss Sallie?"

"I wouldn't do that. Are you sure, Snowball, that this is all agreeable to you? I'd really like it if you'd stay in town so you can be looked after."

"There is one thing, Miss Sallie. If I don't come back in the spring, and if the time comes when you sell off that land, buy Red a new dress and give her a little extra to keep in her pocket. She's been real good to me."

"I'll do that. I'd like a promise from you, too, Snowball. If . . . if you . . . if you go somewhere else . . . you know . . . this winter, tell Cotton I'm doing just fine. Tell him I got myself a high school diploma and . . . and tell him I can read the *whole* newspaper. Tell him I got married, and I have a son."

"I'll be sure to tell him, Miss Sallie. We best be tendin' to business so we can leave before this air scorches out the last of my lungs. The others will be waiting at the general store. I'd purely like to take some of those canned peaches this time."

"As many as you want, Snowball."

Watching the four wagons filled to overflowing, her friends singing off-key at the top of their lungs, was one of Sallie's fondest memories. She stood on the corner of First and Garces Street in the small dusty railroad town on the Los Angeles to Salt Lake City line of the Southern Pacific Railroad until the wagons were out of sight. In her purse was the deed to Black Canyon, a mighty abyss whose sides were steep, near-perpendicular walls more than seven hundred feet high. She wondered, not for the first time, if, as Alvin Waring had suggested, she'd bought a pig in the poke. Only time would tell.

Sallie walked home along Fremont Street, her fingers touching the deed in her pocket. Next week she'd take it and the other valuable papers from her town house safe up to Sunrise and put them in the special safe that was impregnable, believing her future was more than secure.

The morning of the day she was to leave for Sunrise, Sallie packed her bag carefully and emptied the contents of the safe into a bank sack. Just as she snapped the lock, the phone rang. Startled, Sallie picked up the receiver and murmured a cautious hello. She didn't know why, but the telephone terrified her. She never knew what to expect. More often than not, the person on the other end of the phone spoke of bad news. The operator announced it was Philip Thornton and passed him through. "Philip! Where are you calling from? They finally hooked it up! That's wonderful! Now I can speak with you on a regular basis. I'll be leaving in a few minutes if that's why you're calling. I just have to put the presents in the car. I have so much to tell you. So much has been happening here in town. I saved all the newspapers and will bring them with me. I've been so busy, Philip. We'll be talking late into the night. What time do you put Ash to bed? Try and keep him awake so I can see him." She listened as her husband spoke. "I won't recognize my own son? How can you say such a thing, Philip? He can't have changed that much. I fully expect him to look like a little person because he is a little person. Babies grow, Philip." She knew she was on touchy ground with her husband. The change in his voice when the discussion turned to Ash was unmistakable.

Sallie changed the subject. "Do you miss your job, Philip?"

"Not at all. I thought I would, but I was wrong. Taking care of Ash is a full-time job. You will not believe how adept I am at diapering and feeding."

"Yes, yes, I do believe it. I could probably never be half as good a mother . . . I mean father . . . as you are."

"All you need is practice, Sallie. I figured it all out. You just need a system and a schedule. The rest falls into place."

"All right, Philip. I'm going to leave now. I'll see you this evening."

"When you come in the house, Sallie, don't whoop like a banshee in case Ash is sleeping. He reacts to strange noises."

"Good-bye, Philip." Sallie slammed the receiver into the cradle of the phone. Whoop like a banshee? Who did he think he was talking to? She'd never, in the whole of her life, whooped like a banshee.

Sallie's thoughts drifted as she watched her houseman carry her bags and parcels out to the car. Would Philip sweep her into his arms, carry her upstairs and make love to her? Six months without any lovemaking was a long time. If he did, maybe this time it would be different. Maybe this time the heavens would explode the way they did when Cotton took her to bed. She thought about her wedding night; she always thought about it when Philip and their strange relationship entered her mind. She'd expected a wild, passion-filled night. Instead, their lovemaking had been perfunctory, with Philip experiencing his own pleasure, then leaving her high and dry. The same thing happened in the succeeding days. In a fit of frustration she'd demanded her own pleasure. If she lived to be a hundred, she would never forget the look on her husband's face. It was to his credit that he didn't utter the words that were on the tip of his tongue. How was it possible that a man as old as Cotton Easter could make her head spin and a young man like Philip fizzled out after three minutes?

A plan would be good, Sallie thought as she settled herself behind the wheel of the car. She wondered what would happen if she stripped naked in the parlor and did a war dance for her husband.

"Tumi," she called to her houseman, "be sure to take that package on the table over to Red Ruby. Do not, I repeat, do not tell her it's from me. I put a card inside and signed Snowball's name to it. Tell her Snowball said Merry Christmas. Don't say another word, no matter what she says to you."

"I understand, Miss Sallie."

"Good, I'll see you in a few weeks. Maybe sooner. I left all the presents for you and Aieya under the Christmas tree. Don't open them till Christmas morning. Call me if anything goes wrong. I left the number by the phone. You have to talk very loud, Tumi, when you speak on the telephone."

It was pitch-black with more than a hint of snow in the air when Sallie arrived at Sunrise. She tooted the horn three times in rapid succession to signal her arrival. The tiny gold watch on her wrist said it was eight o'clock. She was starved—for food, for sex, for her husband. She almost laughed as she speculated about which one she'd get first.

"It is very good to see you, Miss Sallie. Su Li and I have missed you. Merry Christmas."

"Chue, your English is wonderful. I miss both of you, too. Is the tree beautiful?"

"Very beautiful. Su Li and I wanted to wait till you got here to decorate it, but Mr. Philip wanted to do it."

"Is Mr. Philip being good to you and Su Li, Chue?"

"Mr. Philip has no time for us. He's very busy with the child. We have a small lesson in the evening before bed. I do not complain. Mr. Philip is a kind man. He simply does not *see* us. He sees only the child. His world is his son."

"I know," Sallie said softly.

Inside the warm kitchen, Sallie embraced Su Li. "What's for dinner? I'm starved!"

Su Li made a small curtsy. "For dinner, Miss Sallie, there is sweet potato pie. I say that first because you love sweet things. Roast beef, mashed potatoes, delicious gravy, pickled beets, and coleslaw. I made bread today, and the butter is fresh. Mr. Philip ate some time ago."

"Su Li, your English is remarkable. I am so proud of you. When you and Chue get your diplomas we'll hang them on the wall next to mine. I can't believe Philip didn't wait for me to have dinner. Where is he, Su Li?"

"Where he is every evening at this time. Where he is every hour of the day, in the child's nursery. It is not my place to say this is wrong," Su Li said quietly.

"Would you like to come back to town with me?"

"I would like that very much, Miss Sallie. Go now, wash up, and I will have your supper ready when you come down."

Sallie opened the door to the nursery and walked inside. Two lamps gave the room a soft, yellow glow. The fire in the grate was just right. Sitting next to the fire in a rocking chair, Philip rocked the baby, oblivious to everything and anything. He didn't notice her until she called his name.

"Philip, I'm home. I rather thought you would wait to have supper with me. Why isn't Ash in his bed? Why are you rocking him at this hour of the evening?"

"Shush," Philip whispered, his finger to his lips.

"Don't tell me to shush, Philip. Put Ash in his bed. *Now!* Then I want you to come downstairs and talk to me while I have *my* dinner. I haven't seen you in almost four months. I thought you'd be glad to see me. I don't believe what I'm seeing here is healthy."

"Do you think what you've done is healthy, Sallie? You haven't seen your own son in four months. I'm trying to be mother and father to our son."

"He's *your* son, Philip. You made that very clear to me the day he was born. I just gave birth to him. I know if the child had been a girl, you wouldn't be doing what you are doing now. I saw it in your face that day, and I see it now. All you wanted was a son. God help your son if he grows up to be like you."

"What does that mean?"

"You know damn well what it means. He's going to grow into a prissy child. I will not tolerate that, Philip. You spend all your time here in this room, don't you? You hold him constantly."

"Did Su Li tell you that?"

"No. I figured it out myself. Philip, let's go to our room, rip our clothes off, and make love. I missed you. I want us to be man and wife. Life goes on even after a baby is born."

Philip looked everywhere but at his wife. "What if Ash cries while we're making love?"

"So he cries. Babies cry, Philip. Su Li will stay in the room with him."

"Then she'll be next door to us. Listening."

"Damn it, Philip, then we can go down the hall. We can do it in the kitchen, in the barn, wherever you want to go. Unless, of course, I don't interest you anymore. Is that what this is all about?"

"No. You haven't eaten supper yet. I eat early because it's part of my routine. I told you I have a schedule. I do certain things at certain times. This isn't exactly a picnic, you know. A child is a tremendous responsibility."

"Don't you mean a son is a tremendous responsibility? If Ash were a girl, she'd be downstairs with Su Li in the kitchen in her cradle. You know it, and I know it. You know what, Philip, I'm sorry I came up here. I used to love it here."

"You haven't even looked at Ash. You haven't said one word about how big he's gotten, or how beautiful he is."

Sallie felt tears burn behind her eyelids. "I saw him quite clearly. I noticed his weight gain, and, yes, he's absolutely beautiful. You're right, I didn't pick him up. You don't wake up babies when they're asleep. I'm tired, Philip, tomorrow is another day."

"I don't understand you, Sallie. You aren't too tired to drag me to bed, but you're too tired to pick up your son."

"I'm not going to discuss this with you, Philip. I don't care where you sleep tonight, but it better not be in this room. Su Li will leave her door open so she can hear him if he wakes. I don't want you in my bed, either."

"You don't want me in your bed but you'll take some crusty old miner and roll in the sheets with him, sweet-talk him, and cash in on his death. I'm not good enough for you. I don't fill you with passion. I remember that night, Sallie. You were *wanton*." He took Sallie's slap high on his cheekbone. He flinched, but he stared her down until she stalked from the room, her head high.

In the open doorway, Sallie turned, her eyes filled with tears. "It wasn't like that at all, Philip. I will never forgive you for thinking it was. Never!"

Downstairs in the kitchen, Sallie sat down at the table, her face grim, her eyes sparking dangerously. She picked up her fork and began to eat. Su Li watched her, her eyes worried. When she finished eating, she said, "Please tell Chue to take my bags back out to the car."

"Mine too?"

"Yes. Gather up everything for Ash. We're taking him with us."

"Is Mr. Philip coming with us?"

"No!"

"I see," Su Li said.

"I see, too." Both women smiled at the same time before they fell into each other's arms.

"I think we should wait till morning, Miss Sallie. It's very cold out and the night air won't be good for the child. I can have everything ready by dawn. Are you sure you want to do this?"

"I'm not sure at all. My husband said some very cruel things to me upstairs. He's smothering our child. He's a different person. He blames me for . . . I just keep hearing my mother's voice whenever she spoke about my brother, her firstborn son. He broke her heart into a thousand pieces. I won't let that happen to me. Do you think I'm wrong, Su Li?"

"It doesn't matter what I think, Miss Sallie. It's what you think that is important. A child's life is not something to play with because you're angry. You are angry. Perhaps in the morning you will see things differently. Mr. Philip's heart will break if you take away his son."

"See, you're doing it, too! *His* son. He's my son, too. We'll leave in the morning. Leave your door open in case Ash cries. Philip won't be sleeping in Ash's room tonight or any other night from now on. Good night, Su Li."

"Would you like some hot chocolate before you go to sleep? Or some herb tea?"

"Hot chocolate."

Sallie felt like she was eighty years old when she climbed the stairs to the second floor.

A warm bath and the hot chocolate did not lull her to sleep the way she thought they would. Instead, she huddled in her bed, the covers wrapped around her. Waiting. For what, she didn't know.

Sallie made five trips to the bathroom, taking perverse pleasure in pulling the chain on the overhead tank and listening to the water in the pipes gurgle. She knew the gurgling pipes would wake up Philip. She was so angry she wanted to chew iron and spit out rust. What was wrong with her? Why was she acting like this?

She paced, up one side of the room, across and around the chaise longue until she was dizzy. She finally sat down, her shoulders shaking as she dropped her face into her open palms. She jerked upright almost immediately. What was that strange sound? Ash, of course. In her bare feet, Sallie tiptoed to the door, opening it quietly. Ahead of her, Su Li was walking down the hall, a baby bottle in her hand. Sallie didn't stop to think. She ran down the hall to reach the baby's room at the same moment Su Li did. She reached for the warm bottle.

How strange it felt to hold a baby. She'd held her sisters when they were babies, but the feeling wasn't the same. They'd been thin, bony, wrinkled. This child was plump, contented, well fed and clothed. She smiled as the infant sucked, his cheeks puffing out as he stopped long enough to burp around the nipple. "A regular little piglet," Sallie whispered.

He felt warm, soft, and utterly dependent. "Someday you are going to be a big, strapping young man, and you will have babies who will look just like you. You'll feel just the way I feel right now. All I want for you is for you to grow up healthy and strong. I want you to care about your family and the people around you. I don't ever want you to trample on other people's feelings. It takes very little effort to be kind and caring, and the rewards are enormous. I don't want you to fail me because if you do, that means I failed. I'm going to do my best to make sure you grow up independent, but you will have to cooperate with me. I will love you because you are my son, but you will have to earn that love. When you fall down, you will pick yourself up. You will not whimper or whine to get your own way. I won't allow it. At some point you will think you're smarter than your parents and will find ways to try and get your way by pitting your father and me against each other. It won't work. I'm telling you this now. I realize you don't understand what I'm telling you. You'll understand as you grow up because there will be actions to back up this little talk we're having."

Sallie set the bottle down on the floor as she shifted the baby from her cradled arms to her shoulder so she could burp him. The child smiled at her before his fist went into his mouth.

At that moment, Sallie fell in love with her son.

The moment he nodded off, Sallie placed him back in his cradle. She stood beside it for a long time, her tired eyes devouring her young son. When her own eyelids started to droop, she made her way back to her room.

The last person she expected to see in her room was her husband. "Philip! What are you doing here? I'm tired. I'm not in the mood to talk right now."

"I'm not here to talk to you. I'm here to do this," he said, reaching out with one hand to grasp the front of her nightgown. The sound of the silky material ripping roared in Sallie's ears. She tried to gather the gown about herself and back out of the room at the same time, but Philip stiff-armed her against the wall.

"Philip, let me go," Sallie said. "Tomorrow you're going to be sorry you did this. I can smell the liquor on your breath. Get your hands off me. I mean it, Philip. I'll scream for Su Li. I will, Philip, I swear I will."

"Shut up! This is what you want, so this is what you're going to get. If you want to act like a whore, then I'm going to treat you like one. Ladies don't ask for the kinds of things you want. My mother would die before she'd say the kinds of things you said. Only whores say things like that."

"Philip, don't do this. Please." She did her best to fight him off, but he was too strong for her. She felt her legs being pried apart, heard rather than saw the zipper of his pants go down, and then he was inside her, thrusting himself upward as her body jerked and bounced against the wall, his free hands kneading her breasts.

When it was over, Sallie slid to the floor, her face covered with tears.

"That was what you wanted. I gave it to you. Was it good, Sallie?"

"No," Sallie whimpered. "You raped me, Philip. Get out of here and don't ever come into my room again. All I wanted was for you to make love to me. I wanted you to give me as much pleasure as I gave you. Why is that wrong? Why does that make me a whore? We're married. I'm your wife. I have every right to expect . . .

"This is the last time you will ever touch me."

"I'm taking Su Li back to town with me. I've been sitting here for a long time trying to think about what's best for all of us. I've decided . . . you have a voice in this, too, but hear me out. I want all of us to move back to town. I'll call in the carpenters and have them add to the house. Ash will have a nursemaid. You will go back to doing what you do best. I see what you've accomplished with Su Li and Chue, and myself, of course. Teaching is your calling in life, you can't abandon it to play nursemaid to our son. He needs to grow up in a healthy atmosphere where he has both a mother and a father. I'm certain I can overcome my own shortcomings, or at least come to terms with them. As much as it pains me to say this, I must say it. I did love you in a sisterly kind of way, but I was never *in* love with you. I fooled myself and you, too. It wasn't fair of me. Now we're shackled together, like it or not. We could divorce, I suppose. A divorce would free you to marry someone who will fall in love with you. Who knows, I might find someone who will make my pulse pound. You do not make my heart beat faster, and my pulse doesn't even quiver. You have no idea how sorry I am. What you . . . perceive as my past will always be there between us. So my suggestion is this: We were friends once, and that friendship made both of us happy. I'd like to regain those feelings if possible. If not, a divorce is the alternative. Would you like to think about it and we can talk later?"

"And last night?"

"We'll never speak of it again. You have to live with yourself. That will always stand between us, we both know that."

"I agree," Philip said humbly.

"In total?" Sallie asked quietly.

"In total."

"There's one more thing we need to discuss. If one or the other of us should meet someone whom we think . . . if we decide . . . This is very difficult, Philip, but there's no other way to say it other than to come right out with the words. If either of us should meet someone we want to share certain things with, we agree to be discreet, and if it leads to . . . to . . . other things, we will discuss it and arrive at a decision, which of course would be divorce. Are you agreeable to all of this?"

"Yes. I just want to be in your life. The sweetest times in my life were when we sat in the garden and I read to you, or we played chess or just sat by the fire. I looked forward to waking in the morning because I knew I'd be sitting across from you at the breakfast table, and after that we'd go to the schoolroom where I . . . enabled you to become who you are right now. I wanted so much for you, Sallie. Sometimes I think I wanted more for you than you wanted for yourself. I *need* to talk about last night, Sallie."

Sallie almost took pity on her husband at that moment, but she forced herself to look him in the eye. "I can see why you need to talk about it," she said. "but I don't wish to do so. It's over, it's done with, and I don't ever, ever want to discuss it again. Remember one thing, Philip, and then it's a dead issue. I said no. I said no more than once. You forced yourself on me. I begged you to stop. No means no."

"All right, Sallie. Will you be staying on for the holidays, then? Would you please clarify what my duties are in regard to Ash? He recognizes me, depends on me. He might fuss if I . . . if I stay away from him."

Sallie stared at her husband. In her life she'd never seen a more miserable-looking man. "Why is it, Philip, that you don't listen to me? Maybe you do listen, but you don't *hear* what I say. It's not good for you to hold Ash all day long in the rocking chair. When he's being fed, yes. You don't need to sleep in the same room. He needs to exercise his lungs. He whimpers and you're there. Let him squall once in a while. Let him be the baby he is. Yes, I'll be staying for the holidays. All of us will leave for town the first of the year."

"It's just that he's *my son*."

Sallie's expression froze into place. In a cold, clipped voice she said, "I'm very tired and I want to sleep now. I'll see you at the supper table."

Sallie's last conscious thought before drifting into a troubled sleep was that she was being cruel and heartless to her husband by denying him his twenty-four-hour devotion to their son.

1926

Nine months later, on September 20, 1926, Sallie Coleman Thornton gave birth to a second son named Simon Wilcox Thornton, eight pounds four ounces and twenty-one inches long. The doctor, not known for his patience with mothers who didn't wish to nurse, slapped the squalling infant onto Sallie's stomach while he took care of the afterbirth. "Aren't you going to clean him up?" she demanded.

"Aren't you going to feed him?" the doctor shot back.

"Where's the bottle?"

"Under your chin. Nurse him. Now!"

"I will not," Sallie said.

"Then I guess he's going to starve."

In the wink of an eye, and from long years of experience, the doctor had the infant washed and wrapped in a clean blanket. He placed the child in Sallie's arms and repeated his admonition to suckle the crying baby. Sallie had no other choice but to bring out her breast to the infant, who started to suck immediately. A feeling unlike anything she'd ever experienced settled over Sallie. A smile that rivaled the sun spread across her face. In a world of her own for the moment, she neither saw nor heard the doctor leave.

Sallie bonded with young Simon in a way she'd never bonded with Ash. It paved the way for the rivalry that would divide the brothers in the years to come.

That same rivalry pitted mother against father.

6

1942

Two days after Simon's sixteenth birthday, Sallie stood at the grave site with her husband and two teenage sons, her head bowed in prayer. Alvin Waring had died peacefully in his sleep at the age of ninety-one. She raised her eyes to see virtually everyone in town. Her mind drifted as the minister extolled the attorney's virtues. Where had the last nineteen years gone? How was it possible that it was 1942 and the country was at war? Her legs started to tremble as she thought about young Ash's words the day before. "I want to enlist." She'd looked at Philip, whose face drained of all color. She had almost fainted when Simon repeated his brother's words. Philip had simply said, in a shaky voice, "You're too young, I won't hear of it. Your mother and I will not agree to this. If you get called up, that's one thing, enlisting is something else. I don't want to hear another word on the subject." Ash's young, handsome face had turned angry and sullen. It was the first time his father had denied him anything.

Sallie shifted her weight from one foot to the other. She could sense her son's anger as he stood next to her. She was certain Ash would not let the matter drop. Nor would Simon. A comforting hand to her shoulder jerked her to the present. She turned, fully expecting to see Philip's hand, but it was Simon's. She should have known it would be her younger son. From the day of his birth he'd been in tune with her emotions, and she with his.

"Don't cry, Mom. It was Mr. Waring's time, and he died in his sleep. Remember the good things."

"That's easy, Simon, because there were no bad things," Sallie whispered. "Simon, I need to talk with you."

"I know you do, but, Mom, this isn't the place."

"There is no right place to discuss what needs to be discussed. I want your promise, Simon, right now, that you aren't going to do anything foolish. Please, Simon, promise me."

The sixteen-year-old boy, at six feet two inches in height and weighing 180 pounds, flashed his gentle smile and squeezed his mother's shoulder. "I promise I will not do anything *I* consider foolish."

"You look like you're twenty-five years old," Sallie said inanely.

"I'll take that as a compliment."

"It wasn't a compliment, Simon. Ash looks older, too. If those recruiters get a look at either one of you, they'll snap you up in a heartbeat. I know how it works. Simon, who is that man standing at the head of the line of mourners, do you know?"

"That's Devin Rollins. He's taking over Mr. Waring's practice. I guess he's going to be your new attorney. I heard Pop discussing him with someone from school. After the service maybe you should introduce yourself."

"I'll do no such thing. He's on my payroll, let him come to me. Move, Simon, it's time to say good-bye." Tears rolled down her cheeks. A hankie appeared like magic in her hand. Simon again.

"Don't blow till you pass the coffin. You're a honker, Mom." He squeezed her arm reassuringly.

Standing next to the coffin, with the single yellow rose in her hand, Sallie swallowed hard. She took a full minute, a prayer on her lips, her eyes wet with tears. She felt two strong arms steady her and knew immediately that they didn't belong to her sons or husband. "I'm sorry," she managed to choke out.

"Don't be. Sorry, I mean. This is an emotional time for you, for everyone here. It's all right to cry, to falter. I'm just glad I was here to catch you. Devin Rollins, Mrs. Thornton. I'm Alvin's nephew. I'll be taking over his practice. When the time is right, I'll make an appointment with you to discuss your affairs. Are you steady now?"

"Yes. Thank you." Sallie removed her hat and mourning veil. She saw everything about Devin Rollins in one quick glance. He was incredibly tall, taller than her sons, athletic. He was impeccably dressed right down to the shine on his shoes. His dark hair held a hint of a curl and drooped over his forehead to shade his dove gray eyes. She saw the sinfully long eyelashes, the sharp-chiseled features, the warm smile. In the time it took her heart to beat once, Sallie Thornton fell in love. *This man is my destiny*, she thought wildly. Her heart thundering in her chest, Sallie allowed her son to lead her from the grave site. She wanted to turn for a second look at her destiny, but Simon's grasp on her arm was so tight she couldn't afford to take a wrong step, or she would have landed facedown.

"Are you sure you don't want to go to the luncheon, Sallie?" Philip asked.

"I'm sure. I don't have the fortitude to make small talk and discuss Alvin's life with his friends. If that seems callous to you, Philip, I'm sorry. Feel free to go if you want to."

"Ash?"

"Sure, Pop. I liked Mr. Waring."

"Simon?"

"I'll stay with Mom."

"It would be nice, Simon, to show your respect for one of your elders," Philip said. "Mr. Waring has served this family for many years."

"I paid my respects here at the cemetery, Pop. I don't need to do it twice. I'll stay with Mom."

Ash scowled at his brother. He was about to offer a blistering sermon of some kind when he saw the look of distaste on his mother's face. Over the years he'd seen that look many times when he aligned himself with his father. Ash wondered then, as he'd wondered more times than he could remember, if the hatred he felt for his brother showed on his own face. He tried to compose his features, but knew he was too late. His mother had seen the way he felt.

Simon, Simon, Simon. It was always Simon where his mother was concerned. Simon could do no wrong. Simon was the smart one; Simon was the good-looking one; Simon was the one who was going to be in college at the age of sixteen because his brain power was superior. Simon understood the stock market, counseled and advised his mother on a daily basis. Simon knew the family net worth, while he and his father could only guess. Simon had his own car because he'd graduated ahead of schedule. Simon had everything a person could want. Except a father who adored him. Ash smiled smugly. As early as five years of age he'd realized he had a lock on his father's affections, and over the years he made sure that lock stayed in place.

He stood apart, watching his mother and brother walk away. For some strange reason he wanted to cry. Why couldn't she love him the way she loved Simon? He struggled to maintain good grades, struggled to be the best on the football field, struggled to be the most popular, the most sought-after guy in school. Hell, he had his own private airplane. What no one knew, not even his friends, was he used his allowance and any other monies he could filch from his mother's purse or his father's billfold to pay for private tutors and coaches. He was popular with the guys and the girls because he treated constantly and bought little gifts that he presented with offhand generosity. He knew for a fact that the school yearbook was going to have a picture of him in the center of the book whose caption read: "Most popular, most likely to succeed, student of the year." His father was going to be proud. His mother would probably do little more than glance and smile. She might say something like, "I hope it comes to pass, Ash." What that meant was she was doubtful he could make the grade.

That was all going to change real soon. On Monday he was enlisting in the service. He didn't know which branch yet, whichever one believed he was older than he was, he supposed. He'd show them all.

By God, he'd show up Simon if it was the last thing he did.

The simple clapboard town house was now an edifice that defied description. Sallie had had it done and redone during the Depression years simply to give her construction crews work so they could feed their families. She'd also built four more bingo palaces, a movie theater, a pharmacy, a bakery, and a grocery store that stocked every staple known to man. Her refrigeration system allowed for fresh milk, produce, meats, and cheeses. She'd met with the town council, which approved her plans to clean up the less desirable neighborhoods, not with cans of paint and whitewash, but with new building materials. Her biggest challenge was installing a sewage treatment plant. When the engineers told her the total cost she'd gulped hard, then signed her name to the contract. The day she'd told Philip she owned the sewer system he'd laughed in her face and told her only a fool would do such a thing. He wasn't interested in hearing about the revenues she would receive as each new business tied into her lines.

"Look at it this way, Philip, no one in this town can flush unless they pay me," she'd said smugly. "What was it you used to tell me? Oh, yes, if you can't say something nice, don't say anything at all. Do you remember saying that, Philip? I know you resent me and all the things I've done for this town. I also know, because I overheard you telling Ash, that I'm the acquisitions queen of Nevada. You benefit every single day from my generosity. I have never once said anything derogatory to our sons where you're concerned. You see, I believed you when you said a person should never speak unkindly about another person. Yes, I own this town. What's wrong with that? I don't overcharge, I give more than I take in. I help when it's needed, and if they can't pay me back, that's okay, too."

"My wife, Mrs. Nevada," Philip had said.

"The newspaper gave me that title, Philip. You're still angry about Black Mountain, aren't you? I didn't cheat Snowball. I was more than fair. So the government paid me millions of dollars for the land. So what? Boulder Dam will be here long after you, me, our sons, and their sons pass on. It was needed. I suppose I could have insisted they call it the Sallie Coleman Thornton Dam. You hate it when I include my maiden name, I can tell. Guess what, Philip, I don't care. I don't care about a lot of things anymore. I think we should get a divorce. This marriage is a sham and we both know it. The boys know it, too. They're old enough now to understand divorce. Our lives are empty. When do I get to be happy?"

Philip Thornton stared at his wife, the color leaving his face at the mention of the word divorce. He shrugged and wallked away.

That was a year ago and nothing had changed.

"Simon, I think I'm going to get some things together and drive up to Sunrise. You're welcome to come along if you like."

"I have plans, Mom. I can cancel them if you need me."

"Simon, how upset would you be if I told you I was . . . that I've been thinking about a—"

"A divorce? Mom, I can read you like a book. I guess I'd say, what

took you so long? Don't do it because of me, though. I came to terms
with Pop's favoritism a long time ago. I don't cry myself to sleep anymore, and I still include him in my prayers."

"Simon—"

"Mom, it's okay."

"Ash . . ."

"Ash is Ash. He does what he has to do. Sure I'd like it if we were
close, but we aren't. It's never going to happen, Mom. Not in this
lifetime. I don't want you worrying about me. Promise me."

"How'd you get so smart at your age?" Sallie teased.

"By hanging around you. You're the best. Someday Ash and Pop
will say it out loud. They know it now, but heck, you're a woman
and they're men. . . . Men have a hard time saying things like that."

"You said them."

"I learned from you, Mom. Ash learned from Pop."

"Thank you, Simon. Are you and Jerry going flying?"

"Nope. He's afraid to go up with me. And, I didn't ask Pop or Ash
if I could use the plane."

"You don't have to ask them, Simon. The plane belongs to the
family, not to your father or to Ash."

"It doesn't matter, Mom. When I fly I like to fly alone. It's so
peaceful up there."

"I never thought I'd live to see the day when I owned an airplane.
It just amazes me that both you and Ash can actually fly. You're only
sixteen, Simon. I am so proud of you."

A veil dropped over Simon's eyes. "Age is only a number, Mom.
Everyone who meets me for the first time thinks I'm much older."

Sallie winced. "I'll leave a note for your father. I'll probably be
back in the middle of the week."

"Say hello to the gang for me."

Sallie chuckled. "I'll do that. C'mere and give me a hug."

Sallie looked back once as she climbed the steps leading into the
house. Simon was up to something, she could feel it in her bones, or
maybe it was her motherly instincts working overtime.

Inside, Sallie packed her bag and changed her clothes before she
scribbled off a short note: Gone to Sunrise.

The moment Sallie's car was out of sight, Simon ran to his
mother's room to retrieve the note. He crushed it into a ball and stuck
it in his pants pocket, then printed off a new note that said, Simon
and I went to Sunrise. Be back next week. He scrawled a big S the
way he'd seen his mother do. He knew neither his father nor his

brother would give the note a second glance. He carried it down to the dining room, where he left it on the table in full view.

Upstairs in his room, he reached into the closet for his suitcase, opened it to take out the letter he'd written to his mother. His next stop was her room, where he placed the letter under her pillow.

Five minutes later he was in his car. He beeped the horn at his friend Jerry's house, two zippy sounds that made him grin. Jerry loped down the walkway to the car. "Is everything all set?" Simon asked.

"It's done. I don't mind telling you this is making me real nervous. What are my parents going to say when I show up with this fancy car?"

"Jerry, we worked this all out. Your family thinks you are going to Sunrise with me. They aren't going to call or come looking for you. I taught you to drive, so you won't have any problems on that score. We're driving to California where your twenty-three-year-old cousin, for the sum of $500, has agreed to give me his birth certificate and his college degree so I can enlist. This cousin has sworn to both of us to keep his mouth shut even if he's bleeding to death. How'm I doing so far? And, you, my best friend in the whole world, are going to be the happy recipient of this automobile as payment for getting him to agree to the deal. I've taken care of everything. I explained all of it in a letter to my mother, so no one is going to come and take the car away. You are simply going to tell your parents I gave it to you to take care of till I get back. Foolproof. Did I leave anything out, Jerry?"

"Yeah, you left a lot out. What if you get yourself killed? Then what?"

"Then nothing. It's over. I'm not going to get killed. I promise. I don't want to go to college, at least not now. I can't live in that house one more day with Ash and my father. I'm sick and tired of pretending to my mother that things are fine when they aren't. Jesus, I have to force myself to eat when we're all at the table. Why in hell do you think I invite myself to your house so much?"

"I thought you came over because you liked us."

"Yeah, that too, and I also like your mother's cooking. She makes the best pot roast in the world. Your leftovers are real . . . zesty."

"Zesty? I'll tell my mother you said that." Jerry guffawed. "You gonna write?"

"Every chance I get. Swear on your mother you won't share my letters with anyone?"

"C'mon, who am I gonna share them with?"

"You might get a girlfriend who has a big mouth like you do. Swear, Jerry?"

"Okay, I swear. What if they find out you're only sixteen?"

"If you and that cousin of yours keep your mouths shut, no one will find out. If he squeals, I'll hunt him down and cut off his balls."

"He won't tell. Don't you think you should be referring to my cousin by name so you can be familiar with it?"

Simon roared with laughter. "I keep forgetting what his name is. Tell me again."

"His name is Adam Jessup. He has brown eyes and brown curly hair, a little darker than yours. His hair almost looks black. He's nowhere near as muscular as you are, but he's six feet tall. Nobody's going to notice those extra two inches you have. He's not a sharp dresser, most of the time he looks like a bum. My mother says he's shiftless. My father says he's no damn good. Hey, Simon, maybe you can make a hero out of him. Now, wouldn't that be something? Wonder what he'll do with that $500."

"I've been wondering that myself. Take this envelope, it has another $500 in it. Use it on him if he starts making noises like he's going to blab. Now let's talk about girls. I'm going to go to those canteens. I bet I meet a lot of *older* women."

"Don't go knocking any of them up," Jerry said.

They laughed all the way to California.

"Your mother isn't going to like it that I let you drink all that wine," Philip said.

"Then let's not tell her. I'll go straight upstairs and stay there for a while. I'm going to pass on dinner. I ate too much as it is."

"The house is quiet. Simon is usually blaring his radio at this time of day. What's this?" Philip said, reaching for the folded note on the dining room table. "Don't bother running upstairs. Your mother and Simon went to Sunrise. They'll be back next week. Guess us bachelors are on our own. What should we do?"

"Don't know about you, Pop, but I have a date." At the look on his father's face, he said, "I can cancel it. After all, how often do us guys get a chance to be bachelors on the loose?"

A devil perched itself on Philip's shoulder as he ripped the note into shreds. "How would you like to take a chaperoned trip to Red Ruby's?"

"Pop, are you serious?"

"Yes. Heard she's got some new girls fresh from New York. Of course we won't mention this to your mother."

"Course not," Ash said, his face beet red.

"I think we should wait until it gets dark, don't you?" Philip said.

"Hell, yes, Pop. What if someone sees us?"

"That's what going to Red Ruby's is all about. Sneaking in and sneaking out."

"You've done this before." It wasn't a question but a statement. His father shrugged.

Ash had his ace in the hole now. His father would sign his enlistment papers and he'd get to fuck his brains out for a whole night. How lucky could one guy get?

Father and son crept into the house like thieves in the night. "It was a night and a day to remember, wasn't it, Son?"

"It sure was, Pop. I don't think I shoulda had that last drink. You smell!"

"You don't exactly smell like your mother's flower garden yourself."

Philip wrapped his right arm around his son's shoulder.

"Listen, Pop, let's go in the kitchen and make some coffee. I want to talk to you about something important."

"Sure, Son. How about some eggs while we're at it."

"Great. I'm not doing dishes, though."

"That's why we have a housekeeper."

"Simon dries the dishes for Tulee. He takes out the trash for her, too. He carries the laundry up and down the steps."

"Why didn't you ever do it, Ash?"

"For the same reason we don't have to do the dishes. We pay a housekeeper to do it."

"Simon does it because Tulee is getting old. Simon saw your mother help Tulee one day and he stepped in and took over. Your mother doesn't want to pension Tulee off, and she doesn't want to offend her by hiring a younger person to help out. She's very loyal to her employees. She's never forgotten her humble beginnings. If you'd give your mother a chance, you could learn a lot from her, Ash."

"She never gave me a chance, Pop. I don't want to talk about this anymore. I have my views, you have yours, and Mom has hers. I want to enlist, Pop. Monday morning I'm going to join up. I have to get out of here. I don't want to go to college. I'm never going to be a doctor or a scientist. I want you to sign the papers. If you do, I can be out of here before Mom and Simon get back from Sunrise."

Philip's hands started to shake as he measured coffee into the wire basket. "Ash, ask me to do anything but that. How can I send . . . sign . . . your mother . . . Christ Almighty, son, I can't do that."

"Then I'll take off and enlist somewhere else. Pop, look at me. I want to do this. No, that's not right, I *need* to do this. I need to get away from Mom and Simon. I need to see what I'm made of. Haven't I always done what you asked of me? Well, now, I'm asking you for something. Please, sign the papers."

"Ash . . . your mother . . . God, what if something happens to you? My life would be over."

Ash stared at his father, his jaw dropping. "Pop, don't say something like that. You might . . . grieve for a while, but your life would go on. You have Mom and . . . Simon will be around. Jesus, don't go jinxing me now." He watched his father carefully, his stomach in knots as he waited.

Philip cleared his throat. "Son, if this is what you really and truly want, I'll sign the paper and take the consequences when your mother gets home. I want your promise to write faithfully and to call if you can. Will you promise, Ash?"

"You got it, Pop. Thanks. I'll make sure you never regret this. I'll make you proud of me. I swear to God I will."

"Just come back in one piece, Ash. You hate taking orders. How are you going to handle it when your superior officer tells you to do something?"

"I don't know. I'll let you know when it happens. I'm going to be just fine, so don't worry about me."

There was such jubilation in Ash's voice that Philip could only stare at his son. "Tell me something. Has life here been so unbearable that you can't wait to get away from me . . . us?"

"Not you, Pop. Them. I wouldn't say unbearable, but it certainly hasn't been pleasant. I've contemplated taking off in the middle of the night and leaving a note behind. Then I realized I couldn't do that to *you*. I couldn't have asked for a better father. I'm going to miss you, Pop." His voice was sly, his eyes wary as he waited for his father's reaction. When it came it was exactly what he expected and wanted.

"I'm going to miss you, too. You've been a wonderful son. I knew the day you were born you were going to be someone special."

"I'll make you proud, Pop. Thanks for taking me to Red Ruby's. It was a hell of an experience."

"It's always an experience. Don't get the idea I'm a regular customer. I'm not."

"Ruby told me Mom has style. She said she's one classy lady."

"It's true," Philip said. "I've never heard one person in this town say a negative word about your mother. She's done a lot for this town. Hell, she owns the town. I know she slips Red money from time to time. Anonymously, but Red knows where it comes from. There was a time when Red and your mother . . . well, they didn't like each other."

"Do you have regrets, Pop?"

"Not anymore. I loved your mother very much in the beginning. Things change. I'm still very proud of her. Are you aware that she can speak French, German, and Chinese? She taught herself when she was pregnant with you and Simon. I know a smattering of French, but your mother can speak the language like a native. She has an ear for it the same way she has an ear for music."

Ash felt like crying. He could feel his arms and legs start to tremble. He knew his father was on the verge of tears, too. "Well, I think it's time for me to hit the sheets. Thanks, Pop, for everything. By the way, the papers are under the flowers on the dining room table."

Philip nodded. "I'll clean up so Tulee doesn't have to do it when she wakes up. I'll be up in a few minutes." He waited to see if his son would offer to help. When Ash walked out of the kitchen, Philip drew a deep breath, his heart pounding in his chest at what he'd just agreed to do.

He sat down at the table, his thoughts whirling. A second cup of coffee was called for. He drank it and made a second pot. He found himself looking around the kitchen. He rarely came in here. When had it changed? It was so homey, so cozy. He cringed as he realized Sallie, not Tulee, was responsible. The curtains on the multipane windows were red-checkered gingham with red tassels on the hems, and matched cushions on the wooden chairs. Little red clay pots full of herbs sat on all the windowsills. Lustrous plants in copper pots hung from the beams, their leaves emerald green and shiny. He wondered who watered and trimmed them. On the floor, a huge braided rug lay beneath the table and chairs. Gleaming copper cookware hung from pegs next to the green plants. He noticed the fresh flowers in the middle of the table. He knew they came from the greenhouse Sallie had built so Chue could tend the seedlings that he later transported to Sunrise. The house was always full of fresh flowers.

But it was the huge fieldstone fireplace and the two rocking chairs that drew his attention. The rocking chairs that Sallie insisted on buying, even though her mother would never get to rock in them. For years they had been in the sunroom at Sunrise, a reminder to Sallie of what might have been. Then one day they were gone, and now he knew why.

Philip sat down in one of the rocking chairs, his shoulders shaking. He cried for the would-haves, the could-haves, and the should-haves. What would happen once Ash left? Would Sallie boot him out? Would Simon align himself with his mother? Absolutely the boy would stand by his mother. Not for the first time, Philip compared his two sons. Simon was so like him it was scary. He'd seen his intelligence at the age of four when the boy wanted to learn. Sallie had begged him to help Simon and he'd refused, saying the boy needed the school system. Sallie took it for the slap in the face it was and hired an outside teacher for the child. Simon surpassed his brother early on and skipped two grades. He was shy, loved to read, and wrote poetry that brought tears to Philip's eyes. Poetry for his mother. And what had he done? He'd tolerated the boy because he had to. Ash was his priority. Ash had to be the best, but he wasn't the best. Philip knew it; so did Ash and Sallie. It was Simon who won the honors; it was Simon who could always be counted on; Simon who helped Tulee; Simon who stood by his mother's side. Not Ash. Ash was personable, glib, popular, a good athlete. He was also handsome, well dressed, dashing—all the things Philip never was. Ash was also a liar, a manipulator, and a cheat. Sallie had pointed out his bad traits and in no uncertain terms had told Philip to keep his hands off Simon. *You go right ahead and ruin your son, but keep your hands off my son.* He wished he were able to turn the clock backwards so he could do things differently.

Philip got up from the rocking chair. He cleaned the kitchen, picked a dead leaf off one of the herbs, brought it to his nose. Mint. His mother used to grow mint in her garden.

Then he got angry. He left the house, surprised to find that it was still dark. Where he was going it didn't matter if it was light or dark, Red kept the draperies pulled all day and night. Red had become a good friend over the years. He didn't use her services, even though he paid for them. He sat in the dining room and talked to her, sometimes for an entire night. In the morning she always made him breakfast, and if he wasn't talked out, he'd stay on for lunch or dinner.

Red had a good ear, she always knew the right thing to say at the right time. And, he knew for a fact, she never discussed his visits with anyone else. Red Ruby's was a safe haven.

He wished he knew why he let his son believe he *participated* in the action at Red's. To impress the boy, he supposed.

He checked his pockets for cash. With Red you paid for her girls the minute you walked through the door. Because he was a kind, generous man, he paid for talking, too. After all, Red had a living to make like everyone else.

Tonight he had a lot of talking to do.

"When will you be back, Miss Sallie?"

"In a few weeks. Sometimes, Chue, I can close my eyes and actually believe I'm here. The feeling holds me over until it's time to get in the car to make the trip. Do you miss Su Li?"

"Sometimes. All she does is talk, talk, talk. A man needs quiet."

"Do you regret not going on to college, Chue? It's never too late you know."

"I have no regrets. I love working with my hands. This is what I do best. I can never thank you enough for all you've done for Su Li and all our relatives. The new greenhouse is beautiful. Sometimes I sit out there at night and watch my seeds grow. I see them poke through the soil. It's a wonderful feeling." He turned shy suddenly, his head bowed. "I will marry soon. My bride arrives in ten days. I wanted to tell you sooner, but Su Li didn't call until last evening to tell me the arrangements have been finalized. Do you see a problem, Miss Sallie?"

"Hell no! It's about time, Chue. We'll convert the cottage. We'll put in a modern kitchen, a modern bath with a big tub. Ladies like to take baths."

"It is not necessary, Miss Sallie. My new bride will think my room is a palace as I do. I don't want her to think I'm rich."

Sallie smiled as she wagged her finger under Chue's nose. "Not when I get hold of her. You forget, Su Li taught me Chinese. I will make her into an American in no time at all. You want her to dress like us, don't you?"

"I would like that very much. Thank you."

"It is my pleasure. I love doing things for you and Su Li. Both of you have made me so proud. Well, I have to be on my way."

"Say I said hello to Mr. Simon. I miss him even if he does trample my flowers. He does not have a gentle hand with the seedlings. He is like a bull in a china shop."

"I'll tell him you said that." Sallie could hear Chue's laughter as it followed her down the hill.

It was four o'clock on Wednesday afternoon when Sallie walked into the house in town. "I'm home, Tulee? Simon! Ash! Philip! I'm home." Where was everyone?

"No one home, Miss Sallie," Tulee said quietly. "No one home many days."

"Where did they go? Did they leave a note?" Tulee shook her head. Sallie shrugged. "All right, if they get back, tell them I'm home. I have to go out again. Have dinner ready for six o'clock. Make something really sweet for dessert."

"Su Li come for supper. She call on telly phone."

"Oh, good. I'll be back soon."

When Sallie returned, Su Li was waiting for her, but Sallie's family was still absent. "This is very strange—we always leave notes. Tulee said they've been gone many days. Do you think something happened?" Sallie asked anxiously.

"Of course not. Tulee gets her times mixed up. I looked for notes, but yours was the only one I could find."

"Let me see that. I didn't write this! This is Simon's printing! He wasn't with me. Why would he do this?" Sallie raced through the rooms and up the steps, Su Li behind her. Simon's room was first. "I don't have to look through his things, Su Li. He's gone. The family picture of all of us is gone. He would take that. His suitcase is gone. I shouldn't have forced the college issue. Maybe he's with Ash. That's probably the stupidest thought I've ever said in my life." She was babbling tearfully, her heart thundering in her chest, as she moved to Ash's room.

"Ash is gone, too." Her eye fell on the family picture on Ash's desk. Ash would never take the picture. He didn't have a sentimental bone in his body. His shaving gear, his football trophy, and his bankbook were gone, the important things in his life. "I know where they went, Su Li, and I am going to kill Philip with my bare hands."

"Where, Miss Sallie?" Su Li asked.

"They ran off and enlisted. Philip must have signed the papers for them. My God, Su Li, Simon is only sixteen years old. How could he do this to me?"

"Hush, you don't know any such thing. Maybe they just went away for a few days. Let's go into your room and see if they left you a note. That's where they would leave it, not in their rooms. You go to your room, and I'll check Mr. Thornton's room. How will I know what's missing?"

"I'll check his room myself." A moment later she said, "He didn't go with them. I know everything he has and nothing appears to be missing except him. I don't believe this. Nothing's here, no note, no letter. Nothing."

"Yes, there is something." Su Li handed Simon's note to Sallie. "Simon would never leave without telling you, and this is the place he put his letter. Under your pillow."

A long time later, when there were no more tears, Sallie stood, her eyes cold and hard. "I need to find Philip. Do you have any idea where he might be, Su Li?"

"I can go out and look for him."

"I think I . . . Let me make a phone call first." Sallie picked up the phone, waited for the operator, and quietly said, "2456."

"Red, this is Sallie Thornton. If Philip is there, would you please tell him to come home. It's a family emergency. If he isn't there and you see him, give him the message."

"I'll send him home, Sallie."

"He's at Red Ruby's, Su Li." Suddenly she was so tired she could barely stand.

The moment Philip Thornton walked through the door, Sallie said, "I need you to explain why you allowed our sons to join up. Don't deny it, Philip. Oh, hell, what's the use? It's done. I cannot, I will not, forgive this, Philip."

"Sallie, are you saying Simon . . . ?"

"Don't play me for a fool, Philip. Are you saying you didn't know . . . ?"

"That's exactly what I'm saying. I did sign the papers for Ash. I'd do it again, Sallie. I know nothing about Simon."

Sallie held up her hand. "Do not talk to me, Philip. I'm too upset and I don't want either one of us to say things we'll regret. We cannot undo this."

Philip's shoulders sagged as he walked out of the room.

Su Li walked with Sallie upstairs to her room. "My mother was wrong, Su Li. I was wrong. I thought it was my firstborn who would break my heart, so I took steps to prevent that from happening. It's the second son that breaks your heart. How could I know that? I thought I was safe, immune. I know now how my mother felt. How could I have been so wrong? What did I do to deserve this? Did this happen to me because I don't love Philip? Am I being punished?"

"No, Miss Sallie. Your sons will be fine, I feel it here," Su Li said, thumping her chest. "We Chinese know these things. Believe me. You're weary, sleep."

"You're a wonderful friend, Su Li. I should tell you that more often. Is what you said, true?"

"Yes. Nothing will happen to your sons. I would feel something and I feel only lighthearted. That means they will be all right."

"That sounds like bunk to me," Sallie muttered.

"That's because it is bunk. I've already forgotten the old ways. You made me into an American. Seriously, Miss Sallie, both your sons will be fine. I believe it, and you need to believe it. We'll talk in the morning."

Sallie was already asleep, tears on her lashes.

Su Li settled herself for the long evening ahead.

The following morning Sallie did something she'd never done in the whole of her married life—she cleaned house. Wearing one of Tulee's shapeless housedresses, her hair bound around her head with a clean rag, she plunged into the work at hand. She lined up her cleaning supplies neatly in the hallway before she entered Ash's room. In her hand were three flour sacks. Willy-nilly, she dumped his belongings into the sacks and dragged them out to the hall. She didn't waste a second staring at his mementos or fingering his possessions. When she finished, she dragged the sacks to the stairway and kicked them down the stairs. Later she would have Philip carry them to the basement.

Her next chore was to rip the curtains and draperies from the windows. The bedding was her enemy as she pulled and tugged. The bundle went over the hallway banister to land in the foyer. She scrubbed, then polished. When she was finished with the hand sweeper, she backed out of the room and pulled the door shut. If she had had a key, she would have locked the door.

At the top of the steps she called to Tulee. "Bring me a cup of coffee, please," she said, sitting down on the top step. She sat like an urchin, her legs apart, her scrub dress tucked between her legs as she wiped at the sweat dripping down her face. "And a cigarette. Bring the whole pack along with an ashtray."

Sallie was on her third cigarette and second cup of coffee when the doorbell at the foot of the steps peeled once, twice, three times. She made no move to go down the steps to answer it. Through a cloud of smoke she watched Tulee open the door.

"Devin Rollins to see Mrs. Thornton," she called.

"I'm up here, Mr. Rollins," Sallie said as she blew a perfect smoke ring. "I thought you were going to call first. That is what you said, isn't it?"

"I've been calling for several days, but there was no answer. There are some papers that need to be signed. I brought them along. If this is a bad time, I can come back another day, or you can stop by the office."

"Step into *my* office," Sallie said, pointing to the space next to her at the top of the steps.

Eyes twinkling, a wry smile on his lips, Devin Rollins climbed the steps and took his place next to Sallie.

"Wherever are my manners? Coffee, cigarette?" Sallie said dryly. "Tulee, fetch another cup for Mr. Rollins and a clean ashtray."

"I'll have both. This is . . . ah . . . cozy. I don't think I've ever conducted business on a staircase before. Yes, your knee or mine?" He grinned as he held out paper and pen.

"Mr. Rollins, surely you don't expect me to sign these papers without reading them!"

"Absolutely not. I'll just drink my coffee and smoke my cigarette while you read them. My next appointment isn't until after lunch. Peruse to your heart's content. Signing these papers in no way obligates you to use my services. I'm simply tidying up my uncle's part of the business."

Sallie scanned the papers in her hands. She had no idea what she was reading, she was too aware of the man sitting next to her. He smelled of tobacco, soap, and something else that reminded her of her garden in Sunrise at the beginning of summer. It was an earth smell, clean and fresh. She wondered what she smelled like. Octagon soap and No Worry bleach. A heady combination if there ever was one. She noticed her broken nails for the first time, the polish cracked and chipped. Her hands were already red and dry-looking. She cringed when she looked down at her bare feet.

"They appear to be in order," Sallie said.

"Then you'll sign them."

"No. Leave them, I'll look them over later and drop them off at your office tomorrow."

"Then you just pretended to read them. There's nothing complicated or momentous in any of them. A delay could cost you money. Perhaps you should consider giving your attorney your power of attorney. Time is money, Mrs. Thornton. Just because you have a lot of it doesn't mean you can sit back and do things at your convenience. It's a foolish way of doing business."

"Really," Sallie drawled. Maybe he wasn't her destiny after all. "You're being pushy, Mr. Rollins. That will not endear you to me. I'll sign the papers when I'm damn good and ready. Another cigarette?"

"Why not. Are we having lunch up here, too?" He laughed then, a sound that sent chills up and down Sallie's spine. "I don't think I've ever been called pushy before," he said. "Exactly what does that word mean to you?"

Sallie stared at the man sitting next to her. "It means you're treading on my privacy when I'm in a vulnerable state. You want me to do something I don't want to do. At the moment. I didn't say I wouldn't sign the papers. I said I wanted to read them again, and then you gave me a lecture on time and money. That's pushy. For sure I won't sign them now. I don't like people telling me what to do. When I make a mistake I learn from it, and then I don't make the same mistake again. Do you understand?"

"Point taken. What's for lunch?"

"Crow."

He laughed again—and Sallie shivered again.

"Tulee!" When the old Chinese woman appeared, Sallie said, "Bring us two ham sandwiches and some pickles, please. And some fresh coffee."

They talked as they munched, mostly of Alvin Waring and his years of devoted service. "He told me so much about Sunrise. I'd like to see it someday. He spoke very highly of your sons, Simon and Ashford. These are very good pickles. In fact these are the best pickles I've ever eaten. Not too sour, not too sweet, just right. Do they have a name? Do you mind if I eat yours?"

"Be my guest. I'll have Tulee give you a jar when you leave. When are you leaving?"

"Just as soon as I finish your pickle. You've already forgotten that I said I had an appointment after lunch. Obviously, I interrupted something you were in the midst of. I do thank you for spending time with me."

Sallie didn't know if she should laugh or cry. "I was clearing out Simon's and Ash's rooms. Simon ran away last week and enlisted. I didn't find out until last evening when I got back from Sunrise. Philip   Philip signed the papers for Ash to enlist. He left on Monday. I didn't know. I should have known something was wrong. I didn't. So, as you can see, I'm . . . What I'm doing is—"

"Trying to erase them from your life. You can't do that, Miss Sallie. Oh, you can clean their rooms, put their things in storage, but how do you remove them from your heart? You're just doing physical things to get you through a bad time. Your sons appear to be fine young men. They're doing what they perceive to be their duty. You can't fault them for that."

"It's not that simple, Mr. Rollins."

"It never is. Please, call me Devin. Mr. Rollins is my father and grandfather. I'd like it if you would allow me to call you Sallie, the way my uncle did." Sallie nodded, her eyes miserable.

"When you're done, you aren't going to feel any better, you know."

"I know."

"Why don't you put everything back. *That* might make you feel better. It's something to think about."

"I'll think about it," Sallie said.

"No you won't. My uncle said you were pigheaded at times."

"That won't endear you to me, either," Sallie snapped.

"I wasn't trying to endear myself to you. The truth hurts sometimes. You said something about giving me a jar of pickles."

"Go into the kitchen and ask Tulee to give you one."

"Shall we set up an appointment, or should I just drop by? There's a lot to be said for spontaneity. I enjoyed our meeting. The next time you must allow me to take you to lunch."

Devin was four steps below her, his eyes locked on hers. Instead of being flustered by her appearance, instead of being nervous and jittery at their closeness, she felt exhilarated as he looked deeply into her eyes. "Tell me something," he whispered.

At that precise moment Sallie would have told him the combination to the Sunrise wall safe. "What?" she whispered in return.

"Why do you paint your toenails?"

Sallie's jaw dropped. She pulled her arm up to toss the coffee cup in his direction, but he was at the foot of the steps and out the door. The door opened a second later. "I'll get the pickles another time." She could hear him laughing as he made his way down the walkway.

"Destiny, my ass," Sallie muttered as she walked down the steps. "A pain in my ass is more like it." She knew she was being crude, but she didn't care. Devin Rollins stirred something in her she didn't want to deal with. Something she hadn't felt for many years.

Sallie spent the rest of the afternoon putting everything back into Ash's room. When she was finished she closed the door quietly, her head bowed. She took a deep breath before she walked into Simon's room. She sat down on the edge of the bed and tried to imagine the times Simon had come in here to hide his hurt and anger. Probably as many times as Ash had gone into his room. She said a prayer, then asked God to keep her sons safe. There was nothing else for her to do.

It had been a long time since she'd really looked in here because Simon liked privacy, though he often invited her in. During those times she sat on the chair or on the edge of the bed as she listened to his problems, some of them real, some imagined. Always, though, there was an undertone of unhappiness.

Ash, on the other hand, had an open-door policy. He didn't care if she came in or not. Many times she'd seen him lazing about in his underwear. He'd never been shy or embarrassed the way Simon was. He was messy where Simon was neat and tidy. How Ash managed to go out of the house looking like he stepped from a bandbox was beyond her comprehension. His bathroom was always sloppy with spilled water, wet towels, the mirror dotted with shaving soap, and dirty clothes on the floor. No wonder Tulee was always tired.

Sallie thought about the many mistakes she'd made during these last years, all with good intentions. So many mistakes. Wearily she made her way to the bathroom. She caught a glimpse of herself in the mirror. She looked like a scrubwoman after a long hard day of work. And looking like this, she'd had lunch on top of the steps with Devin Rollins. He liked her pickles. She started to laugh and couldn't stop. When she finally calmed down she started to cry—for the past, the present, and whatever the future held for her.

7

Sallie woke with a headache pounding behind her eyes. It was going to be one of those all-day headaches. A soft knock sounded on her door. She recognized Philip's knock because it was always tentative. "Come in, Philip."

"I thought you might like some coffee. I saved Tulee a trip up the stairs. You have one of your headaches, don't you?"

"I felt it coming on all day yesterday. I'll take a headache powder and it will go away. Do you want to talk about something, Philip?"

"I guess I want to talk about the boys. Sallie, as God is my judge, I believed Simon was with you. He planned it all very carefully. He tricked both of us. I'm more than willing to take the blame for signing the papers for Ash. I don't think it was wrong, Sallie. It might be the best thing in the world for the boy. It just might make a man of him. I'm not blind to his faults, Sallie. I wanted him to be the exact opposite of me. I went about it all wrong. I don't want you to hate me; our relationship is strange enough as it is. We need to talk about that, too. Would you like me to move out or to retire to Sunrise? I can't bear to see you unhappy."

"I've been unfair to you, Philip. I'm truly sorry. What do you want to do? Whatever it is, it will be all right with me. I tried so hard to guard against this happening, but it happened anyway. I don't think I can describe the devastating feelings I experienced. I wish . . . I could turn the clock backward. I feel such . . . a loss. My God, Philip, what if something happens to them? How will we deal with that?"

"I don't know, Sallie. I guess we trust in God the way every other parent does. We aren't special when it comes to something like this. One of the conditions to me signing Ash's papers was that he agreed to write faithfully. I don't know what to say about Simon. I want to believe he'll write, but more than likely he won't. He concocted some cockamamie scheme, and he won't want to jeopardize it. I'm certain he'll call, Sallie. Let's agree to think positive about this."

"All right, Philip. Which brings us back to you. What do you want to do?"

"I want us both to be happy. If we can't be happy together, maybe we can be happy apart. It's going to be hard on both of us now with the boys gone."

"Do *you* want a divorce, Philip?"

"No. I've gotten used to the strange way we live. I always wanted to believe . . . that we would live happily ever after. The joke's on me, though."

"Then let's just let things be. Your job is here in town, so why don't I move back to Sunrise. I can conduct business from there. Since we put in a paved road, I can be here in a little over two hours if I want to come to town. Sunrise is your home, too, Philip. Anytime you want to come up and stay, it will be fine with me. Your teaching friends are here and I know you made a separate life for yourself. It's up to you. Philip, why haven't you ever used the money I gave you?"

"Because you can't buy me, Sallie, and that's what you were doing. You were trying to make up for marrying me when you didn't love me. It's all in the bank. I more or less promised it to Ash. It's a princely sum by now."

"I see."

"This time you really do see, don't you?"

"Yes. Philip, why don't you and I play hooky today and go on a picnic?"

"Now that sounds like a fine idea. Get up, take something for your headache, and I'll have Tulee make us a grand picnic lunch complete with wine and long-stemmed glasses."

"I'm going to wear slacks."

"Great idea."

"We'll drink a toast to our sons. I'd like to do that, Philip."

"Then that's what we'll do. I'll meet you downstairs when you're ready. I'll be the guy in the kitchen reading the paper and drinking coffee."

"And I'll be the dame wearing pants for the first time in public."

"Where shall we go?" Philip asked.

"The one place we both love, Sunrise. We can picnic in the garden and drive back this evening. If we're going to reminisce, I guess we should do it there. The boys were happy there in the summers and during the holidays. Go along, Philip, read your paper and drink your coffee. Oh, I do have to make one stop before we leave. I promised Mr. Rollins I would sign and drop off some papers he left for me yesterday."

Sallie blinked several times before she permitted her eyes to register the changes in Alvin's old offices. In just two weeks, Devin Rollins had transformed the dry, dusty, old-fashioned rooms into a comfortable, colorful suite. The roll-up shades had been replaced with fashionable venetian blinds and pale gray draperies. Deep burgundy threads ran through the window hangings that complemented the rich maroon client chairs. In place of the olive green threadbare carpet was a thick, ankle-hugging dove gray rug. Small mahogany tables held lustrous green ferns and the latest magazines. In the center of the room a shiny mahogany receptionist desk sat empty, but only for a second. A young woman, impeccably dressed, walked from the inner office to take her seat.

Out with the old, in with the new. Sallie couldn't help but wonder where the money came from for all the changes. For a reason she couldn't explain, she felt angry and annoyed.

"Can I help you? Do you have an appointment with Mr. Rollins?"

"No. I'm Sallie Thornton. Tell Mr. Rollins I'm here, please."

"Mr. Rollins is busy at the moment. Would you care to make an appointment or leave a message?"

During all the years she'd done business with Alvin, she'd never once made an appointment, and she wasn't about to start now. "Actually, no, I don't care to make an appointment. Not now, not tomorrow, not any day in the near future. Write that down, Miss . . ."

"Reddington. Do you wish to leave a message, then?"

"Well, in a manner of speaking, I guess I do. *Sit!*" It was an iron command the receptionist didn't question. Half out of her chair, she sat down primly. "Now, stay there until I come out of the office." The folder of papers in one hand, a jar of pickles in the other, Sallie managed to open the door and unscrew the lid from the jar of pickles at the same time.

Devin Rollins, minus his suit jacket, was puffing on a cigarette, his feet propped up on a shiny new desk. His feet thumped to the floor at the sight of Sallie in the open doorway.

"Your secretary said you were busy and wanted to know if I cared to make an appointment. I do not. Nor do I care to leave a message. In the end I was Alvin's only client because he retired and saw to my affairs as a courtesy. What that means is you aren't busy." To make her point, Sallie banged the open jar of pickles down on his desk. She turned on her heel and marched out of the office, her head high, her face burning. In the doorway she turned to face Miss Reddington. "*If* I ever return to this office, you better be prepared to stand on your head and whistle 'Dixie' at the same time. I do not make appointments!"

"Write that down, Miss Reddington," Devin Rollins shouted as he bit into one of the pickles. He laughed as Sallie slammed the door, but he stopped laughing as he watched from the window and saw her get into the car with her husband.

"I just did an incredible, stupid thing, Philip," Sallie said as she climbed into the car.

Philip grinned. "What did you do?" Sallie told him in detail.

"I'd wager that got his attention," Philip said. "Good lawyers are hard to find. I'd heard he was from Boston, but that was just a rumor. He's from Philadelphia. A Harvard man. That means he's one of the best. There's going to be trouble in this town soon. Those gangsters are going to start moving in in droves." There was no apology in his voice when he said, "Red is in a position to hear everything that's going on. She's worried. You know how those mobsters operate. They have their own stable of girls and take a large percentage of the profits. Red gets by because she only takes a small percentage."

"Well, maybe we can do something about that for Red. She's your friend, Philip, would you like me to help her out before those thugs plow her under?"

"Would you do that, Sallie?"

"Of course. Snowball adored her. I've been trying to—"

"I know, Sallie. Red knows, too. You don't have to sign your name to things. You should have seen her in that dress you sent that Christmas. You would have thought you gift wrapped the moon and the stars and threw in the clouds for good measure. That was nice of you."

"Snowball—"

"You would have done it anyway. Don't negate a good deed. Red is not as old as you think."

Sallie nodded. "I'm going to ponder on the matter. I will do something, Philip."

"Have you noticed all the new people in town?"

"I'm up on it, Philip. I have this town under control."

"Now that they've legalized gambling, there could be a whole mess of trouble. I want you to be careful, Sallie."

"Philip, I give you my word, I'll be careful. All my plans are in my head. I think I'm going to build a gambling casino. What do you think of the idea? I plan to give that bug person a run for his money. I'm going to wait until he finishes his project and finds out he has no way to dispose of his sewage, and no way to get his laundry done, and no place to get his ice and no freight company to haul his stuff."

"Jesus Christ! Is that why you bought up all those companies?"

"Yes. I knew this town would boom again. I knew it, Philip, in my gut. You told me everything in life comes full circle at some point. The two ends of the circle are coming together. I don't know why, Philip, but it's important to me for you to be proud of me. If you hadn't been my teacher, we wouldn't be sitting here having this conversation."

"I am very proud of you, Sallie. However, you give me too much credit. You took everything I taught you, all your learning, and built on it by yourself. Jesus, you can speak Chinese like a native. I was never able to do that. Hell, yes, I'm proud of you. Most times I'm downright jealous."

"I like honesty," Sallie said.

"I know you do." Husband and wife shared a friendly, genuine moment.

The outing was one of the few truly happy moments in Sallie's life.

Three weeks from the day of the picnic, Sallie Thornton sashayed into Devin Rollins's office along with an architect, a builder, and Red Ruby. Sallie nodded curtly to the receptionist as Devin literally bounded from his office, his shirtsleeves rolled to his elbows, his tie askew. He made no apologies as he offered his hand first to the architect and then the builder. He smiled at Sallie. "Does this mean I'm your attorney and you're my client?" he whispered as the men preceded him into his plush offices.

"For the moment. Don't get too comfortable in the position. Things change in this town on a daily basis." She smiled to take the sting from her words.

The moment Rollins sat down behind his desk, Sallie felt comfortable with him. From time to time he scribbled a note on a legal pad, his eyes on both the men in front of him. "Let me make sure I have all of this straight. Mrs. Thornton owns a ranch seven miles outside of town. She also owns the acreage that surrounds the ranch. You are going to remodel the main building as well as the two outer buildings. One of the outer buildings will be Miss Ruby's private home. The other buildings will be added on to; you said seven rooms plus a living room, kitchen, and three bathrooms on the first floor, and five rooms on the second floor. A little over ten thousand square feet in the second building, am I right?" The contractor nodded, as did the architect. "Miss Ruby's house will have a front porch, a flower garden, six rooms, and two bathrooms, one upstairs and one downstairs. The ranch itself will be totally remodeled. There will be a gaming room, a solarium, a small theater with a stage for entertainment purposes that have nothing to do with the business at hand. A bar complete with handrails, stools, small tables, and whatever else Miss Ruby wants, will be in the back of the house. There are now twelve rooms that are to be remodeled . . . for . . . business. Two wings branching out left and right will make for fourteen additional rooms. A swimming pool will be added somewhere between the two wings. It sounds to me like a very profitable undertaking. The deed to the property will revert to Miss Ruby after one year. The . . . ah . . . fine details of the contracts between Miss Ruby and her . . . employees will be a separate matter. A special fund for . . . for those who can no longer . . . participate . . . will be monitored by Mrs. Thornton and myself. The percentage of the profits is yet to be decided. I guess that pretty much covers things with the exception of the monies to be paid out as the work progresses. Did I miss anything?"

"I'll be putting all my work crews on the project. We anticipate a completion date of ten months. Since we already have existing structures and Mr. LeVoy's blueprints are finished, I think we can safely say, Miss Ruby's . . . establishment will be operational by our target date."

As one, the men rose, shook hands, and walked through the office to the waiting room, where they held a brief conversation.

The two women stared at one another. "Why?" Red asked.

"Sometimes, Red, you have to give back a little. You're Philip's friend, and I know for a fact that he treasures your friendship. Snowball . . . Well, he wanted me to look after you. Not that you need looking after, think of it more as . . . as . . . you have a friend you can count on if things get . . . you know."

"I know you're the one who's been sending things and the money during the holidays. I wanted to thank you a hundred different times. I do thank you, Sallie."

"This isn't as simple as you think, Red. As you know, there are a lot of strange people in town, and more keep coming every day. Zeke McCabe at town hall calls every day when one of those people comes in to check the land records. The hoods, the thugs, the gangsters are coming, whether we like it or not."

"And you, one woman, you think you're a match for them, Sallie? My God, they use machine guns. Those kinds of people just . . . pop you. If you don't give them what they want, they kill you. I have ears. My girls tell me everything they hear. I'm more than willing to pass it on, but I have to tell you, Sallie, the fear is going to eat me alive."

"That's why I'm moving you out to the ranch. You're going to be running a classy establishment, Red. Clean, healthy girls who get seventy-five percent of the take. You'll put Doc Clayton on your payroll. You need to get some new clothing. Appearances are very important. That's why Beaunell Starr did more business than you. Sometimes, Red, you have to spend money to make money. I learned that the hard way. You are also going to charge outrageous prices.

When something is expensive or out of a person's price range, that person wants it so bad he can taste it. I learned that, too. Your outrageous prices will pay for the swimming pool."

"I don't know if I can pull this off, Sallie. What's that saying, you can't make a silk purse out of a sow's ear."

"In this case that particular saying is all wrong. Do you know anything about chickens, Red?"

"They lay eggs, and the roosters crow very early in the morning. That's it, why?"

"Aside from your own, ah . . . business, you are going to raise chickens, lots and lots of chickens. You'll sell those eggs and chickens to the hotels in town. Think about all that acreage that surrounds the ranch. You can raise cattle and a truck garden, too. I know hundreds of Chinese who can grow anything, but you have to pay them a decent, fair wage. I'll set it all up, it will be a second thriving business. On the books. All you have to do is oversee it. You hire people to take care of the rest. Mr. Rollins will handle the paperwork. You're going to have so much money you're going to get dizzy counting it."

"What do you get out of it, Sallie?"

"Security. When this town takes off, and it is going to boom wide open, I want the power to control it. This is my town, I bought it and paid for it, and no one is going to give me trouble. I own all the land, and my sister Peggy is about to marry the lieutenant governor of this fine state. What do you think of that?"

"God Almighty! Where'd you learn to be so smart?"

"I read, Red. What I'm going to need now is a good set of ears. That's where you come in. Men talk when they're drinking, or in bed. I need an edge, and you're going to give it to me. Can you do it, Red?"

"As long as me and my girls have a place that's ours, I can do whatever you want. Were you serious about giving me the deed? I think about my old age a lot. I don't want to have to scramble and pick pockets when I'm sixty years old."

"That will never happen, Red. You have my word."

"Then that's all I need."

"Good. I want you to go back to your place, pack up, and go out to the ranch. You can all live there while the renovations are going on. I'll have someone bring out food on a weekly basis. Think of it as an extended vacation. Mr. Rollins will put some money into an account for you. You might want to give some thought to going to

Los Angeles to get some new things. He can arrange all that for you."

"What about Beaunell Starr?"

"Beaunell will be moving to Reno very shortly, within the week. Of course she doesn't know that yet. I'm going to be making her the same offer I made to you. She might resist at first, but she'll come around. That's what power is all about, Red. Is there anything else you want to ask me?"

"One question. What happens to all of your plans, to all of us, if something happens to you? I hope you've given that some thought."

"I've given it a great deal of thought. I am doing everything legally, so I don't run afoul of the law. The governor is a personal friend of mine, and he knows everything that is going on. He has some very influential friends. I'm going to do my best to ensure that there is no violence. If that does happen, we'll deal with it. This is my town, and no damn gangster is going to take it away from me. We'll talk, discuss it, negotiate if we have to. I'm not so naive that I don't know I may have to bend a little, and so will they. This town will be someplace you want to come to on Saturday night, Red."

"Is that before or after I pluck the chickens?" Both women doubled over laughing. "I owe you big time, Sallie. Thanks."

"My pleasure, Red."

"Would you ladies allow me to take you to lunch?" Devin asked, coming back into the office.

"I can't. Thank you for the invitation, though," Red said politely.

"I would be delighted," Sallie said.

"You would!"

Sallie laughed. "Did you ask me thinking I'd say no?"

"Not at all. Let me get my jacket and we can be on our way."

"I'll be in touch, Red. By the way, the ranch is going to be called the R & R Ranch. For Red Ruby of course. You do know where it is, don't you?"

"Of course I know where it is. Snowball used to take me on buggy rides out there."

"I know," Sallie said quietly.

"It figures." Red grinned.

"Mrs. Thornton," Devin said, holding out his arm.

"Mr. Rollins," Sallie said as she linked her arm with his.

As they strolled down Fremont Street, Devin said, "I have some business I'd like to discuss with you over lunch. However, I need to know if I'm going to be your full-time attorney. You never did say, you simply showed up."

"I studied your credentials. Mr. Waring thought very highly of you. I see no reason not to use your services. I think we can get along."

"As long as I do exactly what you say, we'll get along, is that what you mean?"

"Pretty much so."

"Then, why do you need me? Why don't you just handle your business yourself?"

"Because I'm not a lawyer. I read everything three times, and then I chew on it for a while, so don't try to put anything over on me. I had this same exact discussion with your uncle at one time. I trusted him. Implicitly. If you want me to trust you, you'll have to earn that trust."

"He adored you, you know. He wrote me a very long, wonderful letter that I will treasure forever. When I finished it, I knew him and you as well. I want to know you better, Mrs. Thornton. He also left a letter for you. He said I was only to give it to you if you hired me. If you didn't, I was to destroy it. I think my uncle was in love with you. His main passion in life, especially during the last ten years, was to make you the richest woman in the country. From everything I've seen and read, it looks to me like he succeeded."

"Did he really leave me a letter? How kind of him. When will you give it to me?"

"After lunch. I thought we were going to call each other by our first names?"

Sallie leaned across the table, her eyes directly on Devin's. "I'm a married woman, Mr. Rollins. What we have is a business relationship like I had with your uncle. I'm Mrs. Thornton, and you are Mr. Rollins."

Devin leaned across his side of the table with only inches to spare between the two of them. "You're flirting with me."

Sallie smiled. "No, I'm not. You want me to, though. When and *if* I ever flirt with you, you'll know it."

"Might that happen?" His grin was so contagious, Sallie laughed.

"Probably not. I told you, I'm married."

"My uncle told me all about your marriage. He felt I needed to know. He put it all in my letter. Don't get angry, a lawyer needs to know things like that so he can represent his client knowing the good as well as the bad. He didn't betray a confidence, he merely passed on his observations to me. Like my uncle, I'm bound by the same legal oath."

"I see." Sallie leaned back against her chair. "Tell me about the business you wanted to discuss."

"A year or so ago my uncle called me and asked me to do some research on an aviation company. A small company with some very lucrative government contracts. It seems the company could use some investment capital to expand. He thought it would be a good idea for you to get in on the ground floor. You could make millions. Airplanes are the wave of the future. I would be more than happy to drop you off, or you can stop by and take all my research back with you. The company is in Austin, Texas. As I said, it's a fledgling business at the moment, but it will take off, with or without your investment. The man who owns the firm is hard as nails. I spoke to him several times. I personally don't like him, but personalities cannot interfere in business. I know for a fact that he will not do business with a woman. He thinks women should be seen and not heard, and they should bake bread, can pickles, and wear aprons."

"I don't own an apron," Sallie said.

"I figured that out myself. It was the pickle part I wasn't sure of." Devin laughed then. Sallie found herself giggling.

"You haven't had much fun in your life, have you?"

"Fun?" Sallie made the word sound obscene.

"I guess what I'm trying to say is, it appears you didn't have a childhood filled with play and laughter. Which is just another way of saying you never had a real childhood."

"I don't care to discuss my childhood, Mr. Rollins. Are you recommending I invest in the aviation company?"

"Based on what I know, I'd say yes. Air travel will be for everyone, not just the rich. Everything goes in cycles, Mrs. Thornton. First it was the railroad, then it was the automobile. Now it's going to be airplanes. Remember the fortune you made on your railroad stock? The same thing could happen with the aviation stock. I guess this all sounds like I'm trying to influence you. I plan on investing myself."

"Is there a time limit on my answer?"

"No. Considering that we're at war, I'd say the government contracts will increase. If the firm doesn't have the capital to buy materials, it could lose out. The sooner the better would be my advice. By the way, just for the record, I don't know a thing about chickens."

"I guess you're going to learn. I want the ranch to be productive, so that no one can take it away from Red. The same goes for Beaunell."

"If I'm doing all this, when will I have time to do my lawyering and see you?"

"Do you have any other clients?" Sallie asked.

"No. That doesn't mean I won't get some at some point."

"Why do you suppose that is? That you don't have any other clients, I mean?"

"Hell, I don't know. All my uncle's clients are dead. The younger people seem to take care of their own problems. Maybe the people in this state don't like lawyers, or maybe they have a preconceived notion that we charge too much."

"You do. I've been meaning to talk to you about that very thing."

Devin groaned. "I'm every bit as good an attorney as my uncle. Possibly better because I'm up on all the latest laws and jurisprudence. No, there is no room for negotiation."

"Okay," Sallie said. "How is it you never married?"

"Whoa. Where did that come from?"

"If you *think* you know everything there is to know about me, then I should know everything about you. Talk."

"I was married when I was twenty-three. My wife drowned in a boating accident. We had no children. I was in law school at the time. I was so devastated I took a year off and literally drank myself into a stupor every day. Uncle Alvin came East and gave me a blistering lecture. He hauled me back to law school and that was it. I never married again. I regret not having children. It would be nice to have a son to carry on the name. I channeled all my energies into my work and made a name for myself in the legal profession back East. I'm more than solvent if that's your next question. I inherited a princely sum of money from my parents, and Uncle Alvin left me his estate. Since I've worked all my life, I have a considerable bank account. Tell me about your sons, Mrs. Thornton."

"You're just like your uncle," Sallie said tartly. "One minute you're talking about one thing, and then you switch in midsentence. I really don't want to talk about Ash and Simon. This was a lovely lunch. I enjoyed everything."

"What did you eat, Mrs. Thornton? No, no, don't look at your plate. Tell me."

"Why . . . I had . . . I . . . Veal," she said triumphantly.

"Wrong. You had lamb with mint jelly."

"It tastes the same."

"It does not. Lamb has a very distinctive taste that cannot be confused with veal. So there, Mrs. Thornton. You're trying to figure out how I fit into your life, and you're confused at what you're feeling for me."

"That's not true. Thank you for lunch." It was true. It was almost as though he could read her mind and see into her soul. Sallie took a deep breath as she got up from the table.

"My mother always told me it was a sin to tell a lie," Devin said lightly.

"My mother told me the same thing."

"What is it you want from life, Mrs. Thornton?" Devin's voice was a whisper. But it was his dove gray eyes that stirred Sallie.

"I don't know. I wish I did." She turned so he wouldn't see her tears.

"I've had enough of that Mrs. Thornton/Mr. Rollins nonsense. It's okay to cry, Sallie. Anytime, anyplace. If it makes you feel better, do it. Don't worry about what I think or what anyone else thinks. Be true to yourself and you'll never go wrong. Come on, I'll give you the aviation packet to study. Thanks for joining me. I'll get on that chicken business right away. It's a damn good thing I don't have any clients; this is going to take all my time. I might even have to raise my rates."

Sallie smiled through her tears as they walked back to Devin's office.

"I could fall in love with you very easily, Mrs. Thornton," Devin blurted.

"Please don't. I told you, I'm married."

"And I told you I know all about your marriage. Tell me the truth now, when you saw me that day at the cemetery, what was your first thought? I'm referring to the moment when we spoke."

Because she'd been taught to be truthful all her life, Sallie didn't think twice before she answered. "I thought I was seeing my destiny."

"Wonderful! That's exactly what I thought. My uncle thought we would be a perfect match. He said so in my letter. How can you stay married to a man you don't love? What kind of life is that for either one of you? Don't you want to be happy?"

"Philip and I are friends. We have a commitment to one another. We've discussed divorce. It hasn't happened. I owe Philip so much. There may not be passion between us, but we have that wonderful thing called friendship. I know I can count on him, and he can count on me. I don't expect you to understand that. It's the way it is. It's all my fault, you see. I married Philip when I didn't love him. I guess I did it because I didn't want to lose my best friend, and he was going to go back to Boston. I told him the truth, and he accepted it.

"All I ever wanted in my life was to be warm in the winter, cool in the summer, and to have a good dress for church. I wanted a family, the kind you read about in storybooks. When good fortune came my way I wasn't prepared. Everything went wrong after that. Money, Mr. Rollins, does not make for happiness. It can bring comfort, security, and possessions, but not happiness. Money allows me to do things for other people. I renovated this town. I consider it mine, but it truly isn't mine. I was just the instrument that modernized it." Sallie paused and took a deep breath. "Define the word happiness, Mr. Rollins."

"It's the feeling you have when you wake up in the morning knowing something wonderful is going to happen. It's doing something kind and good for someone else. Like you just did for Miss Ruby. Now, there was one happy lady."

"I'm promoting prostitution," Sallie said.

"If it wasn't you, it would be someone else. In a town that's going to boom like this one, the profession could get out of hand. You're taking care of the situation by moving it *outside* of the town. Think of it as a separate entity. You aren't going to benefit monetarily. It's the oldest profession in the land, and it is never going to go away. People have choices. Accept the fact that there are things in this world you can't change. You can make them better or worse, but you can't change them. Lunch tomorrow? You will read this report tonight, won't you?"

"Yes, I will read it this evening. Lunch would be very nice. Come to my house, and I'll make sure we open a fresh jar of pickles."

"Would you like to come up to the office, or do you want to wait here while I go and get the folder?"

"I'll walk down the street to the post office. I know it's wishful thinking, but there may be mail from my sons. Don't forget the letter from your uncle."

"I'll be the man standing here with a manila folder in his hand."

"I'd know you anywhere."

"How is that?"

"Because you're my destiny." Sallie winked at the stunned attorney.

"Now you *are* flirting with me."

Sallie laughed. "See, I told you you would know."

"Jesus," was all Devin could think of to say. He knew Sallie Thornton was laughing all the way to the post office. He suddenly felt as if he was eight years old and discovering for the first time that girls were different from boys.

At home, Sallie ripped at the stiff, crackly paper Alvin Waring had always used to write his letters. As she unfolded the single-page letter, she closed her eyes, remembering another time when she'd gotten a letter and how she'd prayed for printed letters instead of script. She found herself smiling at the memory.

My Dear Sallie,

You are the sunshine of my life. I want to thank you for making my life so pleasurable in so many small ways. I hope you will have fond memories of me and speak well of me after I'm gone.

There are several matters I wish to put on paper. The first is a new company I'd like you to invest in. I've given my nephew all the details, and he's promised to research the firm. If his report is satisfactory, I want you to buy in as heavily as you are comfortable with.

The second thing I'd like to address is Devin. Forgive this foolish old man when he tells you he thinks the two of you are meant for each other. Devin has had much sadness in his life, some of it he will talk about, other things he won't discuss at all, even with me. He's a kind, caring man who is capable of great love and devotion, just as you are. You, dear Sallie, need to set Philip free and absolve yourself of the guilt that shackles you. If you don't, you can never be happy. Your marriage is not the kind Cotton had in mind for you. In a way you betrayed your benefactor, Sallie. You need to give this some very serious thought.

That's all I have to say. I'm very tired, dear girl, it's time for me to get ready to go to that place old attorneys go when they can't function anymore.

I hope I served you well over the past years. I want to leave you with my wish for you, dear one. Fill your life with wonderful words, beautiful music, and warm sunshine. Stretch out your arms and embrace all that life has to offer you. Your ever faithful servant.

Alvin Waring, Esq.

Sallie read the letter three times before she gave in to her grief. She wept for a long time.

It was past midnight when Sallie read the last sheet of paper and returned the pile into the folder. Her eyes were wide with shock, her shoulders stiff with anger. "Philip, are you awake?" Sallie shouted, hoping he'd answer.

"I am now. I was just dozing. This book was so dry and boring it put me to sleep. What's wrong, you sound . . . angry. Did something happen, was there a phone call?" He came into her room, his voice so fearful, Sallie herself became frightened.

"No, no, nothing like that. You know the aviation company Mr. Waring and Mr. Rollins want me to invest in. I'd pretty much made up my mind to go ahead. You are never going to guess who owns the company. Never in a million years, Philip."

"For God's sake, who?"

"My brother, Seth Coleman."

"Perhaps it's someone with the same name."

"There's some biographical information on the last page. He's my brother. I know it, I feel it. It says he has a 250,000-acre ranch outside of Austin, Texas. He's married and has a son and a daughter. His son is in the Navy, flying fighter planes. He raises cattle and started up this aviation company. He's rich."

"Then why does he need money?" Philip asked.

"I don't know. If Mr. Waring was here, he'd say the first rule of business is you never use your own money in case you go belly-up. His ranch is called Sunbridge. I inherited a home called Sunrise. Isn't that odd, Philip? They say he's the richest man in the state of Texas. If that's true, why didn't he go back for the family? Why didn't he ever do anything for them? He just lit out and never looked back. What do you think my chances are of buying up fifty-one percent of his company?"

"My God, Sallie, do you want to plow him under? You're angry right now. You need to think this through before you do something you might regret."

"You mean like going there and killing him? That's exactly what I feel like doing. My mother died of a broken heart because of him. Peggy told me his name was on Mama's lips when she died. Seth was the only one Mama cared about."

"Sallie, your mother died because she was sick. I'm not negating what you just said, but—"

"There are no buts, Philip. If he'd gone back once, if he'd sent money, maybe Mama wouldn't have gotten sick. I'd bet my last penny he doesn't even know our parents are dead. Don't even think about defending him, Philip."

"Sallie—"

"Don't Sallie me, Philip. I'm angry. You didn't know my mother. Peggy told me what it was like at the end. My sisters were literally starving. And all my mother wanted was to believe that her firstborn son, Seth, would arrive in time to send her off to heaven. Just a little bit of money, Philip. Five dollars a month. It would have made all the difference in the world. My mother might be alive today if he'd done the decent thing. Don't think for one minute that I won't find Josh, too. I will, somehow, someway."

"The Pinkertons couldn't find Seth. You spent all that money for nothing."

"I tried, Philip. I had to try. You had a wonderful family, Philip. You had a childhood filled with fun and laughter. I never had that. All I can remember is worry about whether I would be cold or hot or hungry. Do you hear me, Philip, I never had a childhood! I can never get it back."

"It wasn't all Seth's fault, Sallie. You had a father. It was his responsibility."

"When my father fell down on the job, it was Seth's place to step in and take over. Instead, he lit out just as Josh did later. It's just like you, Philip, to stick up for Seth because he's a man. Another thing," Sallie raged. "Our son Ash would do the same thing, and you damn well know it."

"I don't want to believe that. You're angry right now. You don't mean it."

"You goddamn well better believe it. I saw it in him every day as he was growing up. He plays both ends against the middle. Ash had to get that from somewhere. I'm not like that and neither are you. It's my bloodline, and don't try telling me differently. I'm thinking about having an affair, Philip," Sallie said in much the same way she would have said, "I think it's going to rain today."

"Is it something you want to discuss?" Philip asked.

"Yes. No. I might, and then I might not. I've never lied to you. I won't be mentioning it again. There is something else I want to talk to you about. I know it's late, but it's on my mind."

"Why don't I make us some hot cocoa and we can sit in the kitchen. How would you like a fried egg sandwich with ketchup?" It wasn't the end of the world; she hadn't said she wanted a divorce. An affair was something he could live with. A divorce would kill him.

"I'd love one, but I want bacon on mine."

"Bacon it is. Cocoa or coffee?"

"Cocoa will be fine," Sallie said, lighting a cigarette. She told him in great detail about everything that happened in Devin Rollins's office and at lunch, leaving out only the personal remarks between her and the attorney.

"I'll bet that made Red's wild red hair stand on end. Chickens, huh? Very clever, Sallie."

"Philip, could you see yourself running a chicken and cattle business? Have you ever thought about giving up teaching?"

"Just about every day of my life now. I don't know anything about chickens. I know less about cows. Milk cows, or cattle for butchering?"

"Both."

"I guess I could learn. I assume you're talking about a lot of chickens and a lot of cows."

"Hundreds, thousands maybe. Instead of a salary you take a share of the profits. What do you think?"

"It sounds interesting."

"You'll do it?"

"It sure beats a stuffy classroom."

"If you're agreeable, that will take some of the pressure off Mr. Rollins. He doesn't know anything about chickens, either. What do you think I should do about my brother, Philip?" Sallie asked, switching the conversation to what was really on her mind.

"Besides killing him? Sallie, you have never been a vindictive person. The past is past. You cannot undo it no matter how much you want to. If you're looking for vengeance, wouldn't the sweetest revenge be buying into his company and not telling him who you are until the right moment? That moment always comes, Sallie. You just have to learn patience. Think it through before you do anything; that's my best advice."

"Okay, Philip, I'll think about it. That was a wonderful sandwich. I'll see you in the morning. Good night." Sallie kissed the top of his head in passing, something she did every night when they parted at the foot of the stairs.

In her room, Sallie flopped down on a chair, withdrew the contents of the manila folder, and spread the papers out on the floor. She picked up the phone and asked to be connected to Devin Rollins's home. His sleepy voice startled her. "You were sleeping, Mr. Rollins." It wasn't a question but a statement.

"It's two o'clock in the morning. I hope you're calling to whisper sweet nothings in my ear and not to talk about chickens."

"I'm calling on business, not about chickens, and I don't whisper sweet nothings into anyone's ear at this hour of the night unless I'm in bed. No, I am not flirting with you. I read all the information you passed on to me. Pay attention to me. Or would you prefer getting a cup of coffee first. I can call you back."

"I'm wide-awake with pencil in hand, Sallie. Do you do this often, call in the middle of the night?"

"Only when I pay outrageous fees to an attorney. I call it getting my money's worth. I want to buy into that company. Is there anyway I could buy the controlling interest? If not now, down the road? If I can't ever get a controlling interest, then I want other considerations. I want you to bargain, to get me the best deal possible. A voice in the firm would be very good. How are you at negotiating? Oh, one other thing, I want my share in the name of S.P. Thornton. My middle name is Pauline. I do not want you ever to allude to the fact that I am a woman. I suspect Mr. Seth Coleman is my brother. I suspect your uncle thought so, too. My brother doesn't even know I exist. All I'm going to tell you about him is he ran off and left our family to fend for ourselves. He never looked back, never sent a penny home, never inquired if we were alive or dead. Do you get the picture, Mr. Rollins?"

"I'll do what I can, Sallie. Don't expect a miracle, though. I told you I spoke with him several times, and I didn't like him. Right off he tried to bamboozle me. Then when he found out I was an attorney, he pulled in his horns. He wants this firm off the ground and in the air so bad he's willing to do almost anything. For some reason he doesn't seem to be able to get investors in his own home state. I'm looking into that. How much money are you talking about, Sallie?"

"Whatever it takes to get me what I want. Use the word cash as often as you need to. You can hand deliver it if necessary."

"What about the chickens?"

Sallie heard the laughter in his voice. "I've taken care of those chickens, Mr. Rollins. Philip is going to give up his teaching job. I told him I was contemplating an affair."

"Jesus Christ!"

Sallie clucked her tongue. "Good night, Mr. Rollins."

The last thing Sallie did before climbing into bed was to drop to her knees and say her nightly prayers. "Please, God, take care of my sons, don't let anything happen to them. Bless this house and all those I hold dear. Tell Mama and Cotton I'm doing my best down here and forgive me for the vengeance in my heart."

Three momentous things happened to Sallie in the last two months of 1942. The first was an unexpected phone call from Simon, who begged her forgiveness and promised to call once a month whenever possible. The second was the beginning of a twenty-year love affair with Devin Rollins. The third was an unexpected visitor in the early hours of the morning on a bright day.

Packing for a weekend tryst with Devin, Sallie at first ignored the doorbell. When the persistent ringing started to give her a headache she walked downstairs to open the door. She looked around for Tulee but didn't see her. "Yes, can I help you?"

"If you're Mrs. Sallie Thornton, yes, you can help me. I'm Benjamin Vallee. I'd like to talk to you about a business matter."

Sallie stared at the man standing in front of her. His double-breasted dark suit, colored shirt with matching tie, and gray fedora shrieked gangster to Sallie. The bulge on the inside of his suit jacket confirmed her suspicions. "You need to speak with my attorney, Mr. Vallee. You caught me at a bad time, I was just about to leave town for a long weekend."

Vallee handed over a small white business card. "Why don't I just tell you what I want, you speak to your lawyer, and when you get back, call me. I'll be in town for a few weeks. I'm interested in purchasing some property you own. I'm willing to pay a fair price."

"What do you consider fair?"

"Double what you paid for it. It's desert, Mrs. Thornton."

"Just because it's desert doesn't mean it's worthless. If it was worthless, you wouldn't want to buy it now, would you? I'm not interested in selling, however, I might be interested in leasing the property. A long-term lease. A very long-term lease. Why don't you think about that while I'm away and get back to my attorney or myself early next week?"

"Lease?"

"Yes, lease. It might be advantageous for you to consider leasing as opposed to buying something I cannot legally sell. The property is tied up in a trust account. An attorney can explain it better than I can."

"Are you telling me all the property the courthouse records show is in a *trust?* You own almost the whole desert!"

"That's not quite true, Mr. Vallee. I own *all* of the desert. What I don't own is not worth owning."

"But you're a woman!"

"How observant of you. Is there something else you want to say?"

"I don't like doing business with women."

"That's too bad. I'm a very good businesswoman. I'm fair and I'm honest. Are you?"

"What kind of question is that?"

"How does this sound? I'm not thrilled and delighted to be doing any kind of business with a gangster, and yes, you are a gangster, so don't bother trying to deny it. The way I look at it is, business is business. You be fair, and I'll be fair. You look out for your interests, and I'll pay someone to look out for mine, like my attorney, or the lieutenant governor, who is going to be marrying my sister very shortly, the police force, and the townspeople themselves. That's another way of saying you can't come into my town—and this *is* my town—and scare me. I will not allow that. That gun you're carrying doesn't scare me, either."

"I'll be back. We'll talk then. Lease, huh?"

"Yes, lease."

"Good-bye, Mrs. Thornton."

"Good-bye, Mr. Vallee. Have a nice day and enjoy the dry desert air."

"Yeah, I will." Sallie heard him mutter as he walked down the steps out to the road. The moment she closed the door she had to fight to take deep breaths. Devin was going to throw an unholy fit when she told him what had just transpired.

"Where are we going, Devin? Why won't you tell me? What's the big surprise?" Sallie asked as she climbed into the attorney's convertible.

"If I told you, it wouldn't be a surprise. Did you miss me this week, Sallie? We haven't seen each other in three days."

"I missed you terribly, Devin. The house here in town is so empty. For some reason I don't even want to go to the bingo palace. I sit curled in a chair and think about you. Where were you, Devin?"

Devin reached across the seat to take Sallie's hand. "Across the border in Arizona. As you know, my uncle left his estate to me. His ranch was badly in need of repair so I had the work done these past months. The workers were putting the finishing touches on everything, and I wanted to be there to make sure it all went according to schedule. That's where we're going. I'm going to carry you over the threshold. I know we aren't married, but it makes no difference to me. Along the way you can tell me what Las Vegas was like in years past. I don't think I can even imagine it."

"If you aren't in a hurry, let's take the scenic route. There was nothing here but tents when I first arrived. I was scared out of my wits. I didn't know what I expected. All I could see were tents, sand, cactus, and bubbling water holes. It smelled terrible. Everywhere you looked there was a saloon that served watered-down whiskey. Crooked gambling was the only kind that went on. There were bust-out joints on every corner. For a while it was a felony to gamble, but the police looked the other way. For the most part the gaming owners went undercover. Operating in the open, the customers played for cigars and drinks. Money changed hands outside, supposedly no more than two dollars a hand. It didn't work that way. I saw what went on because I sang in those saloons. Then came the nickel-in-the-slot, but the gamblers didn't like that. They likened it to playing bingo in the church basement. And, the operators had to be licensed by the local government and they had to pay annual license fees to run their clubs. That caused problems for the state because no one paid their fees. Then in 1931 the Nevada Legislature passed the wide-open gambling bill.

"Turn here, Devin. This used to be where the Oasis stood. It was the town's leading restaurant. Only the elite were able to eat there. They had pretty little Mormon girls from the rural areas serving as waitresses. Later in the evening, after theatergoers left the airdrome, they would stop at the Oasis to get an ice-cream sundae.

"This is Second and Fremont. The post office was on the corner, and there were offices on the second floor. I think it was called the Griffith building. Go down two more blocks, Devin, to Seventh and Bridger. That was the high school. I used to walk by, and I wanted to go inside so bad, but I never had the nerve. Later on they made it into the Fifth Street Grammar School. If you go over a few more blocks you'll see the first service station. I think it was called the Tower Service Station. There it is, between Fremont and Carson Street. In the beginning all they had were drums with spigots.

"Go over to Eighth and Ogden and you'll see where the old hospital was. Doctor Martin converted the Palace Hotel into the hospital. Then he built a new one later on. When they did surgery they had fans blowing over blocks of ice."

"Where did you live, Sallie?"

"In a rooming house. To me it was the grandest room in the world. It was cozy and warm and it was mine, paid for every week with my own money. To this day I miss that little square room. It was the one place I could go to and close and lock the door. I never had an inch of space that was my own, growing up."

"And now you own a whole town. It's hard for me to believe you own almost all the buildings in this town. Those you don't own sit on your leased property. I think I understand you a little better these days. Sallie, are we ever going to talk about Philip?"

"No, Devin, we aren't. I think I've had enough sight-seeing, let's get on with whatever you have planned. One little hint, a small clue. Please."

She's like a child sometimes, Devin thought. *She's so easy to be with, so easy to love.* "All good things come to those who wait."

Wait she did, for a full hour and thirty minutes, until Devin slowed the car and turned onto a graveled driveway. They drove for another half mile before a house sitting far back in a nest of cottonwoods came into view.

"It's beautiful, Devin. Are you happy here?"

"Very much so. I would be a lot happier if I had someone to come home to at night." Seeing the tight white line around Sallie's mouth, he hastened to add, "I didn't change anything on the exterior because I happen to love quarry stone. My uncle told me he personally carted most of the rock and stone from Black Mountain on days when business was slow. I like to think of it as my own miniature castle with those turrets on each end. I love going up those killer steps and looking out those little paned windows. I can actually see Las Vegas from my mountaintop."

"Did your uncle have a name for this place? What do you call it?"

"To my knowledge, no, he didn't. I call it my house."

"Houses should have names. Mine is called Sunrise. My brother calls his ranch Sunbridge. Isn't that strange, Devin?"

"Not really if you stop to think about it. I think both of you, each in your own way, were searching for the sunshine in your life. What's wonderful about it is you both found it. It doesn't matter how it came to you, purchased or inherited, you have it now."

"Still, it should have a name."

"Then let's call it Sallie and Devin's house of happiness. Because . . . when we come here we'll be at our happiest."

Sallie felt her stomach crunch into a knot. What she was doing was wrong. She felt a long sigh escape her lips. Happiness was where you found it, and she'd found hers with Devin Rollins. "Sallie and Devin's house of happiness it is."

Devin put his arm around her shoulder and drew her close. "If I searched the world over, I couldn't find anyone to love more than I love you."

"I feel the same way, Devin."

"Let me give you the grand tour. This is the front door. Note the hand carving. Stained glass in the little panes. Works of art, all done by my uncle. He was very good with his hands as you'll see inside." In the time it took her heart to beat once, Sallie was in his arms and being carried over the threshold. She squealed her pleasure.

"So, what do you think?"

"Oh, Devin, it's beautiful!" She looked around at the lace curtains on the windows, at the hand-carved furniture, which was neither bulky nor manly, at the colorful cushions that matched the hooked rugs on the pine floors. There were vibrant watercolors on all the walls, splashes of brilliant color in silver frames. She stared in awe at the oil painting over a quarry stone fireplace that begged for glowing embers. "That's me!"

"Yes. My uncle had a local artist go to your bingo palace every night when you were singing. He sketched your likeness first and then painted the picture. My uncle was mesmerized by your eyes. He told me once the eyes are the mirror of one's soul. He swore to me he saw your soul, and it was pure and good. The artist captured that, in my opinion."

"Good heavens, Devin, you're making me sound like an angel."

"My uncle thought you were. Mr. Easter thought you were, and so did your friend Snowball and all his friends. Miss Ruby thinks so. It must be true."

"Is this furniture as comfortable as it looks?" Sallie said, flopping down on the nearest chair. "I love the fireplace."

"Will you spend next Christmas here with me? I know it's a long way off, but I'd love to fill this house with evergreens and be here with you."

"Yes, yes, I will."

"I want to make love to you in front of the fireplace. Tonight. Believe it or not, it gets downright chilly here in the evenings once the sun goes down. There's a pile of Indian blankets in that carved chest in the corner. They're softer than feathers."

"You are a wicked, wicked man, Mr. Rollins."

"Only where you're concerned. Come along, I want to show off the rest of my house. This is my dining room. In case I ever have guests. The furniture is store bought. The rugs and the wall hangings are authentic. Note the lace curtains here also. Do they seem out of place to you, Sallie?"

"In a way."

"My uncle told me your greatest joy was seeing curtains billow in the breeze from open windows. He had them hung in case you ever came to visit."

"Truly? I wonder why he never invited me."

"Perhaps his fantasy was all he needed. The windows do open, and the curtains do billow in the breeze. He told me in your heart you're a simple person with simple pleasures. There's nothing pretentious about you, Sallie. I guess that's one of the reasons I love you so much."

"Where's the kitchen. Do you have help?"

"No. I do it all myself. I don't think I could get used to someone living in my house. I like to walk around barefoot and in my underwear."

"I do, too." Sallie giggled.

"Moving right along here, I have a bathroom off the kitchen and one upstairs. I had the back porch screened in so I could eat out here when I want to. All those flowers you see in those clay pots I planted from seeds."

"They're beautiful. I love flowers. I like your dual staircases. You can go upstairs from the kitchen or the living room. Were they always here?"

"Yes. Like a kid I go up one set and come down the other."

"Oh, Devin, this is so gorgeous it takes my breath away," Sallie said as she stepped into the large bedroom.

"It runs the whole length of the house. There is one smaller room at the end of that hallway that leads to the bathroom. For a housekeeper, I guess."

The carpeting was thick and luxurious, soft beige with tiny threads of chocolate yarn woven around the border. Lacy white curtains whispered in the early afternoon breeze, billowing inward in little puffing sounds. Dark earth tone draperies hung at the sides, pulled back with silver pulls. The fireplace, a duplicate of the one in the living room, held a grate filled with logs. The hearth, wide and long, held clay pots filled with plants, whose leaves were shiny and bright. The bed was high and wide enough to hold four people. *A wonderful playground,* she thought wickedly.

"You didn't say anything about the painting," Devin whispered.

"Only because I don't know what to say. It's hard to believe I ever looked that young." Tears sprang to her eyes. Devin kissed them away.

Hours later, Sallie curled into Devin's arm. In her life she'd never been this content, this happy, this satisfied. Devin was everything a lover was supposed to be. She snuggled deeper into his embrace. "I didn't think I could ever be this happy."

"I think God has blessed us," Devin murmured against her hair. Sallie wiped at a tear forming in the corner of her eye.

All through the evening strange sounds filtered through the house and out the open windows. In the early hours of the morning, the little house nestled in the cottonwood grove grew quiet as the occupants fell into a deep, satisfying sleep.

———

Simon Thornton, alias Adam Jessup, sat back in his briefing chair, his eyes on the flight trainer doing the briefing. He tried to look calm, detached. He knew he *looked* as old as the other fighter pilots in the room, but he suddenly felt his real age. His eyes were gritty with lack of sleep, but he was clean-shaven and dressed in open-necked khaki. In front of him was a green-covered table filled with coffee cups and ashtrays. Blue-gray cigarette smoke wafted upward to the metal rafters overhead.

"This is it, gentlemen, so listen up. You're here because you're the best of the best. Because you're the best, you're going to stop the Japs from taking Henderson Field. I don't have to tell you what an important link in the U.S.-Australian lifeline it is. As I speak, the Japs have four carriers, two light cruisers, eight heavy cruisers, and twenty-eight destroyers out there in the Pacific just waiting for you. It's the strongest navy force since Midway. Everyone of you flight jockeys knows how to drop a bomb and hit a target. I expect you to hit your targets dead-on. No bullshit excuses, no misses. I want each one of you to take a minute and pretend your brother is one of those marines at Guadalcanal. Because that marine is your brother, come morning, you are going up there and do the job you were trained to do, blow those sons of bitches right off the map. That's it, gentlemen. Grab some shut-eye and lay off the coffee."

The wardroom was blue with cigarette smoke when Simon scraped back his chair. Maybe he should take the time to write a letter home. Maybe he should sleep and dream about dying. Jesus. Just yesterday he'd had an hour-long talk with the ship's chaplain. He'd really done all the talking, expressing his fear of dying, of killing other people, and then he'd asked for something to carry with him, something to give him comfort. The chaplain, perhaps ten years older than himself, had spoken quietly, told him if he *wasn't* afraid, he didn't belong aboard the Big E. He'd handed over a St. Christopher medal, explaining that it was a medal Catholics carried with them for safety. Simon dropped the medal into his breast pocket and immediately felt better. He held it in his hand now, and he felt as comforted as he had yesterday. Maybe if he kept it in his hand, he would finally be able to get some restful sleep.

"You look a little white around the gills, Jessup. You okay?" Moss Coleman asked. "Look, you're my wingman, I have a right to be concerned about how you're feeling."

"And I have a right to be concerned about you hot-dogging it up there. You're too fucking confident for my liking. Scuttlebutt has it command is worried that you take unnecessary risks with the guys and the planes. If you expect me to cover your ass up there, then you better fly right, Mr. Coleman."

"Up yours, Jessup."

Simon grinned. "Is that anyway for you to talk to the guy who's probably going to save your ass? What if I look the other way, you cocky son of a bitch?"

"Don't even think about it. You do your job, and I'll do mine. Look, all our nerves are a little raw. I'm sorry if I got off on the wrong foot. Let's call a truce. We're here to do a job, so I say let's do it the best way we can. We're the best of the best. Crommelin said so, and I believe him. You're a hell of a pilot, Jessup. Live up to it, and you'll be almost as good as I am."

In spite of himself, Simon grinned. He was the first to stretch out his hand. Moss Coleman's handshake was bone-crushing. Simon neither flinched nor grimaced as he exerted just as much pressure as Coleman. Both men eased up at the same moment.

"Where are you from, Coleman? My mother's maiden name was Coleman."

"Texas-born-and-bred. How about you?"

"Nevada, home of gold and silver. You have a faint resemblance to my bro . . . never mind."

"Finish what you were going to say, Jessup. I'm curious. Maybe we're related."

"You look sort of like my brother Ash. Same high cheekbones, same stance, same body build. I'm sure it's my imagination."

"No, no, the next time I write home I'll ask Pap. What's your mother's name?"

"Sallie. Her middle name is Pauline. She has five sisters, four that she hasn't seen in years and years, and two brothers. She doesn't talk much about her early life."

"Pap doesn't either. He's self-made, pulled himself up by his bootstraps and made a go of it. We have a 250,000-acre ranch back in Texas. I'm real proud of him. How about you?"

"They call my mother Mrs. Nevada. She owns the city of Las Vegas. She had some good luck and things went on from there. I think she owns the whole desert."

"What do you do with a desert?"

"I have no idea, but if there's something to do with it, my mother will figure it out. They say she's the richest woman in the country."

"Are you trying to impress me, Jessup?"

"Were you trying to impress me with your 250,000-acre ranch?"

"Yep."

"Well I wasn't. If I ever try to impress you, it will be with my own accomplishments, not my mother's."

"Touché, Jessup. What about your father?"

"My father is a schoolteacher."

"My mother was a schoolteacher. I'll check it out, Jessup. You got a picture of your brother?"

"Yeah, I do, want to see it?"

"You bet. I have a sister."

The two pilots exchanged snapshots. Moss Coleman was the first to speak. "You're right, I see a resemblance between your brother and me. I also see a striking similarity between your mother and my father. What do you think, Jessup?"

"I think you're right."

"Where's your brother now?"

"I have no idea. He joined up a few days after I did. We aren't exactly the best of friends. I wish it was otherwise, but it isn't going to happen."

"Yeah, I know what you mean. I have a sister . . . I like her, but Pap, he . . . frowns on me having a . . . it isn't worth discussing. Like I said, I'll check this out. I think I need a little more to go on, like where did your mother live exactly."

"In a tenant shack outside of Abilene. She told me her two oldest brothers took off at an early age, and that's all she knows of them."

"Pap came from some pretty humble beginnings himself. I'm glad we had this little talk, Jessup. I'll make sure I look after you up there, you do the same."

"Okay, Coleman." This time there was no bone-crushing handshake. They clapped each other on the back before they went their separate ways, each to write a letter home.

The predawn message was from the headquarters of the commander, South Pacific Force, and signed by Admiral Bill Halsey. Brief and to the point it read:

ATTACK. REPEAT. ATTACK.

Simon stood on the flight deck and watched as aircraft were raised from the hangar bay and rolled to the catapult mechanisms on the runway. Sailors in yellow jackets wearing radio headsets listened for the order to signal takeoff. He could feel his heart thundering in his chest, louder than the thrum of the engines. He looked around trying to gauge the expressions on the other pilots' faces. He thought he saw excitement as well as fear. He knew his own face registered only fear.

His helmet and goggles in hand, his leather jacket unzipped, Simon walked over to Moss Coleman, who was shaking hands with his best buddy, Thad Kingsley. "Good luck, Coleman."

"Same to you, Jessup. I'll see you back in the wardroom."

"You bet. Here comes my plane." For one brief moment, Simon thought he was going to lose his breakfast. The moment he climbed into the *Silver Dollar*, the name he'd christened his plane, he felt as one with the machine. He took another moment to savor the feel of the St. Christopher medal inside his glove. He used up more seconds going over his checklist. Satisfied, he squirmed in his seat, his parachute grinding into his back.

The target was the thousand square miles just north of the Santa Cruz Islands.

Standing amidships, Moss saw the *Silver Dollar* catapult into the air, her wheels barely skimming the deck before she reached the edge. He wondered how it was possible for Adam Jessup to be a better pilot than he was. Better even than Thad Kingsley. He just knew if he peeled off Jessup's shirt, he'd see a pair of wings. The guy was born to fly, just the way he was born to fly. They *must* be related somehow.

"Here comes the *Texas Ranger*," Thad said quietly. "Make damn sure you get back here in one piece, you hear me, you Texas bastard."

"I hear you, you Yankee cracker. I'll be back and you damn well better set your wheels down right behind me."

Navy Fighter Squadron Four took to the air, eight pairs of glinting wings in the early sun. Simon flew starboard wingman for his squadron leader, Moss Coleman, holding slightly in the V-formation. The hunt-and-search pattern was on.

The attack came from the rear with only fifteen minutes of flying time remaining. "Zeros, up-sun, twelve o'clock!" Simon looked up, squinting, and had his first sight of the enemy. His eyes locked on the fuel gauge. He bit down on his lower lip, tasting his own blood as his hand massaged the medal inside his glove.

Curses, some he'd never heard before, were mumbled into headsets as grim and determined faces peered through the cockpit windshields. Explosive firepower flew all about the American fighters.

Coleman radioed their position back to headquarters. The return radio message was curt and to the point. Pursue and attack! Where there were Japanese carriers, there would be Zeros.

"Break formation," Coleman's voice ordered. "Wind around and jump from the rear."

The squadron spiraled portside and dropped to 12,000 feet. The Zeros were still on their tails. Kingsley, second port wingman, broke radio silence. "Squad four, Zeros hanging back. Repeat, two Zeros hanging back. Total seven enemy."

"Jessup, Kingsley, drop back and get them," Coleman commanded.

Simon and Kingsley held back on the throttles, losing air speed, allowing the rest of the squad to shoot ahead. Turning to port, they climbed to seek their Zeros. The Japanese craft flew toward them at a thirty-degree angle, coming from above. Simon saw Kingsley veer to the east. The Zeros trailed him, increasing air speed and losing altitude. Kingsley was a duck out of water. Simon, in that one split second, knew he had to cast aside everything he'd learned in flight school. There was no rule book up here; this was Kingsley's life.

Moss Coleman watched Jessup, his mouth hanging open as he spiraled down, then up and around. He saw the double bursts of fire, swallowed hard, his eyes never leaving Jessup's and Kingsley's planes. "I goddamn well didn't see what I just saw," he muttered. "And the son of a bitch talks about me breaking the fucking rules." His fist shot upward when he saw Jessup's Wildcat circle and head back, Kingsley behind him, but directly overhead of the two burning pyres.

Simon eyed his fuel gauge again as Kingsley's voice rasped, "Zero on your tail, Jessup, head on home, little buddy, one good turn deserves another, I got the bastard covered."

"Like hell you do, you Yankee. Zero four o'clock. I got him. You take care of Jessup's tail, and I'll cover yours. I'm on fumes," Moss said.

The simultaneous bursts of gunfire rocked Simon. He looked down, saw the two Zeros burning like paper lanterns. He looked to his left and then to his right, Coleman and Kingsley giving him the thumbs-up salute. He returned it, the medal warm and moist inside his glove.

"All in a day's work, gentlemen," Moss said flippantly. "Time to go home."

On a course for the *Enterprise,* the three pilots headed home to refuel. It was the beginning of a very long day.

The last sortie of the day found Simon watching Moss Coleman's *Texas Ranger* soar into the gray sky, away from the squadron, and back to the Big E. Something was wrong. He felt his stomach churn when he looked upward to see the fighter pilots from the *Hornet* flying in formation. With four of their own aircraft incapacitated and now Coleman heading back to the Big E, that left only Kingsley, Conrad, and himself to fight off seven Zeros. He felt less than jubilant with the sight of the fighter planes overhead. The St. Christopher medal felt hot in his hand—hot and safe.

They came from all directions, out of the setting sun, their firepower shattering Simon's eardrums. It was worse than all of his wicked dreams put together. He used every ounce of his flying skill to maneuver the *Silver Dollar* up, down, around and then he did a vicious roll, came out of it and fired point-blank at the Zero coming straight for him. He watched the black smoke spiral upward.

"Now that's what I call fancy flying," a lazy voice drawled overhead. "Head back, *Silver Dollar*, the Wildcat to your right looks like she's going down. We'll take over here. If we ever meet up, I'd like to shake your hand."

Simon craned his neck to see the plane on his left. He had time for only one brief look that almost sent him into a tailspin of his own. "Ash, is that you?"

"It's me in the flesh, little brother. Head home, your buddy isn't going to make it."

"Help me, Ash," Simon pleaded. "The waters are full of Japanese, he won't have a prayer."

"I told you to head home, *Silver Dollar*. I can't break formation. Goddamn it, Simon, get the hell out of here. There's a Zero on your wing. I got him. You owe me, little brother."

Simon banked hard left and soared downward, his eyes on Conrad's plane.

"Eject, Conrad, eject!" he screamed into his mouthpiece. "I'll fly in low and drop you a line."

"Get out of here, Simon. Head home. That's a goddamn fucking order, Simon!"

Tears burning in his eyes, Simon's hand straddled the throttle as he soared upward into the sun. Blinded for the moment, he almost missed the sight of Conrad's parachute jerking him upward. He headed home, he had his orders. With only minutes of fuel remaining, he hit the deck of the Big E with expert precision, the St. Christopher medal soaking wet inside his glove.

On wobbly legs, tired to the bone, Simon headed for the debriefing room. All he could think about was Ash and the four meatballs painted on the side of his plane to denote kills of enemy planes. Ash. Ash had called him little brother, had said he wanted to shake his hand. Jesus.

Later, after long hours of battle between ships and aircraft, the Japanese navy retreated, leaving Guadalcanal and the marine bases intact. Simon acknowledged two enemy Zeros destroyed, Coleman two, Kingsley two.

Back in Nevada, Sallie Thornton continued her daily prayers. They were always the same: please, God, bring my sons and every other mother's son home safely. Bless all those I hold dear.

PART TWO

Fanny Logan

1943–1961

8

The 1943 graduating class of Shamrock High School tossed their caps in the air as the band struck up the John Philip Sousa march that would take them outdoors to the football field. A festive party was under way, thanks to the parents and faculty members.

Forty-five graduates clustered in little groups, some tearful, some boisterous. There were manly handshakes, hugs, promises, and more tears.

Fanny Logan circulated among her peers because she didn't have a best friend. She allowed herself to be embraced, clapped on the back, and kissed on the cheek. All she had to do was turn in her cap and gown, providing she could find her cap, eat her hot dog, drink her soda pop, say one more round of good-byes and thank her two favorite teachers for their help during the past four years. Then she could go home to finish packing for her cross-country trip.

"You did it, honey, you graduated in the top three percent of your class. I'm proud of you, cherry button," Damian Logan said as he swept his daughter off her feet and high in the air.

As one, her two brothers said, "Who would have thought a squirt like you could come out on top."

Fanny laughed. "Only because you guys helped me with my homework. Truth is truth. You know me and numbers." They grinned, as did Fanny. "We're gonna miss you."

"And I'm going to miss all of you. I'll write and call, at least once a week. Swear to me you'll take good care of Daddy. Daniel, swear to me."

"I swear, but don't you think it's going to be a little difficult for us to take care of a 220-pound, six-foot-three man?"

"Not at all. Brad, promise me."

"You shouldn't even ask such a thing. We're family, Fanny. Make sure you keep your promise to write and call. We need to know where you are at all times. You've never been outside of Shamrock, so we're going to worry about you. Families always worry when someone leaves the nest. Just because we don't have a mother doesn't mean we aren't like other families. You give us one minute of worry, and I'll come out there and drag you back. Dad's going to be like a wet cat until he knows you're safe and sound. Just remember, Pennsylvania is a lot different from California."

They were wonderful, this small family of hers. She smiled and knew they would all relax immediately when she said, "I love all of you, so very much. I know you and Daniel went to bat for me with Dad. I'm responsible, so you can stop worrying. Daniel, who got you out of that mess with that girl from Pittsburgh who was hell-bent on marrying you? And, Brad, who convinced Dad to let you get that motorcycle? Me, that's who. Although I think that was a mistake. You better not make me sorry I stood up for you."

"Yeah, well, you better not get mixed up with any jerks, Fanny."

Fanny loved it when her brothers blustered the way they were doing now. God, how she loved these three men who had raised her. "Let's not be talking about jerks, Brad. It's time for you to start thinking seriously about Susan and maybe getting engaged. She's going to find someone else if you don't start whispering sweet things in her ear."

Daniel cackled with laughter.

"I wouldn't laugh if I were you, Daniel. You should be married with at least two children. At the rate you two are going I'll have my own children before you do. I want to be an aunt, and Daniel, when I was in the hardware store last week I heard Ellen say she was thinking about joining the WACs. You guys are free now, you don't have to look after me anymore. Listen to me, both of you, I truly, truly appreciate the way you've looked after me all these years. I love it that you are best pals with Daddy. Please, don't be afraid to leave him. I'm doing it, I'm going to make my way. Maybe if the two of you did . . . you know, get married, Daddy would maybe start being interested in Mrs. Kelly. She's certainly interested in him. Give him some breathing room, okay?"

"Eighteen and she knows everything already," Brad said.

"She even has a diploma that says so." Daniel grinned. "Here comes Dad with four hot dogs. They're loaded too. I hope he has four Alka Seltzers to go."

They were handsome, these three men in her life. And the truth was, every available woman and girl in Shamrock had tried to snare her father and her brothers, but they'd taken the responsibility of raising her so seriously, they put their own lives in a holding pattern. She'd been only six weeks old when her mother up and left the family because raising three children was too much for her. Fanny could feel her heart start to swell with love.

"Aahh, jeez, she's gonna bawl now. You're ugly when you cry, Fanny. C'mon, say your good-byes so we can go home and eat that cake Mrs. Kelly made special for you."

"Wait here for me, I'll just be a few minutes." She was as good as her word, returning fifteen minutes later, minus her cap and gown and holding her yearbook. "I'm ready."

In the car, Daniel reached for the yearbook. He chortled with glee as Fanny pointed out the various pictures that had been taken of her during the year. "Hmmmnn, they say you're going to be a successful businesswoman someday. Did you see this, Dad? It was the time they had the carnival and some teacher played fortune-teller. Don't count on it, Fanny."

"I will be someday, you'll see."

"I have no doubts at all," Damian Logan said quietly.

"Daddy, Daniel, Brad, I want you to know I will never do anything that will bring shame on our family. All three of you taught me right from wrong. I just wanted you all to know that."

"Would it have anything to do with all those swats to your rear end, Fanny?" Daniel guffawed.

"A little. I learned though. It's important to me to know I can count on you and that you can count on me."

"Take a good, long look, Fanny. It will be dark in the morning when you leave. This is your last look at Shamrock."

Fanny's eyes misted as her father slowed the car. She looked right and then left, drinking in the sight of the small town where she'd lived her whole life. She had nothing to compare Shamrock to, but she knew it had to be one of the prettiest small towns in the whole world. The streets were tree-lined, the sidewalks wide, perfect for riding a bike without harming pedestrians. The shop doors and wide front windows were shaded by colorful awnings, the shops' wares often displayed outside in the summer months in wicker baskets. Close to the curbs, but between the maple trees, were tubs of bright red geraniums. Men from the fire department watered the flowers and trees every evening when the sun went down. When she was small she'd frolicked in the spray of water along with all the other children in town. It was one of her fondest memories.

It was hard to believe she wouldn't be going to Banebury's drugstore for a cherry phosphate tomorrow. She wondered if she would miss the smell of the Max Factor powder and the scent of licorice that greeted you as you walked in the door. It was harder still to believe she wouldn't be going to Stillwell's bakery on Saturday morning for jelly donuts for her father and brothers. She always ate hers on the way home.

The small A & P with its summer produce under the green-striped awning, compliments of local farmers, was always tempting. More than once she'd snatched a peach or a pear and then when the guilts attacked her, she'd go back, smile, and pay Mr. Oliver who always said, "I saw you, Fanny, I knew you'd be back." She saw a barrel with upended brooms next to the door. Mr. Oliver was getting ready to close. She waved to him. Schoneberg's dress store with the lopsided mannequins was where she bought her summer shorts and blouses. Every other year she got to pick out a new winter coat. Bailey's toy store where she got her first sled and pair of roller skates, the red-and-white post office with the flag blowing in the breeze. Mr. Collins was late taking down the flag today, she thought.

St. Barts, where she was baptized, attended catechism classes, where she made her first holy communion and was confirmed. The church was small and white. The huge front door was solid oak with massive iron hinges. It never made a sound. Inside it was cool, dim, and comforting, and always there was the same familiar smell, candle wax and furniture polish. She thought she could smell it now as her father turned the corner. She didn't crane her neck to look backward. She would never forget this place. Never, ever.

"Home sweet home," Fanny's father said cheerfully.

Home was 333 Bridge Street—a brown shingled house with a white front porch complete with swing and two rocking chairs. This was where she propped her sled in the winter, where she sat on the steps to strap on her roller skates, where she hauled her bike to lean it against the wall. Because there were no children on this particular block, she'd often played on the straw mat on the floor with her paper dolls. She'd hosted hundreds of tea parties whose guest list included her father and her two brothers. When she had her own lemonade stand her only customers were her brothers and her father, but that was okay because they drank the whole pitcher, her brothers paying her from their allowance, her father borrowing the paper boy's money from the sugar bowl.

Sitting on the front porch was Martha Kelly. Next to her on the swing was a cake under a huge dome and a gift-wrapped package. Her father ushered all of them into the house, hanging back to talk in low tones to Martha. "I hope you two are going out after we have our cake," Fanny hissed to her brothers. "Open your eyes and look at the two of them," she continued to hiss. "They're interested in each other. Don't you see it?"

"Yeah, yeah," both brothers whispered.

"It's about time. Daniel you set the table, I'll make the coffee. Brad, get out the silverware and napkins. Put the milk in that little red pitcher and the sugar in the matching bowl."

"You sound like a drill sergeant," Brad grumbled.

"Do you want the Thanksgiving/Christmas dishes?" Daniel asked smartly.

"Of course. This is my last night home. I want to remember eating on the good dishes. When I'm gone I know you lazy bums are going to eat on paper plates because you're too lazy to wash the dishes. You are, aren't you?"

"Yep," Brad said.

"Plastic knives and forks too," Daniel said.

"What are you going to do about the pots and pans?" Fanny teased. This was what she liked best, the light banter, the teasing, the comforting familiarity of belonging to a loving family.

"That's Dad's job. Or, we eat Chinese."

Fanny squeezed her eyes shut as she locked away the memory of this evening. She loved the kitchen, particularly the big, old oak table with the claw feet that took both her brothers and her father to move. She had made the red-and-white-striped cushions in her senior Home Economics class. On the floor by the sink, by the stove, and the refrigerator, were hooked rugs she'd made during one long hot summer when she'd been confined to the front porch with her leg in a cast. Everything was old, but clean and polished. By her and by her brothers. They hadn't made her do all the kitchen work because she was a girl. The boys did their share, and both of them could cook as well as she could. Everything was on a schedule, everyone took turns with the chores.

The moment they finished the cake, and Fanny thanked Mrs. Kelly for the address book, Daniel and Brad excused themselves, saying they had dates. "I'll clean up," Fanny said. "Dad, why don't you and Mrs. Kelly sit on the front porch."

Alone with her thoughts, Fanny washed and dried the holiday dishes. In just a few hours she would leave all this behind her—her family, this house, the town. Her father had given her permission to take a year to do whatever she wanted. At the end of the year, if she didn't find her niche, she was to return to Shamrock and go to college. She had no interest in college. She wanted to taste and experience life. Going all the way across the country was going to be the biggest experience of her life. What she was going to do when she arrived in California was still a mystery. Maybe she would be able to find her mother. Unlikely, but still possible.

Fanny took a last look around the kitchen. She'd fixed the coffeepot for morning, swept the floor, hung up the dish towel. She turned off the bright overhead light and switched on the night-light—things she'd done hundreds of times in the past. In the doorway to the dining room, Fanny turned for one last look at the kitchen. The grape ivy hanging in the window looked exceptionally luscious in the dim light. She'd given everyone in the neighborhood cuttings from the old plant, which she'd tended with care. The thick, glossy philodendron in the red clay pot on the end of the counter beckoned her. She plucked away a yellow leaf. She hoped her brothers would water and trim the plants. Without the greenery, the kitchen would look bare. Her father always commented that the kitchen looked empty when she set the plants outside in the rain. Maybe she should leave a note. "I'm sure I'm going to come back for a visit, but I don't think I'll come back for good, so this is good-bye." She felt silly, even a little guilty, as she walked up the steps to the second floor.

Her room was in wild disarray, but would be neat and tidy as soon as she finished packing. What to take, what not to take? What to throw away, what to take up to the attic?

Two hours later, both suitcases were packed. Her carry-on satchel held a change of clothes, her small pouch of makeup that she rarely wore, several books, her comb, brush, toothpaste, and toothbrush. A writing tablet, pen, several envelopes, and three stamps were in the inside pocket of the satchel. Her purse held her wallet, her change purse, comb, lipstick, tissues, and her keys. She counted her money again. She was just a few dollars short of a thousand. Enough to last her a year if she was frugal and got a job. She had what she considered a fashionable wardrobe, purchased with her baby-sitting money. She was going to be fine.

Fanny turned down her bed. She wished then that she had a best friend, someone she could call to talk about tomorrow, or a mother to talk to, to ask for advice. She didn't regret for one minute, all the time and devotion she'd given to her father and her brothers. She loved them. It was that simple.

She cuddled with her pillow, something she did almost every

night. It was a way of pretending she was grown-up, pretending she was sleeping with someone, pretending all kinds of things. It might have been better to write things down in a diary or a journal, but committing thoughts and desires to paper scared her. Better to hug a pillow and pretend.

By scrooching and wiggling beneath the covers, Fanny made her nest for the night. The position allowed her right arm to snake out to turn off the bedside lamp. One more thing to do and then she could close her eyes. "Bless my mother wherever she is."

The long night hadn't quite relinquished its tentacles when Fanny slid from her bed and raced for the bathroom. Even though it was June, the early mornings and evenings were still chilly. She shivered as she waited for the water to turn hot. She was in and out in five minutes. Huddling in an old flannel robe, she stripped her bed and then straightened the bedspread so it would look like she was going to come home at the end of the day. She planned on leaving her door open when she carried her suitcases downstairs. Closed doors meant a person wasn't coming back. Mrs. Kelly had told her that when her mother left, her father closed the door on their bedroom and slept on the couch. For three long years he'd used the downstairs bathroom and kept his clothes in the hall closet. She was leaving her posters on the wall, her roller skates and ice skates in one corner, her softball bat and glove in another corner. The coatrack Daniel made her in his senior shop class held an old raincoat and an umbrella. She was leaving that, too. The fourth corner stood sentinel over the hockey stick Brad had made for her the year before last. A net bag, saved from a dozen oranges, held sixteen pucks. Her hockey-playing days were over. She wondered if her brothers would be sad when they looked in her room from time to time after she was gone.

The maple dresser was empty. She straightened the crocheted scarf that Mrs. Kelly had made for her years ago. Every spring and fall she washed it and then dipped it in sugar water just the way Mrs. Kelly taught her. She was going to really miss the old maple rocker, too. It was perfect for curling into with a good book on cold winter nights. Because it fit her like a glove, she'd slept in the chair with an afghan more times than she could remember.

Fanny looked at her watch. Time to move. She was dressed in minutes in a swirling lavender skirt, crisp white blouse, and brand-new white sandals. She fluffed out her curly blond hair before she pulled it back into a long, curling ponytail. She needed a fashionable haircut that would make her look older. When she got to California it was going to be one of the first things to go on her list of things to do.

Her arms full of wet towels and sheets, Fanny sprinted down the stairs to the laundry room, where she dumped everything into the washer. The boys could hang out the laundry later in the day. She ran back upstairs and carried down her suitcases, one at a time, and set them by the front door, her new white leather purse on top. She plugged in the coffeepot, got out the toaster, and made everyone's lunches. Ham, baloney, and cheese for Daniel, cheese and baloney for Brad, four slices of cheese for her father placed between the ham and the baloney. Daniel got lettuce and mayo, Brad got mustard, and her father got both mayo and mustard. She wrote their names on the paper bags, and then fitted them into the identical lunch pails. Three oranges, three apples, three bananas, and two cupcakes each were the last things to go in the pail after she filled each thermos. Working in the steel mills required a full lunch pail. Who was going to do this when she was gone? Maybe Mrs. Kelly. She waited for the coffee to perk.

The minute she saw her brothers and father she knew they hadn't slept at all. She looked at them helplessly. "I'm going to be fine. I'm the one who should be worrying. Who's going to make your lunches, who's going to do the laundry? I hate dust and you guys don't know what a dust rag looks like. Will you get someone to come in and clean and cook? You should hire Mrs. Kelly. She could use the money, and she taught me everything I know. I know you aren't going to stretch the curtains, and you aren't going to dip the dresser scarves in sugar water. Well?"

"I already hired her, Fanny." Her father smiled.

"That's a relief." At least she thought it was.

They drained their coffee cups as one. "Time to go, Fanny."

Outside, the early dawn was creeping over the horizon. Everything looked gray and dirty to Fanny. She shivered inside the light sweater she'd thrown over her shoulders. "I hate foggy mornings. I like to see the sun when I get up. The sun always shines in California."

Daniel snorted with laughter. "If you believe that, I know a bridge I can sell you real cheap."

Fanny stood stock-still for a minute, for a long, last look at the brown shingled house. The fog swirling about her ankles spiraled upward, obliterating the brown house. She slid into the family sedan. Daniel reached for her hand.

"You'll get homesick for a little while. Call us, and it will go away. In a way I envy you, Fanny," he whispered.

"I know," she whispered back.

"Swear you won't do anything stupid, Fanny. Swear you'll take care of yourself and swear that you will write and call faithfully. I'll be all right with it if you promise."

"I have never broken a promise, Daniel, and you know that. I . . . I'm going to miss you. I love you all so much."

"Jeez, Fanny, if you start to blubber now, you'll have us sniveling too. Dad's too old to cry."

"You're never too old to cry, son," Damian Logan said quietly.

"Jeez, Dad, I know that. I was just trying to . . . you know . . . I didn't want her to get all choked up. You know Fanny, she thinks we can't get along without her." He turned so that he was facing his sister. "You're probably right. I'm just saying whatever pops into my head so I won't feel so bad. You're going to get on that bus with dry eyes and we're the ones who will be crying."

"Maybe I shouldn't go. Maybe this is a mistake. I didn't think it was going to be so hard to leave all of you."

"It will be all right, Fanny. We'll write and we'll call. You need to do this now, when you're young. I don't want things to go sour for you the way . . . You need to do all the things you want to do when you're single with no family responsibilities. Here's the bus station. Everyone out!"

Her father's voice was so cheerful, Fanny felt herself cringing. "You have your ticket, your money, everything secure, don't you, honey?"

"I have everything in my purse, Daddy. I . . . I think it might be better, Daddy, if you and the boys . . . left. You have to get to work, and you'll be late if you wait for the bus to pull out. I'm just fine. I . . . I don't want to look out the window and wave. Go on, all of you."

"Jeez, after today we won't have to listen to your bossy mouth. You're lucky we're family and put up with you." His hug was so hard, Fanny's eyes started to water. "I love you, you little squirt. Take care of yourself, you hear."

"Okay," Fanny gasped.

"I'm gonna miss you the most," Daniel whispered as he hugged her. "Who's going to sew on my buttons and polish my shoes? I really do like your meat loaf. I just said I didn't to get your goat. Be good, Fanny. I love you so much it hurts."

"Me too, Daniel. I'll be good, I promise."

Both boys walked away to allow Fanny her last moments with their father.

"Daddy, thanks for everything. I know you had to . . . to fight with yourself to let me go. I also know why you finally gave in. I'm not Mama, Daddy. I promise to write and call. I'll never do anything to shame our family. Mrs. Kelly is a real nice lady, Daddy. She's sweet on you. I think you know that, though. Before you know it, Daniel and Brad will be getting married. You need to think about . . . about not being alone."

"Give me a hug and kiss, Miss Know Everything. Remember, anytime you want to come home, we'll be here waiting for you. If your money runs out, let me know. I don't want to worry about you scrimping and just getting by. Promise."

"I promise. I love you, Daddy." She planted a kiss on his cheek and then ran to the bus. She didn't look back.

Three pairs of wet eyes watched the Greyhound bus pull away from the curb.

"So, boys, do you think this might be the right time for us to open our own business? I have all of Fanny's college money we can use as seed money. I think we can make it. I'm tired of the steel mills. How about you? Do you think we can make a go of the construction business?"

"I think so," Daniel said quietly.

"I'm all for it," Brad said.

"Then I say we do it," Damian Logan said as he backed the Nash sedan onto the main road.

Seven years later, Logan & Sons Construction was the biggest company of its kind in the state of Pennsylvania.

Fanny walked down the aisle, taking deep breaths as she looked for just the right seat. She finally chose a window seat near the back of the bus and stowed her small carry-on satchel under the seat in front of her. She carefully tucked her purse into the small opening at the end of her seat and leaned back, a mystery novel in her lap. Now she could take in her surroundings. She'd been on buses before, but they were school buses or the church bus. This bus was elegant, with its scratchy blue seats and paper towels covering the headrests. There was a bar at the bottom of the seat in front of her so she could prop her feet up, and she was only five seats away from the lavatory.

Fanny paid careful attention to the passengers as they boarded the bus. Over the next week—the length of the cross-country trip—

she was sure she would be on a first-name basis with at least a few of the passengers. She was proved wrong. Most of the passengers were of retirement age, and didn't want to bother with a young girl. The three books she'd brought were her only company. When her eyes got tired she napped or nibbled on snacks she purchased along the way.

Fanny finished the book she was reading and stuck it in her bag. An hour to the Las Vegas stop, and then it was on to Los Angeles, her final destination. All she wanted right now was to wash her face and brush her teeth. It was time to put on a clean blouse and change her undies in the washroom when they stopped. Ten more hours, and she would be in California. She could feel the excitement begin to build as she counted the passengers who had boarded the bus in Pittsburgh. Four besides herself. She stared out the dirty window at the dry, cactus-covered landscape. Shamrock was prettier than this barren waste. A lump formed in her throat. For just a moment she wished she was back home in Pennsylvania.

"Ninety-minute layover. Take your time, ladies and gentlemen, and get yourselves a good hot meal. I'll announce the departure time over the loudspeaker so don't wander off."

Fanny grimaced when she entered the washroom. The filling station back home had cleaner bathrooms. She did her best not to touch anything as she washed her face and hands with wet paper towels. She ignored the green soap in the wall dispenser because of the grimy buildup around the edges and the spout. She brushed her teeth, using her hand to cup the water, brushed her hair, changed her blouse and panties. Now she was ready for that hot meal the bus driver spoke of.

Fifteen minutes before the departure was announced, Fanny boarded the bus. She settled herself with the three new magazines she'd purchased. Once or twice she looked up as passengers began boarding. The bus was going to be full.

A man, older than her father, sat down in the seat next to her. Fanny was in awe of his natty attire. Out of the corner of her eye she noticed his diamond stickpin and the diamond ring on his pinkie finger. His nails were bluntly cut, his cuticles clean and neat, a coat of clear polish on his nails. Her brothers and her father had ragged cuticles, and they had to wash and scrub their hands with Lava soap. She could tell that her seat companion had never done a hard day's work in his life. He looked too manicured, too creased, too polished. And he sucked mints.

"Head count," the driver said loudly. "Have your tickets ready."

Fanny opened her purse for the ticket receipt she'd removed when she got off the bus. It was at that moment the commotion occurred. One minute the bus driver was standing in the center of the aisle, the next second he was on the floor, blood spouting from a head wound.

"Do what you're told and no one gets hurts. We want your jewelry and your money! Don't do anything foolish. This is a real gun. I don't want any heroes."

Fanny's fingers worked feverishly with the zipper on her purse. In the blink of an eye she had the envelope with her money in it between the pages of her magazine. Her change purse held $4.33. She held it, along with her birthstone ring, a gift from her father, in her hand.

"Here, girlie, hide this for me," her seat companion whispered. Before she could say yes or no, Fanny found herself holding a stack of money as thick as a sandwich. Without thinking or weighing the consequences, she placed the money next to her own and then folded the magazine.

An elderly lady in the seat in front of them started to cry, begging the man with the gun not to take her wedding ring. "Here's my money, all of it. The ring isn't worth much, but I've worn it for forty-four years, please don't take it."

"Drop it in the bag, lady, and don't give me a story about not being able to get it off."

"Won't somebody help me?"

"Leave her alone, she's an old lady," the man next to Fanny said.

"I didn't ask for your opinion, greaseball," the bandit said. "Sit there and be quiet."

It happened so fast, Fanny later found it almost impossible to explain the circumstances to the police. She felt warm blood splatter on her arms as her seat companion stood to prevent the gunman from hitting the elderly lady. She swore later to the police that she felt the blows her seat companion suffered.

"You killed him! You killed him!" Fanny shouted.

"Shut up, kid. He's just bleeding. Hand it over!" Without hesitation, Fanny handed over her money and birthstone ring. "He needs a doctor. Somebody has to call a doctor," she screamed.

"I told you to shut up. One more peep out of you, and I'm gonna take you with me for a little fun and games. What's it gonna be, kiddo?"

Fanny clamped her lips shut. The man sitting next to her whispered, "Do as he says. Listen to me, call this number and say Jake needs help. Don't call no doctors. My friends will take care of me. Promise, little girl."

"Okay. What's the number?"

"Nine-six-four-two."

Fanny repeated the number over and over so she wouldn't forget it. In between repeating the numbers, she kept asking, "Are you all right, are you all right?"

"No, honey, he is not all right. He's bleeding profusely," the elderly woman said. "It was a brave thing he did. Look, I didn't give up my ring! They're gone. Someone has to call the police and a doctor."

"I will!" Fanny said as she crawled over the man sitting slumped in the seat next to her. "I know what to do."

Fanny raced to the front of the bus, stepped over the driver who was bleeding as much as her seat companion. She jumped down the two steps and ran into the bus stop, dropped her nickel in the slot, and dialed the numbers the man had given her, at which point she completely forgot them. "Jake needs help. He told me to call you. He's bleeding real bad. The doctors are coming as soon as I call them." She quickly rattled off what she'd just gone through. "What should I tell Jake?"

"Tell him we'll be there in five minutes. He ain't dead is he?"

"I don't know. I don't think so. He's bleeding a lot though."

Fanny hung up and called the operator. "Please send an ambulance and call the police." She went through her story a second time. "The driver is unconscious, too."

Fanny ran back to the bus. What kind of person was she that she called Jake's friends before she called the police and an ambulance? The driver was still lying on the floor, the passengers were seated, their faces full of shock. The elderly lady in the back was the only one who seemed to have her wits about her. "Are they coming?"

"They said right away." In her life, Fanny had never been this excited. What if the police took her to the station and . . . and grilled her? Jake had told her not to call a doctor. If he died, would she be held accountable? "He's still alive, I can see his pulse beating in his neck. I never saw so much blood."

"Head wounds bleed more than other wounds. He's unconscious. That's not good. That thug got him right on the temple. He could very well die. Why is everyone still sitting on this bus?"

"I don't know," Fanny wailed. "Oh, look, here comes somebody."

"They look like . . . like . . . criminals."

Fanny stepped aside. "You called us," one of the men said.

Fanny felt something being pushed into her hand. It must be a note that she was meant to read later. She stuffed it into the patch pocket of her circular skirt.

"I hear the ambulance," the elderly lady said.

"Move it, Herbie," one of the men said. "Put him over your shoulder."

Fanny and the elderly lady craned their necks to see where the men were carrying Jake. "That's a limousine. He must be somebody important."

"Bang on the window, lady. I have . . . bang on the window, make them stop," Fanny shouted as she ran down the aisle with the magazine in her hand. "Hey, wait! Wait!" she shouted. It was too late. The tires of the long black car squealed on the pavement just as the ambulance careened around the corner. "Oh, no!" Now what was she supposed to do?

Three hours later, the passengers still sat huddled together in the bus depot. They'd all given their statements to the police, and were waiting word from the bus company. It took another hour before the passengers were told a new driver wouldn't arrive until the following day. Accommodations were available at a local boardinghouse, where dinner and breakfast would be paid for by the bus company. Insurance forms would be handed out first thing in the morning.

"This is a very thrilling adventure," the elderly lady said breathlessly. "Do you know who those . . . those *people* were, young lady?"

Fanny debated a moment before she replied. "No, I don't know who they were." It was the truth. "The police weren't even interested in the man sitting next to me. They only wanted information on the two robbers. I'm glad you didn't have to give up your wedding ring."

"Thanks to that kind gentleman. I do hope he's all right. It's not good when you're rendered unconscious," the woman fretted. "We'll never know if he dies," she added as an afterthought. Fanny blanched. Death was something she was unfamiliar with.

"Ladies, we're going to take you to your accommodations. There's a jitney waiting outside. If you want to take your luggage, see the man in the blue uniform. It will take a while to unload everything. It might be best if you just take your carry-on bags."

Fanny couldn't wait to get into her room and slide the bolt. She unpacked her entire carry-on bag as well as her purse. She removed the envelope with her eight hundred dollars from the magazine and put it back in her purse. Jake's packet of money stared up at her. For the first time she looked at the corner of the bills. Gingerly, with her index finger, she started to count them. One-thousand-dollar bills— and there were about two hundred of them. She dropped the packet and watched it bounce off the chenille bedspread onto the floor, then she kicked it under the bed. Fear, unlike anything she'd ever experienced, rushed through her. She took deep breaths, trying to calm herself.

She had just enough time to wash up before the bell rang for supper. The meal was hearty, conversation at a minimum. Fanny passed on the chocolate cake and returned to her room, where she spent the next hour writing down different combinations of numbers in the hope that one of them would be the number Jake had given her. She would have to stay in Las Vegas, she realized, until she found a way to return the money.

In the morning, Fanny was at the drugstore the moment it opened. She called all the numbers on her list, seriously depleting her pocket change. No gruff, gravelly voice responded. She tried a second set of numbers and then a third with the same results. Maybe if she didn't think about it, the number would come to her.

Outside in the bright sunshine, Fanny looked up and down the business district for the closest bank and the newspaper office.

The Nevada Savings Bank was cool and dim, the brass railings polished to a high sheen. The deep burgundy carpeting and navy blue upholstered chairs displeased her. She decided a man had decorated the bank. The thought made her grimace.

"Can I help you?"

He was tall and thin, with wire-rimmed glasses perched precariously on his nose. He looked like a banker. He also seemed to blend in with the oppressive furnishings. "I'd like to open a safety deposit box."

"Large, medium, or small?"

"Small," Fanny said firmly.

"Come this way, miss. I need you to fill out a form. Will you be the only one with access to the box?"

"Yes."

Fanny filled out the form, signing her name in two places. She paid five dollars for a year's rental, accepted the receipt and the key, and followed the banker down four steps to the vault. She watched carefully as he fit his own key into the lock and then asked for hers. A moment later she had an empty metal box in her hands.

"You can use that room over there," the banker said, indicating three wooden doors to her left. "I'll wait here for you."

Fanny took a deep breath before she opened the box. The packet of money slid from one end to the other when she closed the lid. The box secure in her grasp, she carried it out of the small cubicle.

"Just slide the box into the slot and give me your key again," the banker said. Fanny did as instructed. "Don't lose the key, Miss Logan. If you do, we'll have to drill the box and it will cost $25. We'll notify you at the end of the year when the rental comes due. Is there anything else I can do for you today?"

"Not today, thank you." Fanny slipped the key into her change purse. Her breathing returned to normal as she squared her shoulders and departed the bank.

Fanny's next stop was the local newspaper, where she wrote out an ad to be placed in the classified section of the paper. She was assured the ad would run in the late afternoon edition. She paid for a five-day run. She read and reread the ad before she slid it across the counter. The ad was simply worded: Young lady with magazine is waiting for you to claim it. Identification is required. Call 6643.

Outside again, Fanny crossed the street and walked down three blocks to the bus depot. She was surprised to see almost all of the passengers waiting near the ticket agent's counter. She waited for her turn to speak with the agent. A young girl was arguing with the agent. "I called yesterday and you said that was the price. Why is it five dollars more today? I don't have five extra dollars. That's what you told me. I have to get to Los Angeles, my grandmother is expecting me."

Fanny stepped aside, allowing the person behind her to go in front of her. The young girl had tears in her eyes. On an impulse, Fanny said, "You can use my ticket. I have to stay here for a few days. Don't even bother telling that man. If he lied to you, then he doesn't deserve your courtesy."

"Are you sure? You don't even know me. Why would you give me your ticket? Is there a catch to it?"

"No. I just have to get my bags from the bus. Do you have baggage?"

"Just this bag I'm carrying. I can put it under the seat. If you're serious about the ticket, I'll gladly accept it. Here's the money."

"No, you keep the money, you might need it. I have enough money to get another ticket when I'm ready to leave. Is your grandmother sick?"

"No, she's getting married."

Fanny whooped with laughter. "Are you the flower girl?"

"Yes I am. I love her and she's so happy. I couldn't say no. Thanks again."

"I hope you catch the bouquet," Fanny said.

"I hope so too."

Her bags stowed in the back of a taxicab, Fanny returned to the boardinghouse to wait.

Wait she did, for six straight days. By the end of the week, Fanny thought she would go out of her mind with boredom.

Finally she took the initiative and called the biggest newspaper in Los Angeles and made arrangements to run her ad for two straight weeks. She agreed to wire the money by way of Western Union. She also made the decision to run the ad again in the *Nevada Sentinel*. It was all she could do. Her duties for the day taken care of, Fanny stopped at the Otis Pharmacy, took her seat at the counter, and ordered a ham and Swiss sandwich, coleslaw, and a cup of coffee. While she waited for her food, she opened the morning edition of the paper. Two stools away from her own, a man sat down and spoke to the waitress. "Bess, do you know anyone who might be interested in a temporary job for a few weeks? My secretary is going back East to her brother's wedding. The position might turn into a permanent one if she decides not to return. If you do hear of anyone, tell them to stop by my office."

"I might be interested," Fanny blurted. The man was staring at her with clinical interest. She was glad now that she'd asked the landlady to allow her the use of her iron and ironing board. The mint green linen dress was fashionable, as were her spectator pumps with the small stacked heels. Because of the intense desert heat, she'd piled her hair on top of her head, an arrangement that made her, in her opinion, look five years older. The pearl drop earrings, a gift from her two brothers, were the finishing touch.

"I don't believe I've seen you before. Are you a new resident? Devin Rollins, I'm an attorney." Fanny reached across the counter to grasp his hand. She exerted a full measure of pressure the way her brothers had taught her. She thought she saw grudging respect in the attorney's eyes.

"I'm Fanny Logan. Yes, I'm new here. I don't honestly know how long I'll be staying here, so I would have to say if you're looking for a temporary replacement, I can help you. I have a good secretarial background. I can type over 60 words a minute with no mistakes and my shorthand is about 120 words a minute. I'm staying at Mrs. Hershey's boardinghouse."

Devin stared at Fanny for several minutes. She looked like Sallie—the same bluebell eyes, the same blond curly hair, but there the resemblance ended. This young woman had a heart-shaped face and dimples. "Stop by my office if you're interested. I'm located at 66 Carson Street, second floor."

"Thank you, Mr. Rollins. Will this afternoon be all right, say around two o'clock?"

"Two o'clock will be fine, Miss Logan," Devin said as he finished the last of his coffee.

"I couldn't help but overhear your conversation," the waitress said as she cleared away Devin's dishes. "I know they're looking for kitchen help at the Frontier. The pay is good, I'm told. I'd apply myself, but my father owns this drugstore so I have to work here."

"Thanks for the tip. Do you know Mr. Rollins?"

"He comes in once or twice a week. He's very nice. You said you're new in town, right?" Fanny nodded. "Have you seen the town, the Bright White Way?"

"I haven't been out after dark. I'd like to see it, though."

"Then let's do it. Tonight. You're probably going to get the job with Mr. Rollins, so you can celebrate. I know where you're staying. I'll come by for you if you don't have anything else to do. It's Friday night so things will be going on. Do you want to go? By the way, my name is Bess Otis. Bess is short for Elizabeth."

Fanny eyed the freckle-faced redhead. She liked her infectious grin, the way she swiped at the crumbs on the counter and chuckled when she said, "The ants have to eat too. Pop would kill me if he saw me brush the crumbs on the floor."

"I'd love to go. Do you gamble?"

"Oh, yes, ten dollars every week. One of these days I'm going to win big, real big. Maybe I'll get to be as rich as Mrs. Thornton."

"Who's Mrs. Thornton?"

"Just the richest woman in this state. She might even be the richest woman in the world for all I know. Her picture is always in the newspaper. Mr. Rollins is her lawyer. He's on the town council with my dad, that's how I know. Mrs. Thornton comes in here all the time to buy her sundries. She buys candies by the sack and eats them as she's going out the door. She always wears the latest fashions, and she's so pretty you just want to cry that you're so plain. What time should I pick you up?"

"How about eight o'clock?"

"Okay. Dress up."

"I am dressed up," Fanny said.

"No, I mean fancy. Wear makeup. You're pretty now, but makeup will make you gorgeous. Wait till you see me. I could have any one of those high rollers like this," she said, snapping her fingers. "I don't want them though, I have a steady boyfriend. He shoots pool on Friday nights with his friends, so I'm free. It works out real good. There's no need for him to know *everything* I do. I have a lot of fun, and when I lose my ten dollars I go home. So, do you have any makeup?"

"Lipstick and powder. We didn't wear much makeup back in Shamrock."

"This is Las Vegas, Fanny. I'll come early and we'll put on our makeup together. I even have false eyelashes."

"Aren't you afraid people will think you're . . . *loose?* Aren't you worried about your reputation?"

"Nope. I'm not doing anything wrong, and I'm having fun. I want to have fun now so that when I get married I won't mind staying home and having babies. The way I see it is, I have to get all of this out of my system now. Gambling gets in your blood, though, so you have to be careful."

"I don't think I have to worry about that, I don't have any intention of throwing my money away. Do you ever win?"

"Hardly ever. In the old days the old prospectors kept going up to the hills when they knew they were risking their lives during the winter. They were looking for the big strike, the pot of gold at the end of the rainbow. Some of them even found it and they still kept going back hoping for a *bigger* strike. It's called gambling fever. Once it gets you it doesn't let go."

"Is that going to happen to you?"

"Probably. I'll fight it, though," Bess said airily.

"I like this drugstore, it reminds me of Mr. Banebury's store back in Shamrock. It even smells the same. They have a lunch counter, too, just like this one. The donuts are on a plate under the glass dome. The menu is always the same, egg salad, tuna salad, chicken salad, and ham salad. Mrs. Banebury puts sweet relish in the ham salad, do you do that?"

"No. Maybe I'll try it on Monday. I get so sick of this place sometimes, I want to just sit down and cry. I know there's more to life than making salads and serving customers, I know there is. I want it, too," Bess said.

"The grass is not always greener on the other side of the fence," Fanny said quietly.

"I know that, but it doesn't stop me from dreaming and hoping.

That's half the fun. It's almost time for you to go to Mr. Rollins's office. You can use our bathroom if you want to freshen up. It's the door next to the toothpaste aisle. I'll see you about seven, Fanny. It's going to take us at least an hour to get ready."

Fanny paid her check and left a fifty-cent tip before she headed for the toothpaste aisle. Had she made a mistake in agreeing to go with Bess? Would working for Mr. Rollins, even on a part-time basis, be a mistake? Maybe she should just pack up and go on to Los Angeles and let Jake-whatever-his-name-was find her. The money couldn't be that important to Jake if no one came looking for it. A horrible thought struck her as she was applying fresh lipstick: What if Jake had died? What if the men who came to pick him up didn't know he gave her the money? What if they thought the robbers took it? If that was the case, no one was ever going to claim it. Her heart started to pound, and she had to take deep breaths until she calmed down. What was she supposed to do? Suddenly she wanted to cry. And what should she do with the money in the safety deposit box if she went on to Los Angeles? Should she leave it here in Nevada or take it with her?

Anger started to build within her. This wasn't her doing. She didn't ask to be put in this position, she didn't ask to be robbed. What she should do was turn the money over to the police and forget about it, but she knew she wouldn't do any such thing. She tried to calculate, in her head, the amount of money the bank would charge for long-term rental—like twenty-five years. That was stupid too. The money should earn interest.

An hour later, her typing and shorthand skills put to the test, Fanny waited for Mr. Rollins's decision. "Can you start on Monday morning, Miss Logan? Your hours will be from nine until one, two if you take a lunch hour. Is that agreeable?"

Fanny extended her hand and smiled. She had a job. Her first real job in the business world. Her salary was generous, more than she'd expected. If she were to stay on here, she would be able to get her own apartment, providing she found another part-time job for the afternoon. Maybe she would look into the job Bess spoke of. She shook her head; she wasn't staying on here in this sleazy town; she was going to follow through with her plan to go to California.

Fanny spent the remainder of the afternoon reading on the front porch of the boardinghouse. She was feeling homesick again. She sniffed and then blew her nose. She would not cry, she absolutely would not. But she did. If she was home, she'd be starting supper, probably peeling potatoes and dusting the pork chops with flour, shelling peas or shucking corn if it was ripe. Maybe she'd be squeezing lemons. Daniel loved a pitcher of lemonade on the table, and he drank most of it. Brad always added more sugar. Her father drank strong black coffee with his meal. She herself always spread Mrs. Kelly's homemade strawberry jam and butter on her bread at mealtime. She didn't do that here at the boardinghouse because there was no jam on the table. Maybe jelly bread at mealtime was just something people in Shamrock ate. Since she wasn't sure, she didn't want to risk embarrassment by asking.

Yes, she was definitely homesick.

Fanny was waiting on the front porch when Bess Otis arrived promptly at seven in her father's cream-colored De Soto sedan. She hopped from the car carrying a string bag loaded to the top and hustled Fanny inside and up the steps. "Don't mind me, Fanny, I get like this every Friday night. We can't do any extra riding round because there's just a smidgen of gas. We might even run out. I hate this gas rationing. I just get so excited that maybe this is the night. You know, for something wild and wonderful to happen. What should we do first? Show me what you're going to wear. Fanny, that looks like a church dress. Don't you have anything frilly or lacy? Look at my dress!" Bess pulled a dress out of her string bag—a crimson-colored, off-the-shoulder dress whose ruffles were festooned with little string balls.

"Where . . . where did you get it?" Fanny asked.

"I made it. I took sewing in school. They don't sell dresses like this. You should see my green one. I alternate them. Wait till you see my headdress. I copied it from the flappers. I added my own touches. It's my style, Fanny. I wanted something that said this is me, Bess Otis. If some guy asks me my name I tell them it's Elizabeth Adrian. Adrian is my middle name, so I'm not really lying. So, what do you think?" Not waiting for a reply, she said, "I have to put on my eyelashes and fringe out my hair a little. The makeup goes on last, lots and lots of rouge. Pancake covers most of the freckles."

"My goodness," was the best Fanny could come up with.

Bess took a full minute to assess Fanny's sapphire blue Empire-style dress. "There's nothing you can do with it. We'll have to work on your hair and makeup. I brought an extra pair of earrings for you in case you didn't have any flashy ones. Earrings are a must. I think we should stuff your bra, too."

"Oh, no, I'm not doing that," Fanny said in horror.

"Okay, but I stuff mine. Don't you just love these red shoes? There's something absolutely decadent about wearing red shoes. What color are yours?"

"White. It's summertime."

"You *have* led a sheltered life. Wait till you see some of the outfits in town. Your eyes will roll back in your head. This is your first time, so maybe by next week you'll get a feel for all of it. I could whip you up a dress like that," she said, snapping her fingers. "Of course you have to buy the material."

"I . . . I'll think about it," Fanny said weakly. "I'm not the flashy type, Bess."

"I didn't think I was either. Look at me now!"

Fanny didn't know whether to laugh or cry. She decided to laugh so that her first evening on the town wouldn't be spoiled. She would worry about next week when the time came.

"Can you really walk in those shoes?" she asked.

"I had to practice for months, but yes, I can walk in them. Fast too. Now, let's see what I can do with you."

"Can't I just go like this? Pretend I'm an out-of-town relative who . . . who isn't up on the latest fashion? I need time to . . . to work up to an outfit like you're wearing."

"At least let me do your hair. The earrings and some rouge will help. I see your point, though, so don't worry, you won't embarrass me." Fanny wanted to dive under the bed and hide. Who was embarrassing whom? If Bess showed up in Shamrock wearing her outfit, she'd be run out of town on a rail. The good people of Shamrock would call her a slut without even knowing her. That was the name the town had given her mother when she left her family.

"Rouge is great if you put it on right. I like to blend it high on the cheekbones. You have good bones, Fanny. I didn't put too much on, it goes with your outfit. I like your hair piled high with these little tendrils. It makes you look mysterious. The earrings are perfect, not gaudy. You look great, Fanny. Do you feel comfortable?"

"Do you, Bess?"

"Hell, yes. Let's get this show on the road. Are you bringing any money to gamble? I'll teach you how. Just this once. If you decide to go again, it will be your decision, but tonight I want you to feel a part of the town. Okay?"

"I have ten dollars in my purse. I'm ready. I am excited, Bess."

"You should be. We're gonna have a ball."

"Oh my lord," Fanny said later, her voice filled with awe.

"Isn't it beautiful? It's called the Great White Way."

"Who pays the electric bill?"

"Who cares? Come on, we're going to park the car and walk the rest of the way. I love it when people stare at me. I'd love to be one of those showgirls. I could strut around like that. I know I could. I bet you could, too."

"Never!" Fanny gasped.

Fanny gawked like the tourist she was. No matter where she looked, which side of the street, there were casinos and saloons. The Overland Hotel beckoned on the left, on the right, the music blared from the Boulder Club. In between the larger clubs, bars, cafés and smaller clubs, equally well lit, enticed customers with what Bess called come-ons.

"Come on, Fanny, we're going to the Sal Sagev bar and have one of Mr. Martin's famous sloe gin fizzes. They're delicious. I have one when I get here and one when I leave. Around ten o'clock I go to the White Spot Café for something to eat. You can gamble while you eat. Everyone does it. There's Ronzone's, it's a department store. Even though it's closed at night, it's still lit up. You can come here and shop, they have some great stuff. It's like my dad leaving the lights on at the drugstore at night so people can see in. He says it's good for business."

"What's *that?*" Fanny demanded.

Bess laughed. "That's the Pioneer Club. We're going there after we have our sloe gin fizz. The sign is five stories high. It's a cowboy and his arms swagger back and forth. I bet you never saw anything like that in Pennsylvania, huh? You can see it all along Fremont Street. You can even see it from the railroad depot. You should see the passengers stretching their necks. You ready, Fanny?"

"I'm ready."

Fanny didn't know what she expected, but the noise of the crowds, the loud music, the whirl and thrum of the slot machines pounding at her head, this wasn't it. She thought about the controlled, orderly gambling events in the church basement back home. The fund-raisers were always for church repairs.

"Isn't this great?" Bess said as she slid onto a stool at the bar. "I heard this bar and all the brass in this room cost almost $30,000." She ordered two sloe gin fizzes. "Drink slow, so we can flirt if we want to. Men always want to buy me drinks, but I say no."

Fanny sipped at her drink. It was good. She looked around, amazed at the number of people drinking and gambling. All the women seemed to be dressed like Bess. She felt self-conscious; were people staring at her? She watched as money and chips changed hands. The wide range of emotions on the patrons' faces puzzled her. She saw elation, anticipation, anger, fear, and depression. She mentioned it to Bess.

"Winners and losers. That's what it's all about. Last year a man was in here and he shot up the place. It was in all the papers. He later killed himself because he gambled away all his family's savings. You can't do that. When you come here you have to have a plan. You never gamble more than you can afford to lose. Ten dollars is my limit. If I was addicted to this, I'd be gambling away my hope chest money. I would like to win, though, so I can get some real sterling silver."

"Elizabeth, I've been looking for you." The voice was oily and slick-sounding. Fanny turned to stare at the man next to Bess. He was dapper, his hair greasy and slicked back flat against his head. She thought she saw a trickle of oil running down to his ear. His face was pockmarked, his teeth crooked and yellow beneath a straggly mustache. His suit was dark, double-breasted, his tie cream-colored over a grayish shirt. To Fanny's inexperienced eye, he looked embalmed. She itched to get away.

"Mattie. This is my friend . . . Francine. She's visiting from New York City. She's a schoolteacher."

Mattie nodded his greasy head. "How about me buying you pretty girls some supper?"

"I'm sorry, Mattie, we can't, but thanks for asking. We ate earlier. I promised to show Francine the town, and she has to be home early tonight. Maybe next week."

"You say that every week, Elizabeth." He waved a diamond-studded finger under Bess's nose to make his point.

"I think it just seems that way," Bess said playfully. "We're going over to the Boulder Club. Do you want me to make any bets for you, Mattie?"

Mattie reached into his breast pocket and withdrew ten silver dollars. "You win, we split it, right?"

"Absolutely."

"You ain't won nothing yet. It's been a whole year. You're a lousy gambler. Try the slots tonight instead of poker."

"Whatever you say, Mattie. If I win, I'll be back around eleven-thirty. If not, I'll see you next week. How about Palmer?"

"Ask him yourself, he's coming this way." Fanny watched as Mattie drifted off, his twin approaching from the front. Bess went through her routine again and pocketed ten more silver dollars. She did it twice more before they exited the building.

"See, now I have fifty dollars to play."

"Do you ever win for them?"

"Nope. Like Mattie said, I'm a lousy gambler. Don't worry, if I did win, I'd split with them. That's the deal. All the girls here do it. Mattie and the others, they can't leave. They walk the floors hoping to spot cheaters, that kind of thing. It's that 'grass is greener' thing again. They think the Boulder Club pays off better than this place. Sometimes I do it the other way around. I tap the guys at the Boulder Club and come here to gamble." She laughed. Fanny thought the sound was nervous and fearful.

"Aren't you afraid those men will get fed up giving you money and try . . . you know . . . something funny."

"Heck no. If I won, they'd know in a minute. They know I'm not keeping the money. That's what you mean, isn't it?"

"Not exactly, Bess. They look . . . unsavory."

Bess laughed again. "That's because they are. Listen, would you like to see Mrs. Thornton's casino? You don't see the kind of people there that you see here. I'm not dressed right for her place. Her establishment is very, very classy. There's two men at the door who decide who gets in and who doesn't. You could get in the way you're dressed. Sometimes Mrs. Thornton sings. She hires quality entertainment, and her tables pay off on a regular basis."

"Maybe next time. Let's just go to the Boulder Club so you can gamble."

"It's getting to you, huh?"

Fanny wanted to say, no, it isn't getting to me, I just want you to get rid of your money so I can go home. Instead she said, "Sort of. Before we leave, show me where Mrs. Thornton's casino is. What's it called?"

"The Silver Dollar. She has a bunch of bingo palaces on the side streets. I don't think they play bingo anymore, though. I think most of them are poker parlors now. They're just as spiffy as her casino. Mrs. Thornton has exquisite taste. I'm only repeating what I've heard. Fanny, I just had an idea. If you're looking for a second part-time job maybe you should apply to the Silver Dollar. You'd fit right in."

"I don't think so. I'm not planning on staying here, Bess."

"Maybe you should think about it. Staying here, I mean. What are you going to do when you get to California? Do you have a plan? A job? A place to live?"

"No, no, and no, but I've always wanted to go to California. I'll find a job and a place to live. This place is so . . . garish and . . . artificial. It reminds me of the Fireman's Carnival back in Shamrock. At night it looks exciting, but in the bright daylight, it looks like what it really is. People throwing their money away in the hope they can make a big score . . . is that what you call it? I doubt if this place will ever get in my blood. You told me, Bess, that you don't have a gambling problem, but you do. You're just gambling with other people's money. It's your business, and I won't say anything else. No offense."

"None taken. As long as I only spend my own ten dollars I'm okay with this. Do you have any idea, Fanny, how hard it is sometimes at the drugstore? Some days I don't think I can make another bowl of egg salad, days when I don't even want to look at the same customers, hear their same tired jokes, carry on the same weary conversations. I hate egg salad, I hate tuna and ham salad. I damn well hate the way it smells. Look, I see the worry on your face. I'm okay. I won't let things get out of hand. I bet you were the steady rock in your family. You were the one who kept it all together, am I right?"

Was she? She nodded, a small smile on her face. "So, let's go gamble your money."

Fanny liked playing the slot machines, liked pulling the handle, waiting, holding her breath to see the small pictures flash across the line. She won twice—two dollars the first time, three the second time.

At eleven o'clock, when her arm had started to ache from pulling the lever, Fanny was out a dollar. It wasn't bad for an evening's entertainment. She looked around for Bess. She heard her before she saw her. The bells and whistles followed her shrill shriek.

Bess Otis had won the five-hundred-dollar jackpot!

"Whose money were you playing with, Bess?"

"Mine!" Bess cried excitedly. "I lost everyone else's money an hour ago."

"Will those men believe you?"

Bess turned. Fanny thought she saw fear in her eyes. "Why wouldn't they believe me; it's the truth?"

"Because they're gangsters, that's why. They probably already know you won the jackpot, and they're going to be waiting for you. My advice would be to go back, say you lost track of whose money you were playing with, and divide it up among them."

"I won it fair and square with my own money, Fanny. Why

should I do that? This is going into my hope chest fund. Come on, let's go home."

"Bess, think about it, okay?"

"I have thought about it. Let's forget the going-home drink. I'll open up the drugstore and make us a big banana split. Okay? You're worrying about me, I can see it in your face."

"I'm tired, Bess, I guess it was all the excitement. Let's go get that banana split and go home. Isn't that bag of silver dollars heavy?"

"It sure is, but I don't care if my arm falls off. Oh, Fanny, I'm going to buy my sterling first thing Monday. I saw this lace comforter cover that was exquisite. It had pillows to match and everything. I can get that, too. I can buy so much instead of paying little bits every week at Ronzone's. It takes forever to pay things off. I don't think I've ever been so happy. My boyfriend is going to be happy, too. I'm not going to tell him where I got the money, though. I'll tell him I saved it."

"That's a lie, Bess. You shouldn't start your life off on a lie. Getting married is a serious thing."

Instead of answering Fanny, Bess said, "I think next week, I'll change my style and go to Mrs. Thornton's Silver Dollar. I'd like you to come along, Fanny." Fanny nodded.

It was a wonderful banana split, topped off with cherries, crushed nuts, and a mountain of whipped cream. Fanny and Bess ate every bite and left the dishes in the stainless steel sink under the counter. Then they left the drugstore by the back door, like conspirators in the night.

9

Fanny closed the drawer of the file cabinet, a satisfied expression on her face. She dusted her hands dramatically to show what she thought of her four-day effort at straightening up Devin Rollins's file system. The six drawer cabinet was devoted solely to Sallie Thornton's business. Bess was right, Mrs. Thornton was one rich lady. The only file that puzzled her was the R & R Chicken Ranch and a second ranch in Reno called the B & B Chicken Ranch. She shrugged; it wasn't her place to understand the business workings of Mrs. Sallie Thornton.

"Is there anything else you want me to do, Mr. Rollins?"

"Nothing I can think of. You've done a wonderful job in the four days that you've been here. Is there anything I can do to entice you into staying on full-time?"

"I'm sorry, Mr. Rollins, but I don't think I could live here. It's too dry and dusty for me. I . . . I'm not sure I could ever live in this town's . . . what I'm trying to say is . . ."

"You saw the sleazy, tawdry side of it, eh? Well, it is what it is, and I can't say that I blame you. There is another side, though. Believe it or not, there are families here, children go to school, there are parks and swimming pools, all the things it takes to make a town grow and prosper. The district employs many people, some of those families I just spoke of. In many ways those little communities are like the town you came from in Pennsylvania."

"Tomorrow evening I'm going to the Silver Dollar with Bess Otis. She told me Mrs. Thornton sings on occasion. She also told me there are men at the door who decide who gets in and who doesn't. Will Bess and I have a problem? I have to tell you, Mr. Rollins, I don't have any fancy dress-up clothes with me."

"Tomorrow, remind me and I'll call the casino and tell them to expect you. And, yes, Mrs. Thornton sings at the club on occasion. When she does, it's standing room only. She'll be in some time today, so you'll get a chance to meet her. Maybe you won't. You're about to leave now, aren't you?"

"Yes, sir."

"Perhaps another time. Enjoy the afternoon, Miss Logan."

"Why don't you call me Fanny, Mr. Rollins. I don't mind unless you think it isn't professional."

"Fanny it is."

Fanny covered her typewriter, blew a speck of dust off her desk, straightened her pencil holder. She did like things neat and tidy. Mrs. Kelly always said you never know who's going to come behind you, and you don't want them gossiping about your untidy habits. It was the same principle as, wear your good underwear because you never know if you're going to be in an accident.

She turned, her nose picking up the delicious scent of fresh flowers. She looked up, a smile on her face. "You must be Mrs. Thornton. I'm Fanny Logan, Miss Reddington's temporary replacement.

Mr. Rollins is expecting you." She wasn't just beautiful, she was gorgeous, Fanny thought. Bess would say she was dressed to the nines.

"Sallie! Ah, I see you've met Fanny. Fanny, this is Mrs. Thornton. I cannot tell you how efficient this young woman is. She also makes delicious coffee. We were just talking about you and the Silver Dollar. Fanny and Bess Otis want to go to the Silver Dollar tomorrow evening. She's concerned she doesn't have the proper attire."

"It's not a problem, Miss Logan. Wear whatever is comfortable for you. I'll take care of things. Our show starts at ten o'clock."

Her voice was low, musical-sounding, but it was her smile that Fanny liked. Tongue-tied, she could only nod. She saw the light in Rollins's eyes and the smile on his face when he reached out to touch Sallie Thornton's arm. It was one of those, this-is-mine, this-belongs-to-me touches that she had read about in books. Sallie Thornton's response was a brilliant smile that reached her eyes. She turned, aware of Fanny's flustering movements. She winked roguishly, the smile still on her face.

Fanny left the office believing she knew the biggest secret in the world. Devin Rollins and Sallie Thornton were in love. Maybe someday, someone would look at her the way Devin Rollins looked at Sallie Thornton. She locked the thought away, knowing it would be a measuring guide when and if she ever fell in love.

The following evening, dressed in her best, Fanny was waiting on the front porch when Bess drove up at nine-thirty. "Bess, you look wonderful. Is your dress new?"

"I made it over the weekend. I love emerald green, and the material was a steal. It's appropriate, isn't it?"

"It's perfect. The pearls are just the right touch. You look like a debutante."

"So do you."

Fanny told Bess about her meeting with Sallie Thornton and their brief conversation. She was careful not to mention her own personal observations.

"I'm excited. I think I'm more excited than I was last week. You know, Fanny, I haven't been able to sleep all week. I keep worrying about what you said. I . . . I don't think I'll go back to either one of those places. Having that $500 in my hand, that was the most awesome feeling in the world to me. It was *my* money, Fanny, I swear on my father's life. You were right about everything, and I'm sorry if I was short with you. It's that excitement thing, your adrenaline starts to pump and you're lost. Do you think they'll be looking for me?" she asked fearfully.

Fanny shrugged. "I rather doubt it. I don't know very much about that type of person. Let's not worry about that this evening. I don't think any of those men will be at Mrs. Thornton's place."

"I understand that a lot of the officers from Nellis Air Force Base go to the Silver Dollar. The base is only nine miles away, and they come by the busload. Mostly for the show and to hear Mrs. Thornton sing. Wouldn't that be something, Fanny, if you met one of those good-looking aviators?"

Fanny blushed. "What about you?"

"I have a boyfriend. I told you, I'm just sowing my wild oats. If guys can do it, why can't women?"

"Because society frowns on women doing things like that. Maybe someday things will change, but I doubt it. Men control the world, you know."

Bess snorted, a very unladylike sound. "Listen, Fanny, I'm not about to change my ways. My mother always says, to thine own self be true. She's right. I'm going to go right on doing what I want to do when I want to do it. Life is one big learning experience. God, I'm excited!"

"I am too. You were right, Bess, Mrs. Thornton is beautiful. I hope I look like her when I'm her age."

Bess snorted again. "What else does she have to do except pamper herself, and she has the money to do it? Money can buy anything."

"I don't believe that for one minute." Fanny thought about Jake's $200,000 sitting in the safety deposit box. Wherever he was, she knew he wasn't happy. "Money just buys things and gives you security, Bess. It can't make you happy. That's my opinion."

"Give me a thousand dollars and you'll see one happy person. I'll even sleep with a smile on my face. Just out of curiosity, Fanny, what would make you happy?"

"Finding a person who would love me, someone I'd like to marry and have children with. Someone who would take care of me and the children if I got sick and had to stay in bed. Someone who would bring me a puppy and not complain when it messed on the floor. Someone who would say to me, you look tired, honey, why don't you go take a nice bubble bath, I'll cook dinner and take care of the kids. Someone who would go to church with me on Sunday, someone who knows how to fix a leaky spigot and who doesn't go nuts when it's time to shovel snow. Someone who comes up behind me and says, gee you smell nice. Someone who doesn't carry a grudge and who won't ever go to bed angry. Someone who tells me he wants our first little girl to look like me.

"I'm a simple person, Bess. I'd like to find my mother someday. That would make me happy. Having my own little house and family to take care of would make me happy. A small bank account for emergencies would be an asset. I'd like to be a really good cook, that would make me happy."

"Well, I'd like to be rich and famous. I'll probably be a real stinky wife and mother. I don't know why, but I crave excitement. I love the bright lights and the wild anticipation of things to come. I might never get married. If I decide I can't be what my husband expects, then I'll not walk down the aisle. I might never get done sowing my wild oats. What do you think about that, Fanny Logan?"

"I think, Bess Otis, that you are a very astute young woman. I think you know yourself very well. I like that in a person."

Bess expertly swerved the car neatly into a parking space. Both young women walked sedately to the Silver Dollar entrance, where they were met by an elegantly clad doorman. Behind him, the ornate door with its polished brass and beveled glass, gleamed in the bright lights. "Your names please."

"Fanny Logan and Bess Otis," Fanny said primly. The doorman consulted a list he withdrew from his pocket.

"Mrs. Thornton said you would be coming by this evening, Miss Logan. If you'll wait just a moment, I'll find someone to escort you into the showroom."

"Someone is going to escort us. Well, la-de-da," Bess whispered. "Fanny, I cannot tell you how impressed I am." She stretched her neck to peer through the beveled glass. "Everything is distorted, but I can see a lot of military men, and it might interest you to know we're dressed like schoolgirls compared to what I can see."

"We're just plain, Bess. That doesn't mean our outfits are wrong. Forget about the way we're dressed and enjoy the evening."

"Ladies, if you'll come with me, I'll show you to your table. Mrs. Thornton wants you to have a ringside table, compliments of the house. Dinner is over, but we can accommodate you with dessert and drinks. All complimentary, of course. Our first show of the evening will start in about ten minutes."

"Now, that's a real nice-looking gentleman. Compared to the Pioneer and Boulder Clubs, this is like night and day. This is so elegant," Fanny said, looking around. She touched one of the thick, gold ropes that separated the gaming areas. The ankle-hugging area carpets behind the gold ropes were a perfect color match. Here, too, the gaming was subdued. Maybe it was true that gambling was a gentlemen's game, and everyone knew a true gentleman didn't whistle, stomp his feet, or shout raucously at a win. These gentlemen merely gathered their money and chips and smiled.

"Look at the chandeliers, Fanny. Who do you suppose cleans all those little crystal teardrops? I read in the paper that Mrs. Thornton ordered them from Bavaria. She commissioned an artist from New York City to come here and paint all the pictures. She wanted scenes of Las Vegas the way it looked when she arrived, a long time ago. You have to start at the end of the room and work forward so you can see the changes in the town. I bet she has more money than the government."

"Her taste is exquisite," Fanny said. "I don't think I ever saw so much polished brass and glass in one place."

"Look at the floor, Fanny. That's Tennessee pink marble. This is one classy operation. I didn't know it was by *invitation* only, did you? I guess Mrs. Thornton doesn't care if she makes money or not."

"The place is packed, Bess. That translates into a lot of invitations." Fanny traced her fingers down the length of the linen tablecloth, noting its softness and quality. The fresh flowers and the small candle in a crystal cup all spoke of money. Lots and lots of money.

As if by magic, an elaborate dessert was placed in front of the young women. "Pecan Tulle, made on the premises," the soft-spoken waiter said. "The champagne is compliments of Mrs. Thornton."

"Thank you," Fanny said. She felt out of her depth. Bess felt the same way, she could tell.

The lights dimmed suddenly in the supper club. A single spotlight fell on the stage as the velvet curtains swished to the sides of the small stage. A magician pulled a parrot from his top hat, a comedian made the audience roar with laughter. Then a young singer named Frank Sinatra singing "Night and Day," paved the way for the last act of the evening, Sallie Thornton.

Sitting three tables to Fanny's left was Devin Rollins, his eyes on the stage.

Below the stage a small orchestra prepared for a drumroll. The single spotlight held center stage. The curtains swished open again as Sallie Thornton took her place in the light, microphone in hand. "Ladies and gentlemen, welcome to the Silver Dollar. I hope you all enjoyed tonight's entertainment." A rousing round of applause sounded.

"Tonight, I'd like to welcome the aviators from Nellis Air Force

Base. I'd also like to welcome a new visitor to Las Vegas, Miss Fanny Logan." The aviators were standing, wide smiles on their faces. Fanny half stood and then sat down, her cheeks flaming. The flyers were staring at her. Two of them winked. One of them mouthed the words, I'll see you later.

"I'd like to end the evening by singing a request song. This is not just for the aviators present, but for all our sons who are fighting to keep us safe. I'm sure you know the words, so hum along with me. 'I'll Be Seeing You . . .' "

She was everything a singer should be, Fanny thought. Her voice was pure and high, the tears in her eyes sparkling in the spotlight. The form-fitting silver lamé dress with the slit up the side hugged her lithe body. She was, in Fanny's opinion, Hollywood material. What *was* she doing in this desert town?

"How does she do it?" Bess whispered. "She doesn't move a muscle, doesn't wave her arms, she just sings. Is that a gorgeous dress or what?"

Fanny risked a glance at Devin Rollins, who only had eyes for the woman on the stage.

When Sallie finished her song, she gave a low sweeping bow, and then backed off the stage. The curtains closed and the houselights came up. When Fanny looked to her left again, Devin Rollins was gone.

Fanny and Bess rose, as did the other guests, to file out of the supper club. The aviators, as one, converged on the two young women, offering drinks and other lusty things. Behind the stage curtain, Sallie whispered, "Ten dollars, Devin, that she doesn't fall for their line. She's a good girl, and she's going to stay a good girl. She isn't going to give them a tumble. Bess will flirt, but she won't go with them either."

"That's a sucker bet and you know it, Sallie. All you have to do is look at Fanny Logan and you know what you see is what you get. She reminds me a lot of you. I'd like her to stay because she has my office running so efficiently I could whisk you away to Sallie and Devin's house of happiness in Arizona, right now, this very minute. Let's do it! It's the weekend."

"I thought you said you had to work this weekend."

"The hell with work. I want to make love to you all night long."

"In that case, let me change my clothes. I'll meet you in the game parlor. When was the last time we made love, Devin?" she whispered.

"Last night. I'll be waiting."

Sallie walked back to her office. "Zack, I'm going to be leaving shortly. I won't be back till Monday. I want you to do something for me. I'm going to change and work the room a little before I leave. I'll steer two young women to the thousand-dollar slots. When you see me hand each of them a silver dollar I want you to rig both slots to pay off. Go out on the floor now and put them off-limits until I can get there. We both know I run an honest house, but just this once, I want to . . ."

"I understand, Miss Sallie. We'll never talk about it again."

"Exactly."

"What do you think the odds are of two thousand-dollar slots hitting at the same time?"

"We'll know tomorrow when every club owner in town tries to figure it out," Sallie laughed.

"You're one of a kind, Mrs. Thornton."

"I'm going to take that as a compliment."

Out on the floor, Fanny and Bess walked around, stopping from time to time to watch the outcome of a particular bet. To Fanny, it seemed like mountains of money changed hands. She also noticed that the frenzied-looking gamblers she'd seen in the Boulder and Pioneer Clubs weren't present at the Silver Dollar. It wasn't that the patrons of the Silver Dollar weren't gambling, they were just going about it differently—nonchalantly.

"This is really ritzy, isn't it, Fanny?"

"It sure is. Which do you prefer, Bess?"

"Well, I felt more comfortable last week. I sort of feel like I don't belong here."

"I don't feel that way. My money is the same color as that money on the table. There isn't one person in this room that's better than me. As good as, but not better. I learned that in my eighth grade catechism class. Sister Ann Marie was explaining to us why we had to wear uniforms. It was so we wouldn't be in competition over clothing. We were all equal."

"I think you're a dreamer, Fanny. The reality is these people are hoity-toity and we're the working class."

"What's wrong with the working class?"

"Nothing, if that's what you want to be all your life. I want more. I want it all. I might even get it someday, too."

"I might even be the first female president of the United States someday too," Fanny laughed.

"I'll vote for you, Fanny."

"So will I," Sallie Thornton said, a smile on her face. "I hope you two young ladies are enjoying yourselves."

"Very much," Fanny said. "Thank you for the ringside table and the champagne. I really enjoyed your singing; you have a lovely voice, Mrs. Thornton."

"Thank you, Miss Logan. I'm leaving in a few minutes but I like to give all my guests, at one time or another, a silver dollar. It makes me feel good," Sallie said, steering the girls toward the thousand-dollar slot machines. "I hope you'll come back again. I have to warn you, no one has ever won the thousand dollars since we put the machines in."

Fanny noticed Devin Rollins out of the corner of one eye. When she looked to her right she saw the group of aviators advancing, the light of battle in their eyes. She reached out to accept the silver dollar. Bess did the same thing.

"Do it on the count of three," one of the aviators shouted.

"Okay," Bess shouted back.

"One! Two! Three!"

Fanny and Bess pulled the levers at the same time. When the three clusters of cherries appeared on both machines within seconds of each other, the two aviators in the front grabbed the girls and kissed them soundly as the silver coins rivered from the machines onto the Tennessee marble floor.

"Stop that!" Fanny said firmly.

Fanny didn't know how she knew, but she knew that Sallie Thornton had arranged for the machines to pay off. She looked at Bess, who was still kissing the aviator, at Devin Rollins, who was smiling from ear to ear. Sallie winked at her for the second time in as many days. "Enjoy yourselves, ladies, and come again."

Every eye in the casino was on Sallie Thornton when she walked out the front door, Devin Rollins following her.

The floor manager appeared with a metal tray of money. "The machines only pay out three hundred silver dollars. You can turn it in for paper money or keep the coins." Fanny opted for the bills, as did Bess.

"My God in heaven, Fanny, we won two thousand dollars! What are you going to do with yours?"

"Put it in the bank. What are you going to do with yours?"

"Save some and spend the rest. Fanny, don't leave. Stay here and work full-time for Mr. Rollins.

"I'm ready to go home, Fanny," she said when Fanny didn't answer. "I want to sit on my bed and stare at my money. I can't wait to see the newspaper tomorrow."

"Why?" Fanny said, climbing into the car.

"Didn't you see the flashbulbs? They took our picture! Oh, God, that means my parents are going to see it. And my boyfriend. I'm in for it now. Oh, God, Fanny, what if those aviators are in the pictures. They were kissing us. If my boyfriend sees that, it's all over. What should I do?"

"Go home to bed. In the morning tell your parents the truth. Tell them you were showing me the town. Tell them Mrs. Thornton treated us to the supper show. Tell your boyfriend the aviators were congratulating you. It's more or less the truth. You can't go wrong when you tell the truth."

"See, you always come up with the right answers. Fanny, please stay on."

"I can't, Bess. Well, thanks for the ride. Let me know how things go. Call me tomorrow or stop by."

The following day, the war that Fanny had ignored because she thought it didn't involve her slipped around her like a shroud when she called her father to tell him she was still in Las Vegas and to report her thousand-dollar windfall.

"Daddy, please tell me that's a joke. Why would they up and enlist?"

"Because it's their patriotic duty. People in town were starting to talk. It wasn't just Daniel and Brad that joined up. All the young guys, even the steelworkers with deferments, did it. The mill is hiring women now. Mrs. Kelly got hired yesterday."

"I'm coming home. I'll pack my things and get a ticket this afternoon. I can leave tomorrow. No, no, I can't leave tomorrow, I'll have to wait till Monday."

"Fanny, listen to me. I don't want you to come home. I don't want you worrying about me either. It might even be nice to have the house to myself after all this time. If you want to do something, buy some war bonds, donate some time to the war effort."

"Daddy, are you sure you don't want me to come home? I can go to California some other time. If I come home, I could get a job in the steel mills too, like Mrs. Kelly. I want to do my part. Daddy, are you sure?"

"I'm sure, Fanny. As soon as I hear from your brothers, I'll call you. Don't worry about them, they can take care of themselves. Remember, they were both leaders in their Wilderness Training group."

The chuckle in her father's voice reassured Fanny. On her way back to the boardinghouse she stopped at a newsstand to pick up the morning edition of the *Nevada Sentinel.*

A cup of coffee in hand, the paper spread out in front of her, Fanny settled herself to read up on the war now that her brothers had enlisted. She felt shame and guilt that she knew so little about what was going on in the world. The overlarge headline of the day read; ALLIES LAND IN SICILY, CAPTURE PALERMO. When she finished the article she read the two-column war update.

MacArthur launches Allied offensive in Pacific, Japanese and American navies clash near Bougainville Island, Hitler convinces Mussolini to continue fight against Allied attack, Eighth American Army enters Palermo. American planes bomb Trondheim base in Norway.

Fanny read every printed word, not once, but twice.

She turned the page and read another huge black headline; USE IT UP, WEAR IT OUT, MAKE IT DO, OR DO WITHOUT! Fanny read the article, a deep frown settling on her forehead.

Virtually all consumable goods have a second life, as tin and other metals, paper and nylon are recycled. Kitchen fat is processed for explosives. Rubber, found in inaccessible Asia, is one of the scarcest of commodities. Some municipalities try to ward off rubber thieves by having car owners record the serial numbers of their tires. With gas rationed and a 35mph speed limit in effect, no one takes the car out of the garage much anymore.

Everywhere there is delay. The trains, loaded with enlisted men or hauling war material, are late leaving and late arriving. Lines snake out of grocery stores, restaurants, and bars because there are too few employees waiting on customers.

Yet because manpower—and womanpower—are so much in demand, workers find themselves almost pampered. Factories have introduced coffee breaks, and piped music, fringe benefits, and awards for fine performance. Unfortunately, the sense of delay pervades the workplace; President Roosevelt ordered a freeze on all wages, prices, and salaries, and the mandatory 48-hour week at the war plants is exhausting, coffee breaks or no. There is nothing like just going home at the end of a day, sitting in front of the radio (factories aren't making new ones for civilians anymore), and gulping a small watered-down bottle of beer—not sacrificing a drop.

Additional war updates left Fanny feeling queasy. Now she understood something else about Sallie Thornton and the files she'd read in Devin Rollins's office: Not only was Mrs. Thornton supplying food to the various casinos, she was also supplying chickens, beef, and vegetables to the government war effort. The R & R Ranch as well as the B & B Ranch in Reno were the government's top contributors, along with a man named Seth Coleman from Austin, Texas. The only difference between Sallie Thornton and Seth Coleman, according to the *Sentinel,* was Sallie Thornton *donated* her food to the war effort, whereas Seth Coleman *charged* for his.

Fanny folded up the newspaper and left it on the front porch in case one of the other guests wanted to read. She walked upstairs to her room for her change purse. The long, empty day loomed ahead of her. She might as well make use of her time by making more phone calls. If her efforts were unproductive, Monday morning she would take the money from the safe deposit box and buy war bonds. She would also tell Mr. Rollins she would accept a full-time position. Staying here in Las Vegas for six months or a year wouldn't alter her plans that drastically.

At the newsstand phone booth, Fanny kept the operator busy for two hours as she placed one call after the other, all with negative responses. No one, it seemed, knew of anyone who looked like Jake or knew a man named Jake. Her steps were lighter, her shoulders straighter, as she walked back to the boardinghouse. She'd done everything humanly possible to locate Jake. There was nothing more she could do.

With more hours to fill, Fanny checked with her landlady and got permission to work in her Victory Garden. As she weeded row after row of vegetables, her thoughts were in Shamrock when she used to squabble with her two brothers as they, too, took turns weeding the garden during the summer months. Life, she realized, was going to go on, no matter what she did.

The plane landed neatly, the pilot giving a thumbs-up salute to Lieutenant Ashford Thornton.

"Thanks for the ride," Ash said, saluting smartly.

"Give 'em hell, Lieutenant. Heard you're one meatball away from being an ace. Congratulations!"

"Just one more. I'll get it, too."

Ash was aware of the looks and open stares as he walked across the field, his duffel slung over his good shoulder. The conquering hero returns. He wanted to laugh, but if he did, his shoulder wound might open up. He was home for five days of R & R. It was a beautiful Saturday afternoon, thousands and thousands of miles away from the war he'd been fighting for the past nine months. He could go home now and take a long hot shower that lasted an hour if he wanted to. He could sleep around the clock if he wanted to. He could chow down on food he'd only dreamed about these past months. He could go to town and pick up a passel of women and have an orgy. He could do any goddamn thing he wanted to do for the next five days.

Right now, though, he didn't want to do any of those things. What he wanted to do was barrel into the house and shout his parents' names. He wanted to pick up his mother and swing her high in the air, wanted to grab his father and squeeze him until he yelled for mercy. He wanted to tell them about his four Zeros, of seeing and hearing Simon in the air. He'd downplay the wound he received the day he was forced to drop out of formation and was hit by a wild strafing onslaught. He couldn't wait to tell them what a hell of a pilot his brother was.

Ash hitched a ride into town with a mechanic who dropped him off at his front door. He pulled his duffel from the back of the pickup truck and kicked it up the walkway rather than carry it.

Ash thrust open the front door, bellowing at the top of his lungs. Tulee waddled in from the kitchen, her face fearful. "Where's Mom and Pop, Tulee?"

"Not know, Mr. Ash. You papa not come much anymore. You mama not here, pack bag and leave house last night. Maybe not come back next week."

Ash's shoulders drooped. "Did she go to Sunrise?"

"No Sunrise. Not know. You papa only come visit, not many times."

"Jesus. Okay, okay, I'll find them."

Ash called Sunrise. He felt shaken when Chue told him he didn't know where his parents were. He was more shaken when he found out Chue was married and had a baby son.

"Doesn't anyone in this goddamn family know where anyone else is? What the hell kind of family is this anyway?" he raged. Tulee waddled back to the kitchen as Ash stomped his way up the steps. Now what was he supposed to do? He yanked at the phone near his bed and asked the operator to connect him to Devin Rollins's office, where he was told Mr. Rollins was out of town. Ash swore again as he asked the operator to connect him to the Silver Dollar. He identified himself, asked to speak to Zack, and was told only that his mother had gone away for the weekend. "She does that, says she's going for the weekend and then stays for a week. I'm sorry, Ash, but I don't know where she went. She calls in sometimes. I'll tell her you're home if she does."

"Don't bother, Zack. I don't suppose you know where my father is, or do you?"

"No, Ash, I don't. I rarely see him. I'm sorry, I wish I could help you."

Ash flopped back on his bed, drifting into sleep, up through the clouds to the clear, blue sky, the sound of his squadron all about him. He was flying a Corsair, the most powerful plane in the air, in his opinion. The twin-row engines developed by Pratt and Whitney had so much turning force a plane could almost twist wing over wing if a pilot made a bad landing.

His squadron was searching for a Japanese submarine, forced to look at the sapphire blue water and brilliant blue sky at the same time. Tonight he was going to have one hell of a headache.

"Enemy at two o'clock."

The squadron separated into combat pairs and flew into the formation of the Zeros. Ash heard a burst of tracers as they flashed by him like lightning streaks. He went into a dive and stood on the throttle. He was on the football field again, weaving back and forth the way he'd done during the last game of the season, all to ruin the enemy's aim. "Zero on your tail, Ash. Move it, move it, I got him," Conrad, who in his dream was his second wingman, shouted. Ash veered sharply and headed north, circled, and then roared up to the plane's top speed of 395 mph. He dived down, his finger flicking the cover off his firing button, .50mm fire thudded into the plane heading straight for Conrad at three o'clock. He circled around to see what damage he'd done. A row of slugs in the aft part of the fuselage. He swore, the plane was still intact. He let go with another burst, the slugs hitting the thin armor protecting the engine. His fist shot upward as the Zero turned into a black cloud of smoke.

"I can't do this anymore. I don't want to do this again."

The voice shook him to his very toes. "Move your ass, Ash, you're a sitting duck. Go into a roll, swing out, and veer right. I'll take him for you."

"Simon, I don't want to die. I can't do this anymore."

"I sure as hell don't want to die over some goddamn ocean. Get your ass in gear and get back into formation."

"This is my goddamn dream, Simon, get the hell out of it."

"You're whining, Ash. I'm dropping down now. Do it your way. I'll tell Pop you went out in a blaze of glory."

"You son of a bitch! You can't leave me up here to die!"

"Watch me!" Simon laughed.

Ash fought with the coverlet on the bed, his body bathed in sweat. His shoulder ached and burned unbearably as he swung his legs over the side of the bed. He gingerly removed his uniform and headed for the shower.

"I hate your fucking guts, Simon." He felt like crying again because he knew in his heart he didn't hate his brother. That day late last year when he'd met up with Simon in the air was one of his greatest moments. Maybe someday they could sit down with a beer and talk about it.

Maybe.

Fanny looked at her watch. One more minute and the bank would open. She felt jittery and out of sorts. When one of the bank officers unlocked the door, Fanny was the first customer. She exited the bank ten minutes later, the packet of money secure in her purse. She headed straight to the office, where she found the door locked. Now what was she supposed to do? Go to the drugstore and have a second breakfast of course. Maybe Mr. Rollins was running a little behind schedule or perhaps he was in court.

"Fanny! What are you doing here so early in the morning?"

"Mr. Rollins isn't in yet and the door is locked. I'll have a cup of coffee and some toast. I decided to stay on here for a while, Bess. My father told me on Saturday that my two brothers enlisted. I'm going to buy war bonds with my money. The next time they have a bond rally, I'm going to offer my services."

"Every little bit helps. My mother and father talk about the war all night long. They sit glued to the radio. Hey, I think I just saw Ash Thornton walk by. I heard Dad say he was an ace or going to be an ace, something like that. What that means, Fanny, is he's a cracker-jack pilot. He's killed a lot of Japs. Wonder what he's doing home."

"Where?" Fanny asked as she stretched her neck for a look.

"He walked by. You missed him. You should have seen him on the football field. He went to a different school, so I could only worship him from afar. All the girls were crazy about him. He has a younger brother named Simon, who is one of those whiz kids, perfect scores in everything, real studious, plus he skipped two or three years of school. He's every bit as good-looking as his brother, but in a different way. I heard they both joined up. Ash's name is always in the paper, but not Simon's. He probably got himself stuck somewhere behind a desk."

"I didn't know Mrs. Thornton had children," Fanny said.

"My mother says Mrs. Thornton is a very private person. She always has a funny look on her face when she talks about her. My dad always butts in and says, 'now, Myrtle, I don't want you gossiping about Mrs. Thornton, she's brought this town alive.' Then my mother sort of sniffs, and that's the end of the conversation." Bess leaned across the counter and whispered, "I think she was *racy* when she was younger."

"I guess I better get back to the office. Mr. Rollins seems so professional. I can't believe he didn't tell me he was going to be late. If he isn't there, I guess I'll go home and twiddle my fingers? What's for lunch?"

"Ham salad with sweet relish. The customers like it." Bess laughed.

"Maybe I'll stop back if I get bored."

Bess grimaced. "I'll be here. By the way we're having a sale on Ipana toothpaste in case you're interested. Dad got carried away because the salesperson was a woman, and she flirted with him. All the salespeople are women these days."

"I didn't know that," Fanny muttered on her way out.

Devin Rollins's office was still closed and locked. Fanny tore a page from a small notebook she carried in her purse, wrote a note, and slipped it under the door. The packet of money in her purse stared up at her. Well, she was going to take care of that right now.

After she bought the bonds, Fanny returned to the boarding-house and was told there was a message for her. Her heart skipped a beat as she reached for the short note, certain it was from Jake or his friends. It wasn't—it was from Devin Rollins. The note was brief:

The office will be closed until Wednesday.

What to do? What did she do in Shamrock when chores and schoolwork were finished? She read. Shrugging, Fanny brushed her teeth and washed her hands. She'd ask the landlady where the library was. She could read back issues of the newspapers, find out more than what she'd read over the weekend. She could take out a library card, and, if she was lucky, there might be a new mystery novel on the shelves.

It was a long walk, and she longed for a cool drink by the time she approached the wide double doors of the brick library. Inside it was cool, fans placed strategically all about the two-room building.

Three hours later, her eyes aching, Fanny checked out two books with her new library card. Now she could go to the drugstore and get a cherry phosphate.

Head down, her thoughts on her thirst, Fanny walked straight into a tall young man who wasn't nimble enough to step out of her way. "I'm so sorry. It's my fault, I was . . . my mind . . . I'm very sorry." She looked up at the handsomest man she'd ever seen. And he was laughing. At her.

Fanny backed up a step as the young man's arms stretched out to grasp her shoulders. "Steady there. Are you okay?"

She saw everything about him in one brief moment. He was as tall as her brother Daniel, which meant he was over six feet. Blue eyes were laughing at her. Impatiently, he brushed at the unruly curls crowning the top of his head. She knew he preferred wearing his cap because it flattened out the curls. "Are you sure you're okay? Your head hit me right in the chest. I *felt* it. If I felt it, then so did you." His grin was infectious. It was also wicked.

"I'm fine. It was my fault, and I'm sorry."

"I accept your apology." He held the door for her.

Flustered with his gallant gesture, Fanny tripped over her own feet as she walked through the door of the drugstore. He reached out again and caught her, his face full of pain as he did so.

"Oh, I can't believe how clumsy I am today. I'm sorry. You look . . . you look like you're in pain. What happened? I'm sorry." She was babbling like a schoolgirl.

"Nothing's wrong. I just reached for you with the wrong arm. I've had some trouble with my shoulder. No harm done."

She supposed she should say something. What? She smiled nervously and backed out of the door. "Thank you, and I am sorry. I hope your shoulder improves."

Her tongue thick in her mouth, Fanny took her seat on a red stool at the counter. "Quick, Bess, two really cold cherry phosphates. I might even want a third," Fanny gasped.

"My, God, Fanny, what's wrong? Your face is as pink as this ham salad. Don't drink it so fast, you'll get sick."

"I walked all the way to the library and back. Then I bumped into this . . . the handsomest guy I've ever seen. Then I bumped into him a second time. He was so . . . so . . . Bess, he had the wickedest grin. I got so flustered I couldn't even talk. I acted like I was *thirteen*. That's why my face is so red. I don't know what branch of service he's in, but he had lieutenant's bars on his collar."

"Did you introduce yourself?"

"I did not. He didn't ask," Fanny said, downing the second cherry phosphate.

"If he had, would you have told him your name?"

"In a heartbeat."

"Want a cigarette?" Bess asked.

"Why not?" Fanny said airily.

"Don't inhale. You have to practice doing that in private, or you'll cough your head off. Let me sneak a couple of puffs. My dad isn't looking, is he?"

"Can't see him," Fanny said. Bess sneaked two quick puffs, blowing perfect smoke rings.

"Imagine that," Fanny said.

"Don't forget your Ipana. Do you want to go to the movies with me and Ted tonight?"

"Sure. What's playing?"

"*For Whom the Bell Tolls* with Gary Cooper. We'll stop by at seven. The movie starts at seven-thirty. Do you want me to ask Ted to get you a date? He knows lots of nice guys."

"Why aren't they in the service?" Fanny snapped.

"Ted has very bad eyesight," Bess said defensively. "I don't know why Mike and Joe haven't joined up. Ted says they talk about it all the time. Maybe they're scared. If I was a guy, I'd be scared. Maybe their parents don't want them to go. Does that mean you don't want a date?"

"I don't want a date. Two's company, three's a crowd. Are you sure you want me to go?"

"Sure. I want you to meet Ted. Don't forget your Ipana. Fanny, I have a favor to ask you. Would you mind going to town hall and getting a ration book? With you staying at the boardinghouse, you don't need it. My mother sure could use some extra coupons. I'm sure she'll pay you for them."

"That's dishonest, Bess. Think about what you just asked me to do, and if you still think it's all right, ask me again this evening. We're at war! Think about that. Everyone has to sacrifice. That means me, you, and your mother."

Fanny smiled in the darkness when she saw Ted reach for Bess's hand. She felt out of place and debated leaving. She wasn't a Gary Cooper fan the way Bess was. She wondered if she would ever hold hands with a young man in a movie.

She slumped in her seat, her thoughts everywhere but on the movie. She thought about her boss and Mrs. Thornton. Was their relationship really an affair? Did other people know? What about Mr. Thornton? Did *he* know? Las Vegas wasn't that big. Surely people gossiped here the same way they did back in Shamrock. Even if they were discreet, she'd picked up on it. It was also suspicious that both of them were out of town at the same time. It was none of her business. She tried to push the thoughts away.

Fanny leaned over and whispered. "I've had enough of this movie, I'm going home. You two stay. It's a nice evening, and I'll enjoy the walk."

She walked steadily, her arms swinging back and forth as she stared at the few hardy souls brave enough to take their autos out, using up precious gasoline. Most people were on foot, either in small groups of three or four or couples. She appeared to be the only single person walking. She felt self-conscious as she stood behind a group of chattering girls waiting for the traffic light to change.

The convertible, the ragtop neatly stowed in the back, squealed to a last-minute stop. The couple laughed as both were jolted forward. Even from where she was standing, Fanny could see the woman's breasts spilling out of a tight satin dress. Her hair was bleached, dark at the roots. The streetlight cast both occupants of the car in devilish yellow light that was both revealing and insulting. She wanted to look away, but her eyes were glued to the young man with the lieutenant's bars on his collar. Their eyes locked momentarily. Caught off guard, Fanny inclined her head slightly in recognition. The lieutenant grinned sheepishly.

The light changed and the convertible surged ahead. Fanny stared after it, aware that the driver was staring at her through the rearview mirror. Where were they going? What were they going to do? She wished she knew. In her mind she played out a dozen different scenarios.

The cup of tea and the Agatha Christie novel she'd checked out of the library held no appeal for her now. Maybe she'd sit on the front porch and count the stars.

Fanny stopped rocking long enough to contemplate her blue-and-white-checkered playsuit and white sandals. As a woman of the world, she was a complete fizzle. She cringed when she remembered the day Mrs. Kelly told her she looked *wholesome.* She didn't want to look like a fresh apple or peach or the girl next door. She wanted to look like . . . like . . . Sallie Thornton. They both had the same kind of honey blond hair, the same color eyes, the same lithe figures. Why couldn't she pattern herself after the gorgeous woman? Mrs. Thornton wore makeup, but it was so skillfully applied, it didn't look like she was wearing any at all.

"Fanny, all the guests are in for the evening. If you're going to stay out here, will you lock up when you come in? There's some coffee left if you want some," the landlady said, poking her head out the door.

"No thanks. I'll lock up. Good night, Mrs. Hershey."

Fanny propped her feet up on the banister, tilting back in the rocking chair. Her mind raced. She had good clothes, plain clothes, Shamrock clothes. *Wholesome* clothes. In her Home Economics class she'd learned a thing or two about fashion. Two good dresses were all any woman needed in Shamrock. Quality material, styles that never went out of fashion. And then you added to the dress with a scarf, a belt, or jewelry, or different dickies. Here, it was different. She needed a new hairstyle too.

Obviously, a metamorphosis was called for. She had the money, she could do it tomorrow. She'd kept two hundred dollars from her winnings at the Silver Dollar, and she still had most of the money Mr. Rollins paid her. She'd hardly touched the money she'd brought with her from Shamrock. Just today, she'd paid a month's room and board.

It was time to go to bed and dream about the new improved version of Fanny Logan. It was better than going to bed to dream about the lieutenant and the voluptuous-looking young woman sitting next to him.

Ash Thornton paced the floor. Someone in this damn town must know where his father was. He'd already called everyone he could think of. The only person he hadn't spoken to was Red Ruby, and there was no way he would disgrace the uniform he wore by going into a brothel. He dressed in civilian clothes and walked there, only to find out Red's ricky-ticky building had been demolished. With everyone in town knowing him and his family, he was afraid to make outright inquiries. The information operator had informed him there was no personal listing for Red.

Twelve hours remaining on his R & R.

Who was that girl with the golden hair?

Maybe he could find her.

He cruised, the way he'd done when he was on leave in a foreign port. Sunglasses secure, his cap at a jaunty angle, he stopped on every corner, searching for a glimpse of the girl he'd bumped into outside the drugstore. Ninety minutes into his search, he realized he was getting nowhere. He parked the car and walked into Ronzone's department store. He described Fanny with such detail, the motherly-looking saleswoman smiled.

"I think you mean Miss Logan. I can tell you where to find her."

"You know her!"

"Not personally, but she did some shopping here this morning, then she was going to the beauty parlor. She told me she was going to cut that long hair of hers. I don't think she's been in town very long. She did tell me she's from Pennsylvania. I'll write down the address for you."

Ash took a deep breath. For some reason he felt like he'd just soared to 15,000 feet and he had the sky to himself. His feet barely touched the ground when he left the department store. He was so high on anticipation he barely noticed the two girls across the street as they walked along, their arms linked. He heard them laughing and was curious enough to stare after them. One with curly red hair, one with short blond hair. Not the golden haired girl he sought.

Ash jumped into his convertible, waited for a break in traffic, executed a wide, sloppy U-turn, and roared down the street, tires squealing.

Both girls turned to stare at the rear of the car.

"That's him! That's the guy I was telling you about," Fanny said excitedly.

"I wonder if he flies as fast as he drives."

"If he does, you're in for a hell of a ride, Fanny Logan. That guy is gonna find you. I feel it here," Bess said, thumping her chest.

"I should be so lucky."

"You'll see. I'm hardly ever wrong."

Ash felt like a fool. How long was he going to sit on this damn front porch to wait for a girl he didn't even know? He'd already waited two hours, with the landlady taking pity on him by giving him two bottles of soda pop. He only had a few hours left on his R & R. He had to go home, garage the car, shower, shave, pack his gear, eat and . . . stop by the Silver Dollar one more time before he headed for Nellis to hitch his ride.

Ash opened the screen door and shouted, "I'm leaving now. Thanks for the soda pop."

The landlady waddled down the hall. "Would you like to leave Miss Logan a message? I can't imagine what happened to her. If she isn't going to be here for supper, she calls, and I keep her supper warm in the oven. This isn't like her."

"No message."

"Are you sure, Lieutenant?"

Ash nodded as he backed his way down the steps. What would be the point in leaving a message? She didn't know who he was. He groaned when he remembered the look on her face the evening before when he'd pulled alongside her to stop for a traffic light. For the life of him he couldn't remember the name of the woman he'd been with. He did remember the musty-smelling sheets and the grimy bathroom and makeup smeared on the mirror. He'd seen bathrooms in gas stations that were cleaner.

Rage, unlike anything he'd ever experienced, rivered through Ash. What the hell kind of R & R was this? You defend your country, you get wounded by some yellow Jap bastard, you get leave and what happens? No family, no friends, so what do you do? Not a goddamn thing. He'd pissed away almost a whole week and there wasn't one memorable thing about it. Except maybe seeing the golden-haired girl.

Ash garaged the car that was almost empty of gas, stomped into the house and up the steps to his room, stripped off his clothes, and headed for the shower.

The shower did nothing to abate his anger. Still cursing, the wet towel wrapped around his midsection, he flopped back on the bed. Within minutes he was sound asleep. When he woke, he had four hours left on his R & R. He used up forty minutes shaving, dressing, and packing. The taxi ride, his dinner at the Golden Slipper, ate up another hour and fifteen minutes. He had two hours left.

"Driver, take me to the Silver Dollar. I want you to wait for me, okay? I'll leave my bags in the car if that's okay."

"Sure, Lieutenant. Where do you want to go?"

"Nellis. Thirty minutes, right?"

"Nah, I can get you there in twenty. How much time do you have?"

Ash looked at his watch. "Ninety minutes."

"Get your ass in there and win big, son. Two girls won a thousand dollars each last week. Maybe Lady Luck will smile on you tonight. You'll get a fair shake at the Silver Dollar. I think it's the only honest casino around here. The owner is one sweet lady. She's done her bit for the war effort, I can tell you that."

"That's nice to know. Twenty minutes, huh?"

"On the nose, Lieutenant."

"I'll be here."

It was rare for Ash not to acknowledge the admiring glances he received by a roguish wink or a flip of his hand. Tonight, he walked like a man with a mission, to the upstairs offices. "Have you heard from my mother, Zack?"

"About thirty minutes ago. She's on her way home as we speak. She said to hogtie you and not to let you get away. Here's the number where you can reach your father. I already called it, he's on his way, too."

"I only have," Ash looked at his watch, "eighty minutes. I'm going downstairs. I need a drink. I'll be on the floor. I won't be too hard to find."

"All right, Ash."

Ash strolled the room. He shot craps for fifteen minutes and managed to lose thirty dollars. He played two hands of poker and lost another fifty. He switched to the thousand-dollar slot machines and dropped another twenty bucks. His R & R was down to forty minutes.

He saw her then when he pulled the lever on his last silver dollar, but she looked different. "Hey," he shouted. She didn't hear him. He shouted again, but she was already through the door. He ran then, shouldering and apologizing to the customers as he struggled to get to the front door. She was halfway down the block when he skidded to a stop. "Hey," he shouted again.

Fanny and Bess turned to stare at the man doing the shouting. "That's *him*," Fanny said breathlessly.

"That's Ash Thornton!" Bess hissed into Fanny's ear. "It's you he's calling, Fanny."

"Miss Logan, wait! I need to talk to you. What happened to your hair? I was looking for you earlier and I saw both of you, but you had short hair . . . I liked your long hair. I got home and no one was there. I scoured this town and no one knows where my parents are. I don't even know why I'm telling you this." He was babbling like a fourteen-year-old. Damn, she was going to think he was the biggest jerk alive.

"I accept your apology, Lieutenant. To answer your question, I cut my hair. I'm sorry if . . . if you don't like it."

"It's not that I don't like it, I do. I like long hair better, though. Jesus, where are my manners. I'm Ash Thornton. You're Fanny Logan. I went into Ronzone's and the lady told me where you live. I sat on your front porch for two hours waiting for you."

"You sat on the front porch for two hours!"

"Do you have any idea how long two hours is?"

"One hundred and twenty minutes." Fanny laughed.

"Exactly. Where are you girls going?"

"We were just walking. We're about to head home. Where are you going?"

Ash looked at his watch. He felt a lump settle in the pit of his stomach. He looked around, his eyes wild. "I only have seventeen, sixteen minutes left, and then I have to head for Nellis. I'm on leave, and I have to get back to my ship. I want to see you again."

"How are you going to do that, Lieutenant Thornton, if you only have sixteen minutes, fifteen now?" Fanny said, looking at her watch.

"I should know the answer to that, shouldn't I?"

Fanny smiled. "You could write to me."

"I'll do it. I have your address. The lady at the store gave it to me. Here's mine," Ash said, scribbling on a scrap of paper he tore from the paper that had Fanny's address. "You won't lose it, will you?"

In the time it took Fanny's heart to beat twice, she fell in love, totally and completely, with Lieutenant Ashford Thornton. "I won't lose it. You have to write first, though."

"It's a deal. Where do you work?"

"For an attorney here in town. His name is Devin Rollins."

"Old Devin, huh? Okay. If I can't find you in one place, I'll find you in another."

"This is my friend, Bess Otis, Lieutenant."

Ash smiled and held out his hand. "It's nice to meet you, Bess."

"Likewise, Lieutenant."

A taxi pulled to the curb. "Time to go, son! You don't have a minute to spare."

"I guess I'll see you. One of these days. Sometime." He had one leg inside the cab when he shouted, "Swear you'll write."

"If you write, I'll answer. I promise," Fanny said solemnly.

"I like you. I really like you," Ash said as he poked his head out the moving cab window.

Fanny laughed. "I like you too."

The sound of Ash's laughter seemed to settle around Fanny as she huddled against Bess.

"Wow!" Fanny said when the taxi was out of sight.

"Yeah, wow! I don't know, Fanny, there was something in his eyes. Maybe you shouldn't be so impulsive. Look, there's Mr. and Mrs. Thornton and Mr. Rollins. They look upset. Something's going on. There's that guy from the casino, he's some kind of boss. Look, he's pointing at us. What should we do?"

"Do? Why do we have to do anything? I thought we were going home. I want to go home, so I can go to sleep and dream about this."

"They're coming this way. Get that stupid look off your face, Fanny."

"Miss Logan, Bess, was that Ash you were talking to? The doorman said he saw you and your friend talking to my son."

"Yes, ma'am," Bess said.

"Was he going to Nellis?"

"Yes. The driver said he didn't have a minute to spare."

Fanny stared at the trio in front of her. Sallie Thornton looked angry, the man who must be Mr. Thornton looked sad; she swore she saw tears in his eyes. Devin Rollins just looked miserable. "Your son said he did everything he could to find you," she said quietly.

"Oh, God!" Sallie Thornton said.

"Did he say anything else?" Philip Thornton asked, his eyes pleading for a response.

Fanny told the first direct lie of her life. "He said he didn't realize how much he missed you until he . . . couldn't find you." Devin Rollins recognized the lie and nodded his head ever so slightly. "Good night."

"Good night, Miss Logan," the trio said in unison.
"That's a very sad family," Bess said.
"Yes, I sensed that. Do you think he'll write?"
"Absolutely."
"I can't wait."

10

Fanny Logan received her first letter from Lieutenant Ash Thornton on a crisp day in early October. The moment she saw the red-and-blue stripes on the envelope she knew the letter was from him.

Fanny carried the letter upstairs to her room. Torturing herself was exquisite pleasure as she held the flimsy envelope up to the light. One page. Large writing. She laid it on her pillow, picked it up, and smelled it. It smelled like paper. She started to compose her response. Something to do all night. Pages and pages. Of what? News? There was no news. What would she write about? Silly things? Bess and her boyfriend? Open it! her mind screamed. Not yet. Fanny tried to imagine what the letter said. Guys didn't write much. Her father said her brothers wrote one-paragraph letters and he was lucky he got that much. They were fighting a war, and yet they wrote home and said there was no news. Was Ash like that?

The supper bell rang. Fanny laid the letter on the maple dresser and walked downstairs to the dining room.

"We're having chicken potpie today and fresh garden salad. I managed to get some Crisco this morning. Of course I had to stand in line for almost an hour. They had twenty-four boxes of Duz detergent, but they ran out by the time I got to the front of the line. I did manage to get a pound of coffee and some extra tea." Mrs. Hershey spoke so proudly, Fanny felt like she should stand up and cheer. She thought about it a second and did exactly that, the other guests joining in. The landlady smiled, her face pink with her guests' praise.

Fanny hardly tasted the food. Her thoughts were upstairs with the blue-and-red-striped airmail letter on her dresser. She passed on the strawberry-rhubarb pie.

The flimsy paper yielded to a slight pressure from Fanny's fingernail. She unfolded the all-in-one letter. She was right, Ash Thornton scrawled his letters. Condensed, the letter was like the kind her brothers wrote, one paragraph. Fanny's heart hammered in her chest as she read.

Dear Fanny,

I wanted to write sooner, but it's been one mission after the other. No time. I finally got my fifth meatball, and that makes me an Ace. My CO is trying to get me a five-day leave. So far, no luck. He knows how important leave is or we burn out. I'm counting the days till I get out of this so I can go home. I hope you're still there. If I get leave in December, how would you feel about coming to Hawaii? I could send you the airfare. It would be a way to really get to know each other. Did your hair grow? Write to me when you have time. I look forward to mail.

Sincerely,
Captain Ash Thornton

Fanny flopped back onto her pillows, her eyes wild. *Captain* Ash Thornton. She was up a second later, dancing about the room. God! Did she dare to even *think* about going?

It was a week before she sat down late one evening to compose a letter to Ash Thornton. She convinced herself that it was okay to be a pen pal to a man serving his country. She said so in the first paragraph of her letter. In the second paragraph she explained the position he'd put her in in regard to his mother. She ended the second paragraph with, "I'm not good at subterfuge, and while I do not blurt things out, there is every chance I might say the wrong thing in your mother's presence. My suggestion would be for you to tell her you are corresponding with me. It will make things much simpler on this end."

Fanny continued to write. When she was finished she had three full pages of pure drivel. She read the letter once, twice, and then a third time, then tore it into little pieces and climbed into bed. She'd try again tomorrow. Maybe she'd type the letter at the office if she finished her work on time.

Ten days later, Fanny felt comfortable enough with the letter she'd written to mail it. She licked the airmail stamp and put it on upside down. Bess said if she did that, everyone would know she was Ash's girl and he was her guy.

Fanny was back to waiting, rushing home at lunchtime, and then again at five o'clock, with one thought in her mind: today there might be a letter. Because Ash said he liked to get mail, she continued to write; long, chatty letters, oftentimes clipping articles out of the newspaper to include with her letter. She stopped at the post office every other day to mail them, careful to put the stamps on upside down.

The week before Thanksgiving, Fanny found two letters waiting for her on the hall table of the boardinghouse. One was from Ash, and the second was an invitation from Sallie Thornton. Her heart thumping in her chest, Fanny ripped at the square white envelope that bore Sallie Thornton's return address. It was an invitation to Thanksgiving dinner.

She ripped at Ash's letter and read the contents in what seemed like mere seconds. When she was finished, she was so disappointed she wanted to cry. This was nothing like the letter she'd dreamed of getting—"I think about you all the time, you're on my mind when I'm up above, soaring like a bird, I dream of you, you are so beautiful, you're prettier than any girl I've ever dated. I can't wait till Christmas in the hopes you can join me if I can manage to get leave." Fanny felt like crumpling the letter she'd waited for for so long, and throwing it in the wastebasket.

She picked up the letter and smoothed it out. She knew she'd never throw it away—it would be like throwing away a part of her heart. Maybe she had missed something in the letter, something that held a double meaning. Maybe he was waiting for her to take the lead in the romance area. The thought was so funny, Fanny almost choked.

At least he had asked for a picture of her. He also promised to send one of himself in full flight gear, in his next letter, or as soon as he found someone who had a camera. That had to mean something. Maybe he'd carry her snapshot in the pocket of his flight uniform. She'd just seen a movie where an aviator did that. The only problem was, the guy in the movie died with the snapshot clutched in his hand.

Fanny bolted for the bathroom.

The pilots were weary, their eyes red and bloodshot from the cigarette smoke in the wardroom. Ash Thornton nudged the pilot next to him. "If I fall asleep, give me a kick."

"I was just going to tell you the same thing, Thornton. Christ

Almighty, I can't remember when I've had one full hour of sleep. My body's shot to hell. Right now if I had my choice of having sex with Betty Grable or getting two hours of sleep, there would be no contest."

Ash leaned his head into the palm of his hand. He knew if he closed his eyes, his elbow would slip off the chair, and he'd slide to the floor. He was tempted to try it to see what would happen. Instead, he fired up a cigarette he didn't want and gulped at his cup of cold, bitter, black coffee. "I'm convinced this stuff will corrode the fillings in your teeth," he hissed to the airman on the other side of him.

"That must be why my teeth ache all the time." The airman grinned.

"Mail's in," someone said.

"As usual, Thornton got the most. How the hell many women do you have on the string, Ash? I counted twenty-three letters, and you got that many a couple of days ago. Listen to this roster of names, Adele, Janet, Mona, and Fanny. Fanny writes the thickest letters, pages and pages of sweet nothings, right, Ash? There's one from your mother, too."

"I told you to keep your mitts off my mail, Esposito."

"That's kind of hard to do since I was assigned mail this week. Next time I'll leave yours in the sack, and you can damn well scrounge for it. I don't personally give a shit if you're an ace or not."

"Hang it up, you guys, and listen up," the flight trainer said. "I know tempers are short, and I know you are bone ass tired, but we're fighting a war, and war doesn't allow for siestas and these charming exchanges. You sleep when you can, and you fly when I tell you to fly. Nobody said this was going to be a frolic in a daisy patch.

"You're all being transferred to the *Enterprise*. It's a temporary transfer for a special mission. You'll be briefed once you're aboard the Big E. You'll get to sleep around the clock and I'm told you're going to get some real Texas beef, some fresh vegetables, and fruit for your supper. Chocolate ice cream. You can't beat that!"

"Sounds like a condemned man's last meal," Ash said.

"What's our ETD?" someone asked.

"At 0600 hours."

"That's it?" Ash snapped.

"From me, it is. This shouldn't come as a surprise to any of you, but in case it does, the commander of the Pacific Fleet doesn't confide in me. Don't give me that wide-eyed stare, Thornton. I want to remember you as the cockiest son of a bitch I've ever served with."

Ash gave the flight trainer his famous middle finger salute. It was returned. Both men laughed.

"Is Bill Halsey calling the shots on this one?" one of the pilots asked.

"Looks that way from where I'm standing. One last thing, I want each and every one of your asses back on board this ship in one god-damn piece when your mission is over. In my opinion you're the best of the best. Show those guys on the Big E what you're made of. You have twenty minutes to get your gear together. I want to see letters home before you board that chopper. I'll see that they go out on the next go-round. That's a goddamn order. Good luck."

Ash was last in line. "It's that bad, huh?" he said in a low voice.

"Scuttlebutt has it that it's the biggest mission so far. Keep your eye on Kelly, he's your only weak link. Maybe some sleep and good food will perk him up."

"His wife just had a kid. He's down is all. Once he's in the air he does what he's supposed to do." Ash extended his hand. The hand-shake was bone-crushing.

"Ash?"

"Yeah."

"You're one of the best pilots I ever trained. Don't take chances. I meant it when I said I want to see your sorry ass back on board this ship. You don't have to prove anything to those pilots on board the Big E, or anyone else for that matter. Only yourself."

"Jacobs, if I don't make it back . . ."

"Captain Thornton, I gave you a goddamn fucking order. I told you I want your ass back on board when the mission is over."

Ash favored the major with the snappiest salute of his career. "Yes, sir, Major, sir!"

"Dismissed."

In his quarters, Ash packed his gear. He took five minutes to scribble a note to Fanny and one to his mother and father. He jammed the thick packet of mail into his bag along with all his other mail he hadn't bothered to read. In his haste to get on deck he didn't notice when the letter to his parents slipped from his grasp.

Ash's eyes burned as he stared at the flight deck as the chopper lifted into the air. He wondered if he would ever hit the *Hornet*'s flight deck again with his F4F.

"This place is gorgeous, even in the winter," Bess said in awe. "I can't wait to see the inside. What do you think, Fanny?"

"What I think is, why are we here? Mr. Rollins isn't coming; he went to his house in Arizona yesterday. Mrs. Thornton doesn't really know me. I just don't understand why she asked us. Do you think it's because she saw us talking to Ash that night on the street?"

"Maybe she's just being nice. After all, you are alone in a boardinghouse. She knows Pop closed the drugstore and took Mom to Virginia. He's been telling everyone in town for weeks now to stock up on their sundries and prescriptions. That must be why she invited me."

"Did she ever invite you before, Bess?"

"No."

"Then I rest my case," Fanny said quietly.

Bess stared at her friend uneasily. She'd been wondering for days what the invitation really meant.

Sallie stood in the open doorway dressed in a flowing caftan the color of ripe raspberries. Her hair was done in swirls and curls on top of her head. Diamonds dripped from her ears and throat. "Come, come, it's cold out here. We've all been waiting for you. I'm so glad you could both come. Thanksgiving is such a wonderful holiday. I'm sorry, Bess, that your parents are away. I didn't want you and Fanny to be alone."

Fanny smiled nervously as she extended a small box of gift-wrapped candy. "After-dinner mints," she said shyly.

"That's so nice of you, Fanny," Sallie Thornton said, hugging her.

Fanny wondered what kind of a mother-in-law Sallie would be. Her heart started to thump at the thought.

"They're here, everyone! This is Fanny Logan and Bess Otis. Girls, you know my husband Philip, and this is my friend Red Ruby. My sister, Peggy, and her husband, Steven. On the other side are some very old friends of mine, Zack, Peter, Martha, and Colette. We've been friends for years and years. This lovely girl standing next to me is Su Li and her husband Chen. Both of them are doctors. To her left is Dr. John Noble. Standing next to him is Akia and her husband Chue. Now, what can I get you to drink?"

"Whatever everyone else is having," Fanny said. Bess nodded.

Fanny accepted a wine flute that was so fragile she was certain her teeth would crack the edge.

"I think you should make a toast, Sallie," Philip said.

"Thank you for reminding me, Philip. Let's drink to peace, family, and the return of our sons."

Fanny raised her glass and was startled at the speculation she read in Sallie's eyes. There was no doubt in her mind that Sallie Thornton would be a formidable mother-in-law.

Dinner was delicious. Before she knew it, she heard Sallie Thornton say, "We'll have our coffee in the living room."

Fanny looked around for Bess. Sallie gave her a conspirator's wink as she inclined her head to the left where Bess was talking to John Noble. She'd never seen Bess so animated, so flirtatious. Poor Ted. What was going to happen to the engagement ring? Would he be able to get his money back? Mrs. Bess Noble. It was perfect. Her father would fill all Dr. Noble's patients' perscriptions. He would give the bride away. Mrs. Otis would cry, and everyone would be happy except Ted.

"A penny for your thoughts, Fanny," Sallie said lightly.

"I'm not sure they're worth that much. Bess looks like she's interested in Dr. Noble."

"From where I'm standing, it looks like that interest is being returned. Does that bother you, Fanny?"

"I'm not sure. He's older for one thing. Established. He appears to be . . . sophisticated. Bess is . . . a simple person. I don't mean that in a . . ."

"I know what you mean. Dr. Noble is a fine young man. Perhaps your concern is unwarranted. Do you care for coffee, Fanny?"

"No thank you. You have a lovely house, Mrs. Thornton."

"Would you like to see it? I don't care for any coffee right now either. I don't know why it is that we always think we have to have coffee after a meal. I'd like it if you'd call me Sallie, Fanny. Mrs. Thornton sounds so formal."

"If you're sure you don't mind."

"Come along, we'll start on the second floor. I love showing off my old schoolroom. Philip came all the way from Boston to teach me. To this day, I still learn from him."

The intensity in her tone stunned Fanny.

"So what do you think of my mountaintop?" Sallie asked, pointing to the view from the schoolroom window.

"I don't think I've ever seen anything so pretty. You must love coming here. I think I could live here forever," Fanny sighed.

"I thought that once. It is one of the prettiest places in the world, not that I've seen that much of the world. There might be one other place that is prettier. Perhaps we'll talk about that other place one day," Sallie said, her voice thoughtful and sad at the same time.

"These two rooms belong to my sons. I leave the doors open.

When they were little, they loved coming here. At least I think they did. I never wanted them to grow up. Isn't that silly? Some days I wish time would stand still. Other days I find myself wishing for the future. I'm in a melancholy mood today. Do you get homesick, Fanny?"

"I did for a few days. I call home twice a week. I write, and my father writes back. My brothers write on occasion. I guess you know what that's like."

Sallie nodded.

"This is my bedroom," Sallie said, leading Fanny into the room. Curtains were billowing in the breeze from the open windows.

"I keep the windows open in this room all year long," Sallie said. "The shack I grew up in had no windows. The place where I lived as a child was called Ragtown."

Fanny was at a loss as to how she should respond to these confidences. "If you wanted to, you could go back to that awful place and rebuild it, or you could build a park for children. You could put a statue and a fountain in the park. A big square. You could even name it after your mother or father or whoever you loved best. If it was me, that's exactly what I would do. Loads and loads of pretty flowers, lots of green grass, iron benches, trees, a fountain that never runs dry, and some kind of statue. Maybe a memorial for the young men in the area who . . . who don't . . . return. Am I being too forward?"

"Dear child, not at all. What a marvelous idea! Now, why didn't I ever think of that?"

"Maybe because Ragtown held no pleasant memories for you. But no matter how bad it was, no matter how unpleasant the memories, it was your home. When I think about my father and my brothers, our house is always in that thought. I would be devastated if something happened to the place I grew up in. Houses should be handed down from generation to generation. Some people aren't family-oriented, but I am, and I suspect you are, too."

Sallie hugged Fanny. "I'm going to introduce you to my son when he comes home. I'm going to write him a long letter tomorrow and tell him all about you. Come here, I'll show you his picture."

Fanny grew so light-headed she had to grab hold of the side of the dresser while Sallie rummaged through a stack of photographs. "Ah, here it is. Look at that smile! He flies planes, you know. He can do anything, he's that kind of person. He graduated two years ahead of time. Well, Fanny, what do you think? Isn't Simon the handsomest young man you've ever seen?"

Fanny's head buzzed. *Simon*? Her hand shook as she stared at the young man smiling into the camera. "Very handsome," she managed to say.

"This is Ash. You and Bess were talking to him that night when he was leaving for Nellis. This isn't a very good picture of him. He's not as photogenic as Simon is."

Fanny's tongue felt thick in her mouth. She should say something now about Ash's letters. What should she say? How should she say it? She felt like she'd just stepped into a hornets' nest.

Downstairs, the guests, divided into groups of six, were playing poker. Bess and Dr. Noble were playing checkers. Fanny heard Bess say, "I'm not much of a gambler." She felt like rushing over and slapping the silly expression off her face.

Sallie excused herself. *She's going upstairs to call Devin Rollins*, Fanny thought. She hoped that she herself would never be as transparent as Sallie Thornton when she fell in love. She fought the crazy urge to run over to Philip to console him. The naked hunger in his eyes as he stared after his wife bothered her. She wanted to go home.

When Sallie returned to the living room, she clapped her hands to gain everyone's attention, but not before she walked over to stand behind Fanny's chair. "I have something to tell all of you. Most of you probably won't be interested, but my sister will be. I think I've finally located our brother Seth. I'm going to Texas next week. But, before I go to Austin, I'm going back to Ragtown. Fanny gave me a wonderful idea. She suggested I build a park where we used to live. Perhaps one of Chue's distant cousins would be interested in the perpetual maintenance that will be required. We could build a little caretaker's cottage for him to live in. That way we'll know the park will always be taken care of. We'll have a dedication when it's finished and name it after our parents. What do you think?"

Peggy was quietly weeping. "Only if I can contribute," Peggy said. Her husband moved to her side, his hand on her shoulder.

"I wouldn't have it any other way," Sallie said happily. "I just called my attorney, who will get on it first thing in the morning. By the time I get to Austin, we'll know if the owner will sell the land to us. Chue, do you have a cousin who wants to move to Texas?"

"Many cousins willing to move."

"It's settled," Sallie said happily.

Fanny sighed with relief when Su Li, her husband, and Dr. Noble rose to leave. Bess looked like she'd just lost her best friend.

Sallie was gracious, smiling, hugging everyone as they prepared to leave. "Thank you for coming. Red, I'm going to eat every one of those chocolates when I get into bed this evening with a good book. Shame on you for bringing me *five* pounds."

The trip back to town was made in virtual silence. Bess stared out at the darkness, the dreamy smile still on her face. Fanny poked her on the arm. "What about Ted?"

"Ted?"

"Your boyfriend Ted. That Ted. The same Ted who is going to give you an engagement ring in just a few weeks. The same Ted who is helping you fill your hope chest."

"Oh."

"Oh. That's all you can say is, oh?"

"What do you want me to say?"

"I don't know, Bess. That doctor is too old for you. He must be at least *thirty*. You also told him a lie. You're not much of a gambler! Ha! You eat, drink, and sleep the game."

"You're a real sourpuss tonight. Did someone step on your toes?"

"Now that you ask, yes, in a manner of speaking. Mrs. Thornton, who by the way, has asked me to call her Sallie, wants me to meet her son Simon. Not her son Ash, but her son Simon. I know she's going to send him that picture Su Li took of all us at dinner. I know it, I know it, I know it. I should have told her about the letters. I had the perfect opportunity, and I didn't do it. Are you listening to me, Bess?"

"Of course I'm listening. When you go back to work on Monday, make plans to meet with her and tell her. She said she's going to Texas, so that means she'll be coming into the office. This is just my opinion, but Simon is more suited to you than Ash. That's worthless advice because the same love bug that bit you, bit me. Come over to my house tomorrow, and we'll talk about all this. Obviously, we both need some kind of plan."

"Plan? All we need to do is tell the truth . . . and suffer the consequences. Mrs. Thornton is going to be very disappointed in me. Ted is going to have a broken heart. I know he's going to cry, Bess. He really loves you."

"I know. I realized this afternoon that I must not love him. If I could be so instantly attracted to another man, I couldn't possibly be in love. *In* love, Fanny, is different from just loving someone. My mother explained that to me when I was sixteen. Sallie Thornton loves Philip Thornton. I could see that this afternoon. But, she's *in* love with Devin Rollins who is also *in* love with her. Philip Thornton is *in* love with Sallie Thornton. You are *in* love with Ash Thornton. God, this is all giving me a headache."

"Me too," Fanny said.

"Do you dream about Ash, Fanny?"

"Almost every night. I wish I didn't. I hardly know him and yet . . . yet I feel like I've known him all my life. I've actually created this . . . this fantasy, and yet I can't help myself. I live for those stupid letters that don't say anything."

"You already have your wedding planned, don't try and kid me, Fanny."

"I think about it, that's true. You know what, Bess, I think we're in love with the idea of love. I'm not going to think about this anymore. I hate it when I get one of those frustration headaches. Look, we're home. I'll come over around noon tomorrow, okay?"

"Great."

Fanny stood on the sidewalk until the long, sleek black car was out of sight.

She wished she was back in Shamrock, snacking on leftover turkey stuffing.

Ash Thornton stowed his gear. The bunk looked wonderful, almost as good as a woman beckoning him to her bed. He felt his eyes start to droop and his shoulders begin to sag. He needed to sleep around the clock if possible. But, before he could drop into the arms of Morpheus, he had something to do.

On deck, he singled out one of the sailors. "Can you tell me where I can find the guy who pilots the *Silver Dollar*?"

"Adam Jessup? Sure, Captain, he's down in the wardroom. He was part of the welcoming committee when you came aboard, sir. Guess you didn't see him."

Ash snapped off a sloppy salute before he made his way to the wardroom.

He saw him, feet propped up on one of the green tables, his chair tilted back at an alarming angle, a flight manual open in his lap. Back home he used to study in much the same way, while Ash always had to sit hunched over a desk, reading lamp at just the right angle, his pencil sharpened to a fine point, his notebooks placed just so, his book spine cracked so that the pages lay flat. Simon could study standing upside down.

"Jessup, Ash Thornton," Ash said holding out his hand. For the benefit of the others he said, "I've been wanting to congratulate you since the day we met upstairs. Do you mind if we go someplace where we can talk?"

"Sure," Simon said, his eyes wary.

Outside the wardroom, Ash clapped his brother on the back. "Jesus, I'm glad to see you and to know you're in one piece. They tell me you could well become a legend in your own time. Look, Simon, I don't have any ulterior motives here. I'm sorry about the past. I swear to God I am. I finally realized something. You know how it is when you're up there thinking. All of a sudden, everything seems crystal clear. Maybe it's because you know you're one step away from your own mortality. Whatever the hell it is, I understand it now. This rivalry, the hatred we had for each other, that wasn't our fault. Mom and Pop set the ground rules, and because we were young and stupid, and didn't know any better, we fell into the trap. They're the ones who chose up sides, not us. We were stuck. The whole damn thing just took off and escalated to the point where each of us wanted to kill the other. I regret all those years, Simon, because we can never get them back.

"I see that suspicious look in your eyes, and I don't blame you. If I was standing in your flight boots, I'd probably look the same way. I want to clear the air in case I don't make it back. I didn't tell Mom or Pop about your alias. Hell, I didn't know it myself until a few minutes ago. I could have told them you were on the Big E, but I didn't. You had to do what you had to do, kid." Ash held out his hand again.

"I'm not shaking your hand, you asshole. C'mere," Simon said as he yanked his brother to his chest. "I'm glad you had the guts to come to me. I don't know if I could have done it."

"Yeah, you could have. God, how I always wanted to be like you. You have no idea what it was like, Simon."

"The hell I don't. I would have killed to take your place. I used to lie awake nights and plot your death."

"No kidding! Jesus, I used to do the same thing. I never did it, though, even in my dreams."

"Me either. What's it like to be an ace, Ash?"

"Pretty damn scary. Those little yellow-bellies are out to get me. You're just one short to catching up. I'm calling the shots on this one, Simon. I'd like you to be my wingman."

Simon's jaw dropped.

"None of that noble shit up there, Simon. You fly by the book and take my orders. You got that?"

"Loud and clear."

"You better get off a letter home. You write much?"

"No. They write though. How about you?"

"Same as you. I have all their letters in my duffel. I don't read Mom or Pop's letters. Do you?"

"I hate to admit it, Ash, but I don't read them either. I don't want to read about Mom's guilt and Pop's remorse."

"We've come a long way, Simon. I for one thought this day would never come. What are you going to do when this is all over? Are you going back to Vegas?"

"No. I decided that the day I left. I'm heading for New York and Wall Street. You got any money you want to invest?"

"Yeah, a whole bunch." Ash told him about the bank account his father was going to turn over to him. "I don't want the fucking money, Simon. I'll give it to you to invest, and when it doubles or triples or whatever it does, we'll give it back. Consider it your start-up money. If that makes it better in even a small way, then I'm all for it. I wish there was something else I could do or say. I feel like all our bad times were my fault."

"It's a deal. Remember what they told us in flight training, you never sweat the small stuff. All that's behind us now. Compared to what we're facing, our past is small potatoes."

"Listen, Simon, I have to catch some sleep. I'm not going to be any good to anyone if I don't sack out. You hear any rumors about this top secret mission?"

"Only about two hundred."

"What's the most likely?"

"This is just my opinion, Ash, but we're only a hop, skip and a jump from the Solomons. The enemy is holding Bougainville. They maintain this monster air base at Rabaul on New Britain. The marine pilots have been doing daily missions to escort our bombers en route to their targets. There's this stretch of water that is 250 miles long and 50 miles wide. They call it 'the Slot.' The Japs have an ace pilot who's got twenty-five American kills to his credit. That's who we're up against. I think they want us to take out the base at Rabaul. The bastard, at last count, leads a squadron of forty Mitsubishi A6M fighter planes from the base at Torokina on Bougainville. It might be an either or, or it might be us taking both bases out."

"What's your best guess?"

"I think the powers that be want both taken out. I say we get on with it. I want it over with so I can head for New York. What about you, Ash?"

"I met this girl when I was home on leave. I'm trying to wangle some more R & R and asked her to meet me in Hawaii over Christmas."

"Do you think she'll do it?"

"Hell no! She's a good girl. All you have to do is look at her to know that. Simon, Pop took me to Red Ruby's the night of Mr. Waring's funeral."

"Jesus!"

"Yeah," Ash mumbled. "At the time I thought it was the greatest thing in the world, but there was something screwy about that whole night. I gotta get some shut-eye. Listen, don't let me sleep more than ten hours, okay?"

"Okay, Ash. Ash?"

"Yeah?"

"Thanks. You know, for keeping my secret, for everything. I'm damn glad you're my brother, and I'm damn glad we're on the same side."

"Me too, Simon. Me too."

It was a gray day with dense cloud cover. Ash led his squadron above the clouds in tight formation, every pair of eyes in every cockpit scanning the sea below for the enemy.

Because he was the squadron leader, Ash was first in line to exit a thick cloud bank. He banked hard left, swinging off to the southwest for a quick look at the expanse of water called the Slot. The clouds were thicker now, as far as the eye could see. Ash spotted the first plane and counted nineteen more heading straight up the Slot. His stomach muscles gathered into a hard knot. "Enemy planes, three o'clock," he said tightly.

"Twenty in all," Simon said.

"Okay, you hotshots, you know what to do, go get 'em," Ash said, breaking formation and climbing up, up, to where the Zeros were.

The squadron broke off in sets of two.

"Come and get me, you fired-up rice ball," Ash muttered as he circled wide, coming up behind a Zero bent on sending Izbeckie to the bottom of the Slot's crystal blue waters. The radio crackled to life. "I got ten bucks says Thornton takes the first Zeke. He's hot on his tail."

"That's a sucker bet," came Simon's reply. "Fifty bucks says we cream thirteen of those Zekes in the next forty minutes. Put up or shut up, Orlando."

"You're on, Jessup."

"Twelve more to go, Jessup," came Ash's reply. "Bandits, two o'-clock."

Ash banked left and dived down to engage one of the Zekes. The unblemished sky became a Fourth of July fireworks display as tracers and angry red meatballs erupted. He switched radio frequency, waited a moment, and spoke slowly and clearly, "I'm on your starboard wing, you son of a bitch. Startled at the voice crackling from his radio, the Zeke made a sharp dive to the right as Ash sprayed a row of holes into his wingtip.

"Zero your tail, Thornton, hard left, roll and dive, I got him," Izbeckie's voice roared from the radio. Ash watched as Izbeckie swooped down behind him, a string of firepower-belching flames tearing off the Zeke's antenna. The Jap poured on the coal and whizzed upward, Izbeckie right behind him, but losing ground. The Zeke had the advantage because he could climb at a steeper angle.

"I lost him, I lost him," Izbeckie grumbled.

"He'll be back," Ash said. "Not today, though; you did some serious damage to his plane. He's got no radio to go in on. Good job, Izbeckie. Time to go down below and join the party."

The free-for-all below raged on. The radio was alive with gibes, taunts, and the raunchiest insults known to man. Ash knew they were flying the wings off the Zeros as six of them turned tail and headed back home. He changed frequency, hoping to catch Simon. Instead he heard a Japanese voice call him by name. His hand started to shake. "Speaking," he said.

"I am Captain Nuan Nagoma. I plan on sending you into the Slot, where I sent all your predecessors."

"I'm Jack the Ripper, Nagoma, and it's gonna take a better man than you to send me into those waters. Number one, I'm navy. You've been fooling with the marines up till now. They were just warming you up for us. We're the first string, but I don't suppose you know anything about football."

"I know everything there is to know about American powder-puff pilots."

"Take a look, Nagoma, and tell me we're powder puffs. There go two of your planes now. Notice how neatly they exploded in midair. That's craftsmanship if I ever saw it. Nothing but pieces. Jesus, I forgot, you guys don't give a shit about your wounded, you just let them fend for themselves. To die is an honor. That's bullshit, Nagoma."

"You're mine, Captain Thornton. I've taken out every squadron leader your people have sent up here. You're next."

"Not in this lifetime, bud."

Nagoma was spinning and diving, trying to shake Ash from his tail. Ash held on, growing light-headed with excruciating G-forces. Both pilots whirled and spiraled through the sky, bullets flying. The radio silence was deafening.

Suddenly, Nagoma managed to outclimb Ash and loop over him in a perfect somersault. Ash did the same thing and knew he would come out behind him. It was at this point that Nagoma wandered into Simon's sights as he rolled to the right to escape another Zero. A burst from Simon's six .50mm cannons ripped the cowling from Nagoma's Zero. Thick black smoke spiraled around the plane as it dived downward. It hit the water, leaving behind a plume of white spray.

"You got him, Simon, you got the bastard!"

"I got the plane. The pilot bailed out, I saw his chute."

"That was Nagoma. He's taken out twenty-five of our guys. What do you suppose the Japanese Imperial Navy will think of their ace getting blown out of the sky? You did good, little brother. Time to head home and refuel. Those bombers are waiting for us to lead them. See you on the ground, Simon."

It was the longest day of Ash's life, but at the end, when the sun was beginning to set, he led his squadron back to the Big E, knowing they had crippled both air bases. Air-Sea-Rescue had picked up Neil Tortolow, the squadron's only casualty.

The debriefing lasted an hour, the weary pilots gulping at the black coffee that flowed freely. "Tomorrow your target is Kahili. It's an island base off Bougainville. It's prime, gentlemen. The group before us shot down Admiral Yamamoto, who is considered, by those in authority, the greatest Japanese military mind of all time. We're going to pave the way for another squadron. Our game plan is the same as before—we fly in, circle and draw the Nips out, then we're out of there. The Dauntlesses take over from there. You will engage if it is appropriate. There could be as many as thirty Zeros on the ground according to what Intelligence reports. It's possible they might not all be operational. The Nips like to line their planes up in a nice neat row to make it look like they got more power than they do. One last thing, Tortolow should be arriving shortly. I want a rousing navy welcome. Every last one of you did real good up there."

The tired pilots left the debriefing room in single file, some clapping others on the back, some mumbling to themselves. Simon started to sing "Anchors Aweigh." It was only seconds before the pilots joined in, their voices loud and raucous. More backslapping, more light punches to the shoulders, and then they parted, each man to his quarters, to think and to thank God they'd come to the end of the day.

No pilot looked at the scoreboard tally. It was an unwritten rule that no pilot looked at the board until the total mission was complete. There were three more sorties to go.

Ash held back, waiting for Simon. "Simon, I spoke with Nagoma. I switched frequencies, and there the bastard was. The son of a bitch knew my name."

"I got him, Ash."

"Shit, Simon, he bailed out. He'll be back up there tomorrow. Count on it. It's one thing to shoot down a plane, it's another to carry on a conversation with a guy who's told you right up front he's going to kill you. My blood ran cold. I had the shakes, Simon. I'm a damn good pilot, but that guy is better than me and you put together. He wanted to *chat*. Figure that one out."

"I'd take that as a sign of fear. The Nips are big on saving face, everyone knows that. He has to live up to his own reputation. So he took out every squadron leader. He was lucky. Lucky streaks always break. Didn't you learn anything from Mom?"

"I never had the chance," Ash said.

"Then trust me. The guy's luck is starting to run out. I shot the plane right out from under his yellow ass. That isn't going to look good for him. Nobody, Ash, is infallible. Not you, not me, not Nagoma. I'll keep my eye on you tomorrow, for whatever that's worth."

"I owe you, Simon."

"Put it on the books. Someday I might want to collect."

"Any time, any place."

"I'll remember that. Get some sleep."

The moment the door closed, Ash started to shake. He had trouble making his legs carry him to his bunk, where he collapsed. He was losing his edge, and he knew it. He had to get it back. The alternative was to turn in his wings, which was unthinkable. With his foot, he pulled out his duffel from under the bunk. The thick stack of mail would get him over this rough spot.

He read his father's letters first, serious in tone and then lighter as he explained the chicken business in great detail in letter after letter. When he finished them, he read his mother's letters that were light, witty, and informative. He moved on to Fanny's, putting them in order by date. Some of them he read twice. When he was finished, he felt like he knew Fanny Logan.

Ash propped himself up in his bunk and wrote three long letters, one to his father, one to his mother, and one to Fanny Logan—his girl.

Time to head back to the Big E. Ash flicked on his radio. "Head on home, I can nurse this baby in on my own. I've had engine trouble before. I know it's standard practice to fly cover for me, but I'm okay and the sky is clear. I'll see you on the flight deck."

Ash was just a short distance from the Big E. He eased down to 21,000 feet, leaned back to enjoy the ride. The day's mission had gone perfectly. He'd been as full of piss and vinegar as the rest of his squadron, and it showed during the mission. One more day to go. He had his edge back now. He switched on his radio. "I'm coming home, Mother, have the beer ready," he radioed. All he heard in response was static.

The voice that finally crackled over the radio was familiar and definitely Japanese. Ash felt his forehead bead with sweat. He sensed the Japanese pilot before he saw him on his wingtip. "Want to talk about the weather, Nagoma? Let's cut the bullshit, I'm a sitting duck, and we both know it. Where's the honor in shooting down a defenseless plane?" Sweat dripped down his cheeks. Thank God he'd written those letters last night.

"No one would know."

"You'd know, Rice Ball."

"Is very true, Captain Thornton. We will meet again."

Nagoma banked hard right, his plane pulling away. He offered up a salute that Ash returned.

If one were keeping score, which Ash was, it was Nagoma 0, Thornton 0.

Day three of the mission arrived all too soon. The day was clear, something every pilot wished for. The light cloud cover filtered the bright sunlight, something else the pilots prayed for. They were flying twenty planes in lines of five. Simon led off the first line.

"Keep it tight and dry, and watch out for those wingtips. Stay alert for Zeros. They'll be coming straight down the Slot," Ash radioed.

They flew silently for close to thirty minutes. Down below, an American convoy sailed the clear, blue Pacific waters. Ash, searching for Zeros out the starboard side of his canopy, saw it first: a Japanese submarine.

"Attack!"

Simon needed no second urging. He banked and swooped down first, four planes in his wake.

"We got him off guard. He's expecting an attack from the shore, not the middle of the Slot. Let's show him a little Fourth of July fireworks. I'm buying when this is over," Ash's voice crackled over the radio.

"He's going at flank speed; that means he's going to make a try for the convoy," Simon radioed. "Pour it on, boys."

The first two planes strafed the sub with tracers bouncing round after round off the forward hatch. Ash zeroed in on the conning tower with two long bursts that struck the armor, then bounced off.

"He's trying for a crash dive, get that sucker," Esposito's voice snarled.

Ash flew in low over the water and let loose with a flood of .50mm shells that blew the top off the periscope and snorkel. He fired off another round, this time ripping a foot-long slash in the top of the conning tower.

"He's going under, he's going under!"

"He's coming back up. Get ready. Hit those clouds and dive down. That convoy looks to be five miles out. Pepper that deck, pin those guys down. They don't have enough guns to take us out. The convoy can clean up after us."

Ten minutes later, Ash radioed the convoy to exchange pleasantries with the captain of the destroyer before he headed upward to join his squadron.

"There's no action today, Captain," Davis said into his speaker. "I gotta admit, I never thought I'd help to sink a submarine. When I'm old and gray I'm gonna tell my grandchildren about this day."

"The day isn't over, Davis. Stay alert."

Ash changed frequencies. "Hey, Nagoma, you up here?"

"I'm right behind you. Send the kiddies home, and it's you and me."

Ash craned his neck both ways and saw Nagoma coming in from the side but at a lower altitude. He tipped his wings and gave off his famous middle finger salute, then zoomed by and climbed into the sun.

Twenty minutes later, Ash switched frequencies again. "We're an even match, Nagoma. We both know you have greater maneuverability, I've got greater speed, armor, and firepower. I'm a whizbang at in and out strikes. We can dive, whirl, and twirl, we can jockey for position until our fuel runs out and neither one of us is getting off a shot. Our planes are gulping fuel at a decadent rate. Look around, the sky's full of exhaust. I'm almost out of fuel, Nagoma. I have enough to finish you off, and then it's in the drink for me. You too, I suspect. You want to call it a day?"

"A superior idea. Just remember, Captain Thornton, you're mine."

"Not according to my mother. See you around, Nagoma." Ash peeled off and headed back to his squadron and the Big E. What the hell, they'd junked a sub, that had to count for something. Not to mention leveling the air base on their first sortie of the day.

Tomorrow he was heading back to the *Hornet*. He couldn't help but wonder if he'd ever meet up with Nagoma again. The Nip didn't know it yet, but he'd just lost out on his boast to take out every squadron leader of the Big E. Simon was right, the Jap's luck was running out. "Lady Luck, stay with me," Ash said breathlessly. He just might make it to Hawaii and Fanny Logan in one piece after all.

Christmas Eve morning, Fanny woke to her landlady's knock. "You have a Special Delivery package, Fanny. I signed for it." Fanny leaped from the bed and grabbed the thick envelope, certain it held bad news about her father or her brothers. Her hands trembled as she gouged at the flap, swearing under her breath as she did so. An airline ticket to Hawaii, and a note from Ash Thornton. The note was short, one page. "I'm here and I'm waiting!" Fanny almost fainted. She wasn't going to Hawaii. No way was she going to Hawaii. Only a fool would do something like that. Her father would kill her, absolutely kill her.

Bare feet slapping at the stair treads, Fanny raced down the steps to the phone in the hall outside the dining room. She dialed Bess's number and waited until her friend picked it up. "I need you, Bess, come over here right away. Don't wait to get dressed, just put a coat on and ride your bike. I'm timing you, Bess."

Fanny hung up the phone, squeezed her eyes shut, and dialed Devin Rollins's home number. The moment she heard his sleepy voice she said, "Mr. Rollins, this is Fanny. I'm sorry to be calling you so early in the morning. I think I'm going to Hawaii today. I don't

know when I'll be back. I know the office is closed between Christmas and New Year's. I just wanted you to know. Thank you again
for that lovely Christmas bonus and Merry Christmas, Mr. Rollins.
If I go, I'll bring you a pineapple. Bye."

Fanny bounded up the steps two at a time. She was just *thinking*
about going, that didn't mean it was a fact. Only a fool would go
chasing after a guy she barely knew, a guy who wrote one-paragraph
letters, and who she'd really only had one conversation with. She
must be nuts to even think about it. She was on her way out of the
bathroom when Bess catapulted up the steps and demanded to
know what was happening.

"Oh God, oh God, this is so exciting. Where's your suitcase? You
did buy that lacy underwear we were looking at, didn't you? You
need summer things, where are your summer clothes, Fanny? You
said you packed them in a box. They're going to be all wrinkled, but
they'll get wrinkled in your suitcase, too. God, this is exciting. Liven
up, Fanny, you look like you're half-dead."

"I didn't say I was going. What time does the plane leave?"

"In three hours. That's not much time. Are you scared to fly?"

"I'm petrified," Fanny said.

"You better get used to it, Ash is a flyer."

"Three hours!" Fanny sat down on the bed with a thump. She
watched Bess pack her bag.

"Aren't you glad I talked you into buying all that stuff at the end
of the season? The price tags are still on everything. Jeez. Come on,
Fanny, get dressed. Is he going to meet you? How are you getting
to the airport?"

"I guess I'll call a taxi. Unless you can coax your dad into letting
you have the car."

"I'll just take it. Mom's over at the church preparing things for
the pageant tonight, and Pop's at the store. I'm so jealous. I wish it
was me and John. We talked about it. Maybe for Valentine's Day.
Take notes, Fanny. You are going to ride the waves of passion. They
say it hurts the first time, but after that it's exquisite pleasure. Do you
know the one thing all men want most in this world? A virgin!"

"Bess!"

"It's true. I read it in *True Confessions*. Some guy confessed and
then all his buddies confessed. Therefore, it must be true. They call
it getting your cherry."

"You need to stop reading those trashy magazines, Bess. All right,
I decided, I'm going."

"Attagirl. You are going to have the time of your life. Don't think about anything but the moment. Enjoy everything to the fullest."

"Okay. I'm nervous."

"If you weren't nervous, I'd worry about you. You're supposed to be nervous. Guys expect you to be nervous. They even *want* you to be nervous, so they can be in control."

"What if I do something wrong? What if he compares me to those . . . those other girls he's been out with?"

"If he does, you'll win, so stop worrying. Do you have everything?"

"I don't know, Bess, you packed my bag. Do I?"

"Everything matches. Ten days' worth of clothes. You can buy some stuff over there. They have island dresses, they flow with the breeze and you don't wear anything under them."

"How do you know that?" Fanny demanded.

"I read everything that comes into the drugstore and that includes the travel books. Go downstairs and eat, it's a long trip. I'll go home and get dressed and sneak the car. You better hope Pop put some gas in it. I swear he's got some kind of secret gauge on it. He's got it down to the last drop."

"Go!"

"I'm going, I'm going. Thirty minutes. Be on the porch."

"Okay."

Fanny looked at her bulging suitcase. She was really doing this. She pinched her arm until her eyes watered. She wasn't dreaming. This was real. She was going to Hawaii on a whim. She was probably going to have sex with a man she didn't even know.

Fanny knew, in that one split second, that her life was never going to be the same after today.

"Devin, it's Sallie. I called to say good-bye. I'll see you January second. I'll be counting the hours. I'm sorry, darling, but it has to be this way. Christmas is for family. It breaks my heart that you're going to be alone for the holidays. We'll have our own Christmas when I get back. I promise you it will be wonderful."

"Don't try to snooker me, Sallie. It won't be the same."

"It will be whatever we make it. I love you, Devin, so much my heart aches."

"Sallie, we need to hang up. I want to try and beat some of the heavy traffic. You be careful going up the mountain."

A sob caught in Sallie's throat. "I'll be thinking of you."

"And I'll be thinking of you."

"You ready, Sallie?" Philip called from the foot of the stairs. "Everything's in the car."

"I'll be right down, Philip." Sallie closed her eyes for a moment. She no more wanted to go to Sunrise than she wanted to go to the moon.

On the ride up the mountain Philip talked incessantly about the latest letter from Ash and his trip to Hawaii for the holiday. "I can't even begin to imagine what Christmas is like on an island." He babbled on and on until Sallie thought she would jump out of her skin. If he was aware of her discomfort and unhappiness, he gave no sign.

"Su Li's and Chue's children will be old enough this year to really enjoy the tree. He called last evening and said he cut a monster tree and it's sitting in a bucket of water that turned to ice. He's thawing it out in the greenhouse. We're to decorate it as soon as we get there. It's going to be a wonderful Christmas, don't you think, Sallie?"

"I feel very old, Philip. Su Li and Chue were just children when they came to us. Now they're married with their own families. Do you feel old, Philip?"

"Sometimes. I try not to think about it."

"Is it because you're unhappy, or because the best years of your life are gone?"

"Perhaps a little of both. When the boys get married, how do you think you'll feel?"

Sallie laughed. "I don't know if I'm ready to be a grandmother."

"Have you heard from Simon?"

"I got a Christmas card a few days ago. He wrote a few lines in it. He mentioned a fellow aviator, a Coleman, remember I told you about the possibility he might be related? I'm going to Texas right after the first of the year to meet Seth Coleman. He's got to be my brother. I want to see about the park, too. My goodness, we're here, Philip."

It was nine o'clock when Sallie said good night. Tears burned her eyes when she looked at the glorious tree and the piles of presents underneath. This was not where she wanted to be. She wanted to be in Arizona at Sallie and Devin's house of happiness.

Sallie drew on her fur coat, and crept down the back stairs to the kitchen. She flinched as the cold air struck her face. She knew if she cried, the tears would freeze on her lashes. When she reached the little cemetery, she cleared her throat and swallowed hard. "Merry

Christmas, Mama. Merry Christmas, Cotton. By now you know I'm an . . . adulteress. I did this with my eyes wide-open. I know you're up there wagging your finger and saying, 'Sallie, girl, Sallie girl,' and your eyes are so disappointed in me. Sometimes I'm disappointed in myself. I'm trying not to cry, Mama. I got Christmas cards from Ash and Simon a few days ago. Simon said he shot down some famous Japanese pilot that killed almost thirty of our boys. Ash is okay, too. It won't be long now till both of them come home. Alive and well. Mama, I prayed so much, from my heart, the way you taught me. Merry Christmas, Mama. Tell Pop . . . you know what to tell him."

Sallie moved across the frozen ground to Cotton's grave. "Merry Christmas, old friend. I don't know what to say, Cotton. My sons are fine. I guess that's the most important thing. I just feel . . . empty. I don't want to be here. I hate pretending with Philip. Do you think God is punishing me, Cotton?" When there was no response, Sallie gathered the fur coat close about her. She didn't want to go back in the house. She didn't want to stand here and freeze either.

"Sallie?"

"Philip? What are you doing out here?"

"Talking to you. I heard you going down the steps, then I heard the back door close. I saw you through the window.

"Look at me, Sallie." He cupped her face in both hands, aware of the crystal tears on her lashes. "I'm going to give you a lesson in Philip Thornton's school of logic. Is there any reason why three people should be miserable at this wonderful time of year when one is all that's needed? It's a yes or no question, Sallie."

"No," Sallie murmured.

"Good, I always said you were my star pupil. I'll warm up the car while you grab a bag; you should make your destination by midnight. Oh, here's my Christmas gift to you both." From inside his pocket he withdrew a small tissue-wrapped package. "I'm not even going to make you guess. It's mistletoe. You know what to do with it. Hurry up before you freeze."

"Philip . . ."

"That's my name. Are you going to argue with me?"

"No. Yes. It isn't right."

"Who says it isn't right?"

"We both know it isn't. What about tomorrow and the children. Su Li . . ."

"I can take care of things, Sallie. Everyone will understand. I can put on my Santa suit by myself."

"Oh, Philip . . ."

"You already said that. Get going, Sallie."

"You're going to be miserable, Philip."

"I won't have time to be miserable. Drive carefully."

"I will. I will, Philip. Thank you. Thank you for being the kind, wonderful man you are. Merry Christmas," she whispered before she kissed him lightly on the cheek.

Philip stood in the driveway watching until Sallie's car was out of sight. His shoulders slumped as he made his way back to the warmth of the kitchen. He stared at the tray of liquor next to the phone for a long time. They seemed to go together, the alcohol and the phone. He poured himself half a tumbler of bourbon and drank it before he was calm enough to pick up the phone. He was proud that his voice sounded so normal when he wished the operator a Merry Christmas.

"Devin, it's Philip Thornton. Nothing's wrong." He took a deep breath. "I just wanted you to know she's on her way. She should be there by midnight. Merry Christmas.

"And to the world, a Merry, Merry Christmas," Philip said as he hung up the phone and downed his second bourbon.

Sallie started to blow the horn the moment she swerved onto Devin's property. She continued to tootle the horn until she came to a full stop in front of his door. She ran from the car, up the walk, hardly noticing the evergreen wreath or anything else. All she wanted was Devin and his arms. She raced through the house calling his name and turning on lights. Why was it so dark? Where was Devin? Oh, God, what if he had gone somewhere? She called his name over and over until she was hoarse. She ran through the house a second time, opening and slamming doors, her heart pounding. Oh, God, where was he?

In the kitchen there was no sign of food preparation. Devin had said he was going to make a big turkey dinner for Christmas Eve. Sallie opened the refrigerator. There wasn't even one jar of pickles. She slammed the door and kicked it at the same time.

She walked over to the kitchen sink—and saw colored lights through the window. It took her bare seconds to open the back door. There, for all the world to see, was the most spectacular display she'd ever seen, a thousand lights festooned around an enormous pine tree. Devin stood on the top rung of a ladder, a string of lights around his neck. "What took you so long?" he drawled.

"I came as fast as I could. How'd you get that star up there? Oh, Devin, I love you so."

"It wasn't easy, I had to add on an extension to the tree house. I did it in an hour, after Philip called. I love you more than yesterday, and less than I will tomorrow. God, it's almost tomorrow."

"Come down, Devin," Sallie cried, tears streaming down her cheeks.

She stood in the circle of Devin's arms and sobbed against his shoulder. "Philip . . ."

"I know, sweet, I know," Devin crooned.

"What's for dinner?" Sallie asked a long time later.

Devin pointed to a bathroom towel that served as a tablecloth. "A chunk of cheese, two apples, some bread that has blue stuff on the edges, and some nuts. A feast. Merry Christmas, Sallie."

11

Fanny's nerves jangled as she stepped from the plane. She was alive, in one piece, the long flight behind her. The humidity of the island slapped her in the face as she followed the other passengers across the tarmac. Her hair was going friz, in seconds making her head look like a wild bush.

God in heaven, what would she do if Ash wasn't here to meet her? As Bess would say, switch to Plan B. In theory it was fine, except she didn't have a Plan B. Was he here? She was almost afraid to scan the cluster of people waiting by the iron fencing. Her chest felt tight, her eyes dry, her hands were shaking, and she knew if she opened her mouth to talk, the words would stick in her throat.

She saw him when the heavyset man ahead of her side stepped to the right to wave to someone. He was taller than all the other men waiting at the gates, more handsome. He looked so creased and pressed, she sucked in her breath. She herself was rumpled, and she swore she could feel her hair move outward. He was smiling and waving. She smiled and waved back. Nervously. *What am I doing here?* Following her heart.

He reached for her bag. "I wasn't sure you'd come. I've been standing here for three hours." How deep and mellow his voice was.

Her own voice stunned her; it was normal, flirtatious. "When someone sends me a ticket to Hawaii on Christmas Eve, I'd be a fool to turn it down. Everything looks so green. When did you get here, Ash?" How funny his name sounded on her lips. Funny, yet right.

"Last night. I borrowed a jeep. I had a little trouble with accommodations. Everything was booked. I think every serviceman who has leave is here. I ran into a few guys I know, and one of them steered me to the place I finally found. It's nothing fancy. Hell, what it is is a shack on the beach. The good news is it has some plumbing. You have to shower outside, though, on something called a lanai."

"Does it really matter?"

"Not to me it doesn't, but I thought girls were fussy about things like that."

"Not this girl. I love new experiences." Fanny felt her cheeks start to flame. "How . . . how many rooms does it have?"

"One!"

"One? But . . . what . . . ?"

"We're going to work at it, okay? Let's not put the cart before the horse."

"Well . . . I . . ."

"Yes?" Ash drawled.

"I don't know if I'm . . . what I mean is . . . I'm not sure . . ." she stammered.

"Are you trying to tell me something?" There was such a wicked smile on his face that Fanny burst out laughing.

"Here's the jeep." He stowed her luggage in the back and helped her climb into the passenger seat.

"What I was trying to tell you without saying the words was . . . is . . . I'm a virgin. I never . . . I'm not sure . . ."

"Listen, let's get something straight from the git-go. I am not going to ravage and plunder you. I will not take advantage of you. If things switch up, fine. If they don't, that's fine, too. How does that sit with you, Miss Logan?"

"Just fine, Captain Thornton."

"You see how simple it is once you hit it head-on. We understand each other now. You write some damn fine letters, Fanny. I enjoyed them."

"Ash?" His name still sounded funny on her lips. "About those letters . . . did you ever tell your parents you were writing to me?"

"Yes and no. If you mean did I mention your name, no, I didn't. Should I have?"

"I asked you to. Your mother . . . has taken an interest in me. I told you about being invited to Sunrise for Thanksgiving. I don't want her to think . . . oh, I don't know what I think."

"Don't worry about it. I can handle my mother. Are you a gambling person, Fanny?"

"Not really. Are you?"

"Yes and no. I was going to make a bet with you."

"About what?" Fanny felt her heart take on an extra beat. "How much?" Her heart was pounding in her chest. She wondered if he could hear it.

"Ten bucks."

"Okay. What's the bet, Ash?" Was this purring voice hers?

"That we get married at the end of ten days."

"I don't even know you."

"Then why are you here?" He was laughing at her. Surely he wasn't serious. Or, was he?

"I'm here because . . . because . . . I want to be here. I don't think I'll take that bet."

"Scaredy-cat."

"I am that." Fanny smiled.

"Close your eyes, we turn off here. Our abode is just a quarter of a mile in, maybe not even that far."

When Fanny finally opened her eyes, all she could do was stare at the structure in front of her. Then she burst out laughing. "It looks like an oversize outhouse."

"That was my exact thought the first time I saw it. See, we think alike," Ash said flippantly. "We probably will get married at the end of ten days. I'm hardly ever wrong."

"Hardly ever doesn't count," Fanny shot back.

"In this case it does. I think, Fanny Logan, you are going to be very easy to fall in love with."

"Really," was the best Fanny could manage.

"Yes, really." He was grinning from ear to ear.

Fanny jumped from the jeep. "The flowers are gorgeous. This is plumeria. The scent is reminiscent of honeysuckle. This is more heady, almost intoxicating, don't you think?" She plucked a bloom and held it under Ash's nose. He sniffed and rolled his eyes. "This is night-blooming cereus. It's gorgeous, isn't it?" Fanny said, pointing to the walkway.

"Only half as gorgeous as you are." He tilted his head to allow the warm trade winds to caress his cheeks. "It seems to be a gentle, quiet place," he murmured. "So often of late, I find myself longing for a place like this, a place to sit and think . . . like when I'm flying. When you're up there, you're at peace. Sometimes you think about the past, the future. This place . . . I don't think I'm going to have to think here. I don't know if that's bad or good."

He looks sad, Fanny thought. Without thinking, she reached out for his hand. Ash grasped her hand tightly. A wave of protectiveness surged through her. She was at a loss to explain the strange feeling.

"Let's go for a swim. You brought a suit didn't you?"

"Several."

"You go in and change. I'll wait out here. Don't look at things too closely. I stocked the refrigerator. I thought we'd cook on the beach. We have plenty of wine and beer. I tried to get enough of everything to last ten days. We can go into town to eat if you prefer."

"We can take it one day at a time. I won't be long," Fanny called over her shoulder.

Fanny stared around the shack. Her eyes widened and her jaw dropped. The one room was about nine by fifteen in size. A bed that appeared to be hand-carved took up the center of the room. She checked the bedding, expecting it to be dirty, but it wasn't. The pile of white towels in the center of the bed smelled faintly of soap and bleach. A colorful fiber mat covered most of the floor. A bamboo dresser, a refrigerator, and two chairs were the only other furniture. A paddle fan circled lazily overhead, creating a gentle breeze. On the walls, metal hangers hung from wire hooks. Ash's dress uniform hung from one of the hooks.

Before she undressed, she lowered the bamboo blinds. When she hung her dress next to Ash's uniform, she smiled. It looked right. Side by side. She looked again at the bed underneath the paddle fan. She wondered what it would be like to make love beneath an oscillating fan. She shivered as she pulled on a new lemon yellow bathing suit.

Fanny's face flamed when Ash whistled approvingly. "What'd you think of the place?"

"A veritable palace. It's called pretending. It's fine, Ash."

"Don't go away, Fanny."

Fanny made a point of digging her bare feet into the sand. "I won't budge, Ash."

He was back in less than five minutes. Fanny sucked in her breath. He was perfectly tanned, muscular. Bess would say he was an Adonis. "How is it you have a tan? I feel like a ghost compared to you."

"I like catnapping on the deck of the Big E. Ten minutes here, ten minutes there, it adds up, plus I tan very easily. Your skin looks creamy. Race you to the water."

Fanny sprinted forward, her feet digging into the sand. She dived into the Pacific a scant second before Ash. She surfaced, a huge smile on her face. She looked around for Ash, but didn't see him. Suddenly, she felt him grip her ankles and pull her under the water. They frolicked like children for over an hour, then, giggling, they walked arm in arm up to the beach, where Ash spread out two towels, side by side.

"It's going to be dark soon," Ash said, lying down on his stomach. "What's your feeling on night versus day?"

"I like both. Days are new beginnings. It can never be the same as the day before, so you can always expect something new and wonderful to happen. Nights are nice too, because the day is over and you can reflect on what you accomplished or didn't accomplish. There's a coziness, a safety to the night that I like. I'm a very simple person; I think you need to know that. I like new experiences, but there's a part of me that always wants to return home, to that cozy safe place. I love sitting by a fire with a good book, especially if it's snowing out. Do you like to play ice hockey?"

"I never played hockey."

"So, what do you like best, night or day?"

"I probably couldn't have explained it as well as you did, but I feel the same way. I'm a pretty simple guy myself. We have something else in common." He was on his feet suddenly, reaching down to jerk Fanny to her feet. "Come on, it's going to be dark soon."

"It looks like Christmas," Fanny said happily when the lanai came to life beneath the colored lights that were strung through the high hibiscus bushes. "We even have a picnic table. Everything is just perfect."

"Except for presents," Ash said. "My mother was big on mountains of presents. It used to take us hours and hours to open them all. There was always a lot of tension in our house, though. What was yours like, Fanny?"

"Oh, it was wonderful. My dad always did his best for me and my brothers. We didn't have a mother, so he did everything. We went out together and cut down the tree, then we'd decorate it together and have eggnog and sing carols. We each got five presents— one big one, one silly one, and three that were clothes. Mrs. Kelly, our next-door neighbor, gave us each one, and she baked for us too.

She's a widow and sweet on my dad. I kind of hope they get married one of these days."

"You'd like your dad to get remarried?" Ash asked in awe.

"Yes, but he's never gotten divorced. I think he's going to now, though. I suppose he thought my mother would come back someday. Don't you approve of divorce?"

"Now that you ask, I guess I don't. I used to think about it when I was younger and my parents . . . it's not important. How about this . . . I build a fire on the beach and get the weenies going. Let's sleep on the beach tonight. It's been a long time since I slept under the stars."

"Oh, me too. We had a tent at home and slept out in the backyard when we were little. I always got scared, though, and went in the house at ten o'clock. My dad never went to bed until I chickened out."

"Your family sounds nice and . . . normal. I envy that. I joined up to get away from my family. So did my brother."

Fanny stared at Ash. "To get away? I don't understand."

"All families aren't nice and normal. Guess I better get that fire going. I'm starved."

"Me too," Fanny said lightly as a frown began to build between her eyebrows.

Fanny surveyed her surroundings, the frown deepening. It was suddenly important to her to make a nice Christmas for Ash. She didn't know why. She tried to shake the feeling, but it stayed with her.

She was standing, arms crossed over her breasts, still frowning, when Ash came up behind her. He nuzzled her neck. "Take a look and then say, Ash, how clever of you, that's a magnificent fire."

"Ash, how clever of you, that's a magnificent fire. I can taste those weenies already."

He kissed her until she was breathless. "I think I will marry you," he said airily as he broke away to head inside for the weenies.

"Hey, do that again," Fanny said.

Ash sauntered back to where Fanny was standing. "You really want me to do that again?"

"Uh-huh."

When he released her a second time, Ash was as shaken as Fanny. "I *liked* that," Fanny murmured.

"I did too. We'll do it again later." Fanny smiled. And smiled.

A long time later, when the moon was high in the sky, Fanny

leaned into the crook of Ash's arm. "In my wildest dreams, I never thought I'd be sitting on the beach at Christmas eating weenies and staring at the sky full of stars. Do you think Santa will make it this way? That red suit is going to be awfully hot."

"What time is it?"

Fanny looked at her watch. "Quarter to twelve. It's time to sing. Do you know the words to the Christmas carols?" Ash nodded.

"Then let's sing." They sat next to each other, their shoulders touching, their voices, one high and sweet, the other deep and sad, the gentle trade winds carrying the words out across the deep blue Pacific jewel.

"Merry Christmas, Fanny," Ash said, hugging her.

"Merry Christmas, Ash," Fanny said.

"What do you think your family is doing right now, Fanny?"

"I have no idea. This is Dad's first Christmas without us. He's probably sitting on the couch with Mrs. Kelly. He might even be at her house. How about your family?"

"They're at Sunrise. Every year it's the same. Nothing ever changes. They're probably heading upstairs to bed right now. Wrong! I forgot about the time difference. Eating dinner I guess. Want to go for a walk along the beach so we can watch for the sleigh and those eight tiny reindeer?"

"I thought you'd never ask. It's beautiful, isn't it?"

"It sure is. I'm glad you came, Fanny."

"Me too."

They walked and talked for what seemed like hours. When they returned to the beach, they stretched out on the towels and were asleep within minutes, their arms wrapped around each other.

Day after blissful day passed. On the morning of the sixth day, Fanny finished the lei she'd been working on and placed it around Ash's neck. "I love you." It was said so simply, so gently that Ash's face turned white.

"You do!" he stammered.

"I do. I decided last night. So, if at the end of the ten days you want to marry me, I'm going to say yes."

Ash was speechless. "But we . . . you said . . ."

"I'm ready now."

"You are?"

"Yep. Get ready to ravage and plunder me."

"Jesus, Fanny, it doesn't work that way. I mean . . . not here . . . we'll get sand up our . . . now!"

"I've been living in this bathing suit for . . . this is the sixth day. I'm ready to take it off."

"And I thought girls from Pennsylvania were shy and . . ."

"We are. We also go after what we want. I want you."

"I'm supposed to be the one doing the seducing. This is all mixed up."

"I'm amenable for you to start. Seducing me I mean."

"Well, I don't know if I'm ready."

"Okay. How about this?" In the time it took her heart to beat twice, Fanny's one-piece yellow suit was on the sand. "Are you ready now?" She was really doing this, she was seducing Ash Thornton. She was standing stark naked on a beach in Hawaii waiting for a man she barely knew to make love to her.

The colorful island trunks fell on top of the daffodil-colored suit. Fanny swallowed hard, her gaze shifting from Ash's face to six inches below his waist. She felt blazing hot; even her feet were burning. Her earlobes felt hot enough to spark a fire. Her arms and hands trembled as she reached out to Ash, who gathered her close.

"You're sure?" he whispered.

"Yes," she whispered back. "I don't want to go in the house, I want to . . . here on the beach in the sun."

When it was over, Fanny fell back onto the towel, her body slick with sweat. She was so disappointed she wanted to cry. She'd taken off her suit and seduced this man for *this*? She made no move to cover her nakedness. What was the point? A tear dripped down her cheek. Speak up, Fanny. It was a childhood order her father had given to her on a regular basis when she was disgruntled about something. "I didn't much like that," she said boldly.

"Huh?" Ash said.

"You heard me, I didn't much care for that. You look *satisfied*. Why don't I look like that?"

"Huh?" Ash said for the second time.

"Look at me! Do you see a satisfied look on my face? No, you do not. There has to be more to this act than . . . than . . . what you just did. What do I get out of it?"

"Well . . . I . . . you're a virgin . . . were a virgin . . . didn't it feel even a little bit good?" Ash asked helplessly.

"It hurt. Aren't you supposed to . . . to do . . . *something*?"

"Jesus, I thought I did."

"Obviously you didn't, or I would be looking satisfied," Fanny snorted.

"Maybe you were scared and afraid to let go," Ash mumbled.

"Let go of what? I was looking forward to this. And to think I made the first move. If this is what sex is all about, I'm going to be an old maid." She was off the blanket in a flash and pulling on her suit. She ran down the beach to the water and dived in. Ash didn't bother with a suit, he just ran after her, shouting her name over and over.

"Just a goddamn minute here," he bellowed. When he came up for air, he said, "Listen, I was trying to be careful, I didn't want to hurt you. You weren't . . . relaxed."

"Did you hear me complain?"

"No, but I . . . assumed . . ."

"You should not presume nor should you assume where I am concerned. You're supposed to do *things* to me, to make me . . . hot and bothered. You didn't. You just went in and out."

"You sound like an authority," Ash grumbled.

"I read a lot. If I have to explain it to you, then I guess it isn't going to work." They were treading water now, angry and frustrated.

"Maybe you do need to explain it to me," Ash said quietly. "Tell me what you want me to do, and I'll do it. If I don't know, how can I please you?"

Fanny sniffed. "You're a guy. You should want to . . . to . . . touch me all over, get to know my body as well as you know your own. I expected you to whisper in my ear, *lick* the inside of my ear, that kind of stuff. I know you had sex before, so don't try and tell me you didn't. Is there something wrong with me that doesn't . . . turn you on?"

"Hell no. I couldn't wait. Maybe that was the problem. Look, the women I've had sex with weren't virgins. They just wanted to *do it*. None of them complained."

"Well, I'm complaining. I never did this before. I was willing to do . . . whatever . . . whatever you wanted. I thought it took *hours*. . . . This was so lickety-split, it was over before it started."

"I guess you're saying I'm not a very good lover."

"I suppose you could be . . . with practice."

"We only have three and a half days left."

"I thought we were getting married," Fanny grumbled.

"Jesus."

"Well, are we or aren't we? I think I should know. Isn't there a three-day waiting period or something? Do you have to get permission?"

"Hold on here. You tell me I'm a lousy lover, I don't satisfy you, you said I need practice, and yet you want to marry me. What am I missing here?"

"Me. You don't know me. Do you want to make love to me? Do you want to soar to the heights of passion with me? Do you want to hobble away to the bathroom after we make marathon love? Do you still want to marry me, or was that a joke just to get you through these ten days? I need to tell you it wasn't a joke with me. You can say no and I can leave and we'll probably never see each other again. I'll tell you what, you take a walk up that way, I'll go this way and we'll meet back here and decide. By the way, I don't think I can eat another weenie. I'd like to shower, dress, and go into town to dinner. You know, a date. We never had a date. I don't believe this, we had sex, but we never had a date," Fanny muttered as she stalked off, leaving Ash scratching his head.

It was at that point he realized he was naked.

Ash was the first to arrive back at the designated spot in the sand that Fanny had dug out with her big toe. His thoughts were in a turmoil. He liked Fanny Logan. He might even love her someday, but he wasn't sure. Maybe if she didn't look so much like the way he remembered his mother in her younger days, it might make a difference. A wife would be nice. His own family would be nice. The business about getting married had been a line, and now he was stuck with it. Although Fanny had given him an out if he wanted to take it. Did he? She had guts and more spunk than his mother. Damn, why did he keep harking back to his mother?

"I'm really hungry," Fanny said, flopping down on the towel.

"I am too. Fanny, would you like to get dressed and drive into town for dinner?"

"I'd love to, Ash. Shall we act like tourists and wear our leis?"

"Absolutely. Do you want to shower first?"

"Sure."

"Okay, I'm going for a swim. Don't use all the hot water."

"Okay."

It was midnight when Ash swerved the jeep onto the shale drive that led to the back of the shack. "I had a wonderful evening, Ash. Dinner was scrumptious. The drive up here is just glorious at night. I don't think I ever saw the stars so bright. I've heard people refer to this island as paradise. They might be right. I feel so normal this evening, I think I'm going to sleep in the bed. I don't mind if you do, too."

"That's fine. It was a nice evening, thanks for being my date, Fanny."

Fanny smiled. "It was my pleasure."

"Good night, Fanny."

"Good night, Ash."

It was still dark when Fanny stirred on her side of the bed. She opened one eye to see bright moonlight slivering through the thin slats of the bamboo blinds. The side of the room that she could see looked like it was cast in silver. Not an unpleasing sight. She closed her eyes and tried to go back to sleep. She wanted to roll over, but was afraid she would wake Ash. Instead, she drew her legs up to her chest, hoping the slight cramp she felt in her thigh would go away.

"Can't sleep?" Ash whispered near her ear.

"I was going to roll over, but was afraid I'd wake you. I guess I did. I'm sorry."

"I've been awake for a long time. I never slept with anyone before. I was thinking about how it felt. How about you?"

"I never did either. I read this book not too long ago that described how married couples sleep. They referred to it as spoon fashion. Roll over and I'll show you. I guess in the wintertime it would be real nice."

Ash rolled over, reaching for Fanny. "You look so pretty in the moonlight." He kissed her, gently at first, then more savagely, his hand reaching inside her gown. He felt a smile begin to build within him when he heard Fanny utter a low moan. His hand traveled downward to her belly, his splayed fingers as well as the heel of his hand kneading her, rubbing her, caressing her. A low, throaty moan whispered in his ears.

Fanny's hands reached out to draw his head to her breasts. She sucked in her breath when his mouth made contact with her taut nipples. She moaned again and again as Ash's busy hands explored her body. Her own hand snaked out and reached for his manhood. She was rewarded with a guttural sound of pleasure.

In one dizzying moment she was on her back and then she was on top of him, her flat belly pressing into the hardness beneath her. "Come down on me," Ash groaned. She did, but not before she lowered her lips to his, her tongue spearing into his waiting mouth. The kiss shook her to her toes, her body flaming. She wanted to crawl inside his body, to make them one.

"Ride me, Fanny," Ash demanded, his hands gripping the upper part of her arms. The pleasure was such exquisite torture, Fanny wanted to delay it as long as possible. She slowed her gyrations when Ash gripped her breasts in both his hands. He pulled himself upright, his arms wrapped around her, their bodies glued together. He nuzzled her neck, her ears, kissed her eyes, her throat, his tongue tracing lazy patterns down into the deep V between her breasts.

As one, their mouths clinging, they rolled over until Ash was again on top of her. Fanny opened her thighs. A low moan escaped her as Ash burrowed into the warm softness that belonged to her alone. She raised her hips, daring him, inviting him inside her secret place. He rode her like a wild stallion.

When it was over, when both bodies, slick with each other's sweat, fell back against the pillows, Fanny's breath exploded into a sigh. "The world exploded, I saw stars and rainbows and lightning streaks," Fanny said in awe, her voice a hoarse whisper.

"Jesus," was all Ash said. He didn't mean to say the words, but they tumbled out. He felt like a fool when he asked, "Did I do it right this time?"

"You did."

"You had me worried there for a while." He leaned up on his elbow to stare down at Fanny. "Will you marry me?"

"Yes. Oh, yes."

"Tell me why you love me. I need to know," Ash asked.

"I just do. I love your impetuousness, the way you tracked me down. I like your tenderness, your gentleness, your sense of humor, the way you look, the fact that you enlisted to fight for your country. I love it that you aren't afraid to admit when you do something wrong. I also love it that you had the good sense to ask me to marry you. Does that answer your question? Why do you love me?"

"Yep, it does. I knew you were going to ask me that." Instead of answering her last question, he started to tickle her, their bodies contorting as they laughed and giggled like children. In the end they made love again and again until both of them were limp with exhausted pleasure.

Three days later, on January 4, 1944, two hours before her plane was to leave, Justice of the Peace Malcolm Forrester pronounced Fanny Logan and Ash Thornton man and wife.

Fanny boarded the plane, her eyes full of love for the man she was leaving behind. The love stayed in her eyes as she stared at her wedding ring on the long flight home.

Ash Thornton's eyes were troubled as he stared at his wife climbing the steps to the plane. His heart pounded in his chest when he questioned himself. Did he love Fanny Logan the way a husband is supposed to love a wife? He just didn't know. Was this hasty marriage a mistake? He didn't know that either. He clenched his hands into tight fists.

Sallie Thornton brought the car to a clear stop. She stepped from the Packard to stare at the carved, wooden arch that read SUNBRIDGE. She turned to look at miles of freshly painted white rail fencing. Tall oak trees lined the winding driveway, creating a tunnellike atmosphere. The side lawns were lush and green. Sprinklers thrummed rhythmically. "Very nice," Sallie murmured. "Almost as nice as Sunrise." Inside her purse was a packet of professional photographs she'd had taken to show Seth Coleman. How ironic—she thought, Sunbridge and Sunrise.

Sallie climbed back into the car and drove slowly up the long driveway. If the person who owned this property turned out to be her brother, she was going to be very upset. Only a very wealthy man could afford all this. If this man was her brother, he was going to have some hard explaining to do in regard to her family. She found herself clenching her teeth when the magnificent house came into view.

The house was three stories high. Two extended wings, also three stories high, prairie pink in color, were set back off the sides to create a horseshoelike effect. A wide white veranda supported by pristine white columns completed the picture. The house was beautiful, but only half as beautiful as Sunrise. *This isn't a competition*, she admonished herself.

Sallie climbed from the Packard, straightened the plum-colored skirt of her suit, checked the seams in her stockings, and the soft kidskin shoes for dust. Her gloves and her purse matched her shoes perfectly. She was well turned out, right down to the crisp white blouse under her suit jacket, the three-carat diamond studs in her ears, and the diamond rings on her fingers beneath her gloves.

Sallie admired the ornamental topiary trees and the crepe myrtle that hugged the foundation of the house as she made her way up the verandah steps. She rang the bell and took a step backward, her business card in her gloved hand.

The door was opened by a tall, austere-looking woman. "Yes," she said imperiously.

"I'd like to see Mr. Coleman please. I'm Mrs. Thornton."

"Do you have an appointment?"

Sallie's hackles rose. "In a manner of speaking." She held out her card. The woman took it gingerly between her fingers. She appeared to look at the printing out of the corner of her eye. "I'll see if Mr. Coleman has time to speak with you. Your business concerns . . . what?"

"This particular visit is personal," Sallie said coolly.

"Step this way, Mrs. Thornton," the woman said, holding the door open wider for Sallie to step through. "Wait here."

"And you are . . ."

"Agnes Ames."

Sallie looked around, distaste written all over her face. Everything was dark, manly, from the heavy double oak doors to the massive beams studding the ceiling. The furniture was dark leather, oversize, and worn. The carpets were costly Oriental but dark in color. The panoramic paintings on the walls consisted of burly men doing manly things; breaking horses, branding steers; men in the saddle, Stetsons pushed forward. A man's room. A man's house. Did Seth Coleman have a wife?

Agnes Ames returned. "Mr. Coleman will see you. He said he can spare ten minutes since you made the drive out here."

"How kind of him."

"Mr. Coleman is a very busy man," Agnes Ames said.

"Really. If you worked for me, I would have fired you the minute I walked through the door."

"I beg your pardon?"

Sallie stopped in mid-stride, forcing Agnes to stop and turn to face her. "I'm a visitor and I deserve courtesy. A smile goes a very long way. You don't know what my business is, and since you don't know, it would behoove you to be civil to Mr. Coleman's guests." A devil perched itself on Sallie's shoulder. "For all you know I might be from the bank that holds the mortgage on this house. I might be here to foreclose. Women are doing things like that today while our men are off fighting."

Agnes Ames didn't answer. She proceeded down a dark-paneled hall whose walls held the same kind of pictures as the entranceway.

Agnes knocked on a door, waited for the command to enter, opened the door, and ushered Sallie into the room before she quietly withdrew, her face riddled with wary speculation.

The man behind the rolltop desk rose. Blue eyes glittered beneath a wealth of wiry gray hair. His hand fumbled with his cane as he walked around his desk, but there was nothing of the invalid about this man. Sallie needed only one quick look to know he was indeed her lost brother Seth.

"You look like Pop, Seth. Actually, you're the spitting image of him, just the way I'm the spitting image of Mama. I'm your sister Sallie."

"Don't have no sister Sallie. Guess you made the trip out here for nothin'."

"I was born after you lit out. You and Josh. You remember Josh, don't you? I don't want anything from you, if that's what's worrying you. As a matter of fact, there might be something I could do for you. My son is serving on the Big E with your son Moss. That's how I found you. Our sons talked and compared notes."

"Your boy knows my boy?"

"Yes, he's a fighter pilot. Actually, I have two sons; both are pilots. Seth, I'd like to know why you never went back to Ragtown, why you never sent money home. It would have helped Mama. I did. I was the only one. You have five other sisters, Seth. Peggy's living in Nevada now and married to the lieutenant governor. Maggie has the others and the last we heard they were all living in California. I need to know why you didn't care enough to help. You have no idea how Mama loved you. You don't, do you?" At Seth's helpless look, Sallie told him everything about the day she returned to Ragtown, about the park she was going to build there. "All she wanted was you, her firstborn. Seth this, Seth that. For a while I hated you. I vowed to find you, and I did. I can't say you're someone I want to know. What you did was unforgivable. Doesn't your conscience bother you? I guess it doesn't, or you would have done something."

His voice was gruff, a mixture of molasses and gravel when he spoke. "Pa would have drunk himself to death if I sent money."

"You don't know that for a fact. You should have checked on us. How hard could that have been? Josh, too. I'll find Josh one of these days. He's not going to walk away from this either. I'm so ashamed of you. I cannot believe we have the same blood."

"What the hell do you want from me?" Seth blustered.

"All I want from you is to say you're sorry. We're blood, Seth. Blood takes care of its own. I guess I want to hear you say Mama was pretty, that she was a good mother, that you loved her."

"I did, as much as a thirteen-year-old can love a mother. I lit out so there wouldn't be so many mouths to feed. Josh said he'd look after her. I can't go back and change the past. I was a kid. I busted my ass to get what I have. That doesn't make it right. I'd guess Josh got to the same point I got to, and lit out. You want money, is that it?"

"I don't want money. Most of all I don't want *your* money. I have my own. Probably more than you'll ever have in your lifetime. What do you think of that, big brother?"

"Prove it," Seth blustered.

"You're sure you want to know?"

"I said I did, didn't I?"

"Who was that woman who brought me back here? Are you married? Do you just have one child."

"Are you writing a family history?" Seth demanded sourly.

"One of these days I might just do that. Well?"

"Well what?"

"Are you married?"

"My wife just passed away. She was a weak, frail woman. I have a daughter, a good-for-nothing piece of flesh. That woman who brought you back here is Agnes Ames, my son's wife's mother. She lives here now, with her daughter. Is there anything else you want to know?"

"A weak, frail woman? A daughter . . . like myself, perhaps? I've only known you for a few minutes, but I'd bet you favored your son to the exclusion of all else. No father says his daughter is a good-for-nothing. He'd protect that daughter with his last breath instead of degrading her. I'm sorry about your wife. As for Agnes Ames, she's a haughty, greedy woman."

"You're pretty free with your tongue."

"Yes, I am. I like things right up front. If something is worth saying, say it. I don't lie, I don't cheat, and I don't steal. I ran a check on you and I can read you chapter and verse on some of your escapades. By the way, your wife knew all about them. She knew why you married her. When people are lonely they talk to anyone who is willing to talk with them. I know everything there is to know about you, right down to your bank balance, and I have that to the penny, as of the close of business yesterday. I know about Skid Donovan, too. I know it all, so don't look down your nose at me. I made my mistakes, and I rectified them the best way I could at the time."

"What the hell?"

"Here," she said, handing over a packet of materials. She leaned back and lit a cigarette, her eyes never leaving her brother's startled face.

"So, you're rich. So they call you Mrs. Nevada. What's that got to do with me?"

"What that has to do with you is, you don't talk down to me. Not now, not ever. I can match you dollar for dollar. If I want to, I can call in the mortgage on this house like this," she said, snapping her fingers. "I own fifty-one percent of Coleman Aviation. We're partners. I bought into your company so I could keep my eyes on you, in case you turned out to be my flesh and blood. Women are not worthless. Believe me when I tell you I am not. I'd wager your wife wasn't either. You used her to get respectability. I'd like to shake your daughter's hand because I suspect she stood up to you, but you had only eyes for your son. Am I right? Of course I'm right," Sallie said, answering her own question. "You're going to do the same thing to your daughter-in-law. It's a pattern. People have patterns, did you know that? I don't like what I know about yours."

"I don't know any such thing, and my family is none of your business. What are you here for? Is this some kind of contest? My business should not concern you."

"Damn straight your business is my business. We're blood. I own half of your business. The Pinkertons tell me you *sell* your beef to the war effort, *triple* what it's worth. How can you do that, make a profit from war? You don't need the money."

"I suppose you're going to tell me you *donate* food," Seth snarled.

"As a matter of fact, I do. I wanted to make sure my sons as well as your son, and every other mother's son, had the best food possible. I'm getting weary of this exchange. I hope your son returns home safe and sound. You can keep those materials in case you ever want to get in touch with me."

Seth nodded. "You look like Ma, at least the way I remember her." His voice was gruff with a hint of an apology.

Sallie nodded, her eyes blinded with tears. "Thank you for saying that. She used to call me Sallie girl."

Seth grinned. "She called me Seth boy. It was the same with Josh. You call your place Sunrise?"

"Seems like maybe both of us were searching for some sunshine in our lives. Sunrise is a mountain. Is there anything I can do for you or your family before I leave?"

"You could loan me three million dollars," Seth said slyly.

Sallie nodded. Seth's eyes almost popped from his head when Sallie wrote out a check. "There are no terms, no interest. You pay me back when you can."

"Just like that, no questions asked?"

"Just like that. Wouldn't you do the same?"

"Probably not."

"I respect honesty," Sallie said. "I would, however, like an IOU., duly signed. Legibly, of course."

"I respect your business sense," Seth said, writing out the IOU. Sallie pocketed the slip of paper.

She rose, stretched out her hand. Seth grasped it, exerted as much pressure as his swollen knuckles would allow. Sallie didn't flinch. "I can see myself out, don't get up."

On the walk back to the front door there was no sign of Agnes Ames. A young woman who reminded Sallie of Fanny Logan was at the foot of the steps. She smiled at Sallie.

Sallie smiled back. "I'm Sallie Thornton, your aunt by marriage. Are you my niece, or are you Moss's wife? I should know that, but I don't."

"I'm Billie Coleman, Moss's wife. Amelia, your niece, isn't here right now. I didn't know Moss had an Aunt Sallie. Do you know Moss? I was just going to go for a walk, would you like to join me?"

"I'd love to. This is my first time at Sunbridge. I've been looking for my brother Seth for years and would you believe I just found him. My son and your husband served on the Big E. I think I met your mother when she let me in."

Billie smiled ruefully. "Mother can be rather overbearing. She's very protective of my father-in-law. What did your son tell you about Moss? Tell me what your son said about Moss."

Sallie told her. "Moss and my son Simon agreed that we must be related. I'm so glad it worked out this way. I'd like to extend an invitation to you . . . and your mother to visit my family in Nevada anytime you can. I'd like you to meet our side of the family."

"My mother-in-law died not too long ago. You would have liked her. Moss loved her dearly. Amelia, my sister-in-law, is wonderful, we get along well. I haven't made any friends here yet, I've been busy with my daughter and . . . and things. I'm so glad we met."

"You remind me of a young girl I know back in Las Vegas. I'm going to try and play matchmaker when Simon comes back. The mother in me thinks they would make a perfect couple."

"Tell me about your sons, Aunt Sallie."

Sallie spoke quietly about Ash and Simon—their rivalries, their youth, her hopes and dreams for both of them. Her eyes were as moist as Billie's when she finished.

"You love them very much, don't you?"

"More than you know."

"Where are you staying?" Billie asked.

"I have a flight to catch very shortly. My final destination today is a place called Ragtown. It's where Seth and I grew up. It was a terrible place, but it was the only home I knew."

"I can't wait to tell Amelia about you. I'm sorry she isn't here. If I visit, can I bring her?"

"Dear child, of course you can bring her. I can't wait to meet her.

The next time a holiday comes up, I'll arrange a family party, and you'll come to visit. I'd like you to stay for a while, both you and Amelia. Do you think that might present a problem?"

"If it does, I'll handle it."

They were back at the car. "I wish I could stay longer," Sallie said.

"I wish you could too. It seems like I've known you forever. It gets very lonely here. The house is so dark and gloomy and . . ."

"Manly." Sallie smiled. "It wouldn't be my cup of tea. I like light, bright areas, and I prefer pastel and earth tone colors. I like open windows and lace curtains. Bright lights are important to me; I guess that's why I like Las Vegas. I'll write, Billie. Here's my card. Please, anytime things close in on you, call me. Write. We're family now."

Impulsively, shyly, Billie threw her arms around Sallie. "Thank you, thank you so much for coming today. I needed you today for some reason. You're so pretty. I wish I could look like you."

"Heaven forbid! You're the one who is beautiful. Inside as well as outside. I'm a very good judge of character," Sallie said lightly. "One day at a time, Billie, that's how you get by. I'll pray for Moss every night just the way I pray for all those who are fighting for us. Take care of yourself."

"I will. I promise."

Sallie kissed Billie soundly on both cheeks and gave her one last hug.

Agnes Ames watched the open display of affection from the foyer, her face grim. Seth Coleman watched it from the study window. He snorted his displeasure at the hugs and kisses. "Damn fool women, always hugging and kissing. Can't trust 'em when they start with that sniveling crap." He snapped the window blind back into place before he stomped his way back to his desk where he stared at the three-million-dollar check for a long time, his face sly, his glittery eyes calculating.

Sallie arrived in Ragtown by taxi. Construction contractors, horticulturists, town fathers, the elderly previous owner, all greeted her, smiles on their faces. The amenities over, Sallie walked to where the row of shacks stood. It was impossible to believe several were still standing, twenty years later. Her eyes counted down the straggly row until she came to number four. A strip of the tin roof was still attached to one sagging wall. "How can even one sliver still be standing?" she muttered. *Because,* her heart responded, *it's been waiting for you.*

Sallie walked over to the place where she'd slept, eaten, and cried during her early years. She reached out to touch the sagging wall, turned, nodded to the contractor. She walked away, a red cloud of dust following her in little puffs.

Hours later, after all the meetings, after all the words were said, Sallie took a late-night flight back to Las Vegas, secure in the knowledge the Ragtown Memorial would be a fitting tribute to all the poor families who had once lived there.

Sallie stepped from the plane, her eyes searching for Devin. Instead she saw her husband waiting at the gate. She started to run the moment she saw him. *Please, God, don't let him have bad news. Let my sons be safe.* "What is it, Philip?" she screamed.

"Sallie, Sallie, it's not the boys. They're fine. It's Ash, but it's good news."

"Say it, Philip, what is it? You scared me to death. What? Why are you here?"

"Because I wanted to be the one to tell you. Ash got married."

"Married? Ash? How do you know this, Philip?"

"Because his wife arrived here today, just hours ago."

"His wife? Did you meet her? How did she find you?"

"Ash called before she arrived. Devin was here at the airport, waiting for you, when she arrived. He took her back to town. I told him I'd wait for you. I did talk to her for a few minutes."

"What's she like? Is she nice? Ash got married without telling us? That's unforgivable, Philip. How old is she? Do you like her? Am I going to like her? Answer me, Philip."

"You already know her and like her. She said Ash wanted it this way. It's Fanny Logan, Sallie."

"Fanny! Devin's *secretary*? Philip, how can that be? I don't understand any of this."

"I don't either, but our son is married, and we now have a daughter-in-law. When the shock wears off, it's very easy to accept the fact."

"Philip, this is all wrong. Ash isn't marriage material, and we both know it. Fanny . . . I don't believe that sweet girl . . . how did this happen?"

"They've been writing one another for months. They met when he was home on leave. You remember. It's my understanding they got to know one another through their letter writing."

"I wanted . . . I thought she would be perfect for Simon. I even mentioned him to her, showed her his picture. This is very upsetting, Philip."

"She loves our son, Sallie."

"I want to go on record, Philip, right here and now, that this marriage is a mistake."

"I'll remember you said that, Sallie. Fanny said she was going to continue working for Devin and will stay at the boardinghouse until Ash returns."

"That's not right either. How can we allow her to live in a boardinghouse? Do you know if she has any money?"

"If she wants to continue living in a boardinghouse, who are we to insist otherwise? It's a shock, Sallie. Let's go home and sleep on it. The morning will be time enough to come to terms with it all."

"They aren't suited to one another."

"We aren't either, but we're still married. Ash sounded happy on the phone. Fanny had stars in her eyes. She doesn't strike me as the kind of girl that would rush into marriage. In all the excitement, I forgot to ask you if Seth Coleman turned out to be your brother."

"Yes he is. Let's go home, Philip. I'm very tired. It's all wrong, terribly wrong."

"It's done. We have to make the best of it. Look at it this way, you now have the daughter you always wanted. She even resembles you."

On the ride back to the town house, Sallie kept repeating over and over, "it's all wrong, terribly wrong," to which Philip repeated, "it will work out."

12

Fanny snuggled beneath the covers, her arms clutched around the soft, downy pillow. She squinted at the small alarm clock at the side of the bed—fifteen minutes before she had to get up and go to work. Fifteen, long, wonderful minutes to do nothing but think about Ash and Hawaii and the ten glorious days she'd spent there. She inched her hand out from beneath the pillow to stare at her wedding ring.

It was plain and gold. Ash had promised a better one when he returned home, but she was never, ever, going to take off this ring. Nothing, not diamonds, not rubies, not emeralds, could tempt her. This was the ring Ash put on her finger, and this was the ring that was going to stay on her finger. She thought about the sharp words they'd had when she offered to buy a ring for him. He'd flat out refused. Fanny thought she'd taken his rejection rather well. Her father didn't wear a wedding ring. Philip Thornton didn't wear one, although that was a joke in itself. Perhaps one day, Ash would change his mind when he saw what a good wife she was going to be. She squinted at the clock again.

The buzzer on the alarm clock sounded. This was the real world, not that paradise of warm sunshine and glorious flowers. Today, in the real world, she knew she must call her father again to see if the shock had worn off. She was going to have to talk to Bess and prepare herself for another long discussion with her boss and her new mother-in-law. What was Sallie Thornton going to say? Ash had said his mother wouldn't be pleased, that she didn't believe in hasty marriages because she had married in haste. "Just be yourself, Fanny," was his advice. He'd gone on to say that his mother would either avoid her like the plague or smother her with love and money. "She thinks money can buy anything." His voice had been so tormented she'd reached out for his hand to comfort him.

Fanny applied her lipstick, checked her stockings to be sure the seams were straight, spritzed some perfume on her neck and wrists. Mrs. Ash Thornton was ready for her first day back at work. Mrs. Ash Thornton could handle anything that came up. Mrs. Ash Thornton longed for the lunch hour so she could meet Bess with her news. Mrs. Ash Thornton was deliriously happy.

"Mrs. Thornton, how are you this fine January morning?" Devin Rollins greeted her. "I hate to ask this, but will you be staying on or must I start to look for a new secretary?"

"I'd like to stay on, Mr. Rollins. I'm going to stay on at the boardinghouse, too, and save all my money. It's much cheaper than an apartment. Ash is going to handle all the military paperwork. Have you spoken with Mrs. Thornton?"

"Yes, last evening when she returned. Philip met her at the airport and told her."

"Was she upset?"

"I don't think she was upset as much as she was hurt. Women are funny about weddings, especially the wedding of an oldest son. You might want to give some thought to a church wedding when

Ash returns. Your family would probably like to see you walk down the aisle."

"It's a thought, but it wouldn't be the same. It doesn't bother me, and I know it doesn't bother Ash. I loved our wedding. We wore leis we made ourselves. I had a circlet for my hair and a bridal bouquet. Ash looked incredibly handsome in his uniform. I don't think I want to negate that wedding with a fancy one. We said the words, I have the ring. I told you many times, Mr. Rollins, I'm a simple person. I require very little. I'll be a good homemaker. I'll be very good to Ash. Mrs. Thornton won't have to worry about us."

"It's a shame she never had a daughter, Fanny. By the same token, you haven't had a mother. Perhaps the two of you will become close."

"I'd like that very much. I think Ash would like that too. I guess I better get to work. Oh, what's all this?"

"The blueprints for the Ragtown Park, and the cottage, and of course a stack of bills. Oh, and Mrs. Thornton is going to come by around noon. She would like to take you to lunch if you don't have other plans."

Fanny's heart leaped into her throat. "I'd like that." Bess would have to wait.

It was eleven-thirty when Sallie Thornton walked into Devin Rollins's office dressed in a wool suit the color of ripe blueberries. A tiny pillbox hat of the same color was perched on the back of her head. "You look good enough to eat," Devin smiled. "God, Sallie, I missed you."

Sallie leaned into his embrace. "I was only gone a few days, Devin."

"It doesn't matter. You weren't around the corner where I could reach you if I had to. I panic when you're away. I always have this fear you might not return."

"Why do you think I came back so soon? Let's have dinner this evening . . . and . . ."

"You don't have to ask me twice. Is seven okay?"

"Seven is perfect. Where's Fanny? Did she say anything?"

"Just that she's deliriously happy. She loves your son very much."

"I don't doubt that at all. The problem is Ash. Does he really, truly love her? For some reason I don't think so. Mark it down to woman's intuition. Is she going to have lunch with me?"

"She said she would like to. I sent her to the courthouse to leave some papers for the judge. I think I hear her on the steps."

"Mrs. Thornton . . . Sallie, I . . ."

"You don't have to say anything, Fanny. I'm happy for you and Ash. I hope you have many wonderful years ahead of you."

Fanny thought she saw tears glistening in Sallie's eyes as she stepped into her embrace. "I'll do everything I can to make Ash happy, Sallie. I swear I will. I love him so much, I almost feel sick with the feeling. I promise you I'll be a good wife. I know how to keep house and cook and mend. I can sew and garden. I baby-sat a lot, so I know how to take care of children, even infants. I don't want you to ever be disappointed in me. I can try and be a daughter to you. I might make mistakes because I never had a mother."

"Then we'll learn together. I never had a daughter, so it will work out perfectly. Promise me you'll bring me up short if I start acting like a busybody mother-in-law."

"I promise."

"Now that that's settled, you two beautiful ladies should be on your way so this attorney can get down to work."

"Fanny, I met a wonderful young woman yesterday who's around your age. She's my nephew Moss's wife. The Seth Coleman we spoke about at Thanksgiving really and truly is my brother. I think you two might turn out to be friends. There are no young people at the ranch for her to pal around with. She has a little girl, although I didn't get to see her. I'm going to have a party over Memorial Day, and invite the whole family. In the meantime, I'd like it if you'd call her and get acquainted. I suspect, living in that dark, somber house with a mother who rivals an ogre, and my gruff, harsh brother, she could use a friend. Her name is Billie and she's as pretty and wholesome as you are. I'll give you her phone number before we leave the restaurant."

"I'd like that. How was it to meet your long lost brother? Was it everything you wanted it to be?"

"In many ways it was. Seth is . . . he looks like my father. He's very gruff. I suspect there's a gentle side to him. At first he was suspicious of me. I might be wrong, but I don't think my brother has much use for women. That's the main reason I would like you to call Billie. Here we are, Fanny. I think we should order some champagne to celebrate."

"I never had anything to drink in the middle of the day. Please, if you don't mind, will you tell me all about Ash when he was young? I want to know everything. I want to tell you about how I met him and the letters we've been writing back and forth. I'm so glad it's not a secret anymore."

"We are going to have such a wonderful time, Fanny," Sallie said. She reached across the table and took her brand-new daughter-in-law's hand in hers.

Fanny smiled. It was all going to work out perfectly.

The two Mrs. Thorntons spoke about many things, particularly about Ash and Simon. They drank toasts to happiness and longevity, to workable marriages, and to a houseful of children and pets. By the end of the two-hour luncheon, the two Mrs. Thorntons knew they would be friends forever. Fanny felt like she'd met her very own mother for the first time in her life. She beamed her happiness.

At last, Sallie Thornton had the daughter she'd always dreamed of.

On September 21, 1944, the same day the carrier force in the Pacific launched an air attack on Manila led by Ash Thornton, Fanny Thornton gave birth to twin boys.

"*Two* baby boys!" Sallie said, her eyes round in stunned surprise.

"Two as in one, two?" Philip demanded. "Good lord!"

"Oh, dear," Sallie said, "I have to go shopping. We only have one of everything. Philip, I'm going to need some help."

"Sallie, I would love to stay and help, but I have ten thousand chicks coming in today. I have to be there. They could die if they aren't handled properly."

"You're right, Philip, the chicks are important. Would you mind if I asked Devin to help me? This is family, Philip. I don't want to . . ."

"It's all right, Sallie. I'm sure Devin will be more than glad to help. By the way, where is he? I thought he'd be here."

"Philip! This is family."

"Are you trying to tell me Devin isn't part of this family? So, it's a weird situation, so what? If you need my permission, which you don't, call Devin."

"All right. He feels very close to Fanny, almost like a second father. Which reminds me, I have to call Mr. Logan. I wonder what Fanny will name the boys. Listen to me, name the boys. They're babies."

"Give Mr. Logan my regards and tell him it feels wonderful to be a grandfather."

"Oh, my God, Philip, we really are grandparents. You don't think they'll call me Granny, do you?"

"I wouldn't be a bit surprised." Philip laughed as he kissed his wife on the cheek. "Give Fanny a big kiss for me. I'll try and get back later this evening."

Philip's stomach lurched when he walked through the door to see Devin sitting on the iron bench by the entrance. "Get in there!" he said gruffly.

"It's family, Philip, I don't want to intrude. I've been waiting to see . . . I thought . . ."

"Twin boys! Have a cigar!"

"Two! Oh my God!"

"That's what I said. Take care of things, Devin."

"Philip . . ."

"Sallie's waiting for you."

Devin hesitantly extended his hand. He drew in his breath waiting to see what Philip would do. Philip didn't hesitate; he grasped his hand and pumped it. "Look at it this way, you only have two babies to worry about. I have ten thousand baby chicks waiting for me."

"Thank God you don't have to pick out names for them."

"Oh, but I do. They come in lots of five hundred. I give each lot a name."

"Are you spoofing me, Philip?"

"Not at all. See you around, Devin."

Devin walked into the maternity waiting room and told Sallie about his conversation with Philip.

"He's like that," Sallie said. "Remember last Christmas? He really is worried about the baby chicks. He takes the chicken business very seriously. You have no idea of the money we make from those chickens. Of course you do, you're my attorney. I'm babbling because I'm so excited. The nurse said we can see the babies in a few minutes. They're getting Fanny ready. I don't imagine she's going to feel like having visitors, but I want her to know I'm here. I called her father. He was so excited he could barely talk. I put the wheels in motion for word to get transferred to the *Hornet*. Ash is going to be . . . stunned. The nurse is motioning to us. The babies must be ready."

"They're identical!" Sallie said in amazement.

"They're twins," Devin said. "Are babies always this little?" he asked, his face full of awe.

"More or less. Look at the hair! They're gorgeous!"

"They look like Fanny," Devin said.

"Yes they do," Sallie said happily. "Just like Fanny." *Thank you, God.*

"The nurse is motioning to you, Sallie."

Sallie tore her eyes away from her new grandsons. "We can see Fanny now."

Fanny, her hair soaking wet, was propped up in a nest of white pillows. Sallie tried to remember what she herself looked like when she gave birth. She flinched when she remembered how disgruntled, angry, and miserable she'd been, and how she'd done nothing but sleep for a week. Fanny was bright-eyed, smiling, and anxious to see her new sons.

"Did you see them, Sallie? Hello, Mr. Rollins. What did my father say? Did you get through to the *Hornet*? Are they beautiful, Sallie? Tell me the truth. There isn't anything wrong with them, is there? You were right, I can hardly remember the pain. I only have one of everything, goodness, this is going to take some getting used to."

"You look so pretty," Sallie said as she kissed Fanny on the cheek.

"They fixed me up a little while ago. I feel like myself now, but I'm starving. They said they'd bring me a sandwich soon. I've been trying to pick out names. I just don't know. What if I pick something and Ash doesn't like it? I can't bear for them not to have names. The doctor put little bracelets on their ankles that say, Baby One and Baby Two. Baby One is three minutes older. Can you imagine? What do you think of Birch Coleman Thornton, and Sage Logan Thornton? Those are my two favorites. Now, I don't have to pick one or the other."

"I like them," Sallie said. Devin nodded in agreement. "I like the fact that you want to use my maiden name and your own. That's very kind of you, Fanny."

"Then it's Birch and Sage. They sound strong and rugged; perfect names for boys. Birch is the oldest. I'm so relieved. It didn't seem right to call them One and Two."

"Now that it's settled, you need to get some rest. I'll be back tomorrow."

"Sallie, I want to thank you for everything. I don't know what I would have done without you. I just wanted you to know that."

"I wouldn't have had it any other way. Sleep well, Fanny."

"I can't wait for Ash to get in touch. I'm so happy."

"She's asleep. I don't think I've ever seen anyone so happy and tired at the same time," Devin said. "You should be proud, Sallie."

"I am, Devin, I am. Come, let's go home. We've had a busy day, and now it's our time."

"Our time. It sounds wonderful when you say it like that," Devin said, nuzzling the back of her neck.

"That's because it is wonderful. It was a glorious day, Devin. Going home together makes it perfect. Isn't she the prettiest thing you've ever seen, Devin?"

"Next to you, yes."

"I don't know if I could have handled twenty-one hours of labor," Sallie said, taking Devin's hand and leading him out of the room. "She's going to be a wonderful mother. I hope . . . I hope Ash is half as good a father. I'm going to worry about that, Devin."

"Have you told Fanny about the house you bought for them?"

"No. I'm going to take her straight there from the hospital. I want it to be a surprise. I'll pack her personal things tomorrow or the next day. Do you think she'll like it, Devin?"

"Of course. As belated wedding presents go, I think a house is right up there at the top of the list. What do you think I should get the babies?"

"Fanny will like anything. You have to get two. Isn't it wonderful, Devin? Do you feel like a grandfather, you know, sort of? I know for a positive fact, Devin, that Philip will welcome you as an extra grandfather. I'm sure Mr. Logan won't mind, and I will absolutely love it."

Outside the hospital, Devin hugged Sallie close. "I love you, Grandma Thornton. If we weren't standing in the middle of the street, I'd kiss you till your teeth rattled."

"Will you do that later?" Sallie asked.

"Count on it. I never made love to a grandmother before."

"Do you think it will be different?"

"Better." Devin leered at her as he held the door to the restaurant open.

"Promises, promises."

Helmet and goggles in hand, his parachute slapping him on the buttocks, Major Ash Thornton, newly promoted, saluted his plane as he made his way to his quarters. Midway, he was stopped by a radioman, who handed him a message.

"Congratulations, Major!"

Ash nodded wearily and dropped his eyes to the printed message. It took a moment to digest what he'd just read. Twin boys! He was a father! His stomach started to churn. He was responsible for three people's lives. He turned to go back on deck. All he wanted was to get to his plane and soar up as high as he could, up above the world, where it was quiet and peaceful so he could think. Fanny hadn't said anything about twins. One baby was what she had said. He'd come to terms these past months with *one*. He looked around wildly, his heart pounding in his chest. He thought about jumping overboard. He was a coward. How could he be a flying ace and a coward at the same time?

Ash dumped his flight gear on his bunk. He needed a second opinion here. He headed for the radio room where he asked to send a message to his brother on the *Enterprise*. His message to Captain Adam Jessup, also newly promoted, was brief and to the point. "Dear Uncle Adam, Major Ash Thornton announces the birth of twin sons. Respond so I know it's real."

Ash leaned against the door, chatting with one of the radiomen as he waited for Simon's reply. When it came, he grinned from ear to ear.

"Congratulations, Ash! It doesn't get more real than this. Shooting down Nagoma was a walk in the park compared to two o'clock feedings. Day after day. Night after night. Uncle Adam."

Fatherhood. Well, maybe he'd get used to it. Someday.

Fanny wished she had another set of arms and legs. Anything to help her get ready for Ash's special four-day leave. She must have been out of her mind to volunteer to cook Thanksgiving dinner for her new family. Even with the help of a part-time cleaning woman and part-time baby nurse, she didn't have enough hours in the day.

Now both babies were wailing, Birch with an earache, Sage with a red, sore bottom. The baby nurse was sick and her cleaning lady had said good-bye, she was going back to California. Laundry was piled to the ceiling, she hadn't shopped yet for Thanksgiving dinner, and there was dust and grit over everything. Her husband was coming home in two days, and her waistline wasn't back to normal. Her breasts were overlarge, sore, and dripping. Everything she owned was stained with breast milk.

Sallie found Fanny sitting on the floor, a wailing baby in each arm. When Fanny saw her she cried harder.

Sallie took in the situation at a glance. "Fanny, why didn't you call me? Never, ever, be afraid to ask for help. Tell me what happened." She listened, marveling that the young girl on the floor had managed as well as she had.

"The house is too big, Sallie. The cleaning woman complained. The baby nurse said the boys got on her nerves because they cry too much. I don't think she's going to come back. I haven't shopped for Thanksgiving dinner and I look . . . oh, Sallie, I look like a cow. I do everything the doctor says, and the babies just aren't acting normal. Babies shouldn't cry all the time. That's all they do, Sallie. Sometimes they scream till I think I'll go out of my mind. Ash is . . . I don't want . . ."

"You should have called me, Fanny."

Fanny nodded, her face miserable. "Sallie, it scares me that I'm not coping. Is it because I'm frazzled, or is it because I had the babies too soon after getting married? I'm not sure what it is I'm supposed to be feeling. I can name you all the negative things—frustration, exhaustion, downright anger. There don't seem to be any positives. Why don't I feel love and joy and . . . and all those things?"

Sallie struggled to find the words that would wipe the anguish from Fanny's face. "Motherhood is a totally new experience, Fanny. Once you give birth, you're not the same person you were before. That carefree person who jaunted off to Hawaii on a moment's notice is gone. The responsibility for one little life is awesome, two is double that. I'm skirting around things here. Sons have a way of . . . breaking your heart.

"I love Ash, don't misunderstand, but remember this, Fanny. A son will break your heart if you dote on him, if you coddle him. I can't tell you the times Ash has chipped little chunks from Philip's heart. I know this is not what you wanted to hear, Fanny, but it's the way it is."

"I'm glad you told me. I think I understand a little better now. I'm going to do my best to love my children. I want more, you know. I'd love to have a little girl. Ash never said, but I think he was disappointed that one of the twins wasn't a girl. I know that I was. I feel guilty about that too."

"Guilt is a terrible thing, Fanny."

"I know because I'm riddled with it."

"I'm just sorry you didn't come to me after day one."

"I didn't want to bother you. You've done so much for me already. What kind of wife and mother am I going to be if I can't handle this? Not a very good one. I feel like a failure."

"You are not a failure. You just got off to a slow start. Now, change the babies, get yourself cleaned up. I have some calls to make."

Sallie did what she always did in times of crisis. She picked up the phone. "Su Li, I need help. All the cousins you can gather together. Food. An hour would be good. This instant would be even better. A bag full of your famous herbs. I'm ever so grateful, Su Li.

"We're in business, Fanny. Su Li has the situation in hand. These babies are going on bottles right now. You'll wean them off slowly. I wouldn't be a bit surprised to find out there's something wrong with your milk. We're going to check that out. Get cleaned up, you and I are going out as soon as your help arrives."

"I can't leave the boys, Sallie."

"Of course you can. You're worn to a frazzle. Babies pick up on your tension. They react to it. You need sleep, you need fresh air. You stay cooped up in this house all day and night. It isn't healthy."

"Ash . . ."

"Ash is the least of your problems right now. He will take all this in stride. Your body will return to normal when it's ready to do so."

"He's going to expect me to look . . ."

"Like a movie star. That is not realistic. We have no other choice but to take it as it comes. We're going to do our best to get things back to normal. We'll handle whatever comes up, and that includes Ash." Fanny started to cry again. "No more tears, Fanny. Now, let me see a big smile. It's going to be all right."

They arrived like the army they were, their spokesperson, an elderly Chinese who spoke halting English. Sallie cleared her throat as she struggled to speak the Chinese language she'd once spoken fluently. There were many bows, many bobbing heads, and always there were smiles as Sallie issued her instructions, then guided Fanny out the door.

"When we get back things will be under control. You'll think you stepped into another world. We're going to keep two of the girls, one for nights and one for days, to help with the boys. We'll keep two of the older women for housework, one to cook and one to clean. They'll help you to establish a routine, which is something you lack right now. I'm not criticizing you, Fanny. I couldn't have done it. Two babies is a lot of work. I think the secret is getting them on the same schedule if that's even possible."

"Sallie, I can't afford all those people. Ash is going to have a fit. He wasn't overjoyed that you bought the house for us as a wedding present."

"Ash likes to be comfortable. He likes to snap his fingers and be waited on. He doesn't much care for situations that go awry. He may have changed, but I doubt it. We are not going to worry about Ash.

We're going to lunch. Then you are going to the beauty shop to get the works. After that we're going shopping."

When the women returned home at six-thirty Fanny stood in the foyer, a stunned expression on her face. "Listen, Sallie."

"I don't hear anything."

"Exactly. The boys aren't crying. I don't believe it. Do you think something is wrong?"

"No, everything is very right. Something smells wonderful. Your dinner, no doubt."

"Dinner? There was no food. I've been eating cheese sandwiches."

"My God, Fanny."

"I want to see the boys. The house is so clean," Fanny said, looking around. "There are fresh flowers everywhere. This is wonderful."

"Go along now and see how your sons are doing. I'll check out the kitchen, and then I must be on my way. Let's have a cup of coffee together."

The nursery was dim with only a small lamp burning on the dresser. The old, wrinkled Chinese woman was sitting in the rocking chair, her hands folded in her lap. She inclined her head to the side, indicating Fanny should check on her sons. Both infants were sleeping peacefully. Fanny heaved a sigh of relief that was so loud, the old woman smiled. "What should I call you?" Fanny whispered.

"No whisper. Babies no wake. No tiptoe. Missy make much noise. Run sweeper. Bang door is okay. My name is Moon. You eat, you sleep. Moon stay. Only feed baby once before bed."

Fanny bent over to hug the old woman's shoulders. "My name is Fanny. Thank you for taking care of my sons. I don't know what you did, but you have my permission to keep doing it. I haven't had a night's sleep in two months." Fanny raced downstairs to the kitchen.

"It's amazing, Sallie, the boys are sleeping soundly. Moon is rocking in the chair, and she said she's going to stay. I feel like a thousand pounds have been taken off my shoulders. I'm going to eat, feed the babies, take a long bubble bath, try on my new clothes, and go to bed. Would you like to stay for supper, Sallie?"

"I can't, sweetie, but thanks for asking. Devin wants to go over some of the bills for Ragtown. He just called a few minutes ago to say a letter came to the office from Seth. We'll catch a bite to eat later. It does smell delicious. I asked what it was and they said pork, rice, scallions, a magic sauce of some kind. Fresh snow peas, fresh baked bread, and I believe chocolate cake. Tea. Always tea. All of Su Li's cousins are wonderful cooks. This coffee is delicious. I really have to be going, Fanny. Is there anything else you need me to do?"

"Nothing I can think of. Thank you for everything."

"It was my pleasure. By the way, what time is Thanksgiving dinner?"

"I thought three o'clock would be good. Ash said he'd get here around noon. We can all visit for a few hours. If things change, I'll call you."

"Three o'clock is fine. I'm looking forward to it. It was very nice of you to ask Devin. He was so touched. Philip is comfortable with it. So am I. I just wanted to thank you for that."

"I would do anything for you, Sallie," Fanny said, hugging her mother-in-law.

"I feel the same way. Enjoy the silence, and keep your fingers crossed that it continues."

"It's true," Fanny said. "Silence is golden."

"Amen."

Fanny broke into a sweat as she pulled on the rubber girdle. She stared in the mirror at the bulge of fat above her waistline. Nothing was going to make the twenty extra pounds go away except a diet. The dress Sallie had bought her was cleverly designed, but not enough to cover her offending stomach. The stitching under the bustline and the flowing sweep of the skirt, in her opinion, called attention to her oversize bosom and hinted that there was something she was hiding beneath the flowing skirt. In short, she looked dumpy. The only thing fashionable about her was her new haircut and her makeup. She wanted to cry. Ash was going to be disappointed in her. Even Sallie knew that.

"Fanny, we're here!" Bess trilled from the bottom of the steps.

"Come up, Bess. Tell John to make himself a drink."

"I came early in case you needed some help. I see that things are under control. What's wrong, Fanny, you look like you're going to cry any minute."

"Look at me, Bess. Do I look *anything* like the girl who went off to Hawaii on a moment's notice? Don't answer. I'm twenty pounds overweight. I feel like a cow. I never had thick ankles before. The weight is in all the wrong places. I couldn't get into that lacy underwear if I tried. This dress was the only one we could find that attempted to cover up my . . . deficiencies."

"Fanny, you had two baby boys. You gained sixty pounds. You

lost all the other weight, it's just slow coming off. By the first of the year you'll be back to normal. I wouldn't care at all if I looked like you. John doesn't want me to lose weight; he likes me just the way I am. Do you have any idea how happy that makes me feel? I know you'll be slim and trim in time to be my matron of honor in February. What I'm trying to say here, is, things work out. Trust me."

"Ash is going to be disappointed, Bess."

"Don't start to fret or you'll spoil the whole day. What time do you expect him?"

"He said around noon. It's almost that now. Tell me the truth, how do I look?"

"To me, Fanny, you look beautiful. You look like you're in love with your husband and two sons," Bess said loyally. "I'll go downstairs and sit with John. Finish what you have to do. Can I just peek in at the boys?"

"You can go into that room and beat a drum if you want. You can take them downstairs if you want. I set two cradles up in the living room. I want Ash to see them as soon as he gets here."

"Okay," Bess said agreeably. "I'm so jealous. I can't wait to have a baby."

"Don't do it right away, Bess."

"We're going to try right away. John loves children. He was so proud when you asked us to be godparents. Don't be nervous now. He's your husband, Fanny. Don't make Ash into something he isn't. I don't care if he is a major, and I don't care if the town is going to give him a parade when he gets out of the service. So there."

"So there, yourself." Fanny laughed.

Fanny literally jumped off the couch when she heard the door of Ash's taxi. Her face drained of all color. Should she run to the door? Should she stand in the foyer? Should she stand by the cradles? She looked around at her assembled guests who, as one, were making shooing motions toward the door. Throwing caution to the winds, Fanny ran to the door, Ash's name on her lips as she yanked it open.

Visored cap pushed back on his head, his necktie askew, his duffel over his shoulder, Major Ash Thornton could have posed for a military ad inviting young people to join up for the good of their country.

"Whoa, now that's what I call a greeting!"

If she hadn't been eyeball to eyeball with her husband, Fanny might not have seen the subtle change in Ash's eyes when he held her at arm's length for a better look. She wanted to cry when she felt a burst of warm wetness under her dress. Damn, the gauze pads she'd placed over her sore nipples weren't helping. In five minutes her brand-new dress was going to be soaked. Trying to make the best of it, she linked her arm in her husband's and marched him into the living room, where his mother and father were eagerly awaiting him. "I'll just be a minute," she said hoarsely as she exited the room. Only Bess saw the torment on her face. She followed her friend upstairs.

"What's wrong?"

"Everything's wrong, Bess," Fanny said, lifting the dress over her head. "Look, another minute and my dress would have been stained. Now, wouldn't that look nice!" Two minutes later, she had on fresh clothes. She fussed at her hair for a minute before she took a deep breath. "I saw his eyes, Bess; he couldn't hide what he was feeling. It was almost . . . almost revulsion. I saw it. Damn it, I saw it; he didn't even bother to hide it."

"Come on, you can't stay up here. If what you say is true, then your husband is a creep. Just for today. I don't mean he's a creep all the time. Guys are jerks for the most part, we all know that. Take it slow and easy, Fanny. You might be overreacting. As it is, you're missing Ash's first minutes with his new sons. Shit, why don't things ever work out right?" This was new for Bess; she never said so much as damn. Obviously, John Noble was influencing her life in many different ways.

"Smile, Fanny. Be charming. Talk up a storm. I'll only be an arm's length away."

"What do you think, Ash, do they look like you or me or both of us?" Fanny asked from the doorway.

"I can't decide," Ash said as he jiggled both babies. "I can't tell them apart. If you switched them up and took off their IDs, I wouldn't know them. This one is smiling, this one is frowning," he said, his voice full of awe. "They're little people. I thought babies cried all the time."

"They do cry all the time. They have cried steadily, night and day, for over two months. If it wasn't for your mother and Moon, I'd be in the loony bin. They aren't smiling and frowning; that's gas." Her voice was so flat and dead-sounding, the room grew silent.

"I prefer to think of it as a smile and a frown. What the eye sees is all that's important," Ash said lightly.

"I couldn't agree more," Fanny said. This time her voice was colder than ice. Bess nudged her arm.

"I refuse to pretend. He can't take that look back. I saw it. He just condemned himself with his own words," Fanny said out of the corner of her mouth.

"Dinner's ready," Sallie said, a desperate look in her eyes.

Bess reached for Sage and Fanny reached for Birch. "Go along everyone, we'll just take the babies upstairs to Moon," Fanny said lightly. Ash had no other choice but to relinquish his sons.

When the two young women returned to the dining room the others were waiting to say grace. Fanny took her place next to Sallie, directly across the table from Ash. Bess sat on her right. Philip folded his hands and offered up a simple prayer of thanksgiving as soon as everyone was seated. "I imagine this meal is going to taste very good, Ash. How's the food on the *Hornet?*"

"Pretty good as a matter of fact. Not as good as this, though," he said, filling his plate. "Did you cook any of this, honey?"

"Not one bit!" Fanny said cheerfully.

"Ash just told us he can't stay for the four days he was promised. He has to leave in the morning. He almost didn't make the flight that got him here," Sallie said as she turned to stare at Fanny with puzzled eyes.

"That's a shame," Fanny said, digging into a pile of mashed potatoes on her plate. "Oh, these are good. I guess I'm never going to take off this weight."

"Of course you will. You lost most of it already. I was the same way."

"Sallie's absolutely right. Sallie looked . . . *puffy* for some time."

"Thank you, Philip. I was not *puffy*. I was fat."

Ash looked first at his mother, then at his father. He turned to stare at Fanny. The realization that she was sitting next to his mother seemed to startle him. He could feel his face draining. It was uncanny how much alike they looked. He felt a chill run up his back. Both Mrs. Thorntons were staring at him, waiting for him to say something. "How much weight did you gain, honey?"

"Sixty-five pounds," Fanny said smartly.

"*Sixty-five pounds!*"

Fanny continued to shovel food into her mouth.

An ominous silence fell over the table.

"Tell us, Ash, what do you think of those robust sons of yours?" Devin said, trying to break the silence. Sallie's eyes thanked him.

"I think they're as handsome as their mother and father. When do they start doing things?"

"Any day now," Bess said.

"Like what?"

"You know, standing on their heads, climbing out of the crib, whistling, that kind of thing," Bess said. This man was going to break her best friend's heart, and there was nothing she could do to prevent it.

Sallie forced a laugh. "Bess is teasing you. For now they just eat, sleep, and cry. Around five or six months they *might* roll over and discover their hands and toes."

"You're going to miss that, Ash," Fanny said, reaching for her third dinner roll. She lobbed on a knife full of butter and stuffed it in her mouth. What in the world was wrong with her? So what if her husband looked shocked at her appearance. She herself was shocked each time she looked in the mirror.

"I'm sorry, everyone, this tension here at the table is all my fault. My weight isn't coming off as fast as I thought it would. The next time you see me, Major Ash Thornton, you better hold on to those wings on your blouse because I'm going to knock you for a loop. Please accept my apology, and let's just be a family enjoying dinner."

Sallie clapped her hands, as did everyone at the table. "That's my girl," she said.

"Is that what this is all about?" Ash demanded. "Honey, you look perfect to me. You could be dressed in rags with your hair in curlers and it would be okay. What's for dessert?"

Sallie stared across the table at her son. Philip lowered his gaze so his son wouldn't realize he heard the lie in his voice. Devin Rollins's eyes clearly said, you hurt my women, you answer to me. Ash understood Devin's silent message perfectly.

Fanny's guests excused themselves at six o'clock to allow the newlyweds time alone.

"You call me if anything goes wrong, John and I have the house to ourselves till my parents get back from Virginia," Bess hissed in her ear.

"Call me if there's anything I can do," Sallie whispered against Fanny's cheek.

"Give him a little room, Fanny. Fatherhood is a shock to any man," Philip murmured.

"You're as pretty, maybe prettier, than the first day I saw you at the drugstore. You know where to find me if you need me," Devin Rollins said.

When the door closed behind the last guest, Ash said, "What was all that whispering about?"

"Good wishes, that kind of thing. You look tired, Ash."

"So do you, honey. I wish I could sleep the clock around, but I can't. I have to be up and out of here by three-thirty in the morning. This is really a nice house. Big rooms. Mom always liked big rooms. The bigger the room, the more furniture you have to have. I can see why you have to have all that help. I don't make enough money for all that, Fanny. You're going to have to cut back. We can't keep taking money from my mother; it isn't right."

"I know, Ash. I tried to say no. She insisted. As soon as I can get a routine, a system of some kind, I'll let all the help go. The twins wear me down, Ash. If I get sick, who's going to take care of the boys? I need your mother now because I realize my limitations. I learned a long time ago that you should never fool yourself. We have to settle this now between us so that it doesn't start to fester."

"You're right, Fanny. I want what's best for you. My head must have been in the clouds, no pun intended. We haven't had much of a marriage, have we? I'll make it all up to you when I get out. Let's sit on the couch for a little while and have some coffee and brandy. I want to hear all about my sons and what you've been doing. Ring that damn bell for some service. As long as we have it we might as well use it."

It was nine o'clock when Fanny and Ash climbed the steps to their room. "This is pretty," Ash said, looking around. Did you decorate it, or did my mother do it?"

"I did it. I picked out all the colors. I tried to use neutral tones so you wouldn't think it was a woman's room. You're going to sleep here, too. The boys were here for a while in the beginning, but I didn't think that was a good idea, so I moved them to their own room."

"Commendable. Let's go to bed, Mrs. Thornton."

"I thought you'd never ask."

"This is a lot different from that shack on the beach. I liked it though. I don't think I'm ever going to forget that," Ash said as he nuzzled her neck.

"I loved it. Coming home on the plane I thought I could live there forever if you were with me."

"You can't live in paradise all year long. It's just a place to visit. That's why they call it paradise. I know what you mean, though. Look, Fanny, about before, if I did something or said something . . .

I'm sorry. One minute you were fine and the next you turned to ice. Tell me what I said or did, so I make sure I don't do it again."

Fanny started to cry. "It was the way you looked at me. I looked at myself the same way, but when I saw myself through your eyes, I got angry. I'm sorry. I meant it when I said the next time you see me I'll look like the old me. Half the battle will be over when the boys start sleeping through the night."

"Shuck those clothes, Mrs. Thornton. Speed is of the essence."

Fanny froze. "I'll use the bathroom," she muttered.

"Okay, but don't take forever. I've waited for this day for a long time."

"Me too," she managed to murmur.

In the bathroom, Fanny took off her clothes. It was all she could do not to yelp when she removed the gauze pads from her nipples. Ash wasn't going to understand this. She wrapped one of the large bath towels around her and took a deep breath.

Fanny shed the towel and slipped between the sheets, thanking God as she did so for only the night-light Ash had left on. Did he turn off the lights on purpose so he wouldn't have to look at her body? They'd made love in broad daylight, in the bright sunshine on the beach. They'd left the lights on in the shack, too. The desire she felt for her husband dissipated. It surfaced again when Ash kissed her, his tongue searching and seizing her own as his knee pried her legs apart. He was inside, exploding a moment later. He rolled over, gasping with his exertion. "I couldn't wait. It's all I've been thinking about for days. We'll do it your way in a few minutes. Don't be angry with me. I wanted you so bad I could taste it."

"It's okay," Fanny whispered. "Why don't you sleep now and when you wake, if we want we can . . ."

"Don't let me sleep too long. I have to be out of here by three-thirty at the latest." A second later he was snoring lightly, and Fanny was crying into her pillow. Finally, she too slept.

Shortly after midnight, Fanny was jerked to wakefulness by her husband's body spooning against hers. She did what was expected—she squeezed her thighs hard against her husband's manhood. He moaned with pleasure as he flipped her over. "Get on top of me and do what you did back in Hawaii, ride me like a stallion."

It was a replay of their time in paradise, right down to the part where Ash rolled her over, mounting her, snorting and snarling as he pounded into her. Suddenly she found herself on her side, her husband facing her, "That's what you like, isn't it?" he rasped. She saw his head coming down, saw his mouth open, knew his intent, but she wasn't quick enough to pull and slide away from him.

"What the hell! Jesus, Fanny, what . . . ?" A moment later the bright bedside light came on. "And you were going to let me . . . Jesus Christ!" Fanny felt her own milk splatter over her neck and face. If there was a way for her to die right then and there, Fanny would have opted for death. Instead she tried to grind herself into the mattress and pillows beneath her. She struggled for the sheet and pulled it up to her chin. Ash ripped it away. The naked revulsion she saw on his face made Fanny squeeze her eyes shut. "You're still nursing those babies! When you wrote and told me that, I thought you meant for a week or so." He made it sound like she'd suckled the Devil. "Jesus, the bed is all wet."

"You don't just nurse a baby for a week, Ash. They're on a bottle now, but they have to be weaned slowly. It isn't easy."

"This is 1944, not the Dark Ages. No one forced you to do this to yourself. That's why they make baby bottles. My own mother gave me a bottle, and that was twenty years ago. Jesus, Fanny, every time I think of you I'm going to envision those two babies hanging off . . . I can't handle this. I have to get out of here."

A hundred things flashed through Fanny's mind. Nasty things, explanations, pleas for understanding. She cowered beneath the covers, listening to the sounds of the shower. She wanted to reach out and turn off the light, but she didn't.

Thirty minutes later, Ash exited the bathroom, fully dressed. From the doorway he stared at his wife. "I know I'm probably wrong. Tomorrow or the next day I'll no doubt regret this . . . this . . . whatever it is. I'm sure my expectations were . . . are . . . I expected . . . wanted . . . I need some time to . . . I don't know, I just need time. Maybe we needed to know each other a little . . . I'm confused. I'll write, Fanny."

Fanny lay as still as a statue. Surely this wasn't happening to her. But it was. Her husband was walking out on her because . . . because she nursed her babies. Because she'd gained too much weight. Because they didn't know each other well enough. From somewhere, deep within her, she found the guts to say, "Don't bother."

He was almost to the doorway when he turned and said, "What?"

"You heard me. I said, don't bother to write."

"Okay, if that's the way you want it, I won't. What are you going to do now, call my mother and cry on her shoulder?"

"It doesn't really matter, does it?"

"No, I guess it doesn't."

Fanny closed her eyes as she waited for the door to slam. Instead, it closed so quietly, she had to strain her eyes in the darkness to see that her husband had really left.

13
⁓

Fanny looked at the bedside clock: 6:00 A.M. She lit a cigarette and stared at the messy ashtray. It looked disgusting. The bed looked disgusting, the room looked disgusting. She knew *she* looked disgusting sitting here, huddled in bed like some pariah. Men walked out on their wives every day of the week. Women walked out on their husbands every day of the week. "No matter what, I would never do that," Fanny muttered around a cloud of cigarette smoke. Who *was* that man in bed with her saying those terrible things at two-thirty in the morning? She crushed out her cigarette and fired up another one. So, he wasn't going to write. Well, tough noogies; she wasn't going to write either.

Moon appeared in the doorway, Birch in her arms. Fanny shook her head. "Give him a bottle." Moon nodded. Had she heard Ash's sharp words, heard him leave? Did it matter?

Fanny reached for the phone. "Bess, I want to go Christmas shopping. I want you to go with me. Please?"

"Sure. We'll go in an hour. What happened? Don't leave anything out, I'm your friend, Fanny. I'm on your side, and I can be objective, so don't be embarrassed."

Fanny told her.

"You aren't crying, why is that? Did you cry after he left?"

"No. I guess I was too numb to cry. I'll tell you all about it. Let me get cleaned up and I'll walk over to your house. How does ten o'clock sound?"

"Ten o'clock is fine with me. You're sure you're okay, Fanny?"

"No, I'm not okay. I need some time to . . . I just need some time. Bess, do you think the hurt will ever go away?"

"Time heals everything, Fanny. There might be a scar or two, but time will heal. It's the best I can offer."

"You're such a good friend, Bess. I'll see you in a little while."

It was well past the dinner hour when Fanny returned home. She checked on her sleeping sons, changed her clothes, pumped her milk, and took the second pill John had given her to help dry it up. As John had said, his face full of compassion, the healing process was under way.

At nine o'clock the phone rang. Fanny tripped over her own feet in her rush to get to it. Maybe it was Ash. It was Sallie.

"Fanny, how are you? How are things with the twins? Are they adapting to the bottles?"

"I'm fine, Sallie. The boys are doing just fine, they only cry when they're hungry or need to be changed. They gobble down the bottle and go right back to sleep. If it hadn't been for you, my sons would still be wailing. I feel so stupid."

"Don't be so hard on yourself, darling. These things happen. Did Ash get off all right? Was it as wonderful as you expected. Forget I asked that, it's none of my business. Wait till you hear this, Fanny. My brother Seth and Billie and her mother are coming to Nevada for Christmas. Actually, they'll arrive Christmas Eve. I cannot believe it. Billie can't wait to meet you. She said the two of you have had some wonderful conversations over the phone. She sounded really excited. That's really why I'm calling. I did try calling earlier, but Yee said you'd gone out with Bess. I'm glad you're getting out and about. There is a world outside the house."

"I decided that I would love to go to Sunrise over the holidays if the invitation is still open. Will you have enough room for everyone?"

"Of course. If there isn't, I can always sleep in the schoolroom. Peggy and her husband Steve will be joining us. She's finally agreed to move permanently to Nevada. She liked the freedom of going back and forth to her little house in Texas, but as Steve says, she's a political wife now. I wish Ash and Simon could make it, but I'm afraid this is going to be another Christmas without them. Someday Sunrise will be yours, so it's fitting that the twins spend their first Christmas there. Do you feel that way, Fanny?"

"Very much so. I'm looking forward to the holidays."

"Now that you have house help we can shop till Christmas. It will be so much fun. I'll let you go, sweetie. Sleep well."

"Thanks for calling, Sallie. Have a nice evening."

From long months of habit, Fanny sat down at the desk in her room and wrote a letter to Ash—a letter she would not mail. She poured out her heart on the paper, her eyes dry, her heart sore and bruised. When she finished, she folded the letter and stuck it under the blotter on the desk. Her hand reached for the phone. It was time to talk to Billie Coleman. She placed the call.

"It's Fanny, Billie. Is this too late to be calling you? I need to talk to someone."

"Not at all. Something's wrong, I can hear it in your voice. I'm listening, Fanny. Take your time, I have all night. Maggie is asleep and I was just sitting here reading."

"How are you feeling?"

Billie laughed. "Like I'm six months pregnant, which I am. Most of the time I'm miserable and sick. Seth growls and my mother hovers. They want a boy so bad. I can't tell you how excited I am that we're coming to see you over the holidays. I'm counting the days. Oh, Fanny, it was a battle royal, but I won. I just up and told them I was going, with or without them. Amelia is coming too, I insisted on that. You're going to love her. Seth has been so brutal to her. He disowned her, can you believe that? I want to cry for her, but she's tough. I wish I was more like that. I hate living here, Fanny, I really do."

"Oh, Billie, I wish you were here. All Sallie could do was talk about you after her trip to Texas. Maybe she can get your father-in-law to turn around. I can't wait to see you and your little girl."

The conversation went on for hours. When Fanny hung up at midnight, she felt more like her old self. She knew she would sleep. Billie Coleman had that rare ability to say the right thing at the right time, no matter how miserable she herself was feeling.

Fanny dropped to her knees to say her evening prayers. "Please, God, look after my family and keep them safe. If it's possible, allow Ash to . . . to . . . get over what he feels. It would be a help if you'd let Billie feel a little better. Thank you, God, for hearing my prayer."

Fanny slept deeply and dreamlessly for the first time in eleven months.

"Philip, how terrible! When are you leaving? Are you sure you don't want me to go with you? I will, you know. I know how much you loved your brother. How sad that he should pass away at this time of year."

"Sallie, I appreciate the offer, but you need to be here with Fanny and the boys. Your brother and his family are coming. It's not as though you ever knew my brother."

"I feel like I do, Philip. You talked about him so much. I don't like you going alone."

"Do we need another lesson in Philip Thornton's logic? Isn't it better for one person to be sad than a whole family? Of course it is. Sallie, it's okay, really it is. I wouldn't have much time to spend with you. I'm going to be busy with my brother's family. There are going to be many things I have to see to. I think I'll be gone for at least a month. Promise me you won't worry about me. I'll call when things are under control."

"Philip, are you sure?"

"I'm sure."

"Are you leaving now?"

"Yes. I was lucky to get a seat, this is the holidays, but when I explained the circumstances, they managed to get me on the first available flight. Have a wonderful holiday. Red will drop my gifts off tomorrow. Thanks for inviting her, Sallie."

"The more the merrier. Take care of yourself, Philip."

Philip kissed her lightly, drinking in the scent of her, savoring her soft, gentle lips on his own. "Merry Christmas, Sallie."

"Merry Christmas, Philip," Sallie said with a catch in her voice. "If the boys call, I'll tell them to call you in Boston." Philip nodded.

Sallie watched from the window until Philip's cab was out of sight.

Sunrise hummed with activity as the huge evergreen was brought into the middle of the living room. "No corner this year. I want us all to see every inch of it."

"That's the funniest thing you've ever said, Sallie." Fanny laughed. "There are so many presents, you can't get within two feet of it. I don't think I've ever seen a more beautiful tree. However did you get all these presents, Sallie?"

Sallie laughed. "It wasn't easy. As the days started to dwindle, I called stores, told them what I wanted, and they delivered. Christmas is the only time I'm glad I'm rich. I love to give. How are your driving lessons going, Fanny?"

"They aren't. I'm going to start again after New Year's. You have more faith in my ability than I do, Sallie. I get very jittery behind the wheel."

"That's normal at first. If I can do it, so can you. Joseph was an excellent teacher. Stay on after the New Year and Chue will teach you. He loves to drive. He's a little bossy, but a good teacher."

"Maybe I will. I love it up here. I need to talk to you, Sallie, about all the help. I can't let you keep paying for everything."

"I want to do it, Fanny. It makes me happy to be able to help. I don't want you to have to struggle. I did enough of that to last this family a lifetime. Please, Fanny, let me do this for you, Ash, and the boys. It will make life so much easier for all of you. Take a minute, close your eyes, and try to picture what your life would be like without Moon and the others. Now, open your eyes and tell me what you saw."

"Total disaster. I accept. I'm so grateful, Sallie. Ash will have to . . . come to terms with it."

"Have you heard from him?"

"Not since he left. Not even a Christmas card. He might call if he can get leave, but I'm not counting on it."

"It's going to be a wonderful Christmas. We're all going to be together. What time is it, Fanny?"

"Eight o'clock. They're just a little late."

Sallie's eyes lit up as she smiled from ear to ear. "I hear Devin in the kitchen. He must have come in the back way. Excuse me, Fanny."

Ash, where are you, what are you doing? Are you remembering this time last year? Are you thinking about me? Fanny's eyes filled. That was another time, another place.

When Fanny saw the headlights arc on the living room wall, she ran to the door and threw it open. Billie's name on her lips carried into the crisp star-filled night.

"Fanny! I'd run, but all I can do is waddle."

"I can run," Fanny shouted as she raced across the lawn to the driveway. "I've been waiting all day for you to get here." She hugged Billie as best she could, careful not to press hard on her protruding stomach. "We have so much to talk about. We'll do it later in my room after everyone goes to sleep. My manners are terrible. Mrs. Ames, I'm Fanny Thornton. Mr. Coleman, it's so nice to meet you. And this sleeping cherub must be Maggie. Please, come into the house, it's cold out here. Chue will carry Maggie upstairs if you want to put her to bed. I'll help while the rest of the family gets acquainted," Fanny said, her arms around Billie's shoulders.

"Seth!" Sallie called from the doorway. "Merry Christmas! I'm so glad you could come. You too, Mrs. Ames. Where's Amelia?"

"She couldn't make it," Seth said gruffly.

"Not true," Billie whispered to Fanny. "I'll tell you about it later."

Chue, with Maggie in his arms, led the way up the steps, Fanny and Billie behind him.

Sallie ushered her guests into the huge living room, her eyes amused as Agnes Ames visually cataloged everything in the house with dollar signs. Sallie knew she was comparing each stick of furniture, each painting, each article of clothing on her body, as well as her jewelry, dollar for dollar.

"You have a lovely home, Mrs. Thornton," Mrs. Ames said.

"Please call me Sallie."

"Then you must call me Agnes."

"Call her Aggie. I do," Seth said in his gravel voice.

"Your tree is gorgeous," Agnes said.

"Grown and cut right here on the property," Sallie said.

"How many acres is this spread?" Seth asked.

"Acres? I don't think I'd call it a spread. I own the mountain. To answer your question, I guess I'd have to say I don't know. Tomorrow when it's light you might be able to make a judgment."

"You *own* the whole mountain?" Agnes purred.

"Yes," Sallie smiled. "I'm remiss, let me introduce you to everyone. This is Peggy, your sister. She looks like Pop, don't you think? And you, too. This handsome man standing next to her is her husband, Steven Lawton, the lieutenant governor of Nevada. This is Red Ruby, a personal friend of mine, and this sweet young woman is Akia, Chue's wife. This is Su Li and her husband Teke; both are doctors. Philip isn't here. His brother died, and he had to go to Boston. And, last but not least, this is Devin Rollins, my attorney and friend. The two of you have been corresponding for months now. Everyone, this is Agnes Ames and my brother Seth. Now, what would you all like to drink?"

"Whiskey," Seth said. "A double. Aggie here will have one of those pink blossom things."

Agnes's snoot rose. "Actually, Seth, I'd prefer a double scotch." Her smile was arrogant, an I-guess-I-told-you smile. Sallie thought of barracudas and sharks.

Sallie stepped aside so that her sister Peggy and her husband could greet Seth. She signaled Su Li to offer Agnes a tour of the house, which Agnes readily accepted.

"Where's your office, girl?" Seth demanded. Sallie ignored the question, knowing full well that he was talking to her. Even when he raised his voice and spoke a second time, she ignored him. She had a name.

"Sallie?"

"Yes, Seth," Sallie said sweetly.

"Do you keep an office here in the house?"

"Yes, it's off the kitchen. Would you like to see it?"

"I would, before this whiskey takes hold of my gut."

"Follow me then," Sallie said, leading the way out of the living room, through the dining room, and on out to the kitchen where dinner preparations were under way.

"Is something wrong, Seth? Is it something to do with your son Moss?"

"No, nothing like that."

"He's going to stay safe. You need to have a little more faith. I think you're scaring Billie out of her wits. She's vulnerable right now and she's picking up your negative thoughts. If you aren't careful, she could miscarry. Moss will make it."

"Why in the hell is it that every damn fool woman in the world says exactly the same thing? I love that boy. He's all I got." His voice was hoarse and gruff, almost apologetic.

"Because *every damn fool woman* never gives up until the last second, and even then we keep hoping. I'm at a loss as to why fathers don't think the same way," Sallie said.

Seth snorted. He reached into the breast pocket of his red flannel shirt and handed Sallie a slip of paper. "It's your check. I never cashed it. I was testing you."

Sallie stared at the folded check. "Testing me? For what?"

"To see if you were running off at the mouth or if you had the money to back up my request. I called the bank to verify the amount of money. They were more than willing to cash the check."

Sallie stared at her brother. "I don't mind anything you just said. I don't even mind that you want to give the check back, and I certainly don't mind that you verified the check at the bank. What I do mind is that you're lying to me by saying you were testing me. You need that money desperately. Therefore, I don't understand why you're returning the check. Is it because I'm a woman and your sister? Do you resent it that I'm better off than you are? Why don't we let our hair down and be honest with each other. We're in a closed room, no one can hear, and I do not talk about family business to other people. Whatever we say in this room will stay in this room."

Seth's bushy eyebrows drew together to form a straight line

across his brow. He finger-combed his hair for a few seconds, but never responded.

"I understand," Sallie said softly, her hand with the check extended. "Is there anything else I can do for you? You just have to ask, Seth. Asking isn't all that hard. Who knows, the day might come when I need your help. I'd like to know I can count on you. That's all there is to it. One last thing, Seth; I'd like Billie to stay on for a while. I'll make sure she gets home safe and sound even if I have to drive her myself. She'll be good company for Fanny. Fanny will be good for Billie. It will be nice to have Maggie here, toddling around. However, you can take the barracuda back with you."

Seth snorted with laughter, doubling over and slapping at his knees. In between snorts of laughter, he managed to say, "See you got Aggie pegged."

"You could say that."

"I don't see a problem if the girl wants to stay. She gets on my nerves with all that whimpering and whining. She's not robust. I never expected my only son to marry a sickly girl like this one. Fair makes me want to puke."

"You did. Marry a frail young woman, I mean. That's the funny thing about love. All women aren't broodmares. Thank God for that. There's a saying, Seth, that sons follow in their father's footsteps."

"Smart-ass woman," Seth growled.

"I know you mean that as a compliment, so that's how I'm going to take it. Put the check in your pocket and let's get back to our guests." Impulsively, Sallie reached out to her brother, and hugged him. "That was for Mama. So's this," she said, kissing him on the cheek.

There was no displeasure on Seth's face when he said, "Women, all they want to do is kiss and snuggle and wrap their arms around you. At the end, did . . . Ma . . . did Ma have all her curls piled high on her head like a princess?" He looked away as he waited for his sister's reply.

Sallie heard the choked-back sob in his voice, but pretended she didn't. "She did, Seth, she truly did," Sallie lied with a straight face.

"That's how I want to remember Ma. What's for supper? Don't like eating this late, gives me indigestion."

"Don't worry about a thing. My housekeeper has an herb for everything. If you want to sleep like a baby, just let me know. We're having fresh game hens with all the trimmings. For those who don't like game hens, we're having prime ribs, and everything that goes with beef."

They were almost to the door when Seth said, "Tell me true, girl, and swear on Ma, do you really feel my boy will be safe?"

"Oh, Seth, I do. I truly do. I pray every night. Fanny tells me she does, too. God always listens to women's prayers. I bet you didn't know that, Seth."

"You probably made that up," Seth muttered.

"Do you think we're on good enough terms for me to ask a favor of you."

"Damnation, I knew there was a catch. What is it?"

"Talk to Peggy. Talk to her like she's your sister, and you're her brother. She also needs a sense of family. I'd be very grateful."

"You try the patience of a saint, girl."

Sallie beamed her pleasure.

"Oh, Fanny, how beautiful your sons are. They look like little cherubs." Billie patted her stomach. "I'm hoping for a boy this time, but it feels like a girl. Seth wants a boy so bad. I think part of it is if Moss . . . if Moss doesn't make it back . . . there will be a son to carry on the name. I honestly think if this child turns out to be another girl, he's going to want to give it back. I never saw such desperation. I wish I was back in Philadelphia. He's so . . . so controlling, and Moss always took his side. They treat me like . . . I'm slow-witted. My mother, too. She's aligned herself with Seth. I hate to say this about my own mother, but she's on *their* side. It's all that money. She really thinks she belongs and Seth allows her to think like that. I'm an outsider, Fanny. I'm always going to be an outsider, unless I produce an heir to the Coleman dynasty, in which case they might let me stand on the porch and look through the window. Women simply don't count for anything in that family."

Fanny leaned over the crib Maggie was sleeping in. "Not even this sweet little thing?"

"Seth ignores her. My own mother goes into the nursery once a week or so. She's turned into Seth's right hand. She's got a certain amount of control, and she loves it. She's not going to jeopardize that position. Now do you understand what I meant when I said I have no one?"

Fanny put her arms around Billie's shoulders. "You have me and Sallie. If there's a way to put it right, she'll know how to do it. Why didn't Amelia come with you?"

"Seth wouldn't allow it. She's here from England with her step-son. He's the sweetest little boy, and she loves him dearly. Seth calls him a brat. He's not. He's quiet, well-mannered, and he adores

Amelia. His father was killed. Seth says such cruel things to Amelia. He calls her a slut, a whore, and all because she stood up to him all her life. She wasn't . . . loose. She told me she wasn't, and I believe her. They hate each other. He said she couldn't get a man in Texas, so she had to go to England to get one with a snotty kid. She drove a Red Cross ambulance. Seth said there was no room in the car because I'm so fat, and he wasn't making the trip with a squalling kid. That was the end of it. I cried, Amelia cried, and he turned a deaf ear."

"No, that *isn't* the end of it. Wait right here. Don't move!"

Fanny sprinted down the hall to the back stairway that led to the kitchen. "Fetch Miss Sallie back here right away," she whispered to one of the cooks. "Tell her to come upstairs right away."

"What can I do?" Devin asked, entering the room five minutes later.

"Find a way to get my niece and her little boy here for Christmas morning," Sallie said breathlessly.

"Is that all?"

"How, Devin? What do you mean is that all?"

"Sallie, you are the richest woman in this state, probably the bordering states, too. All we have to do is charter a plane."

A few minutes later, Devin said, "Call your niece and tell her to skedaddle to the airport, the plane is waiting. Tell her not to take the time to pack. You can buy her whatever she needs when she gets here. Do you have presents for the little boy?"

"We'll repackage after everyone goes to bed, right girls?"

"Oh yes," both Fanny and Billie said in unison.

"After dinner I'll go to the airport and wait. I'll bring them in the back way and up the kitchen stairwell. You need to get back downstairs, Sallie."

"Seth is going to . . . Seth will . . ."

"Find out what it's like when someone else takes control," Billie said softly. "He'll have to live with it, won't he?"

"Either that or he's going to leave in the morning."

"Without me and Amelia," Billie said smartly. "I might just stay here forever. I never felt so welcome anyplace in my life."

"Thirty minutes till dinner. Devin is right, we have to get back downstairs. Call Amelia. This man is my white knight in shining armor," Sallie said, leading Devin by the hand.

Fanny turned to Billie. "Hurry up, call Amelia. Good God, I am so excited. What's your father-in-law going to do come morning?"

Billie laughed. "I can't wait to see his reaction. My mother will blame me. So will Seth. Who cares?" Billie said, picking up the telephone.

"Who's Sally Dearest?" Fanny asked when Billie finished the call.

"Amelia's son Rand's stuffed cat. He carried it all through the war. He never puts it down. It was the last thing his mother gave him. She was caught in one of the first bomb blasts."

"Sallie is going to love that name. Time to freshen up and go downstairs. Bright lipstick, Billie, this is Christmas. Some rouge too."

Tears welled in Billie's eyes. "I love him so much, Fanny. My heart is so full of that love, there are times when I feel like I can't breathe. My love for Moss is strangling me, and I know he doesn't love me in the same way. I wish I could turn it off or tone it down, but I can't. If something happens to him . . ."

"You will be strong and do what every other wife does, you will take care of your family and go on, one day at a time. I hope this family dinner goes fast, so we can spend the night talking. Hurry, Billie."

"This is as fast as I move these days. I can't wait till I can see my toes."

Sallie kept the conversation moving during dinner, as did Agnes, whose main contribution was to ask questions. Several times Devin chopped her off at the knees, winking at her as he did so, saying, "Now, those are business secrets, Agnes, and way above your beautiful head."

"That's a polite way of saying it's none of your business, Aggie," Seth growled.

"My apologies," Agnes said. "It's natural curiosity on my part. I'd never been outside Philadelphia until I got to Texas. Nevada intrigues me."

"You could read a travel book, Mother," Billie said.

"And I have one I'll be glad to lend you, Mrs. Ames," Fanny said.

"Shouldn't you be checking on your daughter?" Seth said pointedly to Billie.

"Oh, she doesn't have to do that. Moon has everything under control. Billie is here for a visit and a rest. We're going to spend our time getting to know one another. Isn't that what this visit is all about, Seth, your family and my family?" Sallie said, a huge smile on her face.

"Tomorrow we can do that. I'm heading off to bed if you'll show me where it is. Merry Christmas everyone. Aggie?"

"It's too early for bed, Seth. I plan on having some plum pudding." Seth scowled at her, but headed for the steps, where Khee was waiting to show him to his room. She bowed respectfully before she picked up his heavy bag.

"Seth goes to bed early because he rises early," Agnes said.

"And when he doesn't get his way. Be fair, Mother," Billie said.

"He has a lot on his mind," Agnes said defensively.

"So does everyone else sitting at this table. Aunt Sallie's two sons are flying missions every day just the way Moss does, and Fanny hasn't heard from her husband in a month. We're all coping, we aren't blaming anyone and making everyone around us miserable," Billie said.

"I couldn't have said it better, Billie," Sallie said.

Agnes had the good sense to look embarrassed. She clamped her mouth shut, her eyes everywhere but on Sallie.

Fanny turned to Billie. She mouthed the words, "Good for you." Billie smiled from ear to ear.

"We'll have coffee and brandy in the living room, sing a few Christmas carols, say our Christmas prayer that Simon, Ash, and Moss return home safely as well as every other mother's son fighting this war. We'll admire the tree and go to bed with sugarplums dancing in our heads to await Santa's arrival. I want to thank all of you for coming to share the holiday," Sallie said.

"Good night, Mother," Billie said. She leaned into Sallie's open arm. There was nothing for Agnes to do but head up the stairs.

Sallie flopped down on the sofa next to Billie. "I don't think I've ever spent a Christmas where there wasn't some sort of stress or tension. I expect holidays bring out the best and the worst of most people. I want you to know I am prepared for Seth and your mother to leave in the morning when they see Amelia and her son. I can handle that, Billie, but can you?"

"I have to handle it. Moss loves Amelia, and Amelia loves him. He knows how awful his father is to her. He tries to make it up, but he can't. Moss's mother was always a buffer between Amelia and her father, but she's gone now. Amelia's here in the States to . . . to . . . to get an abortion. I'm sure she'll tell you herself, it's not my place. She's going to need you, Aunt Sallie. She knows . . . someone who has agreed to do it for a great deal of money. She's so frail and fragile right now. Oh, I wish Moss was home."

"Soon, Billie. Listen, I have an idea. Why don't you lie down here on the sofa and take a little nap. While you're snoozing, Fanny and I can rewrap some of the presents to make sure Rand and Amelia have gifts to open."

"I have all the wrapping paper and new ribbon," Fanny said. "Two pairs of scissors."

When they were finished they had trucks, cars, blocks, a pair of roller skates, books, games, a bright red sweater with matching red cap, and a stocking filled with candies, nuts, and oranges for the little boy. For Amelia there was a cashmere sweater set with matching scarf, leather gloves, an alligator handbag with matching belt, a pair of pearl earrings, a peignoir set that was little more than lacy cobwebs stitched together, delightful French perfume, and several new novels.

Sallie leaned back, a glass of wine in her hand. "Merry Christmas, Fanny. I hope we have many, many more. It's Christmas Day. I wonder where my sons are. Dear God, I hope they're alive and well. Moss too."

"Of course they are. How could they be anything less with a mother like you? Wherever they are, I'm sure they're thinking about home and family. You have to think positive. I do; that's the only way I can get through this."

"Put your coat on, Fanny. I have something to show you."

Fanny followed Sallie out into the night air. "It's beautiful, isn't it? Everything is crystal clear. Sometimes I wish I was a child again, knowing what I know today. Come, come, before we freeze."

"Is it a secret?" Fanny asked, her teeth chattering.

"It was." Sallie threw open the door of the garage and turned on the light. "One for you and one for Billie."

"Oh," was all Fanny could say.

"It's a Buick Roadster. I thought you would like yellow because, like me, you like sunshine in your life. I thought Billie would like it too."

"What would Billie like?" Billie said from the open doorway. "I'm sorry, am I intruding? I woke and heard you leave by the back door and thought Amelia was here."

"Of course you're not intruding. I was showing Fanny her Christmas present. Now, you can see yours. Do you like it?"

"I can't drive," both young women said at the same time.

"I rather thought Amelia and you might want to drive back to Texas when you leave. After you have the baby you can take driving lessons. You can take Maggie and go for drives and not have to be dependent on Seth or your mother. Fanny can learn right here when she's ready. Do you like the colors? I picked yellow because it reminds me of sunshine."

"Oh, my goodness. I never, ever thought I'd have a car of my very own. How can I ever thank you?"

"You already have. All I wanted was to see your smile."

"Sallie, I don't know what to say. Thank you doesn't seem to be enough."

"It's enough. You two need to go back in the house now. I want to walk over to the cemetery and visit. I always do that on Christmas Eve. The time got away from me this last evening."

"Seth buried his horse in the family plot. Then he buried his wife right next to the horse," Billie said. "He said when he dies he's going to be buried on the other side of the horse."

All Sallie could do was shake her head. "I don't know why that doesn't surprise me. Merry Christmas to both of you."

"Do you have any idea how lucky you are, Fanny Thornton?" Billie said wistfully. "Wait till my mother sees this car. Her eyes are going to pop right out of her head."

"Before or after she sees Amelia?" Fanny asked. Both women burst out laughing and were still giggling like schoolgirls when Sallie returned to the garage.

"I saw headlights from down below," she said. "I think it's Devin. Come, come, we're going to freeze standing here. They'll be another ten minutes. We can make some coffee and prepare some food. I imagine Amelia will be starving, and I know a thing or two about little boys. I imagine Rand will want some sweets."

Arm in arm, the three women walked to the house. "You really do waddle, Billie. Did I look like that, Sallie?"

"Worse. But, look at you now, Fanny."

In the kitchen, Sallie made coffee and thick sandwiches. Fanny heated Khee's famous chicken soup while Billie cut pie and cake. "I hear the car!" Billie said, struggling up from the kitchen chair. "I'm so glad you did this, Aunt Sallie."

She was tall and thin with tired, weary eyes, a Coleman through and through. A smile warmed her features the moment she saw Billie. "I know I have you to thank for this."

"Welcome to Sunrise, Amelia," Sallie said, opening her arms to the frail young woman. Amelia burst into tears as she stepped into the warm embrace. "Yes, it was Billie's idea. I'm ashamed to admit that I didn't think of it. You're much too thin. Before you leave here, you will have meat on your bones. Smile, you're with people who love you dearly. That will never change, I want you to know that. Now, introduce me to this little fellow. And to the critter in his arms.

"I'm Rand Nelson. And this is Sally Dearest," the little boy said, extending his hand. Sallie shook it solemnly.

"And a remarkable cat it is. I can see that from here."

"He's ... pre ... precious," the little boy said. "Is Santa Claus going to know I'm here? Did he come yet?"

"Not till you have something to eat and go to sleep. When you wake up you'll find presents under the tree. He followed you all the way from England." Sallie smiled.

"Smashing!"

"I'd like to put him to bed, if it's all right," Devin said, when Rand's head started to droop into his ice cream and cake. "Where, Sallie?"

"Is it all right if he sleeps in your room on a cot, Amelia?"

"More than all right. The poor baby has awful nightmares. I like to be close to him."

"Of course you do. Let's finish up here, Khee will clean up in the morning. Fanny, draw a bath for Amelia. I laid out clothes for her. A cup of Khee's special tea along with a few drops of brandy will make you feel like a new person."

A second later, Amelia felt herself swooped into a pair of strong arms and carried upstairs. "Who *is* this wonderful person?" Amelia asked wearily.

Sallie looked at Billie and said softly, "My reason for living."

"*That*, I understand."

Devin set Amelia down by the bathroom door. He steadied her with one strong arm before he let her go. "I imagine you ladies are going to chitter and chat for the remainder of the evening, so if my services aren't needed, I think I'll retire. Call me if you need me."

"He reminds me of Geoff," Amelia said. "Kind and gentle. I felt comfortable with him the minute I saw him. Geoff was like that. I like the smile in his voice. It reaches his eyes. That means he's a good, kind person. Someday I'd like to hear how he fits into the family."

"Why not right now?" Sallie said, perching on the edge of the tub. "He's my lover, my reason for wanting to wake to a new day. He makes me laugh and he can make me cry. He cares about everyone and everything. You're right, there's always a smile in his voice and yes, it reaches his eyes. If I said I wanted the moon, he'd try and find a way to get it for me and he'd wrap it in the stars. Devin is always there, that one-of-a-kind friend you can depend on no matter what. He doesn't judge, but accepts you for who and what you are. I never said that out loud. To anyone. I guess I want all of you to know who I am. I don't want any pretenses with my new family. It's not something I consciously try to hide. Everyone in town knows. For Philip's sake I try to be discreet. He knows. You also need to know I will never divorce Philip. Devin knows that, and so does Philip. Goodness, such a heavy conversation for Christmas morning."

"Billie, are you comfortable sitting on that tufted vanity bench?"

"If it's all right with you, I think I'll go in on your chaise. I think it's time to put my feet up."

The phone took that moment to peal. The women stared at one another, naked fear on their faces. Sallie was the first to move, and then she ran to her room, Fanny right behind her. Did the War Department, or whoever it was that called with bad news, call in the middle of the night?

"It's nothing, Fanny. I know it's nothing. It's probably a wrong number." Sallie rubbed her hands together nervously before she picked up the phone. She worked her tongue around the dryness in her mouth before she could even manage a strangled, hello. She looked up to see Devin standing in the doorway. "Hello," she said more firmly.

"Mom, it's Ash. Merry Christmas."

"Ash! Oh, Ash, it's so good to hear your voice. Merry Christmas, son. Your father isn't here, he had to go to Boston. His brother died. Fanny's standing right here next to me. I'll put her right on."

Sallie tactfully withdrew to the hallway, where Devin was standing. They both heard Billie say, "I won't listen, I'll turn to the wall, it's too much trouble to get up."

Sallie sighed. One minute she was talking to her son, hearing his voice, and the next minute he was gone. Tears filled her eyes. She blinked them away.

"Ash said to tell you he loves you," Fanny said, her voice cool. "I told him to tell you himself, and he said he already did."

"I think we need to rescue Amelia," Sallie said, pretending not to notice how upset Fanny was. "She's either been reduced to a prune or she's asleep in the tub."

Sallie was stunned to see how thin Amelia was. She handed over a long, warm flannel nightgown and slippers. "Come in by the fire, darling. Khee just brought up your tea. Fanny checked on Rand and he's sleeping soundly, Sally Dearest in his arms. I'm so glad you're here," Sallie said, hugging her.

The little boy tiptoed down the steps, his treasured cat secure in his arms. His eyes grew round as saucers when he spied the ceiling-high Christmas tree, the lights still burning. "Ohhhh."

"What are you doing here?"

"Where's your red suit? Did you get it dirty coming down the chimney?"

Seth stared at the small boy with the stuffed animal in his arms. He frowned. How was it possible this child didn't recognize him, and then he remembered. The boy had been sleeping when Amelia first arrived at Sunbridge, the day before yesterday, and on his orders, had been kept upstairs in the nursery. There had been no contact at all between the two of them.

With the aid of his cane, Seth settled himself in one of the chairs.

"You didn't answer my question, sir?" Rand said.

"What question was that?"

"I asked you if you got your suit dirty coming down the chimney?"

Moss used to ask questions like this. So many years ago. "I'm washing it," Seth growled. "Why aren't you in bed?"

"Because I'm awake. I was afraid you wouldn't find me. Are you magic? Where's your sled and the reindeer? Did you get the biscuit I left for you and the glass of milk?"

"Yes," Seth growled again. "The reindeer are having a snack."

"Oh. Are you going to leave soon? Is it far to the North Pole."

"Almost as far as Texas. Where's your pap, boy?"

"His airplane got shot down. He died. He's in heaven. I'm going to fly airplanes someday. Just like my dad. Do you know my dad?"

Seth's stomach started to churn. "Don't know your dad. What happened to your mam?"

"A bomb hit her. She covered me. Amelia found me. I love Amelia. Do you love Amelia, Santa? Can I sit on your lap?" Before Seth could say yes or no, Rand was on his lap snuggling against the big man's chest. Seth's head reared back, but only for a moment. His big, rough, callused hand reached out to stroke the little boy's dark head, so much like Moss's head when he was little and sat on his lap. His faded blue eyes filled. Imperceptively, he started to rock, crooning softly. Before he knew it, Rand was asleep in his arms. Once or twice his hold on the little boy tightened. Tears rolled down his cheeks.

"Yesterday was so long ago, wasn't it, Seth?" Sallie said softly. "You're remembering when Moss was little and you held him like this. He's just a little boy, Seth, with no mother or father. Amelia loves him and he loves her. Are you angry because I brought them here?"

"You got no right to interfere in my family's business."

"I have every right. We're all family. We're all adults with the exception of that little boy. We all have our own minds to make up. You aren't God, Seth. You can't play with people's lives even if you mean well. The sun will be up in a little while. I'll take him if he's too heavy for you."

"My arm is numb is all. He thinks I'm Santy Claus. Wanted to know if my red suit got dirty. Asks as many questions as Moss did. Told me his mam covered him when the bomb hit her. Amelia found him."

"Guess you're going to have to rethink a few things, eh, Seth. I think everyone more or less finds themselves doing that at this time of year. Miracles happen, you know. Moss is coming home. I feel it in every bone in my body. You do too, but you're afraid if you say the words out loud it won't happen. If you have faith and trust in God, it will happen. I think I'll make us some coffee. You sit here and think about what you're going to say to this child when he wakes and finds out you aren't Santa."

"Got that figured out already. Us Texans aren't dumb, we just look that way."

Sallie smiled. "I think you are the biggest phony there is. You're all mush inside."

A sound unlike anything Sallie had ever heard, erupted from her brother's mouth. Such anguished torment. The little boy stirred and muttered, "Don't worry, Santa, Amelia will wash your suit."

"Maybe you better take him, Sallie. I'll go upstairs and shave off this beard. No sense in disappointing the boy."

"Oh, Seth."

"You gonna start to bawl now? I hate squalling women."

"No."

Sallie lifted the little boy from Seth's arms and carried him upstairs. The smile stayed on her face for a long time.

14

Major Ashford Thornton brought his hand up to his forehead and offered his men the snappiest salute of his illustrious career. If his eyes were on the moist side, it wasn't evident to the members of his squadron, whose own eyes were openly wet. "Remember now, we're going to meet one year from today at the Silver Dollar in Las Vegas. That's an order, men! The gig's on me. Now, get the hell out of here, your families are waiting for you."

The date was September 10, 1945, eight days after the Japanese formally surrendered aboard the USS *Missouri.* V-J Day. Victory over Japan.

He was finally going home. Home to his wife and children. No one single word ever sounded as good as the word home.

Impeccably and impressively dressed in his summer whites, his visored cap at a jaunty angle, Ash walked into the waiting arms of his beautiful young wife. His twin sons dressed in blue-and-white sailor suits smiled shyly as they offered their father the salute they'd been practicing for weeks. When he hoisted his sons, one on each shoulder, and took baby daughter Sunny in his arms, his men let loose with shouts, their closed fists shooting into the air.

It was finally over. He was going home with his family.

"Okay, troops, this is the drill," Ash told his family. "We're heading for the nearest hot dog stand so we can get a weenie with the works and an Orange Julius. Say, aye, aye, sir, and we're on our way."

"Aye, aye, sir," three happy voices rang in the air as baby Sunny gurgled her pleasure.

Simon Thornton, alias Captain Adam Jessup, dressed also in impeccable and impressive navy whites, walked away from the San Diego Naval Base. He didn't look right or left. No one was waiting for him with open arms.

Five hours later he was knocking on the door of the *real* Adam Jessup. Simon blinked. Who was this shabby, seedy young man with straggly hair and a three-day stubbly beard? "I'm Simon Thornton, I have something for you."

"Paid the light bill yesterday. Don't want no magazines. Want a beer?"

"No thanks. Do you mind if I come in?"

"Suit yourself. Told you, I'm not buying anything."

"I'm not selling," Simon said as he looked around for a place to sit down. "Do you remember me?"

"You look familiar. Can't exactly place you. I've had a few beers."

"I'm your cousin Jerry's friend. I bought your identity a few years ago. I'm here to give it back."

"Yeah, well, it isn't that easy. Don't think I'm giving you back the money. I spent it a long time ago."

"I don't want the money." Simon opened his duffel and withdrew a manila folder. He held it out to Jessup.

Jessup reared back. "What is it?"

"Your discharge, some commendations, some medals. They belong to you. If you don't mind, I'd like to keep the wings."

"I don't see any wings. What are you talking about?"

Simon sighed. As he explained, he wondered if, when Jessup sobered up, he would remember a thing he said.

Jessup fooled him. His shoulders squared and his eyes lost some of their glassiness. "You were an honest-to-God flying ace? Using my name? Hot damn! Captain, huh? Shouldn't you be paying me for all this? I mean, hell, man, without my name you'd be nothing." His voice turned crafty when he said, "Is it true that a pair of gold wings and dress whites can get you in any woman's bed? Seems to me this should all be worth something."

Simon reached into his duffel for the envelope full of cash, his pay for his years of service minus a few bucks he'd spent on a few weeks of R & R. "You know what, Jessup, you're right." He tossed him the envelope, closed his duffel, and stood up. "We're square, buddy."

"Hey, aren't you supposed to salute me?"

Simon laughed as his middle finger shot in the air.

Simon headed for the nearest drugstore, where he placed a call to his friend Jerry. "Yeah, it's me, Jerry. I want you to clean out my bank account and drive my car here. I'm heading for New York. If you want to come along, I could use some company. I'll be at the Howard Johnson's near your cousin's house. I only have ten bucks and some change on me, so don't drag your feet. I'm going to call the bank now, all you'll need is some ID. Your password is Ace. You got that? Listen, if you have any money of your own, you better bring it along."

It was after eight o'clock when Jerry drove Simon's car into the parking lot. The two friends stared at one another for a long minute before Jerry whooped like a wild Indian, his arms crushing Simon to his chest. "You son of a bitch, you said you were going to write. I made myself sick worrying about you."

"I did write."

"Yeah, one lousy letter. I must have called your mother a thousand times. She cried every single time. The town is having a parade for Ash next week."

"He's home then?"

"Nah, he's in Hawaii with his wife and three kids. The paper interviewed your mother and she was kind of vague. There was a picture of his wife and kids. One of them kind of looks like you when you were little. Jeez, three kids."

"So, what do you say to me shucking this uniform, putting on some civilian duds, and we take on the town, maybe tie one on and then head out for New York tomorrow? You're coming, aren't you?"

"Quit my job this afternoon, cleaned out my almost-nonexistent bank account, and here I am." He paused, looked hard at Simon. "You gonna tell me why you aren't going home, or is it none of my business?"

"That's pretty funny, Jerry. I fought a war using some other guy's name, and you expect me to go home so the papers can dig into what I did? I know what I did, and that's all that's important. Ash knows. We met up a couple of times. We made our peace. Ash made major. He was one hell of a fighter pilot. He downed the Jap's ace flyer. He's going home . . . to take over the management of the Silver Dollar, and if I know him, he's going to build a new casino. Running those bingo and poker parlors along with the Dollar is going to be a full-time job, but I think he's up to it. Time for him to settle down. I, on the other hand, am just now going to start to *live!*"

"How much living do you think you can do on three thousand bucks? I only have a thousand."

"I'll sell the car if I have to. I have a trust fund I can tap into. I don't want to, but it's nice to know there's a cushion there."

"Welcome home, Simon."

It was the only welcome nineteen-year-old Simon Thornton received. He accepted it because it was his choice to do so. From that day on, everything Simon Thornton did would be by his own choice.

On a rare rainy day in early August of 1946, Ash instigated his first serious fight with his wife. He was storming and stomping his way around the bedroom as Fanny stared at him speechlessly.

"I don't damn well get it. You have all this help in the house, and you're telling me you can't go with me to this dinner. What you mean is you don't want to go. You'd rather sit here and talk to your friend Billie in Texas and run up our phone bill. Then, when you're done talking to her you get on the phone and talk to Bess for hours."

"Because you're never here, Ash. You leave here at three in the afternoon and you don't get home till three in the morning. You sleep till one-thirty, get up, shower, eat and repeat the same process all over again. Aside from the children, I have no life. Furthermore, I only talk to Billie once a week, and we take turns calling. You resent my friendship with her because she's from your mother's side of the family. I talk to Bess twice a week, sometimes not at all. Don't lie, Ash, it isn't manly. You're acting like a spoiled brat."

"I know where you got *that*. You spend entirely too much time with my mother."

"What is it you want from me, Ash? Birch has a bad summer cold, Sage has an earache, and Sunny is coming down with the same thing. I can't leave them when they're sick. This isn't an important dinner, it's just a dinner. Do you know what I think, I think you hate this life, I think you compare it to your time in the navy when you were an . . . ace, and you got all kinds of accolades and praise. Civilian life bores you. I bore you, the children bore you, your parents bore you. The business bores you. Bringing up children can be boring. I'm sorry we aren't exciting. I'm sorry about a lot of things."

"What's that supposed to mean?"

"What do you think it means?" Fanny shot back, her stomach starting to churn. The wary look in her husband's eyes told her all she needed to know. Bess was right, Ash was seeing another woman, and trying to make her feel guilty about his infidelity.

"I don't know what you're talking about."

"This is a small town, Ash. I know you're seeing someone. I smell her on your clothes. Everyone in town knows. I was probably the last one to know, but I do know."

"Unlike my mother and Devin Rollins. They don't talk about her, but they talk about me."

Fanny's heart fluttered in her chest. He wasn't denying it. "I deserve better than this, Ash."

"You're spying on me, aren't you?"

"No, Ash, I'm not spying on you. Stay home and spend the evening with me and the children. We need to talk. We need to put our marriage back together, it's starting to fall apart. Surely you can see what's happening."

"What I see, Fanny, is you are a nag. Pick, pick, pick. Nag, nag, nag. When was the last time you fixed yourself up? When was the last time you came into the Silver Dollar? It's been so long I can't remember. Look at you, you're *round*. That's what happens when you sit on your ass all day, eating and reading."

"I don't do that, Ash. Raising three children is a full-time job. I don't have time to sit and eat. I will not let you do this to me. I know your game, you did something unforgivable and you're trying to make me feel guilty. I refuse to live like this any longer."

"Run to my mother, then. She'll buy you a new house, a new car, get you a few more maids, cuddle you, and the two of you can commiserate about your rotten husbands."

"That just goes to show you, Ash, you know nothing about me. I wouldn't dream of going to your mother. I'd be too ashamed. I'll go back to Pennsylvania. My father would love to have me come home."

"Fanny, wait. This is all wrong. That's not what I want, and it's not what you want. We're both being stubborn. We need to work together. Okay, I'm going to stay home this evening. We're going to talk. But Fanny, *you* need to do something. You can't just stay cooped up in the house like you do. Sometimes I think you're someone else, not the girl I married. What happened to her, Fanny?"

"She gave up because her husband didn't want her anymore. She channeled all her energies into her children to try and make up for his lack of attention. When was the last time you made love to me, Ash?"

"Not that long ago," he blustered.

"Six weeks, Ash."

"You're always asleep when I get in. I hate to wake you."

"What about the nights when *I* tried to wake *you*? How do you explain *that*?"

"I guess I was exhausted. You know, Fanny, sometimes I come home and I pray that I can find a way to get a plane so I can fly and . . . everything seems so simple, so peaceful when I'm flying. There are days when I make myself sick in that casino, watching people gamble away their money. I get sick of the smoke, the booze, the whole damn thing. I hate never seeing sunlight, sleeping during the day and being cooped up all night in a smoke-filled room. You were wrong about me getting home at three in the morning. It's more like five-thirty, just in time to see the sun come up."

"It's what you always wanted to do. You said it was all you thought about from the time you were a little boy and when you were in the navy. Now you tell me all you want to do is what you did in the navy, when you were making that very wish. I don't think you even know what would make you happy. If you wanted to do something else, all you had to do was say something. I would have gone along with anything you wanted. I can always go back to work." Right then, at that very second, she almost blurted out about Jake's money. If Sunny hadn't wailed, she probably would have.

"Let Moon take care of her, Fanny, we're talking."

"No, Ash, Sunny is sick. When little ones are sick they want their mothers."

"You coddle them too much. You need to talk about that with my mother. I know firsthand she doesn't . . . didn't believe in all that stuff. I also think you make up the rules as you go along, to suit yourself."

A moment later, Fanny said, "Sunny is running a fever, so you might as well go on to your dinner. Sage is very restless, his fever isn't coming down. Moon and I are going to make a steam tent to help Birch breathe easier."

"How long is that going to take?" Ash asked irritably.

"Probably all night. Go on, go to your dinner. It doesn't matter."

"I thought you said it did matter. Make up your damn mind."

"Ash, did it ever occur to you that you could help me? You're their father. Aren't you concerned?"

"Kids get sick all the time. This is August. People get summer colds, so why can't a kid get a summer cold? For God's sake, Fanny, kids get bellyaches, earaches, snotty noses, and sore throats all the time. Kids run fevers. What they need is to get outside and play in the sunshine, they need fruits and vegetables. Take them to Sunrise. You take them out for an hour a day and give them peanut butter and jelly because they don't want to eat regular food. They control you, Fanny, instead of the other way around. Try running *that* one by my mother and see what she says. As a mother, Fanny, you are a bust, and we both know it. Now do you understand why I don't want to hang around here and hold your hand?" To drive home his point, Ash stomped from the room, slamming the door so hard the windows rattled.

Fanny's shoulders shook as she walked the floor with Sunny in her arms. At midnight, she knew Sunny had more than a slight fever and a summer cold. She handed her over to Moon so she could call Bess's husband to make a house call. "She's burning up, Bess, and the alcohol rubs aren't helping. She's too . . . too lifeless. Please, tell him to hurry."

John Noble took one look at the beet red baby and called Thornton Medical Center to reserve a room in the pediatric unit. Fanny heard him say, "We need an oxygen tent. I'm bringing her myself."

"How long has she been like this, Fanny?"

"She was cranky all day, but she didn't have a fever. She didn't want any dinner. Around seven she started to feel a little warm. The fever started to rise about an hour ago and she got all red in the face. What is it, John?"

"She's on the verge of pneumonia. Her throat is raw, that's why she didn't want to eat."

"Is she going to be all right?"

"Of course she's going to be all right. She's a robust, healthy little girl. Bundle her up. We don't want her getting a chill in the night air."

On the short ride to the medical center, Sunny clutched to her breast, Fanny said, "John, in your opinion, am I a good mother?"

"As good as Bess. That's a high compliment, Fanny. Why do you ask?"

"Ash and I had a row this evening. He said I was a bust as a mother. He said I don't feed them right, I don't see that they get enough fresh air. He said a lot of things. It's funny, isn't it, how a person can say a few words, and suddenly your life changes right in front of your eyes. I actually started to think he might be right."

"Well, he's wrong. You need to start looking beyond the end of your nose, Fanny. When people are unhappy with themselves, they attack other people. Don't pack your bags for a guilt trip, young lady."

"I know about the other women, John. I was so devastated I wanted to die. Why am I talking about this when my child is so sick? Is there something wrong with me, John?"

"It's a nervous reaction. Do you want me to call Bess to come and sit with you?"

"No. I'll be all right. I really appreciate you coming out so late like this."

"I'd be pretty upset if you called someone else, Fanny. What do you think friends are for? Okay, we're here. Just sit still, I'll carry Sunny. After you finish the paperwork, come up to the pediatric floor. She's in good hands, Fanny."

Fanny was dozing in a chair in Sunny's room in the early hours of the morning when Sallie walked into the room. "Fanny, why didn't you call me? You shouldn't be here by yourself. Where's Ash?"

"We had a row last night and he stormed out. He might not even know we're here. Sunny's fever broke an hour ago. It came on her so quick. I thought she was coming down with a cold or at the very worst an earache and sore throat. I was so scared, Sallie. I thought . . . Ash said . . . it's not important."

"What did Ash say, Fanny?"

Tears burned Fanny's eyes. She rubbed at them. "A lot of things. He said things, I said things. It was one of those fights that come up from time to time. How did you know we were here?"

"Bess called. I guess John called her. I stopped by your house. The boys are fine. Moon said they slept through the night. Ash wasn't home. It's six o'clock in the morning, the Silver Dollar closed at three. He wasn't even there last night. Where is he, Fanny?"

"He wanted me to go to a Chamber of Commerce dinner, but I said I couldn't go. I don't know if he went to the dinner or not."

"Those dinners are over by ten at the latest. How long has this been going on, Fanny?"

Fanny shrugged. "I'm going to check on Sunny. If she's sleeping, I'll go home and shower and come back. She'll be frightened if I'm not here. Everything's okay, Sallie," Fanny said wearily.

"I'll drive you home. Bess said John drove you and Sunny in his car."

Fanny rubbed at her eyes. "That's true, I guess I do need a ride home. I'll be right back."

"Sunny is in good hands, Fanny. Look at me," Sallie said, cupping Fanny's face in her two hands. "This isn't your fault. Children get sick all the time. Sky-high fevers aren't normal, but they do happen. You did the right thing by calling John and bringing her here."

"I know," Fanny sighed.

"You're a wonderful mother, better than I ever was. Bess is too. It must be your generation."

They were almost to the lobby door when Fanny noticed the long shadow on the Tennessee marble floor. She started to step aside, felt Sallie grasp her arm just as she raised her eyes. She felt herself cringe before she bit down on her lower lip.

"Well, if it isn't the two Mrs. Thorntons, Senior and Junior," Ash said.

The bite in her husband's voice alerted Fanny that there was more to come. He needed a shave, his eyes were bloodshot, his tie askew, his shirt was half-in and half-out of his trousers. Fanny looked down at her husband's feet. "Where are your socks, Ash?"

Ash looked at the disgust on his mother's face. Both women appeared to be waiting for the lie they knew would be forthcoming.

Ash rocked back on his heels, his arms crossed over his chest. The sneer on his face made Fanny's stomach lurch. "I'll meet you out front, Sallie," she whispered.

"Yes, Mrs. Thornton Senior, Mrs. Thornton Junior will meet you outside," Ash singsonged.

Fanny wished the marble floor would open up and swallow her. She'd been so careful not to involve Sallie in their lives. Now, Ash was making it all public.

"I'm very tired, Ash, I've been here all night. All I want right now is to go home and take a shower so I can come back. If Sunny wakes up, she's going to be frightened. Now, if you don't understand that, I'm sorry. Look, I don't care where you were or what you did last night. Just get the hell out of my way!"

"Just a damn minute! Are you accusing me of . . . are you saying I don't have a right to be here when my own kid has been admitted?"

"Ash, you're making a scene; people are staring at us."

"So what! The Thorntons own this medical center. They aren't going to look too hard."

Fanny brushed past her husband and ran out the door to the front driveway where Sallie was waiting, the car's engine running at full throttle.

The short drive home was made in silence. When Sallie brought the car to a full stop, Fanny leaned over and kissed her mother-in-law on the cheek. "I know how it looks, but it isn't as bad as it seems. Thank you for not . . . thank you for coming to the hospital."

"If you need me, Fanny, call me, day or night. Ring me later and let me know how Sunny is."

Tears dripped down Fanny's cheeks as she made her way into the house. She'd disappointed Sallie, the one person in the world she loved and respected. "Damn you, Ash. Right now, I wish I'd never met you."

Ash stopped in the men's room to straighten his tie, comb his hair, and tidy up. He yanked at his shirt to see if it smelled of perfume. It did. He rinsed his mouth and tried to clean his teeth with a wet paper towel. Where the hell were his socks?

In Sunny's room he sat down in the rocker. He stared at his sockless feet, his thoughts chaotic. He sat for a long time trying to make sense out of his life.

Ash felt his heart start to crumble when he stared down into the crib at his sleeping daughter. She was picture-perfect, a cherub. For some reason he'd expected her to look like Fanny or even his mother, probably because they were females. Instead, Sunny looked so much like him it was incredible. His heart crumbled a little more when he recalled how Sunny came into being—the result of his and Fanny's sexual encounter over Thanksgiving. They'd called her Sunny because she was like a ray of sunshine. He'd been the one to name her since Fanny named the twins. He remembered how Fanny had beamed her pleasure and said it was the perfect name. Even his mother had agreed.

Jesus, what was wrong with him? He'd acted like a first-class jackass last night when Fanny wouldn't go with him to the dinner. In his rage he'd gone out and betrayed all he held dear. And it wasn't the first time.

Ash hunched down, his face eye level with the crib mattress. His daughter. His and Fanny's flesh and blood. Fanny said Sunny would be frightened if she woke in strange surroundings. Did year-old babies know the difference? Fanny said they did, so it must be true. His hand trembled when he reached out to touch the golden ringlets on the child's ears. Sunny stirred, her small clenched fist searching for her mouth. He helped her find it, a wide smile on his face. "I used to suck my thumb, bet you didn't know that," he whispered. "Your uncle Simon did too. Almost every day of my life I learn something about myself. Like today, I learned I'm not a very nice guy. I made your mother miserable. I embarrassed your grandmother. Sometimes it's easier to say mean, nasty things than it is to say something warm and nice. I don't know why that is.

"Take your mother now. She never says mean, nasty things. Don't get the idea that she doesn't have a temper, she does. I've seen her give your brothers a whack on their bottoms for bad behavior. That doesn't mean she doesn't love them, she does. I could have used a few good whacks growing up. I have a feeling you're going to be one of those perfect little girls who never does anything wrong. I think I might have a talk with those brothers of yours as they grow older so they don't put frogs in your bed, things like that. They probably won't let you in their tree house, either. I don't want you to worry about that because I'm going to build you a playhouse in the backyard. Your mother will put curtains on the windows, and maybe we'll give you a doorbell so the boys can come to visit.

"There's something else you don't know. All the time your mother carried you she sewed clothes for you. I'm the first to admit I don't know a thing about little girl's clothes, but your grandmother does, and she said the outfits your mother made are priceless. That means they're special, made just for you. I don't know much about labels, but I understand ladies buy clothes based sometimes on the labels sewn in the neck. Your mother made labels for your clothes. She calls them Sunny's Togs."

Ash's hands itched to pick up his daughter. He got to his feet, his hands clenched into tight fists. Fanny was right, he was a disgrace. He couldn't pick up his daughter after the places he'd been and things he'd done the night before. "God, how do I make this right?" he muttered.

Four days later, Fanny carried Sunny from the hospital, her husband at her side, her sons scampering ahead, shouting, "Sunny's coming home, Sunny's coming home!"

"What's going on?" Fanny asked as she looked around at the circuslike atmosphere on the center grounds.

"The center is having a fund-raiser starting tomorrow," Ash said. "The board wants to raise money for some new medical equipment as well as some other things. Mom wants the community to get involved. She did a huge mailing asking for new things to be donated. Saturday night they're having a big auction. What should we donate?"

"Oh, Lord, I forgot all about it with Sunny getting sick. I'll think of something."

"You could donate some of those things you made for Sunny."

"The second layette. That's a wonderful idea, Ash. I never would have thought of it. They're homemade, though. People like things bought in a store; I'd die if nobody bid on them. Just because I think they're pretty doesn't mean other people will think so."

"Ask Mom's opinion," Ash said, settling the boys in the backseat of the car. "Fanny, I've been thinking. Let's go to Sunrise for a week or so. It will be a lot cooler for Sunny. I promised to build a tree house for the boys. Don't get excited now, it will be low to the ground. Pop is coming up, so he can help. It will be your job to bring us lemonade and sandwiches. Pop got the boys toy tool kits. They'll have Chue's kids to play with. What do you say, Fanny?"

He was trying, really trying. "It sounds like a great idea."

"Now! Now!" the twins shouted from the backseat.

"I guess that's our answer." Fanny laughed. It was so nice when they acted like a family. Her heart swelled. She cuddled Sunny closer to her breast.

Ash swerved the car into the driveway. "All I ever wanted was to see them like that," Ash said, indicating his parents standing together on the front porch. "The only time they were together was holidays, and then there was so much tension even Simon and I could feel it. I don't want that to happen to us, Fanny. Honest to God I don't. If I falter, give me a swift kick."

"They love one another in their own way. Neither one of us has the right to judge them, Ash."

"You're right about that, too."

"She's beautiful, Fanny," Philip said, holding out his arms to take Sunny. "It's amazing how much she looks like Ash. I see Simon in her, too."

Grandfather, son, and granddaughter walked into the house leaving Sallie, Fanny and the boys on the front porch. "Philip tells me you're going to Sunrise. If you want my opinion, I think it's a wonderful idea."

"Sallie, I forgot about the fund-raiser. If I give you twenty-five dollars, will you bid on something for me?"

"Of course. What are you going to donate?"

"That's something else I forgot. Ash had a wonderful idea, though. I'm going to donate the second layette I made for Sunny. If no one bids on it, don't tell me, okay? Don't you bid on it, Sallie. Promise me."

"I promise."

Sallie hugged her daughter-in-law. "Are things okay between you and Ash?"

"Things are okay, Sallie. Why are we standing here on the porch in this heat?"

"Because women do stupid things from time to time." Sallie laughed.

"I'll get the layette ready. I just want to put tissue paper between the garments and then wrap them in more tissue."

"Did you label everything?"

"Yes. It will only take a few minutes to cut those labels. I forgot about that."

"Don't take them out. Let the buyer think Sunny's Togs is the name of the company that made the layette. The labels might fetch a bigger price. I've been meaning to ask you, wherever did you get the idea for that whimsical sun decal you put on all of Sunny's clothes?"

Fanny laughed. "I guess you could call it my signature. When we were little and didn't have money to buy presents for each other, my brothers made their own. Daniel always put the sun on his packages. It's his own drawing. I always cut them off his packages. Each one is a little different. I have hundreds of them in my album. I just picked the ones I liked best and then duplicated them. It seemed so . . . appropriate. I thought about it the minute Ash said he wanted to name our daughter Sunny. I made a toddler overall for Billie's son. She said she'd pay me to make all of her children's clothes. She was just kidding. It was a long nine months, Sallie; it gave me something to do. Would you like to see the other things I made?"

"I'd love to. Good lord, what *is* all that stuff, Ash?"

"The kid's stuff. A man could go to war with less," Ash said cheerfully, as he loaded the car with the boys' things and all of Sunny's gear. "You might have to sit on the roof, Fanny."

"Mommy sit on the roof," one of the twins giggled.

Ash scooped up Sage and swung him high in the air. He plopped him on the roof of the car. "Do you think Mommy should sit up here?"

"Her's too big."

"Yep. Mommy is going to sit by me. It was a joke."

"Daddy said a joke, Birch."

"Me up, Daddy," Birch said.

"Okay, little fellow, hold on."

Sallie closed the door. "He's acting like a real father."

"He's trying, Sallie."

"Show me everything," Sallie said as she watched Fanny rummage in her cedar chest.

"Darling, these are priceless. Sunny is going to be the best-dressed little girl in Nevada. They must have taken you forever. I never saw such fine stitching."

"Mrs. Kelly taught me to do needlepoint when I was nine years old. The stitches are small like that. It took a long time in the beginning, but after I made a few of them, it went faster. Here's the layette. Do you think it's enough?"

"Enough! Fanny, this is . . . these are . . . I haven't seen anything half as good in the stores. I had no idea you were so talented."

Fanny flushed. "You're making me sound like a designer or something."

"Someday you may be one." *Someday you* will *be one,* Sallie said to herself.

"Here it is. I suppose it should be in a box, but I don't have one."

"Not really. We'll display the layette so people can see it. Well, I'm off. Have a wonderful time at Sunrise. I'll call you to let you know how the fund-raiser goes."

"It's so quiet and peaceful here in the garden," Fanny said lazily. "You must have been very happy here as a child."

"At times. Other times it was miserable," Ash said flatly.

Fanny watched her two sons frolic in the small wading pool. She felt like her heart was going to burst with happiness. In the whole of her life she'd never had such a wonderful time. Thirty days of pure bliss with her family. She wanted it to last forever. She said so.

"Fanny, nothing lasts forever. Life would be pretty boring if it did. You have to be open to new things, new ways. You need to make challenges in your life and stride toward them, and when you reach them you have to stretch and embrace those things head-on. That's life. This was our family vacation. Vacations are usually pretty perfect. Like that time you and I were in Hawaii over Christmas. We both knew it couldn't last forever. If it had lasted, we wouldn't be sitting here right now watching our kids and that very fat bumblebee who is going to nip your big toe any second now."

Fanny squealed as she slid backward on the grass. "Are you trying to tell me something, Ash?"

"I suppose. We've all been so happy here, especially the boys. They romp from morning till night, they're eating good, sleeping through the night. That says something to me, Fanny. Look at you, you have color in your cheeks, you romp with the boys, you do your sewing in the afternoon while I nap, it's perfect. I think you should stay up here. I'll come up on the weekends. I'll leave around noon on Friday and stay through Monday noon. I know my mother would love it if you'd stay here. Pop will come up more often to see the kids. Those are the pluses. The negatives are we won't see each other three days a week. What do you think? It's a suggestion, Fanny, that's all. Don't blow it into something else. Invite Bess to come up with her kids for a week or so. You said Billie was going to come for another visit with her kids. Don't think I don't know that you two are planning something. This might be a good time for you to clinch whatever that secret is."

Fanny sighed. "You overheard?"

"I'd have to be deaf not to have heard you squeal when Mom told you your layette fetched three hundred bucks. Then there was all that whispering with Billie, and more squeals."

"It was your idea, Ash," Fanny said.

"Yeah, but I'm not the rich doctor's wife who plunked out three hundred smackaroos to buy the layette. And wants to order more!"

Fanny closed her eyes and rolled over on her stomach. If there was an ulterior motive to Ash's suggestion, she couldn't see it. Yet.

"Okay. I want your promise, Ash, that the weekends are for me and the kids."

In a theatrical gesture, Ash placed his hand on his heart. "I do solemnly swear the weekends are for you and the kids. We need a dog around here, and a couple of cats for the boys. I've got to get my stuff together. I'll have one of the guys at the club drive your car up here next weekend, okay?"

"Sure. You're leaving now. Are you packed?"

"Did it this morning."

"What if I had said no?"

Ash laughed. "Then I would unpack. C'mere, give me one of those sizzling kisses."

Fanny was the first to pull away, her eyes glassy, but not so glassy that she couldn't see there was more to come. She waited.

"Fanny, you know that strip of land Mom didn't lease to those . . . gangsters . . . the one she kept for herself."

"What about it?"

"What do you think about us building a casino like they want to build. They already have a name for it, The Flamingo. We could beat them to the punch. We could sell off the bingo palaces and poker parlors as well as the Silver Dollar. Mom has more money than God."

"Then why would she want to do that, Ash? She loves the palaces, it's how she got started. She likes to sing for the customers at the Silver Dollar. It's her life, Ash."

"They aren't making enough money. That's what I meant when I said you can't stand still, you have to move with the times or you get left behind. I want you to talk to Mom, Fanny. She'll listen to you."

Fanny wanted to cry. She should have known there was a glitch to all this wonderful togetherness. "I can't do that, Ash. I *won't* do it. You need to talk to her yourself. It has nothing to do with me." Her voice was shaking so badly, she could barely understand her own words.

"I don't get it. You'd take from her to start up a baby business, but you won't ask for help for the business she already has."

"Wherever did you get an idea like that? When would I have time to start up a business?"

"I heard you talking to Billie. She's going to come up with the colors for you. What was that corncob yellow, hayride beige, and red wagon business?"

"That was just a fun conversation. Billie and I do that sometimes. I wanted to make some larger-size clothing for Sunny, and . . . it was just a brainstorming conversation. The colors were a point of reference, kid stuff. I won't allow you to throw guilt on me like this. Another thing, Ash, I don't have to explain my phone conversations to you. You had no right to eavesdrop? You were, so don't deny it."

Ash didn't bother to deny it. "You won't talk to Mom then?"

"Absolutely not. That's your job, Ash. You understand the business, I don't. I can't believe you're even asking me to do something like that. Your mother would see right through it the minute the words were out of my mouth. No!"

"Son of a bitch!" Ash said, stomping his foot in front of Fanny. "You're going to regret this. The good life is going to start dwindling, and I'm not going to let you take any more money from my mother. We'll make it on my salary. No more freebies. That means you go back to town and live on my salary, doing all the things other housewives do. You'll have to stretch your food allowance, cut back on your personal shopping, make sure there's enough money to pay all the bills. You might as well make plans now to get rid of all your help. We can't afford it. We can't afford two cars; yours will have to go."

Fanny's heart fluttered in her chest. "What are you talking about? You make good money. Stop spending it."

"You see, you didn't listen to what I said. My mother is subsidizing us. The palaces and the Silver Dollar are barely making it. Mom has to put money in every month to make the payrolls. She knows everyone and won't let them go because they depend on their salaries. She hands me a check. It's never the same amount. Sometimes she's very generous, other times she's stingy. I can't count on the same amount every month. I work my ass off, Fanny. I don't slack off. She tells me I'm running things, but those are just words. She's running things. Every time I make a decision she countermands it. I'm thinking of looking for another job, maybe going with my father. How hard can it be to learn the chicken business? He offered to pay me twice what Mom is paying me."

"Without talking to me? I don't believe I'm hearing this. Your mother will take all of this as a betrayal."

"You don't listen, Fanny. You're just like she is—she doesn't listen either."

Fanny heard the whining tone in his voice. She squared her shoulders. "You need to call your mother and tell her everything you just told me. It's the way you say things, Ash. It's all in the presentation. For once in your life try and be a little humble. This is the way the world is. It's not the navy, where you were this big hero and you lived on your adrenaline."

"Jesus! It's amazing how much you sound like my mother. Get your stuff together, we're going back to town."

Fanny's heart started to flutter again. If she did as Ash wanted, all the rest was a lie. He'd tricked her into coming up here, wooed her, and now this. She thought she could feel something in her die. "No."

Ash's eyes narrowed. "No what? No, you aren't getting your stuff together or no, you aren't going back to town?"

"Both," Fanny said in a strangled voice. "For now." The "for now" was the coward in her speaking. She knew Ash recognized the words for what they were. She wanted to hit him, to wipe the smirk from his face. She clenched her fists and stared him down. It was all she could do.

Fanny didn't move for a long time. She heard the car backfire, heard Ash race the engine for her benefit. He was daring her to come to the driveway to say good-bye, to say, okay, I'll talk to your mother. She clenched her teeth. Her dream was crumbling, and she was powerless to stop it.

So that she wouldn't cry, Fanny widened her eyes to stare at the familiar surroundings, surroundings she loved. The cottonwoods were beautiful at this time of year, the flower beds more vibrant, the carpet of grass, greener than emeralds. The filtered sunlight was just right as it swept through the leaves to create lacy patterns on the freshly mown grass. The scent of the fresh grass and the smell of sagebrush seemed to circle around her, just the way it had yesterday when she and Ash had made love in the gazebo under the stars. She could hear the birds now, chittering as they nestled in the cottonwoods, preparing for the evening. She felt the need to cry. Crying never solved anything.

Fanny smiled when Moon set a cup of tea down on the iron table, and then took the boys inside with her. As she sipped at the hot tea, her thoughts swirled inside her head. She knew in her heart her husband would never work with his father in the chicken business. Ash would consider it demeaning. What he wanted, what he'd always wanted, was to take over his mother's business. What was happening to him?

Dear God, how had things gotten to this point? What was wrong with her? Why did Ash turn on her? Didn't he love her?

Fanny did cry then; for the would-haves, the could-haves, the should-haves. When there were no more tears, she picked up her sewing basket. Maybe this was all she was good for, taking care of children and sewing children's clothes.

Where had all the love gone? Was it ever there? For her, yes. For Ash, she had to admit she didn't know. Whatever it was, it had given her three beautiful children. Her eyes widened suddenly, her forehead beading with sweat. Her knitting basket fell to the ground as she raced into the house in search of a calendar. Her hand trembled as she counted off the days since her last period. The calendar back home in the dressing room was clearly marked, for her benefit as well as Ash's. Three days of sexual abstinence. They had both agreed three children was enough. She closed her eyes as she leaned against the kitchen wall. She was almost 99.99 percent certain that she was already pregnant.

Ash would blame her for this too.

She was so beautiful, all Ash could do was stare at his mother standing on the stage singing for her customers. He looked around at the rapturous looks on the faces of the audience. They loved her. Too bad there weren't more of them. The house was only half-full. Allowing for the month of August, when things were normally slow, regular customers on vacation, plus it was the middle of the week, Ash knew September wouldn't be much better. He hadn't seen a full house since his return. What the Silver Dollar needed was a little skin. Some high-kicking, long-legged showgirls with sparkly costumes. A little boogie-woogie would help too. His mother needed to get rid of the fuddy-duddy atmosphere and spruce up the place with some chrome, glass, and mirrors. Some bright colors would be nice. Bright colors made people move faster, and the faster they moved, the more money they spent. The Silver Dollar's regular customers took *naps* in the lounge. His mother saw it as amusing since they always woke up when she started to sing. He saw it as money going down the drain because no one bought a drink or gambled when his mother began her hour-long act.

Ash waited until his mother finished the last song of the evening. No one, at least no one to his knowledge, could sing "Sentimental Journey," like his mother. When the applause died down and his mother came back onstage, Ash knew she would sing two more songs, "If I Loved You," and "Till the End of Time." The audience would beg for more, but his mother would just smile and walk off the stage, and take her seat next to Devin Rollins. He looked around for Devin, but didn't see him. If Devin wasn't at the Silver Dollar, he might have a chance of cornering his mother to address his concerns.

Ash made his way backstage, nodding to various employees as he went along. It was a dark and dreary area, long overdue for a makeover. He knocked on the door. He noticed his hand was shaking. His mother always did this to him. Anytime he found himself in her presence or even anticipating being in her presence, he either started to shake or he got tongue-tied. Pure and simple, she intimidated him. The moment he opened and closed the door, he jammed his hands into his trouser pockets.

"Ash! How nice of you to come backstage. I hope you're here to tell me you enjoyed my performance."

"I always enjoy listening to you, Mom. As always, you had the audience mesmerized."

"What can I do for you, Ash?" Sallie said as she prepared to remove her theatrical makeup.

Ash drew a deep breath, his hands still jammed in his pockets. "I need to talk to you about a couple of things. The palaces and the Silver Dollar are losing money."

"I know. I don't want you worrying about it, Ash. It's more important that people have jobs and work for someone they like. We aren't losing that much. Actually, according to Simon, we're breaking even. That means we aren't losing, and we aren't winning. I can live with that."

"What does Simon have to do with this?"

"I turned everything over to him months ago. He's come up with some marvelous suggestions and already he's invested certain sums that are showing remarkable gains. You know how he loves to play in the stock market." Sallie smiled at her son in the mirror.

"Play?"

"It's just a figure of speech, Ash."

"And does Simon approve of your break-even way of doing business?"

"No. The gains he's made in other areas pay for the loss of revenue."

"It's time to sell the palaces and the Silver Dollar. If you don't, you're going to get lost in the boom that's starting. You need to move with the times. You need high-class shows, and you need to renovate if you refuse to sell. Do you want this place to be a 'has-been'? The palaces are pure deadweight. You can never tell me they're breaking even. Get rid of them now while you can make a profit. If you have fifty customers a week, it's a lot. Nobody's interested anymore."

"What happens to all those people and their families? They depend on me, and I refuse to just get rid of them. When it's time for them to retire, it will be different. Just out of curiosity, if I were to get rid of them and the Silver Dollar, what would you suggest?"

"Build a big new modern casino on that desert land. You have to stay competitive."

"Why?"

"Why? So you make money. So I can earn more money. I have a family to support. I'm not able to do that the way you pay me. Pop offered me a job at twice what you pay me."

"Is that what this is all about? You want more money? Why didn't you just say so?"

"Because I don't want a handout. I work my tail off. I put in long hours. If I'm running this business, then I should be running it, not you. Each time I make a suggestion you turn it down. Tell me, why do you need me? Or, am I like the employees at the bingo palaces?" he asked bitterly.

"No. Not at all. I thought . . . you have a family . . . you need to spend time . . . give me the bottom line, Ash."

"Sell. Make provisions for the employees. Move with the times. If you insist on standing still, I'm going to have to do more than think about Pop's offer."

"Have you discussed this with Fanny?"

"Yes," Ash lied.

"And she's in agreement?"

"Yes," Ash lied again.

"You're lying to me, Ash. Even as a small boy I could always tell when you were lying to me. I'm your mother, you don't ever have to lie to me."

Ash dug his heels into the carpet. *Son of a bitch.* "Fanny's my wife, she'll do whatever I want. I think she's pregnant, so she won't be interested in business matters."

"Again! My, God, Ash, the poor girl hasn't recovered from her last pregnancy. You're blackmailing me, Ash. I won't tolerate that. Where's Fanny?"

"Sunrise. She'll be coming back any day now. We won't be availing ourselves of your hospitality any longer. I'll take care of my family by myself."

"I see."

"You don't see at all."

"Yes, Ash, I do see. You're doing the same exact same thing you did as a child. If you didn't get your way, you packed up your toys and went off by yourself. You can't do that now, you have a family to think about. This isn't the navy, Ash. We aren't your subordinates that you can order around. You have to stop being so selfish and think about your family instead of yourself."

"I am thinking about them. What the hell do you think this is all about?"

"Taking control away from me. Being in the driver's seat. Isn't that the latest expression?"

"I don't know. That's not what this is all about. I won't be your flunky, Mom. I guess we don't have anything else to say to each other. I'll finish out the night and lock up. Tomorrow you can hire someone else."

"Ash, you need to talk to Fanny about this."

"I'm pretty damn sick and tired of hearing about Fanny this and Fanny that. Fanny does what I want when I want it."

"Ash, do you hear yourself? Fanny is a person. You don't own her."

"Neither do you!" Ash shot back. "I think you think you do, though. You've given her everything in the world. Well, guess what, we're giving the car back because we can't afford two cars. We don't need your household help anymore either. You aren't her goddamn mother. You're *my* mother! It would be nice if you would act like a mother sometime. Shit, I don't know why I even bothered to try and talk to you. Stay out of my life and Fanny's too!"

"Ash . . . wait!"

The slam of the door sounded like an explosion.

Sallie stepped out of the glittery blue stage gown and into street clothes. She was moving around in slow motion, robot fashion. The phone was in her hand. She didn't remember picking it up. "Devin . . . Devin . . . oh, Devin . . . I need you."

"I had no idea this was such a big operation," Ash said, three days later as his father gave him a tour of the R & R Ranch. "I'm sorry, Pop, that I haven't been out here."

"That's okay, Ash. People tend to shy away from you when you tell them you're in the chicken business. It's very profitable. Actually, we bring in more money than the Silver Dollar and the bingo palaces put together. Simon just told me that a few weeks ago. I'm pretty proud of that, Ash."

"You should be, Pop," Ash said, clapping him on the back. "Refrigeration trucks, Pop. Expansion is the way to go. You have to move with the times. Mom can't see that. I tried to explain, but she didn't want to listen. You should be able to cover all the surrounding states. Hell, if you want to spring for a plane, I can make your deliveries. Let's kick that one around."

"I'm your man, son. Let's go into the office and huddle. I'm open for any and all suggestions. Are you sure I'm paying you enough?"

"It's a fair wage, Pop. I'll work my ass off for you, you know that. I have a wife and three kids, maybe four soon, to support. How's the other . . . end of the business doing?"

Philip laughed. "I try not to get involved. Red tells me she can't count the money fast enough, so I guess it's doing okay. Ash, is this going to cause a problem with your mother?"

"Pop, the day I was born I became a problem for Mom. We both know that. I guess so. Then again, maybe not. I'm not going to worry about it. Let's talk about a plane and see how far we're willing to go in our expansion efforts. It's good to be working with you, Pop."

Fanny emerged from the doctor's office in a daze. She was pregnant. She started to cry as she stepped into Bess's waiting car.

"It's only nine months out of your life, Fanny. You love kids, and you're going to love this one too. The twins have each other, and now Sunny will have a sister or brother. It's important for kids to have companions. The time will go fast, you'll see."

"It's not the pregnancy, it's the way it happened. I was careless, but in my own defense, I think Ash planned it all; I just got caught up in the moment. God, I haven't even lost the weight from Sunny's birth. Four months of morning sickness, weight gain, birth, weight loss, crying babies. No more household help. I don't know if I can do it, Bess."

"I hate to point this out, Fanny, but you don't have a choice."

"I could get an abortion if I knew where to go to get it. I've thought about it. Things aren't going that well between me and Ash. To bring another child into the world doesn't make sense. As you know, Ash is working with his father and making twice the money he was making working for Sallie. Philip bought a plane and Ash makes deliveries. He seems to like what he's doing. Philip is ecstatic to have Ash working with him. Ash told me . . . actually, he forbade me to see Sallie. I refused to go along with that, so we aren't speaking. I keep thinking, maybe it's time for me to pack up and go back to Shamrock. I didn't think it was possible to be so unhappy and miserable. Sallie is beside herself. I don't know what to do, Bess."

"When I don't know what to do, I don't do anything. That's the best advice I can give you. Whatever you do, I'm on your side. So is John."

"It shouldn't be like this, choosing up sides. What kind of marriage is this? What did I do wrong?"

"You didn't do anything wrong, Fanny. It's that jackass you married that's done everything wrong. If you start blaming yourself, I swear, I'm going to give you a good kick. Let's go out to lunch, you're eating for two now. My treat."

"I can't, Bess. I have to get home, my sitter has another sitting job for one o'clock."

Left to her own devices, Fanny fed and diapered Sunny and settled the twins with a huge basket of blocks before she picked up the phone to call Billie. The moment she heard her voice, Fanny relaxed.

"Billie, I need to talk with you. Let me just blurt everything out quickly so I can get it over with. I'm pregnant. Ash is working for his father. He sold my car, he forbids me to talk with Sallie, he made me get rid of all my household help. I can't live like this. I refuse to stand around and wait for my husband to make an appearance, to say a kind word. I will never again prostitute myself for a smile or a pat on the head."

"I understand all too well, Fanny. When Moss returned things were wonderful for a little while. Little by little, things started to go downhill. At first I blamed it on his being a prisoner of the Japanese. As time went on I realized Moss is Moss, and he isn't going to change. He's so busy running Coleman Aviation, he doesn't have time for me or anyone else. That isn't quite true—he has time for his father. I take it one day at a time."

"Is there anything I can do, Billie?"

"Be my friend. My greatest joys these days are my children and my friendship with you."

"Oh, Billie, I feel the same way. I don't want to live like this. I need to have a life. You need a life too. If it has to be separate from Ash and yours has to be separate from Moss, so be it. I think I'm ready to go into business, and I want you to be a part of the business. I'm going to need advice, help, and support. Bess is ready to jump in with both feet. Tell me again, Billie, that you think we can do this, tell me that you have faith in me. I need to hear the words."

The words were kind, gentle, and full of approval. Fanny sighed with relief.

"Billie, I need to tell you about Jake. Just listen, okay?"

"Talk, Fanny, I'm listening."

A long time later, her confidence restored with Billie's encouragement, Fanny said, "We can use Jake's money to start up the business. When we begin making a profit, I'll put his money back . . . into an escrow account . . . or something. I want to think of it as borrowing, not just . . . you know, taking it. It's going to work, I can feel it. It will be *ours*, Billie. It will be *our* legacy to *our* children."

Sunny's Togs, the whimsical line of children's wear created in a small sewing room on a mountaintop overlooking the city of Las Vegas, would one day have its shares listed on the New York Stock Exchange.

PART THREE

The Family

1961–1966

15

The town known as Las Vegas had changed greatly in the eighteen
years since Fanny was hijacked at gunpoint aboard a bus bound for
California. Perched on the edge of the Mojave Desert, and on the
edge of the Colorado River, the town was like a shooting star, twinkling overhead, twenty-four hours a day.

Some called the city a gambling mecca with top name entertainment, luxurious accommodations, miles and miles of glittering neon,
showgirls in skimpy outfits, and casino come-ons. Fanny Thornton
and her family called it home.

The Thorntons had changed, too, in those eighteen years as babies passed through childhood into their teen years, and parents read
college manuals and brochures, and began to plan for the day when
there would be only two people at the dinner table instead of six.

Sunrise, now Fanny's, thanks to Sallie's generosity on Fanny's
thirtieth birthday, had also changed. It was no longer a dark and
somber place. These days it was filled with comfortable chintz-
covered furniture, colorful rugs, pastel walls, and sheer curtains.
Green plants were everywhere, thanks to Chue's green thumb. Children's voices, dogs barking, music, television, ringing phones, at-
tested to the fact that this place called Sunrise was finally a home.

Weekdays the Thornton children attended private school in town.
They returned Friday evenings with friends who stayed the weekend to swim, play tennis, or ski. At those times the house rocked with
sounds of laughter and good times. It was the same during the summer months and over holidays. Fanny likened it all to a year-round
picnic minus the ants.

They were older now, these children of hers; Birch and Sage were
sixteen, going on seventeen, Sunny was almost sixteen, and Billie
was fourteen. The girls anguished over pimples, hairdos, boys, and
the telephone, while the boys tried to hide their dismay over their
lack of muscle tone, their skin flaws, and the fact that the phone calls
were never for them, but for their sisters.

The Thornton children were close not only in age, but in their relationships as well. It was okay to fight occasionally, okay to tease, but only within the family. Any outsider who had the audacity to try the same thing found himself not only verbally but physically abused by all four Thornton children. On more than one occasion Fanny had to step between the youngsters to make them apologize and shake hands. Most times there were no hard feelings, and the visiting kids never made the same mistake again.

The twins, Birch and Sage, were normal in every way, regular guys to their friends, jerks to their sisters, caring, loving, respectful sons to their mother. They had chores like their friends, received allowances, made their own beds, helped Chue in the garden and greenhouses, carried out the trash, and in general never complained when Fanny asked them to do something. Each night they kissed and hugged their mother before going upstairs to bed. They were good students, in the top three percent of their class. Their goal was to be accepted to West Chester University in Pennsylvania to study accounting and business management so they could take over the business end of their mother's company, Sunny's Togs, a three-million-dollar-a-year business.

Sunny's Togs, Fanny's fledgling business started in her sewing room, had grown slowly, profitably, over the years, thanks to Fanny's diligence, Sallie's business expertise, and Billie Coleman's knowledge of the textile business.

Fanny referred to Sunny's Togs as a contained business, selling her children's clothing only in Nevada and Texas. Limiting sales to certain states had been Billie's idea, for better quality control, she said. Sallie had taken it one step farther. When something is unavailable, she said, people will do anything to get their hands on it. Expand one state at a time had been her advice. Be good to your employees, be smart enough to know when enough money is enough, and share the rest. It was sound advice, advice Fanny followed to the letter. The result was that in 1955 Sunny's Togs took off like a rocket and exploded into the retail market. A corporate office was established in downtown Las Vegas. Bess Noble, with absolutely no experience, stepped in and took over the operation armed only with Fanny's confidence in her ability. "We're both dumb as dirt, Bess, that's why it will work. We'll both learn from our mistakes, and you know I'll never come down on you for doing something wrong. Someday, Bess, we're going to be known nationally. Mark my word!"

Six years later, net revenues were in the double digit millions.

Sunny, her father's look-alike, was a boisterous, gangly, curly-headed kid who loved to swear and torment her brothers, all the while wearing a perpetual smile. She could shinny up the cotton-woods faster than either one of the twins, and shinny down even faster, laughing uproariously as the boys got tangled in the branches and, more often than not, fell out of the tree. She could pedal her bike faster, run longer distances, swim twice as far, and in general, best her brothers in every endeavor.

Young Billie was an outgoing child whose main interest in life was her mother's business. At the age of six, she discovered paper dolls. Never satisfied with the few cutouts on the pages, she made her own, her chubby fingers drawing and cutting until she had exactly what she wanted. At seven she started designing clothes for her dolls—clothes Fanny sewed for her until the day Sallie showed up on their doorstep with a sewing machine just for Billie. From that day on, every outfit she designed and sewed for her favorite doll Cissie was a work of art. She loved sewing buttons on the sample garments for her mother, loved copying the whimsical suns that went on the patch pockets or shoulder straps, loved packing up the boxes to be taken to United Parcel. When she was twelve and in bed with a vicious cold, she designed a romper suit that she'd cut and stitched by hand. The romper, banded at the legs with miniature sun decals, was the following year's best-seller. The original, tacked, matted, and framed, hung in the workroom with all of her mother's original designs.

Fanny's studio, or workroom as she preferred to call it, was the cottage Chue had lived in before his family started to grow. Sallie had built him a house farther down the mountain the year she deeded the house to Fanny. With Billie and Bess's help, Fanny had renovated the cottage. The workroom was a bright cheerful space filled with easels, drafting tables, stools, and hassocks. Four deep, bright red chairs flanked the fieldstone fireplace. A round oak table covered with swatches, designs, catalogs, and design books sat in the middle. One corner was designated as kitchen area, with a small stove, mini refrigerator, colorful cabinets, and a small wrought-iron table with four chairs. To the far left, twin beds with a small dresser in between welcomed Fanny when she felt the need to catnap or spend the night if she was working late. But it was the fireplace area that was Fanny's favorite place, especially when Billie and Bess were visiting. They would talk about their husbands, their children, their desires, and when they finished with that, they'd switch to business. Other times, it was a gathering place for her and her children when a problem surfaced and needed to be talked out and resolved. Cocoa, a fire, and an open mind made it a sanctuary.

Often she crept down here to "her place" in the middle of the night to sort things out when Ash would come home on one of his rare visits, drunk and angry.

Fanny knew she should have gotten a divorce years ago. Ever hopeful, she'd thought things would change, but they hadn't. Once she'd mentally criticized Sallie for staying in a loveless marriage, professing not to understand the strange relationship, and now she was doing the same thing. Did she still love Ash? The children asked her that all the time, and her standard stock answer was always the same: "of course." Children needed stability, two parents. Not that Ash ever acted like a parent. Oh, he was a big giver, arriving on an occasional weekend with new bicycles, games, toys, outrageous jewelry for the girls. If an item was buyable, Ash bought it and handed it over with a flourish. Then he'd suggest a game of tennis with "the old man" and played the game to the bitter end. It wasn't a game to Ash, it was a battle and there could only be one winner, Ash Thornton. The twins hated the games, but Sunny practiced diligently, went to a month-long summer tennis camp, and walloped her father soundly at the age of thirteen. The twins cheered her wildly, their fists shooting in the air each time she made her father race for her serve. After that there were no more tennis matches.

Fanny's heart started to race the moment she heard the sound of Ash's car on the gravel driveway. She tried to remember the last time he'd been home—six weeks ago, maybe longer. It was the middle of the day. What was he doing here? She ran to the powder room and quickly fluffed her hair and added fresh lipstick. At the last second she spritzed some perfume on her wrists and hated herself for doing it. Her husband was home.

She saw Sunny walk around the corner of the house, wheeling her bike. Even from this distance she could see the smoldering anger on her daughter's face. It could only mean trouble. She remembered that Sunny hadn't been satisfied with her tennis win. She'd challenged Ash to a father/daughter bike race up and down the mountain roads. The twins had set up an obstacle course, a start line, and a finish line with strips of red satin ribbon. She'd heard them planning it.

She watched now as Ash, fit and trim, embraced his children, grinning as he pummeled his young sons. He cocked his head to the side and grinned as the boys raced off to stretch the finish line ribbon between two trees. Sunny was leaning against a tree, stretching her legs and doing squats.

Fanny walked outside just as Ash gave his famous thumbs-up salute and took off like a whiz. Sunny started out slow, her long muscular legs pumping steadily. Every time she passed her father, she gave him a raspberry, crossing the finish line ten seconds ahead of him. She was leaning against a tree, sipping a Coca-Cola, a bottle in her hand for her father, when he finally crossed the line. Ash, his eyes murderous, knocked the soda out of her hand as he threw his bike into the bushes.

Fanny ran after her husband, shouting his name as he headed for his car. She was forced to step back when he ignored her and backed up his car so fast that gravel spewed up, striking Fanny's chest. Still she cried, "Ash, wait, come back!"

Fanny held out her arms, gathering her children together, and headed for her studio, where they sat on the red chairs, not to discuss their father's poor sportsmanship, but to console *her*, to try and wipe away the devastation they saw in her eyes.

"I did it for you, Mom," Sunny said. "At least I thought I did. I hate the way he treats you. I hate it that you put up with it." She turned on her brothers like a tiger. "If I ever see you act like that, I'll punch you silly. You hear me! Look at the both of you, you're six feet tall, you weigh as much as Dad. It's time for you to start acting like the man of the house around here since we don't have one we can count on on a daily basis. There's two of you, how hard can it be?"

"You know what, little sister, you're absolutely right. For once in your life. Starting right now, we are assuming Dad's role." Birch rubbed his hands together gleefully. "This is the way it's going to fly. Sunny, you will set the table every night. Billie, you will clear. Starting tomorrow, you girls will make our beds, meaning me and the other man of the house."

"And while we're doing all of that, what are you two jerks going to be doing?" Sunny demanded.

"Acting like *the* man of the house. Nothing! It's what you wanted. You should have paid more attention when Chue was telling us about all those old Chinese proverbs. Remember the one that goes like this . . . be careful what you wish for because you might get it. I rest my case."

"That's not what I meant and you know it," Sunny sputtered.

"That's enough," Fanny said. "All of you, I appreciate all you've done and said. You worry too much. Your father . . . isn't happy, that's the best answer I can give you. I don't know what it is that can make him happy. I've asked, but he's never given me an answer. He loves all of you. I know this in my heart. Sunny, you're too hard on him."

"In a pig's eye."

"Time to go in and see about dinner," Fanny said, getting up from the hearth.

"I think we should have a big plate of . . . CROW for you guys!" Sunny shouted as she barreled out of the studio, her brothers in hot pursuit.

"I wish I was more like her," Billie said, following Fanny to the house.

"If you were like Sunny, then you wouldn't be you," Fanny said, putting her arms around her younger daughter. "I love you just the way you are."

"Mom, did you ever notice that Dad can never remember my name? He has to do that mental thing, his face goes blank, he starts to fumble for his words and just when you think he's going to give up, he remembers. That doesn't say much for me, does it?"

Fanny was tired of lying to her children about their father. There would be no more lies. "Uh-huh. I think he resents your name a little. As you know, I named you after Billie Coleman, and your father thinks Billie . . . he blames Billie for making me independent. Your father thinks women should stay home to cook, clean, sew, have babies, and wait on their man hand and foot."

"That's slavery," Billie said.

"Some women like doing that, and some don't. I am one of the don'ts. So is your grandmother. I think that part of it is all mixed up in your dad's head. He likens me too much to your grandmother."

"He should be proud of Grandma, and you too. You never told me what he said when my romper turned out to be our best-seller last year. Did he say *anything*? If he didn't, you won't hurt my feelings."

"Sweetie, your dad doesn't concern himself with what he calls my piddly-assed business. Sunny did show him the romper and sang your praises, as did your brothers. He said it was very nice. For your sake I wish he'd been as excited as we all were for you. Sometimes you have to swallow hard and take the good with the bad."

"I understand that, Mom. But where's the *good?*" Her shoulders slumping, Billie walked over to her drafting table and started to sketch. "Call me when dinner's ready. It's my turn to clear, so you and Mazie don't need me right now. What kind of Chinese name is Mazie anyway?" she muttered.

"Show me what you're working on, honey. You've been so secretive these past weeks. You're starting to make me curious. If you don't want me to see it, it's okay."

"It's an idea. I was cleaning out my closet a few weeks ago and I found my old doll. I started to think, wouldn't it be a super idea to make an outfit, a new one like the coverall I'm working on, and make a doll to go with it? A boy doll and a girl doll with the exact same outfit. A small doll to utilize the scraps of material. If we made the coverall a patch garment of different colors, we'd have lots of leftovers. It really has to be a small doll, though, the kind you can stuff into the patch pockets. A bigger doll would be good too. If we made a bigger doll, you know, the kind kids love to cuddle with the way I did, we could sell them separately. A wardrobe for the bigger dolls using the scraps. What do you think, Mom?"

Fanny took a step backward and stared at her young daughter in wide-eyed amazement. "My God, and you're only fourteen! That is one of the best ideas I ever heard. We'll do it! Do you have the sketches?"

"Sort of. I don't want to show them to you yet. Do you really think it's a good idea?"

"Honey, it's a stupendous idea. Is it okay to mention it to Bess, Sallie, and Billie?"

"I'd like to hear what they have to say. Sure, Mom. Promise to tell me *exactly* what they say, okay?"

"I promise a verbatim report. Are you going to tell your brothers and sister?"

"I already did. Birch said I was a genius. Sage said I was a genius plus, and Sunny said she was glad I was her sister because she doesn't know anyone as smart as me. That's exactly what she said. They all hugged me and then Birch pushed me in the pool. He said it was my christening into geniushood. Is there such a word, Mom?"

"Who cares. The title fits you perfectly. Honey, there are no words to tell you how proud of you I am."

"Do you think it will be another best-seller?"

"Absolutely. Now, get to work!"

Fanny walked out into the clear bright sunshine. Just minutes ago she had wanted to kick and scream, to smash something, but her anger had dissipated, the way it always did when her children took over her heart. The looks on their faces after the bicycle race would stay with her for a very long time.

She should have taken matters into her own hands years ago. She made her way to the little cemetery that had always given Sallie such comfort. She sat down under the cottonwoods and hugged her knees.

It was time to make decisions, time to shelve her aching heart and get on with her life. Thirty-six wasn't too old to start over. Billie Coleman was attempting to do the same thing, why couldn't she?

Fanny wept then, for the lost years.

"She's crying," Sunny said as she elbowed her brothers at the kitchen window. "We should do something."

"I think you did enough, Sunny. You started this whole thing. Why couldn't you leave well enough alone? You knew you'd beat him, you knew what he'd do. Why'd you do it? You need to back off a little and get rid of all those burrs in your undies that are pricking you."

"That's easy for you to say. You guys are leaving in a few months for college. Then it will be just Billie and me. It won't be the same without you here. Your size alone always gave me some comfort."

"Oh, my God, she gave us a compliment, Birch," Sage said, his voice full of awe.

"She's getting up," Sunny said. "Look busy."

"Aye, aye, Captain," Sage said, saluting smartly.

Fanny entered the kitchen, her face stony. "Listen, I'm going to clean up and go into town. I'm not hungry, so eat without me. I'll probably stay with Sallie and come back in the morning. Billie told me about her doll idea. It's so good I can't wait to tell everyone and set the wheels in motion. I want to thank all of you for being so encouraging. I don't think you needed to dunk her in the pool, though."

"Yes we did," Sage said. "She loved it!"

"All right, all right. Make sure you eat all of your dinner, not just the dessert. I'll see you before I leave."

As one, Fanny's children looked up from their sprawled positions on the living room floor when their mother came back into the room. For once, the four of them were speechless. Dressed in a simple pale yellow linen sheath that hugged every curve, with matching shoes, Fanny could have posed for a fashion magazine ad. Her hair was arranged high on her head in artful swirls to show off her diamond earrings. A matching diamond pin in a starfish design graced the linen dress a little below the shoulder line. She carried a small clutch purse with a diamond clasp. "What's wrong? Is the pin too much? Is it my hair?" Fanny asked anxiously. "I hardly ever get dressed up anymore. Billie Coleman designed this dress, and she said it would never go out of style. Say something."

"Mom, you look gorgeous. I guess we aren't used to seeing you dressed up. Can you walk in those shoes, the heels are pretty high."

"You look like one of those models in the magazines," Billie said.

"Yeah, yeah," the twins said in unison. They always said things in unison when they were at a loss for words. This gorgeous creature standing in front of them was their *mother*.

"If you're sure I look okay, I'm off. Sage, you need to clean your side of the room. Tomorrow is laundry day. Billie, in bed by ten and no cheating. You're on your honor. Sunny, no fried egg sandwiches at midnight. Absolutely no swimming once it gets dark. Agreed? Come on, you're not too big to give me a kiss good-night."

When the door closed behind Fanny, her children looked at one another. "She's going to blow his socks right off his feet. And then she's going to walk away," Sunny said. "She's angry. Very angry."

"You're imagining things," Birch said. "She didn't look angry to me."

"Trust me. I'm a woman, I know," Sunny said.

"Woman my ass. You're only fifteen," Sage said.

Birch swallowed his own retort when he noticed that Sunny had started to cry, her shoulders shaking. He stared at her helplessly.

"Why can't we just be a family? Why does it have to be him against us? He goes out with other women. He cheats on Mom. Did he ever kiss you, Birch, or hug you, or even say he was proud of you?"

"Guys aren't into that mushy stuff, Sunny. But to answer your question, no."

"He's not a guy, Birch, he's our father. Mom does all those things every day. I think we take it for granted sometimes. Do you want to end up like him and be estranged from Mom the way he is from Grandma?"

"No," Birch muttered.

"He doesn't care, Birch. He doesn't care about any of us. In your heart you know it's true."

Birch watched as Sage and Billie headed for the kitchen to start supper. When they were out of earshot, he went to Sunny and put his arm around her. "Sunny, I want to talk to you like a big brother. Look at me," he said, cupping her freckled face in both his hands.

"You aren't alone in all this. I want you to stop pretending you're this . . . tough guy. I know why you do it, but the others, they think you're really what you're pretending to be. It makes you less a girl if you know what I mean. I'd like it if you'd muzzle that mouth of yours too. I don't want you to get a bad reputation, you're my sister. It's okay for you to excel in athletics, in fact that's good, but you need to temper that win-win attitude of yours. Yeah, you can beat the pants off me and Sage, and yeah, you whopped Dad's butt, but look what happened. You set him up, Sunny, and he walked right into the trap. Don't be proud of that. Jesus, he's old, he must be at least *fifty*, and you're fifteen."

"I just want us to be a family."

"It ain't gonna happen, at least not the way you want it to happen. When something doesn't work, you make do, you pull up your socks and get on with it. You'll get up to bat when it's your time. Sit down."

Sunny's heart fluttered in her chest. She'd never seen such a serious look on her brother's face. She put her hand over her chest and took a deep breath.

"What's going on?" Billie asked from the doorway. "Want some cocoa?"

Birch nodded. Then, alone again, he put his arm around his sister's shoulders. "Look, last year Sage and I went to town to have a talk with Dad. We had seen Mom crying out in the studio, watching his car go down the mountain. She called Aunt Billie in Texas. Yeah, we eavesdropped. We know what Dad said because she repeated everything. Dad said if she tried to get a divorce, he'd say she was unfaithful and sue for custody of us. He called her all kinds of names and said she was like Grandma and that he was sorry he ever married her, stuff like that. She told Aunt Billie she still loved him. Sage and I couldn't figure that out, so we called Uncle Simon."

"You told Uncle Simon!"

"I told you, we didn't know what to do. He's a great guy, I wish he was our father," Birch said wistfully. "You don't need to go blabbing this, but we call him all the time. He told us to go talk to Dad. He didn't tell us what to say, he said we'd know when we got there. The only other thing he said was to remember that Dad was our father. We took that to mean we had to show respect, which we did. That's where we were going that day you heckled us for wearing suits and ties. Jesus, it was like standing in front of the principal. Something died in me that day, Sunny, I swear to God. Dad looked at us like we were strangers. The funny thing was we were eyeball-to-eyeball. He had this wary look, like he just discovered we were all grown-up and we matched him in height and weight. He took a step backward. Because there were two of us, I guess. Maybe he felt threatened. The worst thing I said, I swear to God, was that I wished he was more like Uncle Simon. He whacked me so hard across the face I thought I was going to black out."

"What else did you say to him?"

"We told him we heard Mom's conversation with Aunt Billie. We told him it was all bullshit about him trying to get custody of us. We flat out told him we wouldn't go with him. He said he'd get Billie. She'd just turned thirteen and we weren't sure if that was true or not, so we kind of backed down a little. He called us sneaks, little turds, things like that. The whole thing was damn awful."

"You shoulda told me," Sunny muttered.

"Maybe I should have. Let this be a lesson in patience to you. Stop going off half-cocked and stop all that cussing."

He gave her one last hug. "Friends?" he asked.

"Yeah," Sunny said.

"Sallie, I need to talk to you about something," Philip said. "Do you have some time this afternoon?"

"I always have time for you. You can come over now if you like. I'll give you some lunch."

Sallie saw immediately that her husband was worried. "Let's be decadent and have some wine with our chicken pie. It's Ash, isn't it?"

"You always could read me. The boy isn't happy, Sallie."

"Ash isn't a boy. He's a man, a married man. A man who has ignored his marital responsibilities. I can't condone that. Tell me what's bothering you, maybe I can help."

"Actually you are the only one who *can* help. Ash came to me the other day and told me something that shocked me. I guess I've been so caught up in the chicken business that I haven't paid too much attention to what's been happening in town."

"What did Ash tell you?" Sallie asked, with an edge to her voice.

"He told me he stopped by the Silver Dollar on Wednesday evening and there were only three people in the lounge when you sang, and one of those three people was Devin Rollins. The palaces are no longer productive, Sallie. Ash was right when he told you years ago that you needed to move with the times. The other places have headline shows, classy decor, new equipment. Your operation is outdated. It's 1961, Sallie, not 1923. It's thirty-eight years later and you're pretty much in the same place as you were then. That shouldn't be."

"I don't like change, Philip, you know that."

"What does that mean?"

Sallie's eyes burned with unshed tears. "I guess it means I don't know what to do."

"That's not true. You do know what to do, you just don't want to do it. I don't see that you have many choices right now."

"What do you suggest?"

"Go to Ash, and you will have to go to him. He'll never come to you, you must realize that. He was right, but he won't rub your nose in it. Be honest, sit down and talk. You can still be a viable contender in the gaming business if that's what you want. If it's not what you want, close up shop, retire, and help Fanny with her business."

"What about all my people?"

"I can give a lot of them jobs, but they'll have to work for their money. You don't owe them anything, Sallie, you carried them these last ten years."

"Just like that?"

"Just like that. By the way, Ash doesn't know I'm here, and I'd like to keep it that way. If you decide to go ahead and make changes, he needs to believe it was all your idea. He's a hard worker, and he has good ideas. I don't much care for what he does in his personal life, but he's a man, and if he wants to screw up his life, I'm not going to change his mind."

"He's a rotten husband and a miserable father. Don't get the idea Fanny runs to me with tales, she doesn't. I'd have to be blind not to see what's going on. How is it possible to be blind to one thing and not another? Don't bother to answer that, Philip. I'm glad you had the guts to come here and tell me this. Why didn't Devin say something?"

"I guess because he loves you too much to want to hurt your feelings," Philip said in a choked voice.

"I guess I should thank you, Philip. How . . . what . . . ?"

"Do what your heart tells you, Sallie. Meet your son halfway, and the rest will fall into place. Know this though, if you turn things over to Ash, you have to step aside and let him do things his way. You can't interfere the way you did before."

"We didn't even touch our lunch," Sallie said.

"Another time."

Sallie allowed herself to be kissed on the cheek before she walked back to her sitting room and rang for a pot of tea. She sat quietly all afternoon sipping her tea and smoking. She was still sitting when the sun started to set. She waved away her housekeeper when she announced dinner, but she did accept another pot of tea. She was still sitting in the dark when the doorbell rang at nine-thirty and again at ten-thirty.

At eleven o'clock when she climbed the stairs to her room she felt old beyond her years. She wished she could cry so she would feel better, but her eyes were dry. She should call Devin and ask him a few questions. She took a deep breath, then dialed his number.

"Did I wake you, Devin? No, that's good. Devin, I need to ask you something. Philip was here this afternoon and we had a long talk. Listen and tell me what you think."

A long time later, Sallie said, "Devin, how did I allow this to happen? Do you know? Am I a fool? I thought I was being . . . I thought my customers would be loyal and come back when all that . . . that . . . neon, that noise . . . It won't ever wear off, will it? People like that kind of atmosphere. Ash was right. The question is, what do I do now? Devin, why didn't you say something to me?"

"Because you were so happy. I didn't want to spoil that for you. It was selfish of me. It's not too late, Sallie. Shift into high gear and take charge, make hard decisions and don't look back. Call Simon in the morning and talk with him before you commit to Ash. It might be a good idea for both of us to take a stroll through the casinos to see what you're up against. We'll do it when you're ready."

"I want you to shut everything down first thing in the morning. Give all the employees a month's severance pay."

"Good for you. That's the first step. And then?"

"I don't know. I'm going to Sunrise. I'll call you in a few days."

"Now you're talking."

"I'm going to hang up now, Devin, I have a lot of thinking to do."

"I'm here if you need me. I love you, sweetheart. Remember that."

Sallie looked around her empty bedroom. There was a huge four-poster with a lacy canopy that matched the lace curtains on the window, brocade and satin chaise longues, a dressing table with an exquisite skirt, hand-sewn by Fanny, hand-carved night tables, a magnificent Bavarian crystal chandelier. It would always be an empty bedroom, no matter how much furniture there was. An empty room—empty of emotion, empty of love. Empty.

Sallie blinked when she reached for the petit point pillow Fanny had given her for Christmas so many years ago. She counted the pillow among her few rare treasures. She'd cried that year, cried because someone cared enough to try and preserve a memory for her. How appropriate it was that Fanny had been the one to do it. Her sister Peggy had sketched a drawing of Ragtown just after Sallie's visit home, and mailed it to her. It was so detailed, so perfect, right down to the rags stuffed in the door, that she had to run from the room to be alone. Fanny had taken the drawing and stitched it to perfection. Sallie cradled it to her breast now, her eyes filled with tears.

Her past. The past that had brought her to this point in time. If only she knew what the future held for her.

"Sage, wake up. Sage, get up," Sunny hissed into her sleeping brother's ear. She shook him, yanked at his covers, and then swatted him on the face. "Get up, come out to the hall. This is important."

"What time is it?"

"It's four in the morning. C'mon, get up."

"Go away. Why are you whispering, Birch sleeps through anything."

"C'mon, I want you to see something. I'm losing sleep too."

In the hallway, Sage rubbed at his tousled hair. "So, show me already so I can go back to sleep. This better be good. Does your hair always stand straight up in the air when you sleep?"

"Shut up! I haven't been to sleep yet."

"Huh?"

Sunny pushed her brother into her room and closed the door. "Watch where you're walking. I can't turn the light on. Look! I thought it was Mom when the car's headlights arched on the wall. It's Grandma!"

"What's she doing in the cemetery at four o'clock in the morning? Something must be wrong."

"Sage, you don't think something happened to Mom, do you?"

That was exactly what he did think. "No, of course not. How . . . how long has she been out there?"

Sunny stretched her neck to look at her bedside clock. "Forty-five minutes or so. I sat here and watched her for a while. I didn't know if I should go down . . . what's she doing there?"

"I don't know. It must be important . . . to her. I don't think she would appreciate it if we . . . intruded. People who go to cemeteries in the middle of the night must want privacy."

"I already figured that out," Sunny snorted. "I wish Mom was here."

"She doesn't appear to be moving at all. How can anyone sit that still?"

"Maybe she's in shock. Maybe it's something terrible and the cemetery is giving her comfort. Her parents are buried there. That's part of what I always try to tell you guys. You only have one mother, one father and . . . and you always in the time of need go back to that one person who loved and comforted you. I think that's what Grandma is doing. I don't think it has anything to do with Mom. What do you think we should do?"

"Nothing. I think Grandma wants to be alone. Why else would she come here in the middle of the night?"

"She's crying, see her shoulders are shaking."

"This is your show, kiddo," Sage said. "What do you want us to do?"

"Nothing. I think we need to sit here and watch so that she - doesn't . . . she would . . . we need to watch. I can go downstairs and make some coffee. I can do it in the dark."

"Toast too."

"If she moves or . . . or anything, run down to the kitchen, okay?"

Sage nodded.

The two kept their vigil. They were still sitting on the floor by Sunny's window, their eyes glued to their grandmother, when they heard the sound of their mother's car just as dawn began to break.

"Whatever it is, it's going to be all right now," Sunny said in a re-lieved tone. "Don't go back to bed yet. Let's see what happens."

They watched as their mother sat down, Indian fashion, opposite their grandmother.

Fanny's heartbeat quickened as she sat next to her mother-in-law under the massive cottonwood tree. "I'm a good listener, Sallie. I stopped by your house twice last night but there was no answer when I rang the doorbell."

"I didn't feel like . . . I'm sorry, Fanny. I was wondering, would you mind if I stayed with you for a little while? I won't be in the way, I'll sleep in my old schoolroom."

"Of course you can stay, as long as you like. The children will love it that you're here. We're family, Sallie, this is where you belong. How long have you been out here?"

"I wasn't paying attention to the time. At eight o'clock, Devin is going to shut down the Silver Dollar and all of the bingo palaces. I screwed up, Fanny. Isn't that how the young people today say it?"

Fanny nodded. "It's not a bad thing."

"It means I failed. Because I was stupid and vain. I think it broke Philip's heart to tell me."

"What can I do?"

"Be my friend."

"Always," Fanny said.

"What were you doing in town last night?"

"Ash and I had a row. Actually, that isn't true. The children . . . there was this bike race and Sunny beat him. He threw his bike in the bushes and took off like a dragon was on his heels. All of a sudden I couldn't take it one minute longer. I looked for him all over town. I called the ranch, but Philip said he was here at Sunrise. I went by your house, and then I sat on the front porch all night long waiting for him to come home. I spent hours making excuses for him, lying to myself, searching for things that would make things right again. I don't think they were ever right and that's why I . . . It's a big mess. It doesn't matter anymore. I feel confident that I can go it alone as long as I have my children. We can talk about me anytime; you have a crisis in your life, and we need to work on that. I see you brought the pillow with you."

"It gives me great comfort, Fanny, because it was from your heart. There are very few things in this life that I truly treasure. Money can't buy happiness, Fanny."

Fanny thought she'd never heard a sadder voice in her life. "I know that." She had told Sallie, finally, about Jake and the $200,000. The two women had laughed together; each of them had had a windfall of money. Then they had stopped laughing, remembering that neither windfall had brought happiness.

"Are you getting a good return on your money?" Sallie asked, as she had often asked before.

"It's not my money, Sallie. But, yes, it is getting a good return."

"We should get Simon to invest the money for you. I'm sorry you never got to meet him. I wish he would come home more often. I can count the times on one hand that he's been here in the last eighteen years. Three times. All three times you were in Pennsylvania visiting your family. At least he got to meet the twins, and then the girls. I might call him to come home. All of this . . . is too important to discuss on the telephone. Do you still love Ash?"

Fanny picked at a blade of grass. She placed it between her two index fingers and brought them to her mouth. An ear-piercing whistle was the result. "Try it, Sallie."

"So that's where Sunny learned to do it. Is this one of those things that takes practice?"

"Depends on how loud you want to whistle. You should hear my brother Daniel. Your ears ring for hours when he does it."

"I never wanted Cotton's money, Fanny. It scared me out of my wits. I tried to do what he would have wanted me to do. I married a good man so he would give me children. The only problem was I didn't love him. Cotton didn't say anything about loving him. It enabled me to do things for other people. I wanted to be as good and kind to others as Cotton was to me. The single most wonderful thing was helping my sister and finding Seth. I still haven't found Josh, and I don't know why that is. I guess I shelved it and . . . I'm making an excuse for my laxness."

"I understand, Sallie. I never really initiated a search for my mother. I wrote a bunch of letters, that's the sum total of what I did. I didn't follow through. Life got in the way, that's the best way I can explain it."

An ear-piercing sound ricocheted around the cottonwoods.

"Sallie, that was wonderful! Let's do it again. You a betting woman, Sallie?"

"Two bits," Sallie said.

"You're on. On the count of three!

"It's a draw. Again," Fanny said.

"One more time," she said after the second try that resulted in another tie.

"Three out of three," Sallie said.

"And the winner is . . . Sallie." Fanny whooped.

Upstairs behind the curtains, Birch grabbed Sunny by the neck. "You got me out of bed to watch our mother and our grandmother *whistle*?"

"You are so stupid. I can't believe some college is letting you in their doors. Mom just made it right for Grandma. The whistle is like when she used to give us a Popsicle. Remember how good it felt when she smiled and handed it to us? No matter how bad it was, that always made it right. Whatever happened down there was serious."

"Okay, I'm gonna give you that one because in your own cockamamie way you make sense. Is it okay if we go back to bed?"

In the garden, Fanny sat back on her haunches. "If I knew somebody worthy of my affections, I'd contemplate an affair."

"It's not the answer. You have to deal with the problem first. I know what I'm talking about, Fanny."

"Sometimes I ache, Sallie. I'm not a cold, hard person. I have feelings and needs, and I don't know what to do."

"When it's right you'll know. You have to make decisions where Ash is concerned. That's where you have to start."

"What about you, Sallie?"

"I don't know. I have a lot of thinking to do."

"I learned something a while ago. When something disastrous happens, something good usually happens right afterward. If you aren't too caught up in your misery, and you keep your heart and your eyes open, you can usually see it. I'm probably not explaining this right. It doesn't have to be a big major happening, it could be something as simple as seeing a rosebud open or a child's drawing made just for you. In this case it's Billie. Come along, Mrs. Thornton Senior, I have lots to tell you about your youngest granddaughter. We need your advice. First, though, we're going to have a big, whopping breakfast."

Sallie smiled. "Lead on, Mrs. Thornton Junior."

16

"I think this is what I've missed the most during my life," Sallie said, indicating her boisterous grandchildren. "I'm glad they get along so well. You're going to miss the boys when they leave. I know I'll miss them."

"Just two more days and they're off to college. Give me a kick if you see me start to blubber, Sallie."

"Who's going to give *me* a kick?" Sallie asked.

"Me," Fanny said sprightly. "You're excused, don't slam the door!"

The two Mrs. Thorntons watched indulgently as the four youngsters hurtled through the kitchen door, shouldering each other out of the way in their hurry to ride down the mountain to Chue's, where a baseball game was scheduled for one o'clock.

"I should leave, Fanny. I've been here six weeks. It's time for me to . . . it's time."

"Have you made any decisions?"

"No."

"Have you called Devin?"

"No."

"He must be a very patient man, Sallie."

"Among other things. Have you heard from Ash?"

"No. I was going to call him today to remind him the boys are leaving, then I said to myself, why should I do that? He's their father, he should know. I'm so glad Simon is coming. I long to meet him, after all these years. The boys are really looking forward to driving cross-country with him. Do you think they badgered him into doing it."

Sallie chuckled. "I wouldn't be surprised. I guess they were astute enough to know their father wouldn't make the trip and grown boys don't want their mother showing up with them to hold their hand and then wailing her head off when it's time to leave. It was my understanding that this was all arranged early in the summer. It doesn't surprise me that you and I are the last to know. Simon always waits till the eleventh hour to make announcements. Is everything ready for the party?"

"The Colemans arrive tomorrow, sometime before lunch. At first Seth said he couldn't make it, but I think Agnes talked him into it. They're all coming in the Coleman plane. One minute I feel elated and the next minute I feel like I'm losing . . ."

"Your children. Life goes on, Fanny. Sometimes I think it would be nice to be able to stop time. It seems to be moving so fast these days. I remember the day the twins were born so clearly. Now look at them! They're going to be campus idols, or whatever good-looking young men are called these days. What will we do if Ash is a no-show at the party?"

"Try to gloss over it I guess. What else can I do?"

"If he knows I'm here, he might not come. I'm sure Philip has told him I've been staying here. Maybe I should . . ."

"Don't even *think* about leaving, Sallie. I wish you had allowed me to invite Devin. He's part of the family and he adores the boys. It's not fair, Sallie."

"I fibbed to you earlier, I did call Devin this morning. Simon will bring him up this evening."

"That's one positive thing you've done since you've been here."

Sallie smiled, but the smile didn't reach her eyes.

"In two weeks the girls will be leaving for school. I hope I didn't make a mistake, Sallie."

"They'll be home the first weekend of every month. It's the best school in the state. Mentally, both of them are ready for it. Sunny

needs a big dose of discipline as well as a few lessons in . . . in la-
dylike behavior. Billie needs children her age. Don't get selfish on
me now. Think of it in terms of independence. You'll also have more
time for your business. You said you wanted to go to New York and
to Hong Kong. It's time for Fanny to think about Fanny. You need
a life beyond Sunrise."

"I have the business . . ." Fanny said lamely.

"Yes, you sit here designing and make sample garments. Bess
runs the offices and Billie takes care of the Texas end of things. You
need to involve yourself more. It's your business, Fanny. You gave
birth to it, you nurtured it, and you watched it bud and blossom. I
don't want to see you make the same mistakes I did. You did this
with nothing but guts. What I have was given to me. There's a big
difference. You can't do it halfway, the way I did. Either you take
hold all the way or you sell now while you can make a big profit.
My advice would be to talk it over with Simon. I don't know if you
know this or not, but Nevada is a community property state. What
that means is Ash is entitled to half of everything you have. You
might want to give some thought to that."

"I'll talk to Simon." *For the first time*, Fanny thought. She could
hardly believe she was going to meet this paragon at last. What
would he be like?

"How many people are coming?" Sallie asked.

"Around a hundred. I have things planned for the older people,
the middle-aged people, and the youngsters. Birch is going to orga-
nize a baseball game. Sunny is the shortstop, whatever that is. Sage
says she can catch a pop fly better than any of the guys at school
when she's in the outfield."

"I'm almost afraid to ask this, but do you know if Moss is coming?"

"As of last night, Billie didn't know. She said she refuses to beg
him. She and Moss aren't . . ." Fanny stopped herself. This was not
the time to discuss Billie's problems. "She did say Thad Kingsley,
Moss's best friend, was coming, but in his own plane."

"I'm looking forward to seeing Simon. I miss him terribly. He's
so independent, so unlike Ash. I ask myself often why he's never
married, and the only answer I can come up with is he didn't like
Philip and my marriage, and he's afraid the same thing might happen to him. He would make such a wonderful husband and father."

Fanny made a production out of getting up from the table to
allow Sallie time to wipe at her wet eyes. She wanted to cry herself
at the change in her mother-in-law in six short weeks. All the life,
the spontaneity, and the sparkle seemed to have gone out of her.

Would Devin or Simon be able to bring it back? Perhaps seeing Seth might help.

She doubted her own thoughts as she led the way up the winding stairs.

"Fanny, what time is it?"

"Ten minutes past ten."

"Simon should have been here by now. I worry about him; he drives the way he flies a plane."

"What? And he's going to be driving my sons cross-country! I thought you said he was the stable one of your two sons."

"He is. I will caution him as you will, too, to drive sedately. Simon is responsible.

"I hear a car." The panic on Sallie's face was almost comical. Amused, Fanny watched as Sallie ran into the house to freshen her makeup. Maybe she should do the same. Too much trouble, she muttered to herself as she got up from the front steps where she and Sallie had been sitting for the past hour.

"Fanny, I don't believe you've met Simon," Devin said, climbing from the car.

Fanny wished she had followed Sallie into the house to freshen up. She knew stray tendrils of hair had escaped the rubber band that pulled her hair back. She'd eaten off her lipstick hours ago, and there was no powder on her face, so she knew her nose was shiny. Her blue jeans, oversize shirt, and sneakers were hardly fashionable. She wished that she had listened to Sallie when she suggested she change into a sundress to show off her golden tan.

"It's so nice to finally meet you," Fanny said, extending her hand.

"No, no, we aren't going to shake hands. I'm your brother-in-law. That means we're family." Before Fanny knew what was happening she was in Simon's arms and he was hugging her tightly as he kissed first one cheek and then the other. She was aware of the heady scent of his woodsy after-shave, the faint odor of pipe tobacco, and the clean smell of him. In that one brief glance she knew exactly what he was wearing even though the porch light was dimly yellow. She took a moment to marvel at the thought before she stepped aside, her cheeks flushed, her heart racing. This was a man. Her heart continued to race.

"Mom, you're looking better than ever," Simon said, lifting his mother high in the air and swinging her around. He turned till he was facing Fanny and said, "I could do this to you with one hand. You're skinny as a rail. Mom, make her eat."

"She eats like a truck driver. It's all in the genes," Sallie said happily as she linked her arm with Simon's.

"You didn't tell me she was so gorgeous," Simon said in a loud stage whisper.

Fanny felt her entire body grow warm as she followed Sallie and Simon into the house. "Devin, would you like something to drink? Simon?"

"A cold beer would be nice. A sandwich would go real good with the beer," Simon said.

"Don't forget the pickles," Devin said.

In the kitchen Fanny leaned against the counter to take deep breaths. Something was happening to her, something she hadn't felt for a very long time. In a few brief seconds she found herself attracted to a man she'd never met before. She should run upstairs to the bathroom to comb her hair and put on lipstick. No, too obvious. She pulled a turkey and a ham from the refrigerator. She sliced and sliced, and when she was finished she had two sandwiches that were five inches high. She added potato chips and pickles along with the beer to the tray.

He was so tall he dwarfed her when he reached out to take the tray. He smiled when he said, "Now that's what I call a sandwich. Mom used to make them like that." His voice was deliciously husky. Fanny shivered in the oversize shirt.

"I know," Fanny said. In her life she'd never seen a more handsome man. She sat down next to Sallie and immediately got up. "I imagine you have lots to talk about. I'll say good-night."

"No, no, stay," Simon said.

"Darling, Devin and I are going to take a walk in the garden. Keep Simon company."

"Devin, your sandwich . . ."

"I'm taking it with me. I love eating in the garden and listening to the night sounds."

"Oh, let them go. It will give us a chance to get acquainted. Where's Ash?"

Fanny stared into cobalt blue eyes. "I have no idea," she said.

"Oh. Is that one of those questions I shouldn't have asked?"

"You can ask anything you want. Ash doesn't live here anymore. On occasion, he visits. Is there anything else you want to know?" Her voice was colder than chilled milk. Why was that?

"I'm sorry. I didn't know. It's been a while since Ash and I have spoken."

"Are you saying you haven't spoken to your brother in five years?" Fanny asked.

"No, not at all," Simon said warily.

"Well, that's how long this has been going on."

"Ash isn't exactly the confiding type. He plays everything pretty close to his chest. I didn't mean to stir something up here. I apologize, this is none of my business."

"Don't apologize. Everyone knows, now you know. We work around it."

Simon finished his sandwich. "Would I be out of line to ask why you don't do something about it?"

"I was going to do something, but Ash said he had a list of men as long as his arm who would swear they had an affair with me. In case you're wondering why I'm telling you all this when we just met, it's because . . . I'm sick of the lies, sick of covering up, sick of the whole damn thing. Tomorrow . . . he could . . . what he could do is . . . is show up, make a scene, and ruin everything. I panic just thinking about it. I worked hard on this party, to give the boys a nice send-off."

"I don't know what to say," Simon said, leaning over the coffee table to stare at her.

"That's pretty much what everyone says. But, I can top that. I don't know what to say, either."

"What does Mom say?"

"I do my best not to involve your mother. She has her own problems with Ash. She's going through a very bad time right now. I'm glad you came, she needs you. More than you'll ever know. I also think it's pretty shabby of you not to visit more often. Your business can't be that time-consuming. Everyone gets a vacation. Are you a selfish person?"

"Jesus. You are outspoken, aren't you?"

"Pretty much so. I didn't used to be, but I am these days. When you say it right up front there's no room for doubt. I had to learn the hard way. If you don't feel like answering my questions, don't."

"I didn't say I didn't want to answer your questions. My business is very time-consuming. I do take an occasional vacation. No one has ever accused me of being selfish, at least not to my knowledge. It's possible that I am, and I'm too dumb to know it. I call my mother twice a week. I'm not much of a letter writer, but I do write. It works for us."

"It works for you, you mean. It doesn't work for Sallie. I know this. She would never say anything to you, but that doesn't mean I can't say it for her. You should have come here right away when . . . when things started to go bad for her. That's my opinion of course."

"Wait just one damn minute. I offered to come, she said no. She said she was coming up here to Sunrise to get herself together."

"Those were just words. She wanted you to care enough to come on your own. She watched the road for days. Sometimes people say things and mean something else. Sallie is your mother—you should be able to figure her out."

"This is one of those women things, right?"

"Sunny always says, and this is a direct quote, 'Oh, that's one of those penis things, right?' If it helps you to believe that, it's okay with me."

"I'll be damned," Simon said, throwing his head back and laughing until tears gathered on his lashes. "I think you made the right decision to send her to that academy for young ladies. She might have to repeat a term or two if she doesn't conform."

"I know. She's what she is, and she isn't changing." Fanny laughed.

"I was trying to make a good impression," Simon said.

"Me too. Guess I didn't. How come you haven't married?" Fanny asked, propping her feet up on the coffee table. She lit a cigarette. Suddenly she was very comfortable with this man with the salt-and-pepper hair and the wonderful voice that sent chills up and down her spine.

"Why do you want to know? I didn't know you smoked."

"I was making conversation. It seemed like a good question. You know, get it out of the way early on. Should someone have told you I smoked? Does it even matter? You smoke. I do a lot of things these days that I never did before. I chew gum when I'm designing, and I gobble peanuts by the bag."

Simon laughed. "I'm glad you told me that. I almost got married twice. I'm the one who broke it off both times."

"Oh. Do you miss having children?"

"I do. I want to thank you for sharing your children with me. I'm very fond of all of them."

"I don't think it's any secret that they adore you. Ash has a hard time with those feelings."

"I didn't know that. He does know I'm driving the boys to Pennsylvania, doesn't he?"

"I don't know. I hate to keep saying that, but we don't communicate. I'm sure the boys told him."

"I hope so, I don't want to step on toes here and cause a problem. Where are the kids?"

"Down at Chue's. They like to shoot baskets in his driveway in the evening. It's a nice evening, would you like to walk down?"

"Sure. Should we tell someone where we're going?" Simon asked, a devilish glint in his eye.

"You can if you think it's necessary. I'm of the opinion we're both old enough to go out at night as long as we're home before midnight. When I was growing up my father always made us be home when the streetlights went on. It was to teach us responsibility. We didn't have watches in those days."

"And did it?"

"Oh yes. I've tried to bring my own kids up the same way. Sunny is the rebel. She absolutely refuses to conform as you put it. No amount of punishment can make her change her mind. Next year she'll be going off to college and then it will be just Billie and me. I don't know how I'm going to handle that."

"One day at a time in the beginning. I imagine you'll do what I did when I left. You throw yourself into whatever it is that makes you happy. Happiness is very important."

"You sound like you aren't too happy, Simon."

"I'm not sure I know what happiness really is. Since I don't know, I guess I'm not."

"I think happiness is kind of nebulous. People, myself included, tend to think it should be this euphoric feeling that cloaks you and makes you immune to all other emotions. In my opinion, happiness is little bits of things. For me, for example, it was the birth of all my children, then it would be something they did or said, a small gift that made me smile. Sage used to bring me dandelions. One year Sunny gave me a handmade gift certificate that said she would rub my neck and shoulders every night for a month. She did too—she never missed a night. She guaranteed me a smile every night for a month. I feel happy each time I see Billie sitting at the drafting table. One of Chue's flower arrangements for the dining room table gives me happiness. There's a little brown bird that nests in one of the cottonwoods in the cemetery. It trusts me and will perch on my finger. That gives me happiness. I believe each person is responsible for their own happiness. To depend on other people to make you happy is a mistake. That's just my opinion of course. Your mother and I talked about this a while ago. I think she agrees with me. What's your view?"

"I don't think I have a view. I can't say I ever gave it much thought. That's not to say I'm miserable. I don't think about it. I try to stay busy. My life is quite full."

"You sound defensive," Fanny said.

"You're pretty brash for just meeting me for the first time," Simon said with a chuckle. "Actually, I kind of like it, it's refreshing to meet someone who doesn't say five different things when they don't mean any of them. I'm almost an expert at interpreting people's conversations these days. The key word is almost." The chuckle stayed in his voice.

"Would you listen to those kids!"

Simon charged ahead, apologizing over his shoulder as he leaped for a basketball that Birch threw to Sunny. He intercepted the ball, loped up the driveway to sink the ball with his first shot!

"For an old guy that was pretty good," Sunny yelled. "How'ya doing, Uncle Simon?"

"Who are you calling old? I can beat you with one hand tied behind my back wearing weights on my ankles."

The twins hooted with laughter. "Put up or shut up, Sunny. My money is on Uncle Simon. Let's make it interesting and make a pot here. All bets for Uncle Simon go on this side, Sunny's stack goes on this side. We'll take IOU.s."

"Can we bet on ourselves?" Sunny asked.

"Why not. I'm going to beat you," Simon grinned.

"Not on your best day!" Sunny shot back. "You're bettin' on me, right, Mom?"

"Fifty bucks," Fanny said generously.

"Put me down for fifty too," Billie said.

"Does she have fifty bucks, Mom?" Birch demanded.

"Yes, she does. I don't approve of gambling."

"A Thornton who doesn't believe in gambling. Shame on you!" Simon yelled.

"Birch and I are each betting fifty bucks on Uncle Simon," Sage said.

"I'm betting a hundred on myself," Simon said.

"Ah, this is getting real sweet," Birch said. "Chue, what are you in for?"

"One hundred dollars on Miss Sunny," Chue said smartly. "How does this work, Miss Fanny? Do they have enough to pay off if Miss Sunny wins?"

"I'm covering all bets," Simon said.

"In that case, Chue, let's decide what we're going to spend our money on," Fanny said.

"Spoilsport," Simon said as he took his place in the middle of the driveway to face Sunny. Sage held the ball aloft. "On the count of three. Ten shots. Okay, ready, one, two, THREE!"

"Is she really good, Chue?" Fanny whispered.

"She's hot stuff."

"Really," Fanny said. The pride in her voice was unmistakable.

They were whirlwinds racing up and down the driveway. Sunny laughed as she forced her uncle to use muscles he'd forgotten he had.

"C'mon, c'mon, Uncle Simon, you can do it!" the twins shouted as Simon lagged behind.

"You got him, Sunny, he's huffing and puffing," Billie shouted. "Dribble, dribble, he's no match for you. Go! Go! Wow! Did you see that! Yeah, Sunny!"

Fanny clapped her hands. "Ooohhh, I can't wait to spend my money! Good girl, Sunny, you're wearing him down. It's seven–four. You're in the lead, honey!"

"She's gaining, Uncle Simon, c'mon, make her work for her money. She can't last forever. She's a girl! Get that ball! Oh, no," Birch groaned as Sunny sank two baskets one right after the other.

"Nine–four," Fanny screamed. "You won, Sunny! Pay up," she said, holding out her hand. She turned to Chue. "Did you see that, we won!"

"You are the marvel in marvelous," Simon said, hugging his niece. "I don't think I ever saw such fancy footwork. Congratulations!"

"You kept up with me. That's good for a guy your age. I don't mean that disrespectfully," Sunny added hastily. "It's a compliment."

"And a sincere one too," Simon gasped. "God, I feel old."

"Come along, it's almost midnight. Chue needs his sleep."

"Cocoa and fried egg sandwiches. I'll make it," Sunny said.

"Don't look at me like that, Simon. She has this thing about fried egg sandwiches and cocoa at midnight. It wasn't bad enough that she wanted it, she got the others hooked right along with her. As early as seven I had to sleep with one eye open because she'd try and do it herself."

"I don't think I ever had a fried egg sandwich at midnight," Simon said, laughing.

"With ketchup and crispy bacon. You have to spread butter on the bread first, then ketchup, then you put the bacon on and the egg goes on top of it. The yolk has to be semisoft so it dribbles down your chin. The cocoa has to have marshmallows and be hot enough to melt the marshmallows. Trust me, you'll love it!" Fanny laughed.

"In the kitchen everyone! Billie, see if Grandma and Devin are in the garden. They love my fried egg sandwiches."

Midway during the feast, Fanny poked Simon on the arm. "This is one of those small moments called happiness." Simon nodded, understanding perfectly. "I want to thank you for being so kind to Sunny when she beat you." Simon's eyes were puzzled as he nodded. *That*, he didn't understand.

"I cooked, you guys clean," Sunny said.

The kitchen was suddenly filled with good-natured kidding and laughter as everyone had an excuse for not doing kitchen duty.

Sunny saw him first, the laughter dying on her face.

"Looks like I missed a great party," Ash said. "Simon, it's good to see you. Mom, Devin, good to see you too." He ignored his wife as he walked around the table to shake hands with Simon and Devin. He clapped his sons on their backs before he took a seat at the table. "What were you celebrating?"

"Sunny beat me shooting baskets down at Chue's. This daughter of yours is pretty fast on her feet."

"Good night, everyone," Sunny said. In her haste to get out of the room she knocked over her chair. As she fumbled to right it, her face miserable, she managed to upend Sage's half-full cup of cocoa. In a dither she tried to mop it up with napkins, her brothers scrambling to help her. "Oh, shit," she muttered under her breath. It was Devin who saw Ash's raised arm and moved accordingly. It happened so fast, Fanny could only gasp.

"Sorry, old man, I didn't realize you were moving. Did the chair get you on the leg?"

"Yeah, it's okay. Sunny, come here. What did you just say?"

"She didn't say anything, I said, 'oh shit,' " Birch said.

"I heard him," Sage said.

"So did I," Billie said.

"What the hell. When in Rome . . ." I heard Birch say it too," Simon said. "If my memory serves me right, I think that was your favorite expression when you were Birch's age."

Fanny felt like she should stand up and cheer. "Thank you," she whispered to Simon. "Time for bed," she said then. "Tomorrow's a big day. I'll clean up."

"Who's going to make me a fried egg sandwich?" Ash asked.

"Good night, everyone," Sallie said as she followed Devin from the room.

"Don't look at me, I can't cook. I'm more than willing to dry if someone else washes," Simon said.

"Don't look at me either," Fanny said coolly. "I'll wash, you dry," she said to Simon. She turned her back on her husband to fill the sink with hot soapy water.

"Well, I had a rough day, so I'm off to bed," Ash said. "Don't be too late, Fanny."

Fanny shuddered as she plunged her hands into the soapy water. She didn't acknowledge her husband's comment.

Fanny didn't speak until she was certain Ash was upstairs. "I'm sorry you had to . . . lie like that and to hear . . ."

"Listen, it never happened, okay. I need to know something first, though. What would have happened if Birch hadn't stepped in? Then we won't speak of it again," Simon said gently.

"I don't know. Obviously Birch didn't know either and that's why he . . . said what he did. I'm surprised Sunny didn't get right in Ash's face and tell the truth. The fact that she didn't, stuns me." A tear dropped on Fanny's cheek. "I'm not going up there. I'm not. There's no way I'm going up there. I absolutely refuse."

"Okay, we've established you aren't going up there. Is it okay to ask where you *are* going to go?"

"I have any number of places I could go . . . can go. I can sleep with Sunny or Billie. I can go down to Chue's house. I usually end up at the studio. I had dead bolts put on both doors a while ago."

"Jesus. I'm a good listener, Fanny, and I never judge. What went wrong? I was under the assumption you and Ash had one of those heavenly marriages. I can tell you I was damn jealous for a long time."

"Now that's about the funniest thing I've heard in a long time. I suppose I should laugh. I don't know what went wrong. Probably everything. A lot of it I think has to do with your mother. He thinks I look like her and act like her. He resented the help Sallie got me when the twins were born. Then I got pregnant again and things didn't get any better. Ash wanted a stylish, beautiful wife like the showgirls in town, and there I was, and . . . he started having affairs, staying away, coming home drunk, and being abusive. He was never around for family things, never around for the kids' events. I was a single parent. I swear to God, I never complained. I bit my tongue, made excuses, lied . . . you name it, I did it. All in the name of family. I don't know why I'm telling you all this . . . maybe you should just go up to bed and forget about us."

"You're telling me because you finally got the courage to talk to someone. Even though we're related, I'm pretty much a stranger. For now. Whatever you say will never go any further than me. Go on."

"I started to sew to keep myself occupied. Billie, your mother, and my friend Bess persuaded me to start up the business. They all helped. Ash blames Billie for making me independent. He never liked Bess, and you know the situation with your mother. No matter what I did, it wasn't right. I couldn't please him. He drinks too much, and he's nasty. Things got worse when your mother deeded Sunrise to me on my thirtieth birthday. I stayed up here and he stayed in town. It became a way of life."

"I'm sorry. At least now I understand why the boys have called me so much. Did you know they called?"

"No. It doesn't surprise me, though. They need and want a father. You're the next best thing and please, don't take that the wrong way."

"Never," Simon said. "How will you deal with tomorrow and the day after tomorrow? I'd like to help if that's possible."

"I don't know. I pretty much take it as it comes and try to deal with it at the time so things don't get out of hand." Fanny took her hands out of the soapy water and grasped the edge of the sink. She turned to face Simon, her eyes locked with his. "Do you ever feel like you want to chuck everything and run away? You know, when things start to pile up. My mother did that to my brothers and me. She just up and left us. She never came back. I think I can understand her now." She paused. "Do *you* ever get restless?"

"Twice a day. Someday I might just up and leave, too. Someday I'm going to wake up and say the hell with all of this. Then I'm going to buy a boat, christen it *Someday*, and sail away and not look back. I have a list of people who want to sign on as my crew. Put your name in now if you want to come along."

Fanny dipped her finger into the soapy water, withdrew it, and made a big X on Simon's shirtfront. "Count me in." Her knees felt weak when he smiled at her.

"Can I walk you to wherever you're going?" Simon asked, hanging up the dish towel.

"If you like. I'm going to my studio."

"Mom told me about it. She called it your sanctuary."

"You really felt the need to share that with me, huh?" Fanny laughed.

He loved her laugh, loved her easy stride, loved the way she looked, loved her tell-it-like-it-is attitude. Ash had to be the biggest fool alive. "We're here. I'll wait until you lock the door."

"Good night, Simon. Thanks for walking me home. I think I can truthfully say no man or boy has ever walked me home before. It's a nice feeling. When I was in high school I always wondered what it would be like to walk home with a boy I really really liked, you know, have him hold my hand under a harvest moon with the scent of autumn in the air. I love the smell of burning leaves. Good night, Simon. I'll see you in the morning."

"You bet." He waited until he heard the sound of the dead bolt shooting home before he started up the path to the main house—the house he'd grown up in. He sat down on a low brick wall in the courtyard. It was new—Chue must have built it sometime during the past few years. He looked back at the dim yellow light in the studio windows. He wanted to run back down the path and bang on the door. And do what? He fumbled for a cigarette and lit it. He blew three perfect smoke rings, one right after the other. *What a big, major accomplishment,* he thought sourly. Since he wasn't going to go back down the path, maybe he should go upstairs and put his fist through his brother's smirking face. What he should *really* do was get back in his car and head for home before things got out of hand.

Even before the thought hit him, he knew he wasn't going to do it. What he was probably going to do was take the boys to Pennsylvania, garage the car, and hop a plane back here the next day. He'd stay until he was either asked to leave or until he couldn't stand it a minute longer. Whichever came first. It sounded like a reasonable game plan. A workable game plan. He could stay as long as he wanted. He had capable people working for him, making him money. All he had to do was call the office and say, you'll see me when you see me. Period.

And then what? Did he stay with his mother? Everyone would want to know why he was suddenly smitten with Nevada after all these years. Who would be the first to figure it out? Ash, of course.

Better to go back to New York where he belonged and forget about the person who put a big soapy X on his shirt, that person who signed on for his runaway cruise.

Sallie and Fanny stepped from the car to sharp whistles of approval. Ash added to the scene by putting his arm around his wife's shoulders and whispering, "You look gorgeous, honey." Fanny tried to shrug off his arm, but it only tightened more securely. "We need to talk, Fanny, and I don't mean later. I mean now."

"Ash, I'm down to the wire. I have so much to do and the Colemans will be arriving soon. I'll talk with you after the party. We'll talk in the garden the way we used to do."

"All right, after the party. Don't stand me up, Fanny."

"Don't ever threaten me, Ash. Those days are gone forever."

"You like my brother, don't you?" Ash said coolly.

"He seems like a very nice man. Yes, I like him. The children like him, and children, for the most part, are shrewd judges of character."

"I guess I'm supposed to make something out of that statement. The kids like him, but they don't like me, is that it? You like him too. Simon the Savior," Ash snorted.

"Maybe you need to pay more attention to your brother and try to be a little more like him," Fanny snorted in return. "I want a divorce, Ash. I don't want to live like this any longer. Think about that before we meet in the garden."

"I told you . . ."

"I know what you told me. I was afraid of you then. I'm not afraid of what you can do any longer. The children have a voice now. Your slimy friends and their testimonials don't bother me. Your mother knows every judge in this state. If I have to, I'll appeal to her. You think about that too."

"Fanny, I don't want a divorce, I never did. You say you do each time we have a falling out. What happened to us? We were meant for one another, you said so yourself. You think about that until we meet in the garden."

Fanny stared at her husband with her mouth hanging open. "What happened to *us*? There is no *us*. It's just you. The marriage didn't work from the beginning, and we both know it. I at least tried. This is the end of the discussion. Don't look at me with those narrowed eyes, Ash. I'm not buying into your silent threats. Get it through your head, you can no longer intimidate me. Now, I suggest you put on your party face and act like the host you're supposed to be."

"Hurry, Fanny, we need to get ready," Sallie said from the kitchen doorway. "Sweetie, I couldn't help but hear. I'm so sorry. Abide by your convictions, and you'll never go wrong. That's all the advice I'm going to give you. Sage just finished hanging the paper lanterns. They're going to look so festive when it gets dark. The band arrived while we were in town. Mazie tells me everything is running smoothly. I didn't know there was such a thing as a portable dance floor. I guess I really am behind the times. So, tell me, what did you think of Simon?" Sallie asked on her way up the back stairway.

"It's hard to believe Simon and Ash are brothers. They're so different. I like his sense of humor and his forthrightness. I can understand why he's such a successful businessman. He gave me the impression he was going to come back. It wasn't anything he said, just an impression."

"If that's the case, then things will run smoothly. Simon has that rare knack of making things right. He knows what to say at just the right time. When you walk away from Simon you always have a smile on your face. Ash always makes me grit my teeth. I notice you do the same thing."

"It's all wrong, Sallie. I think it was wrong from the beginning. Let's not talk about this today, okay?"

"Okay. I'll see you in twenty minutes. You look gorgeous, Mrs. Thornton."

"And you, Mrs. Thornton, look ravishing. I plan to dance all evening if someone will dance with me," Fanny said airily.

"I'll be right behind you," Sallie said just as airily.

Twenty minutes later the two Mrs. Thorntons met in the upper hallway.

"Ravishing," the young Mrs. Thornton said.

"Gorgeous," the elder Mrs. Thornton said.

"I'll second that," Simon said, whistling his approval.

"A man of discriminating taste," Sallie said.

"Allow me," Simon said, extending both arms. Sallie took one, Fanny the other.

Fanny allowed a small smile to tug at the corner of her mouth as she winked at her escort. She would not think about the meeting in the garden with Ash. This day was for the twins, and for her too.

"They're here," Sunny bellowed at the top of her lungs. "Ohhh, Mom, would you look at Riley. Is he a hunk or what? Too bad he's our cousin. Do I look okay, Mom? I'm getting my ears pierced, did I tell you that? He's changed so much since I saw him last. Did I change, Mom? Wow, Uncle Moss is here too. That should tell us all something. Aggie's wearing those pearls, and this time she has matching earrings. Her snoot is higher than ever. Billie looks as pretty as you, Mom, but you're prettier. Uncle Seth looks like he just sat on a beehive." She wound down like a clock whose batteries were low. Fanny stared at her helplessly.

"Look at it this way, Fanny, she's starting to notice things," Simon hissed in her ear. "Excuse me, ladies."

"Moss, it's good to see you," Simon said, extending his hand. "Just think, if it wasn't for our conversation that day on the Big E, none of us would be standing here now."

"Every time I see you I want to call you Jessup. You're lookin' good, Simon. This place looks better each time I see it. Reminds me of Sunbridge."

"Billie, you look beautiful," Fanny said, hugging her tightly.

"Moss decided to come along as we were getting in the car," Billie whispered in her ear. "How's it going? I had no idea Simon was so . . . so . . ."

"I didn't either," Fanny whispered in return.

"I could use a drink," Seth growled.

"I have two waiting, with your name on both of them," Sallie laughed. "It's good to see you again, Seth. Agnes, it's nice to see you too."

Ash joined them. His mood was expansive, his smile affable, as he shook hands, complimenting Agnes, who preened like a peacock.

From that point on the guests began to arrive, car after car.

The party was under way by noon, music rocking across the mountain, young people whooping and hollering as they frolicked in the pool to the loud music. Relatives visited and watched the youngsters with indulgent smiles on their faces. Some of the friends and business associates from town discussed the casinos until Sallie playfully waved her finger under their noses, indicating this was a social gathering. Texas beef, compliments of Seth Coleman, sizzled in the open pit manned by Chue and a cousin. Philip's plump chickens twirled on a spit, browning to perfection. The gay red-and-white-striped tents held long tables with outrageously beautiful flower arrangements, thanks to Chue and his greenhouse. Adding to the fun theme were clusters of colorful balloons and gaily wrapped going-away presents piled to the top of the tent. It would take the boys hours to unwrap them all.

Agnes Ames, resplendent in a bright blue designer outfit, walked the property, her eyes cataloging and calculating the cost of the party, all the while comparing it to one of Seth's Texas barbecues. She needed to come up with a dollar amount because it would be the first thing Seth would ask on the way home. She watched out of the corner of her eye as Seth cornered Philip. She smirked, knowing exactly what he was asking: did chickens bring in as much money as beef? Then he'd want to know the cost of chicken feed. She'd hear all the details the moment they started for home.

Agnes sucked in her breath as her eyes traveled across the yard to where her son-in-law Moss was standing with Ash, Simon Thornton, and John Noble, Bess's husband. She'd never in the whole of her life seen four such handsome men in one place. She looked around for her daughter and was dismayed to see her huddled with Fanny and

Fanny's friend Bess. She could just imagine what they were talking about. Her stomach started to react. It would be just like Billie to decide on the spur of the moment to leave Moss because of his philandering ways. And exactly where would that leave her? She fingered the pearls at her neck. She was the Mistress of Sunbridge, and she had no intention of giving up the title. Not now, not later, not ever.

She wasn't blind to her son-in-law's infidelities, infidelities that Seth condoned. Her job was to hold Billie in line, to make sure her daughter didn't do something foolish like file for divorce and take young Riley, heir to the Coleman dynasty, with her. She knew that was what Billie intended to do. The question was, when would she do it? She stared now at her beautiful daughter, who was talking animatedly with Fanny Thornton. Two beautiful women who had come into their own, *on their own*, each giving support to the other. Ash Thornton, she knew, was an alley cat, just like her son-in-law. She'd learned that by eavesdropping, something she did on a regular basis. And then she raced to Seth and reported her findings. She hated herself for betraying her own daughter, but she was too old to give up the good life she'd grown accustomed to.

Agnes didn't like the way the three young women were huddling, didn't like the speculative looks in their eyes. They were comparing husband notes, and the men were coming up drastically short. She needed to do something, but what? She could feel Seth's eyes boring into the back of her head. Mustering all the willpower she could, she turned and marched across the yard to where Seth was sitting with Sallie. He looked like an ugly predator ready to snatch his grandson from her daughter's arms if a divorce was imminent. She hated herself for aiding and abetting this cantankerous old man. She swallowed hard, her fingers on her pearls when she took her place next to Seth.

"Are you enjoying yourself, Agnes?" Sallie asked.

"Very much. The air is so crisp and clean up here. It reminds me of the Allegheny Mountains in Pennsylvania. It's different here now—things have changed in the past few years."

"Absolutely. A family lives here now. There are nicks and scratches everywhere, dogs and cats, bicycles and baseball bats. Some days you can't get in the front door. It's good to hear the laughter and even the squabbling. The only problem is, this little family is lopsided. My son doesn't participate much. I find it particularly amazing that Fanny has managed to keep it all together. I imagine you both must feel the same way about Billie, proud of her plans to start up her own business. Fanny and Billie work so well together. They trade strengths. One day, mark my word, Billie will be a famous textile designer."

"And where's she going to get the money to do that? My boy isn't going to approve of his wife starting up her own business. She belongs at home with the family. Ain't that right, Aggie?"

Agnes decided to travel the low road. "Billie hasn't said anything to me about it. I'm her mother, I think I would know."

"No money for such foolishness," Seth growled again, not liking Agnes's response.

"That's not true, Seth. Fanny is going to back her. Bess and John are prepared to buy into it too. I don't think money will be an issue. The way I see it, Thornton money is just as green as Coleman money." Sallie leaned closer to her brother. "She's had enough, Seth, just the way Fanny has had enough. I'm not proud of what my son has been doing these past years. I don't see where you have any right to be proud of what your son is doing to Billie. She's a wonderful young woman with brilliant ideas and the energy to put those ideas to use. Neither you nor Moss will be able to hold her down. If you try, you'll regret it. As you know, I'm a gambling woman. If you'd like to place a small wager, I'm more than willing."

"That's the biggest damn fool thing I ever heard," Seth snarled. "Aggie, what do you have to say to this?"

"Not much, Seth," Agnes drawled. Maybe she was backing the wrong horse. Sallie was right, Thornton money was just as green as Coleman money, and there were indications there was more of it. Maybe she should switch gears and head for the high road right now. Common sense dictated she straddle the center line, for now, to see if it was going to be a Texas wind or a Nevada bonanza. Her long fingers with the manicured nails caressed her pearls.

"What in the goddamn hell is that supposed to mean. I want an answer, Aggie. She's your daughter, ain't she?"

"I gave you my answer, you simply didn't like it. In case you haven't noticed, Billie has a mind of her own. It's been a long time since she's listened to either you or me. You can't lead her around the way you lead around your horse." There was such distaste in her voice that Sallie's eyes widened.

"Leave my horse out of this. You better rein in that little gal of yours real quick, Aggie."

"Or what, Seth?" Agnes asked coolly.

"This is supposed to be a party, and here we are discussing family problems. Our children have minds of their own and they'll do whatever they feel is right for them. I, for one, support them. That's my last word on the subject. Here come the girls. I guess I should say here come the young ladies since they aren't girls any longer. That does make us older, doesn't it, Agnes?"

"Yes it does. I, for one, like being a grandmother," Agnes said.

"And I love it too," Sallie said.

"Mother, are you enjoying yourself?" Billie asked.

Agnes smiled weakly. "Of course. Where's Moss?"

"I have no idea. He doesn't tell me where he's going or what he's going to do, as you well know. Why don't you ask Seth, he knows everything," Billie said with a bite to her voice.

"I'll be right back, I want to check on something in the house," Fanny said.

Fanny blinked as she walked down the corridor toward the kitchen, blinking again so her eyes would adjust to the dimness inside after the bright sunshine. She stopped outside the study door when she heard Moss Coleman's voice. She did something then that she'd never done in the whole of her life: she eavesdropped, her heart flip-flopping inside her chest at what she was hearing.

"Alice, I had to come, the old man said it was one of those mandatory things. I couldn't get out of it. You know I do. I can top that, I count the hours. I'm leaving tomorrow. I'll tell Pap tonight. I can catch the first plane to New York around ten-thirty. You'll be in my arms by six-thirty. Trust me, I'm real good at explaining things to Pap. Billie will stay on here with her friends. When it's time for a divorce, you'll be the first to know. Now, tell me again what it is you're going to do to me when we . . ."

Fanny turned and fled in the other direction. At the end of the hall that led into the sunroom, she bumped into Billie.

"My God, Fanny, what's wrong?"

"No . . . nothing. I think coming in from the bright sunlight made me . . . light-headed for a moment. I'll be all right in a minute."

"Well, well, what have we here?" Moss Coleman said jovially. "I hope you don't mind, Fanny, but I had to use the phone. What's up, honey?" he said addressing his wife. "Did Thad get here yet?"

"No, not yet," Billie said, eyeing the hallway and the room Moss had exited, and where it ended.

"I think I'll check on Pap and wait for him. Great party, Fanny. I'm glad I could get away. I heard Birch organized a baseball game for three o'clock, guys against the gals. The bets are going to be heavy so think about that. See you later, honey." A moment later he was gone.

"He's gone, Fanny, now tell me what you saw or heard and don't expect me to believe that sunshine story."

"Billie, it's just the way I said it was."

"It's okay, Fanny, I know what he's all about. Isn't it better for me to know than to have me speculate, and perhaps be wrong? You were going down the hall toward the kitchen and Moss was in the study making a phone call. It wasn't business, it was monkey business, right?"

Fanny nodded miserably. "I never eavesdropped before in my life, Billie, I swear on my children."

"It's all right, Fanny. Now, tell me."

"He was talking to someone named Alice and . . . and he said he was leaving in the morning and would . . . would be in her arms by six-thirty. He said . . . he said Seth made him come here today. That's all. I'm so sorry, Billie. You should know, but I hate it that I was the one to tell you. Do you know Alice whoever she is?"

Billie nodded. "She's a Broadway playwright. Moss has been having an affair with her for years. I found some letters recently. It's hard to believe I didn't know. Years, Fanny. My God, how could I have been so blind? He knows I know. At least now he's being a little more discreet, or I thought he was. We are not going to let this ruin our day. We are going outside and act like the ladies we are. I'll deal with this in my own way in my own time. Wipe that awful look off your face."

"I'm so sorry, Billie. I know how bad it hurts. I know," Fanny repeated.

"Their loss," Billie said.

"Their loss," Fanny said, echoing her friend's words.

17

The baseball game was over. Mazie and her crew of cousins had cleared away the dishes and silverware. Now, Chue turned on the colored lanterns, and the band laid down the portable dance floor. Music echoed across the mountain.

"I don't see Sunny anywhere, and where's Sallie?" Fanny asked.

"I haven't seen either one of them for almost an hour. I just love listening to music and watching the kids, don't you, Billie? I'm sorry,
how thoughtless of me. I keep forgetting . . . well not really forgetting, I just never seem to know what to say about your daughters,
Maggie and Susan."

"It's all right, Fanny. Maggie will make it when she's ready to stop
fighting the world and her father. Susan wanted to go to England
with Amelia to study her music. I guess it was meant to be. I have
Sawyer and Riley. I just checked on Sawyer, and she's sleeping
soundly. Oh, oh, you wanted to know where Sunny was. Well,
Fanny there she is."

"Oh, my God, that . . . that . . . beautiful creature is my daughter.
Ah, so that was where Sallie was, fixing her up. That looks like one
of your dresses, Billie."

Billie laughed. "It is. I sent it to Sallie a month ago. I thought
Sunny might want a party dress for when she goes off to school. You
know, a fancy one that isn't too fancy. She looks beautiful. Look how
everyone is staring at her. Be careful what you say, Fanny, this look
she's showing off is very important to her."

"A couple of hours ago she was just a kid with skinned knees and
a fat pigtail down her back. Oh, my!"

"Mom, what do you think?" Sunny asked, twirling around for her
mother's benefit.

"I like it, honey," Fanny said. "The pearl combs in your hair are
just the right touch. They match all those seed pearls on your dress.
Summer white with your tan is glorious. If you had a dance card, it
would be full. You look so grown-up, Sunny."

"Ah, Mom, you aren't going to cry, are you?"

"Of course not. Can you dance, you never told me."

"Mommmmm."

"Go!"

Go she did. She was all over the dance floor, smirking at the girls
as the boys lined up to dance with her.

"She's flirting. I never did learn how to do that," Fanny said.

"Me either," Billie said.

"She's taking center stage," Sallie smiled. "It was worth it just to
see the twins' faces. Look at them—they can't believe it either.
Tonight will make a wonderful memory for Sunny. It's better than
a debutante ball. I hope you aren't upset, Fanny. Sunny enlisted my
aid a month or so ago. Actually, she got the idea the day the dress
arrived. We practiced with the makeup and hairdo for hours and
hours. She couldn't make up her mind. Then she practiced her danc-

ing until she got blisters. When that girl puts her mind to something, she accomplishes it. She takes after you, Fanny."

Fanny beamed as her daughter danced her way over and whispered in her ear. Fanny smiled. Sunny glowed.

"She said," Fanny lowered her voice to a bare whisper, "Ted Alexander said she looked like a Greek goddess. A first year cadet at West Point, no less."

Suddenly Fanny felt a hand on her shoulder. "Your daughter is making a spectacle of herself out there, Fanny. I don't see anyone else dressed like that, even the older girls. What were you thinking of? She looks like a goddamn floozie. Take her in the house and wash her face."

"Ash, don't be ridiculous. You've been drinking, and you're going to spoil everything. Leave it alone."

"Ash, Fanny is right," Sallie said quietly. "There's nothing wrong with the way Sunny looks, and there's nothing wrong with her having a good time. She's being a proper young lady."

"Well, you should know a thing or two about proper young ladies, Mother."

"That will be enough of that kind of talk, young man. Now, go inside and get some coffee," Agnes said.

"Who do you think you are to give me orders in my own house?" Ash blustered.

"Whose house, young man?" Agnes demanded.

"Nasty old biddy," Ash snarled.

"I'm going to take that as a compliment," Agnes said as she took his arm and forcefully turned him around. "There will be no scenes at this party. Good night, young man."

"Mother," Billie wailed.

"Mother, what? Did you think I would allow him to talk like that about Sunny? Sallie and Fanny have to be tolerant, but I don't. I apologize for my . . . take-charge attitude, but lately I find myself doing it with Seth. If I don't, he walks all over me. I don't like it when men demean women. Sometimes it appears that I do, but I don't. I hope I haven't offended you."

"I feel like giving you a medal, Aggie," Sallie said. "I don't think anyone has ever taken Ash to task quite like that."

Agnes knew she'd just endeared herself to the Thornton women. Men were so incredibly stupid sometimes the way they underestimated women.

"Mom, we're turning over the dance floor to you guys. We're going into the tent to get our cake and open the presents. They're gonna play that old fogy music you like. Boy, this was some party, thanks, Mom, Grandma. Sunny was a knockout, Mom. You're gonna have to watch her, she's all grown-up now. Ted Alexander is going to ask her to go to West Point for his Christmas formal. Don't let her go, she's too young."

"Okay."

"Mrs. Thornton, would you do me the favor of having this dance with me?" Simon said as he bowed low in front of Fanny.

"I'd love to, Mr. Thornton."

"I like this song," Simon said, leading Fanny onto the dance floor. "No one can sing 'Because of You' like Tony Bennett."

"Hmmnn," Fanny murmured as she settled herself in Simon's arms to glide across the dance floor. She couldn't ever remember feeling this good.

"You smell good," Simon said.

"Thank you, so do you. Did you have a good time, Simon?"

"You throw a hell of a party, Mrs. Thornton. Everybody had a good time. All you have to do is look around. I never saw such a bunch of happy kids. This was my first real family gathering. It was nice, Fanny. I still can't believe you girls beat us at baseball."

"We cheated," Fanny said.

"What?"

"Sure. Sunny figured out that you guys were drinking, and she said sun and alcohol didn't mix. We stalled for an hour and then, voilà!"

"I'll be damned. I'd like to come back, Fanny, if that's okay."

"Of course it's okay as long as you come for the right reasons. I don't need you to be a buffer between Ash and me. If you want to come because you like being here with us, that's fine. We'd love to have you, and I know Sallie will be delighted. Your dad will like having you here too."

"I'll call you from New York. I have a few things I want to set in motion. When I go away I like to go with a clear mind. Mom said you wanted to talk to me about something. Is it something we can talk about over fried egg sandwiches and cocoa?"

"That sounds like a great idea. It's business. You're a good dancer."

"So are you." Fanny felt herself being drawn closer. She allowed it because it felt good, and right. The song ended and the band swung into "I Love Paris." "Have you ever been to Paris, Fanny?"

Fanny laughed. "The extent of my travels is Pennsylvania, Texas, and within the state of Nevada. I guess I'm not very cosmopolitan. Do you ever have the fear that you'll somehow change and you won't be the same person? I guess that sounds kind of silly to you."

"The truth is, yes. I lived with someone else's identity for a long time. That isn't exactly the same thing, but yes, there are days when I wake up and I *know* I changed while I was sleeping. It's not a good thing, to try and hold back change. You don't strike me as the timid type."

"I know. But, when you stick your neck out, someone is out there waiting to chop it off."

"Are you talking about Ash?"

"It always comes back to Ash," Fanny said wearily. She told him about Agnes and Ash, laughing in spite of herself.

"That lady has some grit. It worked, and Ash is probably asleep. I watched him today, and he drank a lot. Dad tried to cut him off, but Ash has a mind of his own. When he started pounding Kentucky bourbon with Seth, I gave up. Want to take a walk in the garden?" Simon asked as the band set aside their instruments to take a break.

On the periphery, Sallie nudged Devin, a smile on her face. She inclined her head in her son's direction. "It's beginning."

"I see that. It's a can of worms, Sallie. A very big can of worms."

"I know. Fanny is a woman now, Devin. She's not the starry-eyed young girl who married Ash. I prayed every night that it would work because Fanny loved him so much. He didn't love her enough, if indeed he ever loved her at all. Fanny stayed married to Ash for the children. Children cannot save a marriage. I know this firsthand.

"Look. The guests are starting to leave. I'll not disturb Fanny. Agnes will stand in with me to say our good-byes. She's a feisty lady, Devin. I like her. At first I didn't. She was too austere. Today she let us see who she really is. I like it when a person lets you see what makes them who they are. I won't be long, Devin. By the way, did anyone say what happened to Admiral Kingsley?"

"He called earlier and asked for Moss. Seems some type of emergency came up. That's all I know."

"It's enough to tell me why Billie became so quiet. She's very fond of Admiral Kingsley. We all make such messes of our lives, don't we, Devin?" Sallie said sadly.

"We do the best we can. Everyone makes mistakes. One needs to learn from those mistakes. If you don't, it's a screw up you can't fix. Say your good-byes."

In the garden, Simon led Fanny to a bench. "Tell me what I can do for you."

She wanted to tell him to kiss her, to take her in his arms and hold her. She wanted to tell him to whisper things in her ears, things only lovers said in the darkness. Her lips tingled when she said, "When I first arrived in Nevada . . ."

A long time later, Simon said, "Remarkable."

"That money wasn't mine, Simon. I still feel guilty about borrowing it even though I paid it back with interest. Sunny's Togs owes its success to Jake. I don't know what the statute of limitations is."

"The money is yours, Fanny. Statutes usually run seven years. I can invest it for you."

"I don't feel right about it. I swear to you, I tried everything to find Jake. I didn't tell anyone but Sallie and Billie. I . . . I never told Ash. I don't know why. I guess I thought he would try and talk me into spending it. I could be doing him a disservice by thinking such a thing."

"What are you going to do, Fanny?"

"I was supposed to meet Ash in the garden after the party. He wanted to talk about us. There is no us. I told him I wanted a divorce. As usual, I'll take it one day at a time. Right now all I can think about is tomorrow, when the twins get in the car with you. Next week Sunny and Billie leave. I have a feeling Ash wants to come back, knowing the children will be gone."

Simon clenched his fists. "And . . ."

"And I don't want that to happen. Ash can be . . . what he can be is . . . forceful. No one knows better than me that I have hard decisions to make."

"I'll be just a phone call away. You can count on Mom and Devin. Dad, too, to a degree. This is probably not the time or the place, but I find myself very attracted to you. I'm not going to do anything about it, because you're my brother's wife. I just wanted you to know."

Fanny wanted to say something, but the words wouldn't come. What was so hard about saying, yes, I'm attracted to you too? She was still a married woman. She could not be the one to muck up her marriage. If and when she walked away, she wanted to do it with her head high, knowing she'd done everything possible to make the marriage work.

"It makes me a failure," Fanny whispered.

"How can you even think you're a failure with those four great kids? You made a wonderful family. Look at what you've done with this house, these grounds. And while you were doing all that you managed to start up a business that earns megadollars. There's no way you're a failure. Ash's problem is Ash's problem. As a kid, I found out that I had to stand firm with him. He used to try and intimidate me. Before I got wise, it worked. Once I got in his face and called him on whatever it was we were dealing with, he backed right down. He doesn't deal well with confrontations when the confronter is as tough as he is. Tuck that away for future reference."

Fanny nodded. "It's nice out here in the evening, isn't it? I can't tell you how often I come out here once the kids are asleep. I try to count the stars. I watch the moon and try to find a face. Twice I saw a shooting star. I made a wish both times. Neither came true. Simon, I'm afraid of what the future holds. If I had a wish right now, this very minute, I'd wish for time to stand still. I'd wish for star-filled nights, warm summer breezes and someone to . . . to . . . talk to, someone who understands me and cares about what I think and feel. When I was little, I'd wish on a star at night for my mother to come home. I wanted a mother so bad. Why in the world am I telling you this?"

"Because you trust me," Simon said lightly.

"I do, you know. Isn't that strange? I just met you. I have a confession to make. Sallie showed me pictures of you. She had them in a big box and kept them in one of the closets. When we moved here for good, I put the box in my closet and from time to time when I needed an immediate friend, I'd get the pictures out and line them up. I'd tell Ash's picture what I thought of him, and then I'd ask your picture for your opinion. It was a stupid, silly thing to do, but it got me over some very bad times. I used to study those pictures for hours at a time. I saw so many different emotions in both of you even though you were smiling for the camera. The last time I looked at the pictures I felt like I really knew you. Are you going to laugh at me now?"

"No. I even understand it."

"You do?"

There was such amazement in Fanny's voice that Simon laughed. "We should be getting back. I imagine our guests are long gone. Are we going to do the fried egg thing?"

"Hard to tell. Depends on the kids. This is their night. I wouldn't be a bit surprised if they all went down to Chue's house to play basketball. Especially if Seth and Agnes have gone to bed."

"Will I be out of line if I ask where you're spending the night?"

"The studio. I gave up my room to Seth and Moss. Ash is sleeping on the third floor as you are. I meant to tell you that earlier."

"That's fine. I can sleep anywhere, anytime."

"Really. Sometimes I'm like that too. I'm a light sleeper, though. That's because when the kids were little, I slept with one ear and eye open. Sometimes I have been known to take a nap."

"No! I do too. I have an old leather couch in my office. The leather is all broken in and is softer than butter. I can lie down and snooze for thirty minutes. Do you like peanut butter and jelly sandwiches with mashed banana?"

"Oh, yes. Have you had one with melted marshmallow on top of the banana? Sunny calls them Fiendish Delights. She only makes them for the boys when she wants them to do something for her."

"What a wonderful family you have, Fanny. I'm glad you shared all of them with me even if it was for just a short while. I don't want you to worry about the twins. West Chester isn't that far from New York. I'll go up every so often. Once they get into the swing of things and make friends they won't want me visiting. I'll take them into the city and show them around. I have a cabin on a lake in the Poconos. I can take them there too." They approached the house; the door stood open.

"Everyone's gone!" Fanny said.

"We're still here," Agnes called. "We've been visiting and getting to know one another. I want to thank all of you for a wonderful day. I think it's time for me to head upstairs. Unless you need some help cleaning up."

"Mazie and the others will clean in the morning. Go to bed. That was a great baseball game you played today, Agnes," Fanny said.

"That's what Billie said. Then she hugged me. She hasn't hugged me since she was a little girl. It was nice. Good night, everyone."

"I'll walk you home, Mrs. Thornton," Simon said.

"People are going to start to talk, Mr. Thornton."

Simon heard the smile in her voice. "Let 'em," he said.

At the door to the studio, Fanny said good night, her voice husky with emotion. Simon's voice was just as husky when he said good night.

"I'll wait until you're inside. Sleep well, Fanny."

"You too, Simon."

The sun was barely up when the twins crept down the steps. "One last look, one last walk around the property. It won't be the same when we come home again. We'll be college men," Sage said.

"Where'da think you two are going?" Sunny demanded from the kitchen doorway.

"Yeah, where are you sneaking to?" Billie asked.

"Here," Sunny said, holding out a sandwich. "I made them just for you. You won't get any for a long time. We just came down thinking you'd want us to . . . you know . . . walk around with you. If you don't, we can stay here in the kitchen. We wanted to say good-bye here so we won't embarrass you later. Do you want us to write, you never said."

"Heck, yes. Write and tell us everything. You can call us too. Look, we're going to miss you as much as you're going to miss us. Come on, you can walk with us. I don't want you trying to talk Mom into letting you go to West Point, Sunny. Ted Alexander is . . ."

"A real drip," Sunny said. "I was flattered, though."

"Okay. You looked pretty good last night. All those guys are going to be sniffing around you. You be careful. Don't go teasing them, either. Guys don't like that."

"Yeah, yeah," Sunny said.

The walk was leisurely, consisting of scuffing feet and lots of, do you remembers. "If you use up all of your allowance I can float you a loan," Sunny offered. "They say dorm food is awful and the kids eat out. That's where your money goes. You have to budget."

"Thank you for sharing that. Well, this is it. Want to sit on the front steps for a few minutes?" Sage asked.

They lined up, their faces solemn as they stared at their Uncle Simon's car.

"What have we here?" their father asked jovially.

"Nothing. We're just waiting for Uncle Simon. He said he wanted to get an early start," Sage said.

"He's having coffee in the kitchen. Is the car packed up?"

"Uncle Simon did it earlier. Mom shipped our trunks out last week," Birch volunteered.

"Well, everyone is up to make sure you get a good send-off. Any misgivings about going off on your own?"

The twins shook their heads.

"You'll write and call?"

"Sure," the twins said in unison.

"You're young men now. I expect both of you to conduct your-selves properly."

Birch looked pained. Sage squeezed his eyes shut. Sunny bit down on her lower lip. Billie put one hand on Birch's shoulder and one on Sage's. She squeezed hard.

"I'll get your Uncle Simon," Ash said, retreating into the house. For some strange reason he felt like crying. Rebuffed by his own children. And it was all his own fault. Suddenly he didn't want to walk into the kitchen, didn't want to see his brother or his wife, his mother and father. If he did walk in, conversation would stop. They would all look at him with blank faces as much as to say, what are you doing here? They wouldn't say, you don't belong, but that's what it would mean. He needed to get out of here. Now.

Ash walked back to the front door, opened it, and walked down the steps. "Take care of yourselves. Remember to call your mother. If you need anything, let me know." A moment later he was gone, his car roaring down the mountain. The Thornton children exhaled as one.

"Time to hit the road," Simon bellowed from the other side of the door. "Ah, they can't wait to leave this lush paradise; they're all ready. I don't want to hear any weeping and wailing."

Fanny swallowed hard as she hugged her sons, her eyes bright with unshed tears. "Be good." It was something she always said when her children walked out the door. The response was always the same: Okay, Mom.

"Okay, Mom."

"I'm allowed to be misty-eyed, I'm your grandmother," Sallie said. The twins hugged her, their own eyes misty.

Philip hugged his grandsons, a wicked smile on his face. "You're gonna love it, boys," he said heartily. "Make sure you write often."

Devin extended his hand as did the Coleman men. Billie and Agnes kissed them lightly on the cheek.

"Where's your dad?" Fanny asked.

"He said good-bye and left," Sunny said.

Billie started to cry as she hugged her brothers, a pitched keening wail that raised the hackles on the back of Fanny's neck. "It won't be the same anymore."

"Shhhh, honey, they'll be home before you know it."

"Why are you standing there like two big boobs? Get in the damn car and go," Sunny said.

"Jesus," Simon said. "Get in the car! Everyone's going to call and everyone's going to write. Everybody say good-bye."

A chorus of good-byes rang across the mountain as Simon slipped the car in gear. Fanny cried into a tissue as Sallie put her arms around her.

"I might as well say my good-bye now, too," Moss Coleman said. "Chue was kind enough to lend me his truck. I'll leave it at the airport. It was a great party, Fanny, thanks for inviting me. Pap, I'll see you back in Texas in about a week. Riley, look after your mother and grandmother." He waved airily in Agnes's and Billie's direction.

"Sun's up. Seems to me it's time to eat," Seth growled. "I'd like some steak, potatoes, and eggs. Easy over. Take care of it, Aggie."

"Would you like me to bring it to you here on the porch?" Agnes snapped.

"Kitchen table will do just fine," Seth said as he stomped his way into the house, his cane making a loud thumping noise as he went along.

Three days later, Seth set his bag down in the foyer and bellowed for Agnes. "It's time to go, Aggie."

Agnes bellowed in return, "We have a full hour before we have to leave. Cantankerous curmudgeon," she muttered under her breath. "Now, Billie, you stay as long as you like. This will be good for Sawyer. You need to stop coddling her so much. A few bumps and scrapes is what she needs. And a firm tone. I'll call when we get home."

"Agnes, I'd like to give you a little going-away present," Sallie said.

"Goodness, Sallie, that isn't necessary. I can't tell you how much I enjoyed this visit. Seth did too, but he won't admit it. I'm looking forward to the time you all come to Texas so we can show you some of what Seth calls down-home Texas hospitality."

"Seth invited us all for Christmas," Sallie whispered.

"Did he now? That should be a feather in your cap, Sallie. Seth never invites anyone to the ranch except his cronies, who stink up the place with their smelly cigars. You simply wouldn't believe the condition of the walls at Sunbridge. It took me years, but we finally got them clean. What was the *little* present?" Her face started to twitch when Seth bellowed again.

Sallie withdrew a small velvet box from the pocket of her slacks. "It pleases me to give this to you, Aggie, because I know you'll wear it. My taste sometimes still runs to the gaudy and this little trinket is more . . . genteel."

Trinket. Agnes wondered if it meant the dime store kind or if trinket was just a word a wealthy woman like Sallie would use. She opened the box and gasped. "My goodness, Sallie, I can't accept this. Why this must have cost a fortune. If I wore it, I'd be scared to death I'd lose it." *Fifty thousand if it cost a dime.* Agnes felt dizzy and disoriented at the thought.

"There's a safety catch on the back. You can't lose it. The appraisal and insurance receipt are folded in the bottom of the box. You'll need to insure it in May of next year."

"I don't know what to say," Agnes said, at a loss for words for the first time in her life.

"Thank you is more than enough," Sallie said. "Would you like me to pin it on your jacket lapel? Diamonds show up nicely on black and navy blue."

There had to be at least a *hundred* small diamonds in the star lapel pin. Agnes grew light-headed as Sallie pinned the "trinket" on her jacket. "Oh, my," was all she could utter. Seth's eyes were going to pop right out of his head.

"Oh, Mother, it's gorgeous," Billie said. Fanny concurred.

"Thank you, Sallie."

"My pleasure. Have a safe trip. Be still, Seth, she's coming," Sallie called down to the foot of the stairs. "Good lord, is he always like this?"

"Worse," Billie said. "Mother, when Moss gets home, tell him I don't know when I'll be back."

"I'll tell him, Billie. Stay as long as you like. You deserve this respite."

"Take care of your grandmother," Billie said, hugging Riley.

"Okay, Mom."

Everyone waved wildly as one of Chue's cousins drove Seth, Riley, and Agnes down the mountain.

"I'll be going too, Fanny," Sallie said. "It's time for me to get back to town. Thank you so much for letting me stay as long as I did. Anytime you feel the need for bright lights come down and we'll have dinner at Peridot. A night out with just us girls."

"That sounds wonderful," Billie said. Fanny nodded.

"Now that we're alone," Fanny said later, "let's see if we can't get into some trouble. Delicious trouble with a happy ending. We have until six o'clock, when Chue gets back with Sawyer."

"What do you have in mind?"

"Well, for starters, I thought you could call Admiral Kingsley and I could call Simon. Just to talk, of course. I'm not very good at this and I know you aren't either, so we need to come up with an excuse we're both comfortable with."

"Moss wanted to have sex with me the night before he left. He was going off to New York the next day to meet Alice. I felt like a whore, Fanny."

"Did you do it?"

"I wasn't exactly an active participant, if that's what you mean. I've never refused him. I should have told him I knew where he was going, but I couldn't because then he would have known you overheard him on the phone."

"You could call him on some pretext or other. Or, if you want to catch him you could head for New York right now. I can take care of Sawyer. There's a plane for New York right after lunch. Around one o'clock. You'll be there by six. The desk clerk will give you a key to the room. After all, you are Mrs. Moss Coleman. How could they refuse?"

"Fanny, if I do that, if I actually catch . . . him . . . see him with Alice, then I have to do something about it. Hearing about his infidelity is one thing, seeing it is something else. A part of me will always love Moss. It's a small part, and it gets smaller by the day. One day it won't be there anymore and then . . . then I'll do what I have to do. I know that makes me a fool in your eyes. As a woman I guess I'm a fizzle."

"If that's true, then this fizzle recognizes your fizzle. I guess we aren't glamorous enough. We're mothers. Maybe that has something to do with it. Ash told me once I was used. I was too ashamed to ask what he meant. He can be very cruel sometimes, and when he's like that, he convinces me I'm not good enough, and I hide out to lick my wounds."

"I can relate to that. It's the power and the money behind them. Moss feels he deserves whatever he wants. He offers no apologies because he's entitled to whatever it is. Seth agrees with him. In your wildest dreams would you ever think a man would bury his horse next to his wife? Moss thought that was just fine. I want to take Sawyer and run as fast as I can. Riley too, but I know he would opt to stay with his father. It would tear him apart if he had to leave Sunbridge."

"You need to sign on for Simon's runaway cruise on his boat called *Someday*." Fanny laughed. "I did. I'll go if Simon ever gets it under way. I swear, Billie, I could walk out of here and not look back. Ever. It's the kids that bother me. Lately, more and more, I've been thinking about my mother and why she left me and my brothers. My father was a good man . . . is a good man, but I don't know how it was between them. I saw him through a child's eyes, not a woman's eyes. To this day, he's never divorced her. I can't figure it out."

"Then don't try. Of course I'll sign on. Just give me two days' notice. I like Simon. It's amazing how two brothers can be so totally different. God, I feel so . . . *free*. What shall we do?"

"Let's go to the studio, and I'll make us some coffee. I'd really like to call Simon. I know it's wrong, but I can't get him out of my mind. Tell me about Admiral Kingsley. Everything."

"As you know, he's Moss's best friend. He's my friend too. He's a kind, gentle man who cares about people. Moss calls him a Yankee cracker. He helped me a lot with my daughter Maggie when she got pregnant at the age of fourteen. Moss and Seth . . . it was so awful. Thad found a place for unwed mothers and they took wonderful care of her during the whole time. He cared. Seth and Moss saw only the shame of it. She was so rebellious, all she wanted was attention from Moss, and he was too damn busy to give it to her. Seth wouldn't even look at her, that's how bad it was. If it wasn't for Thad, I don't know what I would have done. During that . . . that bad time, Thad and I . . . this sounds corny, but I like to think we had a meeting of our minds, kindred spirits, that kind of thing. I find myself attracted to him. When I see something or hear something, *he's* the one I want to share it with. I don't, because like you, I'm still married. I don't know, Fanny, if I will ever have the guts to leave Moss."

"We've given them our youth, the best years of our life. If we don't do something soon we're going to be old women who sit on rocking chairs moaning and groaning on what might have been if we only had the courage to act on our feelings. We're cowards, Billie. I feel like such a failure. Simon says I'm not, but if that's true, why do I still feel like I am?"

"Only in our choice of men," Billie snapped. "Do you really think I should go to New York?"

"If it was me, I would. If it doesn't feel right, don't do it. Why don't you give some thought to moving out so he doesn't . . . you know."

"I'm living in the cottage at the end of the property. It's big enough for Sawyer and me. I can work on my textile designs. Most times I don't even go to the house for meals. I fix something for us in the little kitchen. Seth almost went up in smoke when he saw me move my things down to the cottage. Riley actually cried. My mother didn't say anything, but I think she approved. Technically, I am living apart from Moss. They make a mockery of what I'm trying to do. They pretend to be indulgent. You know, the dumb little female who doesn't have anything to do so let her mess with her paints and swatches."

"What have you done with the money you earned from Sunny's Togs?"

"Gave it to Simon to invest at Sallie's direction. The account is *very* healthy. You should have seen Moss's face when he filed our income tax return. Thanks to you, Fanny, he knows I can leave him and not depend on him to support me. He did a lot of stuttering and sputtering. He even suggested I put his name on the account. He said accounts should always have two names, so I put Sawyer's name right next to mine. We even got her a social security number. Moss didn't like that at all. Something good has to come out of all of this, Fanny. To me, it's Sawyer. She's my last chance, Fanny. I won't fail where Sawyer is concerned. She's mine. Maggie didn't want her, my husband and father-in-law didn't want her. I'm all she has. Isn't she a pretty little girl, Fanny?"

"As pretty as her grandmother," Fanny said sincerely. "I think your mother is coming around, Billie. She acted real ... you know ...*human*. She loves you a lot. I think she just has a hard time showing it."

"She got sucked into the Coleman way of life. Most times I consider her one of *them*. I'll never be one of them. If I ever get a divorce, I'm going to take back my maiden name. I don't know why women have to give up their name when they get married. It's not fair."

"Tell me something in this life that's fair. Enough of that stuff. We came down here to the studio to do something ... meaningful, so let's do it."

"All right. I'll call Thad. To tell him he was missed at the party. I'll tell him about the baseball game. Just a short conversation. Nothing ... no hidden words, no nuances, nothing like that. Simply a straightforward conversation between two old friends. We *are* old friends, Fanny. When I talk to him I feel good for days."

"You call him and I'll run into the house and bring down some food. Take your time and enjoy your call. I'll ring Chue from the house to check on Sawyer."

Forty-five minutes later Fanny walked into the studio. Billie was sitting in one of the red chairs, her feet propped on the round table, a beautiful smile on her face. "Your eyes are sparkling, Billie. You look ... dreamy."

"That's how I feel. When I told Thad about our baseball game he laughed so hard he couldn't get his breath. He asked about everyone. He's going to try and come for Thanksgiving. He said he might get transferred to someplace near Hong Kong. He offered to send me some silks. He's so incredibly thoughtful. It's what he didn't say that's more important. I ... I told him I knew about Alice Forbes. He didn't admit it, but I think he knew. He's Moss's friend. No matter what he thinks or feels about me, he would never betray Moss. Never."

"What if you were divorced?"

"I don't know, Fanny. Okay, it's your turn. I'll go to the green-house and pick some flowers. We'll fill this place with all kinds of blossoms, light some candles this evening, have a little wine, and . . . and . . ."

"Cry," Fanny said softly.

"Yes. For all our lost years. Tell Simon I said hello."

Fanny reached for her Betty Crocker cookbook. In the middle of the book was Simon's business card, the same card he'd printed his home phone number on. First she called the office and was told Simon was on vacation. She tried his home phone number and smiled from ear to ear when she heard his voice.

"It's Fanny, Simon. I don't know why I'm calling you. For no rea-son really. I think I just wanted to . . . to hear your voice. Everyone left, but Billie and Sawyer stayed on. Billie says hello. I don't sup-pose the twins called again?"

"No. They're fine, Fanny. They were so excited they forgot I was there. They're rooming together, so that's good. How are things at Sunrise?"

"The same. How are things in New York?"

"The same. I could pack up and be there by tonight."

"I know. You can't."

"I know. We were just dreaming the other night, right?"

"Yes. Billie invited us all for Thanksgiving. She asked me to ex-tend the invitation. It's okay if you want to think about it. It's months away."

"Tell her yes."

"She wants to sign on for *Someday*. Is your crew full yet?"

"I'm being selective. The line gets longer every day. I wish I had kissed you that night."

Fanny's eyes started to water. "I wish you had too."

"I don't feel like doing anything. I sit here and stare at the walls."

"You need to get a dog, Simon. They're always there for you, and they love unconditionally."

"Are you trying to tell me something, Fanny?"

"I'm not free, Simon. I shouldn't even be calling you. I don't know what possessed me to do this. It simply isn't right."

"We could hang up."

"We could," Fanny agreed.

"I miss you."

Fanny drew a deep breath. She wanted to say she missed him too, had begun missing him the moment he drove the car down the mountain, wanted to tell him how she had to fight the urge to run after the car, not because her sons were inside, but because he was going away from her. "You need to get a dog, Simon." It was probably the stupidest thing she'd ever said in her life.

"Okay, I'll get a dog. Male or female?"

She was on safe ground here. A smile crept into her voice. "A female of course, males lift their legs. They're a tremendous responsibility. Maybe you should start off with a cat. They more or less take care of themselves if you provide a litter box."

"If I get one, can I call you for instructions?"

"I'll send you a book on pet care." No commitment there.

"I'd like that."

Such an inane conversation. If it was so inane, why was her heart beating so fast?

"I'll look for a good one the next time I'm in town."

"Are things okay?"

"Things are the same. Billie's great company, and Sawyer is adorable. Sunny and young Billie have packed and unpacked their trunks eighty-seven times in the past few days. They're actually excited that they're going to live at school in a real dormitory." *I can't wait to see you.*

"Have you thought about me?" Simon asked.

Every hour of every day. To lie or not to lie? "Yes," she said breathlessly. "I'm going to hang up now, Simon. This makes me very uncomfortable. I need to . . . to . . ."

"When will I see you again?"

When? "When I need you the most," Fanny whispered, breaking the connection.

18

When Fanny heard the crunch of gravel and the sound of the high-pitched engine, she knew Ash was on the property. She started to tremble and her mouth grew dry as she realized how alone she was with the children gone. Staring up at her was a note pinned to her drafting board, reminding her of her appointment with an attorney in town to discuss the divorce she intended to file within the week. An attorney Devin Rollins had recommended.

Fanny slipped off her stool and went to the door. She didn't want Ash in this place that was hers, didn't want him touching her things, sitting in her chairs. He no longer belonged here. She walked outside into the October sunshine, the key to the studio secure in her pocket.

It was amazing, Fanny thought, how Ash never seemed to change. He was still tall and slim, athletic, impeccably dressed even in the middle of the afternoon. His hair wasn't thinning the way most men's hair thinned at his age, he wasn't jowly, and there was no sign of a paunch. He still looked like the dashing young pilot she'd fallen in love with. God in heaven, where had that love gone?

How ironic that the sun was shining, that the skies were a perfect blue, that the clouds were marshmallow white and the grass was still green. It was almost like some other being knew Ash was going to arrive and decided to take a brush and paint a perfect day. For the return of the wayward husband. Fanny shuddered. What *did* he want? She inhaled deeply, growing light-headed with the sweet scent of the sagebrush. Birds chittered in the cottonwoods as much as to say "Intruder, intruder in our midst."

Fanny steeled herself for whatever was to come as she walked to the paved area near the garage. She gave no thought to her appearance, a sure sign that she no longer thought of Ash in any romantic way. She rolled up the sleeves of her smock, which was full of thread, paint smears, and safety pins. She wore no makeup, and her hair was pulled back and tied into a ponytail with bright yellow yarn. She wore wool socks and fuzzy slippers because her feet were always cold. She thought suddenly about Simon; she always thought about him when she found herself stressed out or under pressure. "Ash, what brings you up the mountain on such a beautiful day?" That was polite, noncommittal, an I-don't-care-what-you're-doing-here statement.

"I thought we might go pumpkin picking. It's only a few days till Halloween. I know how you love to decorate. You're having your usual party, aren't you?" Not how are you, I missed you, Fanny.

"As a matter of fact, Ash, I'm not. The Primrose School is having a party and the girls aren't coming home this weekend. They've planned a hayride and a square dance. It's going to be a coed event with the young men from the Addison School."

Ash's face grew thoughtful. "This will be the first year you've missed having a party."

"It's no big deal, Ash. The children are grown now. Sunny will be going off to college next year. Billie isn't interested in parties, she never was. I think they all pretended Halloween was a big deal because they thought I liked it. In the scheme of things it really doesn't matter."

"You sound so matter-of-fact. Doesn't anything bother you anymore? You don't even look like the same person." His voice sounded fretful and whiny. "I came to ask if you would be interested in attending my annual reunion with my old squadron this month."

"No thank you. My calendar is booked with work."

"Fanny, I want us to try again. Nobody knows better than me what a heel I've been. I want to put that all behind me. I want us to be a family again. I swear, Fanny, I won't let you down. That day when the boys drove off with Simon . . . left a mark on me. I've wanted to come up here so many times and tell you how and what I felt that day, but I didn't want you to . . . toss me out on my ear. I do have some pride."

"What about my pride, Ash? Everyone in town knows your reputation. How do you think I feel when I go to town and know people are looking at me with pity, asking what kind of woman I am who would stay with a man who betrays me? And what about the kids, they had to listen to the snickers and the sly looks?"

"I know. I'm sorry. It's just a word as you've said many times. I've said some mean, rotten things, Fanny. I regret every single one of them. I wish I could take them back, but I can't. All I can do is start over if you'll give me a chance. I can still work at the ranch and come home every single night. I make it up here in forty-five minutes since they paved the road. Will you at least think about it? I'll come up next weekend and we can . . . we can start to rebuild our lives."

"I was forced to rebuild my own life, Ash. A long time ago."

"You're the best thing that ever happened to me, Fanny. I was just too dumb and stupid to know it. I'm even going to go to a psychiatrist to talk things through. I need to resolve things about my mother and father. I'm trying. If it doesn't work, I'll try harder. Listen, I have to get back to the ranch. Dad has a bunch of young tom turkeys coming in late today, and I don't want to leave him to handle it by himself. Chickens are one thing, turkeys are something else entirely. Get a mental picture of three thousand turkeys in one place. They're a giveaway. Dad is going to give all of them away for Thanksgiving. He amazes me the way he does things sometimes. By the way, am I included in the trip to Texas for Thanksgiving?"

"Billie said family. If you consider yourself family, I guess so."

"You're so cold, Fanny. This isn't like you."

"You don't know the first thing about me, Ash. You have no clue as to how bad you hurt me and the kids. You stomp us. You come in like a storm trooper, you pummel us, and then you go away. We try to gather our lives together and just when we start to make it happen you come back and do it all over again."

"I'm not going to do it again. You have my word. I swear, Fanny, I'll work night and day to make it up to you and the kids. I won't give you one moment of grief. I'm going to dedicate myself to this family."

"Do I dare ask what brought about this miraculous change?" Fanny asked, an ice-cold edge to her voice. She'd heard it all before, a hundred times, a thousand times.

"I told you, it happened when I saw the boys getting ready to leave. All of a sudden they were grown-up, as tall as me, young men. I asked myself where did all the years go, and I had no answer. I'll come up next weekend and we can sit and talk. I'll abide by your decision."

"Good-bye, Ash."

Fanny waited until she was certain Ash was really driving away, then she ran back to the studio and, with fumbling hands, threw the dead bolt. In a frenzy she pulled the drapes and turned on all the lights. Hugging her arms close to her chest, she started to shiver. In her life she'd never been so cold. She untangled her arms long enough to throw two huge logs on the fire. She slid to the floor beside one of the red chairs and rocked back and forth, shivering.

Hours later, when the room was stifling hot, Fanny walked on stiff legs over to the little kitchen, where she made a pot of coffee. She drank it all and smoked half a pack of cigarettes. She wanted to call someone, someone who would listen and not judge her, but there was no such person. She longed for a dog that was hers alone, a dog she could talk to, who would listen and watch her with dark, adoring eyes. Two dogs, so they could keep each other company. A friend who would sleep at the foot of her lonely bed, a friend who would welcome her when she came in, a friend who would take long walks with her. "Some one to love me unconditionally," she whispered.

If she wanted to, she could call Simon. She'd told him to get a dog and a cat. Maybe she needed to take her own advice.

Was it possible for someone like Ash to change? Did age mellow a person? Was Ash sincere? The best years for her young family were gone. What good would it do any of them to patch things up? The children were accustomed to a one-parent household. Going back with Ash would change her life and their lives too.

Fanny curled up in one of the red chairs. She cradled her head in the crook of her arm and was instantly asleep. When she woke hours later, there were tears on her lashes. She made more coffee and drank it all. She moved about the studio like a robot as she tidied up her work area, her eye going to the note reminding her of her legal appointment. What to do?

Fanny showered and climbed beneath the covers. Maybe tomorrow things would be more clear. Maybe . . .

Ash's steps were hesitant when he walked away from his parked car, his eyes wary as he watched Fanny on the front steps. He stood quite still at the bottom of the steps, his eyes level with his wife's, since she was sitting on the top step. "It's a nice day, isn't it?"

"A lovely day."

"Is it a day for a new beginning or an ending?"

Fanny waited a long time before she answered. She probably would have waited longer if she hadn't seen the tears in her husband's eyes. "I called the kids. I know this is my decision, but they have a voice, too, and I wanted to hear it. They all said, and this is a direct quote, 'No, don't let him come back.' " Her heart thumped in her chest when she saw Ash's shoulders slump. "I have to admit, their answer surprised me. Children as a rule are very forgiving. I guess I underestimated how deeply you hurt them. They went on to say whatever I decide to do, it will be all right with them. I'm willing, Ash, to try one more time. But with certain provisions. You need to hear them all before you decide if you want to stay or not.

"First, I have an appointment this week with an attorney in town to file for divorce. I'm going to go ahead and have him draw up the papers, but I'm going to tell him not to file those papers. That's because I don't believe you, Ash. I don't trust you, either. I'm agreeing to do what you propose because I don't ever want to have to look back and say, maybe I should have, why didn't I at least try one more time. I don't want that to happen. This is what I propose. Yes, you can move back here to Sunrise. You can try and act like the father you are when the girls come home on weekends. We can interact the way husbands and wives do, but I will not sleep with you. Not now. We may never go back to being husband and wife in the true sense of the word. Regardless, I expect you to be faithful. I suppose you're going to view this as punishment. I don't much care. Whatever you expect from me will have to be earned. I'm not comfortable with this at all. One last thing, and I want your word, Ash, that you understand: my studio is off-limits. Someday that may change. For now, it's what it is."

"I agree to everything. You have my word. I'm bound to make mistakes. Mistakes can be fixed, Fanny. Will you agree to that?"

Fanny digested the words. She nodded.

"Is it okay to bring my stuff into the house? You won't regret this, Fanny. I want to be open and right up front with you. I don't blame you for not trusting me and not believing anything I've said. I won't let you down, I promise. Look, would you like to go for a walk after I lug this stuff in?"

"Sure."

"You would?" There was such surprise in Ash's voice that Fanny smiled.

"Of course. I get lonely, Ash. Days go by sometimes when I don't talk to a soul, not even to Chue."

"You know what, Fanny, I get lonely too. I don't expect you to believe me, but I'm going to tell you anyway, I can be in a room full of people and still be lonely. I don't know why that is. It is. Let's include pumpkin picking down at Mr. Ogden's ranch. You have to pay for the pumpkins, but that's okay. We can make jack-o'-lanterns tonight. Remember how we used to do that?"

Of course she remembered, but she wasn't going to admit it. It was safer that way. "Vaguely," she said shortly. "While you're taking your things in, I'll put on my hiking boots. I'll meet you here by the front steps."

"Are the girls coming after supper or before?"

"Actually, Ash, they aren't coming at all. They're going to your mother's for the weekend. Su Li just came back from a trip to China with her husband and she brought presents for them. Chue and his family are going down too."

"Why aren't we going?"

"We weren't invited," Fanny said quietly.

"Oh. Don't you mean I wasn't invited?"

"No, that's not what I mean. We were not invited," Fanny said.

"If you want to go, it's okay, Fanny. Really."

"Ash Thornton!" Fanny screamed. "Listen to what I said. I said we were not invited. Your mother does not include me in all her plans. You need to start listening when I say something. It won't work otherwise. I'm not trying to be hard-nosed about this, but part of our problem is you never listened to me. Obviously you thought

I never had anything important to say. You like to hear yourself talk to the exclusion of all else."

Ash turned from one of his many trips up the stairs to stare at his wife. "Do I really do that? I'm sorry, Fanny. You might be bringing me up short for quite a while until I get the hang of things."

"I can do this. I will do this," Fanny muttered over and over as she made her way to the studio. On her way back to the front of the house she kept muttering, "I don't want to do this, but I'm going to do it anyway. I have to do this, I will do this. I want to be able to look at myself in the mirror and know I did everything I could."

Fanny wanted to laugh when she saw her husband walk out of the house. Then she did laugh. The impeccable Ash Thornton in flannel shirt and blue jeans and baseball cap. "I never saw you dressed like that."

"This is how I look every day at the ranch. With the exception of the boots. I wear rubber boots at the ranch because of all the chicken poop. Now that you mention it, I guess I do look peculiar." His voice was good-natured.

"Tell me again, Ash, why we're doing this? Halloween is over."

"Thanksgiving is coming. You used to decorate the front porch with bales of straw, scarecrows, and pumpkins. We're going to do the same thing. After Thanksgiving we'll get out all the Christmas things and do up the front porch. There's a specialty store in town that has big straw reindeer. They even have a sleigh. If things work out between us, Fanny, I'm going to play Santa this year. You still have my suit, don't you?"

"It's in the attic."

"Mazie said you didn't give her instructions for dinner so I took the liberty of asking her to roast a chicken and to make giblet gravy. I brought some chickens Dad packed in ice. That was okay, wasn't it?"

"You already did it, so I guess it has to be okay. I normally don't eat a big dinner anymore."

"You were always a big eater, Fanny. A good eater as I recall. Mealtimes are very important, you shouldn't skimp."

"I guess it was all that criticism you heaped on me about my weight. I changed my eating habits. I starved myself for a while. It wasn't a good time in my life, Ash."

"I'm sorry, truly sorry."

"Why don't we make a pact not to bring up the past. You're going to get weary saying you're sorry and I'm going to get tired of throwing things in your face. Today is today, not yesterday. We're going

forward. It might not work for us, Ash. Both of us need to be prepared."

"If it doesn't, it won't be for lack of trying on my part. How about
you?"

"I'll react to you. It's all I'm willing to do, Ash. I'm sorry if that's
not the answer you want or expect."

"It's good enough for now."

"I want your word that you won't crowd me, pressure me, or take
advantage of me."

"You have my word." His voice was solemn, his face serious.
Fanny found herself cringing inwardly. She'd heard it all before.

Fanny snapped the locks on her suitcase. She looked around to
see if she'd forgotten anything. She felt uneasy for some reason and
couldn't figure out why. It couldn't be the trip to Texas because
she'd been looking forward to it for weeks. Ash was doing everything he'd promised and more. She was actually enjoying his company. If he wasn't a perfect husband, he was at least a model one.
Maybe it was because Simon was taking the boys skiing in Colorado
over Thanksgiving—a plan that was formulated, according to Birch
and Sage, after he found out Ash was living at Sunrise again. She
shrugged. It wasn't Simon. It wasn't the girls, either. What was it?
She looked around, expecting an answer to fly in front of her. When
it didn't happen, she sat down on the edge of the bed—the bed she
was now sharing with Ash.

There were no sparks, no shower of stars, no passion. Pure and
simple, she pretended. And she ached. She'd tried everything she
could think of, even fantasized, but she wasn't able to release the
years of yearning and longing. "It is what it is," she murmured to
herself.

Fanny closed her eyes and roll-called the prior days. Ash got up,
they had breakfast together, he kissed her good-bye, he drove down
the mountain, she walked across the yard to her studio. At four-
thirty, Ash arrived home, they'd go for a walk, talk about their day,
have a drink, eat dinner, read or play a game of chess. Regardless of
the weather, they'd take another walk around the yard before turning in. She should remember how it happened that she ended up in
bed with her husband, but she couldn't. She had agreed to go upstairs with him. When the realization hit her that she no longer loved
Ash, she'd been stunned and had cried for days. Now she was committed to a loveless marriage, and it was her own fault.

Candlelight dinners, a fresh rose from the greenhouse, small gifts, hand-holding—she'd accepted it all with a smile and tried harder. How was it possible that Ash couldn't see through her? Fanny sighed.

The nagging feeling that something, somewhere, was wrong stayed with her as she checked Ash's luggage. Sunny and Billie's bags were already downstairs by the front door. Her womanly intuition, her sixth sense, stayed with her as she walked downstairs to the kitchen for a cup of coffee. She had another hour before it was time to drive down the mountain to the airport to meet Ash, who would then fly the family to Texas in the Thornton plane.

More jittery than before, possibly due to the strong black coffee, Fanny picked up the phone to call her sons. After much shouting and yelling on the other end, she finally heard Birch's voice. "Mom! What's up?"

"Nothing really. I just wanted to let you know we'll be leaving within the hour. If you need me, you can call me in Texas. I wanted to be sure you had the number. What time is Simon picking you up?"

"He's here now, downstairs in the lobby. The flight leaves out of Philadelphia in an hour. I won't forget to call you the minute we get back to the dorm. Uncle Simon is bringing some lady with him. Her name is Kathryn. Hey, Mom, you still there?"

"Yes ... I ... I'm still here. That's nice," she managed to say. *Kathryn.* That would certainly explain her uneasiness today. "Well, have a good time. Say hello to your Uncle Simon for me. Give Sage a hug and have him hug you for me. I love you."

"Love you too."

Fanny poured the rest of her coffee down the sink. She called for the girls. "Let's leave now. I don't like the way the sky looks."

"Those clouds look like dirty melted marshmallows. Is that descriptive, Mom?" Billie asked.

"I suppose so, but couldn't you come up with something better?"

"I'll work on it. Actually, Mom, if you *really* look at them they look like Sage's dirty sweat socks."

"Why not a flock of gray mourning doves?" Sunny grunted as she lugged her mother's suitcase to the front door.

Ten minutes later, Sunny stuck her head in the door and yelled, "Everything's in the trunk. Everyone think, did we forget anything?"

"Phone's ringing," Billie said.

"Then answer it. It's probably Dad," Sunny said.

"Tell him we're leaving right now," Fanny said, gathering up her purse and scarf.

"It's Grandma," Billie said. "I think something's wrong. She's crying."

Fanny grabbed for the phone. "Sallie, what's wrong?" She listened, her eyes growing wide. "It's going to be all right. We're on our way. We'll meet you there. We were ready to walk out the door. Fifty minutes and we'll be there. Maybe sixty, I have to call Texas. Listen to me, Sallie, it's going to be all right. I'm hanging up, Sallie."

"Philip . . . your grandfather is in the hospital," she told the girls. "They think . . . they aren't sure . . . but there are indications he's had a stroke. That certainly doesn't mean he's going to die. Stroke victims recover and lead very productive lives. We aren't going to . . . to think negative thoughts. Bring our luggage back inside while I call Texas and then we'll leave for the hospital."

An hour and ten minutes later, Fanny and her children walked into the private suite at the Thornton Medical Center. Sallie was sitting alone in a gray chair, smoking, tears rolling down her cheeks. "I don't want this cigarette, Fanny. I must have lit twenty of them just to have something to do. Ash is on his way to the airport, they're trying to reach him. Red brought Philip in about two hours ago. He was in the turkey pen and they attacked him. No one really knows what happened to him. Su Li and John Noble are with him. Su Li brought in two specialists. Everything that can be done is being done."

"Do you want me to call Devin, Sallie?"

"God, no! He can't come here, surely you realize that, Fanny."

Fanny wanted to say, at this point, does it matter, but she didn't. She nodded. "How about if I drive the girls over to your house, Sallie."

"Do they want to go?"

"I don't know. It might be better for them. There's nothing they can do here. I can call them every hour or so. I'll tell them to bake some cookies or brownies for Philip. It will make them feel like they're doing something important. Sunny will see right through it, but she'll do it for Billie."

"If you feel it's best for them, okay. What if he dies, Fanny?"

"He isn't going to die, Sallie. You can't think like that. Philip is strong, he's got a long life ahead of him."

"I should have spent more time with him. I should have been kinder to him."

"Sallie, you can't undo the past. You and Philip did what you had to do. It worked for both of you."

"It worked for me. It never worked for Philip. I know that in my heart. He was . . . is such a good pretender. I feel like my heart has been ripped out of my chest. I did this to Philip. I did."

"You did no such thing. I don't want to hear you say such things. You can't blame yourself. You've been with Devin for almost twenty years. Those early years . . . if something was going to happen, it would have happened then. This is not your fault, Sallie."

"Call Devin and tell him for me. Be sure he doesn't come here. I couldn't handle that. Someone should have come out by now to tell us how things are going. It's been so long."

"Fanny, Mom," Ash said, his face white. "I came as soon as I heard. How is he?"

"We don't know," Sallie said.

"We're waiting. It's all we can do. Do me a favor, Ash, take the girls to Sallie's and tell them to bake some cookies and brownies for Philip. They need to keep busy. I don't want them here if . . . if things change. Please, Ash."

"What about Simon? We need to call him."

Fanny looked at her watch. "He's airborne. I can call the airport in Colorado and leave a message. I doubt if he can get here before morning unless he charters a private plane."

It was eight o'clock before Su Li and John Noble came into the waiting room. Su Li wrapped Sallie in her arms. "The bad news is, Philip has had a stroke. The good news is he is alive and in stable condition. We'll know more in the morning. He's in the Intensive Care Unit and has his own private nurse."

"He's being monitored very closely," John Noble said quietly. "This is an early opinion on my part, but I think with therapy, Philip will mend. He won't be quite the same old Philip, but he'll still be with us. The alternative isn't something we even want to think about. I'm going to let you see him through the glass, and then I want you to go home. Su Li and I will stay here through the night."

"I don't want to go home," Sallie muttered. "Things . . . things happen in hospitals."

"I didn't ask you if you wanted to go home, Sallie. I told you to go home. There's a difference."

"This is my medical center," Sallie said.

"I know. It makes no difference. There's nothing you can do for Philip, and you'll just be miserable sitting here. If you would rather get another doctor . . ."

"No. I'm sorry. You're right. I want to see him."

"Of course you do. Come with me."

Fanny thought her heart would break when she heard Sallie whisper, "I'm here, Philip. I'm so sorry. I'm here." She tapped lightly with the tips of her nails on the window. "Please, Philip, if you can, let me know that you know I'm here. I can't leave otherwise. I'm going to make this up to you, Philip, I swear I am." When there was no response from the still figure in the bed, Sallie turned away, her shoulders shaking with uncontrollable sobs.

"He moved his hand, Sallie. I saw him," Fanny lied.

Sallie whirled around, her hands pressing up against the window. "I'll make it right, Philip. I will. I truly will." Her voice was a hoarse whisper that only Fanny heard.

Fanny held back to allow Ash to put his arm around his mother's shoulder. Sallie leaned heavily against her son. Maybe something good would come of this tragedy. Fanny felt saddened that the *tragedy* was Philip's condition. She felt as if cement blocks were tied to her ankles as she trailed behind Sallie and Ash.

In the parking lot, Fanny stood aside as Ash helped his mother into the car. When she saw movement out of the corner of her eye, she turned to see Devin Rollins. She shook her head slightly before she climbed into the car. At that moment she didn't know who she felt more sorry for, Sallie or Devin.

The days and weeks dragged on. The children returned to school and college, only to pack up for the Christmas holidays. Sallie insisted Fanny return to Sunrise to take care of her family the day her sister Peggy arrived. Ash took control of the R & R Ranch with a great deal of fear and trepidation. He later expressed his opinion that no one could fill his father's shoes, but he was going to do the best he could. Simon flew in for one day, arriving early in the morning and leaving late in the afternoon when he realized there was nothing he could do for his mother or his father. Fanny was devastated that she'd missed Simon by fifteen minutes, so devastated she cried for hours in the privacy of her studio. Another small piece of her life had been chipped away.

Three days before Christmas, Sallie brought Philip home from the hospital and up to Sunrise, the one place he loved above all else. Fanny stood on the steps to welcome them, a smile on her face. The urge to cry was so great when Philip tried vainly to smile in return that Fanny bit down on her lower lip and tasted her own blood. Sallie wiped at the drool on Philip's chin and adjusted the pillow behind his neck so his head wouldn't loll to one side.

Fanny ran down the steps and hugged Philip, babbling as she did so. "I didn't know there was such a thing," she said, indicating the specially equipped van with the electronic device that lowered and raised Philip's wheelchair. The chair itself was motorized; maybe someday Philip would have the use of at least one of his arms and be able to maneuver himself around.

The month of hospital care, with intravenous feedings, had taken its toll on Philip. He was thin to the point of being emaciated. He muttered something Fanny could only guess at. The children used to talk like this when they were first learning words, she thought. Behind the chair, Sallie mouthed the words, "Sallie promised to fatten me up." "If anyone can fatten you up it's Sallie, Philip." He struggled to smile. Sallie again wiped at the drool with a lace-edged handkerchief. Philip uttered another word. Sallie mouthed the word, mashed. "I make real good mashed potatoes, Philip. Sometimes I put turnips in them, lots of butter and salt and pepper. You're going to love my mashed potatoes."

"Let's get you in by the fire, Philip," Sallie said.

"Chue installed the ramp by the back door. He finished it yesterday. He even put hand rails up for you, Philip. He did a good job."

Sallie walked into the kitchen hours later. "He's sleeping on the sofa. He hates the chair. It's difficult for me to get him in and out of it."

"Sallie, why didn't you call me? He's too heavy for you. Chue's in the greenhouse. You look exhausted."

"I am, but in other ways I feel exhilarated. I can finally do something for Philip. I'm heartsick that this is what it is, though. I wish I could do more. He seems to panic when I'm out of his sight."

"You need to get a male nurse, Sallie. You'll kill yourself. I'm more than willing, but even with the two of us, it's going to take its toll. Chue isn't exactly robust."

"Right after Christmas, a male nurse and a therapist will come in by the day. Philip understands. We used sign language a lot in the beginning. It was the only way I had of knowing if he truly understood what I was saying. He gets frustrated easily. Don't say it, Fanny, I know how hard it's going to be. I'm prepared. I see doubt on your face. Trust me, I can handle this. I'm so grateful, Fanny, that you want us to stay here."

"Sallie, this will always be your home, but Philip is consuming your life. If you have help, it might be easier. You cannot allow another person to take over your life. If you do, you will cease to be who you are. This might not be any of my business, but what are you going to do about Devin? He's called hundreds of time. He deserves some kind of response from you, Sallie."

"I know that. I was sitting at the hospital the other day and I remembered the year Philip told me to go to Devin on Christmas Eve. He gave me permission to go and then he called Devin and told him I was on the way. I tried so hard, Fanny, to love Philip the way he wanted to be loved. The feeling wasn't there. I couldn't manufacture something I didn't feel, the way you're doing with Ash. I was honest with Philip from the beginning. I never, ever, lied to him. Not once. I won't lie to him now, either. But, to answer your question, I will arrange a meeting with Devin after the holidays. Ever since this happened, I seem to play that game called, 'do you remember' with myself."

"I play the same game, Sallie. The past is past. We can't bring it back and we can't change it."

"I know Ash. So do you. It's difficult to change. Listen, I want to ask how you feel about something. Would you have any objection to my building a cottage at the bend in the road? Not too close to Chue's house and not too far from this one. Just four or five rooms with a kitchen and a special bath for Philip. A nice wide front porch with a ramp. A garden on the side and flowers in the front. Philip loves to watch things grow. I think that was why he did so well with the chickens. He got them as chicks and nurtured them along. I hate those damn turkeys. Philip was full of bites from head to toe. It's a good thing Red got him out. She let those turkeys go, all of them. God only knows where they went. That's all Philip was worried about. What happened to the turkeys? I told him the truth."

"But, why, Sallie? We have all the room in the world right here. I won't interfere, and Ash is only home in the evenings. The Primrose School made the weekends so full and interesting the girls hardly ever come home. The twins won't be home till summer. Right now it might seem a little noisy and crowded, but that will change the day after New Year's."

"I think a separate house will be best. As Philip progresses, and I'm certain he will progress, he's going to want some small measure of privacy. It's not this house that he loves, it's the mountain. Right now he doesn't much care about anything. At least that's my perception. John and Su Li both said he's going to get stronger with each day. I'm hopeful he'll be much improved by spring, when the cottage will be done. I've spoken with a building contractor and he assures me he can put it up in three months, possibly sooner if the weather holds, but I wanted to talk with you first. Do you need to speak with Ash?"

"I don't need to, but I will. I know he'll be in agreement."

"Is Simon coming for Christmas?"

Fanny sucked in her breath at the mention of Simon's name. "I sent him a note and invited him. He didn't respond. I suppose it's possible he called the boys, but I doubt it."

"Simon usually goes some place where it's warm for the holidays. As a child he loved Christmas, more so than Ash."

"Maybe he wants to be invited by you, his mother. Did you ever think of that, Sallie?"

"Really. Are you saying I should *invite* my son? The door is always open to one's children. With Philip . . . I thought Simon would be here to . . . to . . . help. I guess that was wishful thinking on my part. He did come that one day—maybe I should be grateful for that."

Fanny wanted to say, no, that's not the reason. He won't come because Ash and I are together again. She looked at her mother-in-law and realized she didn't have to say the words. Sallie already knew why Simon wouldn't join them at Christmas.

Sallie was simply making conversation.

In the privacy of their room, with the door closed, Fanny whispered to Ash about Sallie's plans. "I took the liberty of telling her I didn't think you'd mind. You don't, do you, Ash?"

Ash sat down on the edge of the bed, dropping his head into his hands. "I hate seeing him like that. I can't bear to look at him. I don't know if I can live with him until the cottage is ready. Jesus, I'd do anything I could for him, he's my father, but every time I look at him I see this strange . . . his eyes seem to pierce right through me. It's like he wants me to do something. I don't understand a damn thing he says. It's just gibberish. I pretend I understand and he knows I don't. I feel like I've been kicked in the gut."

"That's a pretty damn selfish attitude, Ash. You used the word 'I' eleven times. How do you think Philip feels?"

"I know and you're right. I don't know how to handle this. Where in the hell is Simon? He should be here. Have you heard from him? Is he at least coming for Christmas?"

"I sent him a note, but he didn't respond. I don't know, Ash. You need to be patient with your father."

"I don't have any patience, Fanny, you know that. I get goddamn sick looking at him. I hate myself for feeling this way."

"Guess what," Fanny hissed. "I hate you for feeling that way too. You're going to have to develop patience. I refuse to accept less from you, Ash."

"Don't tell me what to do and feel, Fanny—he's my father, not yours. I feel bad enough as it is. You don't need to rub my nose in it."

"Obviously you don't feel bad enough. The man is your father. He's seriously ill, and he's trying to make the best of it. Can't you even begin to imagine how a vital person like Philip feels at being so incapacitated? If you're going to stay here at Sunrise, Ash, you will not, by word or deed, show any adverse feelings to that poor soul in that wheelchair. Let's settle it now, Ash, and get it over with. I don't want this hanging over everyone's head for Christmas. You've already ruined too many of them for this family."

"I knew this was too good to be true. Are you telling me you want me to leave?"

"I didn't say that. The choice is yours. This is what you always do, Ash, we have a fight and when it doesn't go your way, you pack up and go. Know this though, if you go this time, you can never come back."

"You're a damn dictator, Fanny."

"No, Ash, I'm not. I'm your wife. I see how restless you are. Coming home every night has to be a real chore for you. I'm also aware that each day it gets later and later. You're working weekends, but are you really working? I've called the ranch and Red says you're never there on the weekends. So, tell me, who's fooling whom here?"

"Are you spying on me?" Ash said through clenched teeth.

"Yes." Fanny walked over to her jewelry box and withdrew a matchbook. "Who's Rosalie?"

"I have no idea."

The sneer on her husband's face made Fanny cringe. "Oh, I think you do. I called Miss Rosalie and pretended to be your sister. She was very helpful. Now, do you have anything to say?"

"Yeah, I do. At least she doesn't lie in bed like a damn cardboard doll."

"Is that what marriage is to you, Ash—just sex?"

"A good part of it."

Fanny watched as her husband started to throw things into his suitcases. She gave no thought to telling him to stop, to beg him to stay. What she felt was an overwhelming sense of relief. Christmas would at least be peaceful.

Fanny's tone was conversational when she said, "Just so I understand, Ash, are you leaving because I lie in bed like a cardboard doll, because of Rosalie, or because of your father?"

"All of the above," Ash snapped.

"You do remember what I said when you first came back. The divorce papers are ready to be filed. I'll call my attorney first thing in the morning. I'm sorry it didn't work out, Ash. You're walking out, and by doing so you are throwing away this family. I will never forgive you for that. You're also going to break your father's heart. That in itself will never give you a moment's peace. Someday, Ash, something could happen to you, and who will be around to take care of you? If you don't have a family, there's no one left. Nothing else matters in the end. Damn it, don't you know how important family is?"

"I can't say that I do, Fanny. Ours was sour, my own family was kind of shitty if you know what I mean. You do that family thing real well, so keep on doing it. Yeah, I'm sorry too that it didn't work out. Look, I'm not even mad. It didn't work. You tried, I tried. Sometimes things aren't meant to be. I can't handle Dad. I have to accept whatever that makes me. I'll call the kids on Christmas. There are presents in the hall closet. Is there anything else?"

"One thing, Ash. Since we're being civil here, I'd like to know if you ever loved me. I know I asked you once before, but you were angry at the time. I truly need to know, Ash, because I loved you so much, my heart was so full with feeling, and then it went bad. How do feelings just die like that? I don't want us to hate each other. We share four very wonderful children. We'll always have that between us, so for their sake, let's at least try to be friends."

Ash walked back into the room to face his wife. He put both his hands on her shoulders. "No, I don't think I loved you. It wasn't a good time in my life. I thought I had things under control, but I was wrong. I handed you a line, and then you took me up on it and proposed. I was very fond of you, but sexually, we just never . . . it wasn't what I expected. It was okay, but I guess I wanted more, you know, swinging from the chandelier, doing it backward, that kind of thing. I care about you, I want you to believe that. I'm also jealous that you've been successful with your business. I feel proud of you and jealous of what you've accomplished all the while raising a family. Many times, Fanny, I tried to tell you I wasn't marriage material, but you didn't listen. I'm not father material, either. I like bright lights, excitement, pretty, sexy women. I want that feeling I have when I'm flying, and I can't get it if I'm shackled. I thought I could change, but I'm not going to, and neither are you. The only thing left is for us to split. I sense a relief in you now that it's over. Or, is it my imagination?"

"No, you're right. Good luck, Ash."

"The same to you, Fanny. Jesus, do we shake hands or what?"

"A hug and a kiss on the cheek would be nice," Fanny said, fighting back the tears.

"Don't cry, Fanny, I'm not worth it. You should have married Simon. This is just a guess on my part, but I think he's already in love with you."

Fanny's heart leaped in her chest. "Birch said he's going with someone named Kathryn. She went on the skiing trip with them. I understand she stayed on in Colorado."

Ash threw back his head and laughed. "Kathryn! Kathryn is Simon's right hand. She's been with him since he started up his business. This is just a guess, but I'd say Kathryn is at least seventy-three. She has family in Rocky Mountain. She probably was going to visit her family and flew with them as far as Denver."

Fanny flopped down in the middle of the bed, Indian fashion. She looked around, there was no sign that Ash had ever inhabited the room. He'd known, just as she'd known, that it was temporary. Had it been permanent, he would have hung his flight pictures on the walls. She crawled off the bed to look at herself in the mirror. How had she gotten to this point in her life and never been loved? She felt beaten and wounded. She stared at the phone. It would be acceptable now for her to call Simon. She was free to do as she pleased. She didn't even have to look up the number; she knew it by heart. Not because she called it often, but because she had thought about calling hundreds of times. Maybe thousands of times. She looked at the clock. It was later in New York, Simon would be asleep. Maybe not—he said he was the proverbial night owl. What would she say?

The phone was in her hands—a magical instrument that would allow her to hear Simon's voice from a thousand miles away. A sleepy voice with the hint of a smile. She dialed the number and waited. Six rings, seven, eight. "This better be good whoever you are. Do you have any idea of what time it is?"

"I'm . . . I'm sorry, Simon. I'll hang up and call you tomorrow."

"Fanny? Fanny, is that you?"

"Yes, but I can call back tomorrow."

"No, no. I thought you were someone selling something—ency-

clopedias, cemetery plots, water filters. I was stalling for time, trying to get my wits together."

"In the middle of the night?"

"Hell, this is New York. You don't sound right. Is anything
wrong. It isn't Dad, is it?"

"Your mother brought him up to Sunrise today. He's going to
need a lot of care, Simon. He tries very hard to talk, but the words
don't come out right. Your mother understands him perfectly. If
there's a way to make him whole again, your mother will find it.
She's going to build a cottage for the two of them off the bend in the
road. It would mean a lot to them if you would come for the holidays. Do you have other plans?"

"No, but I'm not sure I'll be able to get a flight at this late date."

"Why don't you charter a plane? Or rent one and fly it yourself.
It would be money well spent."

"Do *you* want me to come, Fanny? What about Ash?"

Here it was, the question she'd been dreading. Fanny cleared her
throat and said, "My divorce papers will be filed tomorrow morning. Please don't ask me any questions because I really don't want
to talk about it. We parted friends, that's all I'm going to say."

"I'm sorry, Fanny. I know you wanted it to work. I'll tell you
what, I'll see about getting to Nevada as soon as it gets light. Nothing's open right now. As soon as I know, I'll call you. One way or
another, I'll get there. Good night, Fanny."

Fanny undressed for bed and crawled beneath the warm flannel
sheets. She scrunched the pillow under her head and struggled to
get comfortable. She should be devastated that her marriage was finally going to be dissolved. She'd tried but failed. Everyone was still
sleeping soundly, the earth hadn't tilted on its axis, the sun would
come up in the morning and set again in the evening. Time wasn't
going to stand still for her, for Ash, or for anyone else.

Her options were few. She could choose to get on with her life,
whatever it would hold, or she could hunker down, suck her thumb,
and let that same life pass her by. If there was anything to be thankful for, it was that she and Ash had parted with civility between
them. They might not be the best of friends in the days to come, but
they would at least be friends.

A moment later, Fanny was sound asleep.

Fanny escorted Simon into the living room as though she were
about to present an Academy Award nominee. "And we have,

standing at my right, Mr. Simon Thornton who will be gracing Sunrise with his presence for the holiday season."

"Oh, Simon, it's so good to see you. Philip, look, Simon is here." Sallie moved his chair slightly so that Simon was facing his father.

Simon dropped to his haunches. "Hi, Dad. It's good to see you here at Sunrise again. I'm going to be here for a few days so we can . . . do whatever . . . or just sit and talk." He got up and gave his father an awkward hug.

Fanny watched father and son and wanted to cry when Philip's eyes searched the path in front of him. *He's looking for Ash, wondering where he is. He doesn't care about Simon.* The thought jolted her. She hoped Simon hadn't picked up on his father's intense gaze.

Simon stepped back when his father mouthed a string of unintelligible words. He stared at his mother, a blank look on his face.

"I think so, Philip. I know you don't like the chair, but you have to sit up for a while. I don't suppose it will hurt if we have Simon move you to the couch, but you have to sit up."

"He wants to be moved, is that it?" Simon whispered to his mother. Sallie nodded.

Five minutes later the twins came into the room. "Okay, we're playing chess with Grandpa. This is our time so you guys can do whatever you have to do. Keep your eye on Birch, Grandpa, he cheats. If you want anything, wink."

Fanny, Simon, and Sallie left the room and headed for the kitchen.

"The boys will monitor Philip," Fanny said. "When their stint is up, Sunny and Billie will take over. It was their idea, not mine. They have all kinds of sit-down plans as Sage calls them."

"I had no idea," Simon murmured. "He was looking for Ash. Isn't anyone going to tell him?"

"I thought I would lie and tell him there was some kind of emergency at the ranch. Or we can tell him the truth and hope it doesn't give him a setback. I have to defer to you, Sallie," Fanny said.

"Simon, what do you think?"

"I always opt for the truth. It saves wear and tear on the emotions. It should be Fanny who tells him. That's just my opinion. I think he'll handle it." Sallie nodded.

The phone rang in the kitchen.

"Isn't anyone going to answer it?"

Sallie and Fanny looked at one another. Both of them shook their heads.

"Ash?" Both women shook their heads.

"Devin?" Sallie looked away, her eyes wet. Fanny picked at a loose thread on the sleeve of her shirt.

"I guess this is one of those things that's none of my business," Simon said. He watched as Sallie moved to the kitchen window, her back to her son and daughter-in-law. "Uh-huh, well, when I don't know what to do or when I'm at a loss for words, I eat."

"Eating's good," Fanny said, opening the refrigerator.

Sallie sat down at the table and started to cry. Simon's eyes grew wide. He'd never seen his mother cry. He looked at Fanny, who could only stare at him, a turkey carcass in her hands. She set the platter on the counter. "I'm going to see if the kids want an early lunch." When she returned forty-five minutes later, Simon was alone in the kitchen, picking white meat off the bones of the turkey.

"Where's Sallie?" Fanny asked.

"I told her to go to town and talk to Devin." Fanny could tell that he was struggling with his emotions. "I didn't tell her what to say. He's a very kind man and he loves Mom," he said, almost in a whisper.

"And your mother loves him. But it's over now. That's what she's going to tell him." She paused, moved closer to him, almost reached a hand to his shoulder. "The kids don't want anything to eat."

"I don't either."

Fanny put the turkey back in the refrigerator.

"Wanna go for a walk?" Simon asked.

"Sure. What about Philip's lunch?"

"I told Mom I'd feed him. She said he needs a bib, and not to worry if I don't get much in him. Life isn't very fair sometimes, is it, Fanny?"

"Everything has a price, Simon. Life wouldn't be worth much if it was free. It's like that saying, let's see, how does it go, oh, yes, how can one appreciate happiness if one never experiences unhappiness? All we can do is our best."

"I knew I liked you for a reason," Simon said, taking her by the arm. "Twice around the yard to clear the cobwebs and then we'll trot our frozen bodies back to the house so you can make us some hot tea. Tea makes everything better. Mom always said that."

"Mothers are always right," Fanny said.

"I've heard that," Simon grinned.

Sallie felt older than her years when she sat down in Devin's waiting room. She looked around, trying to see everything, printing it on her memory so that when she left this place she could recall it at a moment's notice. Today, with the winter sunshine filtering through the blinds, the room looked cheerful. Maybe it was the small Christmas tree on the coffee table. The office was cozier now, the room broken in with years of clients passing through. She knew people coming into this suite of rooms were worried, and when they left they were smiling. "Their steps are lighter," Devin's secretary had told her. "Mr. Rollins has shouldered their problems."

She heard his voice and started to tremble.

"I don't want you to worry about a thing, Mr. King. I'll file the necessary papers and when we have our response my secretary will call you and make an appointment."

Devin whirled around the moment he closed the door. "Sallie! I've been going out of my mind. I called the medical center every day. What can I do? Tell me and I'll do it. How is he, darling?"

"Not good, Devin. I'm hopeful that intensive therapy will help. John Noble, Su Li, and the specialists say he'll never be the same. He's alive, so I'm grateful for that. We'll take it one day at a time."

"Sallie . . ."

Sallie shook her head. "I came down to . . . to say good-bye, Devin. It isn't just Philip's life that will never be the same; mine won't either. I have to take care of him. Me, not other people. I did this to him. Perhaps not directly, but I did it. It's the only way I can make up for all those years of . . . of anguish I've caused him."

"No, I can't accept that. I won't accept it. I love you. You love me. You can't do this, Sallie."

"Yes, Devin, I can. We . . . we had our time in the sun. Together we had more than most people get in a lifetime. I have to give back now. I can't do it halfway."

"I . . . I won't know what to do without you, Sallie." Devin's voice tore at her already-bruised heart. "You became my life. How can either of us go on?"

"I don't know, Devin, but we have to put it behind us. I realize it isn't going to be easy. I lived for you too, my darling, but nothing is forever. I'm trying to make it easier for both of us and botching it all up."

"No. You make perfect sense. If Philip . . ."

"No, Devin. He isn't going to recover to the extent that he will be able to take care of himself. I am all Philip has. He's totally dependent on me, and I can't fail him. Ash . . . Ash and Fanny have split up. Ash can't handle his father's disability. Philip makes him sick. I have to reconcile that mess in my mind too. There's no room left for you, Devin. Please, I promised myself I wouldn't cry and carry on."

"Can I call you?" Devin asked brokenly.

"No, darling, it has to be a clean break. I can't handle anything else. We'll have our memories."

"I don't want memories, I want you! There has to be a way around this. Boston has medical marvels, doctors that are . . . the best. You have the money, Sallie, get the best there is."

"The damage can't be undone, Devin. Su Li called in two specialists at the very beginning, one from New York and one from Boston. It's what it is, Devin. I've accepted it, and you must too."

"No."

"Yes. There are no choices. I wish it were otherwise."

"You're giving up your life to a man who . . . a man who can't recover. I can't believe Philip would expect or want you to do this. Not the Philip I know. This is so wrong, Sallie."

"No, Devin. It's right. Till death do us part. That's what I signed on for. I didn't love, honor, or obey. That part of it . . . Philip and I agreed to that part of it. I can't talk about this anymore. I can't afford to fall apart. I need to be strong for Philip. He needs me. He tries so hard to smile when he sees me. He would do anything in the world for me. I can't . . . won't do less for him. He's my friend as well as my husband."

"Sallie . . ."

"I have to go now, Devin." Sallie choked back a sob. What she wanted to do was throw herself in Devin's arms. "I will always love you, Devin. Always, forever, into eternity." Then she turned and left the room.

Devin walked into his office and closed the door. He looked around at the life he'd created for himself, recalling the early days when Sallie was his only client. He leaned back in his chair, closed his eyes, and brought his most precious memories to the forefront of his mind. When he had tucked away his final memory, Devin stood up. He tried to see beyond the moment, to tomorrow, the day after. He saw nothing but total blankness. What was the point in going on?

He worked steadily for the rest of the day, sorting through files, calling other attorneys, making plans. At the end of the day he wrote out a check, placed it in an envelope, and put it in the center of his secretary's desk. The last thing he did was place a call to Dr. John Noble, asking him to stop by the office on his way home from making evening rounds. He spent the next hour writing personal letters, letters he left in the outgoing mail basket. He rummaged for a cigarette, saw that there was one in the crumpled pack.

That was okay, he only needed one.

Fanny was alone in the kitchen. Simon, the twins, and Sallie were preparing Philip for bed. Sunny and Billie had gone down to Chue's to make Christmas cookies.

She sat at the table, her hands cupped around a mug of coffee. She knew if she drank it, she'd not sleep all night. The same feeling she had the day Philip had his stroke was with her once again. She gulped at the coffee, burned her tongue, and swore softly. She gulped again, this time more cautiously. What could possibly be wrong? This was the Christmas season, nothing goes wrong during the Christmas holidays, she thought. Somewhere, though, something was wrong.

When the phone rang fifteen minutes later, Fanny bounded out of the chair to catch it on the first ring. Her voice was hoarse and gruff when she said, "Hello." Her voice turned to a whimper when she heard John Noble identify himself. "Please don't tell me something happened to Bess. Please, John, don't tell me that."

"Bess is fine. Fanny, I want you to sit down. I'm going to tell you something, and then I'm getting in my car and driving up there. I want . . . I need to prepare you so you can take whatever steps are . . . are necessary. Is Ash with you?"

"No, John. My attorney filed for divorce this morning. What is it, John?"

"It's Devin."

"Devin? *What's wrong?*"

"Devin . . . died in his office earlier this evening. I'm going to hang up now. I should be there in a little less than an hour."

Tears burned Fanny's eyes. Devin *dead?* Sweet, kind, wonderful Devin, who gave her her first job, the man who loved Sallie more than he loved life?

Fanny poured a fresh cup of coffee and gulped at it. She was staring into the bottom of the cup when Simon walked into the kitchen.

"I know, you're a tea leaf reader in disguise. Tell me," he said dramatically, smacking his palms together, "will I meet a tall, blond, willowy lass who has millions and who can't live without me?"

"John Noble called. Devin died. He didn't say how, but I think . . . he's on his way up here now."

"God, Fanny, I told her to go to town to talk to him."

"Don't blame yourself. I've been telling her the same thing for days. Each time she called, I'd ask her if she spoke to him. I gave her every single message he left. She'd look right through me when I was talking. She heard me, but she didn't hear me, if you know what I mean. Where is she now?"

"She said she was going to bed, not to sleep, but to read. She looked exhausted. Even with the twins' help, it was hard to get Dad undressed and into bed. Brushing his teeth was a horror. Poor guy, he tries to fight it. He wants Mom to do everything. I tried to explain to him, but I don't know if he understood. Mom weighs 110 pounds, Dad weights 180. I think he was embarrassed that we had to diaper him and the boys saw . . . helped. They were real good about it, Fanny. I saw the way Sunny and Billie were with him this afternoon. They didn't let up at all. They put in their time, gladly, willingly, and I even think they enjoyed what they were doing. Believe it or not, Sage and Billie can decipher what he's saying. You can be proud of them, Fanny."

"I feel like I should cry. I want to cry, but I can't. Someone has to cry for Devin. Do you think your mother will, Simon?"

"No. I don't know why I say that, either."

"Devin has no family left. He was talking about that just a few months ago. He said the Thornton family was his family. I guess that means we have to make . . . do . . . you know . . . take care of things. Sallie told me once Devin wanted to be cremated. I'm a Catholic, so I'm not too comfortable with . . . that. If you do that, there's nothing left, that person is totally gone. Sallie got such comfort from visiting in the cemetery. There won't be a place to go. A memory isn't good enough, not for someone like Devin. I'll keep the ashes if his will says he's to be cremated. I will, I'll . . . what I'll do is . . . I don't know what I'll do, but I'll do something. No scattering, Simon."

"Maybe . . . maybe we could bury the . . . whatever the ashes are in . . . in the cemetery."

"He's not family."

"Cotton Easter wasn't family, either," Simon said.

"Yes, but this is . . . was . . . Easter land. Oh, Simon, the kids are going to take this real hard. They adored Devin. Christmas is going to be very difficult."

"Only if we make it difficult. We have a lot to be thankful for. Dad's alive. Christmas isn't just packages with red ribbons. If I have a vote, I say we go ahead with the plans for the tree and the Christmas Eve dinner. I'm sure you've got all your gifts wrapped. I don't think we should tell Dad about Devin."

"I agree."

"I'd like some coffee," Simon said. "I hear a car." He went to the door to wait for John Noble.

"I'll make the coffee," Fanny said.

"Where's Sallie?" John asked from the open doorway.

"In bed reading," Fanny said. "We didn't tell her. She's in a fragile state right now." Fanny looked him straight in the eye. "Was it . . ." John nodded.

"Did he leave a letter or anything?"

"Everything was on his desk, the letters, his will, his insurance policies. Letters of instructions to other attorneys regarding pending cases. Sallie's affairs, as I'm sure you know, were separate, in the second room off the hall. Everything was packed in boxes, properly labeled, and a name of an attorney who he thought would handle her affairs as well as he did. I scanned his will to see if there were any burial wishes. He wanted to be cremated. I had him moved to the mortuary awaiting your decisions."

"How . . . ?"

"He shot himself. He used a pillow so . . . it was a tidy death, for want of a better word. It was so like Devin to do it this way."

Fanny held out a mug of coffee to him.

"I'll have it after I talk with Sallie. Is she in the same room?"

"Yes, at the end of the hall on the left," Fanny said.

"We'll wait here," Simon said.

John knocked softly on Sallie's door. He waited for the command to enter. "You don't seem surprised to see me, Sallie."

"I take things one day at a time, John. It is rather late for a house call, isn't it?"

"I have bad news, Sallie. There's no easy way to say this, so I'm just going to say it. Devin committed suicide this evening. He called me earlier. I guess he wanted me to be the one to find his body."

Sallie closed her eyes. "I appreciate you coming all the way up here to tell me."

"I don't understand, Sallie."

"It's not terribly complicated. I had to tell Devin that my place was here now with Philip and that I couldn't see him anymore. I never thought I could love someone so much, and Devin felt the same way. It's rare, John, for two people to find the kind of love we shared. My life is over, at least my life as I knew it, before Philip had his stroke. I owe so much to Philip, and I can't turn my back on him. I couldn't share my life with Devin any longer. I explained it to him, and I thought he understood. I never said in so many words that I felt dead. Devin knows . . . knew me so well. When two people love one another, they are very attuned to one another. He didn't want to go on, and I understand why he did what he did. I'm not being vain, John, when I tell you he couldn't live without me. Because I feel so . . . I hate to keep using the word dead, but I must, because I feel as I do, I know I have to take care of Philip. When Philip . . . goes, I will do the same thing Devin did. If the situation was reversed, I would do what Devin did. Thank you for coming up here, John. I think I'll go to sleep now."

"He left you a letter. Shall I put it on the dresser?"

"Yes. Good night, John."

John walked down the stairs, accepted a cup of coffee, and repeated his conversation with Sallie. "I'm leaving now. I want to be with my family. If you need me, call."

The following day, at twelve o'clock noon, the Thornton family, minus Sallie, Philip, and Ash, carried Devin Rollins's ashes to the private cemetery on the side of the mountain, where Chue had a small square opening waiting. Simon bent to lower the urn, his touch gentle, reverent. The family watched as Chue covered the urn with the hard frozen ground, packing the soil down with the back of the shovel.

Simon said a prayer. The others bowed their heads, their eyes filled with tears.

Inside the warm, cozy house called Sunrise, Sallie Thornton watched the simple burial. Her eyes were dry, her heart barely beating. A fine white snow was falling. She pressed her forehead to the windowpane, the palms of her hands flat against the grids. "Wait for me, Devin. I'll be there before you know it." The whispered torment in her voice was so intense, Philip started to jabber. Sallie turned around, her face totally blank. "It's snowing. I guess we're going to have a white Christmas after all."

More jabbering. "Where is everyone? Outside. They're going down the mountain to pick out just the right tree. Simon said he'd chop it down. I think Chue might be a little annoyed. He's been doing it for forty years, so he's going along since he claims to have an eye for height and width. I had no idea there was so much work involved in getting a Christmas tree. Did you know, Philip, you have to bore a hole in the base of the trunk and then set the tree in a bucket of water? According to Chue, you can actually see the tree suck up the water. I find that amazing."

A long stream of fretful gibberish permeated the room. "What in the world makes you think I'm babbling? What could possibly be wrong, it's Christmas Eve? I know you want everyone here in the room with you all the time, but it can't be, Philip. We're never going to leave you alone, someone will always be here, but you can't expect *everyone* to be here all the time. Please don't upset yourself. There's no reason for you to be fearful.

"Devin? No, Philip, Devin won't be joining us for Christmas this year. Now, let's talk about something else, or would you rather I read you the morning paper? No. Oh, I see, Birch is going to read it to you later. Does he really put more zip into his words? I'll work on that, Philip, so that when he goes back to school and I take over, I do it right. Sage is very good with the funnies. I'll have to listen to see how he does it. My work will be cut out for me. Yes, the way yours was when you first came to Sunrise. It was so long ago, Philip, and yet it feels like last week."

Sallie lowered herself to the floor to sit next to Philip's chair. She dropped her head into her husband's lap, tears rolling down her cheeks. She made no sound. Philip's eyes blinked furiously as he focused on the window and the falling snow. A tear formed in one eye, then in the other eye. He knew they were dropping onto his wife's curly blond head he so dearly loved, and there was nothing he could do about it. Just as he couldn't do anything about what lay beyond the window.

He struggled, sweat beading on his forehead, to move his arm, his hand, his fingers. He felt the sweat mingle with his tears. He struggled harder, and then he said the only prayer he could remember. Christmas was a time for miracles if one believed. He'd always believed. He wanted to say the prayer again, but the words were gone from his memory. He knew his hand had moved, knew it was touching soft, silky hair. Sallie hadn't lied to him after all. He'd moved his hand.

A miracle.

19

The wide front porch of the cottage was of verandah proportions, and painted a soft yellow. "You need a soothing color," John Noble had said. And, because John was a friend as well as Philip's doctor,

Sallie had the porch painted the same color as the early spring daffodils. The wicker furniture was a pale green, the same color as the stems of the spring flowers, also a soothing color, according to John. Right up until October, lush green plants hung from the beams—plants for Philip to see when he lay on his back on the portable therapy table. Two swings, one on each end of the porch, were also painted a soft green. Philip had requested the swings, so that Sallie could watch his intense therapy, his body pummeled and massaged by the New York therapist who charged $150 an hour, six hours a day, seven days a week.

The therapy started early in the morning, usually right after breakfast. It had been going on for three and a half years. Sallie's dedication, Philip's endurance, the therapist's greed, and John Noble's expertise were proof that the body could recover. Philip was now walking with the aid of a cane, his speech was intelligible, his motor skills greatly improved. At times he had memory lapses, and sometimes he would start a sentence and stop in the middle, forgetting what it was he was trying to say, but that happened less and less often.

Sallie sipped at her coffee from her position on the swing. She hated the array of medical equipment that lined the walls of the porch—the wheelchair, the canes, the walkers, the crutches, the therapy table, the stack of weights, the poles used for range of motion exercises. A wicker table held towels, ointments, liniments, medical books, and a telephone for emergencies. She hated sitting on this porch nine months of the year. She hated this house, hated this porch. More than anything, she hated her husband. She finished her coffee and moved off the swing.

"Where are you going, Sallie?" Philip asked.

Sallie schooled her face to blankness. "You ask me that every morning, Philip. I'm going into the house."

"What are you going to do?"

Sallie felt her shoulders grow stiff. Her standard answer for the past three and a half years was always the same, "I'm going to the bathroom." Today for some reason she didn't feel like making the same response. Instead she said, "I'm going to bake a cake and then I'm going to eat the whole thing."

Philip's voice was a whine, full of self-pity. "I want you out here with me. I don't want any cake."

"Philip, I said I was making the cake for *myself*. I didn't offer to share it with you. I've watched you every single day for three and a half years. I think you've punished me enough. John said you don't need this therapy every day. He said we could have stopped it ten months ago. Once a week is sufficient from now on. Your new, local therapist from the medical center will come up on Mondays and work with you for four hours. He will give you a list of instructions to follow. What that means, Philip, is, you're ready to start taking care of yourself. I've been your slave for the past three and a half years. No more. Chue will be up later to move all this stuff to the barn at Sunrise. You're going to have to relocate because the porch and the furniture is going to be painted."

Philip started to cry, his shoulders shaking. "Why are you doing this to me?"

In a frenzy, Sallie tossed her coffee cup off the railing, then crossed the porch to where her husband was sitting. "You're a man, act like one," she said. She knew that the disgust she felt finally showed in her face, something she'd hidden since Philip's stroke.

"Can I watch you bake the cake?"

"No! You don't get it, do you, Philip?"

"Get what?"

"This sick devotion you're demanding of me. The guilt you put on me. I can't take it anymore. I *won't* take it anymore. You're well enough to work. Three different specialists have said so. I don't mean you should get out in the pens with the chickens, but you can handle the office end of things. You can start out a few hours at a time and build up to whatever you can handle. You're too young to give up on life. Everyone needs a purpose in life. I am not your purpose. It's time for you to do for yourself."

"I'm afraid," Philip said as he started to wring his hands. "What if . . ."

"What if . . . what? It happens again? I can't stop it, Philip. I would think the chances of it happening again would be greater with you sitting here whining and feeling sorry for yourself. You need to move about, you need to do things, have an interest in life. I can't do it for you, you have to do it yourself. You have to *want* to do it. Don't think for one minute that I don't know what your game is. You've shackled me to you. You have a rope around my neck and you try to reel me in each time you think I might be getting away. You're punishing me for not loving you the way you want me to. In spite of yourself you couldn't hate Devin because he was a good, kind man. You're making me pay for Devin. I paid, Philip, and paid and paid. I have the wherewithal to walk away from you. I wouldn't look back, and I would never come back. Ever. Look at me, Philip, read my lips, I-don't-like-you!"

"You're a bitch!" Philip said under his breath, but Sallie heard it clearly.

"Perhaps. If I am, you can take credit for it. And you can cut out that bullshit that you're afraid. You don't have an ounce of fear in your body. What you have is vindictiveness, anger, and a host of other emotions. I want to remind you one more time, *I* wanted a divorce. *You* said no. You better be listening to me, Philip, because . . . I won't put up with you any longer."

"I didn't mean to call you a bitch."

"Yes you did. It's okay, that was an honest emotion on your part. Now you negate it. You make me sick, Philip."

"I'll change. I'll do what you want. I'll go to the ranch and start out slow. Don't leave, Sallie."

"I don't want you to do it for me. I want you to want to do it for *yourself*. I have nothing else to say, Philip."

In the kitchen she picked up the phone. "Chue, it's Sallie. I want you to come now and move the things from the front porch. If Philip is sitting in one of the chairs, paint over him."

Sallie dusted her hands dramatically. Time to bake a cake. She ate it while it was still warm, the frosting dribbling down the sides. She guzzled two bottles of soda pop before she headed for the living room to get rid of Philip's indoor equipment, equipment that was meant to wrench at her soul. According to the specialists, the therapist, and John Noble, all Philip had to do now was take long walks with weights on his ankles and wrists. She shoved the box of weights into the closet after she pushed and shoved all the things in the living room out to the front porch.

Now it was time to walk out to the cemetery. She needed to talk to those she'd once held near and dear. It was finally time to shed her guilt. Her step was light, her shoulders less heavy with her decision.

It was time to take her place in the sun again.

PART FOUR

The Thorntons: The Second Generation

1975–1978

20

Fanny looked at the date with the big red circle on the calendar hanging in her office. June 14, 1975. Five days till the big party to celebrate Sunny's Togs going public and Philip's seventy-fifth birthday. Where had the last twelve years gone? One minute she was packing up Billie's trunks to send her off to the Fashion Institute of Technology in New York, and the next minute her company was listed on the New York Stock Exchange. She remembered the day Simon and the twins had come into her small cluttered studio and said, "It's time to go public." Then Simon had sweetened his announcement by saying Billie Limited, Billie Coleman's textile business, was going on the big board too.

So much had happened these past years. Philip's illness, Sallie's withdrawal from life, her own failure to follow through with her divorce from Ash, the love she held close to her heart for Simon that she denied every day of her life. Sunny's Togs had rocketed to the top of the retail business. Riley Coleman, Billie and Moss's only son, had died in a foreign land, flying a defective Coleman plane. Then, one year later, in 1970, Seth and Agnes died together, in a freak accident. Finally, Moss's death from leukemia, eighteen months ago.

No one could say that either the Coleman or Thornton family was blessed.

Today Fanny was feeling maudlin. Today she was going to have to deal with the drastic change in Philip's health and the vacant stare in Sallie's eyes. Today she was going to ask questions and not be put off with Sallie's vagueness about her own illness, about her plans, if she had any. Today she was taking Sallie down the mountain to town for a lunch outing—if Sallie didn't cancel. There was no reason to believe that after spending fourteen long years as Philip's slave, she would agree to leave the mountain today. Sallie spent her days reading incessantly, either to herself or aloud to Philip. Not once in the fifteen years had Fanny heard her mention Devin Rollins's name. As far as she knew, Sallie hadn't gone to the cemetery either, unless she went in the middle of the night. Mrs. Philip Thornton was a mountain recluse who no longer cared how she looked or what she wore. The sophisticated, well-groomed woman of yesteryear was gone. In her place was a blowsy, carelessly dressed person who tied her hair in a knot on top of her head and chain-smoked every waking hour of the day. Her beautiful, crystal clear voice was now harsh and husky from alcohol and cigarettes.

Fanny tidied her work area so that when she returned she could sit down and start to work. As she stacked swatches, designs, and patterns, she wondered about the big announcement Simon said his mother was going to make at the party. Fanny had been stunned that her mother-in-law was even planning to attend. Maybe today Sallie would give her a clue. Maybe a lot of things. Like, maybe tomorrow she could go up to Simon and tell him she loved him, that she would go away with him. She thought of Sallie again and her blood literally ran cold. In her own way, she was doing exactly what Sallie had done. So much for role models.

Fanny checked her makeup, added fresh lipstick, ran her fingers through her new short wash-and-wear hairdo. Her dress, a summer print, said she was a classy matron on her way into town. She made a face at herself in the mirror. "You better be ready, Sallie, because if you aren't, I'm dragging you by your hair into town anyway," Fanny muttered as she climbed behind the wheel of her car.

Fanny sat in stunned surprise when she brought the car to a halt in front of the small cottage. Sallie was dressed in a light summer pantsuit with a long-sleeved sweater under the jacket. She looked *bulky*. A wealth of jewels rode high on her neck and in her ears. Her fingers and wrists sparkled in the bright sunshine. Sallie was taking the trip to town seriously.

"Surprised?"

"Not exactly. I was prepared to drag you by the hair."

"I know, that's why I decided to make it easier on you. I'd like to skip the lunch, though, and take you someplace. Someplace very special. You drive, and I'll give you directions."

"Okay. Anything to get you out of that house. How *do* you stand it?"

"I stand it because I have no other choice, Fanny. It's a way of life. I've had so many 'ways of life' I am now immune. I'm seventy-one years old. I never thought I'd end up like this. I've been thinking about going for a face-lift. What's your opinion?"

Fanny could feel her heart take on an extra beat. Something important was happening here, and she didn't understand it. "Well, personally, I don't think I'd go under the knife for something as vain as a face-lift. Why would you want to do that, Sallie, at your age? I think I read somewhere that you have to diet first. Tell me why."

"I want to look good when I die."

Fanny swerved the car, almost going off the shoulder of the road. "You aren't going to die for a very long time." She waited, but Sallie didn't answer her, just stared straight ahead, her mouth set in a grim line.

They rode in silence for almost an hour.

"We're almost there," Sallie finally said. "Make a right when you see a dirt road. I imagine it's overgrown, but there was a mailbox of sorts on the side of the road."

"Where are we going, Sallie?"

"I told you, to a very special place."

"What makes it special?" Fanny asked.

"There it is, turn right. It really is overgrown. They're just weeds and grass, it won't hurt the car. It's not far. The cottonwoods are more beautiful than I remember. Smell the sagebrush, Fanny. It's very sweet this year, isn't it? You can stop the car and we'll walk the rest of the way. I think I might have Chue come here and clean this up. Do you think that would be wise, Fanny?"

Fanny's heart thundered in her chest. She stared at her mother-in-law, trying to fathom the strange look on her face, the singsong quality of her voice, and the questions she was asking. It didn't seem to bother Sallie that she wasn't responding.

"It's beautiful, isn't it?"

Fanny stared at the small house nestled in the cottonwoods. "Oh, yes, Sallie. Whose house is this?"

"It was Devin's house. He left it to me in his will. I'm giving it to you today. I don't want to put it in my will. I signed over the deed a few weeks ago. I cannot think of another person besides yourself who will love this place as I did . . . do. Devin christened it the Sallie and Devin's house of happiness. Alvin Waring left it to Devin. I'd like it if you wouldn't tell people about this place. Tell Simon, but no one else. I want you to have it . . . as a place of solitude, your own private place. In the years to come you might need a sanctuary. I'm not a doomsayer, but one never knows what the future holds. The stock market could crash tomorrow. Interest rates could drop. One needs a little nest. That's how I always thought of it, my nest. I loved keeping the secret, so did Devin. When we came here, no one knew where we were. For a long time there was no phone. Come along, I want to show it to you."

"Why today, Sallie?"

"Because I wanted to be able to come here one last time. I wanted to be the one to show it to you. I didn't want to tell you about it or have you read it on a piece of paper. I'm . . . going to die soon, Fanny. Very soon."

"Take that back, Sallie," Fanny said, too loudly.

"Now look what you've done, you've scared the birds out of the trees. Darling Fanny, I can't take it back, it's true. I can't wait. I know you don't understand, but . . ."

"What do you mean, you can't wait?"

"It's time for me to go, Fanny. Mama and Cotton and Devin, they're waiting for me. It's been too long. Devin and I had many talks over the years about what we would do if something happened to either of us. I knew Devin couldn't live without me. He knew I wouldn't walk away from my responsibility in regard to Philip. I tried, and you see what a mess I made. Devin did what he had to do, just as I did."

"You were killing yourself taking care of Philip. You should have let the trained professionals do it. You didn't do this to yourself, Philip did it to you. Philip was fine two years after his stroke. You coddled him for another year and a half. Bess told me that. The doctors said he wouldn't walk again. Philip walked. Those same medical marvels said his speech would be defective. Philip talks almost as well as you and I. He fooled us all, and by doing so he shackled you to him, and you allowed it because you felt guilty."

"He made me atone for Devin. I paid the price, Fanny. I've paid in full. Now tell me, is it true what you said about dieting before a face-lift?"

"Yes," Fanny said.

"How long do you think it will take me to lose thirty pounds?"

"Twenty years. I don't want to talk about this, Sallie."

"I'm serious."

"Six months, maybe longer."

"I don't have six months. I need your help, Fanny."

"I can't talk about this. People don't get a face-lift when they're . . . they're . . ."

"Dying? How do you know they don't? I'll eat lettuce and carrots and take lots and lots of vitamins. I should be able to drop the weight in two months. A week later, I'll get the face-lift. That leaves me three weeks. The doctors could be wrong, I might have longer. Philip is the living proof that they can make mistakes. Of course I might not be able to . . . be up and about, but that's okay, a face-lift can heal in bed."

"Shut up, Sallie. You're making me crazy. How can you be so goddamn matter-of-fact?"

"Because I've lived with this for a long time. I didn't want to burden anyone."

"What do you think family is all about, Sallie? Not for just the good times, the bad too. I could have . . . been there to listen, if nothing else. I would have come to the cottage more, but I thought you didn't want me there. Every single night I cried for you, and every single night I said a prayer for you. It was all I could do."

Sallie sat down in the weeds. "I love you like a daughter, Fanny. Will you help me?"

"Of course I'll help you. Did you think I wouldn't even for a minute?"

"No. We need a plan."

"We need more than a plan. What's wrong with you, Sallie?"

"Everything. What kind of plan? A face-lift takes fifteen years off my life. I saw that on television. I should look just the way I did when Devin . . . when Devin saw me the last time. Think about how remarkable that is, Fanny."

Fanny sat up in the tall grass and hugged her knees. "I miss you already. What will I do without you?" Tears dripped from her eyes.

"You'll come to your senses, get a divorce, and marry Simon. You should have done that fourteen years ago. The nice thing about families, Fanny, is, you live on through your children. You'll see me in Simon every day of your life. The best of me is in Simon. I don't know how that happened, but it did. That's my legacy to you, that and this house in the cottonwoods. It hurts me to see you cry for me. Come on now, I said I wanted to show you the house. Then we'll make plans for my diet and the face-lift. Oh, you have to cancel the party. There's no time for a party. Philip didn't want one anyway. I already called half the guest list and canceled. You'll have to do the rest or have Sunny and Billie do it."

"You're telling me this now, at the eleventh hour? Sallie, it's too late."

"No, it isn't. It's never too late. Simon always does things at the eleventh hour. Philip has gone into kidney failure. He won't last the week. God must not think I'm such a bad person after all. He's going to take Philip first, so he won't be a burden to anyone after I'm gone. It's amazing how things work out."

Fanny followed Sallie through the waist-high grass in a daze as she tried to comprehend everything Sallie had just said.

"What do you think? Isn't it wonderful?" They stood in front of the house together, arm in arm. "Let's go inside. It's quite charming. Devin made some of the wooden tables."

"Why don't we come back another day. I'll . . . I'll keep the tables, I won't change anything. I give you my promise, Sallie." Fanny hung back. Somehow, she couldn't bear the thought of going inside.

"You're right, we need to get back. I want to check on Philip. I need to call Ash and Simon. What will you do with the cottage after we're both gone?"

Fanny jerked open the door of the car. "Do?"

"I'd like you to burn it down."

"Burn it down. You want me to burn it down?" Fanny said, a stupid look on her face.

"Yes."

This wasn't happening. She was dreaming. This was a nightmare and she was going to wake any second. "All right."

"Make it look like an accident. Don't claim it on the insurance. I wish I could tell you how much I hate that cottage. Make sure the wind is right or you'll burn down the mountain."

Oh, God. Oh, God. Fanny nodded.

"When I go, Fanny, I want you to dig up Devin and mix our ashes. You might need help doing that. Sunny or Billie Coleman can help you. No one else."

Fanny lowered her head to the steering wheel. She cried as she'd never cried in her life.

"I guess you're sorry you suggested this outing," Sallie said. Fanny's head bobbed up and down. "Is it too much for you to handle, Fanny? I've always believed that God never gives a person more than they can handle."

"No, no, I can handle it. I don't want you to die, Sallie. I'm selfish—I want you to live forever. I don't know how to handle death. I don't know where Billie got the strength to go on after her mother, her husband, and her only son died. A mother isn't supposed to bury a child. I don't think I have that kind of strength, Sallie. I'll fall apart and you'll . . . you'll be up there saying you screwed up by picking me to . . . to burn your house down and . . . and . . . all that other stuff."

"I know strength and character when I see it, and I saw it in you the minute I met you. Simply put, dear Fanny, there is no one else I would trust. We need to get back on the road, dear."

Hell yes, they needed to get back on the highway. Fanny's tires squealed as she barreled out to the road, her foot heavy on the accelerator. All she wanted was to get back to her little studio, lock the door, and crawl into one of the big red chairs.

Fanny brought the car to a full stop in front of Sallie's cottage. "Would you like me to come in, Sallie? Is there anything I can do?"

Sallie's voice was cheerful. "Not a thing, Fanny. Here's the list of names for you to call to cancel the party. I put a check next to the ones I called. I'll come over to the studio early this evening, and we can work on my plan. Will that be all right?"

"Of course. You don't have to ask, Sallie. Can we stop being so polite to one another?"

Sallie walked around to the driver's side of the car. She leaned in and hugged Fanny. "You are the dearest, sweetest person walking this earth. I would do anything to see you happy. I see the shadows in your eyes, and that bothers me. You deserve happiness, and it makes me sad that I won't live to see you truly happy. We need to work on that before I go. I'll see you later."

Fanny bolted to the studio, her hands trembling so badly she could barely shoot the dead bolt. She ran to the oversize red chairs, curled herself into a tight ball, and cried, her shoulders shaking with grief. A long time later, exhausted with all the crying she'd done that day, she reached for the phone. Her voice was barely recognizable as her own, raspy and hoarse. "Mr. Tinsdale, please. This is Fanny Thornton." When the attorney's voice came over the wire, Fanny squared her shoulders. "Mr. Tinsdale, file my divorce papers. I know it's been fourteen years since you drew them up. I'm ready now. It's very important to me that they be filed today. No, I will not change my mind. I appreciate your patience with me. Yes, I'll give your regards to Sallie. Good-bye."

Fanny's next call was to John Noble. When his comforting voice came over the wire, Fanny felt so relieved her tense body relaxed immediately. "John, I need to talk with you about something very important. I just want you to listen . . . and when I'm finished, tell me if . . . if it can be done."

Ten minutes later, Fanny cleared her throat. "I know I can handle it, but what will it do to Sallie?"

"Fanny, I have always been of the opinion that when a person is nearing the end of their life, their wishes should be taken into account. Sallie is a very strong-willed woman. If she wants a face-lift, let her get a face-lift, but she should get it now. If she wants to diet, let her diet. She's going to do it anyway if she's as determined as you say she is. Do you want me to get in touch with a plastic surgeon I know and make the arrangements?"

"Yes. Call me when you know the date and the time. There is Philip to . . . to consider."

"Yes," John said, "there is Philip to consider."

Philip Thornton was laid to rest on a clear sunny day. Only the immediate family and the employees of the R & R Ranch were in attendance.

"When I die I want you to play Dusty Springfield's rendition of 'If You Don't Love Me,' " Sallie whispered to Fanny. "Promise me?" Fanny nodded.

As a buffet lunch was being served, Ash drew Fanny aside. "So you're really going through with the divorce." It wasn't a question, but a statement. "Fine."

"I didn't think you'd mind. I feel compelled to say I didn't think you'd show up today."

"Jesus, Fanny, that's pretty low even coming from you. Why wouldn't I show up, he's my . . . was my father?"

"Where were you in the early years when he had to be fed and diapered? You ran then. I don't think he ever forgave you, Ash."

"This is not the time to pick a fight, Fanny. What's done is done. We'll see if he forgave me when it's time to read the will."

"Philip's will is one paragraph after all the legal stuff that goes before the bequests. He left everything to Sallie and a small bequest to each of the kids. That's it, Ash."

Ash stared at Fanny in stupefied amazement. "He wouldn't do that. What about Simon? Who gets R & R?"

"R & R goes to Red Ruby. I think it was hers all along. The chicken business is . . . was . . . Sallie's. Philip got a salary and a bonus. That's the way Philip wanted it. I thought you knew all that."

"Well, I didn't. What's that mean, I'm out in the cold?"

"You need to discuss business with your mother. Things may have changed over the years. Sallie has never confided in me with regard to her business or her finances. I know you think she has, but she hasn't. Excuse me, Ash, I want to say good-bye to Red and the others."

Ash found Simon in the cemetery, sitting on a low stone wall under the cottonwoods. He hung back when he heard Simon's low voice. When there was a break in the monologue, Ash called out. "Simon?"

"Here, Ash. I'm talking to Pop, saying all the things I wanted to say for over forty years. It's not that I didn't try over the years, I did, but he didn't want . . . he didn't like confrontations. I spoke with him a week or so before he slipped into his coma. I was looking for some small measure of comfort. Needless to say, I didn't get it. Ash, have you taken a good look at Mom?"

"Yeah," Ash said, sitting down on the wall next to his brother. "I tried talking to her about a month ago. I wanted her to give me the go-ahead to build that casino and hotel I talked to you about. She stared at me like I was an alien from another planet. I realize now she probably knew Dad didn't have long to live. Fanny told me Dad left everything to Mom and a few small bequests to the kids."

"I didn't know that. I wasn't expecting to inherit anything. Were you, Ash? Guess so, you were Pop's golden-haired boy."

"Yeah, I was. I want to build that casino."

"Do you need money?"

"Megadollars. Fanny filed for divorce. She's finally going to go through with it."

"It might be best for both of you. You don't want to end up like Mom and Dad, do you?"

"Fanny has this family thing. I wish I could be . . . I'm not what she needs. To be honest, I don't know what she wants. I believe in my gut that Mom warped her mind along the way just the way they both warped us."

"Jesus, Ash, that's a terrible thing to say."

"Have you ever seen anyone more like Mom? I swear, Fanny patterned her life after her. She denies it of course. She even looks like her. That's a crazy fluke, I know, but there it is."

"Ash, about Mom . . . I talked to John Noble this morning. He wouldn't tell me anything specific. It was what he didn't say that scared me. He as much as confirmed that she's . . . terminally ill. I think we should both go to him and make him tell us . . . whatever it is he's keeping from us."

"Simon, we just buried Dad. I don't think I want . . . hell, I *know* I don't want to know if Mom is that ill. I don't think I could handle knowing. Can you?" He puffed furiously on his cigarette, the smoke making his eyes water.

"You always need to be prepared," Simon said quietly.

"You can't prepare for something like that."

"Don't you want to make peace with her?" Simon asked.

"Like you did with Dad?"

"I tried. You need to try, Ash. If you don't, that means you're going to have one more demon riding on your shoulders."

"I got a whole flock of them now. What difference does one more make?"

"Okay. I'm going to stay on for a while. What are you going to do?"

"Go back to the ranch. Dad had some things on the drawing board we didn't get to . . . we didn't get around to when his kidneys started to go. What's your opinion of packaged frozen chicken dinners?"

"Speaking as a single guy, great. Single women would probably love it. Hell, married people with kids might love it too. Did you test-market the idea?"

"Yeah. We got great percentages. However, that was five years ago. If we had gone ahead and done it, then we'd be at the head of the pack. Now we have competitors."

"Thornton chicken is right up there. You should be able to crack the market. I'd do it."

"I think I will. You know, Simon, in my wildest dreams I never thought I'd be running a chicken business. Hell, I never thought I'd have four kids and be divorced, either. Who ever would have thought Moss Coleman and his son would die? You just don't know what life holds. I have some good years left, and I intend to live them. What about you?"

"I take things one day at a time. I like to deal with the problem, solve it, and go on so it doesn't hang over my head. I've got a good life, it's comfortable, I have my own house, money in the bank. I have good friends and my brother. My best friend Jerry has nine kids. I'm godfather to four of them. Good old Jerry. Most of the time he's in a fog. How the hell do you put nine kids through college?"

Ash grinned. "You wait for godfather Simon to make an offer. You paid for the four, right?"

"You know me, I threw in two others. They're good kids. I'd rather do something like that than piss the money away."

"Was it your idea to have Sunny's Togs buy the Silver Dollar for its corporate headquarters?"

"No. Actually, it was Sage's idea."

"Well, I gotta get back, Simon. If you're staying on, give me a call and maybe we can do the town." Simon nodded. "Are you going to . . . stay here in the cemetery?"

"Yeah, for a little while. I still have some things I need to say."

"You aren't going to get any answers," Ash said, clapping his brother on the back.

"I'm not looking for answers, Ash. I think I'm trying to be a good son after the fact."

"Forget it, little brother. Death isn't going to make a difference."

"To me it does," Simon said quietly. "See you around, Ash."

As per Sallie's instructions, she'd been spirited into the medical center after dark, her surgery scheduled at five in the morning. She spent five hours in the recovery unit and then was transferred to Sunrise. An intern was to stay with her until the surgeon removed the sutures from the eye area and the pressure bandage wrapped around her head.

"I want to know how we're to keep this little . . . sojourn from Simon," Fanny said, settling Sallie in after driving her home. "Oh, God, Sallie, I cannot believe you did this to yourself. Do you hurt?"

"Not at all." Sallie spoke with her teeth clamped together. "Tell him I'm in a cranky mood and don't want visitors."

"He's not going to believe me. He already knows something is wrong. He's staying on, that was the first clue. I see him sitting on the steps, staring at your cottage. I also saw him talking, very intently, I might add, with John Noble the day Philip was buried."

"How bad do I look, Fanny?"

"You're swollen and you're black-and-blue. Simon is going to start to quiz me."

"Su Li brought herbs up last week. I've got everything ready. Poultices, Fanny. I'll be able to wear makeup and wash my hair in four days. I want you to come for lunch tomorrow, I have things I want to discuss with you. Do you have the time?"

"I'll make the time. Nothing on my calendar is more important than you."

"Not even Simon?"

Fanny smiled. "Not even Simon. I'll be there at noon."

Outside in the bright sunshine, Fanny looked around. Everything looked the same, the sun was shining, the clouds were as pretty as they were yesterday, the grass just as green, the flowers as brilliant and fragrant. Overhead the same birds chirped and chittered among themselves. Yet everything was different. Her shoulders started to slump as she climbed behind the wheel. She wanted to cry.

Simon rapped on the car window, two bottles of beer in his hands. "I heard the car. We're going to sit on the steps and drink this beer, and you are going to tell me exactly what's wrong with my mother. I mean it, Fanny. Let me tell you what I know, and you can take it from there. No bullshit, okay?"

"Okay." Fanny climbed out of the car and followed him.

"Mom's dying. You took her to the hospital last night. Why?"

"Simon, I can't talk about your mother. I want to, but I can't. I gave my word. Yes, she's very ill. I can confirm that."

Fanny watched, her eyes filling, as Simon crumpled into himself. "I want to be there for her. How do I accept that she doesn't want me around?"

"Will it help if I tell you that when she's . . . gone, you'll understand?"

Simon looked at Fanny, disgust written all over his face. However, his voice was gentle when he said, "No, Fanny, it won't help. I want to know now, while she's alive. I want to do something, whatever that something might be. If there's nothing I can do, that's okay, but I think I deserve more than a phone call when it's . . . when she's gone."

The torment in Simon's voice tugged at Fanny's heart. She almost gave in and told him everything. Instead she reached for his hand and brought it to her cheek. "She wants it this way. It's not so terrible. She's . . . she's okay with the . . . the dying part. She really is. In the beginning, and Simon, the beginning wasn't that long ago, two weeks at the most, I had a hard time with it. I've accepted it because I don't have a choice. I love your mother too much not to respect her last wishes. She probably wants to spare you more grief. Your father just died, and . . . you're going to need to recover from that. I'm sure that's what's on her mind."

Simon caressed the hand on his cheek. It felt soft and gentle. "How long does she have, Fanny?"

"Not long at all," Fanny said in a choked voice.

"Are we talking weeks or months?"

"When I asked her, she said soon. She seems optimistic that she can . . . several months. My own assessment wouldn't be that generous."

"Hypothetically, what would your assessment be?"

"A month. How did you know?"

"My God, Fanny, all I had to do was look at her. I tried to cover up my shock, but she saw it. She patted my hand and said . . . and said . . . Fanny is going to need you, so be strong, Simon. What would you take that to mean?"

Fanny didn't trust herself to speak for a long time. "When Sallie is laid to rest, I'm going away. My divorce will be final in another month. It's time for me to . . . to as Sunny put it, spread my wings."

"Can I come along?" Simon asked.

"I'm not free, Simon. Do you remember the day Alvin Waring died?"

"Yes."

"I saw Devin Rollins look at your mother that day, and then again on another occasion, and I said to myself, I want a man to look at me like that someday. That look had everything. It literally stunned me. In the beginning I wanted Ash to look at me like that. He never did. I'm glad now that he didn't. Devin and your mother looked at one another with naked adoration. There was love, protectiveness, passion, gentleness, that, I-can't-wait-one-more-minute-to-take-you-in-my-arms look. There was no way to hide it. It seemed so right, and yet it wasn't right. Your mother never told me what went wrong between her and your father. I never judged her. I don't think anyone did. At least no one that I know. Devin told me once that Sallie said the first time she saw him she knew she was looking at her destiny. He said he felt the same way. I'm sorry, Simon, I shouldn't be saying these things, your father just died. It seems sacrilegious."

"My father was like a stranger to me. I never really knew him. I regret that. I didn't even have a surrogate growing up. I had no male figure. I didn't want that to happen to your kids. I tried to pick up Ash's slack. He's going to fall apart when Mom goes. We always think our parents are going to live forever, and we have all the time in the world to right old wrongs. It never works out that way."

"Ash won't fall apart. He'll be too busy counting the money he thinks he's going to get. He'll jump in with both feet and start that casino he's always wanted to build. That alone will take the edge off your mother's . . . passing. I'm glad you decided to stay on, Simon."

"Me too." He squeezed her hand.

"Are you going to town in the next few days?"

"Tomorrow. Can I get you something?"

"A record if you wouldn't mind. Dusty Springfield singing 'If You Don't Love Me.' "

"But I do," Simon smiled. "Wasn't she appearing at one of the casinos recently?"

"I don't know. Ash would know. He knows everything that goes on in town. Is it important?"

"Nope. Just making conversation." He paused, then took Fanny's hand in both of his. "You're my kind of gal, Fanny Thornton. You're supposed to say, you're my kind of guy, Simon Thornton."

"I promise to say it when the time is right."

"Ah, promises, promises. My lot in life."

Fanny smiled, and smiled. "Think about the time when those promises come true."

Simon grinned.

Fanny walked around to the back of Sallie's cottage when there was no answer at the front door. She smiled when she saw her playing gin rummy with the young intern. "He cheats," Sallie said. "He says I owe him three thousand cookies plus ten dollars. The pressure bandage came off at noon. I still haven't looked in the mirror. What do you think, Fanny, your honest opinion?"

"One more day and I'd say you're going to look like the old Sallie."

"Su Li's herbs are what did it. Even Tyler here agrees. He wants to order the herbs by the bushel."

Tyler was a handsome young man with sandy hair, chocolate brown eyes, and a firm, no-nonsense chin. A smattering of freckles danced across the bridge of his nose. He was tall, well over six feet, muscular, with an infectious grin. "I hear you have a beautiful daughter . . ." he said, standing to greet Fanny. "Sallie said she's gorgeous, and has a mouth with no equal. I'm looking forward to meeting her."

"Not until you break off with that nurse you're seeing," Sallie said. "I don't want my granddaughter compromised."

"I agree," Fanny said, looking from one to the other. *What was going on here?*

"Sunny can do anything. She can fly a plane, she graduated in the top three percent of her class," Sallie said.

"I'm sold!" Tyler said. "I can't wait to meet her. This nice lady made me promise that face-lifts for all the females in the family are *free* if we get together. That was the jackpot last night when we played poker. She threw in the Coleman women this morning. Tell me she doesn't cheat!"

"Never!" Fanny said dramatically.

"I'll leave you two to discuss your business. I'm going to hike down the mountain. I'll be back by noon. Can I get you anything from the kitchen before I go? How about a nice strawberry milk shake?"

"Leave! Any minute now I'll start to moo like a cow."

When he was gone, Sallie leaned across the table, her eyes bright and intense. "We have to do this just right. We'll invite Sunny up here and have Tyler ignore her. Sunny hates to be ignored. He's going to make a wonderful doctor, Fanny. He's charming, he's handsome in a casual kind of way, his bedside manner is divine, and his sense of humor is contagious. He reminds me of Devin. I think he's capable of a very deep love. I see things in him that remind me of Devin."

Sallie leaned back in her chair and closed her eyes. A moment later she opened them and sat up straight. "Down to business," she said matter-of-factly.

Fanny nodded. "Enough of this silly matchmaking. You need to talk to Simon and Ash. They're your sons, Sallie. Don't leave this earth with things in turmoil. They have to go on."

"Ash couldn't care less. Simon knows. I don't want anyone hovering. They should have hovered years ago. Now it's too late. I'm getting tired, Fanny, so I'm going to rush through this. My will is current. This is the combination to that monster safe at Sunrise. Until this moment, no one had it but me. It's your responsibility now. I'm leaving fifty-one percent of my estate to your children. You are the sole trustee. What you say goes. You will distribute it as you see fit. Twenty-four and one-half percent goes to Ash, the same to Simon. I had the attorneys set aside three and one-half million dollars for Ash to build his casino. When it's completed it will belong to Thornton Enterprises. Ash and Sunny will operate it, if she agrees, and I think she will. The fashion business is beginning to bore her. I know that three and one-half million isn't enough to build the casino. It will be up to Ash to secure the financing. His twenty-four and a half percent won't be that much help. Most of the money is gone now—the sewage and power plants took most of it. Yes, revenues come in, but the big money days are gone. Believe it or not, Thornton Chickens is my best moneymaker. Ash will want to sell the business. The decision will be up to you."

"Sallie . . . why don't you lie down for a while. I can come back after lunch."

"That's too risky. I could . . . go in my sleep. I can nap all afternoon." Her voice was weaker, her eyes slightly glazed. "I'm leaving all my jewelry to you. Everything is in a box in the living room along with the insurance policies. They're paid up until next year. Pass it along to Sunny and Billie when they get older. My sister Peggy told me over the holidays she wanted nothing left to her. I'm going to respect her wishes. There's a bank account in Texas that I started with a million dollars. It's in her name. She doesn't want that either, so I put your name on the account. The bankbook is in the jewelry box. I've given Chue his house and some extra property for his children. He didn't want me to do that. He cried. Actually, we cried together. The greenhouses are his. He made a nice little business out of his seedlings. He and his family can live out their lives in comfort. Su Li, like Peggy, refused to accept any kind of gift. Red has been taken care of. See that she gets my fur coats. She's always admired them. I would like you to keep Sunrise in the family. Your children love it here. Soon they'll have children of their own, and this place was meant for a family. There's so much room on this mountain that five more houses will only be dots on the landscape."

"I'll do whatever you want, Sallie."

"Sooner or later there will be trouble in town even though I've tried my best to ward it off. In the jewelry box there is a small leather folder with a phone number. If there's ever a problem with the casino or with those people, call the number."

"Who do I ask to speak to?"

"The man who answers the phone. Remember, Fanny, if there's trouble, you will have the power to shut down Las Vegas. All you have to do is turn off a valve and no one flushes. You snap a switch and the Bright White Way goes dark. Use that power carefully, and only as a last resort. Did I forget anything?"

"No, Sallie."

"The truth now. How do I look?" Sallie asked, her voice thinner and more weary. "What . . . what should I wear?"

"Wear?"

"When I go to meet Devin. You know my wardrobe, what would be appropriate? Do you think my summer flowered dress would be good? With my pearls."

Fanny bent over to tie her shoelace that didn't need to be tied. She broke her fingernail in the process. The crazy urge to upend the table and smash everything in sight swept over her. She righted herself and was saved from a reply when she saw that Sallie was asleep in the chair. She couldn't help but wonder if Sallie was confusing her mother's burial dress with her own.

She tiptoed into the house to check Sallie's closet. Her hand flew to her mouth when she saw a sheer flowered dress with a delicate lace collar. She fingered the material: voile. The price tag still hung from the hem of the sleeve. In all the years she'd known Sallie Thornton, she'd never seen her in such a dress.

Fanny leaned against the doorframe, her shoulders shaking. She heard the front door close, and stood straighter.

"Is there anything I can do?" Tyler asked quietly, his hand on her shoulder.

"If you could work a miracle, I'd appreciate it. How much longer do you think she has?"

"I don't know, Mrs. Thornton. It amazes me that she's as lucid as she is with all the medication she's taking. I think, Mrs. Thornton, you should have the family close by."

Fanny nodded, choking back her tears.

"I've come to love your mother-in-law," Tyler said. "I'm sorry it's under these circumstances."

"Me too. This is tearing me up. I feel so helpless. She's handling it so well. My God, she has everything planned, she's taken care of everything."

"Some people do that. My own father did the same thing to make it easier on my mother and us kids. Sallie—and by the way, she's the one who told me to call her Sallie—is a public figure. I think the whole town will want to come out to pay their respects. She told me how much she loves the Cotton Easter Memorial Church. She told me she used to sing in that church."

"Yes she did. She had a glorious voice. She wants Dusty Springfield to sing at her service. A record. Simon got it for me. I'm trying to do . . . this is my first experience with death. I'm afraid I'm not handling it very well. I wish . . . so many things."

"You're handling it very well, Mrs. Thornton. Everything you're doing and feeling is natural." The young doctor patted her back reassuringly. "Let's go see if Sallie is awake. By the way, Mr. Thornton is sitting on the front steps. I saw him when I came around the back. He looked to me like he was in the need of some comforting."

"He's wary about coming in. He doesn't know about the face-lift and . . . and the other stuff. Sallie wanted it that way. I feel terrible for him, and I don't know what to do."

"I'll talk to her. I think she actually respects my opinion."

"Oh, thank you. I'll go outside and sit with him. Call us when . . . when it's okay to come in the house. If Sallie isn't comfortable with this, just tell me. I don't want to upset her in any way."

"Hi," Fanny said, sitting down next to Simon. She reached for his hand. "Your mother is sleeping. I stayed with her while Tyler hiked down the mountain. Tyler is going to try and persuade her to . . . receive visitors."

"My God, Fanny, is that what I am, a visitor?" The pain in his voice was palpable.

"Simon, I think it's the medication your mother is taking. She says strange things and acts . . . unlike herself."

"How is it you always know the right thing to say at the right time?"

They sat in comfortable silence, smoking. From time to time they squeezed each other's hand.

An hour later, Tyler beckoned them from the door. With no words needed between the two, Simon helped Fanny to her feet. "Let's go see Mom."

Simon's eyes started to burn when he bent to hug his mother. He worked enthusiasm into his voice. "You're looking gorgeous as usual, Mom. I don't know how you do it. You don't look a day over twenty-one. Okay, thirty-one," he said when his mother quirked an eyebrow upward.

"It must be this new makeup. It guarantees a dewy complexion. A bloom in your cheeks, but I had to add rouge. I'm seventy-two, Simon. I did like your compliment, though," Sallie said in her new frail raspy voice. "Are you staying long?"

"A month or so. Wall Street gets to you after a while. I was thinking of taking the boys on a camping trip to Big Sur in California."

"You had better take Sunny with you. She was a Girl Scout." Sallie made a sound in her throat that was supposed to be laughter.

"I wouldn't have it any other way." Simon laughed.

They visited for the better part of the afternoon, reminiscing, talking about the future, and finally about the gaming industry. Sallie dozed off and on while Fanny and Simon struggled to keep the conversation going, with Tyler poking his head in the door every few minutes to check on his patient.

"I hate to mention this, Fanny, but what does this guy know about Mom's condition? Didn't you say he was interning in plastic surgery?"

"Sallie adores him. At this point that's all that matters. Su Li has been coming up every day to help Sallie take a bath. She's quite frail underneath all those layers of clothing. She's struggling very hard to be positive and upbeat. She never says a word about her condition," Fanny whispered behind her hand.

Sallie woke, her eyes going immediately to Fanny and Simon. She smiled. "I think you should mow the grass, Simon. Chue's been too busy this past week. I like it to look like a velvet carpet."

"Sure, Mom. Is there anything else you want me to do?"

"If I think of something I'll call you. Fanny and I will visit."

"What did you forget to tell me, Sallie?" Fanny asked, leaning closer to her mother-in-law."

Sallie's shaky hands fumbled with the pocket of her skirt. "This letter came the other day from that private detective I hired so long ago . . . to find my brother Josh, your mother, and that person Jake you met on the bus. He's been working on this for what seems like forever with no results. He says he might have a lead on my brother, but only dead ends on your mother and Jake. I promised him a sizable bonus if he could find them. Will you promise to follow through when I'm gone?"

Fanny folded the letter and stuffed it in her pocket. "Of course."

"If you find Josh, tell him all about Seth, and tell him how long I've looked for him. He could be dead, but if he is, he might have left a family. If they need anything, Fanny, I'd like it if you'd help them out."

"I'll be more than happy to do that, Sallie."

"If that detective does succeed in finding your mother, you give her a piece of your mind for going off and leaving you like that. You tell her I loved you more than she did. Promise me you'll do that."

Fanny choked back a sob. "I promise, Sallie."

"Simon never mowed a lawn in his life," Sallie said as she struggled with her laughter that left her gasping for breath.

"You're tiring my patient," Tyler said from the doorway. He was carrying a tray with a glass of water and some pills.

"I'm not taking any more pills," Sallie said. "Don't try to sweet-talk me, and don't think you're going to mix them in my orange juice. I don't want to be all drugged up when it's time to go. Throw them away."

"Okay," Tyler said, tossing the colored pills into the wastebasket.

"I like it when you do what I tell you," Sallie said. She was asleep again within seconds.

"Those were just placebos," Tyler said. He and Fanny had moved to the front porch for a breath of air. "I mix the *real* pills in her mashed potatoes. This is the part I don't like about being a doctor. I think that's why I decided on reconstructive surgery. My second choice would have been dermatology. I can't be objective. Dr. Noble says you never learn to be objective."

Fanny found herself trying to comfort the young doctor when he sat down on the steps next to her. "I guess we have to think in terms of pain and going to a better place. You must know by now that Sallie is most . . . anxious to . . . to go. There are days when I wonder if she was ever truly happy. She's a very simple person with few wants and desires. All the money and responsibility frightened her. That's why I think she built the sewage treatment and the power plants. I personally think it's a wonderful legacy. Would you look at what he's doing to that lawn!"

Tyler burst out laughing. He was off the steps a moment later, running across the yard. "Let me show you how a *real* gardener mows the lawn. I worked summers mowing lawns and delivering newspapers for eight years. You're wasting time and energy because you left strips down each mowed section. Now you have to go back and go over them." The young doctor cast a critical eye over the lawn.

"Are you trying to tell me this is a piss-poor job?" Simon said, wiping sweat from his forehead.

"Why don't we ask for an unbiased opinion from the young Mrs. Thornton," Tyler said. "Is her daughter really . . . you know . . ."

"That girl is one of a kind. Has Sallie suggested . . . I can't believe this . . . Just remember something, my eyes are going to be on you if you meet her. I remember what it was like being your age." Simon relinquished his hold on the lawn mower. "Let's see you do this lawn in twenty minutes, and remember, I already mowed six strips."

Back on the steps, Simon repeated his conversation to Fanny. "He fell for it."

"See, you think like a man. He's letting you *think* he fell for it. Actually, he felt sorry for you, and that's why he's doing it. He probably thinks you're an old man and he doesn't want you to have heatstroke. Young people really think like that. I know you're a virile, muscular man, but he only sees your gray hair. To him, you're *old.*"

"And what are you, the female equivalent of virile?" He winked at her.

"I hope so," Fanny said.

The Coleman jet set down at McCarran International Airport, the lone passenger heaving a sigh of relief when the wheels touched the ground. She closed her sewing basket, securing the lid with a security latch. Like a doctor who was never without his medical bag, Billie was never without her sewing.

"You can deplane now, Mrs. Coleman. There's a limousine waiting for you on the tarmac."

Billie exited the plane, her eyes searching for the Thornton vintage limousine. "Over here, Aunt Billie!" Sunny shouted.

"Darling, you look more gorgeous each time I see you. When is some nice young man going to snatch you up?" Billie said, hugging the young woman. "How's your grandmother?"

"Mom said to tell you she got up this morning and put on the flowered dress and pearls. I took that to mean time is of the essence. Mom called Dad to come up when she saw that flowered dress."

"I worry about your mother," Billie said.

"She worries about you. Is it going okay, Aunt Billie?"

"It goes one day at a time. The absolute worst time is when it's time to go to bed. My thoughts go to Riley and I know I'm never going to hear him say, 'Yo, Mam, where are you?' then I cry myself to sleep. I don't expect it ever to get better. I don't want it to get better. I don't want to forget about my son." Nothing was said about Moss. Sunny understood perfectly.

Sunny struggled for words of comfort. "You know of course that Grandma will take him under her wing, no pun intended, when she gets *up there*. Devin too."

"Oh, Sunny, thank you for saying that. I never thought of that. It gives me comfort."

Sunny, her eyes wild, said, "Grandma is talking about this like she's taking a *trip*. Don't be surprised if she says strange things. Everything has a meaning, you just have to figure it out. I haven't been up there for a week, but I call her three times a day. Mom said if I went up, Grandma would view it as hovering. She said it would be better for me and Billie to stay down here. Birch, Sage, and Billie went up this morning."

"Your mother is going to be so lost. The divorce is scheduled for Friday and now . . . this."

"Mom's okay, but she's not okay if you know what I mean. She's strong, like you. I guess you know she's going away for a month."

"Yes, I know. It will do her good. Who's at the house, Sunny?"

"Dr. Noble and Aunt Bess, Su Li, Chue, and Red Ruby. Uncle Simon has been there for a while. I really don't know if Dad will show up or not. I'm so glad you're here."

"I'm so glad you met me, Sunny."

At the cottage, the greetings were subdued. "How is she, Fanny?" Billie whispered.

"She can barely talk. I know she's in pain, but she won't take anything. She . . . she says she wants to be alert . . . when . . . She's holding on very tightly. I get the feeling if she . . . if she closes her eyes, it's all over. When I saw the flowered dress this morning I knew that today was the day."

Fanny pointed to Tyler. "Come along, Billie, say hello to Sallie. I want you to meet Tyler."

"Tyler Ford, I'm your future husband," Tyler said, loud enough for Sallie to hear. He extended his hand to Sunny. "Will you marry me?" He winked.

Sunny winked back, then looked the young doctor over, from top to bottom and then from side to side. "So what do you have going for you?"

"Not much. I owe over a hundred thousand dollars to banks for my education. I have three hundred bucks in the bank, one good suit, and a rinky-dink car that hardly ever works. I can throw in a facelift. Later on, when you get old," he added hastily.

"What about a boob job and a fanny lift?"

"That too."

"When?" Sunny said.

"When what?"

"When do you want to get married?"

"I have a day off in November and one the day after Christmas and not another one till March," Tyler said, following Sunny's cue.

"The day after Christmas sounds good. The day after is always a letdown. A wedding would perk things right up. I could wear red velvet trimmed in white fur. You okay with that date?"

"Fine. You got a dowry?"

"Nope, but I have more than four hundred bucks in the bank. I won't have to buy any clothes for a year. My car is four years old, but it runs smooth, real smooth. Do I get free prescriptions?"

"Hell yes."

"It's a deal. You can kiss me later. Thanks for looking after my grandmother." She dropped the bantering tone and led him out of the room. "I mean that part."

"I know you do. Sallie said you were wonderful. Besides, it was my pleasure. She's that rare person you call friend." He spoke in a quieter tone. "All that stuff . . . was just for her benefit, right?" he said nervously.

"I committed. Are you saying you don't want to marry me now?"

"No. I didn't say that. I don't even know you."

"I don't know you either, and I'm willing to marry you the day after Christmas."

"You think I'm easy, huh? Just because the day after Christmas is a letdown don't think you can use me and then throw me away like an old . . . shoe, or is that old newspaper?"

"Does it matter? I just promised to cherish you. I'm not big on that obeying part. Well!"

"This family of yours is certainly different. Your brothers sure are big. Are they typical older brothers? You know, protective and all that?" His voice was even more nervous-sounding.

"Are you kidding! They're petrified of me. Don't let on you know that little fact. They still think of me as a bratty kid who could whip their butts with one hand tied behind my back. Now that I'm this ravishing grown-up, they aren't sure if my skills still prevail."

"Modest too, I see."

"Are you saying you don't think I'm ravishing?"

"Good God, no. I think you're the prettiest girl I've ever seen," Tyler said, his face and neck beet red.

"Pretty is good. I find you . . . wholesome. In a virile kind of way. You're gonna have to have two best men. I can't show favoritism."

"Wait a minute. The groom gets to pick the best man . . . men. I don't even know your brothers."

"You'll grow to love them the way I do. My sister Billie will be my maid of honor."

Tyler sniffed. "Okay, but only because I haven't made any friends here. Listen," he whispered, pushing Sunny back into Sallie's room, "I'm going to kiss you, right here, right now. That will perk Sallie right up. Don't bite my lips."

"I'm not a damn cannibal."

Fanny nudged Sallie's spindly arm. She leaned over and whispered, "They set the date for the day after Christmas."

"I told you it would work out. He's a fine young man. Tell my attorney to pay off his student bank loans. Promise me, Fanny. Simon . . ."

Fanny smiled.

"Ash isn't coming to see me, is he, Fanny?"

"Of course he is, Sallie."

"Seth didn't show up either. I knew he wouldn't. I thought Ash would . . . Why should I be different than my mother?" Sallie said, her words a thin, barely audible whisper. "It's all right, Fanny, Ash can't break my heart. I prepared myself for this moment all my life." Fanny recognized the lie in her voice, but said nothing when she saw the way her mother-in-law's eyes kept going to the road that led down the mountain.

Sallie held out her hand to Sunny as she struggled for words. "So very pretty. I love you so much, child." She was trying desperately to draw a deep breath. "Promise me . . . to take care of your mother. I don't see your father . . . It's getting so dark, we need to turn on the lights. I want to go outside, on the porch, before it gets dark."

"I have to get some lightbulbs, Sallie," John Noble said as he eased Sallie up from her chair and half carried her out to the porch.

"No need, the light is coming over the mountain. Look how bright it is, John. That's so I can find my way. Oh, Mama, my dress is just like yours. Mother and daughter outfits. Fanny makes them all the time. Thank you for saying that, Cotton." Sallie's voice was suddenly high, rich and strong, carrying clearly. "I tried to do everything you asked me to do. Look at my wonderful family. There's one missing, Cotton. I'm sorry. Devin's going to carry me over the threshold, Mama. I wanted to come sooner but I couldn't. John must need new glasses, this light is so pretty and bright. Are you proud of me, Mama?" Sallie turned, her eyes seeking out the road leading down the mountain. "Tell Ash I said good-bye, Simon. They're so impatient. I'm coming, I'm coming. . . ."

The plaintive wails of the Thornton family's grief carried across the mountain late into the afternoon.

It was Simon Thornton, the second son, who carried his mother's frail body into the cottage.

The sun was setting behind the mountain when the family gathered once again to watch Sallie Thornton's last ride down the mountain.

The small, somber group returned to Sunrise, their spirits low, their eyes sad. Fanny led them around to the back of the house, where Mazie had a light supper spread out on a long table. "I feel like I should make a toast or . . . something," Fanny said. "I just lost my best friend. Simon lost his mother, and my children lost their grandmother. Sallie did so much for all of us and she never asked for anything in return except maybe our love. She helped everyone, friends, strangers, the whole town. Sallie didn't know what the word no meant. She was always the first one to say, what can I do? This might not be the right time to say this, but I'm going to say it anyway because Sallie . . . what she said . . . what she made me promise, right there at the end, which just goes to prove what I said previously . . . and I'm babbling here, was that I was to pay off Tyler's school loans. She gave all her life to those she cared about. Shh, Tyler, don't say anything, she's listening somewhere."

"You must accept, Doctor," Su Li said in her gentle voice. "To do otherwise would be to insult the kindest, the most gentle, generous woman who ever walked this earth. I know firsthand, as does my brother Chue, what giving meant to Sallie. You will say no more."

"Well . . . I . . ."

"Oh, oh, I hear a car. It must be Dad," Sunny said, whirling around.

Birch, Sage, and Simon were on their feet in an instant. "Please, everyone, sit down. I'll handle this," Fanny said, getting up off her chair, her back ramrod stiff.

"Maybe I should leave," Tyler said.

"Maybe you shouldn't," Sunny said.

"You will stay, Doctor," Chue said as he clamped a hand on the young man's shoulder.

Ash Thornton, impeccably dressed in a dark suit, pristine white shirt, and colorful tie, walked up the two steps to the porch. He allowed his gaze to swivel around the table. The red-rimmed eyes, the somber faces, the uneaten food, and his wife's angry face told him all he needed to know. He was too late.

"I called you at seven-thirty this morning, Ash. You could have made it up this mountain in thirty-five minutes the way you drive. We all want to hear your excuse."

"I had meetings. I tried . . . I wanted . . ."

"You son of a bitch! I should kill you for this, but then I'd rot in jail and you aren't worth it, Ash Thornton. Your mother waited . . . tried to wait . . . she hung on . . . her last words were your name. She said you wanted to break her heart, but she prepared herself and wouldn't let that happen. If that was your intention, you failed, you miserable bastard. You don't belong here." In her blind fury, Fanny reached for the broom resting against the kitchen door. She rammed the handle into her husband's stomach, again and again, as she exploded with every curse she knew. Too stunned to move, the others could only sit and watch Fanny poke at the man in the dark suit. They continued to watch as Ash tried to retreat, Fanny running after him. When they heard the sound of breaking glass they ran to the driveway to see Fanny throwing handfuls of pebbles at the windshield of Ash's fancy sports car. The car skidded out of control, almost hitting a tree.

"The service is at ten o'clock at Cotton Easter Memorial," Fanny yelled after him. "If I were you, I'd sit in the back pew."

The wheels of Ash's car squealed on the gravel as they sought traction.

"Is your family always this . . . explosive? Where I come from the most exciting thing that happens is milking the cows," Tyler said.

"I see. Well, don't go thinking *my* family is weird. Do you have a sedative you can give Mom?"

"I'm all right," Fanny said. "I'm sorry, everyone. I don't know what got into me. Oh, God, I'm sorry. There's no excuse for what I just did. Sallie must be . . ."

"Clapping her hands," Tyler said.

"There you go. See, you fit right in with the rest of us," Sunny said.

Billie Coleman wrapped her arms around Fanny. "Shhh, it's okay, Fanny. You did what every woman wants to do at some point in her life. I'm sorry for Ash. He has to live with his actions, not you. Let's get a bottle of wine and go to the studio, just you and me, and tie one on."

"That's the best offer I've had in months. I need to apologize . . ."

"No, you don't. Everyone here understood. Go down to the studio and I'll bring my things and the wine. I'll explain to the kids."

"You're such a good friend, Billie."

"So are you. Do you think that broom hurt him?" she whispered.

"It hurt like hell. I saw his face. The reason I threw the rocks was I could smell his car, it reeked of that shitty perfume I told you about. He was out with some bimbo while his mother was dying."

"We'll talk in the studio. A nice warm soothing shower always works."

Fanny nodded.

21

Fanny leaned heavily on her sons as they walked alongside her, out of the small church. So many people had come to pay their respects! The church had been crowded, people standing three deep in the back. Outside, the line circled around the block, three abreast.

"I wonder if Grandma is watching," Birch whispered.

"Damn straight she's watching. She wouldn't miss this for anything," Sunny said. She adjusted her sunglasses to hide her red-rimmed eyes.

"I didn't know so many people knew Grandma," Sage said, his voice full of awe. "I don't recognize half of these people. I saw Dad in the back row. People are going to talk about *that*."

"I don't think anyone here cares," Sunny snapped. "Can we please hurry? I want to go home. Are you okay, Mom?"

"I didn't think it would be so heartbreaking. I want to go home, too. I *need* to go home."

"Uncle Simon is going to stay here with Dad to talk to those who came to pay their respects. They'll come up later with the lawyer to read the will. Whose idea was it to do something like that today? Couldn't it have waited?" Sage said.

"It was your grandmother's idea," Fanny said listlessly. "She . . . she wanted everything done quickly. To get it over with, I guess."

Birch helped his mother and Billie Coleman into the car. "Your intended is calling you," Birch said, pointing across the street to where Tyler was standing. "You're driving up with Billie, right?" he asked Sunny.

"Sure. What do you guys think of him?"

"I think he's on the ball. Grandma adored him. She couldn't wait to get you two together. I'd snap him up if I were you. That dumb magazine you read says someone your age is an old maid. Go for it!" Birch said.

"He was a good sport about it, going along with the charade," Sunny said.

"I like him," Sage said. "Nobody else is knocking on your door, Sunny. Birch is right, snatch him up before someone else grabs him."

"He's someone you can call a friend," Fanny said wearily. "Give him my regards."

Sunny nodded. "I won't be long. Billie and I will see you at Sunrise."

Fanny leaned back in the seat next to Billie Coleman. "I'm so grateful that you're here with me. Sallie knew . . . she wanted you here to . . . to help me. She knew you'd understand. Today must have brought back painful memories for you. I'm sorry you have to go through this."

"It's all right, Fanny. I can handle it. Sallie told me once that God never gives you more than you can handle."

"Yes, she said that often. It must be true."

"Fanny, was Sallie ever happy? Do you know?"

"I truly don't know. I know she loved Devin as much as a woman can love a man. Her wealth overwhelmed her, and I think that's why she gave so much of it away. She made mistakes along the way, the same way we all do. Most times she didn't correct them. Her mother's death and Seth . . . those two people left lasting scars on Sallie. Those same two people caused her to react to her own family's problems, problems she didn't want to deal with. Sometimes I sit quietly by myself and try to figure out where and how . . . never mind, I don't want to talk about it anymore."

Fanny closed her eyes, her head against the headrest. Billie did the same. Tears slipped down their cheeks from time to time.

The attorney cleared his throat, his gaze sweeping around the dining room table. He shuffled his papers, adjusted his glasses, sipped from his coffee cup, and finally barked, "Are we all assembled?"

"Can we just get on with it," Ash barked in return. "Skip the legal mumbo jumbo and get to the heart of the will."

"Hrumph," the lawyer said as he wrestled with his papers. "I don't conduct my business in that manner, sir. You will all have to listen to the legal mumbo jumbo." He started to read, his voice a boring monotone. Fanny's sigh was loud in the otherwise quiet room when the attorney paused, his gaze again sweeping around the table. "And now for the bequests. To my son Ash, the sum of three and one-half million dollars to begin building the casino he's always wanted to build. The casino, to be called Babylon, will become part of Thornton Enterprises. The stipulation to this bequest is that my granddaughter Sunny operate said casino. Ash will work the floor, something he's always said he wanted to do. If either party disagrees with this stipulation, the bequest is null and void and the three and one-half million dollars will revert to Thornton Enterprises.

"The balance of my estate is to be divided in the following manner: fifty-one percent to my grandchildren, Birch, Sage, Sunny, and Billie, to be held in trust by my daughter-in-law, Fanny Thornton. She is to have sole discretion as to distribution. The remaining forty-nine percent is to be divided between my two sons, Ashford Thornton and Simon Thornton. To my niece Billie Coleman, I leave my sewing basket. To my friend Red Ruby, I leave all my furs and any other personal items she may want. To Dr. John Noble and his wife Bess, I leave the sum of fifty thousand dollars and the wish that they take a trip to Monte Carlo. To my beloved daughter-in-law, Fanny Thornton, I leave my first bingo palace, the one thing in my life that gave me true joy."

Fanny burst into tears as she ran from the room. Billie Coleman followed her. Together, they wrapped their arms around one of the stout pillars holding up the roof of the front porch. "There are twelve one-carat diamonds and six perfect emeralds on the clasp of the sewing box. It's trimmed in solid gold. Devin gave it to Sallie on her fiftieth birthday. She treasured it more than any of the jewels she owned. She must have loved you a lot to leave it to you," Fanny said.

In between her sobs, Billie said, "She left you the thing she treasured most in the whole world, the bingo palace. What will you do with it?"

"Oh, God, Billie, I don't know. Refurbish it, make a museum out of it, turn it into . . . into . . . I don't know, a free bingo parlor for older people."

"I hope you're satisfied," Ash said coming up behind her. "You worked on her, didn't you? She was old and sick, and you took advantage of her. Sole discretion as to distribution! Ha! I'll contest the will, I'll break it. I'm going to fight you on the divorce too, after I press assault and battery charges against you. You weaseled your way into her life and look what you got for your efforts. Sunrise, the bingo palace. That piece of property is a gold mine and you ended up with it. You!" He made her name sound obscene.

Fanny sat down on the top step. "Go away, Ash. Do whatever you have to do. You have to live with yourself. My conscience is clear. I'm sorry things didn't work out between us. Can't we act like normal human beings for the benefit of the children?"

"With you controlling fifty-one percent! Now that's got to be the joke of the year. Like I can really build the kind of casino I want to build for three and a half million dollars. If I go to a contractor with that amount in mind he'd laugh his head off. I can't stand it when you play dumb, Fanny."

Fanny didn't mean to say the words, but they hurtled out of her mouth so fast she thought she was thinking them until Ash's jaw dropped. "How much would a casino cost?"

"Ten times that much, maybe more."

"Fanny . . ." Billie gasped, "think . . ."

"I think you need to mind your own business, Mrs. Coleman," Ash snapped.

"All right, Ash, the divorce goes through, I give you the balance of the money, and you let all of us alone. The part about Sunny stays, it's what Sallie wanted. I don't ever want to see you again until we meet in court."

"You have something up your sleeve, I can smell it," Ash snarled.

Fanny wiggled her arm. "See, no sleeve. I'm trying to do what you want. If money can make up to you for what you think your mother did to you or what you did to her, then I'll give you every cent I have. I know how to live on nothing. I know how to make do. I'm not afraid to start over. You're the one who made me independent. I don't need help from anyone. You are the father of my children. I owe you something for that . . . them. I even know I'm being a fool. Take it or leave it, Ash."

"I'll call you tomorrow."

"No. Call my lawyer. I don't want you to ever come here again. I'm going to have an electric fence installed, the kind people put up to keep criminals out. Good-bye, Ash."

Both women watched as Ash slid into his car.

"Fanny . . ."

"Shhhh, Billie, don't cry for me. It doesn't matter. Ash is just someone I used to know."

They were weeping conspirators, their shoulders shaking with their grief. Billie Coleman held the flashlight as Fanny jabbed at the soft earth with the shovel. "Chue's going to know what we did . . . are doing. I can't get the grass back to . . . the way it was," Fanny said.

"He won't let on he knows. He'll fix everything. I saw beds of sod in the greenhouse. We can't worry about Chue. I'll dig for a while, you hold the light." Fanny gratefully relinquished the shovel.

"Tell me again why we're doing this," Billie said.

"Sallie wants . . . wanted . . . Devin's ashes and hers together. Do you think there's some kind of protocol for this?"

"If there is, I don't know what it is," Billie said through clenched teeth. "I hit something. You have to help me lift it. I didn't know Chue put the urn in a concrete block. It's heavy, Fanny."

"They make them . . . Chue said they're made special for the urns. Okay, we got it out," Fanny said, sitting back on her haunches. She wiped sweat from her brow with her sleeve.

Billie's voice was just short of hysterical. "Okay, the lid is back on. Do you want me to turn on the record player now?"

"Yeah. Yeah, do it now. I put new batteries in it this afternoon." Dusty Springfield's voice soared over the mountain.

"Look, Fanny, look! A shooting star! Do you think it's Sallie?"

"I hope so. I want her to know I'm doing everything she asked me to do."

Fifteen minutes later, Sallie and Devin's ashes swirled across the mountain to the strains of Dusty Springfield. "Rest in peace, Sallie," Fanny whispered.

"Oh, God, look, Fanny!"

Fanny raised tear-filled eyes to see not one, but two shooting stars, so close together they appeared as one. "I take that to mean our night's work met with their approval."

"I'd say so," Billie said breathlessly. "Fanny, do you . . . do you believe . . . ?"

"Yes. Yes, I do."

A long time later, Billie said, "What time is it, Fanny?"

"Ten past midnight. It's a relatively still night. I think it's safe to burn the house now. I listened to the weather forecast and . . . and I think it's okay. If anything goes awry, I'll live with it."

"Where's the gasoline?"

"On the front porch. I bought three five-gallon cans. As soon as it really starts to burn, we'll go down to Chue's and get the hoses ready . . . just in case. I hooked ours up this afternoon. Would you like a cup of coffee or a soft drink first?"

"No. Let's just do it."

"Okay."

"It's such a pretty little cottage. I like simple things," Billie said as she poured gasoline over the living room carpet.

"Sallie hated it. And yet she lived here for fourteen years. I will never understand how she did that. You light a match in the kitchen and I'll light one here. Close the door tight and run around to the front, okay?" Billie nodded.

The two women stood in the middle of the road, their arms around each other. "It's going to burn real quick. The wind is holding steady. If I were a pyromaniac, I'd be real happy with this."

"Let's go down to Chue's. As soon as he sees the flames he's going to be heading this way," Billie said. "Oh, oh, here he comes."

Fanny reached out a hand to Chue. "It's okay, Chue. Sallie asked me to burn it. We waited until the wind was right. I don't think it will spread."

"Why, Miss Fanny?"

"Sallie said the cottage was a blight on the mountain. She said you should clear the rubble when it cools, and plant grass and flowers. It's all right, Chue, if you don't understand. Some days I don't understand it either. I promised."

The three of them sat on the shoulder of the road, their arms wrapped around their knees, watching the flames shooting upward.

In the predawn hours, Chue dragged hoses from his cottage and from Sunrise to spray the smoldering ashes in case the wind whipped up. When the sun crept over the horizon, Fanny and Billie, soot-blackened from head to toe, headed for the main house.

Sallie Coleman Thornton's last wishes had been respected. To the letter.

"Have a safe trip. Call me as soon as you get home."

"I will." Billie smiled as Chue turned the truck around. Fanny waved wildly until the truck was out of sight.

"I miss her already," Fanny said, sitting down next to Simon on the steps. "Bess and I used to be close the way Billie and I are. We're still great friends, I would do anything for her and she would do anything for me, but we lead different lives now. She's involved in all the activities at the medical center, she has her children, she helps her father out in the drugstore, and she still manages to put in a full day at Sunny's Togs. I wish it were otherwise. True friends are so rare these days."

"You're feeling nostalgic," Simon said. "Do you want to talk about what else is bothering you?"

"Yes, and no. Ash was so ugly, so hateful. I've been trying for the past several days to figure out . . . I should say try to figure out where it all went wrong. I get such a raging headache I then try to put it out of my mind. At this stage I don't even know why it's important to me."

"Ash is the father of your children. He was the center of your life for many years. You don't just cast that aside and not think about it. No matter what happens, he will always be a part of your life. One day at a time, Fanny."

"Ash is going to fight the divorce. Out of spitefulness. I'm giving him the money for the casino. I have to call my attorney this afternoon. I need you to sell off everything as soon as possible. Not Jake's securities, though."

"You didn't ask for my opinion, Fanny, but I'm going to give it to you anyway. You're making a mistake to give Ash so much money all at one time. Spend the money for a real tough financial man to come in and oversee everything. I know several I can recommend. Ash has no head for financial matters. Some smart-ass contractor could come in, hear the name Thornton, and jack the price up double. You can't let that happen. Ash could go through the money in a year. Contractors usually want a real healthy chunk up front, then they schedule payments according to the progress of the building. Ash likes to gamble, bear that in mind."

"What would you suggest? I gave my word to Ash. How can I switch up now? For sure he'll fight the divorce."

"Listen, Fanny, I want you to give serious thought to controlling any monies you give Ash. I can set up a separate fund your attorney can oversee. You and Sunny should be the only one who can sign checks. No one else. Will you think about it?"

"Of course I'll think about it. I never thought of it in those terms. I think you're right, Simon."

"Okay, let's go to town and have some breakfast. We'll make a day of it and check out the other casinos. I'd like to see what Ash is up against, building wise."

"I'd like to visit the bingo palace. Sallie loved it, more than she ever loved Sunrise or her house in town. The second-best thing that she loved was the church she built for her friend Cotton. Your mother was such a simple person, Simon. Not many people knew that."

"I didn't know it for a long time. I love you, Fanny. I never said it aloud before. I don't expect you to say the same thing in return."

Fanny drew in her breath. This kind, gentle man truly cared about her. He deserved a response. "I think I fell in love with you the first time I saw your picture. Are you my destiny, Simon?" she asked softly.

"I believe so. I feel . . . like . . ."

"Giddy?"

"Yeah, giddy. Here I am, 48, going on 49, one year away from the half century mark, and I'm feeling the same way I felt when I was seventeen."

Fanny smiled. "Your heart doesn't know you aren't seventeen. I feel the same way. And then I look in the mirror and see my gray hair, the lines in my face. It doesn't change the way I feel. I find myself wanting to go roller skating with you, sleigh riding, skiing, all the things I did as a teenager. Did that make sense?"

"Oh, yes. Your kids probably would have trouble with it, but I understand perfectly."

"A whole day to spend together, Simon. Just you and me. I can be ready in fifteen minutes. Casual dress, okay?"

"Sure. I'll bring my things with me and catch an early flight out tomorrow morning. Then I'll be waiting. I'll wait forever, Fanny, if I know that you and I . . ."

"Shhhh," Fanny said, placing her index finger over Simon's lips. "We have all the time in the world. One day, Simon, when the time is right, I'm going to take you to a very special place. It's a simple place, but its simplicity is wondrous. I want you to hold on to that thought."

"We're going to make it, Fanny. We might be old and gray, but we're going to make it. You hold on to *that* thought."

"I will, Simon."

"Now we both have something to hold on to," Simon said.

The office was luxurious, consisting of green marble, dark shiny mahogany, stained glass windows, and ankle-deep carpeting. The lone figure in the elegant waiting room was impeccably dressed, appearing a part of the costly furnishings. One tasseled loafer tapped a path on the green marble that led to the carpeted area where comfortable chairs waited for wealthy clients.

Fanny Thornton and her attorney entered the room. Fanny stopped in her tracks to view the surroundings before she marched up to where her husband was sitting. He was so handsome, so incredibly polished, Fanny had to take a moment to gather her wits. "Your legal fees better not be coming out of any monies from me, Ash."

"Are you going back on your word?"

"Talk to my attorney through your attorney, Ash, but I repeat, I am not paying for these offices. I don't think the White House has such an elegant waiting room. The president of the United States probably makes less money than these attorneys you've hired. Just so you know, Ash. I'm giving you and these fancy attorneys exactly seven more minutes. Our appointment was for 10:00 A.M. It's now five minutes past the hour. Attorneys bill by the quarter hour. I'd hustle if I were you. These days I'm not known for my patience."

"Mr. Thornton, Mr. Tinsdale, Mr. Palmer will see you now."

Fanny sat down on one of the comfortable chairs. *Mr. Thornton, Mr. Tinsdale.* Was she invisible? She had been the one to schedule the meeting, she was the one with the money, she was the one who agreed to a meeting at this office to accommodate Ash. Blind with fury, Fanny stood up and addressed the modellike secretary Ash was eyeing greedily. "This meeting has just been canceled. It will take place fifteen minutes from now, in Mr. Tinsdale's office. Excuse me, gentlemen."

Outside the offices, in the marble hallway that was as elegant as the waiting room she'd just been in, Fanny took a deep breath. She thought about Devin's suite of offices on the second floor and Sallie's first experience with Devin's secretary. She had learned a thing or two from Sallie. She was sick and tired of men and secretaries classifying women as second-class citizens. Her head high, she marched to the elevator. She entered it just as Ash barreled through the office door, Mr. Tinsdale behind him. His rage-filled face was the last thing Fanny saw before the elevator door swished shut.

Fanny walked out of the legal building and around the corner to where Harry Tinsdale's offices were located. Her back was stiff, her eyes angry when she settled herself to wait. She was looking pointedly at her watch when her attorney, Ash, and his attorney entered the room. "Fanny Thornton, Mr. Ettinger. Time is money, so let's get our meeting under way."

Ettinger has more teeth than a shark, Fanny thought as she followed her attorney down a long hallway to his offices.

It was a long meeting, with three temper tantrums thrown by Ash Thornton and much cajoling on the part of Samuel Ettinger before the meeting broke up with Fanny's last words being hurled over her shoulder as she exited the office; "Take it or leave it, Ash. It's my only offer, and there will be no negotiating."

"What the hell was that all about, Fanny?" Ash blustered. "Moving that meeting."

"Common courtesy goes a long way, Ash. Don't worry about it, that long-legged beauty will probably end up in some chorus line, and you'll get to see her again. If she worked for me, she'd be walking the streets right now looking for a job."

"Is that what this is all about?" Ash snorted. "I didn't think you had a jealous bone in your body, Fanny."

"You're right, I don't. She didn't invite me into the meeting, she invited you and my lawyer. Since I wasn't included, I opted to conduct business on my own turf, in this case, my attorney's offices. I'd appreciate it if you'd get out of my way. I'm running late. No terms, Ash, until you agree to the divorce. I have no intention of ending up like your mother and Philip."

"Unless you agree to my terms, that's *exactly* how you're going to end up. I know you, Fanny, you won't allow yourself to get involved with anyone unless you're free. Well, guess what, you aren't going to be free. Don't forget, that assault and battery charge is still looming. I haven't dropped the charges."

"As I said to you once before, you don't know me at all, Ash. I'm not that stupid, starry-eyed girl you married thirty years ago. If I feel like having an affair, I'll have an affair. If I feel like hopping between the sheets with some pit boss, I'll do that too. Being married to you will never stop me. I will do what I want when I want. You go ahead with your assault and battery charge, stall the divorce. You're the one who wants to build a casino, not me. I have all the time in the world. I'm leaving the country in a few days, so don't drag your feet. If you decide to hold out, it will take that much longer. Your choice. Sallie's will is unbreakable. All that attorney is doing is taking your money. Get a second opinion."

"Fanny, wait a minute. Let's go get a cup of coffee and talk about this like the civilized adults we are."

"No." Fanny opened her car door and slid inside.

"What do you mean, no."

"What part of 'no' didn't you understand?"

"No you don't want coffee or no you won't reconsider?" Ash said, his face murderous.

Fanny shifted gears, her eyes straight ahead. "I'll send you a postcard from the Orient."

Fanny's heart pumped furiously. How was it possible that Ash could still get to her? Tears ran down her cheeks as she drove through traffic. She was going home, the home she'd created for the children and herself. Home to lick her wounds, and cry for what might have been.

The phone rang, just as Fanny lugged her bags to the top of the steps. She ran back to her bedroom to pick up the phone. "Sunny! How are you honey?"

"Real good, Mom. Just called to say good-bye. Have fun and bring me a present."

"Now, did I ever go anywhere and not bring presents?" Fanny laughed.

"You might have such a good time you'll forget. Everyone wants to say good-bye. What are you going to do for a whole *month?*"

"I'll sightsee, eat, sleep, shop. I don't have much time, honey, put the others on, okay?"

"Okay, love you, Mom."

"Love you too. Birch, watch out for everyone, you are the oldest. Sage, before you can ask, yes, I have a window seat. You know I love you. If your dad calls . . . just be respectful. I'll call and give you a phone number as soon as I know what it is. Love you. Bye!"

"This is everything, Chue. Goodness, I don't have much time, do I?"

"Plenty time."

"Did anything good come in the mail?"

"Lots of letters. I put them in the car so you could read them on the way to the airport."

Fanny settled herself and immediately ripped open the one from her attorney. When she finished reading she heaved a sigh so loud that Chue asked her if she was all right.

"Better than you'll ever know, Chue," Fanny said happily. Ash had agreed to her terms and the divorce would go through. By the time she returned from China she would be a free woman. What did one do when divorce became final? Did women stand up and cheer, did they cry and wail, did they celebrate? What was she going to do?

Fanny leaned back in the seat of the car, her eyes closed, her heart thumping in her chest. In just a few hours, in Honolulu, she would be meeting Simon. Then she would travel halfway around the world with him.

They would board a flight for Hong Kong. Together. Fanny's eyelid twitched. She was going off with a man for an . . . assignation. Sunny would call it a tryst. She couldn't help but wonder now if she had made a mistake by not telling her children Simon was going with her to the Orient. What would they think, what would they say? Because she didn't want to know their opinions or their attitudes, she'd kept quiet. According to the letter from her attorney, her divorce would be final in seven days. The countdown had started yesterday. Not counting today, she would be a free woman in six days. Today, and into tomorrow, was a travel day. One minute after midnight, on the seventh day, she would finally be liberated. She could do whatever she damn well pleased. She could go to bed with Simon Thornton. She could *marry* Simon if she wanted to, providing he asked her.

Mrs. Simon Thornton. A smile tugged at the corners of her mouth. If she was into monograms, which she wasn't, she would have no need to change hers.

"We're here, Miss Fanny. Take care of your ticket, and I'll check your bags," Chue said. "The trunk with my things is going to cost extra. I have the money right here."

Fanny placed a gentle hand on his arm. "No, Chue. I want to do this for you. I have all the messages in my purse along with telephone numbers, addresses, and even some pictures. Should your relatives have presents or mementos for you and your family, I'll bring them back in the same trunk."

"Give Mr. Simon my regards." Chue smiled.

"Chue! How did you know?" Fanny asked, flustered that this kind, gentle man knew what she was up to.

"I see it in your eyes. I see the same thing in Mr. Simon's eyes. He is a good man. When he was a small boy he worried that I worked too hard. He would try to help in many small ways."

"I don't want you to think . . ."

"I do not think anything, Miss Fanny. Life is very short here on earth. One must be happy and content. I wish much happiness for you and Mr. Simon."

"I wish that too," Fanny said, hugging Chue. She accepted her baggage claim tickets, stuffing them along with her ticket into her purse.

"When you return, the remains of Miss Sallie's cottage will be gone. I have the sod and many beautiful flowers to plant. Each time we look at the bend in the road, we'll think of Miss Sallie and her goodness. For many days I did not understand. Will there be a stone?"

"Just a simple wooden cross. She said one of your cousins would carve it."

"But everyone else has a stone," Chue said, "Even Mr. Devin."

"Sallie said . . . what she said was . . . if she was just plain old Sallie Coleman, all she would have was a wooden cross and be lucky to have that. A wooden cross it is. It will read: Sallie Coleman. She said she disgraced the Thornton name. I couldn't talk her out of it, Chue. You might want to think about a large stone with her name chiseled on it, in the flower garden you're going to create. How do you get butterflies? What kind of flowers do they like? A garden for butterflies. Sallie would like that. All kinds of butterflies."

"I will look into it, Miss Fanny."

"I know you will, Chue. I'll bring you a present. A Chinese yo-yo for your collection."

"Have a safe trip, Miss Fanny. Call, and I will meet you here on your return."

Fanny watched until Chue's truck was out of sight. She felt dizzy with her freedom. She hadn't traveled alone since her trip to Hawaii to meet Ash over thirty years ago. She'd been a girl then. Now she was a woman ready to meet her destiny.

Simon was her destiny. Sallie had said so. Simon had said so. She believed.

He was walking toward her, his eyes searching the milling passengers as they walked the concourse. Fanny stopped, forcing people to walk around her. She didn't apologize, her mouth was paper-dry, preventing any words from escaping. She remembered another time when a young lieutenant dressed in navy whites had met her at this airport. She shook her head to clear the thought away. This was Simon, wonderful, wonderful Simon. He was a vision to her weary eyes, dressed in a crisp white shirt, open at the throat, with rolled-up sleeves, creased khaki trousers, and tasseled loafers. A lightweight summer jacket was folded over his arm. He was more handsome than the young lieutenant dressed in navy whites she'd remembered a moment ago.

"Simon," Fanny said breathlessly.

"Fanny! I was starting to panic. I must have walked this concourse five times. I thought you might have . . . changed your mind." His voice was hoarse, his eyes drinking in the sight of her.

"Never." Her voice was still breathless.

"Tired?"

"I'm too excited to be tired. I am hungry, though."

"We have two hours, so let's head for the nearest restaurant. I'm all checked in, so we can cut it right down to the wire. How about you?"

"Me too. We're seated together. The passenger scheduled to sit next to me decided at the last moment to wait until tomorrow to travel. I told the ticket agent you were my husband but coming from another direction. I hope you don't mind."

"Not likely. I planned to crouch in the aisle next to your seat until they made me move or took pity on me and ousted the person next to you."

"I can't believe we're here. Together. It's like a dream. Sallie always said, 'all good things come to those who wait.' I think it must be true."

Over bites of well-done hamburger, soggy french fries, crunchy pickles, and greasy potato chips, Fanny repeated, verbatim, the letter she'd received from her attorney. Simon stopped chewing long enough to stare at her. "What's the trick? Ash never gives in."

He had to agree; otherwise, he doesn't get the money. Ash signed off on everything. In five more days I'll be free."

"That's good enough for me."

"They're calling our flight, Simon. We're really going to get on that plane together, aren't we?"

"Yes we are. Allow me," Simon said, extending his arm.

"Simon, I'm giddy."

"Look at my feet, Fanny, they aren't touching the floor. From this point on, we are not going to talk about family, friends, or business. This is *our* time, yours and mine. We've waited a long time for this and now that time has arrived. No clocks, no calendars. Agreed?"

"Oh, yes, Simon. Yes, yes, yes."

"This, my dear, is the Peninsula Hotel, the finest hotel in all of Asia. It's the home away from home of queens and kings, grand dukes, heads of state, divas, captains of industry, and, I'm told, CIA Agents. I read everything I could get my hands on in regard to Asia.

"See that man dressed in white, the imperious one. He's a majordomo. The young boys are pages. This is a serious business to all of them. No one smiles. We're going to register, have tea here in this golden room, go for a walk, have an early dinner, go to bed, in separate rooms, catch up on our jet lag, and get up in the morning and *do it*. By doing it, I mean we're going to do Hong Kong."

Fanny giggled. "I knew what you meant. Does Queen Elizabeth really have tea here?"

"So I have heard."

"I feel important," Fanny said as a white-clad waiter ushered her to a seat at a small round table.

"And well you should," Simon said smartly. "I believe the man to your left, the one in profile, is Prince Charles."

"Who cares?" Fanny said airily. "I'd rather look at you."

"Ah. This is Lushan Yun Wu tea. By the time we leave here, we'll be drinking it with gusto."

Fanny made a face. "I find that hard to believe. I prefer Lipton Tea bags. Does that mean I won't fit in?"

Simon threw back his head and laughed. The Prince Charles look-alike frowned at this uncouth outburst. Simon laughed harder. Fanny smiled. She loved the sound of Simon's laughter, loved the merriment in his eyes. Loved sitting here with him at this little round table where queens and kings had tea. Loved him. Period.

"Tomorrow we'll have tea and crumpets," Simon said, the laughter still in his voice.

"Tomorrow we'll have Coca-Cola and potato chips. If we're going for a walk, Simon, we should go now before I fall asleep."

"We can skip all that, Fanny. I'm tired too. Maybe we should check in, go to our rooms, sleep, and meet up for breakfast. Tomorrow is another day."

Fanny yawned. "That's the nicest thing you've said to me all day. Let's do that. Nine o'clock in the morning for breakfast. We'll meet in the lobby, okay?"

Simon matched her yawn. "I'll check us in."

Fanny slept for twelve straight hours, waking at 6:00 A.M. Hong Kong time. She felt groggy and disoriented as she slid her legs over the side of the bed. Her voice sounded thick and hoarse when she spoke with room service. "Coffee and orange juice. Immediately."

Fanny opened her traveling case to remove her robe and stared at herself in the huge bathroom mirror. Who *was* this person staring back at her, this person with the flyaway hair sticking up at all angles, this person with the smudged makeup and dry skin? It was true then what frequent travelers said; pressurized cabins sucked all the moisture from one's skin. She winced.

The coffee was strong and black. Fanny sipped leisurely as she fired up her first cigarette of the day. When she finished her third cup of coffee she felt like the Fanny Thornton who left Nevada the day before. She turned on the television to see American subtitles. She turned it off; it was better to sit here and daydream about spending the next four weeks with Simon. She looked at her watch. She would see him, in two hours, sit across from him at breakfast, walk with him hand in hand. She was going to share her life with Simon for a whole month. She wanted to think beyond the month, but caution prevented her. One day at a time.

The last thing Fanny did before leaving the hotel room was to prop up a pocket calendar against the lamp. The countdown to her divorce was under way.

Dressed in a simple yellow linen shift that showed off her summer tan to perfection, Fanny stepped from the lift at five minutes to nine. She knew she looked good because she felt good.

"I've been here since seven-thirty. I could float out of here on the coffee I consumed," Simon said.

"You should have called me, Simon. I was up at six. If it will make you feel better, I consumed an entire pot of coffee myself. We can float away together. That thought makes me very happy. Let's just walk."

As Simon said later, "We did Hong Kong on foot."

The day passed in a literal blur for Fanny as they made their way through hordes of people, none of whom smiled. They took the Star Ferry, sitting close together on the slatted seat, holding hands. On solid ground again, Simon took her arm. "Want rickshaw ride?" a wizened man queried.

"Mercy, Simon, the man is so old, I can't in good conscience let him haul us around. It's too sad."

"You ride rickshaw? I take you, roads go wiggly, wiggly. Taxi no go wiggly wiggly. Much far. Where you want go?"

Fanny consulted her notes. "Cloth Lane."

"Okay, Cloth Lane it is," Simon said, helping Fanny into the rickshaw. "I'll give him a big tip," he whispered.

The old man was right, the road went wiggly wiggly. He trotted along at an even rate of speed, coming to a stop at the beginning of the lane. Fanny gasped in awe at the hundreds of colorful banners and metal signs hanging overhead, blocking out all traces of sunlight.

"I guess our best bet is to walk up one side and down the other. Exactly what are you looking for?" Simon asked.

"Materials for the new Rainbow Babies line and perhaps some new patterned fabric. I applied to the government for permission to travel to Zhejiang on the east coast. Billie told me the silks coming out of the famous Silk City as it's called, are clear as water, beautiful as poetry, like clouds in the sky and flowers on earth. I don't want to miss the mulberry trees and the silk experts in the Zhejiang Province. I wish I knew someone with clout who could intercede for me."

"We can stop by the embassy tomorrow. Perhaps they can expedite your request," Simon said.

They walked from shop to shop, getting the knack of haggling by the time they visited the fifth shop, where Fanny bought two silk robes for the twins with dragons belching fire appliquéd on the back. For Sunny and Billie she bought pale pink silk robes with ap-pliquéd flowers around the bands of the sleeves and the hem. They ate noodles, rice cakes, and egg rolls and drank the awful Lushan Yun Wu tea by the cup.

Late in the afternoon, walking down Nathan Road, on their way back to the Star Ferry, they found themselves caught in a horde of people watching a Dragon Boat Festival whose lead Dragon Boat belched fire. Simon snapped pictures, one after the other. When they were allowed to proceed to the ferry, Fanny pointed to the camera, her face full of laughter. "You ran out of film after the first shot."

"No!"

"Uh-huh. At least you got one shot."

"What would I do without you?" Simon asked.

"Oh, Simon, I don't ever want to find out the answer to that question."

At the American Embassy, Fanny's countrymen helped her locate the families on Chue's list. Written messages were sent, and phone calls were made. On the evening of the fourth day, Chue's gifts were dispersed and a pile of gifts was offered to Fanny to take home for Chue. Fanny showed pictures of Chue, Su Li, and their families. The relatives' smiles were the only ones she saw during the entire time she spent in Hong Kong. The trunk was full again.

One more day until her divorce was final.

Day five was spent taking the Kowloon–Canton Railway—the Peak-tram—thirty kilometers to a height of 397 meters above sea level. Fanny and Simon had a picnic.

Dinner at Gaddi's lasted three and a half hours with two bottles of wine. Simon and Fanny parted company at her door a little after ten, promising to meet for breakfast at nine the following morning.

Fanny removed her makeup, changed into her nightgown, and crept into bed. Tomorrow was day seven. Tomorrow she would be a free woman. Suddenly she sat up, bolted from the bed to race to the dresser where the small pocket calendar leaned against the lamp. Her mind raced. Tomorrow was day seven. *Day seven in the United States.* Day seven here in Asia was half-over. Hong Kong was twelve hours ahead of US time. Her divorce hearing was scheduled for 9:00 A.M. on the morning of the seventh day. Lordy, Lordy, Lordy, she was already divorced! She was free to go to Simon. Now. This minute.

Later, she had no memory of putting on her robe and slippers, no memory of opening her door, no memory of walking down the hall, five doors away, to Simon's room, no memory of knocking on his door. When the door opened, she stared at Simon for a full minute. "Hong Kong is twelve hours ahead of the United States. Simon, I'm *free*."

Fanny's feet left the floor as Simon yanked her into the room. His voice was hoarse when he said, "How did that slip by us?"

"Simon . . ."

"Shhh," he said, kissing her.

"Oh, my, do that again. I *liked* that."

"You should see what else I can do. That was just a teaser," Simon murmured.

Fanny nibbled on Simon's ear, her tongue tickling the inside. "You should see what else I can do. That was *my* teaser," Fanny said.

"I can be out of these pajama bottoms in a heartbeat," Simon said.

Fanny's nightgown was on the floor and she was in the bed before Simon had his left leg out of his pajama bottom.

"There's a lot to be said for speed," Simon grinned.

Simon looked at her naked body with the eye of a lover and a connoisseur. "You're beautiful," he whispered.

"You talk too much. Come here, I want to feel you next to me. I want to feel all of you against all of me."

He knelt over her for a long moment, his eyes drinking in the sight of the long, sweeping lines of her body. His gaze traveled up the length of her thighs to the perfection of her molded breasts. The blaze in his loins raced to his head, making him light-headed, knowing a deep, aching desire. Fanny held out her arms to him, and with a sound close to a moan, he lay down next to her, entwining himself around her. His arms drew her close.

Fanny's head was swimming with exhilaration. Her body was ready, arching, needing, wanting, eager for his touch. She didn't know how she knew, but she knew Simon would be slow and artful. He would give and take and finally, claim her for his own. And when he was deep inside her, then he would take her, joining her to himself.

Their mouths touched, his tongue spearing into the warm wetness of her mouth. His arms wrapped around her, anchoring her body to his while her senses soared and took flight. Her world, upside-down, focused only on those places covered by his hands and lips.

She moved to cup his face in her hands. She kissed his mouth, his chin, his ears, her tongue trailing kisses down his chest, down, down, down. She felt herself being moved, felt his lips on hers, forcing her to arch her back, her head moving back and forth on the pillow as though to negate the exquisite demand of her sensuality. Their lips met, lingered, tasted, and met again. She felt a prisoner, loving the feeling.

His hands grasped her hips, drawing her against him, filling her with himself, knowing his own needs, demanding she fulfill them. Her breathing was as ragged as his own, his chest heaving to the same rhythm as hers. He moved within her, rhythmically, insistently, rocking against her, forcing her to tighten herself around him, bringing each of them closer to their sunburst climax, where each of them would surrender to the other.

Gasping and panting, Simon covered her body with his own, quieting her shudders, calming her spasms. When he finally withdrew from her, he cradled her to him. He whispered words only lovers knew until they slept in each other's arms.

22

Fanny sucked a long noodle through her pursed lips at the same time Simon did. It was a silly thing, but both of them laughed and did it again.

All their shopping had been done, the gifts and mementos packed in two large trunks. Their visit to the Silk City had been accomplished. They'd had half of the silks sent directly to Billie Coleman in Texas, the other half to Sunny's Togs in Las Vegas.

They headed for a small park they'd found by accident. Simon carried a string bag with a blanket, cheese, apples and Coca-Cola. Fanny carried a book and a day-old copy of the *Wall Street Journal*. Together they spread the blanket and then removed their shoes. Both of them rolled over on their stomachs with the easy familiarity of a couple in love. They spoke quietly, softly to one another so as not to disturb the many young people studying under the trees.

"We haven't made any kind of a plan," Simon said. "I need to know, Fanny, was this just a vacation to you? Are we going home to . . . what? I live in New York. You live in Nevada. How are we going to handle that?"

"I don't know, Simon. This has been so perfect. I've tried not to think about it. Inevitably when you make a plan, things start to go awry. I don't want anything to go wrong."

"We're talking about the rest of our lives. You're free. I'm free. What are we going to do about it?"

"What would you like to do?"

"Marry you of course."

"Simon, it's too soon. I've only been divorced a few weeks. I don't want to . . . rush into anything. I'm thinking about the kids too. It would bother me tremendously for them to think you and I were having an affair while I was still married to their father. I realize they aren't kids any longer, they're adults, but even adults have a problem when their parents get divorced. You should be able to relate to all of this, Simon. How did you feel when your mother and Devin . . . when they started keeping . . . company, for want of a better word?"

"My parents had a very strange style, Fanny. Dad was one place, Mom was someplace else. We got together on holidays. I accepted it because I didn't know any other way. I knew it wasn't normal because I had friends who had normal families, like Jerry. I had already enlisted when Mom and Devin got together. Jerry wrote and told me what was going on. Mom kind of talked around it in her letters. I really liked Devin. He could make Mom smile, make her eyes sparkle. Dad could never do that. Your kids are no different than I was. They'll accept me. I think they like me as much as I like them."

"They more than like you. They adore you. You're their father's brother. That's the difference. They don't think of you and me in romantic terms."

Simon rolled over onto his back, his hands laced behind his head. "Are you saying you won't marry me because of the kids?"

"For now. I can go to New York twice a month. You can come to Nevada twice a month. We'll see each other every weekend. It will only be for a little while. Simon, I worked so hard to keep my family together, I can't take the chance . . . I *won't* take the chance that something could go wrong. You can't just walk away from a business that has taken you all your life to build. I would never ask you to do that. Please, tell me you understand."

Simon leaned over on his side, his chin propped in the palm of his hand. He stared at the woman next to him, the woman who had given him such happiness over the past month. He felt like crying. "I do understand, but, Fanny, I need something I can look forward to, something to hang on to."

"Oh, Simon, oh, Simon, you're looking at me the way Devin looked at your mother. Oh, Simon. Thank you, thank you." She was in his arms, smothering his face with kisses. "I do love you. So much I can't imagine my life without you in it. Be patient with me. We'll make it work."

"I don't think I could live without you," Simon whispered.

"Don't say that, Simon. Don't ever say that to me again. Promise me, swear to me you'll never say that. Devin said that to your mother and then he shot himself." Her voice was almost hysterical, her nails digging into the fleshy part of his upper arms.

"I swear, I promise. It's okay, shhh, it's all right. They were just words, Fanny. I would never take my own life. Not in a million years. Let's just lie here and compose a song about the two of us, a song we'll hire Dusty Springfield to sing for us the day we get married."

Fanny rolled over and laughed. The bad moment was over.

Fanny walked through the door of Sunrise, aware of the silence that surrounded her. For the past month her ears had been full of strange sounds in a strange land. The silence that now engulfed her made her heart pound in her chest. She missed Simon. Her heart started to ache the moment he walked away from her, toward his plane. The only thing she wanted to do was to go inside, pick up the phone, and call him, but she couldn't do that for five more hours. Her shoulders slumping, Fanny shouldered her way inside to the shouts of, "Surprise! Surprise!" Stunned, she stared around at her family and friends. A huge banner stretched across the dining room arch read WELCOME HOME! A smile worked its way around the corners of her mouth . . . until she saw Ash shoulder his way through the small knot of people.

"Welcome home, Fanny! It's good to see you! You look gorgeous. Tired, but gorgeous."

"Ash! What are you doing here?" she managed to ask. Guilt settled over her like a shroud.

"The kids invited me. You won't believe the time the five of us have had this past month. It was like opening up an umbrella, Fanny. We told each other all kinds of things. Everything just came out, we dealt with it, and now we're all good friends. We want to include you," he whispered.

The shroud of guilt tightened. "How nice." She wanted to run to the studio and lock the door. She pulled herself together, instead, and tried to smile. "Chue's bringing in the trunks."

"We'll talk later. Sunny made her peanut butter, jelly, banana, and marshmallow sandwiches. Just a small welcome from all of us to show you how much you mean to everyone. We all really did miss you. We tried calling Simon this week, but his office said he was on a business trip. Oh, well, his loss," Ash laughed.

"Boy, did I miss you, Mom. Tyler's coming any minute now. He's always late. Dad likes him, Mom. Dad spread the peanut butter on the bread. He was right at home in the kitchen. Mom, he turned over a new leaf, he's been so good," Sunny said brightly.

Fanny fought the urge to slap her daughter's face. What was happening here?

"How was it, Fanny?" Bess asked, hugging her.

"It was wonderful. Now, this. My God, Bess, what's been going on?"

"I tried to stop this little get-together but my excuses sounded lame, even to my own ears. It's my understanding, from your two daughters, that your husband, now that you're divorced, has seen the error of his ways, and is intent on courting you in the hopes of getting you to remarry him. Not one of them has a clue about Simon, Fanny, so be careful."

"This can't be happening. No. This is wrong. I won't allow this. I absolutely will not."

"Fanny, the kids . . . they want this. Be careful of what you say and how you say it. Kids can turn on you in the blink of an eye."

"It just might come to that, Bess. Thanks for warning me."

The shroud of guilt tightened another notch. Surely, God, in his infinite wisdom, wouldn't make her choose between her family and Simon. Or, would He?

Fanny steeled herself to get through the next hour, sickened at the way her children hovered over their father, patting him on the back, Sunny kissing Ash's cheek from time to time, Billie smiling tightly. Their light, teasing banter, that didn't include her, brought an angry flush to her cheeks. She had to get through this. She *would* get through this. She almost yelped in sheer joy when Bess said, "Party's over, Fanny is dead on her feet. She needs to go to bed and get over her jet lag. C'mon, everyone, party's over. Gather up your presents and head down the mountain."

"Sure. Mom, how about if we all come up this weekend? We haven't had a picnic in a long time. Dad said he'll bring the ants. Is that funny or what?"

"I'll call you. Thanks for the party."

"Mom, what's wrong, you look . . . strange," Sunny said, wrapping her mother in her arms.

Fanny stiffened. "What could possibly be wrong?" *Look at me, do I look happy? Are you blind? Can't you see what this party with your father has done to me? Open your eyes and look at me.*

"I guess you're just tired. Tomorrow you'll be fine. I'll call you."

Guess what, Sunny, I won't be answering the phone. I take betrayal very seriously.

"Oh, Mom, I'm so happy. Things are going great between Tyler and me. And now we have a chance to be a real family again. Isn't it wonderful? Dad told me I had really good ideas about the casino and that he's looking forward to working with me. The twins are switching up too, Mom. We aren't leaving you in a bind or anything. Bess and Billie have it all under control."

Fanny shook off her daughter's arms. She wanted to cry, to scream at her children. *Don't you get it? He wants your inheritance! That's what this is all about and you're buying into it.*

"What about you, Billie?" Fanny asked her youngest daughter.

Billie hugged her mother. She whispered, "It's a crock, Mom. The two of them can't see it, but I can. I pretended for a little while to see which way it was going to go. Now I know. I'm sorry it had to be today on your first day home. Mom, don't answer the phone tomorrow or the day after, and scratch the picnic."

"Okay, honey. I'll call you and we'll talk, okay?"

"Take it easy, Mom." Fanny nodded.

"Thanks for the robe, Mom," Birch said.

"Yeah, me too, Mom," Sage said. He hugged her, whispering in her ear the same way Billie had done. "Sometimes the eye fools you, Mom. Seeing isn't always believing. If you're counting, the score is two, two."

"Good-bye everybody," Fanny said as she neatly sidestepped Ash's outstretched arms.

"Good-bye, Mrs. Thornton," Tyler Ford called from the doorway, his eyes puzzled at her cool behavior toward her family.

Fanny walked through the house toward the kitchen and out the back door, where she followed the path to her studio.

Her sanctuary.

She put on a pot of coffee to perk while she showered. Dressed in her old, tattered robe, she curled into one of the big red chairs, the clock on the table near her drafting table directly in her line of vision. She nibbled on crunchy pretzels she didn't want and drank cup after cup of strong black coffee. The hands on the Big Ben clock moved torturously slowly.

At ten o'clock eastern time, Fanny picked up the phone to dial Simon's number. She started to cry the moment she heard his voice. "Simon . . . Simon . . . I . . . Oh, Simon . . ."

"Okay, we've established that I'm Simon. Take a deep breath, honey. Whatever it is, we'll make it right. Are *you* all right? I had a god-awful flight, turbulence all the way. My stomach is still heaving. You didn't answer my question, Fanny."

"I'm fine. I need to talk, Simon, and I need you to listen. Let me ramble on until I wind down, okay? I need to do this." Simon mumbled something unintelligible.

Fanny's words tumbled out so fast, Simon had a hard time following the runaway conversation. "Sage said if I was counting, the score was two, two. Do you believe this, Simon, because I can't. I know what Ash is doing. Obviously, Billie and Sage know also. He wants the money in the trust. That's what this is all about. I wanted to slap Sunny's face; I would have too, but Bess stopped me. Birch made me sick the way he fawned over his father. Do you hear how I sound, Simon? I'm so ashamed of these feelings. Maybe today was just the wrong day. It hit me in the face the minute I saw Ash. It went downhill after that. I don't know what to do."

"When you don't know what to do, the best course of action is to do nothing. You can ride this out. You've been through worse than this. If you want, I can be on the next plane out of here and be there by morning."

"No, that isn't necessary. Talking to you has helped a lot. Who am I to demand my children ignore their father? They were so happy, Simon. I wish you could have seen Birch and Sunny. It was like someone gift-wrapped the moon and the stars for them. At some point, when things don't go his way, Ash is going to turn on them. I can feel it in every bone in my body. What happens then?"

"You'll be there for them, Fanny, the way you're always there for them. They're all grown-up now. They aren't little kids any longer."

"There aren't Band-Aids big enough to cover the wounds Ash is going to inflict. I feel like they're standing on a cliff, ready to go over, and I can't stop them. It's terrible to feel helpless. I don't expect you to understand, Simon, you aren't a mother."

"I'm not a mother *or* a father, but I understand. Whatever happens, Fanny, we'll deal with it. Please, don't torture yourself. Sometimes you just have to stand back and let life take care of life."

"I'm going to say good-night, Simon. There are no words to tell you how much I love you."

"And I love you more. I'll call you tomorrow, Fanny. Sleep well."

"I don't plan on answering the phone tomorrow. I'll call you after dinner."

"You can't hide or bury your head where this is concerned, Fanny."

"Just for a few days, Simon. Good night."

The following morning, as soon as the offices of Sunny's Togs opened, Fanny called Bess to leave a message for her children. "Write this down verbatim, Bess. There is no room in my schedule for a picnic this weekend. Furthermore, your father violated the agreement we had never to set foot on Sunrise property. I resent the liberties you took upon yourselves in bringing your father to the mountain. Please do not do it again. When I want you to come to Sunrise, I'll invite you. Until that time, please respect my privacy."

"This is pretty . . . harsh, Fanny. Are you sure you want me to give this to Sunny? I don't want you to regret it later on."

"I rather doubt that I will. Ash is setting them up to get control of their money. How can I tell them that? First of all, they wouldn't believe me. They want to believe in their father, they *need* to believe in him, and Ash knows that. That doesn't mean *I* have to fall into line. What kind of monster would throw his ex-wife into the pot? Sallie was right, Bess, your firstborn will break your heart. In the end I don't think it matters what order a child is born in. Any one of them can break your heart. I have to get to work. Let's have lunch one day next week. Give my regards to John." She was trembling all over when she hung up the phone. She picked it up again, listened for the dial tone, then laid the receiver on the small table near her drafting table. The phone would be silent for the rest of the day.

Fanny walked out into the sunshine. Now that her head was a little more clear she wanted to see what Chue had accomplished with the grounds, and to inspect the progress of the electric fence. Chue was weeding a lovely flower bed when she rounded the bend in the road.

"Oh, Chue, it's beautiful. Sallie would be so pleased. The grass is perfect. It's the first thing you see when you come up to the bend. It's a veritable rainbow."

"Thank you, Miss Fanny. The electric company is waiting for you to call them. The fence is finished. The gates are open, you must decide on the combination. I will set the code. You will then enter by pressing a small appliance. I had them install a manual gate in case of an electrical failure. Even though we have a generator, one never knows. The small walk-through gate is hidden in the mountain shrubbery. I have two keys. Everything can be operational today if you call now."

Fanny stared at the fence. They'd done just as she instructed. Fourteen-foot iron spears embedded in a concrete base. "I hope no one is foolish enough to impale themselves on one of those spears. It does look . . . prisonlike, doesn't it? I'll call the electric company as soon as I go up to the house. Perhaps we should plant some vines, ivy or something, to take away that . . . institutional look. Whatever you think best, Chue. Only you and I will have the code. Not my children. If they ask, tell them to press the button to speak with me through the intercom. Under no circumstance are you to allow them to pass through the gate unless I tell you so. Does that make you uncomfortable?"

"No, Miss Fanny, it does not. What about Mr. Simon?"

"Just you and me, Chue. I don't care if the children bang and holler, blow their horn, whatever, do not open the gate."

"I understand, Miss Fanny. Thank you very much for the gifts. My family was most grateful. Did you know the yo-yo glows in the dark?"

"No, Chue, I didn't know that."

"My wife says she is going to tie it onto my big toe when I sleep because I am all over the bed."

Fanny laughed all the way back to the studio. She used the telephone to call the electric company, and gave her order. She broke the connection, listened for the dial tone before she laid the phone back on the little table.

A coffee cup in hand, Fanny sat down at her drawing board. Three hours later she gave up in disgust, crunching designs into tight little balls. She threw them, one by one, into the trash basket at her side.

Elbows on her drafting board, chin in her hands, Fanny contemplated the matters at hand. She realized what she was experiencing was *fear*. Fear that what had happened in Sallie's life was now happening to her. How could their lives parallel each other like this? Was this Sallie's legacy to her?

What should she do? Call the telephone company and request a hookup and an unlisted number. She followed her own instructions and at three o'clock, a shiny new phone was installed in the studio, the old phone disconnected. That number would still ring in the main house, where messages would be recorded on an answering machine. There were no extensions to her new phone, the number was unlisted. She called Simon immediately to give him her new number. They talked for an hour. Finally, the conversation shifted to business.

"The Bernsteins are going to have something to show us in a few days," Simon said. "You'll need to give some thought to where you're going to get a baby to model the outfits. Do you know anyone or would you like me to call a professional modeling agency?"

"I was thinking of using Bess's newest grandchild. She's eight months old. She'll be perfect for the outfits. I'm going to stitch the model this afternoon. I have a meeting scheduled with Bess for tomorrow. Right now, I'd say we can get our first shipment out in time for Easter. Bess hired quite a few qualified people, to the kids' dismay, while we were away. She said everything is on schedule. Orders are starting to come in already, mostly from our Sunny's Togs customers. I miss you, Simon."

"Let's remedy that right now. I can come there or you could come here. If you come here, we can set up the meeting with Audrey and Mike here in the city. How about this weekend? Better yet, how about if you pack and leave this evening?"

"I'd love to, but I have some things I want to take care of. I'll plan to leave on Friday unless something comes up. I'll call you this evening to say good-night. Simon"—her voice was suddenly shy—"I think about us all the time. You're in my thoughts every minute of the day. You're what's making this bearable."

"Fanny, I didn't know . . . that love . . . could be so all-consuming. I didn't exactly think my life was going to be over when I approached the fifty-year mark, but I never expected it to change so drastically. You've made me feel young again. I thought those feelings were gone. Jesus, I love you. More than life itself. By the way, I took all sixteen rolls of film to be developed. I should have them by Friday. I'll console myself by staring at them."

"Wonderful. I can't wait to see them. Bye, darling."

Fanny felt all the built-up tenseness leave her body the moment she hung up the phone. Just talking to Simon made her feel good. She stared out the window over her drafting board. Daydreaming was a wonderful way to pass the time. She was frolicking with Simon on a sandy beach in Baja, California, in her daydream, when a thunderous-sounding staccato noise rocked the walls of the studio. Fanny gripped the edges of her drafting table, her eyes wide with panic. The noise sounded a second and then a third time and seemed to be coming from the panel near the door. The intercom. Someone was at the gate. She ran to the door to try and adjust the volume. She should have read the operator's manual. She thought she could make out the words, "Open the damn gates! What the hell kind of fence is this? All you need is rolled barbed wire on top! Jesus Christ!"

Ash!

"Fanny, open the gate! Sunny is here with me. We want to talk with you. Honey, are you there? Chue says he can't open the gates."

"Mom, it's me, Sunny. Are you home?"

Fanny stared at the square white panel with the blinking lights. What to press? Maybe she should walk down to the gate and talk to her daughter and ex-husband. On the other hand, maybe she shouldn't. She walked back to her work area and dialed Bess's number. "Did you give Sunny and Birch my message?"

"Yes, I did, Fanny. At 9:00 A.M. when they both walked in. Neither one of them said a thing. Why?"

"Ash and Sunny are at the gate. I don't know how to work the panel. I guess I have to read the manual. I could walk down to the gate, but I don't want to do that, either."

"You're the boss, Fanny. Don't do anything you don't want to do. The message was quite clear. Sometimes people have a hard time accepting unwanted news. I think that's the case. Or, maybe Ash is going to try and charm you again. Don't fall for it, Fanny."

"I won't. I'm going to hang up and read the manual. Want to know something, Bess? I feel safe and powerful. Those gates . . . I'm glad I did it. Ash said I should put rolled barbed wire across the top. Maybe I should do it. Just kidding. But I had told Ash not to come here anymore. I told him I would put the fence up. We're divorced. That gives him no rights. So, what does he do? He brings my daughter here, thinking because she's with him, I'll relent. If I don't relent, that makes me a bad guy in front of Sunny. I'm going to New York this weekend. If you need to reach me, call me at Simon's. No one needs to know where I'm going."

Fanny hung up the phone. The silence hammered at her ears. The tears she'd been fighting flowed to the surface, her clenched fists pounded her drafting board. She watched a Granny Smith apple teeter and slide off the board. Whose idea was it to come to the mountain? Ash's of course. She knew this was Ash's first step in getting the children to turn on her, and she was playing right into his hands. "If he could, he'd suck the blood from my body," she muttered.

Fanny changed her shoes. Time for some fresh air and a nice long walk with a stop at the cemetery to calm herself once again. Key in hand, she headed for the walk-through gate. Outside the gate, a note was pinned to one of the cottonwoods. She pulled it off, her face registering disgust when she saw Ash's scrawled signature at the bottom. She whirled at the sound of Chue's soft voice.

"Mr. Ash was very, very angry. Miss Sunny cried. Mr. Ash asked for a nail to hang the note. I offered to deliver it to you, but he said no. Is there anything I can do, Miss Fanny?"

"Actually, Chue, there is something you can do. It must be one more secret for you to keep. Are you amenable?"

"Most certainly."

"Are you aware of the small cottage in Arizona?"

The Chinese nodded. "Once, many years ago, Miss Sallie had me install some screen doors."

"Sallie deeded the house to me a little while before she died. The grounds are overgrown and I'm sure the inside needs a lot of work. It's been standing empty for over fifteen years. Do you think you and your sons could . . . do whatever is needed to make it habitable? I'd like to keep everything just the way it is."

"I will take my sons tomorrow. I will need directions and an address." Fanny nodded. "I understand, Miss Fanny. You are thinking a fence such as this will be no deterrent to Mr. Ash."

"Something bad is going to happen, Chue. I'm not intuitive or psychic or anything like that. It's something I feel, not in my gut, but here in my heart," she said, putting her hand on her chest.

"Miss Sallie always listened to her heart. She told me this."

"The butterflies are beautiful. Why is beauty always followed by something ugly?"

"I do not know, Miss Fanny."

"The fence is very ugly. It's a shame, this is such a beautiful mountain. I feel like I'm desecrating it. I can't give Ash an inch. If I do, he'll trample me. I'm going for a long walk. Thank you, Chue, for everything, for being my friend, for being here. Just for being."

"All that I am, all that my children will be, is because of Miss Sallie and you." He bowed graciously. It had been years since he'd reverted to his Chinese ways.

To Fanny it was symbolic.

Fanny parked her car on a side street. Her plan was to meet Bess and walk to the building site where Ash's new casino was under construction. "I feel like a sneak," Fanny said.

"I don't. They've made a lot of progress. It's almost a year since your return from Hong Kong. I can't believe Ash is still dogging you. He won't give up, will he?"

"Ash hates to be ignored. I thought when I didn't respond in any way he'd give up, but if anything, his letters, calls, and visits to the gate have intensified. I don't read the letters, I burn them. The moment I hear his voice on the recorder I erase it. I think he's getting nervous because the money is going out very fast. I saw the financial report yesterday. My eyes almost popped out of my head. I have a complete set of blueprints and the spec sheet. He's putting gold-plated faucets in the bathrooms and whirlpool tubs. The penthouse suites are going to have sunken tubs and fireplaces. I've been getting a lot of my information from Simon. Last week, Simon said Ash wanted to sell Thornton Chickens. Thirty-three million dollars, Bess. Every time I think of it, my heart jumps into my throat."

They looked like tourists with their straw hats, dark glasses, and casual attire. It was Bess's idea to go in disguise. Fanny stared up at the iron girders from the roped-off area near the street. "My God, Bess, is this all that's been done in eleven months? All that money and they still have fifty percent to go? Am I crazy, or am I just not seeing something here?"

"You're seeing what I'm seeing, Fanny. Take a good look because this is what you sold your stock for. Oh, Fanny, I could cry."

Fanny's back stiffened. "It proves my point. He wants . . . needs the kids' trust money."

"Don't you dare give it to him. If you do, I'll kick you in the pants. How much is this going to cost?"

"God only knows. Where is he going to get the money if I don't give it to him? The bank won't lend it to him if he can't put up collateral."

"Loan sharks?"

"Ash isn't *that* stupid. Simon hasn't said anything to me, but I wonder if he'll lend Ash money if he asks for a loan? You know, out of guilt. What do you think?"

"Not likely. Simon has nothing to feel guilty about. You and Ash are divorced. Let's get out of here, okay? Sage and Billie are waiting for us."

"Just a minute. I want a few more pictures."

"Come on, Fanny, you have enough pictures. Two hard hats are walking toward us. Walk fast, one of them might be Ash, I can't tell from this distance." The two women scurried away, trying not to run in their haste. They were breathless when they arrived at Peridot, where Sage and Billie were waiting.

"Gee, Mom, you look like a tourist," Billie said, hugging her mother.

"You're lookin' good, Mom." Sage grinned as he accepted her embrace. "You always look good, Aunt Bess."

"Absolutely," Billie concurred.

"I knew I loved these kids for a reason," Bess said.

Lunch was a bit tense, Sage and Billie chattering nonstop. It was obvious to Fanny that something was wrong, and both her children were waiting for the right moment to bring it up. She decided to help them along.

"Okay, what's the problem?"

"Dad's pissed off," Sage said. "That's the only word to describe him at this point in time. Birch is . . . angry. Sunny is . . . she cries a lot. All she does is huddle with Birch. I can't remember the last time Birch spoke to me. He goes out of his way to avoid me, just the way Sunny avoids Billie. It's awful, Mom."

Fanny stared at her children. "What would it take so that it isn't awful?"

"Ask Aunt Bess. I can't remember the last time either Birch or Sunny did any work. You're paying them a salary to watch Dad swing around on those girders like some damn monkey. Sunny is there with her clipboard, Birch is there with Dad in his hard hat. I'm damn tired, Mom, of working sixteen hours a day trying to cover for Birch. Billie has been putting in as much time as I have. Aunt Bess won't tell you, but she's in the office at six in the morning and doesn't leave until nine or ten. It's not fair."

"No, it isn't. Bess, change the locks on the offices and draft up Sunny and Birch's termination papers. Make it effective tomorrow. I'm running a business here. I'm sorry it isn't possible to keep it in the family. This will not happen to Rainbow Babies. I guarantee it. I'm moving that operation to Sallie's bingo palace."

"Jesus," Sage hissed. "Dad's been showing that property to people like he owns it. It's prime real estate, Mom. You could name your price if you want to sell."

"I have no intention of selling. The palace meant everything to Sallie. I think she'd like to see Rainbow Babies take over the building. Where did your father get a key to show it?"

"From Sunny. I don't know where she got it, maybe she had a

locksmith make a key. You can do that you know," Billie said. "If Dad says jump, Sunny says, how high? Birch too."

"I see. Bess, I want you to help me set up shop. No more late hours. You should have told me what was going on."

"Fanny . . . I didn't mind."

"I mind. That's not how I do business. Now, let's put our heads together. Rainbow Babies is our top priority. We four are not in the casino business. One more thing," she said, addressing her son and daughter. "Do you two want or expect me to release the trust fund monies?"

"No way," Sage said.

"Absolutely not," Billie said.

Bess beamed her approval as she nudged Fanny's ankle under the table.

"Down to business," Fanny said.

Seven months later, shortly before Easter, Audrey Bernstein, dressed in a gorgeous flowered dress, her husband Michael at her side, stood next to Fanny and her small staff to watch the first televised commercial for Rainbow Babies. For a full ninety seconds all eyes were glued to gleeful cherubs reaching for Rainbow Babies attire attached to colorful rainbows. When it was over, Audrey said, "There is nothing more interesting to a mother than a baby or a puppy. Wait till you see the commercial with two fat puppies and six babies. What do you think?"

"I love it!" Fanny said. "I think I'm glad Simon found you two. My biggest concern right now is that demand might exceed our production. Su Li has offered to set up shop in Hong Kong. She said she can hire as many people as needed, at a fair salary, and absolutely no sweat shop conditions. No twenty-five-cent-an-hour labor either. She knows everyone there is to know in her country and can get this company moving quickly. What's more, she understands the import export business like a professional. My vote is yes. How about the rest of you?"

"I want to see numbers!" Mike Bernstein said. "Audrey and I were CPAs, still are for that matter, before we went into the advertising business. I love big numbers. Rows and rows of big numbers. This blitz will last for a full ten days. It's costing, but as you know, in order to make money, you need to spend money. We're headed back to New York. We still have the print side of things to get under way. New York, which I think is going to be one of your biggest markets, is featuring our ads in the subways, buses, and on giant bill-boards. Every major newspaper in the country will carry a full-page ad in the Sunday and Wednesday editions. It's been a pleasure doing business with you, Mrs. Thornton. Here's our bill."

Fanny did a little jig. "Those are knockout commercials. Bess, your granddaughter stole the show. We have an exclusive contract with her now. You wait, offers are going to be pouring in for her. Don't even look at them."

"Mom, don't look now, but Sunny is coming into the building. I bet she saw the commercial. Do you want us to disappear?" Billie asked.

"No, of course not. I don't want you being nasty to her either, she's your sister."

It was an awkward meeting. Fanny tensed the moment her older daughter walked into the room. "Sunny, it's nice to see you," she said, holding up her face for Sunny's light kiss. She pretended not to see the tears in her daughter's eyes.

"Hi, Mom. I just . . . wanted to stop and . . . congratulate all of you. I saw those commercials early this morning. They were wonderful!"

"Thank you, Sunny, I know you mean that. We've been working round the clock to get it all under way. How are you? How's Tyler?"

Sunny shrugged. "Mom . . . I . . ."

"If you're trying to apologize, it isn't necessary. You did what you felt you had to do, and I did what I felt I had to do. Why don't we just leave it at that."

"I don't like that fence."

"I know you don't, Sunny. It's ugly, even with the morning glories climbing over it."

"It means keep out."

"Yes, that's what it means, Sunny. Do you really want to have this conversation?"

"Yes. You said you always wanted a family."

"I had a family once. No matter what I did, I couldn't hold it together. A family doesn't choose up sides, they don't betray one another. You and Birch forced me to make a choice, Sunny. I'm sorry if it wasn't what you wanted or expected."

"Dad tried so hard, Mom, and you wouldn't listen . . ."

"Sunny, don't spoil this visit. I don't want to discuss your father, not now, not later, not ever. He's not my husband any longer. Would you like to join us for lunch. We're celebrating today."

Sunny looked at her brother and sister, then at Bess. She looked away, not wanting to deal with the anger she saw in their faces. "I can't. I'm meeting Tyler. He has a few hours off today. I should be going. I'm probably going to be late as it is."

Fanny's shoulders slumped when her daughter walked out of the office. Her voice was husky when she said, "Don't read anything into this other than what it was. Sunny was sincere, and it took a lot of guts to come here, but she did it. Sunny is still her own person, and right now she doesn't like the person she is. That's just my motherly opinion. One day that might change. Until that time comes, it's business as usual. I'm off now to the airport to pick up Simon, who is going to celebrate with us. We'll meet you at Peridot."

Fanny waved frantically, her eyes misting at the sight of Simon. *Dear God, how I love him.* "Oh, it's so good to see you. Seeing you is like receiving a precious present, one you've wished for, longed for, all your life. Do you have baggage?"

"Just this backpack. It's a present for you."

"Really, Simon! Tell me. I don't like surprises. I mean I like surprises, I just don't . . . What is it, Simon? Can we stop right here so I can see it?"

Simon stopped and pretended to think. "It might cause a stir. Airports don't like it when funny things happen. People might stop to stare. This is one of those one-of-a-kind gifts, the kind you can't return, no matter what. Do you want to think about it, or do you really want me to open this bag here and now?"

Fanny smiled. "After that little speech, I want to see it more than ever. Hurry, Simon, there's no one around."

Simon dropped to his haunches and unzipped the canvas bag with the mesh sides. Fanny peered inside, squealed her pleasure, kissed Simon so hard his eyeballs crossed before she picked up the tiny fur ball inside the bag.

"Her name is Daisy. She's third generation, Fanny. Today is her first day away from her mother, so she's going to need lots of tender loving care. You're going to go into shock when you see how much gear you have to buy for this one little dog. We'll stop at a pet store before we go up the mountain. Now, tell me, how did you like the commercials?"

But Fanny wasn't thinking about business—about anything except the little dog cuddled under her chin.

"Do you want to know what's really happening, Fanny?"

"I don't know if I *really* want to know. It's more like I *should* know, because of the kids."

"Ash is down to the wire. Fanny, the money is going out so fast it makes me dizzy. A month from now he's going to be hard-pressed to make his payroll. He sold your old house in town and Mom's town house. That money is gone. He wants to sell Thornton Chickens. I refused to commit until I talked to you. I'd like to keep it because Dad started that up and built it to the company it is today. I'm not discounting Ash's help, but it was already thriving when he jumped on board. He's mortgaged the R & R Ranch with Red Ruby's approval. He promised her something when Babylon is finished. Why Red would do something like that is beyond me. People do strange things at times. So, you really like Daisy, huh?"

"I love her, Simon. I always wanted a dog. Ash never wanted one. Did you lend Ash money, Simon?"

"He hasn't asked. The last time I talked to him he told me he applied for several loans at different banks. The interest is going to kill him. Dad had an account with Ash's name on it. I didn't even know about it until he told me. It's all gone too. The balance of the money you turned over will last another six weeks. That's it."

"What will he do, Simon?"

"I have no idea."

"What about Birch and Sunny? Do they know how serious this is?"

"Birch should, he's the financial man. I'm sure he's told Sunny. If you turn over the trust fund to them, Ash might make it."

"It isn't going to happen, Simon. Do I put Daisy in her bag and take her in the restaurant?"

"She's family now. I say bring her."

"Okay, sweet baby, in you go," Fanny crooned as she placed the little dog inside the canvas bag.

The greetings inside the restaurant were sweet. Simon basked in his niece and nephew's adoration. He embraced Bess and kissed her on the cheek before he held Fanny's chair and then Bess's. "This is my treat for a job well-done," Simon said. "Ask Fanny to give you a peek at her congratulatory present." He grinned from ear to ear at the oohs and aahs. Daisy slept on, curled against a fuzzy teddy bear that was bigger than she was.

Fanny was about to dip her spoon into her Pecan Tulle when she noticed Birch and Sunny standing by the front door, their eyes raking the room. Sunny's face was ashen, as was her brother's. Fanny laid her spoon down and said, "Something's wrong."

Sunny weaved her way between the tables. She opened her mouth to speak, but no words came out. Birch said in a voice Fanny didn't recognize, "Dad fell from one of the girders. They rushed him to the medical center. He's unconscious."

Fanny reached down for the canvas bag and put it in her lap. "Go," she said to her children. "You too, Simon."

Sunny found her voice. "Aren't you coming, Mom?"

Fanny reached under the table for Simon's hand, a gesture that didn't go unnoticed by Birch. She glanced at Sunny and read the open speculation in her eyes. "I'll come if you want me to, but I don't think your father will want me there. If he sees all of us there, he might think . . . He could never abide any kind of ailment, even head colds."

"We need to show support, solidarity," Birch said in a strangled voice. "Did you hear what I said, Dad fell nine floors. He could die. He could really die."

"What the hell was he doing up on the girders?" Simon demanded.

"Keeping his eye on things," Birch said. His voice was so defensive-sounding, Fanny blinked.

"Things have been going wrong. Dad was trying to put his finger on what it was that was delaying things," Sunny said. "He was more than agile." Her voice sounded as defensive as her brother's.

Simon laid some bills on the table. "Let's go, we'll follow you."

Bess embraced Fanny. "I'll stop by the medical center later on. Don't do anything . . . don't let those kids put pressure on you, Fanny. And for God's sake, don't start feeling guilty. Are you listening to me, Fanny?"

"Yes, Bess, I'm listening. What if . . ."

"There are no what ifs, Fanny. Whatever will be will be. The kids are going to need you to be strong."

Fanny felt light-headed when she took her seat in the waiting room. She remembered another time, years ago, when she sat in this same room, in this same chair, waiting for news of Philip.

They waited throughout the day, drinking coffee, smoking cigarettes, and pacing.

"It's almost midnight," Sunny said. "Somebody should have come out here and told us something by now. Where's Dr. Noble?"

"I don't know," Fanny said wearily.

"You sound like you don't care either," Sunny snapped. Fanny ignored her.

"Simon, I'm going outside to walk around. Do you want to come along?"

"Sure. Come and get us if you hear anything," he said to the children. Sage nodded.

"I thought it would be cool out here. It's hotter now than it was at noon when we arrived. It doesn't look good, does it, Simon?"

"We don't know that, Fanny. Dad made a recovery and we all thought . . ."

"For some reason, Simon, I don't think that's going to happen this time around. I have a terrible feeling about all of this. I heard Birch say Ash let his health insurance lapse. He tried to reinstate it, but he doesn't know if it's been accepted. I thought he was under a master policy for Thornton Chickens. Do you see what I mean, Simon? Something so very important, Ash . . . can't be bothered to keep up. He scrimps on pennies and squanders thousands. He was always like that. I want to get married now, Simon. Tomorrow . . . today really."

"No," Simon said. His voice was so gentle, so sad, Fanny started to cry.

"I don't understand. You said you wanted to marry me, you asked me hundreds of times. I'm saying yes, and now you're saying no." Her shoulders shaking, Fanny lifted the puppy from the canvas bag and set her on the ground. She piddled immediately. "If that's the way you feel about it, maybe you should leave. I guess I should apologize."

"Fanny . . ."

"I don't want to hear an excuse. Since you aren't going to leave, I'll leave. I don't even know why I'm here. Ash and I are no longer married. Do you want your dog back?"

"Of course not. This isn't the time or the place to be talking about getting married. You know I want to marry you more than anything in the world. You're reacting to Ash's accident. I think you should go home. There's nothing you can do here."

Fanny's back stiffened. "You had your chance, Simon." She gathered up the puppy, slipped her into the canvas bag. Her head high, her eyes smarting, Fanny entered the medical center. In the waiting room she announced her decision to leave as she gathered up her purse and jacket. Daisy whimpered inside the canvas bag.

Sunny's face registered outrage. "You're leaving not knowing how Dad is?"

"I believe that's what I said. I don't owe any of you an explanation, but out of courtesy, I'm going to give you one anyway. I'm tired. Actually, I'm extremely tired. I've been working around the clock for the past three months. I'll say a prayer that your father comes out of this whole. Good night."

"Fanny, wait!" John Noble called, Bess at his side.

"Is there news?" Fanny asked.

"Yes and no. I'm going to give you all an update and then I want every person in this room to go home. The good news," he said, addressing the twins, "is that your father's fall was partially broken by some rolls of insultation. The bad news is Ash has a fractured skull, internal injuries, and both legs are broken, as is his right shoulder. He's done some serious damage to several discs in his back. He's conscious, but in excruciating pain. His condition is critical. I don't have to tell any of you that everything humanly possible is being done. Now, go home. That's an order!"

Fanny started to walk away, Bess at her side. Out of the corner of her eye she saw Simon walk toward John Noble. Even a five-minute conversation would give her time to get to her car to head for the mountain. Once she was inside her fortress, Simon wouldn't be able to get in. She said so to Bess, as she ran to her car. "He told me no, Bess. He damn well told me no. Once a fool, always a fool. I'll call you. If you run into Simon, stall him so I can . . . get away."

"Fanny . . . I'm sure there's a reason . . ." Whatever else she was about to say was drowned out by the sound of the car's engine. She watched as Fanny floored the gas pedal to roar out of the parking lot.

The moment she drove around the corner, Fanny stopped the car to pick up Daisy to snuggle her inside the jacket. The little dog's whimpers stopped immediately. In a choked voice she said, "You're supposed to be man's best friend. Being a modern woman, I expect the same friendship. It's just you and me, Daisy. No one knows this about me . . . well, maybe Simon knew, I have so much love in me, and I'm going to give it all to you. Hang on, little girl, we're going to burn some rubber."

Forty minutes later, Fanny roared past Chue's house, past the bend in the road, and up to the gate that was standing open, thanks to the remote control on her visor that she pressed the moment she approached the curve in the road. The low-slung sports car sailed through the open gates at the same speed Fanny used driving up the mountain. Fanny brought the car to a screeching halt at the back of the house. She ran, the puppy jostling inside her jacket. Inside, she removed her jacket, cradling the puppy in both hands. She talked to her then, crooning as she scrambled an egg and filled a water bowl.

She soaked some cornflakes in warm milk, waited for them to soften before she mixed them with the egg. She set the puppy down on the floor and watched, mesmerized, as the little dog did her best to eat as both front paws vied with her tongue.

The phone shrilled. Fanny almost jumped out of her skin. From off in the distance, she could hear the loud sound of a horn. Simon. Soft-hearted Bess had probably lent him her car. The phone continued to shrill. Daisy skidded around as she tried to eat the strange food in front of her. In a frenzy, Fanny yanked at the phone wires. The two holes in the wall glared at her. The silence was reward enough. Daisy squatted and peed.

"Obviously, we need a system here. We'll work on that tomorrow. Right now, I'm going to make some coffee, and then we're going to snuggle together in one of those red chairs." The horn was still blowing as though someone was leaning on it. "Wear out your damn battery, see if I care."

At some point during the long night, it occurred to Fanny that if something happened to Ash, no one would be able to reach her. She squinted at the clock. Three-fifty-five. An hour and a half till the sun came up.

In her robe and slippers, Fanny scooped up Daisy and headed for the main house. She set her down by the back door and watched as she peed a puddle as large as a dinner plate. "Good girl. We're going to get along just fine if you keep doing that. Ah, you want to explore, is that it? Okay, but I have to tell you, it's been years since I walked around in the middle of the night. We have moonlight for your first stroll. That's a plus."

Fanny found herself smiling as the puppy leapfrogged ahead of her, turning ever other second to see if she was following. "You're growling. A little thing like you knows how to growl! Remarkable." She saw the huge black shadow in the moonlight. A car by the gate. Simon of course, sleeping in his car. Or was he walking the perimeter, trying to get over the fence? He'd laughed the first time he saw it. She wondered if he was laughing now. She bent down to pick up the dog and entered the house by the back door. She looked to see if the red light was blinking on the answering machine. No messages. She made fresh coffee while Daisy walked around, sniffing her new surroundings. Fanny looked at the clock again. Four-fifteen.

Everyone she knew was an early riser. Bess and John got up at five in the morning. Chue was up and doing things by five-ten, which probably meant he got up at four-thirty. Mazie was up at five also. In forty-five minutes she could start making phone calls. The first one to Bess, the second to Chue for dog food and to tell him to ask Simon to leave.

Once again she found herself a prisoner of her own making. A prisoner of her own love. It sounded like a prelude to some kind of torch song. She snorted at the idea.

Her life was changing in front of her eyes, changing even as she sipped at her cup of coffee. Her life had been so wonderful up until yesterday. After years of unhappiness, she had finally been happy. Now, that happiness was gone. She'd been rejected by both Thornton men. She cringed in shame. What was wrong with her?

Fanny bolted upright in the kitchen chair when she remembered that she had been the one to propose marriage to Ash. He'd accepted the proposal. Simon was just the reverse. Rejection felt the same, no matter how many times it happened. "As soon as you stick your neck out, Daisy, someone chops it off." The little dog tilted her head, her ears at attention. She pawed at Fanny's leg to be picked up. Fanny obliged her, cuddling her to her chest as she hummed a childhood lullaby. Daisy snuggled in the crook of her arm and was instantly asleep.

Animals love unconditionally. Why can't people do the same thing? No. Simon had said no in such an explosive voice there was no mistaking what he meant. Today could have been her wedding day. Could have. She continued to torment herself. She thought about the last fifteen years of Sallie's life that were filled with such bitterness, about Philip's bittersweet revenge on his wife. Somehow, someway, Ash would do the same thing to her. She knew it just as she knew her name was Fanny Logan Thornton. She'd been so sure it wouldn't happen to her, that's why she'd given in to Ash and gotten the divorce, so she would be free. "Oh, Sallie, I wish you were here. I need to talk about this. How did you do it all those years? How did you live without Devin?" A tear dropped on Daisy's head.

Fanny looked at the clock. Five minutes past five. She dialed Bess's number. Her friend picked up the phone on the first ring. "It's Fanny. Is there any news on Ash? I wish you hadn't given Simon your car."

"I didn't give Simon my car. He borrowed Sage's. John got home at three o'clock. He's showering. Are you all right, Fanny?"

"Of course not. I feel like someone sliced a chunk out of my heart. I'm up at the house. I ripped the phones out of the studio walls.

Simon blew the horn for hours. Bess, the same thing that happened to Sallie is going to happen to me, I feel it . . ."

"Fanny, here's John. Don't hang up when you finish speaking with him."

"There's no change, Fanny. I have to be honest, it could go either way. We have him heavily sedated. There's no point in coming to the center. There's nothing you can do. I wish I had better news. Simon and your children are devastated. You need to be strong, Fanny."

"No she doesn't, John. She's not married to Ash anymore. Don't tell her something like that!" Bess could be heard in the background. "She's given up enough of her life to that man. I mean it, John, I don't want to hear you say things like that to Fanny."

"My spouse has spoken, Fanny. My apologies. She's right of course. You do whatever feels right to you. I know what you're thinking, Fanny. I saw it in your eyes last night. You are *not* Sallie Thornton. You are Fanny Thornton. No one can make you do anything you don't want to do. No one, Fanny. I'll call when I have something to report."

Bess was back on the line. "Don't mind John, Fanny. Where's Simon?" The words were asked in a half whisper.

"I think he's still outside by the gate. I don't want to talk about Simon."

"Do you want me to come up, Fanny?"

"No. I need to do some thinking, and I need to be alone to do that. You can do me a favor, though. Since I ripped the phones out of the studio I have to come up here to the house for messages. Keep checking with John and call me here, and I'll call you back. Ash isn't going to die. I'd feel something if he was. Thanks for being such a good friend, Bess."

"It's easy to be your friend, Fanny. Things will work out. Remember Sallie's famous words, God never gives you more than you can handle. Believe that, and you'll be okay."

"Mazie!" Fanny bellowed, after hanging up the phone. "I'm sorry, Mazie, I didn't mean to yell like that. Will you please fry up some hamburger and mix it with rice for my new friend here. Bring it down to the studio when it cools off. Make up a whole bowl so it lasts me a couple of days. Call Chue and ask him to get me some puppy food. Don't answer the phone. Let the machine take the messages. I think I'd like some stuffed peppers for dinner this evening."

"Come on, little lady, time to go home," Fanny said, putting the puppy down by the door. She watched as Daisy scurried outside, squatted, waited for approval, which Fanny gave happily. Together, they walked back to the studio.

From the front window of her studio, Fanny stared at the horizon that was as bleak as her life.

23

Fanny entered the Thornton Medical Center, Billie Coleman at her side. It looked the same as it had thirty days ago, when Ash had his accident. She glanced around at the framed desert scenes on the walls, at the bluish gray, heavy-duty carpet and matching drapes. Something should have changed. "Take a deep breath, Fanny." Billie said. "You can do this. I'm here, and Bess will be meeting us in the waiting room. I think we make a pretty united front. I forget, who are we trying to intimidate?" she asked in a light tone.

Fanny shrugged. Her shoulders straightened, her head went up a notch. Directly in her line of vision was a portrait of Sallie Thornton, the medical center's benefactor. "I wonder if she knows what's going on. What would she do? Would she stand quietly and listen to that gaggle of doctors or would she ask questions and make her own decisions? How would she handle the kids? Billie . . ."

"It's Simon you're worrying about. He's respecting your wishes. Isn't that what you wanted?"

"It's what he wanted, Billie. Would you feel any differently if you had asked Admiral Kingsley to marry you and the word no exploded from his mouth?"

"Of course not, but I do think I would listen to *why* he said no."

"Perhaps. I needed to do it, to get married, right then and there. I'm lost now, Billie. I'm chained to Ash all over again. I know it, you know it, the kids know it, the doctors know it. The whole damn world knows it. Who else is there to take care of him? You don't think for one minute the kids are going to put their lives on hold and do it, do you? Simon isn't going to do it. I don't see anyone standing in line to offer their assistance. I'm the only one left. If Simon had agreed to marry me, I wouldn't be in this position. I'm Sallie all over again, and it's scaring me. I think I'm entitled to feel bitter."

"Of course you are," Billie said soothingly. "There are options, Fanny. We have a fine rehabilitation center in Austin. There must be one here that's associated with the hospital. We can look into it before we leave today. You don't have to make any kind of decision right now, Fanny. Thad always says you have to get all of your ducks in a row and then you make a decision. I think it's sound advice. Here comes Bess. We need to fix her up, she's starting to look dowdy."

"She's frazzled, Billie. I left it to her to deal with the business, Simon, and the kids during my thirty-day . . . hiatus. It wasn't fair. Bess has too much on her plate, too many irons in the fire. We could try, though. What do you suggest?"

"How about a pajama party. A little wine, some good rich food, some high-spirited conversation, sharing secrets. A shopping expedition. Fanny, we're all free; we can do as we please. We earned this time in our lives. Just once, let's set aside commitment, responsibility, and do something for us. We can moan and groan about it later. Personally, I'd like to see all of us go away together for a week or so. Just us girls. I need to do some wound licking myself."

"I think the Coleman, slash, Thornton families are jinxed. Sallie saw it early on, why didn't we?"

"I guess because each of us has to find her own way. Sallie was a guide. It was up to us to decide if we wanted to follow her."

"Anything new, Bess?" Fanny asked. Bess did look frazzled.

"Simon's here. I don't think I've ever seen a more miserable human being. Your kids are picking up on it."

"Ask me if I care."

"They're rolling out the proverbial red carpet for you, Fanny. All those top-notch doctors Su Li recruited are waiting to talk to you in the doctors' lounge. John will be there too."

"They should be talking to Simon and the kids, not me. How did this happen?"

"I don't know," Bess said. "If I had to take a guess, I'd say Ash got to the kids someway. He wants you."

"Doesn't *anyone* understand that we're *divorced?* Let's get this over with."

Nothing in the world could have prepared Fanny for the hostility on her children's faces, or for the misery she read in Simon's face. Her step faltered. Billie reached for one arm, Bess the other.

Introductions were made. Fanny nodded curtly, her eyes on the doctors. They took turns speaking. Fanny listened. When they were finished, Fanny let her gaze rake the room. "Let me be sure I understand what you've all just said. Mr. Thornton, my *ex*-husband, refuses to go into a rehabilitation center for therapy. He thinks he will get better care from me, his ex-wife, in my home. Because there is plenty of room on the mountain, Mr. Thornton feels the therapists can 'live in' and give him twenty-four-hour care which will speed up his progress. It's my understanding that Mr. Thornton has a nine-room penthouse apartment here in town. It would seem to me that live-in therapists would have plenty of room in a nine-room penthouse apartment. It would also seem to me that this fine medical center should be more than willing to write off Mr. Thornton's medical bills. If they aren't, I'll have to take a hard look at the funding of this fine institution. What role do you see Mr. Thornton's brother and children playing in Mr. Thornton's recovery? Isn't anyone going to answer me? No. Well then, gentlemen, I think I've said all I have to say."

"Bravo," Billie Coleman whispered.

"That goes for me too," Bess whispered.

John Noble's voice was sharp when he said, "Bess . . ."

"Don't say it, John. You know my feelings. You sit on one side of the medical table, and I sit on the other. Don't make me choose up sides here."

Suddenly they were all talking at once—her children, the doctors, and Simon. Fanny's heart was shattering inside her chest. She looked down at the floor, certain she was going to see bloody pieces of her heart at her feet. She felt Billie Coleman cringe at her nieces' and nephews' vitriolic words.

Birch spoke first. "Dad will die. He'll give up. How can you refuse him? He was right about you, wasn't he, Mom? You are cold and heartless."

Fanny sucked in her breath. She would not cry, she absolutely would not. This was her oldest son, if only by a few minutes, speaking to her like this. She'd labored to bring him into the world, nurtured him, loved him as only a mother can love a son. She was about to speak when Sunny advanced a step and shouted. "Birch only said the half of it. Dad knew you were fooling around with his brother. He never said anything because he hoped you'd come to your senses. He said everyone makes mistakes, and he was willing to forgive yours."

Fanny could hear Simon's angry voice beyond the thundering in her ears. She could feel Billie and Bess's fingers digging into her arms. Again, her step faltered, but her voice was strong when she said, "What your father told you isn't true. I can forgive you, Sunny, and you, Birch, because you're my children, and I will love you no matter what. However, what you've said is unconscionable. Your father lied to you. Doctors, I apologize for my children's rude behavior and for my own as well."

Su Li moved then, as did her colleagues—four of the finest doctors in the country—to stand next to Fanny. She spoke, her well-modulated voice circling the room. She addressed herself to the children. "Your mother spoke the truth. One should never speak in haste. Do not ask for my help again."

"Well, la-de-da, and whose family was it that pulled you and your brother out of the gutter? Whose family paid for your years of medical training? You and Chue have been on a gravy train from the time my grandmother took you out of the laundry. This is how you repay our family by siding with *her!*" Birch snarled.

Fanny shook off Bess and Billie's arms. She turned, walked back across the room to stand in front of her son. The sound of the slap Birch took high on his cheekbone bounced around the room. *"That I will never forgive."*

"What the hell kind of family is this?" Simon bellowed.

"You tell me, Simon," Fanny shot back. "I rue the day I ever set eyes on your brother."

Outside in the heat of the day, Fanny doubled over. "I want to throw up and take a bath at the same time," she moaned. "My God, that was my family! Can we just go home?" Fanny said brokenly. "No, not home, someplace else. Someplace Sallie knew I would need someday."

"Fanny! Fanny, wait!"

"Go away, Simon. Go back to New York and take your brother with you or leave him here for his children to take care of. Just go."

"Fanny, please, you need to listen to me. I love you. You love me. We're destroying each other and for what?"

"For your brother. I told you this would happen. I knew it, that's why I asked you . . ."

"It wouldn't have changed anything, Fanny."

"It was important for me to believe that it would. Now I'll never know if it would have or not. I just want you to know something, Simon. I loved you more than I ever thought it was possible to love a man. You should have trusted me. You know your brother as well as I do. You should have been prepared for this."

"Fanny, I didn't mean I didn't want to marry you. I meant not that instant, not that day."

"Well, I *needed* to do it *that instant, that day.* Send me a Christmas card. Good-bye, Simon."

Fanny slid behind the wheel of the car, tears sliding down her cheeks.

"There were tears in his eyes," Billie said.

"He really and truly loves you," Bess said.

"It doesn't matter," Fanny said. "Do either one of you think . . . Ash will . . . give up and . . . and die?"

"Do you really expect us to answer that, Fanny? You know what cynics we are."

"He wants that trust money. In his condition, he's still fighting me. Obviously there is nothing wrong with his head, even if it's fractured. He's insidious enough to go right down to . . . what do I want to say here, dying, his deathbed, and then when I capitulate, he'll make a miraculous recovery?"

"Where are we going, Fanny?" Billie asked.

"To a place no one knows about. A place Sallie gave me for just this reason. Sallie said I would need it someday. I think this is the someday she was talking about."

"What's it called, Fanny."

"It had a name once. The Sallie and Devin's house of happiness. Maybe someday I'll give it my own name. For now, it's a sanctuary. For us."

In a room filled with flowers, on the top floor of the Thornton Medical Center, Ash Thornton stared at his brother and his children. "She said no." His voice was a low whimper.

"That's what she said, Ash," Simon said. "I'm leaving here when I walk out of this building. Before I do that, I want you to tell your children you were . . . mistaken when you told them Fanny and I were having an affair while you were married. It's not true, and you know it isn't true. I would do anything humanly possible to aid in your recovery. The one thing I cannot do is force your ex-wife to take care of you. If you don't tell your children the truth, you and I are finished as brothers. You owe me, Ash, and it's time to pay up. You need to let it all go, Ash, and get on with your life. I'll help in any way I can."

"I don't want or need your help, Simon. If you say you didn't have an affair with my wife, that's good enough for me. I can't speak for the kids. Sunny, sweetie, see if you can cajole the charge nurse into giving me my pain pills a little early."

"Sure, Dad." Sunny turned to her Uncle Simon. "I'm willing to take your word for it. I was taught early on that Thorntons don't lie."

"I guess that means you owe your mother an apology for your outburst in the doctors' lounge."

Ash was the consummate actor when he said, "Sunny, you promised me you wouldn't do or say anything to hurt your mother's feelings. Did you break that promise?" He closed his eyes, struggling to take deep breaths.

If he had been certain that Ash wasn't putting on an act for his benefit, Simon would have felt sorry for him. "Now, what, Ash?"

"I don't know, Simon, one day at a time. The boys have been keeping me apprised of what's going on with the construction. Things are almost at a standstill. Did you make a decision yet about Thornton Chickens?"

"I haven't had a chance to talk to Fanny. The last time I mentioned it, she said she wants to keep it in the family."

"Why did Mom give her control, Simon? Do you know?"

"Because she loved Fanny, and she didn't trust either you or me. The account is almost dry, Ash."

"I know. I have some ideas. There are places where I can get financing."

"I know the kind of places you're talking about, Ash. Don't do it. If you do, you'll be selling them your soul. I can lend you some money."

"How much?"

Simon's eyebrows shot upward at his brother's snappy question. "Compared to what you need, a spit in the wind. Two million with a promissory note."

"You got it."

"I'll transfer the money when I get back to New York. When are you leaving here?"

"I was scheduled to leave tomorrow, but since Fanny didn't agree to helping out, we have to make other arrangements."

"Ash, your kids owe Fanny a huge apology. I hate to leave here thinking they were acting on your orders. I was ashamed of them. You might notice I'm not addressing them, because they don't deserve any kind of recognition for what they did. I know you and I have two different views of family life, Ash, but trust me when I tell you those kids were shameful. Call me, if I can help in any way."

Sage approached his father's bed when Simon left the room. There was wary speculation in his eyes when he said, "You backed down. Did he or didn't he have an affair with Mom?"

"It got us two million dollars, didn't it? Sunny, where are the pills?" Ash said, ignoring his son's question.

"The nurse said no. She said they can't risk you getting addicted. It's just ten more minutes, Dad."

"It doesn't matter. What does anything matter? We're going to lose the casino, we're just weeks away from filing for bankruptcy. We'll all be out in the street. I'd like it if you'd all leave now. No father wants his children to see him cry."

Outside in the waiting room, the young Thorntons looked at one another. "I'd like to hear someone say something," Billie said. When no one spoke, she said, "I'm damn sorry I sided with the three of you. I must have been out of my mind. Do you have any idea what we all did to Mom? Did you see her face this morning? My God, what kind of people are we turning into?"

"Aren't you forgetting Dad back there in that room? There's every possibility he won't walk again. He's in constant pain," Birch said, refusing to meet his sister's eyes.

"That's not Mom's fault," Billie said. "I feel like crawling on my hands and knees to her and beg her to take me back. I won't do that, though, because I'm too ashamed. I don't know about the rest of you, but I need a job, my savings are almost gone. It's a pretty sorry state of affairs when your family fires you. I'm going to New York this afternoon to look for a job. I don't care what the rest of you do."

"What about Dad?" Birch said.

"What about him, Birch? Didn't you catch that little scene he played out for us. What was it he said, oh yeah, it got us two million, didn't it? My ears snapped open at that. Why are you all looking at me like I suddenly sprouted another head?"

"You're going to New York? You're leaving us here with . . . Dad! That's a pretty shitty thing to do if you want my opinion," Birch said coldly.

"I didn't ask for your opinion. I like to eat. I like a roof over my head. In order to have those things, I need a job. We're old enough to stand on our own two feet and earn a living. You all can keep diddling around with Dad or whatever you want to do. Know this though. Mom is not going to touch that trust. No matter what Dad does. That's what this is all about, and you all know it—you simply refuse to say the words out loud."

"Like you know everything," Sage blustered. "Dad was hurt, we rallied around. That's what families do."

"That's what *normal* families do. We are not a normal family. Dad has always had ulterior motives. Mom did her best to keep things as normal as possible. We screwed it up. Well, I'm bailing out, cutting my losses. Someday I hope Mom and Uncle Simon will be able to forgive my part in all of this. I guess this is good-bye."

"Little shit," Sunny said.

"Take off your blinders, Sunny. Dad's using you, he's using all of you. When I get settled, I'll send my address."

"She's bluffing," Sunny sniffed.

"No she isn't. I saw her packed bags in the car this morning. She's leaving this afternoon. Of the four of us, whoever would have thought it was Billie who had the guts. Dad's out of the woods now. He's recovering. I'll be leaving myself next week. I have enough money left to enter the Master's program at UCLA. I can work part-time while I'm going to school. I might even go on to get my doctorate. Whatever I do, I'll do on my own. This might be a good time for me to say good-bye too. Being around you two just reminds me of what we've become. There's no way to make this right. I don't like any of us," Sage said.

"What is this, rats leaving a sinking ship?" Birch blustered. "C'mon, Sage, we can work this out."

"Billie was just upset, she'll come around. Come on, Sage, we need you," Sunny pleaded. "Dad needs you. How can you turn your back on us, on him?"

"The same way he turned his back on us years ago. I just walk away. I'll let you know where I am in case you want to stay in touch. Sorry, Birch, there's no working this one out."

"Who's going to tell Dad?" Sunny asked.

"Let's not say anything to him for a while," Birch said. "I'd like to see how long it takes Dad to notice Billie and Sage are gone. Sage and I have never been separated."

"For God's sake, Birch, you make it sound like you and Sage are joined at the hip. He's always been jealous of you."

"Sage doesn't have a jealous bone in his body. It takes guts to do what he and Billie are doing."

"Birch, I'm scared. What are we going to do? Dad isn't going to recover and get the use of his legs again. We both know that. The damage to his back was too severe. When he finds out he's going to be confined to a wheelchair . . . I don't know what will happen. Mom could make that right, you know. Where can we get money, Birch? I don't want to file for bankruptcy and lose Babylon. Everything got out of hand so fast. I'm really scared, Birch. Are Sage and Billie right about Dad and the trust?"

Birch sat down and dropped his head into his hands. "I'm afraid so, Sunny." Suddenly all his bluster was gone.

"All that stuff he handed us was a *lie?* I refuse to believe that." Sunny cried.

"Then don't believe it. When did you ever know Uncle Simon to lie? He was always painfully honest. I do think he likes Mom. A lot. I thought you knew what you were talking about when you said he and Mom were . . . we all believed you. We've destroyed what was left of this family. Take a damn good look at us, Sunny. You tell me what we're going to do."

"You're blaming *me* for all of this!" Sunny sputtered.

"I don't see anyone else around here, do you? You conned me, and I fell for it because I'm a stupid jerk. You know what, I'm sick and tired of being a stupid jerk. I'm sick and tired of kissing Dad's ass so he might smile at you or me or someone. I'm sick and tired of those construction guys and I'm sick and tired of the gambling business. And I'm sick to my soul at what we did to Mom. Like Billie, I'm too ashamed to go to her and apologize because I know she'd . . . say okay, I forgive you, and kiss me on the cheek. Jesus, she slapped me. In my whole life she never did that, not even a pat on the behind. I don't deserve one kind word from her and neither do the rest of you."

"You're leading up to something, Birch. Why don't you just spit it out and get on with it," Sunny said.

"I'm going with Sage even though he didn't ask me to join him. I don't want to be a part of this any longer. I didn't think anything could be worse than the day Mom fired us, and then the day I saw that damn iron fence. Today makes both of those things pale in comparison. I want to live with myself. I hope it works out for you, Sunny."

"What about Dad?" Sunny asked tremulously.

"Mom laid it out this morning. It doesn't matter where Dad gets his therapy as long as he gets it. It isn't even going to start until all three of his body casts come off. That's at least two or three weeks away. Mom doesn't owe Dad anything. There's nothing more I can do for him. If there was, I'd do it. I don't know the first thing about the construction business. And I don't want to learn, either. I'm a CPA. Would you like some brotherly advice?"

"Sure, why not?"

"You were always Mom's favorite. It's okay, Sunny, we didn't mind. Jesus, you even have a business named after you. Find a way to make it right with Mom. She's probably hurting real bad. If Dad's awake, I'll say good-bye. If he's sleeping, tell him I said good-bye when he wakes up. Look, Sunny, if you really want to know which way the wind is blowing, tell him you're not going to beg Mom to release the trust monies. His attitude will tell you everything you need to know. I hope it works out for you. Tell Tyler I said good-bye."

Sunny watched her brother walk down the hall, and then watched him come back. "He's sleeping. See you around."

Tears streaming down her cheeks, Sunny nodded. "This reminds me of the day you and Sage left for college. I felt so lost that day."

"We were kids then, Sunny. We're adults now, we have to take whatever life dishes out. Don't go bawling on me now, okay."

"Okay."

"All right," Birch relented, "a couple of tears won't hurt."

Birch cradled her against his chest, his own eyes wet. "Jesus, I'm gonna need my raincoat if you keep this up. If Billie writes or calls, let us know where she is so we can stay in touch. We're family, and don't you ever forget it."

Ash woke four and a half hours later, his face bathed in sweat. His eyes were glazed as he looked around the room. "Where is everyone?" he asked groggily.

"Everybody left, Dad," Sunny said.

"What time is it?"

"Almost six. They'll be bringing your dinner soon."

"I refuse to eat that slop. I don't much care if I ever eat again. What time is everyone coming back?"

"They aren't coming back, Dad. Billie left for New York this afternoon. Sage and Birch are going to California next week, maybe sooner. I'm the only one left."

A tear rolled out of the corner of Ash's eye. "I appreciate your loyalty. What brought this to a head?"

"The way we treated Mom. That's not exactly true, it was the way I treated Mom."

"Are you blaming me, Sunny?"

"To a degree," Sunny said, her voice ringing with honesty.

"Do you want to leave your old man too?" Another tear rolled down Ash's cheek. His mouth was even tighter than before. "This isn't much of a family, is it?"

"No. Most of it's your fault, Dad."

"I know. I came to my senses, though. I thought if we all started over, it would work. I didn't know your mother hated me so much."

Sunny cringed at her father's pitiful tone. "I don't know if she hates you or not. I know she hates what you did to our family. We all hated that. We've gone over this a hundred times, Dad. I'm tired of it. When something's over, it's over. I guess what I'm trying to say is, Birch, Sage, and Billie don't want Mom to release the trust monies. I told them I'd go along with their decision."

"So, you're turning on me too. What do I have to do or say to make you believe I'm not that person anymore? Take a good look at me, Sunny. What's going to happen to me? What's my life going to be like? Do you think I don't know my chances of walking are less than slim? That casino is what's kept me going. If I have to work the floor in a damn wheelchair, I will. I waited all my life for this. Now, when I need my family the most, you all cut and run. *I might even die!*" More tears rolled down his cheeks. "I love you kids more than life itself. If you don't want me in your lives . . . well, I guess you'll have your Uncle Simon to take my place. He's in love with your mother. I had a hard time believing that at first. Now it all fits together. Why would your mother want a cripple like me when she can have Simon?"

There was desperation in Sunny's voice when she said, "Mom's not like that, Dad."

"You're the one who told me something was going on between them. Are you saying you lied to me?"

"I was mistaken."

Sunny stood up.

"Don't go, Sunny. Stay with me, talk to me. I'm scared. I hate to admit it, but I am. What if I lose . . . what if I never walk again . . . ? What's going to happen to me, to us?"

"I don't know, Dad."

"You're all I have left, Sunny. God, I don't want to lose you too. Help me, tell me what to do."

"Dad, I don't know. You need money to finish Babylon. I hate that contractor you hired. Sage and Birch tried to tell you the guy was robbing you blind, but you wouldn't listen. You wouldn't take advice from anyone. You must realize every time you make a change the architect has to go back to his drawing board to make those changes. That costs money. Sage pretty much summed it all up when he said you think you know more than the builders. You don't, Dad, and this is the result. I don't know where you're going to get the money."

"Your mother could make this right. Babylon would belong to Thornton Enterprises, it's not like she's giving the money to strangers. She'll recoup, and Simon can reinvest the money. I want to see Babylon up and running before I die. I am going to die, Sunny."

It was too much for Sunny. She ran from the room.

Ash leaned back into his nest of pillows, his eyes cold and hard. With his good arm he reached for a bag of popcorn on his night table. One by one he popped the kernels into his mouth. Will she go to Fanny, won't she go to Fanny? The last kernel went into his mouth. Hell yes, she would, and Fanny would come around. Sunny was Fanny's Achilles' heel.

"It's so hard to say good-bye," Fanny said, hugging both Bess and Billie Coleman. "I'd rather say hello anytime. I can't remember ever spending a more restful time. I just know Sallie is up there, beaming down at us."

"And now, back to the real world," Bess said. "Back to listening to John groan and grumble about women who have careers and are never home. He himself is never home, so I don't know how he knows when I'm not home. Oh, well, remember how Devin used to tell us not to sweat the small stuff?"

"I remember," Fanny said softly.

"Well, it's back to Texas for me and the battle Sawyer is raging to build Moss's dream plane," Billie said. "I'm a phone call away, Fanny. I can be here in a few hours if you need me."

"The same goes for me, Billie. Just last night when I was falling asleep, I asked myself what my life would be like without you two in it."

"And what was your answer?"

"Dreary. Lackluster. Boring. You've both made my life so rich. We'll always be here for one another, won't we?"

"You can count on it," Billie said.

"I'd give up John before I'd give up this friendship," Bess said.

"Be careful driving down the mountain, Bess. Have a safe trip, Billie. Call me when you get home, both of you."

"Yes, Mother," both women said in teasing voices.

Fanny stood in the driveway watching as her two best friends in the whole world drove away. When the car was out of sight and the monster gates closed with a loud clang, Fanny turned to walk back to her lonely life. Her footsteps dragged, and then picked up speed as she headed for the cemetery.

She had so much to tell Sallie.

The following day, Fanny woke with an ominous feeling in the pit of her stomach. It wasn't going to be a good day. She wondered why as she sat down to eat her breakfast. As she chewed her toast she thought about Simon because she thought about him every waking hour of the day. Where was he? What was he doing? What was he thinking?

Today was a workday, a day to get back to the business at hand. The first thing on her agenda was to carry the mail down to the studio and go through it. She needed both hands to carry the heavy shopping bag Mazie had filled with the week's mail.

The ominous feeling was still with her as she pawed through the catalogs, shopping flyers, bank statements, bills, and charitable requests. The first class letters went into their own pile. Only three of them held her attention. One from her daughter Billie; one whose return address read Birch and Sage Thornton. The third letter bore the business address for Simon Thornton. Where, she wondered, was the letter from Sunny? She decided to save Simon's letter till later because she knew it would make her cry. Saving it for later would give her something to look forward to at the end of the day. She decided to read Billie's letter first. What in the world was Billie doing in New York?

Dear Mom,

I love you. I want to say that first. The second thing I want to tell you is I'm sorry. I know, it's just a word. Because it's just a word, I couldn't bring myself to call you or come up to Sunrise. I am so ashamed, Mom. Perhaps someday you can forgive me for what I know you consider my betrayal. I decided to come here to New York to get a job. My savings were getting dangerously low. I found a nice apartment and got a job yesterday in the garment district. As soon as I get

*my nerve and guts together, I'm going to call Uncle Simon and apolo-
gize to him. I'm not sure when that will be. Soon I hope.*

*I really am sorry, Mom. Take care of yourself. I don't have a phone
yet. Maybe by next month. Thanks for being my mother. I love you.*

Billie

Fanny opened the twins' letter, amused at their large scrawl.
They were in California! Her heart took on an extra beat.

Dear Mom,

*Guess you can see by the letter that we are in California. We de-
cided to use the last of our savings to go back to graduate school. Sage
has a part-time job in an accounting firm. He's going to try and get
me into the firm too. I'm waiting tables in a cafe for the time being.
It's working. Who knows, maybe we'll get so carried away we'll decide
to go for our doctorates or open a restaurant.*

*We're sorry, Mom. There aren't any other words, no other way to
say it. Maybe someday you can remember the good days and think of
what we did as "that time the twins went insane." If you need us,
Mom, just let us know. We're selling our cars, but we can be there in
a few hours by plane. I guess you thought we didn't love you. If I were
you, I'd think that too, but it's wrong. We do love you, bushels and
bushels. Sage is writing a letter of apology to Uncle Simon while I'm
writing this one. We just wanted you to know that. Take care of yourself, Mom.*

Birch and Sage

Fanny reached for a tissue before she folded the letter to return
it to the envelope. She pressed both letters against her heart. She rifled through the mail again to see if she'd missed a letter from Sunny.
She sighed deeply. Sunny wasn't a letter writer. Her gaze swiveled
to Simon's letter. With her index finger she pushed it farther away.

She thought she could feel her heart starting to heal.

The morning passed swiftly as Fanny devoted herself to the work
at hand. Shortly after the noon hour, as she munched on an apple,
the phone rang. Chue's excited voice came over the wire. "Miss
Fanny, Sunny is outside the gate. You better come quick. Her engine
is going very fast. She backs up, starts, stops, backs up. Hurry, Miss
Fanny."

Fanny ran out the door, up the path, around the house to a small grove of cottonwoods that gave her a clear view of the driveway and gate. She could see Sunny, but Sunny couldn't see her. *She's going to smash the gate.* She watched, horrified, as Sunny backed her car farther down the road. The roar of the engine sounded like a jet plane to Fanny's ears. She moved then, out of harm's way, to stand at the far side of the gate, the apple still in her hands. She sucked in her breath when she heard the tires squeal on the asphalt. Fifty, sixty, seventy, *eighty* . . . The monster gates flew sideways, sparks shooting in every direction. Sunny roared past her.

The car came to a screeching halt as Sunny scrambled from the driver's seat, her face bone white. She saw her mother then, leaning against an ancient cottonwood, munching an apple.

"That was a hell of an entrance. What do you do for an encore?" Fanny said.

"I didn't think that far ahead," Sunny said in a jittery voice. "I hate that fence."

"Yeah, me too," Fanny said. "Did you just come up here to smash my gate or did you have another reason?"

"Let's sit on the front steps, Mom. I want to talk to you. Listen, I'm sorry about the gate . . . no, that's a lie, I'm not sorry. I'll pay to have it repaired."

"That's okay. I've wanted to smash it myself many times. The gate was put up for a reason. It's no longer important. Sooner or later I would have gotten around to taking it down. You saved me the trouble. Now, how can I help you, Sunny?"

"Mom, I'm sorry. I have no excuse. I don't think I can ever make it right. I've been thinking about it for days, maybe weeks, I've lost track of time. Billie, Sage, and Birch, they just took off because they were too ashamed to come up here. I'm ashamed, too, but I'm here. I need you to rub it in my face. I need to hear you tell me off. This thing . . . whatever it is, is making me sick. It's all I can do to get through the day. I started with Uncle Simon. I went to New York last weekend and . . . apologized. He took me to lunch, showed me around his offices. He was so nice to me I spent the whole time bawling my head off. You're a fool, Mom, if you let him go. I don't know if you want to know this or not, but he looks like shit. He's lost weight, he has dark circles under his eyes, and he just picked at his lunch that was outrageously expensive. He didn't say one word about you. He . . ."

"It's over and done with, Sunny."

"No, Mom, it's not over. I'm here to ask a favor. I never asked you for a favor in my whole life. That's what's giving me the courage to ask you. I will understand if you feel . . . if you want to say no. Will you hear me out, Mom?"

"Of course, Sunny."

"God, I don't know where to start. I'm just going to blurt this out. Mom, let Dad come up here on a temporary basis when he's ready to leave the hospital. Just until he comes to terms with his life. I'll come and help out. Mom, I didn't know you didn't love Dad any-more. Every time we asked you, you always said, of course I love your father. I swear to God, I didn't know. I thought you just got fed up and were going . . . going to end it. I guess I thought . . . wanted to believe you would love him forever. I'm afraid to marry Tyler be-cause I don't want it to go wrong. He's getting fed up with me. Back to Dad. I swear to you, he doesn't know I'm here. He's in constant pain, Mom. He's not eating, and the only time he sleeps is when they medicate him. I don't know if he'll make it long-term. I want . . . I need to know I did everything I could where he's concerned.

"Mom, I want you to let me finish Babylon. I can do it. I know I can. All I need is ten months and that baby will be up and running. There's too much money riding on that building to let it go down the drain. Dad doesn't know I'm asking for this, either. I'll work my ass off, Mom. I won't let you down. I can't do it unless you release the money from the trust. I think Grandma would approve. I gave that a lot of thought, Mom. The first thing I'll do is fire that jackass Dad hired to put the building up."

Fanny finished the apple. She stared at her daughter until Sunny started to squirm. "Only if the trust retains fifty-one-percent control. Things will have to be sold. Your father is in no condition, physically or mentally, to have any control at all. I don't think he'll agree to any of this, Sunny."

"If he knows Babylon is going to be finished, he'll agree. He knows how ill he is, Mom. I know now that you don't love him, but, Mom, if anything happens to Dad, don't you want to know you did everything you could?"

"I already know that, Sunny. I gave one hundred percent. All right. I have conditions. Your father can come here for six months. Six months, Sunny. Not one day longer. His therapist can live in. The therapist will be responsible for all his needs. I'll live in the studio. That's as far as I'll go, Sunny."

"Thanks, Mom. You won't be sorry."

"I'm sorry already. I don't have a good feeling about this at all. I trust you, but I don't trust your father. I'd like a legal contract with you, Sunny. You take your orders from me, and only me. Is that going to be a problem?"

"Not at all. I was going to suggest the same thing. Someone's coming up the road."

"It's the kennel people, they're bringing Daisy home. I boarded her because I've been away. Is there anything else, Sunny?"

"Mom, will it ever be like it was before?"

"No, Sunny." At her daughter's devastated look she said, "That's not to say it can't be better. Six months, Sunny. The therapist sleeps in the same room as your father, the nurse sleeps in the little room at the top of the stairs. All the other doors will be locked. One bathroom for all of them. The nurse cleans it. Mazie isn't young anymore, and she doesn't need any extra duties. I'm not being cruel. It would be just like your father to sue me if something goes wrong. I want to be sure he gets twenty-four-hour supervision. By the way, who's paying for this?"

"Dad's health insurance was picked up. Everything is covered. I swear, Mom, I'll find a way to make this up to you. I want you to be happy, I really do." But Fanny had stopped listening.

"Daisy, you grew!" Fanny laughed as the small dog leaped into her outstretched arms. "Oh, I missed you. Look, Sunny, she has a kerchief around her neck. Ah, kisses, kisses. You are a love, aren't you. You missed me, huh?"

Sunny watched as her mother snuggled the little dog. Her eyes filled with tears. Would she ever hear love-filled words directed at her again? Would her mother ever hold out her arms to her the way she just did for Daisy? She dropped her head between her knees and wept, her shoulders shaking. She jerked upright when she felt a gentle hand on her shoulder.

"Be careful driving down the mountain, Sunny."

"Dad doesn't like dogs," Sunny said.

"Yes, I know. That's not my problem, is it?"

"No, Mom, it isn't," Sunny said wearily. "Well, guess I'll be going. I'll call you when I'm ready to bring Dad up."

Her heart in her eyes, Sunny waited. Would her mother smile and hug her?

"Come here, Sunny." Sunny didn't have to be told twice. She ran to her mother. "Shhh, it's all right. We have a lot of tomorrows ahead of us. We'll take at it one day at a time. If our expectations aren't too high, we can make it work," Fanny crooned.

"Thanks, Mom."

With Daisy in her arms, Fanny watched her daughter back up her car. "Wait till she gets the bill for the front end damage," she said to the dog. "Oh, well, that's not our problem either. Come on, sport, let's head back to the studio. I have a whole box of dog treats that have your name on them."

Inside the studio, Fanny busied herself getting out dog food, settling Daisy with a basket of dog toys in the middle of the floor. Anything so she wouldn't have to think about what she'd just committed to. In a frenzy she ripped open Simon's letter.

Dear Fanny,

   This is just a short note to tell you once again how much I love you. I deeply regret our misunderstanding. I want you to know that I will always be here waiting for you. Always means forever, Fanny.

                                        All my love and affection,
                                        Simon

"Forever is such a long time, Simon," Fanny whispered.

Address book in hand, Fanny picked up the phone to call Simon's office. "I'd like to leave a message for Mr. Thornton. This is Fanny Thornton in Las Vegas. The message is this, sell everything in the trust and transfer the money into the Babylon account. Find a buyer for Thornton Chickens ASAP. The code words for my account are Cotton Easter. Please advise me when the funds are transferred. Thank you."

"I know I'm going to regret this, Daisy. I guess I'm just one of those foolish mothers that love her children too much."

On a crisp autumn day in mid-October, Fanny watched Ash's arrival from her studio window. She continued to watch as a motorized lift swung up and out, lowering Ash in his wheelchair to the ground. A young man and a middle-aged woman followed. Therapist and nurse. Sunny climbed from her own car parked behind the van. She motioned for the trio to follow her. Even from this distance, Fanny could tell that Ash was balking at something. He looked incredibly thin and drawn. She struggled to find something good to remember about the man to whom she was once married. Courtesy demanded she go out and at least say hello.

Fanny took her time, walking slowly, Daisy at her side. "Good morning, Ash."

"Where are the goddamn ramps, Fanny? You invite me here and there are no ramps. Jesus, can't you get anything straight?"

Fanny looked at the embarrassed faces surrounding her. She dropped to her haunches, her hands on the wheelchair arms. "There are no goddamn ramps unless you brought them with you. You won't be here long enough to justify the expense. That's another way of saying, don't get comfortable, Ash. Let's get one thing straight right now. I did not *invite* you here. Your daughter asked me if she could bring you here to the mountain for a little while. I said yes. I did it for her, not you. For six months. Not one day longer."

Daisy took that moment to leap onto Ash's lap. He recoiled, slapping at the little dog, who only wanted to lick his face. Fanny picked up Daisy who was whining softly. "Touch my dog again, and I'll push you off this mountain. That's not a threat, Ash, it's a promise. Sunny, see that your father is made comfortable. By the way, I'm Fanny Thornton," Fanny said, extending her hand to the nurse and therapist. She thought she read approval in their eyes. Sunny looked miserable as she contemplated how best to get her father up the steps and into the house.

"Who's going to do the cooking?" Ash bellowed.

"I don't know, Dad. You're at home in the kitchen. Everything's within reach. The doctors said you have to start doing things for yourself."

"Damn quacks."

"The best money can buy. They got you this far, didn't they? It's up to you to follow through." She lowered her voice when she said, "We have to do what's best, not necessarily what he wants, okay? If he gets too abusive, threaten to leave. He'll snap around because he knows my mother won't help him. I'm sorry he's so . . . overbearing."

Sunny sat in her car for a long time before she turned the key. She offered up a small prayer that things would work out. Her gaze swiveled to the studio and then to the cemetery. "She deserves better than this. She deserves everything good and wonderful." She raised her gaze upward. "Help her. Please."

24

Fanny stirred, aware of a heaviness on her chest. Her first conscious thought was she was having a heart attack. Her eyes snapped open to see Daisy sitting on her chest, her short tail swishing back and forth. "Thank God," Fanny muttered. "Who told you we were going to be bed buddies?" The little dog whimpered in response. "You gotta go, huh? Okay, let me get my robe and slippers."

The air was dark and chilly, the young sun struggling to creep up from the horizon. Fanny loved watching the sun come up. In the old days she referred to it as AA, which meant After Ash, when all she had was time and the hope things would get better. Watching a new day begin was, in a way, her own new beginning.

"Let's go up to the big house, get some coffee, and watch the sun, Daisy," Fanny said as she scooped up the little dog into her arms. "We've regressed a little, but things will get better."

Fanny rounded the house as she walked toward the lacy, lavender shadows that proclaimed a new day. She saw him then, in profile, sitting in his wheelchair on the deck, in the same spot she'd always sat. His shoulders were slumped, his hands clutching the arms of the wheelchair. How vulnerable and beaten he looked, this man who was once her husband. Where was the mean-spirited arrogance of yesterday? Fanny closed her eyes for a moment, trying to imagine herself sitting in the wheelchair with the same injuries. Her heart seemed to skip a beat. She could feel her eyes start to burn.

Obviously Ash thought he was alone. Should she make some noise to attract his attention or should she simply walk up and say hello? Daisy whimpered. Ash turned to stare at her.

"It's my favorite time of day. I used to sit out here every morning, even in the winter, after you left, wondering if today would be the day you came back. You never did. When I saw you sitting here I was tempted to go back to the studio, but I wanted to apologize for yesterday. We . . . I got off to a bad start. When things look the most bleak, the most dark, it can only get better. I can make some coffee if you like."

"I'd like that, Fanny. I'm sorry too. Especially about the dog. He's cute."

"She. Her name is Daisy. Simon gave her to me. Would you like to hold her. She's really docile."

"Sure."

Fanny watched as the little dog snuggled into the crook of Ash's arms. His movements were just as clumsy as when he'd held their babies years ago. Her eyes started to burn again as she entered the house. When she returned with two mugs of coffee, Ash was stroking the sleeping dog's silky head. "Do you want me to take her?"

"No. It feels good to have something warm in my arms. I get very cold sometimes, even when it's ninety degrees. Why didn't we ever get a dog, Fanny?"

"You refused to allow a dog in the house. Most of the time you weren't a nice person, Ash."

"Why did you allow me to come here, Fanny?"

"I've been thinking about that a lot. I guess I could say it was because of Sunny. She drove up here and smashed right through the gates. That's how important it was to her for you to come here. I was already leaning in that direction anyway. To deny you the right to come here would have put me on the same level as you, and, Ash, I'm nothing like you. In my soul-searching I realized that I took away the only home you knew as a child. I didn't ask for Sunrise . . . to this day I don't know why Sallie deeded it to me. Sunrise should belong to you and Simon. When things get back to normal for you, I'm going to deed it back to you with one condition, and that is that you keep it in the family and not sell it. Don't ask me what I'm going to do or where I'm going to go, because I haven't gotten that far."

Ash nodded. "Part of me loves this place and a part of me hates it. All I could think about after the accident was coming here. I try not to think about the possibility of not walking again, and it scares the hell out of me."

"Then don't think about it, Ash. Think about today and what you have to do so that doesn't happen. That's how I handle unpleasant things."

"You always had a handle on everything. You were too good for me, Fanny. I'm not just a son of a bitch, I'm a weak son of a bitch. I always start off with good intentions, and then something goes awry. I'm also selfish."

"I know."

"Yeah, I guess you do. About the kids . . ."

"Each of us has to find our own way, Ash. Our kids are no different. I think they're going to be fine. All I ever wanted was a close-knit family. Do you realize, Ash, that you and I never, that's as in never, ever, tucked the kids into bed? We never stood together looking at the miracles we both created. We never went to recitals, ball games, or picnics together. That was a priority for me."

"That's why I never did those things. You did it better alone. I would have screwed it up someway. Hell, I did screw it up. Take right now for instance, here we are together, actually talking civilly to one another, and you know what I'm thinking? I'm thinking I'm never going to fly again, I'm never going to get the chance to manage Babylon."

"You need to think positive. Try and cut down on the painkillers. Endure what you can, try to hold out. I know, I know, I don't feel what you feel. I'm just telling you to try, Ash. Listen, I'll call Mazie to come back, but don't overwork her, Ash. I'll have Chue start on the ramps. Is there anything else I can do for you?"

"Don't hate me. Be my friend. I don't have any friends."

"Ash, I don't hate you. I hate what you've done to this family. One small part of me will always love you. There were many times when I almost hated you. Like the day of Sallie's service."

"I dream about that day. I started up this mountain three different times and three different times I turned around in the middle of the road and went back. In my heart I wanted to come, but my mind wouldn't allow it. You know, when I was a kid and she ignored me or she acted the way she did, I'd plot her death. I used to tell myself I'd dance on her grave, sing the kinds of songs she used to sing to those drunken miners. My mother the whore. I never worked my way past that. Simon did though. Simon was the smart one. Mom loved him so much. When she looked at me she'd look right through me. Are you in love with Simon?"

"That's none of your business, Ash. And don't try making it your business. Oh, one other thing, you can stay as long as needed. I'll be the judge of when it's time for you to go. Do we agree?"

"Sure."

"If you aren't too tired after dinner, I can come up and play a game of chess with you. I've gotten quite good over the years."

"It's a date. Do you want your dog back?"

"Hell, yes, I do. Don't try stealing my dog's affection, Ash. I waited a long time for her."

"Okay, Fanny. Listen, thanks for . . . letting me hold your dog."

Fanny laughed. "My pleasure. Remember, she bites on command."

It was Ash's turn to laugh. "Yeah, as she's licking you to death."

On the way back to the studio Daisy trotted along beside her. "If you have the desire to meander up there from time to time," she said to the little dog, "I won't hold it against you."

Fanny packed up the Christmas ornaments in tissue, aware that Ash's eyes were boring into her back. The fine hairs on the back of her neck prickled. Today wasn't going well for her ex-husband. "Would you like some tea, Ash?"

"No. You're upset with me, aren't you?"

"I think that's a fair statement. Ash, you cannot keep firing the people who are here to help you. You need to control your temper. You've gone through four therapists and six nurses. There is not an endless supply of people who are willing to come to the mountain. Tell me, please, what you're going to do now?"

"With you, Mazie and Chue, we can manage."

"No, Ash, we can't. Mazie and Chue are old and none of us are qualified. If we can't find help, you'll have to go back to town. Face it, the mountain is a drawback."

"They're all worthless and I'm not one damn bit better. If anything, I'm in more pain now than I was before. Jesus, I can't remember when I slept all night."

"You fire them because that puts you in control of the medication. Ash, you're taking too much. You're doped up all the time. Let's give some serious thought to a rehabilitation center on a temporary basis."

"Absolutely not. Those places are like prisons. I'm not ready for that. I can do a lot of things myself."

"A new team is coming up. This is the last time, Ash. I'm scheduled to leave on a business trip in two weeks, so you would be advised to 'make nice' to the new team."

"You didn't tell me you were going away."

Fanny threw her hands up in the air. "Ash, I have a life, personal as well as business. I cannot be here with you. I hate to keep reminding you, but we had a deal. Everyone is doing what's best for you." She watched in horror as Ash swallowed what looked like a handful of pills.

"Okay, okay. We'll do it your way," Ash said. "You're the boss as you keep reminding me. Sunny was supposed to be here two hours ago. Did she call?"

"I imagine there's snow on the road. If Sunny promised to be here, she'll be here."

"None of them cared enough to spend the holidays with us."

Fanny's tone was sharper than she intended. "How many holidays did you spend with Sallie and Philip?"

"Okay, Fanny, I get the point."

"Do you want me to get you a book? Some new ones came last week."

"I'm sick and tired of reading. I'm sick and tired of watching television, and I'm sick and tired of listening to the radio. I wish I'd died when I fell."

Fanny had heard it all before, many times. She chose to ignore the self-pity, the whining voice, the glazed eyes. She continued with what she was doing.

"Did you hear me, Fanny?"

"I'm sure Chue heard you down at his cottage."

"Let's pack up and go to Hawaii. It's warm there. We could see if that shack is still there.

Fanny closed the box of ornaments. "That was another time and another place. We're divorced. I'm going back to the studio now."

"You're leaving me here alone?" Ash asked, his voice full of outrage. "I don't like to be alone. Leave Daisy."

"If Daisy wants to stay, she can stay." At the sound of her name, Daisy ran to the door and woofed. "Guess she doesn't," Fanny said, slipping into her jacket.

"I think I hear a car. Yep, it's Sunny. I'll see you at dinner if I finish my work."

She looks bone tired, Fanny thought, when her daughter hugged her. "Happy New Year, Mom. You too, Dad." Ash grunted. Fanny rolled her eyes. Sunny's face went totally blank. "I'll come down to the studio before I leave," Sunny whispered.

"Dad, where's the nurse and therapist?"

"They're gone. I terminated their employment. Let's get down to business. Did you bring the new blueprints?"

"Dad, this is the holiday season. The architect didn't work between Christmas and New Year's. I told you that last week."

"Fire the son of a bitch! So, nothing's been done?"

"That isn't going to be easy, Dad. No one wants to pick up behind someone else. If you give up on the indoor pool, we can get back on track and save a fortune." Sunny took a deep breath. "You can't keep making these changes, Dad. I'm an engineer, I know what I'm talking about. We've failed every single inspection. I had to bring new people in to correct everything. We're so far over budget I'm starting to worry. Mom can pull the plug if she wants to. When she sees this latest batch of specs, she's going to hit the ceiling."

"Then don't tell her. Let's keep it between us."

"Oh, no, I'm not playing that game. Scratch the pool and those marble floors. We don't need ten miles of Italian marble."

"It's one of a kind. No one else has it. It stays. Babylon is one of the seven wonders of the world. People will come from all over the world to gamble in my casino. The hanging gardens will have no equal. When a customer walks through the golden doors he has every right to expect the most sensual experience of his life. That's exactly what I'm going to give them."

"What happens when the money runs out?"

"There are places to get money," Ash said vaguely.

Sunny snorted. "I know about *those* places. If you do that, you'll be selling your soul to the devils of Las Vegas."

"It's my soul," Ash snapped.

"So it is. However, it isn't mine. I made the decision to go with the regulation locks on the doors. The first eight floors have been done. We signed off on them."

"You had no goddamn right to make a decision without asking me."

"Yes, I did. I only had thirty days to return the hardware. We were fifteen days past that time. The security locks you wanted were double the cost of the ones we had. People aren't ready for credit card locks anyway. They aren't ready for bidets, either."

"If I wanted regulation, I would have ordered regulation. I want new, different, sizzling, sensuous. I want men to think Babylon is the ultimate aphrodisiac, and I want women to think they're part of it. The women will love the bidets, the security of the credit card locks. Women like that sort of thing. Those same women will love going into a grotto pool under the stars. I know what I'm talking about. I traveled in those circles for a long time."

Shaking with fury, Sunny struggled into her coat. "You're out of your mind. I must be out of mine too to even be arguing with you. Happy New Year!"

Sunny ran to the studio and burst through the door. "Mom . . . I can't . . . Mom, he won't listen. Just let me blurt everything out. He . . . he's over the edge, Mom. He wants the architect fired. This whole thing is turning into a joke. There's some heavy betting going on in the street. The heavy hitters are nine to one Babylon goes into Chapter Eleven. The damn barracudas are lining up. He refuses to budge on the pool. Ultimate aphrodisiac my ass!"

"What do you suggest we do?" Fanny asked.

"Two sets of books, blueprints, one set for him, one for us."

"And when he sees the finished building?" Fanny said gently. "I can't be a party to deception, and I don't think you want to, either."

"So what you're telling me is to go along with whatever Dad wants, which includes dumping the hardware in favor of those cockamamie locks?" Fanny nodded. "And the architect?"

"If you can't find another architect, there isn't much you can do. You work with what you have until things change. Do your best, Sunny."

"Mom, have you *really* looked at Dad lately? I see junkies on the strip every day that look better than he does. He took six pills while I was there."

"I can't stop him, Sunny. He lies about how much he takes. He says the bottle dropped, or the pills spilled in the toilet. He has more excuses than you can imagine. I tried telling John, but he said he couldn't call him a liar nor could he deprive him of the medicine. It's a Catch-22. A new nurse and therapist are due momentarily. This couple will not be fired. Ash will have to buckle under and go by the rules. If he doesn't, we'll have to transfer him to a rehabiliation center. I told him so this morning."

"Have you seen any improvement, Mom?"

"None. Your father can walk, but he's in incredible pain when he does. One day he actually passed out. The therapist grabbed him in time to break his fall. The orthopedic surgeon is now saying the back operation is too risky."

"What's going to happen to him?"

"I don't know. We've had the best doctors and surgeons in the country. Everything that could possibly be done, has been done. His broken bones have healed. One can survive without a spleen. He has medication for his violent headaches and medication for the pain in his back. He receives therapy every day. His nutrition is good. He says he doesn't sleep. The nurse says he does sleep. I'm doing my best."

"I know that, Mom, but his attitude has changed drastically in just a few weeks. He's becoming abusive."

"I had a thought, Sunny. What would you think if I called my father and brothers to come here and oversee things? We wouldn't necessarily have to mention that to your father since they wouldn't be taking any money. Consultants if you will. Perhaps those contractors are taking advantage of you because you're a woman. My brother Brad will find out in five minutes. Since your father isn't living in his penthouse apartment, I thought they could stay there while they're here. We won't mention that to your father, agreed?"

"Oh, Mom, I knew you'd come up with something. That's the perfect solution. I won't breathe a word." The relief on her daughter's face was so total, Fanny knew her idea would work.

"I'll call my father this evening. I did suggest Ash use them in the beginning, but he didn't want any part of *my* family working on *his* casino. Can Babylon be finished by the Fourth of July the way your father planned?" *Why am I doing this?*

"If the crews work around the clock, if materials come in on time, if the inspections go off as scheduled, and if there's enough money to make the draws, it's possible," Sunny said.

"Your father says all you need is six months."

"With no change orders, maybe. Labor Day seems more likely. That's my target date, and it's a realistic one. If we finish by the first of August, we'll have a month to prepare for the grand opening. Entertainers need six months' notice. He's promising people *the world.* When it's time to pay off I don't know what he's going to do. Reputation, as I'm finding out, is everything in this business. The smart money refers to Dad as a nutcase. I gotta get going, Mom. I have to find a way to recycle $200,000 worth of gold-plated doorknobs. I have a 6:00 A.M. meeting with the design architect for the pool. You know what, Mom, men always look good at six in the morning. Women just look tired. I'll give you a call tomorrow."

"How's Tyler, Sunny?"

"I haven't seen him in two weeks, and the last time I did see him I fell asleep over my egg rolls. I keep telling myself this will be over soon and I can pick up my old life. See you, Mom." She left the way she had arrived, a whirlwind of motion.

Fanny curled into her red chair, her glasses perched on the end of her nose. Pencil in one hand, calculator in the other, she worked the numbers, adding, subtracting, multiplying. So much *money.* Sallie, Sallie, did you really think Ash could build a casino for three million dollars? Was this your legacy to me? She shook her head wearily as she continued with her addition. Eight months and millions to go. The only problem was, the millions were gone. What was left? Sallie's jewelry, the bingo palace, and the little house in the cottonwoods. Sunrise. If she deeded the mountain back to Ash and Simon, Ash would find a way to sell it.

Simon. She started to cry. Daisy leaped on her lap to lick at her tears. Once Ash had said she was the stupidest woman walking the earth. He'd clarified that by saying, next to his mother, she was the stupidest. He must be right. Who in their right mind would do what she did to Simon? She cried harder. Daisy whimpered at these strange sounds. She could call him on some pretext or other. If she wanted to. Just to hear his voice. Just to know he was alive and well.

Fanny set aside the papers she'd been working on. From the cabinet under her drafting table she withdrew Sallie's box of photographs. She cried harder when she lined up Simon's pictures. When there were no more tears, she blew her nose and straightened her shoulders. She'd made the decision, no one else. Now, she had to live with it. She closed the box and pulled out Sallie's magnificent jewelry box. The jewelry was ornate—gaudy, but priceless. She had no idea what it was worth, surely a small fortune. If she added her own jewelry to the pile, maybe, if she was lucky, she could get three, maybe four million dollars.

She was on her knees, the baubles spread out on the red chair. The jewelry box alone must be worth close to fifty thousand dollars. Her hands were clumsy as she lifted the box to see if there was any kind of engraving or tag on the bottom. It slipped from her hands to land on the carpet, the red velvet trays askew. As she tugged at the trays she noticed two pieces of paper. She spread them out, adjusted her glasses. An IOU. signed by Seth Coleman for three million dollars. Fanny gasped. The second piece of paper was the combination to the monster safe in the main house. The special key to the room was among the jewelry. She'd meant to go into the room so many times since Sallie's death, but other things seemed to take priority. She thought it strange that she'd never shown any curiosity in regard to the safe. It was Sallies'; therefore, it was off-limits, the same way Jake's money was off-limits. Legally, the house was hers, but the schoolroom and the safe room, as Sallie called it, were always her mother-in-law's.

Her curiosity was aroused now. She fingered the heavy brass, one-of-a-kind key, made especially for the one-of-a-kind lock, according to Sallie. A lock that couldn't be picked and a key that couldn't be duplicated. Once Sallie had told her the door was solid steel with a wooden veneer. Impregnable. Well, she had the key and the combination. If she entered the main house by the front door, she could go up to the second floor undetected. Her heart started to pump furiously. *Do it! Do it!* An inner voice challenged. *It's yours now, you have the right to go into that special room and open the safe.* Fanny didn't argue with herself. Instead, she told Daisy to guard the family jewels.

The early evening darkness allowed Fanny to blend with the shadows as she walked around to the front of the house. She shivered in the night air, not so much from the cold mountain air, but from fear. Of what, she didn't know.

The front door opened soundlessly. Fanny tiptoed inside. She waited a moment to see if any sounds were coming from the living room. She heard low-voiced conversation and the lower voices of the television set. Good, all present and accounted for. Aware that the fourth step from the bottom creaked, Fanny stepped above it, the thick carpeting muffling any sound she might make.

Upstairs, Fanny walked down the hall to the room at the end. She fit the heavy brass key into the lock and turned it. She had to use her shoulder to push the heavy door inward. Total darkness greeted her. Her hands fumbled for a light switch. There wasn't one. Light from the hallway spilled into the room. To the right of the door she saw a large black flashlight. When she turned it on instant bright light flooded the room. She pocketed the key, but not until she was certain the key would open the door from the inside. The door closed soundlessly.

Fanny panicked for a second when she realized there were no windows in the room. The key inside her pocket felt warm against her leg. It should be cold, she thought crazily. She moved the flashlight in a wide arc to see the ugly, black, floor-to-ceiling safe. The round silver circle in the middle reminded her of a Cyclops eye.

Fanny placed the flashlight on the floor, the light shining directly on the lock. She fished in her pocket for the tattered piece of paper. How long could she stay in this airless room? Her heart pounding in her chest, Fanny twirled the dial. It took her four tries before she finally heard the click that told her all she had to do was grasp the handle and open the massive door. She pulled and tugged. She tried using her rear end, her shoulder, her hip, and finally she managed to pry the door open. She leaned against it, her back pushing the heavy door. She was left breathless with exertion.

Flashlight in hand, Fanny played it around the inside of the safe. There's no dust, she thought inanely. She stared at the six long shelves, three of which were filled with burlap sacks. They appeared to be identical and equally heavy. She untied the knots on two of them. Gold nuggets, different sizes. Fanny reached for the heavy door for support. The third shelf held four stout wooden boxes. The word EXPLOSIVES was printed on each box. Fanny lifted one of the boxes off the shelf. She dropped to her knees. She took a deep breath before she opened it. Stock certificates—railroad stocks, mining stocks—bundled tightly in neat piles. Land deeds, bundled into thinner piles. War bonds, stacks and stacks of them. She closed the lid and replaced the box on the shelf. Expecting to see the same thing in the second box, she was stunned to find thick bundles of old, very dry money. She rifled through a stack. Thousand-dollar bills, two hundred to a stack. She almost fainted when she counted the stacks. Her hands were shaking so badly it was all she could do to close the box and replace it on the shelf. She took a deep breath before she opened the third box. What she saw brought tears to her eyes. Photograph albums, one for Ash and one for Simon. Baby caps and baby shoes. Mementos of Sallie's children that she'd kept. Tears trickled own Fanny's cheeks. On the bottom of the box were twelve leather-bound diaries, each with Sallie's name embossed in gold on the cover, and the years the diaries covered. Taped to the first diary was a long white envelope with the name Fanny scrawled across the front. She pushed the box closer to the door. She would take this box with her when she returned to the studio.

Fanny struggled to lift one of the sacks off the shelf. How much did it weigh? Ten, twenty pounds? Since she couldn't lift it above her knees, it had to weigh much more. By pushing and tugging she managed to get it onto the bottom shelf. Maybe seventy pounds, she estimated. Gold sold by the *ounce*. Mercy! She counted sixty-five burlap stacks. She had to sit down with her head between her knees.

Fanny looked at her watch. Ash would be having dinner now. If the television was still on, she could make it out of the house without being noticed. The box wasn't heavy, but it was bulky. Fanny tiptoed to the top of the steps. She leaned over the railing, straining to hear the sounds of the television. A small sigh escaped her lips as she started down the steps, the box firmly clasped in her hands, careful to avoid the fourth step from the bottom. She held her breath until she was outside in the crisp evening air. The moment she had her wits about her, she began to run. Inside her studio, she slammed the dead bolt home. Daisy ran to her.

Fanny dropped to the floor, the dog in her lap. "I betcha this is how criminals feel when they leave the scene of a crime." She hugged the little dog until her heartbeat returned to normal.

"I'll put the jewelry back, make you some dinner, make myself some coffee, and we'll sit here and try to figure out what I'm going to do."

While Daisy ate her dinner, Fanny slapped a wrinkled piece of cheese between two slices of dry bread. She carried her coffee and sandwich to the big red chair, poked at the fire, and added another log. Now, she was set for hours. The intercom buzzed near the front door just as she was about to sit down. Ash.

"Yes?"

"Fanny, you missed dinner. Do you want me to have Mazie send something down?"

Fanny looked at her cheese sandwich. "I ate, Ash. I wasn't hungry this evening."

"Are you coming up?"

"No, not this evening. I have something I have to do."

Ash lowered his voice. "This therapist is a jerk, Fanny. The nurse is like something from a Godzilla movie. This team isn't going to work."

"It has to work. You know what the alternative is."

"Stop threatening me, Fanny. Come up and meet them. We can play a game of chess."

"Maybe tomorrow. Ask the nurse or therapist to play with you. If they aren't chess players, play checkers. Good night, Ash."

Fanny spent the rest of the evening working her calculator and talking to Bess and Billie Coleman. The last thing she did before climbing into bed was to look through the wooden box a second time. Dear God, she'd forgotten about the letter with her name on it.

Fanny withdrew the letter and smoothed it out on her bedspread. It was written on Sallie's flowered paper and smelled faintly of lilacs. It was dated three months before her death.

My Dear Fanny,

If you're reading this letter, you have finally opened the monster safe. There are no words to tell you how that room, and the safe itself, intimidated me the first time I saw it. I prayed that I was dreaming, that I would wake and it would all be a bad dream. It wasn't, as you know. I only used one bag of the gold and some of the money for investment purposes. My fortune was mostly made on my own, and of course the money from the sale of Black Mountain to the government. I always thought of the contents of the safe as Cotton's money, never mine. It's the way you thought of Jake's money. I used two boxes of the money to pay for the power and sewage plants, because Cotton would have liked that.

By now, I imagine Ash is over his head in debt. Convert the contents of the safe into cash and bail him out, Fanny. When Ash first came to me with the idea of Babylon, I looked into it. The cost made my eyes water. If, as I suspect, you opened the safe because you've used up all the available monies, this will lighten your burden. Parcel it out carefully, Fanny, because Ash has no money sense.

When the time is right, give my sons the contents of the box. Everything is clearly marked. You, Fanny, are the caretaker of my life.

One last thing. In the bottom of the box with the stocks and bonds, there is a special letter. Again, when the time is right, in your opinion, I want you to follow the instructions in the letter. I hope I haven't put too heavy a burden on your shoulders. You and Devin are the only two people in the whole world that I ever trusted. I understand now how Cotton must have felt when he entrusted his fortune to me. When Babylon is finished and you have the dedication ceremonies, I'd like it if you'd dedicate separate rooms to Cotton, Devin, and Philip.

Be happy, dear child, for life is so very short. Follow your heart, the rest will fall into place.

> *All my love and affection,*
> *Sallie*

Your rump and shoulder will be sore for a week. I think you should blow up that ugly safe the first chance you get.

Fanny smiled through her tears.

25
〜

Fanny picked at her salad, her eyes on her daughter. "This is a very nice restaurant. The food is even good."

"If it's so good, why aren't you eating?" Sunny chided.

"I guess for the same reason you aren't eating. I'm too excited. Thirty days till Labor Day. The only word to describe that building is magnificent. I'm very proud of you, Sunny. How are the grand opening plans going?"

"On schedule. A lot of money changed hands on the strip. Oh, those naysayers, they're eating their nasty words these days. I hate to admit this, but I had Tyler place a bet for me. We're going to use the money to pay for our honeymoon."

"Sunny, you finally said yes?"

Sunny beamed. "We're getting married the week after Christmas, just like I promised Grandma. Thank God, I didn't tell her *which* Christmas. Everyone is coming for the grand opening. Our whole family will finally be together at one time—Grandpa Logan, Mrs. Kelly, Uncle Daniel and Uncle Brad, the Colemans. When was the last time that happened?"

"Never. Someone was always missing." She hated herself for asking, but she needed to know. She tried for a nonchalant tone and knew she failed when Sunny's eyes sparked. "Is your Uncle Simon planning to attend?"

"Of course. He groaned when I told him it was black tie. He asked about you, Mom."

"I'm sure he did. It will be nice to see him again."

"That's exactly what Uncle Simon said." Sunny made a little face. "Mom, guys like Uncle Simon and Tyler only come along once in a lifetime. Don't blow it for some silly reason. I know you love him. Hell, everyone, including Dad, knows you love him. You aren't getting any younger, Mom."

"Thank you, Miss Know-It-All."

"What are you wearing to the opening, Mom?"

"Billie is making me something outrageously beautiful. She's bringing Admiral Kingsley, Riley, and Amelia. It's all going to be so wonderful."

"How's Dad? I've been afraid to ask. He said he was coming to town this week. Was he just saying that?"

"What did he say when he came to town last week?"

"He found fault with everything. Grandpa Logan settled his hash, though. I like that saying and Grandpa did it so slick Dad didn't even know what was happening. I miss them already and they just left yesterday. Mom, there's no way Babylon could have come in on schedule without Uncle Daniel and Uncle Brad. Your brothers are just like you, Mom. Grandpa had his finger on everything. I knew he would make things right when he fired everyone on the site and brought his people from Pennsylvania."

"He's getting salty in his old age," Fanny smiled. "From the time I was a little girl, I thought he was perfect. I'm more convinced than ever."

"Do you know how wonderful that sounds, Mom? I wish I could say something like that about Dad."

"I wish you could too, Sunny. Hey, just out of curiosity, whose idea was it to install handicap ramps at the casino?"

"Uncle Daniel's. He saw how difficult it was for Dad when he came down here. If Dad is going to work the floor like he said he was, he's going to have to have maneuverability. One whole floor is designated for the handicapped. The *Nevada Sun* did a write-up on us last week. Just yesterday I heard the other casinos are scurrying to do the same thing. We have the edge, though. Ten months, Mom, and we did it! I feel like I'm going to bust wide-open. I just wish Dad had said one kind word. Just one."

"He knows, Sunny. It's hard for your father to see all this and to know he lost control."

"There you go, Mom, making excuses for him again. The day of the grand opening he'll be Mister Charm himself. I sent invitations to the guys in his old squadron. Do you think that was a mistake?"

"For Mister Charm? He'll pull it off. I can't even begin to comprehend how an operation this size is all going to come together in a mere thirty days. How do five dining areas . . ."

"Very carefully, Mom. We have a five-star chef for starters. Good management people. I managed to snag some of the employees, mostly women, from other casinos. I'm going to give them a chance to move up the ladder. Women are loyal, Mom. They hate that bullshit they have to take from male employers. Someday, Mom, I'm gonna be the biggest, the best, the most respected *powerful* woman in this town. That's a promise too. It won't be men that get me there either, it will be women. Wherever she is, I want Grandma Sallie to be proud of me. She set it up, so I have to think she knew I could do it."

"I know it too, Sunny," Fanny said.

"Everything's under control. Aunt Bess has been a tremendous help. We've got good experienced casino people working for us. You can go back to the mountain and not give another thought to the opening. All you have to do is show up." She paused, then reached out to hug her mother. "Bye, Mom. Think about calling Uncle Simon, okay."

Fanny didn't answer, but she hugged Sunny back.

The moment Fanny parked the car she knew something was wrong. The door to her studio was standing open and Daisy was nowhere in sight. She whistled for the little dog and called her name. A chill ran up her back. She went inside, knowing Ash had been here going through her things. Thank God she'd taken the important things back to the safe. How had he gotten in? Did she forget to lock the door? Every inch of floor space was covered with bills, estimates, change orders, canceled checks, memos from her brothers and father.

Fanny ran to the house. The nurse and therapist's cars were gone. The specially equipped van was standing in the driveway. She opened the back door and walked into the house through the kitchen. She called to Daisy and to Ash. She found them both in the living room, staring at the television. The volume was muted. "Ash?"

Daisy squirmed from Ash's lap and ran to her, leaping into her arms. "Ash? Where's the nurse and therapist?"

"They're gone. I paid them off and kicked them out. I'm moving back to town tomorrow. I can take care of myself."

"Ash, have you been drinking? You know you can't drink with that medication. What happened?"

"Like you don't know what happened? Your goddamn family is what happened. You went behind my back."

Fanny sat down. "Ash, it was the only way to bring the building in on time. I asked them to come here for you. For you, Ash, because I knew how important Babylon is to you. Does it really matter who finished up? You can be proud, Ash. You'll be king of the strip. There's not another building that can come close. Sunny told me all two thousand rooms are booked for the opening."

"You fucking lied to me. You sneaked behind my back. You knew I'd say no, so you did it anyway."

"I didn't lie, I simply didn't tell you because I knew you'd say exactly what you just said. I'd do it again too."

"Jesus, do you have any idea how much I hate your guts?"

"I think I have a pretty good idea. I'm sorry about your accident. I hate seeing you in such agony. If there was something for me to do for you, I'd do it. If you needed a kidney transplant, I wouldn't hesitate to donate one of mine, but I can't free you from the pain. My God, I wish I could. I wish that more than anything. I'll drive you down the mountain tomorrow. What were you looking for in my studio and how did you get in?"

"I wanted to see what was so fucking wonderful about that hole in the wall. You left the door unlocked. You never once invited me down there. It's a damn dump, the furniture is old and worn, the appliances are even older." His voice was spiteful and whiny.

"I told you way back in the beginning that I was a plain, simple person. I don't need or want all those fancy things you crave and need to exist. That was the *one* thing Sallie and I did have in common. I think this might be the right time. I'll be right back. I have something for you."

Fanny ran to the studio for the key to the secret room, and then back to the house. She galloped up the steps and down the hall to the room with the safe. She rummaged through the box, laying the things Sallie left for Simon on the floor. She didn't bother to close the safe, but she did lock the steel door leading to the hallway.

"This is for you, Ash. Sallie left it to me to give you when I thought the time was right. I don't think there will ever be a more right time than now. I want you to know I'm taking all the liquor out of this house, and your medication. I'll leave what's needed for the night. I'll have Mazie fix you some soup and a sandwich. I'll be up first thing in the morning to drive you down the mountain. Ash, did you hear what I just said?"

"Go away, Fanny. I don't want to look at you anymore. I'm in so much pain I want to die. How the hell do you know I was drinking?"

"Because I can smell it. The doctors warned you not to drink while on your medication. Ash, I'm not a paramedic, I won't know what to do for you if something happens. You can't put that kind of burden on my shoulders. It would take an ambulance an hour to get here. I can't live like this anymore."

"I can't either. I'm going to do something about it."

A knot of fear formed in Fanny's stomach. "I don't like the way that sounds, Ash. If you're trying to scare me, you're succeeding. I also want to know who that strange man is who's been coming up here three times a week. The one you meet in the kitchen."

"He's a supplier. You try to make something out of nothing all the time." Ash's voice was so defensive, Fanny knew she was on to something.

"He's a drug dealer, isn't he?" Her heart started to pound inside her chest at Ash's wary look.

"Where in the hell did you get an idea like that?"

"From you, Ash." Before he could respond, Fanny was standing over the wheelchair, her hands rummaging in the side pockets. "I knew it!" she shouted triumphantly. She held up two thin packets wrapped in butcher's paper. She moved away from the wheelchair and Ash's outstretched hands. "My, God, Ash, what are you doing to yourself? This is going down the drain."

"Fanny, no! Please. You don't understand. The pain . . . The pain is unbearable at times. I can't handle it. It doesn't take the pain away, it just dulls it so that I can . . . live with it. I need it. If you never believed anything else I've ever said to you, believe that."

"There has to be a better way," Fanny said desperately. "Listen, Ash, I heard about this clinic in Boston that is supposed to be the best of the best. It's Leahy or something that sounds like that. I can look into it, and I'd be more than willing to take you there for an evaluation. They make new discoveries every day. It will be a week out of your life, Ash. We could do it now, or we could wait until after the opening. If there's even a remote chance, take it. Anything, Ash, will be better than sitting in this chair and becoming a drug addict."

"I've had all the tests I can handle. We both know nothing can be done, so why are we even discussing it? Give me back the stuff."

"No. Can't we at least try?"

"Why are you being so damn thickheaded, Fanny? Su Li, the paragon of the medical profession, brought in the top doctors in the country. Hell, I even went through that acupuncture where they stick needles all over you. Nothing works. Don't you understand, nothing goddamn works!"

It was true, and Fanny knew it. Did she have the right to destroy the one thing that gave him some measure of comfort? If she returned the drugs to him, if she turned a blind eye to what he was doing, did that make her an accessory?

"If I give these back to you, will you promise not to drink?"

"Hell, no."

"Then I can't let you go back to town. Sooner or later someone will find out what you're doing. People will use it against you, Ash. I know it's considered fashionable to take drugs at parties these days, but what you're doing goes beyond that. How do you plan on working at the casino looking like a rag doll with glassy eyes? Have you given any thought to that, Ash?"

"Jesus Christ, Fanny, all I do is think. Do you have any idea how many times I thought about taking my own life? Thousands, millions of times. I don't have the guts. I don't want to die, no one wants to die."

"You have to stay here, Ash. If I'm going to be a party to this, you have to be where I can keep my eyes on you. I don't want the kids to know about this, Ash. I want your promise."

"I'll promise anything you want. I'm going to have real bad days, Fanny, days when the street drugs won't work. I go crazy when that happens. That was bullshit about me going to town. I know I can't make it on my own. I know I'm dependent on you. I'm giving you my promise in good faith. Now, can I have my packages back?"

Fanny handed them over. She wondered how she was going to live with this dangerous, dark secret.

"What's all this stuff, Fanny?"

"Things your mother left for you. I'm going to leave you now, Ash, and go to the studio to clean it up. I'll speak to Chue. You'll have to manage on your own this evening. Can you do it?"

"Yeah. Yeah, I can do it, Fanny. I'm sorry about the mess I made in your studio. Can we play some chess this evening. I think I have a new move."

"I'll see, Ash."

Ash waited until he heard the door close before he wheeled his chair to the couch. By gripping the arm of the sofa, he lifted himself onto the cushions. His face was beaded in sweat when he leaned back against the cushions, the box at his side. At first his eyes were puzzled at the assortment of things inside the box. Then he understood. Small things from every year of his life. His christening hat, his first baby shoes, his report cards, his football letter, his first pocketknife, whose blade was so dull it wouldn't cut Jell-O, the horn from his first bicycle. His hands trembled when he picked up the packet of photos. They chronicled his life, from the day he was born until his return from military service, at which point his mother had relinquished his life's mementoes to Fanny.

The photographs brought tears to his eyes. When they overflowed and rolled down his cheeks, he made no move to wipe them away. When his vision cleared, Ash picked up one of the diaries, realizing they were in chronological order.

His mother's life.

His life.

Together in the same box.

Did he have the guts to read the diaries? His body started to shake. Here it was, right in his face. The answers he'd longed for all his life. How ironic that it was given to him now, at the worst time of his life. Maybe that was why Fanny chose today to give it to him. She said today was the right time. He couldn't help but wonder how she knew.

The first diary was nothing more than a small notebook that seemed to cover the first three years of his mother's life, when she first arrived in Nevada. Thereafter, the journals were leather-bound and embossed in gold. Each diary covered five years.

He forgot about the pounding inside his head, forgot the searing pain in his back. He didn't see Fanny standing in the doorway nor did he see or hear Mazie when she brought him his dinner.

It was past midnight when Ash closed the last diary. He rubbed at his eyes as he placed the treasures back inside the wooden box. He struggled to an upright position, reached for his canes. The first jolt of pain was horrific. He clenched his teeth, but kept on walking, through the living room, to the hall, out the front door, down the walkway, around the corner, and on to the cemetery. He was breathless with the effort he expended to get here, to this low brick wall.

He dug his canes into the soft earth to give him the balance he needed to lower himself to the wall.

He looked around, marveling that he'd made it this far on his own. The pounding inside his head had abated, the searing pain in his back was a dull ache. He found himself marveling at that too.

What was it Simon had said that day so long ago? You simply open your heart and you talk. He did, the words tumbling out so fast he had trouble keeping up with them.

With Daisy in her arms, Fanny stood sentinel, a safe distance away. "If there's a way, Sallie, for you to give him a sign, some-thing . . . anything, this is the time to do it. Between us, maybe we can save him from himself." Daisy whimpered softly in her arms. "Shhh, it's going to be all right."

The sign she requested, if it truly was a sign, came a few minutes later in the form of two shooting stars. She thought she gasped, but a second later she realized it was Ash who had made the noise. Even from this distance, the moonlight allowed her to see his clenched fist shoot in the air.

"Thank you, Sallie," Fanny whispered. She stepped deeper into the night shadows when she saw Ash prepare to get up. She watched, her eyes wide in disbelief when he leaned his right cane against the wall. He straightened to his full height, and offered up the snappiest salute she'd ever seen. To his mother.

In the kitchen, Ash leaned against the sink while he fumbled in his pockets for the two packets of drugs. He turned on the water and dribbled the cocaine down the drain. The marijuana followed. He let the water run for a long time to make sure the leaves and seeds didn't clog the drain. He walked back to the living room and the sofa. He stretched out and slept deeply and dreamlessly.

It was his first drug-free sleep since the day of his accident.

The newspapers described the opening of Babylon as the biggest event in the history of Las Vegas. The Thorntons did their best to take it all in stride as they gathered outside the golden doors of Babylon for the ribbon-cutting ceremony.

"You did it, honey," Damian Logan whispered in his daughter's ear.

"We're kind of proud to call you our sister," Daniel said.

"I'm just glad I had the good sense to call you guys. Thanks seems so inadequate."

"That's what families are for, pulling together, helping one another during the good as well as the bad times. We have over two dozen job offers we're turning down," Damian said. "No offense, honey, but this town is too frisky for me."

"Sunny did all the decorating; in fact, she's totally responsible for this opening. All the liquor, all the food in all five dining rooms is on the house. It was her idea to give each woman a single red rose. There are fresh flowers in all two thousand rooms, thanks to Chue. Chue also gets credit for those magnificent hanging gardens. He said he has to beat off potential customers with sticks. The gold plate, the Persian carpets, the Bavarian crystal chandeliers, it just boggles my mind. The sculptures, the fountains, the fresh flowers, all those miles of Italian marble, the rare orchids, the sunken pools, the water-falls . . . It's all so . . . decadent."

"That's what people want, Fanny. Ash knew that. The crowd is lined up around the block. I've never seen so many limousines in one place in my life," Billie Coleman said. "This is stupendous. The ice sculptures are fantastic. What's Ash going to say, do you know?"

"He hasn't told me. The usual I guess. He'll thank the mayor, the governor, etc. . . . and then thank the people for coming."

"It's a night of beautiful people," Sunny said. "There's so much glitz and glitter you need sunglasses. Look, Mom, that showgirl is hitting on Uncle Simon. He's eating it up."

In spite of herself, Fanny looked in the direction her daughter was pointing. The showgirl was incredibly gorgeous and *young*. Simon looked . . . wonderful. She turned away, her heart pounding in her chest.

"Ladies and gentlemen, welcome to Babylon!" Ash said as he took his place in the center of the golden ribbon stretched between two pillars. He was flanked on the right by the governor, the mayor on the left. Gold shears found their way to his hands. "Please, may I have your attention. I want to thank all of you for coming today. My special thanks go to the Logan family, who brought this building to fruition. As most of you know, I wasn't able to . . . finish what I started. My brother Simon and I . . ." he motioned for Simon to take his place next to him, "want to dedicate this building to four wonderful people: Sallie Thornton, our mother, Philip Thornton, our father, and to Devin Rollins and Cotton Easter." The public watched as Ash's shaking hands cut the golden ribbon.

Simon clapped his brother on the back. "It's a hell of a building, Ash." Simon looked into his brother's eyes. "You okay, Ash, you look kind of white around the mouth?"

"Fanny wants a private dedication ceremony later for the four penthouses. She said Mom wanted it that way. It's time for me to sit down. Would you mind helping me?"

"Where's your chair?"

"In the office. I can make it, just walk next to me."

Fanny suddenly found herself standing next to her twin sons. It was the first time she'd seen them since they'd left the year before. She smiled and opened her arms. At six-two, they dwarfed her, smothering her with their arms. "It's good to be back," Birch said huskily.

"I dreamed about this day," Sage said, a catch in his voice.

"I wish you'd stay. I've missed you. My, you're handsome."

"Mom . . ." the twins said in unison because they always said important things in unison.

"You don't have to say anything. You're here, I'm here. Nothing else is important."

"In that case . . ."

"They'll stay," Sunny chirped, coming up behind her brothers. "That's two down, one to go. Where's Billie? She was here a few minutes ago."

Billie Coleman laughed. "She went inside to check the material on the drapes and bedspreads. So tell me, what do you think of my fella?" She cut her eyes to Thad Kingsley.

"Very distinguished," the twins said.

"Handsome," Sunny said.

"I like him a lot, Billie," Fanny said. "Anyone who can put stars in your eyes has my vote."

"Let's go for a walk, Fanny. I want to see this fabulous establishment." She waved airily to Thad. "Now, tell me, have you spoken to Simon?"

"We said hello."

"I saw three different young women sidle up to him. He was polite, nothing more. Come on, Fanny, you've carried this far enough. You've done everything you said you weren't going to do. When are you going to do what you want to do?"

"Soon. I'm going to talk to Ash tomorrow. Then I'm going on a trip. By myself. Lord, you can't hear yourself think in here. Let's go outside and walk in one of the gardens. I have something I want to talk to you about."

"Don't complain about the noise. Those sounds represent money. Ooops, sorry, I wasn't watching. Oh, it's you, Simon. I need to find Thad before some starlet whisks him away. I'll catch up with you later, Fanny."

"How are you, Fanny?"

"I'm fine, Simon. And, you?"

"Fine."

"We're such liars," Fanny smiled. "How's Ash?"

"He's in the office resting. He told me he's moving back to town. He wants to be closer to the casino."

"We discussed it. He's never going to get much better than he is right now."

"He admitted that to me a little while ago. This place will help. I love you, Fanny. I believe you love me, yet we're standing here like two polite strangers. Why is that? If it's my fault, I'll take the blame. If it's your fault, I'll take the blame for that too. See how broad my shoulders are. I told Ash how I felt about you. He told me he knew. He also told me I could search the world over and not find anyone better than you. He didn't exactly give us his blessing, but it was implied."

"Ash said that?" Fanny gasped.

"I also told your kids. They were more verbal. That means they approve. All I need is your approval, Fanny. This is the point in time when someone should say to us, live happily ever after."

"I need some time, Simon. I've decided to go away for a while. This past year has been . . . very hard. I need a clear head. I need to get back all those feelings I lost. I realize that I merely existed for the past two years. Don't ask me where I'm going or how long I'll be gone, because I don't know. I just know I have to go."

"But you're coming back?" The worry in Simon's voice was palpable.

"I can't promise that, Simon."

"You're breaking my heart, Fanny."

"I'm sorry, Simon. I wish . . . things were different. One can only work with what's at hand. I do love you, I want you to know that."

"Why doesn't that make me feel better?"

Fanny shrugged.

"I'll wait, forever if necessary."

"That's good to know. I think we should circulate and put some money into this business."

"I feel lucky tonight," Simon said. "Oh, oh, the family is lining up for some pictures. Come along, Fanny, and smile pretty for the camera. You're tomorrow's news. It's front-page stuff."

When the photographer finished, Fanny walked, alongside Ash, back to the office. Ash reached for her hands. "Thanks, Fanny. For everything."

Fanny smiled. "I know you mean that. That's all that's important.

The kids are back. Things will work out. I'm going away for a while, Ash."

"I understand. Is Simon going with you? I'm sure my opinion isn't important to you, but it's okay if he is."

"Nope. Just me and Daisy."

"Do the kids know?"

"I'll tell them tonight."

"Can I do anything, Fanny?"

"Be my friend."

"You got it," Ash said, hugging her.

Simon turned away, his eyes burning. Some things just weren't meant to be.

They were lined up like soldiers—her sons, her daughters, and her ex-husband. They were here to say good-bye.

"I feel like I should salute." Fanny laughed.

She tossed her two suitcases in the backseat. "Come on, Daisy, hop in."

"Will you write and call?" Billie and Sunny asked.

"Nope," Fanny said, settling herself behind the wheel of the car.

"Will you send presents?" the twins asked at the same time.

"No way." The engine turned over. "You're on your own."

She blew the horn three sharp blasts. She didn't look back.

"There goes our life force," Sunny said, tears streaming down her cheeks. "She'll write and call. She just said that."

"No, she won't. Mom never says anything she doesn't mean," Billie said.

"She'll be home by Christmas. Mom loves Christmas," the twins said in unison.

"Like you all came for Christmas last year. You guys broke the chain of tradition, so don't count on it," Ash said.

The Thornton children, as one, looked at their father and spoke at the same time. "Is she coming back at all?"

"I don't know. I hope she does. If I were your mother, I'd probably think we weren't worth coming back for. I have an idea, I know it's not midnight, but let's have some fried egg sandwiches."

"Mothers don't leave their children," Sunny grumbled as she headed for the house. "If she's not back by the middle of December we'll go look for her, okay?"

"Okay," everyone said.

"To Mom," Billie said, holding her cup of cocoa high in the air.

"To Mom."

Epilogue

December 10, 1978

Simon Thornton opened the messengered letter, his heart beating so fast he had to struggle to take a deep breath. Why would Fanny have her letter delivered by a special messenger? Read the damn letter, Thornton, and find out!

Dear Simon,

Please meet me at the address listed at the bottom of this letter. I'm in town for a few hours and I would like to see you.

Affectionately,
Fanny

Simon didn't stop to think, didn't bother with his overcoat even though the temperature was in the low thirties. He barreled through the offices, out the door, and down the steps. Elevators were just too damn slow. Outside in the bracing air, he ran to the road and hailed a cab. Shivering, he gave the driver the address from the bottom of Fanny's letter. He sat on the edge of the seat, his imagination running wild. At one point he rolled down the window to the chagrin of the driver.

Thirty minutes later, the driver skidded to a stop. "Here you are, buddy. You want me to wait?"

Did he? He didn't know? "No." He shoved bills in the driver's hand.

Simon looked around, his eyes wild. What the hell was Fanny doing at the harbor?

"Simon! Over here!"

Jesus, where was over here? He looked around. He blinked. Fanny, Bess, Billie, and Admiral Thad Kingsley. All of them were dressed in sailor outfits. It was a bad dream and he was going to wake up any minute.

He saw it then, pristine white in the early morning sunshine. *SOMEDAY.*

"We're your crew," Fanny called. "We brought Thad along because he knows about boats . . . ships. Sallie asked me to do this for you. Say something!"

"Where are we going?" he managed to ask.

"Wherever you want, Simon. There's a real crew on board, so don't panic. I thought we'd sail to Bermuda if you have no objections, drop off our guests, and then you and I can hit the high seas. What do you think?"

Simon swung her high in the air. "I say, what are we waiting for?"

"I do like a man who makes instant decisions," Fanny said.

"And I do like a woman who allows me to make them. God, I love you, Fanny."

"And I love you, Simon."

"Tallyho!" Billie said.

"No, it's all aboard," Bess said.

"Wrong! It's anchors aweigh," the admiral said.

"Whatever," Fanny and Simon said in unison.

Coming soon from Kensington Books

VEGAS HEAT

For a sample chapter of the next book in the
Thornton family's story, just turn the page . . .

PART I

1980–1985

1

Those in the know said Babylon was a one-of-a-kind gambling casino. Those same people in the know said the Thornton family, owners of the casino, had overextended themselves. The big question, though, on the Bright White Way, was how Ash Thornton, a man confined to a wheelchair, a man whose body was racked with pain twenty-four hours a day, was going to operate a business like Babylon.

The windowless counting room, an inner sanctuary where the money washed through daily, bore testament to how well the wheelchair-bound man managed. Ash said he experienced the ultimate thrill when he became immersed in the sight, smell, and touch of money—tons of money, stacks and bundles of coins so heavy Ash had been forced to buy a hydraulic lift to move it all around the counting room.

It was amazing to Fanny that rather than counting the money, Ash had the cash counted according to denomination and *weighed.* Her daughter Sunny had told her a million dollars in $100 bills weighed 20.5 pounds; a million dollars in $20 bills weighed 102 pounds. A million dollars in $5 bills weighed 408 pounds.

There was even a name for the electronic coin-weighing scale, the Toledo Scale. Sunny had laughed, a tinge of hysteria in her voice, when she said a million dollars in quarters from the slots weighed twenty-one tons. A fortune passed through Babylon every day of the year, so much money it had to be weighed instead of counted. What was the world coming to?

What *was* she doing here? *I'm trying to justify my mother-in-law's faith in my ability to safeguard the Thornton family fortune. I'm trying to help her family and to keep my own family intact.*

Fanny Thornton hated the opulent, decadent casino known as Babylon. Today, she should have called ahead to arrange a meeting someplace or, at the very least, made a luncheon reservation as far away from this fool's paradise as possible.

Fanny, her face grim, knew floor security had announced her entrance the moment she walked through the door. Ash was probably watching her from one of his top secret peepholes. Birch and Sage were probably on their way to intercept her while Sunny sat with her feet propped up on an open desk drawer, awaiting her arrival. She too would have been notified that Fanny Thornton was in the casino. The big question to all of them would be, why?

Knowing what was ahead of her, Fanny quickened her step, refusing to look at the acres of slot machines and banks of poker tables. Directly in her line of vision, striding toward her, were her handsome twin sons. Dressed in dark suits and pristine white shirts, they could have posed as Wall Street bankers. They were smiling, but only Sage's smile reached his eyes.

"Mom! What brings you down here? Try and work up a smile, or the customers will think Babylon hasn't been kind to you." Birch leaned over and kissed her lightly on the cheek to soften his stern admonition.

"Mom, it's good to see you." Sage hugged her as he gave her a smacking loud kiss on the cheek. "Do you have time for lunch, or at least a cup of coffee?"

"I have the time. How's your father?" Her voice was polite, nothing more.

"Is that one of those polite questions that doesn't require an answer, or is it one of those questions whose answer doesn't matter?" Birch asked as he cupped her elbow to lead her through the casino.

"Both."

Sage laughed, a sound of genuine merriment. Birch's features tightened.

Fanny looked from one of her sons to the other. The twins were like night and day. Sage was loving, open, warmhearted and always the first one to ask, what can I do to help? He was so much like her he scared her at times. Birch was cool, noncommittal except where his father was concerned, selfish, and arrogant, possessing all the same traits that his father was known for. Her husband and brother-in-law all over again.

Fanny shook off her son's hand, a motion that caused Birch's lips to tighten. She didn't care. She had every right to expect loyalty from her children. "If it's your intention to lead me to your father's office, forget it. This may surprise you, but I don't require an escort."

"Mom, why are you always so difficult when you come here?" Birch asked.

Fanny stopped in mid-stride. "That's a very amusing statement, Birch. I've been to this casino exactly twice in eighteen months. The first time was at the grand opening. The second time was when Sunny fainted and Sage called me. The first time I was here I spent so much time smiling I thought I would end up with TMJ pain. My second visit was spent putting cool cloths on Sunny's forehead. Perhaps you have me mixed up with someone else."

"Mom, Birch didn't mean . . ."

"Yes, Birch means exactly what he says. I don't like this place. I have never liked it even when it was on the drawing board. Those feelings have not changed. The only reason I'm here is because of business. Now, if you don't mind, I can find my way to Sunny's office by myself. Fetch your father, please."

"Mom . . ." Birch watched his mother walk away, her shoulders stiff, her ears closed to whatever he wanted to say.

"When was the last time you called her just to say hello, how are you?" Sage asked quietly. "She hasn't forgiven us for choosing up sides two years ago. I can't say that I blame her. It was the worst kind of betrayal. You know it, and I know it. We're damn lucky she even talks to us."

"This is bullshit. We're running a business here. There's no room for 'he said, she said, I don't like this, and I don't like that' crap. What's the point in calling, she's never home. She's always off somewhere with Simon."

"Uncle Simon, Birch. Show some respect. Mom can do whatever she pleases. She doesn't owe any of us explanations. She's fifty-four, and she's independent. She makes more money than this casino does. Go ahead, defend that one."

"I don't have to defend anything I say or do to anyone. I don't kiss ass and take names later like you do, Sage."

"Where the hell did that come from? Mom walks in here, and she has every right to do so, and that invisible alarm goes off. Dad gets in a flap, Sunny goes white in the face, and you look so damn brittle it wouldn't surprise me to see your face split wide open. Am I the only one who's normal around here? Scratch that, and add our sister Billie to the normal list. Don't forget for even one minute where the money came from for this fancy-dancy casino. Or is that what's eating you?"

"Let's not get into this now, Sage. I'll get Dad and meet you in Sunny's office. Where do you suppose Uncle Simon is? Dad calls him *her* shadow. He says they're joined at the hip. Actually, he didn't say hip."

"I know what he said. I was there. That crap is getting really old, Birch. Why can't you accept things for what they are? You're turning into Dad's clone. I just want you to know I hate what I see."

"Ah, the good son. Mom's good son. I'm the bad seed, is that it? Because I hate it that our uncle has taken over Mom's life? Dad hates it too. He still loves Mom."

"That's about the biggest crock I've ever heard. You're even more stupid if you believe it. You need to start lining up your ducks, Birch, before it's too late."

"Jesus, Sage, that almost sounds like a threat. Cool it before Dad gets upset."

"It's whatever you want it to be," Sage said, turning on his heel. "I wouldn't make light of this to Dad. Whatever it is that brought Mom here must be serious. Hey, isn't that our youngest sister making her way in our direction?"

"What the hell! Is this a family reunion?" Birch demanded.

Sage grinned. "I think it's one of those things that's going to require a family vote. Billie, you're lookin' good!" Sage said as he hugged his sister. Birch followed his brother's actions, but not with the same enthusiasm.

"You handsome devil! You still beating the women off with a stick?" Billie teased as she tweaked Sage's cheek. "If you'd wipe that scowl off your face, Birch, you'd be just as handsome. What's up? Mom just said to be here at noon."

"Your guess is as good as ours."

"How's our little mother to be? I can't believe Sunny is going to have a baby."

"Dad can't believe it either. He's taking it personally. He thinks Sunny is having this baby to embarrass him. He won't allow her out on the floor," Sage said.

"What?"

"You heard me. You wouldn't believe the crap that goes on here."

"Sure I would. Sunny takes it?" Billie said, her eyes wide with disbelief.

"She doesn't want to make waves. She says she learned her lesson that time when we all turned on Mom. In addition, I don't think she's feeling all that good. Tyler asked me to keep a close eye on her. I worry about her. If she doesn't shoot off her mouth, something is very wrong. Birch . . . Birch seems to take some kind of perverse pleasure in baiting her. It's taking a toll on her, Billie. So, enough about us, how are you doing? You still seeing that guy?"

"Yes, and don't ask me any more questions. My love life is my own. Tell me about yours."

"Her name is Iris. She said her mother named her after her favorite flower. She reminds me of Mom. Really down-to-earth, wants a family. She just got a professorship at the university. Is that the right term? She's so smart she makes me look like a dummy." Billie hooted with laughter. "Sunny told me you told her that Rainbow Babies is making so much money, you guys can't count it fast enough."

"Kid clothing sells. We're doing well. Why does it have to be us guys versus you guys? I hate that, Sage."

"Because that's the way it is. This family has always been divided, and it will probably remain that way as long as Dad calls the shots around here. I don't see any changes on the horizon."

"Is there anything I can do, Sage?"

"Sure, have dinner with me and Iris over the weekend. I'd really like you to meet her. Bring along what's his name." Sage dropped his voice to a whisper as they approached the door to Sunny's office. "Billie, I want out of here. I gave it my best shot, but it isn't good enough. This was supposed to be a four-way operation, but Dad and Birch call the shots. Sunny and I are just their flunkies. I hate getting up in the morning knowing I have to come here."

"Then do something about it. The Dutch have a saying, Sage. 'If you can't whistle on your way to work, you don't belong in that job.' Do you whistle?"

"Hell no, I don't."

"There you go. Is there anything I can do?"

"If there is, I'll call you. I just know this is going to be one of those spill your guts things. Everyone is going to say things they'll regret later on. The wedge will become wider. One of these days we're going to be strangers to one another. Wanna bet?"

"No thanks." The door to Sunny's office opened. "Mom," Billie said, "you look wonderful. Sunny, you look terrible. Are you taking your vitamins?"

"Of course I'm taking my vitamins. I'm married to a doctor. I just called down to the conference room to get it ready. We're going to need to spread out. The kitchen is sending up some coffee and sandwiches. How's what's his name?" Sunny asked, leading the way out of her office.

"What's his name is just fine, thank you. So, Mom, what's this all about?" Billie asked as she linked her arm with her mother's.

"Family business. Serious business. I'm going to stop by the offices later. I haven't seen Bess in three weeks."

"Sunny's Togs and Rainbow Babies aren't the same without you. Bess misses you, Mom. She's just like you and Aunt Billie. You really are lucky to have such a good friend."

"I know that. We're like sisters. Actually, we're closer than sisters. I'm worried about Sunny, Billie. Has she said anything to you?"

"Only that she's taking her vitamins. Get her out of here, Mom. There aren't any windows, she's indoors all day, sometimes for twelve hours. It doesn't look to me like she gets any thanks for all her hard work, either. Wouldn't it be something if she had twins?"

"Bite your tongue, Billie," Fanny said.

"Are you going to give us a clue as to what this meeting is all about, Mom?" Sunny asked. "Pop's smack in the middle of winding up all the details for the World Series Poker Championship. The emperor of Las Vegas, as he's called these days, will view this meeting as a thorn in his side."

Fanny snorted. The World Series Poker Championship was what Wimbledon was to tennis—the oldest and most prestigious of all the tournaments. Players came from all over the globe to compete. For three straight weeks, twenty-four hours a day, people would line up and play, right up to the main event, the $10,000 buy-in no-limit tournament that would last four days until a new champion was crowned.

"Fanny, what a pleasant surprise."

Fanny stared at Ash Thornton, the man who had once been her husband. The man who didn't know the meaning of the words husband, father, son, fidelity. In her eyes, Ash was a name-only person. She'd given 110 percent to the marriage, and Ash had given zero percent. It wasn't enough. Two hundred percent wouldn't have been enough. There were no regrets. Not now, not ever.

Wheelchair-bound, Ash was impeccably dressed, manicured, and coifed. "Ash," Fanny said coolly, acknowledging the man in the chair.

"Whatever this is about, Fanny, can we make it quick? I'm up to my ears with the final details for the championship. This tournament is a real feather in my cap. Thousands of small details need to be taken care of. There aren't enough hours in the day." His voice was syrupy, the way it always was when he thought he could charm her, wheedle her into doing what he wanted.

"Dad, I offered to help," Sunny said. "Sage . . ."

"Forget it, Sunny. The customers don't want to see your big belly. It's a turn-off. Men don't want reminders of home and hearth when they come to paradise."

Fanny sucked in her breath when her daughter's eyes filled with tears. "That was unnecessarily cruel, Ash, and you need to apologize to your daughter."

"It's okay, Mom," Sunny said.

"No. It is not okay. It wasn't okay when your father said the same things to me years ago, and it's not okay now. This is not *your* casino, Ash. It belongs to Thornton Enterprises. Sunny has a role here, and if you forgot what it is, I can have my attorneys refresh your memory. I also don't give a damn about your championship gambling tournament, and I certainly don't want to hear about those percentages you are forever throwing out to justify whatever it is you do. Now, I came here to discuss something very important."

"You're really trying to stick it to me, aren't you, Fanny? Where's Simon? Shouldn't he be here?"

"Why is that, Ash? He doesn't belong to this immediate family even though he is your brother. But, to answer your question, I don't know where he is. Before we get down to the reason I'm here, outline what Sunny can do to take part of the burden off your shoulders, some of those thousand details. *Now*, Ash."

"Mom, it's okay. Really it is."

"Ash? Birch? Sage?" Fanny said. The three men stared at Fanny, blank looks on their faces. "I see, no one knows what's going on. Well, we'll change that right now. Sunny, you are in charge of the championship. You will report to Billie and me at the end of each workday. If it's too much for you, hire some help. Now that we've settled that little matter, let's get on with it."

"Just a goddamn minute, Fanny. You can't waltz in here and tell me how to run this business. I won't stand for it. Do you hear me?"

"I just did. We've moved on, Ash. What part didn't you understand?"

"You're deliberately screwing this up, Fanny. The minute you get your fingers on something, it goes to hell."

"I made a decision, Ash. When I do that, I don't look back, and I don't back down. If I did, I wouldn't be in business and you wouldn't be sitting here in this . . . this obscene den of opulence. As I said, I came here for a reason. I'm giving you all the courtesy of asking your opinion. I'll weigh what you have to say very carefully." Fanny drew a deep breath as she stared at the faces of her family.

"What is it, Mom?" young Billie asked gently.

"Billie Coleman needs our help. As you know, your grandmother Sallie bought into Coleman Aviation years ago. The stock has been holding its own until now. Ash, I know Moss talked to you about the plans he had for his new plane before he died. I also heard you say you would help in any way you could. Simon also agreed. The Colemans are tapped out. They have nowhere else to turn. They've come too far now to let it all settle in the dust. I think we should do all we can to help Billie bring Moss's dream to life the way we all worked to make this dream possible for you, Ash. I'd like to hear your thoughts."

"Charity begins at home, Mom. What have the Colemans ever done for us? Uncle Seth didn't give a damn about Grandma Sallie. His own *sister*. I don't plan on forgetting that," Birch said.

"What happens if they go belly up?" Ash asked. "Where does that leave us, Fanny? What exactly do you want from us? Our cash flow isn't that strong. Or are you saying you want to mortgage everything. That's it, isn't it? Jesus Christ, Fanny, we could lose everything on some cockamamie dream of Moss's."

Fanny's heart hammered in her chest. She waited.

"Aunt Billie is family. Families stick together. If this is a yes or no vote, then I vote yes," Sage said.

"Me too," Billie said without hesitation.

The score was two to two. If Sunny didn't vote, it would be up to her to break the tie. The turmoil on her daughter's face tore at her heart. Once before Sunny had taken a stand and made a decision she couldn't live with.

"What are you waiting for, Sunny?" Ash demanded, his eyes boring into his daughter.

Fanny shivered at Ash's tone as she too waited for her daughter's response.

"I love Aunt Billie. I love all the Colemans. I say what's ours is theirs. I know in my heart Aunt Billie would do the same for us. Whatever Uncle Seth did or didn't do in regard to Grandma Sallie, has nothing to do with us. I'm voting the way Grandma Sallie would want me to vote. I vote yes."

"That's just dandy. And when that plane doesn't get off the ground and we're hiding out from our creditors, where will you all be?" Ash snarled, his wheelchair burning rubber as he pressed the electric control.

"You're a jerk, Sunny," Birch said. He followed his father out into the hall.

"No, you are not a jerk," Billie said as she wrapped her arms around her sister. "I know what it took for you to do that." This last was said in a hushed whisper.

"So, what's the game plan?" Sage asked.

"I'm going to talk to Simon. He's our investment man. I don't think he's going to agree. This could go either way. Sage said it best. Families need to stick together. It's possible we could lose our shirts."

Billie's voice was flippant. "The sign on my door says I'm the head designer of Sunny's Togs and Rainbow Babies. If it comes down to that, I'll design us new shirts."

"Attagirl," Sage said, pounding her on the back. "C'mon, Sunny, sit down. You don't have any color. Are you sure you're okay?"

Fanny's head jerked upward at the concern in Sage's voice. Did these children of hers know something about Sunny's condition that she didn't know? "I'm taking all of us to lunch at Peridot. Billie, call Bess and ask her to meet us there. Sage, ask Birch if he wants to join us. There's no point in asking your father, but do it anyway. I'll meet you at the front door. I want to call Billie and tell her the good news."

The moment the door closed behind her children, the phone was in Fanny's hand. She would call Billie, but first she was calling Sunny's husband, Tyler Ford.

"Dr. Ford here."

"Tyler, it's Fanny."

"What's wrong, Fanny?"

"That's what I want you to tell me. Sunny looks like death warmed over, and that's a kind statement. Aside from morning sickness, a pregnant woman usually has a wonderful sparkle in her eyes, color in her cheeks. She's a happy woman. This is not the case with Sunny. And another thing, she shouldn't be working twelve hours a day."

"You're right about everything, Fanny. Were you ever successful in changing Sunny's mind or getting her to do something she didn't want to do? I've spoken to her doctor and he tells me she's fine. He said if she wants to work, she should work. She eats well, she exercises moderately, she takes her prenatal vitamins, and she sleeps through the night. She tells me she takes an hour nap in the middle of the afternoon. She makes sure she takes breaks and walks outside. She didn't have morning sickness. She's never been one to complain. My personal opinion is she's under a lot of stress at the casino with her father and brothers. Did something happen, or did you just call to ask me questions? Whatever we say, Fanny, will go no farther."

"I know that, Tyler." Fanny told him about the brief meeting and

Sunny's vote. "She looks so . . . fragile, so washed-out. She appeared a little wobbly to me. If she's willing to come up to Sunrise for a week or so, would you have any objections?"

"None at all. I've suggested the same thing to her, but she's married to that casino. I hate that goddamn place."

"Not as much as I do. Maybe I can work a little mother magic. How's everything going otherwise, Tyler?"

"Reconstructive surgery is not glamorous, but it is rewarding to make someone feel whole again. I love what I do as much as Sunny loves what she does. So, you see, I'm the last person who should even make suggestions where her job is concerned. I'm being paged, Fanny. Call me if you think there's something I can do. Not that my vote counts, but I think you're doing the right thing where the Colemans are concerned. Tell Billie I said hello when you talk to her."

"I'll do that, Tyler. She adores you, you know. She said you remind her of her son Riley."

"That's one of the nicest things anyone has ever said to me. Look, you do what you feel is right and don't let anyone make you back down. Families need to stick together. We'll talk again."

Fanny's fingers drummed on Sunny's desk. She should be feeling better after Tyler's reassuring words, but she didn't. Her motherly intuition was telling her something was wrong. She dialed Billie Coleman's number in Austin, Texas.

"Fanny, is everything okay? Every time I hear the phone the word disaster rings in my head. Before you can ask, we're facing a brick wall. Money just pours out of here. I don't know what to do. If I don't finish this project, then Riley's death and all those other boys who died in Coleman aircraft will have been in vain . . . how can I live with that? As sick as he was at the end, Moss worked tirelessly to perfect this plane. How can I do less?"

"You can't. The Thorntons are going to help, Billie. I'm at Babylon right now. We voted and the money will be on the way by the end of the week. If it isn't enough, we'll go back to the drawing board. Please, Billie, don't cry. Be thankful your granddaughter Sawyer is the aeronautical engineer on this project."

"We're all obsessed with this plane, Sawyer more so. My own children . . . Fanny, how is it possible for a mother to be estranged from her two daughters? I never, ever thought such a thing would happen to me; how can my daughters fight me on this plane? All they want is the money they say we're wasting. They say a new plane won't bring Riley back, and they're right about that. Riley was their brother and I know they loved him. When this is all over, perhaps I'll be able to understand. On a more pleasant note, I just know Sawyer is going to explode when I tell her about your offer. That child has worked for months now, getting by on three hours' sleep a night. She eats, sleeps, and dreams about her grandfather's dream plane. She's going to get it off the ground too, thanks to you. Fanny, I wish there were words . . ."

"Words aren't necessary, Billie. We're family."

"We could lose our shirts."

"Well, guess what? Your namesake said if that happens, she would design us new ones. You can't beat an offer like that."

"No, you can't. How are things going on the Bright White Way? How's Sunny? Is Birch still giving you heartache?"

"I'm in the conference room here at Babylon, Billie. I'll call you this evening. I'm taking the kids to lunch at Peridot."

"That place where you and Sallie used to go?"

"Oh, Billie, I miss her so much. She had such faith and trust in me. I hope I can live up to all of her expectations. I know in my heart she would approve of what we're doing. Family, Billie, is what life is all about. Sallie always said our families' destiny was in your hands and mine. Together, we'll work toward that end."

"We won't fail, Fanny. You can take that to the bank. Do I dare ask about Simon?"

"Tonight, Billie. Give everyone my love. Now, take a nap, okay?"

"At ten o'clock in the morning?"

"Why not? Aren't we independent women? If we are, then we can take a nap anytime we want. Actually, we can do *anything* we want. Both of us have earned that little perk. Talk to you tonight."

The Peridot restaurant was as old as Las Vegas itself. It was also Fanny's favorite restaurant for the very reason Billie Coleman had mentioned earlier.

"I love it when my brother finally acts like a grown-up and holds our chairs out for us," Billie said.

Sunny's voice was blunt yet sad when she said, "You're leaving, aren't you, Sage?"

"I want to. I'm willing to stay until you have the baby and get back into the swing of things. We're just flunkies, Sunny. You know it, and I know it. I glide around the floor trying to look important. I'm not sure what you do behind those closed doors. I don't know if you're aware of the latest developments. Is anyone interested?" The women nodded just as Bess Noble, Fanny's second-in-command, joined them.

"I heard that," Bess said as she kissed everyone before taking her seat. "Now, tell us what the latest development is."

"Dad and Birch want to buy riverboats in Biloxi, Mississippi, for gambling. He planned to apply for a mortgage, but you beat him to it, Mom. At least I think you did. Dad and Birch can be secretive at times. Those riverboats are a great big can of worms. I spoke up and said it had to be put to a vote, but they ignored me. At the risk of repeating myself, what the hell kind of family is this? Tell me, Mom, what you want us to do to help Aunt Billie."

"I'm going to call Simon this evening and discuss everything. We'll sell off all our shares of Rainbow Babies and Sunny's Togs. Simon never sold them. He fibbed to us about that transaction. Thank God he did. We're going to move out of Sallie's bingo palace. It will go on the market tomorrow. It's prime real estate, so it will fetch several million. I'm going to mortgage Babylon. By tomorrow the news will be on the strip and the sharks will start to gather, so be prepared. I'll empty out that monster safe in Sunrise. I'll *mortgage* Sunrise. I'll sell all the jewelry Sallie left me. That's already in the works. I'll borrow what I can to make up the difference. The only monies we'll have coming in will go to make the mortgage payments. I did have a thought, though, and I'd like your opinions. Sallie never raised the rates for the other casinos to tie into her sewage and electrical systems. It's time for a hefty increase. Those fees, I believe, will keep our heads above water." The sighs of relief could be heard around the table.

"Good thinking, Mom," Sunny said.

"It's about time," Sage said.

"This might be a good time to unveil my latest creation," Billie said as she dug into the voluminous bag she was never without and pulled out two soft dolls. "Meet Bernie and Blossom. I showed them to a few of our salespeople who took them on the road. Guess what! We already have orders for ten thousand. The big question is, how are we going to market them? The next question is, where do we get the money? Do we form a separate company, or do we license them under Rainbow Babies or Sunny's Togs? I thought we could hire the Bernsteins to get our publicity started. We can have a million of these on the market by next Christmas."

Sage stared at his sister, his face full of awe. "Just like that! Where are you going to manufacture them?"

"Made in the good old U.S. of A. Forty bucks a pop or $39.95. People like to walk away with change even if it's only a nickel. We learned that in marketing class."

Fanny held the soft fabric doll in her hands. As always, she marveled at her younger daughter's abilities. "The scraps from Rainbow Babies, right?"

"Yes, but each face is different. I know eight people that come to mind who will be willing to work on the faces. The doll itself and the garment can be made for under a dollar if mass-produced. The faces are what will cost, and labor of course. Sign on, Sage, we can use your expertise. You said you want out of Babylon. So, what do you all think?"

"I think this is one of your best ideas," Bess said, a calculator in hand.

"Billie, these dolls are priceless. I wish I had your talent. Can I have the first one off the line for my new baby, Bernie if he's a boy? If I have a girl, I'll take Blossom. They are so adorable. Raggedy Ann and Andy will be passé."

Billie reached into the bag again and withdrew two tissue-wrapped bundles. "I already made them for you. I wanted something special for you. That's where I got the idea, Sunny. Think about it, Sunny; you have a clothing company named after you and now you're the inspiration behind these two dolls. I don't think we're headed to the poorhouse just yet."

"This calls for a celebration," Fanny said.

"Let's have some of that same wine you and Grandma Sallie had that famous day when you met her for the first time. Tell us the story again, Mom," Sage said.

"It was wartime and I was meeting your grandmother for the first time . . ."

The moment the door closed behind Ash Thornton, he went into a rage. "Now, do you see what your mother is capable of? She undermines every single thing I do. If she'd keep her nose out of the casino business, things would be just fine. Do I interfere in her business? No, I do not. Your mother has to dabble in everything. She's not content to own two of the biggest clothing companies in the country, she has to make her presence felt in everything that concerns me. I'm not going to let that happen. We're going to go ahead with those riverboats. I want you in Mississippi tomorrow. Get everything under way. She won't stop us. If she does . . . I'll deal with it then and there. When Sunny comes back from lunch, send her in here. She's out of here until that kid arrives. I have enough problems without her jinxing me. Why are you looking at me that way, Birch? Business is business. We're on top, and I plan on staying there. So I already took a mortgage out, so what? I got a good interest rate and cut Tisdale's markers to half. That's how you do business in this town. I love bankers who gamble. Hell, the governor was in here two weeks ago, and he shot a load that made me blink. You suck up to these people, and you can get anything you want. You have to know how to play the game. Your mother doesn't know the *name* of the game much less how to *play* it. I even know what her next move is going to be. She's going to raise the rates on the sewage and electric plants. That won't endear us to the rest of the owners. The dark stuff will start to fly. Anything can happen in this town and take my word for it, something will happen as soon as those rate hikes go into effect. Your mother talks a good game about tightening our belts and all that crap. Don't kid yourself, son, it's what Fanny wants when Fanny wants it. Thanks for sticking up for me. They'll eat our dust yet."

"Dad, this is all wrong. Why in the hell does it have to be like this? The past is past. Can't we let it die and make things better? I know you can't go back, but you can go forward and make it better than it was. Sage is going to walk. I could see it in his face."

"Sage is not a team player. Neither is Sunny. You and me now, we have the same goals. We'll make those goals too."

Birch watched as his father swallowed a handful of pills. He could feel his shoulders slump. Sage was his twin, his other half. He never felt quite whole unless Sage was close by. He adored Sunny, always had. It was all getting away from him, just like the last time when they sided with their father against their mother.

"You can't tell Sunny she isn't needed right now. If we do that, Mom will shut this place down so fast we won't have time to blink. She'll do it, Dad. I'd hate to see you make the mistake of pushing her to the edge. If you do that, she won't jump over the edge, she'll plow you right under. She takes her commitment to Grandma Sallie and this family very seriously. You're wrong about Sage too. Sage has the charisma to make this place work. He works the floor like a pro. Any casino on this strip would hire him and pay him five times what we pay him. He'd be worth every dollar too. Don't mess with Sage, Dad."

Ash eyed his son, his one remaining ally. His thoughts were scrambled with the pills he'd just taken. His chaotic thoughts reeled back in time when he was Birch's age. He'd been just as tall, just as good-looking, just as virile, just as mobile. He stared at the replica of himself and wanted to cry. "Sage is weak," he mumbled.

"You're wrong. Sage has more guts than the two of us put together. I'll walk out of here before I let you put Sage down."

Ash stared at his son and knew he meant every word. He waved him out of the room. When the door closed behind Birch, great wrenching sobs tore at his wasted body the custom tailoring couldn't hide. "I hate your goddamn fucking guts, Fanny," he sobbed.

In his office, Birch sat down behind his desk. His head dropped to his hands. He wished he could turn back the hands of the clock to the day he and Sage left for college with Simon behind the wheel.

He knew the story behind his father and his uncle Simon. He'd heard his father's version, his grandmother's version, Simon's version, and then his mother's version. Somewhere in between was the *real* story. Late at night in the college dorm, he and Sage had put their own spin on the story and came up with one they could both live with. Now, fifteen years later, history seemed to be repeating itself. He was his father and Sage was Simon.

Deep shudders ripped through him when he remembered how his uncle Simon had come out the winner from all the different stories, even their own. That meant Sage was a winner and he was . . . his father all over again.

It was three o'clock when Birch closed his briefcase. "Biloxi, Mississippi, here I come," he muttered. The knock on his door startled him. "Come in," he called.

"Nah. I don't think so," Sage said from the open doorway. "I stopped by Dad's office to drop this off, but he was asleep. He'd just tear it up anyway. You can do whatever you want with it. It's my resignation. You going somewhere? Let me guess, Biloxi, Mississippi, right? Big mistake, Birch."

"Come on, Sage, we go through this at least once a week. You always back down. This thing is going to blow over the way these things always blow over. This is our business. We need to pull together."

"That's really funny coming from you, Birch. I've had it. What we voted for was right for all the right reasons. I don't have any regrets. All I want is a life, and I'm damn well going to get one. Uncle Simon walked away and got his life. I've got the guts to do the same thing."

"Let's not forget that good old Uncle Simon walked off with the queen of this parade. Our mother."

"Mom's personal life is none of our business. Justify what happened with Sunny, Birch. Don't tell me nothing happened either. I know how you and Dad do things."

"Sunny belongs at home taking care of herself. Mom stayed home and took care of us. Why isn't that good enough for her?"

"The why of it doesn't matter. It's her choice. We made a pact early on. You can't slough Sunny off. You're gonna do it, aren't you? I refuse to be a party to anything that hurts one of us. What the hell happened to you, Birch? For months now we've been at opposite ends of the spectrum. I miss the old Birch, my buddy and my pal. Where'd he go?"

"Get your ass in here and stop telling the world our business. What about Dad?"

"Ah, the emperor's son has spoken. The queen's son is speaking now, the son who is his own man, and he says, fuck you, Birch." In a dramatic gesture, Sage threw his hands high in the air. "Jesus, do you have any idea of how good I feel right now? Because I'm in such a good mood, I'm going to give you some advice for free. Forget those riverboats, they're going to sink to the bottom of the Mississippi River. Give some thought to buying a gondola. Isn't that what emperors ride around in or sail in . . . ? Whatever. See you around."

"Sage, wait. We need to talk. Sage, get in here. What the hell is bugging you? Come on, we can talk this through and make it work."

"Sorry, Birch, not this time."

The sound of the door closing behind his brother sounded ominous, final. Birch cried then for what he'd allowed himself to become: the emperor's son.